REG RAWLINS, PRIVATE INVESTIGATOR

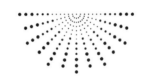

REG RAWLINS, PRIVATE INVESTIGATOR

CASES 4-6

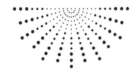

P.D. WORKMAN

ISBN: 9781989415887 (Kindle)

ISBN: 9781989415894 (ePub)

ISBN: 9781774681305 (KDP Print Paperback)

ISBN: 9781774681312 (Ingram Paperback)

ISBN: 9781774681329 (Ingram Hardcover)

AND MORE AT PDWORKMAN.COM

NIGHT OF NINE TAILS

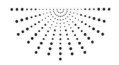

REG RAWLINS, PSYCHIC INVESTIGATOR #4

CHAPTER ONE

R eg climbed out of bed, the dread from her nightmare still squeezing
her heart so tightly it hurt. It had been a long time since she had felt
that anxious without knowing what it was she had to fear. She was keenly
attuned to the possible dangers in her life, always staying one step ahead of
the authorities or anyone who might have figured out her latest scam, but
the heart-squeezing dread was different. It wasn't connected to any specific
risk she could identify.

She could write it off as the vestiges of her nightmare, but she didn't
want to ignore the warning. It could be something that her subconscious
was trying to warn her about. If something was bothering her, she needed to
know what it was to address it. If it was time to leave Black Sands… she
didn't want to, but if it were the only way to stay safe, then she would.

Starlight was sitting in the window looking out at the back garden. He
looked over at Reg and let out a low, mournful howl. Reg went over to him
and petted him and let her tuxedo cat rub the top of his head against her
chin and neck.

"What's the matter, Star? Did you have a nightmare too?"

He sat back and started to wash, giving her the cold shoulder. She felt
his rebuff keenly. She knew very well that he wasn't unhappy because he'd
been having a nightmare. She was being silly, but in doing so, she had made

light of his problem, which, as far as he was concerned, was far more important than her petty human problems.

"Okay, I'm sorry." She stroked him again. "What is it?"

She peered out the window. She could see Sarah working in the garden, something that lifted her heart just a little. Not so long ago, she had been worried that she was going to lose Sarah for good. Suffering the effects of losing her powerful emerald amulet, Sarah had been on the brink of death. It had been a hard-won battle to bring her back. Seeing her puttering around in the garden was something that Reg had never expected to see again and it warmed her heart.

She kneaded the back of Starlight's neck. "Are you looking for your friend?"

This time he didn't rebuff her. She could feel the warmth of his confirmation, but also the emptiness and longing that the other cat had left behind.

Reg had only seen the black cat he watched for twice. Then, Reg's mind had been on more important things; finding the emerald and proving that she wasn't the one who had stolen it. It wasn't easy for someone with a past like Reg's to prove her innocence. While no one in Black Sands knew her full history, both Corvin and Detective Jessup had a pretty good idea that she had stolen and fenced jewelry and other valuable goods before.

"I'll ask Sarah if she's seen any sign of him," Reg told Starlight, kissing his velvety black ears.

He stared at her reproachfully with his mismatched green and blue eyes. Reg coughed and corrected herself.

"I'll ask Sarah if she's seen *her*."

She chuckled as she grabbed a housecoat to pull on over her shorts and t-shirt and walked out to the kitchen. Starlight remained in the window watching for any sign of the black cat rather than following Reg into the kitchen and demanding breakfast. He really was worried about the black cat.

Reg turned on the coffee machine. She looked at her phone for any new mail or messages while she waited for it to brew a pot of coffee, trying to immerse herself in something other than the tightness around her heart. If she just ignored the feeling, it would go away. If it was just general anxiety, then distracting herself with something else should help.

But even before she filled her first cup of coffee, she knew that it wasn't going away. It wasn't just the vestiges of a bad dream, brought on by imagination or watching TV too late into the night.

Something was really wrong.

She just didn't know what it was.

~

Reg slipped on a pair of pink flip-flops and went around the cottage to the garden, where Sarah was standing, hands on well-padded hips, looking at the bent and broken plants, shaking her head. She glanced at Reg and shook her gray head.

"It looks like a hurricane was through here."

Reg sipped her coffee, which was really still too hot to drink.

"I'm sorry," she acknowledged. She wasn't apologizing for something she had done wrong, just saying that she felt sorry for the state of things. She was sorry that Sarah was feeling bad.

It was, in fact, not Reg or a hurricane that was responsible for all of the beaten-down plants in the garden. The damage had been done by Sarah herself, in a demented frenzy as she had tried to chase off the black cat that Starlight was looking for as he sat in the window. Reg hadn't seen it—hadn't seen her—since.

"I half-remember doing it," Sarah said, her forehead wrinkling into frown lines, "but it's like it happened a long time ago to someone else. I know I was angry, uncontrollably angry, but I can't remember feeling that way. Not… really."

"You were not well. But now you're feeling better… and I bet it won't be long before you have everything whipped back into shape again."

"I think it's taken a bad enough beating already. I need to remove all of the detritus and tie up some of the plants until they are strong enough… a lot of them won't bloom again this year. It's such a meaningless loss. It didn't have to happen at all…"

Reg tried another sip of coffee. "Do you want a cup?" she offered Sarah. "I just brewed a pot."

"No, dear. I have found that since my… reanimation… caffeine just puts me over the top. I have more energy than I know what to do with."

"I could make you some tea."

"I'm fine. I've had my breakfast and I don't need anything else. I just need to figure out how to get started here." Sarah sighed. "You're up early. Do you have an appointment?"

"No. I'm just having nightmares. I thought I might as well get up."

Sarah nodded. "I could make you a potion to help with nightmares."

Reg shook her head. She assumed that Sarah just meant some herbal remedy with valerian and whatever other brain-calming herbs she could think of, but Reg wasn't about to swallow anything called a potion. She wasn't that far gone yet.

"It's okay. I'm sure they'll pass in a few days."

"You need to make sure you get a good sleep. It can affect your productivity. Especially your psychic abilities."

Uncomfortable, Reg changed the subject. "So, I was wondering if you saw that cat around here again."

"Which cat?" Sarah frowned and motioned to her wrecked garden. "The one that caused all of this?"

It certainly hadn't been the cat's fault that Sarah had freaked out, trying to beat it with a broom and flattening most of the garden.

"Uh, yes. The black cat."

"It's a stray," Sarah said dismissively. "It will be in someone else's yard."

"Well, probably," Reg agreed. "I'm just looking for it... Starlight is looking for it. Her." She looked at the cottage window. "He's sitting there watching for her. But I haven't seen her since that day."

"I don't want another cat wandering around here. Starlight is inside, and that's fine; I don't want a cat out in the garden chasing away my birds."

"I know. But Starlight is very... convincing. He really wants me to look for her."

"You're not going to become the neighborhood cat lady, taking in all of the strays in the neighborhood. Not while you're living in my guest cottage."

"I don't want more than one cat."

"Then what are you going to do when you find it?"

"I don't know." Reg just knew that Starlight wanted her to look for his new amour. "I guess... maybe I would find a good home for her, and I could take Starlight there sometime to visit with her?" She rolled her eyes. "I don't really know anything about cat relationships. Do you?"

"No. Nor do I want to."

"So, you haven't seen her around anywhere?"

"No, I haven't. And if I do, I'll chase her away again."

Reg nodded. When Sarah said that she didn't like cats, she had meant it. Even though she was polite to Starlight and would even feed him when she came to see Reg, she was still not a cat person and didn't want them anywhere near her birds.

There was a loud crash, and Reg whirled around, putting her hands up, ready to defend herself. But there was no imminent attack. Just the rattle of a truck as it continued to drive down the street in front of Sarah's house. It had hit a bump or a pothole along the way, that was all. Sarah raised her brows at Reg, amused.

"A little jumpy today?"

"I just thought…" Reg trailed off. "Yeah, I guess I'm a little jumpy today. I don't know what is going on with me… I'm feeling anxious all the time… like something is going to happen. Something is wrong."

Sarah picked up a ball of twine, finally deciding where to start on her garden refurbishment.

"Well, you could help me with the garden. It's a very relaxing hobby."

"I'm not really looking for a hobby. I need to stay focused on my business if I'm going to support myself."

"Are you worried about failing? I thought that your psychic services business had been going quite well."

"It is. I can't complain about that. You've been a real help to me with all of your contacts and I'm always getting new clients. It's just that… I don't think this anxiety is related to my business; it's something else."

"But you don't know what it is?"

"No."

Reg watched Sarah as she approached a droopy, bent-over plant and lifted its branches tentatively as if trying to gauge whether it were still alive or beyond repair. She started to tie it to a nearby stake.

"Maybe you're picking up someone else's anxiety, then. Maybe it's not even your own."

Reg still had a hard time believing she actually had a psychic gift. She was good at reading people, that much was certain, but all of the other odd things that had happened since she had moved to Black Sands seemed like magic tricks. Someone using sleight of hand to gaslight her into thinking that she really did have unexplained powers. But she couldn't think of a way to explain everything that had happened using science or illusion.

She couldn't deny that she was often influenced by others' moods, though. Maybe that's all that Sarah was saying. She had recently met with someone or been around someone who had been very anxious, and she had just taken on those emotions herself without realizing it.

"Yeah. Maybe that's it."

"Have you had a client recently who was worried about the future?" Sarah suggested. "I imagine that a lot of the people who hire you are concerned about the future. That's what tends to worry humans the most. Not knowing where they are going."

"I can't think of anyone offhand, but there must have been. That must be what I'm doing. I'm just... empathetic."

"Exactly," Sarah agreed. "Maybe have a nice, calming cup of tea instead of caffeine in the morning, take some time to meditate and center yourself. I'm sure it will help to smooth away your anxiety. And if not... I do know some recipes. Or I could help you to find a healer who could help you if you don't trust my skills."

"Oh, it isn't that. I'm just not used to... magical solutions." Reg tried to explain it in a way that wouldn't offend Sarah. "I'm sure that your potions are just as good as the other charms and protection spells around the property. You're very good at what you do."

Sarah sighed, tying up another branch. "I think I'm going to have to find someone who can fix gardens. It's going to take forever to repair one plant at a time, and then to wait to see how they respond. I need a spellcaster who is good with flora."

Reg couldn't offer much help in that direction. "Maybe... Letticia would know someone."

"I'm sure I have a name in my Rolodex. I'll just have to take a look. It's been a long time since I needed to hire someone to do this." She put her hands on her hips again, surveying the minuscule amount of work she had done. "I really don't want to be tied to my garden all day. I want to be out, having a good time."

For a woman who, according to Jessup, was several centuries old, Sarah had a remarkable level of vigor, which had grown with her recent healing.

If Reg hadn't known that taking the emerald away would kill Sarah in short order, she might have been tempted to have it for her own.

CHAPTER TWO

Once Sarah decided to get someone else to come and help her to put her garden in order, she headed back to the big house, and Reg returned to the rental cottage to report to Starlight on her non-progress.

The cat made a snorting noise that suggested to Reg that she wasn't trying hard enough and finally left his perch on the windowsill to yowl around his bowl, insisting that Reg find something better than the stale kitty kibble that remained in his bowl. He rubbed against Reg's legs and then the fridge to encourage her to make the connection between the cat and his need to eat something tasty and nourishing from the fridge.

"I'm not that stupid," Reg said, "I actually do know what you want."

He sat back and looked at her, his gaze steady. If she knew what he wanted, then why did it take her so long to comply with his requests? How hard was it to go to the fridge and use her huge paws with their opposable thumbs to get him something good to eat?

Reg sighed, shook her head, and did as she was told, poking through the leftover fast food boxes and Tupperware containing offerings from Sarah. She found some beef stew that she needed to get rid of one way or another. She spooned some into Starlight's dish, and he pushed his head in to start eating before she had even finished dishing it up.

Reg watched him chow down noisily for a few seconds, then picked up her coffee and watched the house, feeling for Sarah. She knew without having to see that Sarah was going out again. Since her miraculous healing, she had been going out nearly every day. She was meeting with this friend or that new beau or somebody else who Reg had never heard of. Having decided that she wasn't going to do the garden work herself, she was now free to go gallivanting off yet again.

It was pretty sad that a centuries-old woman had a better social life than Reg. Reg didn't have a boyfriend, though she wasn't sure that she wanted one. And she didn't have very many people she could actually call friends. There was Sarah, of course, but she and Reg didn't see each other socially unless Reg happened to be eating at The Crystal Bowl, which was where Sarah usually ate, or they were both at a community event together. There was Detective Jessup, but Reg was not happy with her, primarily due to the fact that Marta Jessup had considered Reg the prime suspect in the investigation of Sarah's missing emerald. It was true that multiple witnesses and Reg's past had all made her look guilty, but she *wasn't* guilty, and if Jessup had been a friend, she would have known that.

But that was fine, because it wasn't a good idea for Reg to have a friend who was a cop. She knew that there were a lot of cons and cops who were close friends, but she had never understood how it worked, and she couldn't see herself fully trusting anyone who had anything to do with law enforcement. Back in Bald Eagle Falls, her foster sister Erin's boyfriend was a cop. But Erin had a legitimate business baking gluten-free products now. The fact that she kept finding bodies or getting involved in police investigations didn't help matters, but in spite of all of that, she seemed to have a pretty good relationship with Officer Handsome.

Reg needed to find some new friends. She was usually good at making friends quickly. She had been moved around a lot as a kid, so she'd had to develop some good social skills if she wanted to play with anyone other than her imaginary friends.

Corvin had suggested that Reg's imaginary friends hadn't been invented, but ghostly, but Reg thought he was either pulling her leg or he was mistaken. She hadn't learned until later in life that she could pretend to talk to dead people and get money for it. As a child, she had just been entertaining herself by peopling her surroundings with interesting characters, like a writer writing a book. The psychologists had always said that she had a vivid imagination, if they could just get her to put it to good use.

Which was precisely what Reg was doing.

After Corvin's hearing, a security guard had walked Reg out to her car. He hadn't been an unattractive guy and had shown an interest in her. He had given her his card, but she couldn't remember what she had done with it. She tried to remember what she had been wearing that day. It was probably still in her pocket or her purse. She wouldn't have thrown it out.

She tried her purse first, but it was the sort of cavernous bag where miscellany went to die. Who knew what kind of crud had collected in the bottom of it. She was always putting little things in there for an emergency or to put to good use later, and could never find them again when she wanted them.

She looked through the top few layers, including pulling out her wallet and checking to see if she had put the card into one of the slots, but there was no sign of it. She didn't want to dig all the way to the bottom or to dump it out, so she decided to try her pockets instead. She always put her clothes back in her dresser or closet if they didn't need washing. She couldn't see the point of washing an item every time you wore it if you didn't sweat or spill and it still looked fresh and unwrinkled. Her wardrobe was pretty small, and she didn't want to have to do the laundry every two or three days.

She was pretty sure she had been wearing pants, not one of her gypsy skirts when she went to the trial. She had driven to Letticia's house that day, and it was a long way through the woods. She hadn't known whether she was going to end up having to hike up a trail or something else requiring a full range of movement, so she had worn pants rather than a skirt.

Reg went through the pockets of a couple of pairs of pants. She hated how women's clothing so seldom had pockets and refused to buy any without pockets. It was easy to sew pockets into a skirt, but tailored pants were another story. It was much easier to hide things quickly if one had proper pockets. What else was she going to do, stuff something down her bra? While that might work for smaller items, something larger would end up looking odd.

In the second pair of pants, her fingers touched a card. Reg pulled it out, feeling a warm rush of satisfaction over having found it. She turned the card over to look at the name on it. Damon Knight. She didn't know much about him, but it sounded like a magical name. He had appeared to have some magic the day of the trial, able to put out a small fire with his powers without even turning a hair. And he hadn't escorted Reg to her car because she was causing trouble or because he wanted to protect her from an ugly mob. He'd walked her to her car because he wanted a chance to spend a few minutes alone with her and to give her his number.

Reg left her bedroom and walked over to the wicker couch. She had left her phone on the coffee table in front of it. She didn't have any appointments in the next couple of hours, so the time was hers to use as she liked. She sat down on the couch and curled her feet up beneath her, trying to get comfy. The wicker couch always seemed to be lumpy or poky somewhere. But it was a piece of furniture that she hadn't had to buy herself, so what did she have to complain about?

"Come on over, Starlight."

The cat was washing in a bright sunbeam. He stopped and looked at Reg as if he couldn't believe that she had interrupted his ablutions.

"Come on." Reg patted the cushion next to her. "I'll scratch your ears."

He looked at her for another minute, then consented to join her. He jumped up beside her and accepted the pets and cuddles and ear scratches. She touched the white spot on his forehead, the star that gave him his name. His third eye, Sarah called it.

"What do you think?" she asked him thoughtfully. "Think Damon will answer the phone, or will it go to voicemail? He might be working. I don't know if he works regular hours or only special events. He could be an accountant or something boring the rest of the time."

Starlight rubbed against her hand, purring, lapping up the attention. Reg focused on him for a few more minutes before picking up her phone to call Damon.

"Here, lay down now and cuddle," she encouraged, patting the couch to encourage him to lie down. Starlight continued to rub and bump against her. She rolled her eyes and tapped Damon's number into her phone.

It only rang once or twice before a click told Reg it had connected. It was so fast that she was sure it had gone to voicemail and she was trying to think of what she wanted to say in her message. Did she even want to leave a message, or should she try him again another time so that they could actually talk to each other and judge each other's temperature?

"Damon," he said.

Reg waited for the rest of the recording, then realized that was it. She wasn't talking to a machine; she was talking to the warlock himself.

"Oh, hi, Damon. I don't know if you remember me, but I met you at Corvin Hunter's hearing…"

"Reg Rawlins," Damon said, a smile in his voice.

Reg smiled back. "Yes. That's right. You do remember."

"I was hoping you would call."

"Well… I did." Reg rolled her eyes at her response. How quickly the conversation was dwindling to something she was likely to have had in sixth grade.

"How are you?" Damon asked politely. "Did you hear the verdict about Hunter?"

"Yes, I did. I got a delivery."

"Good. They're supposed to notify all of the concerned parties, but sometimes someone gets missed. Whether by accident or on purpose…"

"So they decided to shun him."

"Yes."

"Are you… part of Corvin's coven?" Reg asked tentatively. She didn't know how big the magical community was and whether there were multiple covens or just the one. Were all warlocks automatically admitted to the coven, or did they have to qualify to get in? Or did they have a choice as to what coven they wanted to go to?

"No." Damon gave a low chuckle. "I'm more of a lone wolf. Which is one of the reasons that I can work security at something like that. You couldn't do security if the warlock on trial was someone from your own coven. Too close of a relationship."

"So the two of you are not friends?"

"No. I don't have anything to do with Hunter. Not because I have anything against him… he was just never my type. You know. The kind of guy that I would associate with."

"What kind of guy do you associate with?"

"Well, as I say, I'm sort of a lone wolf. So… not a lot of people. I have a couple of close friends, but other than that… my circle is pretty small."

"Mine too," Reg admitted. "I need to make some new friends."

"Old ones just not holding up?" he teased.

"No." Reg let out a sigh that was all too real. "I need someone I can hang out with. I haven't had a lot of luck in making friends here. I mean… I haven't made enemies, but I'd like to get to know some people who are… more like me."

"Psychics?" Damon suggested.

"No way," Reg said immediately. She had only associated with one other psychic so far, and Marian was not the kind of person she wanted to be around. She didn't want to be around anyone who was going to try to read her or to influence her feelings. Marian was good at manipulating people, and Reg wanted to stay in full control of her own thoughts and feelings.

"No way?" Damon repeated, laughing. "You sound pretty adamant about that!"

"Have you ever been in a room where everyone is trying to read everyone else?" Reg asked. "I'd go crazy. I'll keep my thoughts to myself."

"That makes sense." Damon didn't say anything for a moment, and Reg tried to figure out how to take control of the conversation and steer it in the direction she wanted to go. "So did you decide to take me up on my offer?"

Reg frowned, trying to remember the conversation. What offer had he made?

"Umm... I..."

"I offered to take you out to dinner, show you around town. I didn't hear from you right away, so I thought maybe you weren't interested."

"Things have just been a little crazy with me lately. Well, forget lately, they've been a little crazy ever since I hit town. But yeah, I would be interested in getting out... getting to know Black Sands a little better."

"Excellent. Are you free tonight?"

"Let me take a look at my appointment book. Hang on. I should have done that before I called you, but I forgot."

"Sure."

Reg went to the kitchen, where her appointment book was lying on the island. She kept it out where Sarah could access it so that if Sarah happened to make an appointment for her, she would not be surprised. She opened the calendar and quickly found the day.

"Yeah, it looks like I'm free tonight. About seven onward?"

"Seven it is," Damon agreed. "Can I pick you up at your house?"

"No, you don't need to do that. Why don't we meet somewhere?"

CHAPTER THREE

Reg had been expecting Damon to suggest a restaurant. Dinner and a date, it seemed the natural choice. But instead, he had suggested a bowling alley. Did people even do that anymore? It brought to mind pictures of Fred Flintstone dancing up to the alley and throwing his stone bowling ball to knock down the pins. She wasn't sure what to do when she got there. Damon found her standing on the worn red carpet looking around at the various counters, baffled.

"Hello, stranger! You're looking a little lost."

"Yeah. What exactly am I supposed to do here?"

"Come with me; we need to get you a ticket, shoes, and a ball."

"Can't I just wear my own shoes?"

"Not unless you have bowling shoes, and I gather by your expression that you are not a regular bowler."

"I don't like wearing other people's shoes."

With all of the foster homes she had been in, Reg had put up with all kinds of hand-me-downs, and shoes were the worst. She hated putting her feet in someone else's stinky shoes.

"No one does," Damon agreed. "But they sanitize them. You won't get someone else's foot fungus."

"Ugh." Reg was seriously reconsidering a date with Damon. She hadn't even thought about foot fungus.

"Come on. Try it once. If you don't like it, then you know for next time, and we'll do something else instead. You choose next time."

"I don't know."

"Just try," Damon urged. "It's a lot of fun."

Reg shook her head, but she followed Damon to the ticket counter, then the shoe counter where she got the ugliest flat red-laced shoes she had ever seen. They didn't feel right on her feet. Of course they wouldn't, since other people had been wearing them. Who knew how many people.

The bowling balls were cool. There were a lot of different colors, and she liked the sparkles and swirls that some of them had. Damon helped her to pick out the size he thought she should use, and got a slightly bigger one for himself. At least he hadn't brought his own ball, so she knew he wasn't too crazy about bowling. If he'd brought his own... she would have known that he was too far gone and she couldn't ever go out with him again.

"So you've never bowled before?" Damon asked as he led her to the alley they had been assigned and pointed out their seats and the computer that would keep track of their scores.

"I think I might have once or twice when I was a kid, but I don't remember very well." Reg had an impression of crowds of kids yelling and throwing their balls down the alley. Bright lights and loud music and way too much sensory input. Since most of her foster families had not had the money to do much, it had probably been through one of the organizations that took disadvantaged youth places. She had gone to all kinds of camps and movies and other events with community outreach organizations.

"Okay, let me just walk you through the rules and the scoring then. I'm assuming you don't watch it on TV or already know all of that?"

"Assume I don't know anything," Reg agreed.

He gave her a warm smile and put an arm around her shoulder. Reg tensed. She wasn't ready for physical contact yet. Especially with a warlock whose powers she knew nothing about. She gave her shoulders a little shrug to dislodge his arm.

"Sorry," Damon said, raising an eyebrow questioningly.

Reg moved an inch away from him to regain her space and took a deep breath.

"Corvin Hunter," she said.

He looked around, but since she didn't actually mean that Corvin was there, he looked back at her, even more confused.

"The only experience I've had with romance with warlocks was with Corvin Hunter," Reg explained, her face getting warm with what she knew would be a bright red flush to match her red box braids.

"Ah." Damon nodded. "But not all warlocks are like him. He's... special."

"Oh yeah, he's special," Reg agreed. "And I'm not going to walk into anything like that again. So you can expect me to be Miss Prim and Proper until I know you better and know what your powers and your motives are."

He smiled reassuringly. "You don't need to worry. As I'm sure you've been told, Hunter's powers are very rare. And dying out, with any luck. You don't need to worry about running into another warlock who can steal your powers like that."

"Just because they are rare, that doesn't mean there aren't any more. And who knows what other powers I need to worry about. It seems like the magical community doesn't like to talk about the bad stuff, so they're not going to tell me if someone else like you has powers that I should be concerned about."

"No one warned you about Hunter?"

Reg sat down to retie her shoe. She grimaced. "Well, a few people told me to be careful of him or to stay away from him, but they didn't tell me why or what I needed to be careful of. So I was warned... but I wasn't warned."

"And you are the kind of person who doesn't take well to being told what to do?"

Reg hoped that her face wasn't going to keep burning the whole night. She shook her head. "No, I'm not. My parents were always frustrated with not being able to tell me anything. But I guess all of that came out at the trial. Now everyone knows that I'm not the kind of person who listens to warnings, however well-intentioned."

"Not everyone in the community was at the trial," he reassured her. "It wasn't that big of a crowd. And I don't think that's what they got out of the trial."

"Oh, what do you think they got out of it?"

"That you are a strong, independent woman who isn't going to be pushed around by the patriarchy."

Reg coughed. She checked the lace on her other shoe and stood up.

They still didn't feel right. "Well, I guess you got that part right. You wouldn't happen to be psychic, would you?"

"No, just very sensitive."

She looked at him and shook her head. She wasn't sure that a sensitive man was what she was looking for. Damon's grin back at her was too mischievous to take his words seriously. He didn't consider himself a sensitive man; he was just teasing her.

"Oh, you're a handful," she told him.

Damon's grin got wider. "You are a psychic!"

Reg snorted. "Okay, why don't we play? I want to get this over with."

"Really? I'm hurt. If you knew how much fun this is, you wouldn't be in such a hurry to get out of here."

"Prove it."

"Why don't you go first?" he offered, motioning to their alley.

Reg looked at the other bowlers playing nearby. "Since I'm the newbie here, why don't you show me how it's done? I want to see your technique."

"Ladies first."

"Age before beauty," Reg countered.

"Oh," Damon put his hand over his heart. "What makes you think I'm older than you are?"

"From what I've seen so far, all of the witches and warlocks are older than they look. So I'm assuming you're at least seventy."

He laughed. But he picked up his bowling ball and didn't argue.

Reg watched him closely as he strode forward, swung back, and then delivered the ball in a smooth forward motion, his leg jutting out behind him at an angle as he squatted low to the floor. He knocked down a few of the pins but did not get a strike. Reg tried to put herself into his body as he took another turn, trying to feel what it must be like, how each action would naturally flow into the next. The rest of the pins went down, so according to the rules he had given Reg, that meant it was her turn.

She picked up her ball and held it in one hand. Could she connect psychically to a bowling ball? Lately, when she'd been angry, things had been breaking or falling around her. She still wasn't sure that she believed it was anything to do with her mood, but if the others were right and she could affect physical objects telekinetically, than why not to direct a bowling ball down the lane?

She took a deep breath and tried to imitate Damon's approach and release. When she reached the line and released the ball, it went directly into the gutter and rolled down to the end. Reg watched it in dismay.

Damon laughed. "Don't look so heartbroken. It was only your first try."

"Yeah, but... I thought... I just thought I would be better than that."

"Just get a feel for it first. Don't try to use perfect form; just get a feel for what it feels like to roll it."

Reg went to the ball return machine and waited for her ball to pop back up. The midnight blue ball returned and she picked it up.

"I get another try, right?"

"Yes, one more this frame."

"And then it's your turn."

"Right."

Reg tried again, this time not trying to imitate Damon's form, but just to get the ball closer to the center instead of throwing it directly into the gutter. She tripped over the toe of one shoe and just about did a faceplant before reaching the line.

She dropped the ball with a crash that made everyone turn and look at her, and it didn't even go down the lane, but rolled back to her feet and looked up at her like a lost puppy. Reg covered her face.

"Can I leave now?"

"No, you can't leave. You're just getting warmed up. Don't worry about what anyone else thinks. This is your first time. You're going to be just fine once you get settled in."

Reg groaned and picked up the ball, eyeing the people on either side of her that were glaring like she had intentionally broken the rules by dropping her ball. She didn't try to approach the alley again, she just threw it down the lane, making it crash again as it hit the polished wood floor, and it rolled most of the way down the alley before falling into the gutter.

"Can I just give up now?"

"Be patient. Don't be so hard on yourself."

"I don't like this game."

"You don't know yet. You've only bowled one frame."

"I know already."

Damon took his turn, getting a strike. He sat back down before she even had a chance to sit down.

"How long have you been doing this?" Reg questioned. "It isn't fair to bring me to something that you're already a pro at."

"I'm not a pro. I just do it for fun now and then. I'm not in a league or anything."

"Is this where you bring all of your girlfriends on a first date?"

He cocked his head, looking at her. "Believe it or not, I don't date very much. And you're the first girl that I've brought here... at least in a couple of years."

"Then why me? Why not take me somewhere else instead of humiliating me?"

"Are you really feeling that badly about it?"

Reg rolled her eyes. "No. I'm dramatizing—a little. I don't like being shown up like this. If I'd said that I liked to bowl or was good at bowling... then I'd forgive you for bringing me here. But it seems a little... show-offy to bring me here just to show me how good you are when I'm so awful at it."

"You're really not that bad. You've only bowled one frame."

Reg picked up her ball and walked toward the lane.

"If you still hate it by the end, I promise I won't try to bring you back here," Damon promised.

"Yeah. I heard you."

Reg retrieved her ball. She looked at the lane, closed her eyes, and rolled the ball. Nothing bad happened. She waited a few seconds before opening her eyes, just in time to see the ball hit the last pin on the right-hand side of the triangle.

"There you go!" Damon encouraged. "That wasn't so bad, was it? You knocked one down."

"Just one," Reg groused. But secretly, she was encouraged. She had managed to hit one pin without even looking. It hadn't gone into the gutter every time. Maybe there was some hope for her after all.

She again closed her eyes and released the ball. It wobbled back and forth down the lane, weaving this way and that until it reached the end, and it knocked down the front pin and a couple of others.

"See that?" Damon crowed. "You're a natural. Center pin."

Reg shook her head, but was pleased. At least she hadn't put every ball in the gutter. Damon took his turn, not getting a strike, but ending up knocking down all of the pins except for the outside two. He pouted dramatically, but she didn't feel at all bad for him.

Reg picked up her ball again.

"Do you want me to show you the proper form?" Damon offered, approaching her without waiting for her answer, and putting his arms around her to readjust her position. Reg flailed, knocking him in the gut with her ball and then dropping it on the ends of his shoes as she pulled out of his grasp. Damon went white and gasped for breath while trying to lift both feet at the same time to clutch at his toes. He ended up on his butt on the worn, dirty carpet, holding the ends of his shoes and drawing in a big, wheezing breath. Reg was horrified, but at the same time angry that he had touched her after she had already warned him once.

She bent down to talk to him, aware that everyone around them was laughing or watching her closely, eager to see what was going to happen next.

"Are you okay?" She offered him a hand to help him up, but then pulled it away before he could take it. "I'm sorry, I didn't mean to…"

He rubbed his toes through the shoes, hunched over to protect his stomach. "No, my fault," he said in a strained voice. "You did tell me once already…"

"I know, but still, I didn't mean to hit you or to drop my ball."

"It's your turn. Why don't you go ahead and take your turn?"

Reg turned to look for her ball and picked it up. "Really, I didn't mean to wreck everything…"

"I think maybe next time we'll do something else. Something that doesn't include a built-in weapon." Damon groaned and pushed himself back up to his feet.

"Are you okay? I mean, really?"

"I'll be fine. Just a small bowling mishap. Happens all the time."

"If this is what it's always like, then maybe we shouldn't do it again," Reg agreed.

Damon gave a weak laugh. Reg looked at the pins and walked forward, not even aiming, just wanting to get her turn over with and be done with the night. The faster she could finish, the sooner they could be out of there, away from all of the prying eyes. The ball made its way straight down the alley and hit the front pin. Reg was turning away, then stopped and watched as they all fell down. She glanced aside at Damon, then back at the pins as they all toppled over and the machine lowered to reset the pins.

She blinked, and the pins were all upright again.

"Your turn," she said to Damon, trying to sound casual. He looked at her; one eyebrow raised inquiringly.

"You have to take your frame first," he reminded her.

Reg looked at the pins and at the screen showing the scoring. She was going to tell him that it was her turn, she'd just gotten her first strike, and then she realized that her ball was still in her hand. She looked down at it and frowned, trying to reconcile what she was experiencing with what had just happened.

"What the...? But I bowled. I got a strike..."

"You got a strike?" Damon repeated. "I think I would have noticed that."

"But... I did."

He motioned at the scoring screen. Reg signed in exasperation. He hadn't been paying attention, and for some reason, the scoring machine had missed it. Her first strike, and it had gone unnoticed. Except that didn't explain why she was still holding the ball in her hand. If she had already bowled her frame, then it should have been in the return slot, and Damon should have been stepping forward to take his turn.

She shook her head and stepped forward to roll the ball again. She didn't want Damon thinking she was a complete lunatic, so she didn't argue it any further. It must have been some brain glitch or deja vu.

Not deja vu, but prescience. She had seen what was going to happen next.

Reg swung her arm and released the ball and watched it blast down the center of the lane and hit the front pin. But it knocked down only a couple of pins, and the rest remained standing. Reg sighed and shook her head. If that was the level of her prescience, she'd better not be laying any bets based on her visions of the future.

"Good job," Damon praised. "That was a nice throw. It was just a quirk that it wasn't a strike. Sometimes that happens. Nothing you can do about it. Try again, maybe you'll get a spare."

Reg looked at the pins standing on either side and shook her head. Not likely. How was she supposed to hit pins on both sides at once? She'd have to bowl down one side the first time and then down the other side. If she was lucky, she could wipe them all out in two more shots. But she wasn't expecting to get lucky.

She retrieved her ball and tried once more. She tried to aim it just left of center where most of the pins were, but the ball just went straight through the hole that she had created the first time. Reg shook her head. Damon didn't try any encouraging statements this time. She had missed her shot at a spare. There seemed to be an awful lot of technical language for something as simple as rolling a ball into some pins.

She flashed back to bowling as a child on one of those youth group field trips. She could see one of the supervisors who had escorted them there helping her with her stance, reaching out as Damon had to readjust her positioning. His hands on her shoulders, brushing her legs, encouraging her to pull in her belly. His warm body pressing up against hers as he gave her one last squeeze and encouraged her to go for it.

Reg felt suddenly sick. She turned and ran for the restrooms. She had seen the ladies room next to the shoe rental counter when they had been getting everything they needed.

"Reg?" Damon called after her, his voice concerned.

But she didn't care what he thought of her taking off like that and didn't have the time to stop and explain what was going on. She just ran for the bathroom without looking back.

CHAPTER FOUR

She had thought that she was going to throw up, the pain that had seized her in the gut had been so intense. But once she made it to the bathroom stall and hovered there, the feeling passed, and she was just anxious and uncertain. She didn't want to throw up, but she felt like she wouldn't be able to get rid of the memory if she didn't. It would keep pressing in on her, wrecking her night. She didn't want to be there bowling. Why had she agreed to in the first place? Who did Damon think he was, dictating that they had to play a game that Reg knew nothing about and he was so expert at? He was just showing off. He was doing some kind of macho positioning thing, showing his superiority, and she didn't need to play along with him like that. He knew her feelings about being pushed around by a man. He had first met her as she defended herself and explained what had happened between her and that predator, Corvin Hunter.

Hunter was a good name for him. Reg didn't know why she'd never thought about that before. He was a hunter, just like his name suggested. He looked for those with powers, and he hunted them down so that he could take it from them. She should have been warned just by his name.

Damon. Did his name mean something too? Should she know by what his parents had named him what kind of a person he would grow up to be? Did Damon mean demon? Was he black and evil inside, and she was supposed to be warned by his name? She drew a blank on his last name and she hadn't brought the business card with her to check it.

It had been a bad idea to come out on a date. She obviously wasn't up to it. Maybe the nightmares she had been having signified that she wasn't safe in Black Sands. She should leave. Or at least, not have anything else to do with warlocks. There had to be plenty of non-magical people in Black Sands. Why did she have to pick someone who had powers?

Reg stayed in the bathroom stall for an extended time, waiting for the pain and the profuse sweating to go away. She didn't want to go back out and have to face Damon until she was sure she was settled down and calm again. She didn't want to play the part of a hysterical woman. She wasn't *hysterical*. She took the flashback as a sign that she should not be dating Damon. And she should not be bowling. She should have listened to her instincts in the beginning and refused. She shouldn't let someone talk her into something she didn't want to do just because she wanted to please him and not cause a social scene.

Next time, she would cause the scene. After all, that was what she had ended up doing anyway. She had ended up attracting more attention to her and Damon than she would have if she'd just insisted that she wanted to do something else.

Finally, Reg flushed the unused toilet and walked back out to the sinks, where she washed her hands and splashed water on her face, then sponged it off with a scratchy paper towel. She was just fine. She was perfectly calm. There was nothing to be concerned about. She would tell Damon it was a mistake and she was going to go home. The date was a failure. How was she to have known that without trying? Sometimes a person just had to try and fail.

She took one more deep breath and then walked out of the restroom.

She had thought that he would still be in their bowling lane, but Damon was hovering near the bathrooms. His attention was distracted the moment that she exited the bathroom, looking over at something at the shoe rental table, but then he turned his eyes back toward the ladies' room and saw that she was out. He hurried toward her.

"Reg? Are you okay? Are you not feeling well?"

"No, I'm not." She latched on to the excuse. "I should go home. Sorry to wreck our evening together, but…"

"I was having a good time. I'm sorry you're not feeling very well."

He was having a good time? Getting hit in the gut with the ball and having her drop it on his toes? Or watching her toddler-like struggles to figure out how to roll a ball down an alley? Did he get off on watching her fail, on exulting over how superior he was to her at the game? It was a stupid game, anyway.

"I think I should go home."

His mouth was turned down in a frown. "Do you want to go out somewhere? Maybe we should get you something to eat. You may just not be feeling well because you're playing on an empty stomach. We could go out and get something to eat. Or we could eat here," he motioned to the commissary. "I was going to take you out somewhere to eat afterward, so I didn't order any snacks, but we could have something here. We could have a snack here so that you were feeling up to bowling the rest of the set, and then we could go out somewhere fancier to eat…"

"I really don't want to play anymore. I don't think I can."

He looked disappointed, but he nodded and didn't argue with her about it. Reg was momentarily angry with herself. Now she was playing the part of the weak female and putting him into the role of protector? Why would she do that, when he was the one who had made her feel the way she did? He wasn't an innocent party, who just happened to be there when she got sick. He was the reason that she wasn't feeling well.

In fact, she felt just fine. The initial nausea had passed. She just didn't want to bowl anymore.

It wouldn't teach him anything if he thought that she was just sick and that everything had been going fine between them. The next time, he would just choose mini golf, and he would put his arms around her to readjust her stance, and she would have to jab the golf club into his gut to make him back off.

"Look, I'm not enjoying myself," she told him, making her voice strong. She had the right to her feelings and didn't have to cave to his just because he was a man and she didn't want him to think she was a witch. "I'd just like to go home."

His eyes widened, and she could read how startled he was. He'd really thought that she was having fun, or that she would have at least changed her mind about bowling by the end of the night.

"Oh. I didn't realize… I thought that…" He tried to find a way to put it back on her, to indicate that it was her fault for not communicating with him. But she had said from the start that she didn't want to bowl and that she wasn't comfortable there.

Reg bent down to untie her shoes, and slid them off. She was glad to get out of them. They felt oppressive to her. She knew how it felt to have to strip off her clothes and put on a uniform. How it was supposed to make her feel vulnerable and uncertain and to make her more likely to do what she was told by whatever authority was over her. Stripping off her shoes felt like taking back her control. She wasn't that little girl who'd had to stand there and let the supervisor put his hands all over her under the guise of helping her bowl. She had a voice, and she could use it.

"I don't like it," she told Damon in a quiet, firm voice, "and I'm not going to stay here."

The music and other noise of the bowling alley were too loud. Reg looked around in irritation. She just wanted quiet. The piped-in music stopped abruptly. All of the bowlers stopped talking and looked around to see what was going on. Reg could hear someone behind the commissary counter calling out to whoever was in charge of the music equipment to fix the problem.

"I'm leaving," she told Damon.

"Reg—" He reached out to catch her shoulder and stop her, then froze and didn't touch her. "Let me take you out to eat. If that's okay. Bowling was a stupid idea. I'm sorry. You told me you didn't want to do it and I should have just listened. Okay? I screwed up."

"Well… I don't know…"

"Let me make it up to you. You can choose the place. Where do you want to eat? We can even go out to the city if there's somewhere nice you'd like to go."

Not that Black Sands didn't have some nice restaurants. But the city did offer more options.

"Okay. If you're sure you still want to hang out with me. Your night hasn't exactly been all fun and games either."

He looked surprised that she should suggest such a thing. As if punching him in the gut and dropping a bowling ball on his toes hadn't made any impression on him.

"No, I'm having a good time. I mean… I don't mean it that way. I'm not having a good time if you're not happy. But I could be having a good time. If you were happy." He trailed off, knowing it must sound pretty lame.

Reg rolled her eyes and laughed. "Let's just get our shoes on and go."

They retrieved their shoes and returned their rented balls and shoes, advising the ticket person that their lane was available for use. She frowned at them, then shrugged and cleared the scoring screen.

They went back and forth on what restaurant to go to. Reg wasn't familiar with a lot of the eating establishments. She went to The Crystal Bowl, which was where Sarah frequently went for dinner and where she occasionally saw Corvin or others she knew from the magical community. And Corvin had once taken her to the Eagle Arms, but that was a fancy, expensive place, and Reg didn't want to suggest that Damon should take her somewhere so highbrow. They probably required reservations to be made two weeks ahead of time or some significant name-dropping in order to get a table.

"What do you like?" Damon asked. "Seafood? Burgers? Italian?"

"I'm pretty good with anything." Reg shrugged. Having been on the skids from time to time, she would eat pretty much anything that was put in front of her. After rejecting Damon's choice of activity, she didn't want to be pushy on the restaurant choice.

"There's a cool little diner on the west side," Damon said. "They have an all-day breakfast menu and make great waffles."

"Sure, that sounds good," Reg agreed. She could handle a waffle and syrup piled with strawberries and whipped cream. It was like having dessert for dinner.

"Yeah? You're sure?" Damon checked.

Reg nodded. "I'm sure. Waffles would be good."

So he took her to Wickedly Waffle, a charming 50's-style diner that was popular, but not too busy. Reg opened the menu and was pleased to see that nothing was in cursive writing and there were plenty of pictures as well as the written descriptions. She preferred not to have to read an entire book to figure out what she wanted to eat. The breakfast section of the menu was a few pages long, and Reg found what she was looking for, a picture of a waffle smothered in berries and cream. Damon took longer to choose what he wanted, flipping back and forth between pages. And it sounded like he'd already been there enough times to know what he liked.

Once they had both made their choices, they relaxed and made an effort to start the evening over fresh.

"So, have you always lived in Black Sands?" Reg asked Damon.

"Most of my life. I wasn't born here, but my family moved here when I was just a kid."

"And I don't know how this works… is everyone in your family magical, or…?"

"We all have certain gifts… things that come more naturally. But not everyone has decided to pursue them. My mother was always very involved with her coven. My dad wasn't big on developing his gifts. I have five older brothers and sisters, and I'm the only one who decided to go all-out in pursuing my powers."

Reg nodded, fascinated by this little window into the world of magic and how people chose to live with their gifts when they knew about them from birth, or whenever they knew that they had gifts. Out of everyone in Damon's family, only two chose to be part of the magical community. She would have thought that anyone with paranormal powers would be interested in developing them. At least, if they lived in a place like Black Sands where there was a big magical community. For Reg, growing up without knowing anyone else who had that kind of gift, she hadn't understood her abilities and it had been safer to be like everybody else. Was the same true in a place like Black Sands? Was it still best for children to lie low to keep from being bullied or abused? Despite the extensive network of magical persons, was it still something that was frowned upon?

"So is it impolite of me to ask you about your gifts?" she asked tentatively. "I haven't worked out the etiquette yet."

"I don't mind you asking. But I don't share very much. I work private security and, as you saw at Hunter's hearing, I do have the ability to deal with minor magical curses and psychic phenomena. I'm good at calming people down, deescalating violence. Abilities that have led me to the position that I'm in."

Reg nodded slowly. She ran her finger around the rim of her glass, thinking about that.

He had been able to hold off her angry reactions to Corvin and to calm her down enough to let the hearing continue, though it had been pretty much over by the time Reg blew a gasket. He had kept her feeling calm as it came to an end and had walked her out to her car. She had felt good being around him.

But what about bowling? He had not been able to keep her calm throughout their game and had not been able to convince her to stay and finish. Was that because he hadn't used his powers on her, or because she had been able to overcome them? She looked at him speculatively.

"It isn't polite to use your powers on someone without their permission," Damon said as if he were reading her thoughts. "It's different when I'm at work. Kind of like it's okay for a cop to arrest you and put you in handcuffs when you've broken the law, but if he breaks out the handcuffs when you're having an intimate moment, then he'd better have your permission before he slaps them on."

Reg laughed. She liked the picture that came into her head as he described it.

"So if I wanted you to help me to calm down, you could do that? But you wouldn't do it without my permission unless I was causing a stink at an event you were working?"

"Yes."

She took a sip of her water, thinking about that. "And what Corvin does, taking someone's powers away for his own use, that's why he's supposed to get his victim's consent before doing it."

"Yes. Exactly," Damon agreed, studying her with his dark, serious eyes.

"But who would ever consent to him taking their powers? No one would if they really knew what he was doing."

"I'm just the security guard at these things. I don't have to make the decision about whether someone is guilty or not."

"You don't like Corvin, though, do you?"

"Why would I like someone who takes advantage of women, even if it is his inborn nature?"

Reg couldn't help liking the guy, even if he had made her bowl. She smiled at him and took another sip of her water, hoping that the waffles would arrive soon. "So you think that Corvin could control himself, if he wanted to, and not take advantage of women?"

"I wouldn't like to speculate. I don't have anyone in my family like him. But I do know that in my family, we have each chosen whether we wanted to pursue our magical nature or whether to live normal lives."

"You think he had that choice too?"

"I don't know." He shrugged. "It's not my problem. Whether he did or whether he didn't, the results are still the same, he preys on women and I don't have to accept that."

Reg's stomach rumbled. She put her hand over it, hoping that Damon hadn't been able to hear it.

"Well, I guess we should have planned dinner before anything else," Damon observed. "You should have told me you were hungry."

Reg looked away, embarrassed. But the conversation made her think more about Corvin.

"I felt Corvin's hunger," she told Damon. "Two times. And it's…" She shook her head, trying to find the words. "It's overwhelming. It's like a hole eating right through him. I don't see how anyone could ignore something like that. That's why I don't know what to think of him. He's not just a predator… he's human too, and he has human emotions, and he has this driving need to fill his hunger. I don't think I'd be able to deny it."

"But you don't have to. And neither do I. That's his curse. Not ours. We all have our own troubles. No reason we should have to be responsible for his too."

"No, I don't mean that. I just mean…"

"You feel sorry for him."

"A little, okay. Yes. It's true. It's a dreadful feeling."

"But he might have just projected that onto you. You don't know that's what he was feeling."

"He couldn't give it to me if he didn't feel it, could he?"

Damon raised an eyebrow. "Couldn't he?"

"Well… I don't know. I don't know enough about magic or the way it all works…"

"I don't know much about psychic abilities. That's your wheelhouse. But I think he could make you think he's worse off than he is."

Reg hadn't thought of that. She had just assumed that what she had felt had been the true state of how Corvin felt. And not only on that day, but from one day to the next, always on the brink of starvation because he wasn't allowed to feast on anybody without their permission.

"Have you found Hunter to be… an honest and open person?" Damon prodded.

Reg shook her head, laughing, even though it wasn't really funny. "An honest and open person? No. Definitely not. He's always hiding something, holding something back. He's always trying to convince me to do something I don't want to, and he uses every bit of guile to do that. The time that I actually gave him permission…"

Damon waited for her to finish the thought. Blood rushed to Reg's face until it felt like it was on fire. She didn't want to finish. She had no intention of telling him about that experience. Her tongue had gotten ahead of her brain. Something she could not allow to happen.

"I… I don't want to talk about that."

Damon shrugged. His eyes were curious, but he had to understand why she wouldn't want to talk about such an intimate subject and to tell him exactly what he had done to get her cooperation. Another wave of heat went over Reg's face, and she took a drink of water to cool it. It might work better if she splashed it on her face. She was going to turn a permanent beet red if she kept it up.

The waitress arrived with their dinners. Or their breakfasts. Whichever they were, they provided a welcome distraction from Reg's embarrassment. She exclaimed over her waffles with rather more enthusiasm than would typically be expected, and while the waitress smiled and nodded, there was a little crease between her eyebrows as she looked at Reg, obviously wondering what planet she came from.

Reg remembered how Marian had tried to influence her feelings on more than one occasion, and tried to send reassuring feelings toward the waitress. The crease smoothed out. The woman nodded once more and left them to their food.

"Sorry. I'm feeling a little… off balance tonight," Reg tried to explain, as she sank her fork into the waffles and consumed her first few bites.

Damon appeared to be enjoying his stack of pancakes topped with a fried egg. He shrugged his shoulders. "I don't think you have anything to apologize for. You haven't done anything wrong or inappropriate."

"No?" She looked at him for reassurance.

Damon shook his head. "Would I lie to you?"

"I barely even know you. I would guess that if you had a good enough motive, you would."

"Well, I'm not lying to you, okay? Try to relax and enjoy yourself. You're... trying too hard."

"Am I?" Reg thought about it and decided he was probably right. Why was she trying so hard to impress him and make him think that they were a good match? What if he wasn't a good match for her? She didn't want to end up caught in a relationship that didn't work. She'd rather know early in the relationship if they were not right for each other. If she wanted to know whether or not they were compatible, the best policy was to be herself.

"Okay. I'll try to calm down."

She did her best to relax and enjoy herself, but that nagging feeling of foreboding was still sitting in the back of her mind, dark and cold.

CHAPTER FIVE

The rest of the evening had been as enjoyable as it could be with the feeling of dread still probing at the edges of her consciousness and with the poor start it had gotten off to. Reg tried to forget about the childhood memories and her anxiety over the possibility that Damon would try to magic her as Corvin had. She tried to pretend that it was just a regular date like she might have been on before she moved to Black Sands. But she found herself trying to read Damon's face and body language, to see his aura, and to feel the feelings that he was projecting. It was hard to be relaxed when anything could happen. She had no idea what to expect from him.

Eventually, they had finished eating dinner, had drunk their after-dinner coffee, and it was time for them to go their separate directions. Reg had insisted on arriving in her own car because she didn't want to be put in the position of having to invite Damon into her cottage or to send him away. She didn't want an awkward doorstep kiss or expectations.

Damon insisted on walking her to her car, as he had the day of the hearing. Reg tried to remember how she had felt with him beside her, how she had been happy to have the company and someone who seemed to be on her side instead of siding with Corvin's accusations. At least someone had stood by her.

It was dark. Reg felt all the more worried as they moved from one circle of light pooled beneath a streetlight to the next. She was in an unfamiliar neighborhood with an unfamiliar man, and it was darker than she would have liked.

The oppressive feeling was getting closer and thicker, pressing in on her like a wolf pack circling in the darkness, just outside the pool of light. Without even thinking, she grasped Damon's arm and moved closer to him, seeking safety in someone bigger and stronger than she was. He put his hand comfortably over hers for a moment, nice and warm and secure. He reached to put one arm around her shoulders, but paused before setting it down.

"Is it okay? Do you mind if I...?"

Reg grasped his hand and wrapped his arm around her like it was a warm scarf. She nestled against his side and looked around. He would think she was a coward for being so nervous. There was no one around them who was a danger to her. A few people walking on their own, a few walking with a friend or partner. No one who looked the least bit threatening.

So why did she feel so threatened?

Reg forced herself to separate from Damon when they reached her car.

"It's been a nice night." She hoped that her smile looked sincere. It didn't feel natural. It had been a nice dinner, but not spectacular. She didn't get swept away by him like she did by Corvin, but that was a good thing. She didn't want to lose herself or to lose control of the situation.

"Sorry about the bowling," Damon apologized, moving a little closer to her again and trying to put his arms around her waist or his hands on her hips or some other intimate gesture that would seem natural. But he wasn't sure how she was going to take it, so it was awkward. Reg took both of his hands in hers. Friendly, but not too friendly.

"Yeah... sorry about that. Just... some bad memories. I don't think... I don't think I ever want to go bowling again."

He gazed into her eyes. He did have nice eyes. He was taller than she, with a five o'clock shadow that gave him a rugged, manly look, but it was his eyes that were the most striking.

She could see herself getting involved with him. Ending the date with a kiss of promise instead of just holding hands and saying empty words. She could almost feel his lips on hers.

It was only with an effort that Reg was able to pull herself away from the imagined scene and see what was really before her. He had a slight cleft in his chin. And beautiful dark eyes.

"We'll do something else next time," he promised. "You can tell me what you like to do. No more bowling."

She sensed, though, his sadness at this promise. What emotional attachment did he have with bowling? Maybe he had gone with his parents as a boy, or maybe that was where his parents had met and fallen in love, and he saw it as something fun and romantic rather than a pointless game. She didn't let his regret change her mind.

"I'll call you."

She let go of his hands and turned to unlock her door and get in. As soon as her back was turned, she sensed a shift in the atmosphere. Danger loomed up so strongly that she whirled around, hands up to defend herself. Damon was just standing there and stepped back in alarm at her sudden movement.

Reg darted a glance back and forth, looking behind him and in the periphery. Something that set off her internal alarm. There was some danger close by. But it didn't seem to be Damon himself.

"What is it?" Damon asked.

"Something... I don't know what it is." She searched for some sign of it. "Something in the shadows."

Reg couldn't help pressing her foot to the gas a little bit too hard. She knew she was speeding and hoped that she wouldn't get pulled over by the cops, but she was more worried about what was behind her than about the police. If the police came, then maybe their weapons and lights would scare off whatever was behind her.

As a child, she'd been pursued by a nameless darkness more than once. It followed her from one home to another. She thought that if she moved around enough, she would leave it behind, and eventually, she had. She had always expected it to return, but it never did.

But it was back.

She looked in the rear-view mirror, watching for any glimpse of something dark. There had to be others in the magical community who could see or feel it. She couldn't be the only one.

Unless she were going crazy. Maybe the stress of the last few months was getting to her. Her brain couldn't handle all of the crazy stuff anymore and she had cracked. Now she was seeing bogeymen where there wasn't anything. They would end up locking her up. She would no longer be in control of her own life and they could keep her there for years, until they decided she had been cured.

There was nothing unusual in the rear-view mirror. No shapes in the darkness. Just that feeling of dread.

It only took fifteen minutes to get home. Reg didn't see anything or get pulled over. The feeling didn't go away, but she didn't feel like it was quite as imminent. Maybe it had stayed behind with Damon. Or maybe it had tried to follow her but hadn't been able to keep up with the car. Spirits could travel long distances, but if it were something tangible, it might not be able to move quickly without a vehicle.

Damon.

Demon.

Could demons drive?

Damon wasn't evil. He was just a warlock; one who had been nice to her, but who had terrible taste in his choice of recreational activities. He wasn't a dark wizard, trying to catch her in his net of evil magic.

Was he?

CHAPTER SIX

S he sat in her car for a few minutes before getting out, looking around and watching for any unusual activity. Feeling her way ahead of her, as she had learned during the past few investigations. There was no need to run straight into trouble. Not when she could psychically scan Sarah's house and the guest cottage in the back yard to make sure that there were no monsters or demons there waiting for her.

Sarah was in her house. No one was in Reg's. She could sense no traps.

Reg got out, locked the doors of the car as soon as she was out, and walked at a brisk pace around the house and down the path in the backyard to her door. She flicked her eyes around before going in her door, looking for the black cat. But it did not appear to have returned.

She put her hand on the cottage door and reached out once more before putting her key in the lock and letting herself in. Nothing. Starlight was there, snoozing peacefully. No one else. No disturbances.

She swung the door open silently and reached over to turn on the inside lights before stepping in. Nothing appeared to have been touched. She pulled the door shut behind her, locking it securely. She often left it unlocked for Sarah until she went to bed, but not on a night there was a nameless shadow skulking around Black Sands. Sarah had a key. Or she could ring the doorbell. Reg didn't know whether Sarah could unlock doors with magic; she'd never had a reason to ask. Were there practitioners who

NIGHT OF NINE TAILS

were able to unlock doors without a key? Maybe her cottage wasn't as secure as she had thought.

But Sarah had set wards for Reg's protection. Hopefully, they were strong enough to keep out the dark force.

Starlight jumped off of Reg's bed with a soft thump and wandered out to the kitchen, where he meowed inquiringly at Reg, wondering what had taken her so long to get home and why she seemed so disturbed.

"It's nothing," Reg said. "I'm sure it's nothing. Just letting my imagination get away from me."

Starlight looked at her sharply, as if she had said something worrisome instead of something reassuring. Reg went to the fridge, even though she was not hungry after the meal at the diner. She was just looking for something to soothe the stress away. She'd had plenty of sugar and fat, but maybe if there was chocolate… Failing that, she might try one of Sarah's soothing teas. Maybe that would settle her down enough that she would be able to sleep without dreams.

Starlight jumped up on the island counter behind her. Reg turned and looked at him.

"You know you're not supposed to be up there."

She reached toward the tap to turn on the water and flick it at him. Starlight gave a cross yowl. She looked at him, sensing something more than his usual impatience with her. She looked at the island, where her appointment book waited for her. Starlight pawed at something underneath it. Reg slid the appointment book to the side to reveal a few flyers. Sarah was still trying to get her to go to community events so she could meet more of the Black Sands residents and be more involved. Reg wasn't sure she wanted to be more involved. She seemed to have enough on her plate already.

She looked through the flyers to make sure there was nothing important. One of them was not advertising an event or special sale, but had a picture of a black cat photocopied onto it. Reg scanned the 'lost cat' headline, the brief description of a cat named Nicole, and a few details about the area she might be in and three different phone numbers at which to reach Nicole's owner.

Black cat, female, no markings, no tattoos or identification. Why had Nicole's owner let the cat out without any tags or identification? That wasn't very responsible pet ownership.

Of course, Starlight had escaped not that long ago, let out by Sarah when Reg was away. He hadn't had any tags either. Though he had been tattooed by the animal shelter in case he was ever brought in again.

"Nicole," she said to Starlight. "Is that your friend's name? Are you looking for Nicole?"

He sat looking at her. Reg sighed. "I suppose I should call in the morning and let them know that she's been around here. But I haven't seen her lately, so I don't know whether that will be of any help."

Starlight flicked his ears and didn't have anything to say about it one way or the other.

Reg tossed and turned, trying to find a comfortable position in the bed, to turn off her brain's constant replay of the date with Damon, and to push away the feeling of darkness and dread that threatened to overwhelm her. She'd had two cups of one of Sarah's soothing teas, but that just made her have to run to the toilet after an hour of waiting for it to have some effect. She wanted desperately to get to sleep and to escape the oppressive feelings, but it just wasn't helping.

Eventually, she gave up. She couldn't bear lying in bed and trying to shut everything out. It made her body ache and her head throb. She could be sitting up watching a late movie, or posting to community websites to drum up more clients. She could bake a cake. Anything was better than trying to sleep when it was far beyond her ability to shut off her brain and find rest.

She was a psychic. She did midnight seances and readings. She was used to being up late. So why bother going to bed so early? She could wait until two or three and try again when she was suitably tired.

Starlight made a noise as she got up out of bed, a soft, startled purr-meow. He was in the window again, looking out into the garden for Nicole, the missing cat. When she walked out to the living room, he jumped down and followed her. He went over to the fridge and rubbed against it, suggesting that things would be better if she made them both a midnight snack. Reg resisted at first. She turned on the TV and surfed through a few channels. The TV was small and she rarely ever used it. She kept busy with other things, and when she wanted to watch something, she often watched on her phone screen, which was even smaller.

Starlight kept calling to her and, eventually, Reg got up and joined him in the kitchen.

"Don't you know that anything you eat this late at night goes straight to your hips?" she demanded. "Your body doesn't have a chance to burn it off before you go to sleep, so it goes straight to storage. We'll both get as fat as pigs."

Starlight was a nocturnal animal. He wasn't going to sleep. He was at the active part of his day. So why shouldn't he eat at night? Feeding him in the morning before his sleep was more likely to make him fat, if she were to follow her own logic.

"Fine, fine, let's see what's in here," Reg conceded.

She was trying not to eat too much high-calorie food. She ate out a lot and too much fast food did not do her body good. But the picture of a nice chocolate cake was stuck in her mind, and she wanted something sweet and calorific.

She hadn't had dessert at the restaurant.

But who wanted dessert after a pile of syrup, strawberries, and whipped cream? And a waffle was more like cake than a sandwich. When she thought about it, she'd had dessert for dinner. So her snack should be something savory and healthy. Exactly what she didn't want. She went through the containers in the fridge and pulled out the remains of a fried chicken breast sandwich. She removed the meat from the soggy bun and put it on the cutting board to cut into strips for Starlight. He purred and rubbed around her legs, opening his mouth so that his purr filled the room.

"Okay, okay, I know, you like my choice," Reg laughed, looking down at him. She swiftly cut the chicken breast up for him and put it into his bowl. She licked off her fingers and watched him. That was one problem solved. She still didn't know what she was going to eat. She didn't have any cake, but that was what she was craving. She looked in the fridge once more, but no chocolate cake had magically appeared there and none of the other offerings appealed to her.

"Why don't I ever buy cake?" she groused aloud.

Starlight looked up from his chicken, then went back to chawing it down.

Reg grabbed an apple and closed the fridge.

An apple wasn't what she wanted. But it was what she had, so it would have to do. She sat down again and looked at the TV.

News. Yuck.

She started flipping channels again. A late-night black and white zombie movie. No. A sports station showing—believe it or not—a bowling tournament.

No.

She kept going, looking for something to occupy her mind until she could get tired enough to fall asleep in spite of her anxiety.

Maybe she should see a doctor. She'd had anxiety pills prescribed in the past and she knew it wouldn't be hard to get them again. But she didn't want pills. She wanted the feeling to go away without any pills. She wanted to be normal. She always felt so defective when a doctor suggested that she needed medication to control her anxiety or her wild, runaway-train imagination. She was normal. She just happened to have a highly active brain.

The sound of her phone ringing just about sent her rocketing out of her seat. Who would be calling her so late at night? Yes, she was often up into the wee hours of the morning, but etiquette usually dictated that people call closer to regular business hours. She wasn't running a psychic hotline that people could call late at night to get a reading. Though that wasn't such a bad idea if she were going to be staying up late every night. She could refuse to schedule anything in the morning, and shift her schedule so that she was always sleeping in the morning instead of at night. Maybe she wouldn't feel so anxious about sleep if the sun were up and she didn't have to worry about shadowy shapes in the darkness.

It was as bad as when she had been a kid and thought that there were monsters under the bed. Or ghosts. Or vampires. Or some other supernatural but equally frightening force.

The phone rang again, and Reg jumped again. She knew it was going to keep ringing, so why would she be startled that it did?

Reg picked it up from the side table and looked at the screen.

Corvin Hunter.

What was he calling her about? Especially in the middle of the night? She never encouraged him to call her. And she had certainly never called him at that hour.

Well, maybe she had encouraged him to call. In the early days, before she knew what he really was. That the attraction she felt to him was part of his powers, not just the usual chemical attraction to a handsome man.

She swiped to answer the call. There was no reason she should want to talk to Corvin Hunter, knowing how dangerous he was, but she wanted someone to talk to, and he was available. He would distract her from the unsettled feelings.

"Hello?"

"Regina." The way that he said her name, correctly pronouncing it Reh-JEE-nah rather than like the Canadian city, never failed to send a shiver of pleasure through her. Even though he wasn't in the same room as she and therefore couldn't send his rose-scented pheromones and charms in her direction, she still felt the little tug at her heartstrings, like watching a Hallmark commercial.

"What are you doing calling me so late?" Reg demanded, keeping her voice stern, not letting him know how close she was to turning to mush just at hearing his voice.

"What are you doing up so late?"

"I could be doing a seance, you know. You could be interrupting something very important."

"I assume that if you were doing a seance, you would have your ringer turned off."

That wasn't a bad idea, but Regina had never bothered to turn her ringer off for one. "I don't plan on people calling me this late, so no, I don't usually bother."

"Well, since you answered, I assume that either you aren't holding a seance, or the spirits don't mind. Maybe they'd like someone else to talk to."

Reg snorted. "They wouldn't want to talk to you."

"Trust me, there are plenty of spirits who would be interested in talking to me," he assured her, ego as big as anything.

"So why did you call? What do you want so late at night?"

"What I always want." He let that statement sit and fester for a few seconds. Reg's face heated as she considered the statement. "Just a chance to talk to a friend."

"We're not friends."

"Reg." The voice he put on was hurt, but Reg knew enough not to take it seriously. "You wound me. We're not friends? After all that we've been through together? After all that we have shared?"

"We haven't shared anything. You've taken."

"I don't think you're remembering correctly." His voice took on a velvety tone that reminded her of the night that they had spent together. It had been an incredible night and she couldn't deny that they had been connected more intimately than any other relationship she'd ever had. Maybe that was why it was so hard to leave him alone, even knowing what he was.

She cleared her throat. "Why did you call? You just wanted to chat? It's a bit late for that, don't you think?"

"I knew you were up. I saw your light on."

Reg glanced uneasily toward the door. "Stay away from here."

"I'm not there. I just drove past and happened to see your light. I wondered…" His voice was serious, dropping the teasing, intimate tone. Reg waited for him to finish his question, goosebumps rising on her arms for no reason.

"Wondered what?" she prompted.

"I wondered if maybe it was keeping you awake too."

CHAPTER SEVEN

Reg frowned at the phone. She didn't say anything right away. Corvin wondered if *what* was keeping her awake? She remembered when she had first moved to Black Sands and had been struggling to deal with a new environment and Warren's restless spirit. Corvin had said he was having problems sleeping due to a disturbance in the spiritual balance of Black Sands.

"What are you talking about?"

Corvin answered carefully. "There is something… dark at work."

Reg breathed into the phone. Starlight jumped up beside her on the couch. He nosed at her, trying to get her attention.

"Tell me what you mean." Reg struggled to keep her voice steady.

But Corvin probably read all he needed to from her response. "I thought that if anyone else in Black Sands could feel it, it would be you."

"What is it?" Reg didn't bother denying that she had felt something too.

"I don't know yet. But it's very powerful."

"Is it like when Warren was unconscious? When Hawthorne-Rose was operating?"

"Yes… but more powerful than that. Like someone or something has moved into the neighborhood."

Reg nodded her agreement. She scratched Starlight's ears. He rubbed his head on the bottom of her chin and scraped his jowls against her phone.

"It's really…" Reg tried to put it into words. "It's really creepy. I feel sick and worried all the time. And when I was with Damon…"

"Damon?" Corvin repeated sharply.

"Yes."

"What were you doing with Damon?"

"None of your business."

"Okay… then… when you were with Damon, what? What happened?"

"I thought it was coming after me. I felt it… closing in."

"Hmm." He didn't sound like he doubted her. More like he was concerned. "Damon didn't feel it?"

"No. Nothing."

"He's not sensitive, but I thought if it was that close, maybe he would have felt something."

Reg made a murmur of acknowledgment. It was hard for her to believe that with how strongly she'd felt the presence, Damon had felt nothing at all.

"When did it start?" Corvin asked. "When did you start to feel it?"

"A day or two after we got Sarah's emerald back. I thought… it would just go away. I was hoping that it was just from a nightmare, or just because so much had been going on lately, and once I got into something else, it would just disappear."

"But it didn't."

"No. When did you notice it?"

"About the same time. I had given Sarah a lot of energy and had just gotten notice of the tribunal's decision, so it seemed natural that I'd be having bad feelings. But as you said, it didn't go away. I replenished my energy, I ramped up my business with people outside of the coven and kept myself busy. But it didn't work. The feelings just kept getting…"

"Worse?"

"Yes. Growing. Like something is gathering power. Or multiplying. It's not a good feeling."

"No," Reg agreed. She stroked Starlight's fur, thinking. "So it's not just after me? I thought… that it might be looking for me."

"Looking for you? I don't know. Why would it?"

"I don't know. It's just that… I've felt this before, and last time it followed me. For a long time."

"Can we get together to discuss this?"

"No." Reg immediately pushed him away in her thoughts. He said he had seen her light on, so he had been past the cottage. He might have returned. Or he might have been there the whole time, lying about just having driven past. She tried to put blocks up around her. She hadn't learned how to protect herself against psychic or magical forces, but she really should. She didn't want to be so vulnerable around Corvin. Or around anyone else. She needed layers of protection.

"Regina. I really do want to discuss this. But I don't think it is something that we can flesh out over the phone. You know that I'm not just making it up. You've felt it too. The two of us need to get together. If we're the only two who are aware of this force, it's our responsibility to at least try to find out what it is. Find out if we need protection, and how to stand up against it."

"You and I can't get together. You know that. You know that as soon as we do, you'll be tempted to steal my powers, and I'll be subject to your charms. Things can never end well for us."

Corvin was silent. Reg reconsidered her statement. It could never go well for her. But for Corvin… if she succumbed to his charms, then he would get exactly what he wanted.

"We can go somewhere public. Invite someone else who can help to… make you feel protected. We could figure this out and get ahead of it. We don't know what kind of havoc it might create in Black Sands if we don't confront it early. You can't let these things get a foothold."

Reg had tried going to public places with him before. She had been places where she thought she would be safe because there were other people around. But somehow, she kept falling for him.

"Reg…" Corvin pleaded. "We need to do this. Do you want *that* to take over? Do you want it to gain power here?"

"How do I know this isn't something that you've engineered just to make me let down my guard with you? It could be something… a curse you put on me to make me think that there was some danger in Black Sands. That… *being* in the parking lot could have been you. You might have been manipulating me this whole time."

"Why would I do that?"

"Because you want my powers. And maybe because you want a friend since you've been shunned from your coven. Those are two really big incentives."

"Okay, so maybe I would do that," he admitted. "It would be a good ploy. But I promise you, I haven't. I haven't put any spell or curse on you. We haven't even seen each other, so how could I have? And I couldn't have been near you the whole time you have been feeling this. It's been too long."

Reg sighed. Unfortunately, he was right.

CHAPTER EIGHT

R eg? Are you still there?"
　　　Reg tried to pull herself out from her dark thoughts to focus on
the conversation.

"You expect me to help you out with this after the garbage you pulled at
the tribunal?"

There was an intake of breath. "Uh…"

"You tried to blackmail me into speaking on your behalf instead of
talking about what you had done to me. You attacked my character. You
even tried to bring up stuff from the past."

"Well—" he tried to protest.

"Stuff from before I even came here," Reg pointed out. "And that means
you went digging into my past."

He cleared his throat. "I can see how that might bother you, but in all
honesty, the reason I looked into your past wasn't to attack you, it was to
find out more about who you are and where you came from. Where your
psychic powers came from. I've told you before, and I know others have as
well, that you are very strong. Your powers are significant. Powers like that
don't just show up randomly. It came from somewhere. *You* came from
somewhere."

Reg didn't want to know where she had come from or where her psychic
gift had come from. She was her own person, strong and independent.

"You still snooped around in my life without my permission, and you tried to use it against me at the tribunal. If I hadn't—"

"If you hadn't set me on fire, I would have succeeded?" Corvin said dryly.

Reg swallowed. She didn't know whether to laugh or to yell at him. She had been so furious at the time, but she could see the humor in it now. She had fought back against him unconsciously, exercising powers she didn't even know that she had—if it had been her doing and not that of someone else in the room—and she had put a stop to his inflammatory words.

She giggled.

She couldn't help it. It was just a stress relief valve. All of the anxiety and darkness had been building up inside her, and the giggle was just a way to bleed off a little of the pressure. It *had* been funny. Seeing imperturbable Corvin tearing off his cloak and his jacket as they each burst into flames. The glare of exasperation he had leveled across the room at her when she had disrupted his testimony and nearly derailed the hearing. He had gotten his comeuppance.

"How about this," Corvin continued in his stiff, dry tone. "If I try anything, then you can simply light me on fire."

"I don't actually know how to control it. And if you charmed me, I don't know if I could."

"We need to get together."

"Not tonight. Everybody else has already gone to bed. We'll try to sort something out tomorrow."

"Witches don't go to bed by midnight. I suspect there are more magical folk awake than asleep at this point. In the morning, they will all be heading to bed. Call someone. Call all of the witches you know. Put us all in a room together so that they can keep track of me and make sure I don't try anything with you."

He was being overdramatic, and he knew it. He was trying to force her into action, and Reg didn't understand why it was vital that it be right away. She looked at the black window behind her and felt a wave of cold that raised goosebumps all the way up her arms and down her back.

Whatever was out there, it was getting stronger. Corvin was right; they couldn't keep arguing when the force was growing stronger and gathering in power. Who knew what its goal might be and what kind of destruction it might have planned? If it were, as Reg suspected, something that she had known in her childhood, if it were focused directly on causing her harm, then shouldn't she have as many on her side as she could get? So far, Corvin was the only other person who seemed to be aware of the dark force at work, so he was the only one who could help to protect her. He was the only one who could help her to convince anyone else that there really was something at work in the darkness and it wasn't just her imagination.

Starlight prowled around as Reg got ready to leave, not liking her going out so late at night. Reg wasn't so sure of it herself. There she was, afraid of the dark, so she was going to go back out into the night where she was unprotected?

Corvin didn't seem to think that she would have any problems on her way over to his club, but Reg wasn't so sure. There weren't any protective wards on her car like there were on the cottage. And something *had* been following her earlier.

"There will be a lot of people over at the club," Corvin had assured her. "You don't need to worry about being alone. You bring along whoever you want for personal protection. I'm not trying to take advantage of you. I want to meet and see whether we can figure out what is going on."

"How about Starlight?" Reg teased. Starlight seemed to have some power over Corvin. Even though Corvin claimed not to be able to hear Starlight telepathically, he still spoke to the cat as if he knew exactly what Starlight was telling him.

"Familiars are not generally welcomed at the Club," Corvin said stiffly, "I realize that we took Starlight there once, but that was out of necessity."

Reg hadn't been serious about taking Starlight anyway, but she enjoyed goading Corvin however she could.

Starlight being out of the question, Reg decided to call Damon to see whether he would oversee things at the club. She'd tried to rely on women to supervise before but, of course, Corvin had some influence over them as well, even though it didn't seem to be as strong as his ability to charm Reg. She had a feeling that a male escort would be a different story. Damon wouldn't let Corvin get away with anything. And he wouldn't trust Corvin if he didn't have eyes on him at all times. He was a security guard by trade, so who better to provide Reg with some magical protection?

She walked quickly back to her car, looking up and down the street for anything out of the ordinary. The presence was still there, in the background. Not the feeling that she'd had in the parking lot with Damon when she'd been afraid it was going to attack. She got into the car and locked the door and turned on the headlights before putting her phone in its holder and calling Damon on speakerphone so that she could drive safely.

"Hi," Damon said, surprise in his voice. Reg couldn't tell whether she had woken him up. He didn't sound too fuzzy, but if he hadn't been asleep for very long, it probably wouldn't take much for him to wake up enough to answer the phone. "I wasn't expecting to hear back from you so soon. To tell the truth… I wasn't sure whether you would call me at all, after the bowling thing…"

"Yeah. Something has come up, and… I have to go out. I don't want to be alone. Are you already in bed, or could you come and… act as my escort to make sure that nothing happens?"

"Of course," Damon said immediately. She could hear him start to move around as he spoke. He hadn't said whether he'd gone to bed yet, but she imagined that soft background noises she could hear were the rustling of his sheets and clothing as he got up and dressed. "So… what exactly came up? What's going on? Does it have something to do with what you… felt in the parking lot?"

"Yeah. Sort of. Someone who might know a little bit more about what is going on. But I don't want to meet with him alone."

"No, that wouldn't be a good idea. Who are you meeting with?"

Reg cleared her throat. She knew he wasn't going to like her answer. "Corvin Hunter."

"Hunter?" His voice held disbelief. "Why are you meeting with Hunter?"

"Like I said, he might be able to shed a little light on whatever it is that's going on. It's not just a nightmare or the stress of living in a new place. It's more than that. He can feel it too."

"So he says. What makes you think that he isn't just trying to con you? He could very well be the one making you feel so anxious. He could be following you around, casting some spell to make you uneasy, even when he isn't around."

"I thought of that. He said he isn't, but… I don't exactly trust him. It doesn't feel like him. But I want to have someone with me, whether he's got anything to do with it or not. Even if he says he just wants to help me, I know what's going to happen the minute we're in the same room together."

Damon growled something under his breath and Reg didn't bother asking him to repeat it. She could guess. He'd heard the testimony at the hearing; he knew her history with Corvin.

"Where are you meeting him? Somewhere public, I hope? Not his own lair?"

"This club he belongs to. He said there would be plenty of people around, but that I could bring whoever I wanted to along for protection. So I thought…"

"I'm happy to help. You do not want to be getting mixed up with this guy. Not again. I'm not sure why you would even agree to meet with him again."

"I know."

"Tell me where it is."

Reg was a little surprised that Damon didn't already know where Corvin's club was, but Corvin had said before that it was exclusive. Even Jessup, a police detective, hadn't known anything about it. She gave Damon the address and directions and described the entrance door, which was a small, nondescript side door that no one would think led into such a lavish, exclusive place.

"Okay. Got it. Are you on your way over there now?"

"Yes."

"It will take me a few minutes to get there. Stay in your car until I call you back. I'll walk you in."

"I can go in ahead and wait for you. There are staff."

"No. You stay in your car until I'm with you. If I'm going to provide you with protection, you have to follow the rules."

Reg felt like a scolded child. But she had asked him for his help; she knew she needed to do what he said.

"Okay. I'll wait for you."

"Good. I'll see you in a few minutes."

Reg hung up the phone. She was reaching for the gear shift when she saw a shadow down the street. She squinted, trying to get a better look at it. Was someone out there, watching her and waiting for her to leave? Or was it just an animal? A stray pet or wildlife? She didn't like to think of what things could be lurking in the treed areas around the houses. There were more than just raccoons and foxes like back in Maine where she'd grown up. There were things like alligators and snakes.

But it wasn't slithering across the road. It scurried like a cat or a fox.

She pulled out, keeping an eye on the spot where the shape had merged into the shadows.

As she was watching, a cat darted out from under one of the cars, making her jump and swerve before hitting the brakes. The cat stopped in the road and looked back at her.

A black cat. She couldn't see whether it had any markings or tattoos, but it certainly could be Nicole. Reg rolled down her window.

"Nicole?" she called softly, trying not to spook it. She made kissy calling sounds to see if it would come to her.

The cat continued to look in her direction but did not approach the car or react to the name. There were probably a lot of black cats in Black Sands. Cats were a common familiar for witches and warlocks and, of course, a black cat was the stereotypical witch's companion.

Reg released the brake and the cat dashed away. Reg tried to relax her shoulders and then the rest of her muscles. It was just a black cat. Maybe it was Nicole and maybe it wasn't. She would call or text the owner later and describe what she had seen, and the owner could come over and look around and call for her.

If the cat in Sarah's garden had been Nicole, she'd been out on her own for a while. The cat had been skinny and had obviously been outside for more than just a day or two.

Trying to put any other distractions out of her mind, Reg focused on her driving. She had only been to the club once and was relying on the GPS to get her there, but the GPS wasn't always reliable. If she lost satellite reception, she'd be in trouble, and she didn't want to be driving around aimlessly late at night with whatever had been following her.

She made it to the club and sat in the car parked on the street, since she didn't know how to get access to the underground parking that the members were allowed to use. She scanned the road for any activity and then looked down at her phone. Damon wasn't there yet, so she'd have to sit there and wait for him. She knew it would be safer inside the club. She hadn't told him how close it was to the pixies' realm. Maybe that would have made a difference. She knew that the pixies didn't like the sun, so they were probably out in force at night, scurrying around her in the dark. She looked up again, searching for any sign of movement. Still nothing.

She closed her eyes and reached out with her mind. She could sense the presence of magical powers in the club, a sort of a warmth that throbbed around the building like a beating heart. Corvin was probably in there already, though she had a hard time picking his signature out of the rest of the warlocks in there.

She opened her eyes again, sighing to herself.

She nearly screamed when she saw the dark shape outside her window.

But she hadn't felt the evil presence there and, when she was able to look more closely, she saw that it was Damon.

Unlike earlier, at the bowling alley and the restaurant, he was dressed in a long black cloak, a peaked hood pulled up over his head that hid his face, making it hard to see him until he shifted his head and a streetlight fell across his features. Reg put her hand over her pounding heart. She opened the door.

"You scared the hell out of me! What are you doing sneaking up on me like that?"

"I wasn't sneaking."

"Well… you should let me know you were there. I just opened my eyes, and you were standing there, I thought that you were…"

He raised his brows. "Thought that I was Corvin?"

"No. A… I don't know. Something else. Something… dark." Reg climbed out of the car, glad that he couldn't see how flushed she was.

He cocked his head to the side slightly, then shook his head, bemused. He couldn't feel the dark presence, so of course he was confused. He didn't know what was out there.

"Did you see anything?" she asked, looking around. She shut her car door. She didn't want to be taken unaware by pixies or by the dark force. She shouldn't have agreed to meet Corvin at night. What had she been thinking? She knew it was a bad idea, but she had let herself be talked into it. She always let him talk her into things.

"No, I didn't see anything." Damon took a glance around, but his manner was loose and unconcerned. "Our crime rate in Black Sands is pretty low. It's good to be careful, but I'm more concerned about what you're going to face when you go inside than I am about what could happen out here. You are not likely to get mugged. But Hunter... no one likes him or his ilk. I don't trust any club that would allow him membership."

"I thought... it was a place that all warlocks went. I mean, I know he said it was exclusive, but all guys like to make themselves look important. Exclusive usually just means no women allowed or they have really expensive fees."

"I don't know what kind of place it is, but I'm not a member, and I don't think anyone else in his coven is. It's best to stay away from places where beings like him gather."

Reg suppressed a shiver. She and Damon walked up to the door that Reg had previously used. Maybe she should take Damon's advice and not go inside. She could call Corvin and tell him that she'd come to her senses and they would have to meet somewhere else, somewhere of her choosing, in the daylight. With lots of other people around who were not 'his kind.'

Reg couldn't imagine what it would be like to be surrounded by them. How could she raise any defenses against a coordinated attack, when she couldn't even protect herself against one warlock? Did she think that having Damon there would be enough protection? Corvin might not be able to charm another warlock the same way as he could influence Reg, but she was sure that he had other magic too. He had to make a living in the magical community, and he didn't do that just by stealing powers from unsuspecting psychics.

Reg took one more nervous look around, then raised her hand and knocked on the door. There should at least be some weird Victorian door knocker on the door. Something magical and mysterious looking. It didn't seem right that she should have to use her fist to knock. Maybe a doorbell that made deep chimes within the building to set the mood.

The door opened almost immediately. A tall, slim, pale woman stood before them. She had a smile of bright red lipstick that looked like an artist had applied it. Her dress could have been painted on by the same brush, it was so form fitting. Reg averted her eyes, embarrassed by the fact that she would have been able to see any lines from the woman's undergarments, but there were none.

"Miss Rawlins, so nice of you to visit again," the woman greeted pleasantly.

It was good that she recognized Reg since Reg was so tongue-tied, she had no idea what to say to the hostess. It wasn't the same woman as she had seen there before, so she shouldn't have been able to recognize Reg, but she supposed that Corvin had told her he was expecting a guest, and there weren't too many people around town with red hair in braids like Reg's.

The woman's eyes turned to Damon. "And we are happy to welcome you here...?"

"Damon," he told her crisply. "Damon Knight."

She nodded but showed no recognition of his name. If he was hoping to make an impression on her, he appeared to have failed.

"Mr. Knight. We are always happy to welcome new guests. I'm sure Mr. Hunter will be happy to host you."

Reg snorted. Mr. Hunter would definitely not be happy to host Damon. He had repeatedly suggested that Reg could bring whatever witches she wanted to. He had not suggested that she bring a warlock or an actual security guard.

"Mr. Hunter is waiting for you in a private room. I will take you there..."

Reg stood inside the doorway and shook her head. "No. He said it would be in public. Where there were a lot of people around. Not alone in a private room."

"Well, you won't be alone, you have Mr. Knight."

"No. You must have a dining room here, or a game room or library where people get together to talk. Take us there. You can tell Corvin to come to us."

She looked at Reg, clearly dismayed. They were sworn to do whatever it took to keep the club members happy, and this was not going to make Corvin happy. She tried again.

"You will be perfectly safe in the private room. There is nothing to fear. We take our guests' security very seriously here."

"You take your *members'* security very seriously. I am not convinced about your guests'. My friend was nearly assaulted here. And I'm sure you know that Corvin isn't the safest guy to be around. I am not meeting him in private. He agreed to meet in public."

"You'll be more comfortable in the private room. I can bring you drinks. We can provide whatever you need. In one of the public rooms, you won't be able to have the privacy that you desire for your discussion..."

"No. Is this going to be a problem? Because I can just leave now."

The woman reached out and touched Reg's arm. "No!"

Damon shifted forward, his big frame crowding Reg and the hostess in the entryway. His eyes were like lightning. "Don't touch her."

The hostess withdrew her hand immediately, eyes wide.

"Don't try that again. Are you going to accommodate Miss Rawlins, or are we going to leave?"

"Please don't leave." She seemed almost afraid. Would she face severe consequences if Reg decided it wasn't safe and walked back out? Would she be fired or physically punished? Something even worse? The woman swallowed and tried to keep a calm demeanor, but even though she managed to control her face and her voice, Reg could still feel the emotions pouring off of her.

"I'll stay if you take me to one of the common rooms, where there are other people," Reg asserted. "Then you can go talk to Corvin and tell him that you convinced me to stay, but that he's going to have to come down off of his high horse and meet me in front of other people like he promised."

The hostess nodded woodenly. "Please come with me. I will update him on the situation after you are settled."

CHAPTER NINE

The dining room that Reg and Damon were escorted to was not full by any measure, but it wasn't empty. There would be other witnesses if Corvin decided to do something threatening. Reg wasn't sure anymore whether that would be enough of a protection. Obviously, the other people who frequented the club were going to be just as privileged and self-centered as Corvin himself. They would be loyal to their own kind, not to someone like Reg who came from outside of the community and barely knew which way was up in the magical world. She didn't know what kind of reputation Damon might have, but the hostess had not recognized him or his name. He had said that he was a lone wolf. She hadn't thought about it before, but that meant that he didn't have the weight of a coven behind him. He didn't have anyone watching his back. They were just two people against Corvin and the staff of the club and the other members and their guests.

Conversations ceased when they were escorted in. People didn't recognize them, and they weren't there with another member, so Reg supposed that was worthy of note. She explored the emotions of the room, looking around at the diners and trying to discern who they needed to be careful of and who might be friendly. Some people were naturally the protectors of strangers and the weak, but she didn't get that vibe from any of them. They were curious. Some of them were irritated by the introduction of strangers into their ranks. But no one was there who cared whether something happened to her. She might be fractionally safer in a room with other people than she was in Corvin's private room, but Reg sensed that it wasn't by much.

Damon looked around, assessing whatever angles he had been trained to. When the hostess indicated one table, he shook his head and selected another empty table instead.

"We'll sit here."

Reg couldn't see any difference in safety between the two. She suspected that he was just showing his control of the situation. He wanted them to know that he had the upper hand and they weren't going to be calling the shots. Reg sat down where Damon indicated. They could both see the door that Corvin would enter through. Reg was aware that there was also a kitchen door and an emergency exit. She couldn't watch them all at the same time. Damon glanced around and sat down.

"Nice little place he's got here," he commented.

"Yes. It must be really expensive. And from what I understand, they'll go to any lengths to satisfy their members' needs."

"I'm not sure I find that reassuring."

"No. Me neither."

"Are you sure you want to go ahead with this? You can change your mind. If you don't feel safe here, you can dictate the terms. You can tell him that you'll meet him at another time and place."

"I know. But I want to get this over with. I want to find out what he knows about this force. What's going on in Black Sands."

"I doubt you'll get any answers out of Hunter. He'll pump you for what you know, or try to get whatever it is that he invited you here for, and you'll leave here none the wiser. Hunter looks out for one person, and that's himself."

"I get that."

He gazed at her for a minute, then nodded. "I guess you do."

Low lights and flickering candles lit the dining room. Damon's hood was still up over his head, his face mostly in shadows. He looked rugged and dangerous. Maybe a match for someone like Corvin, who seemed to be more refined and careful.

It was a few minutes before Corvin appeared. He was not escorted by the hostess. Of course, he knew where the dining room was and didn't need her to point his guests out.

His jaw was clenched. He sat down in the seat next to Reg at the round table rather than the one across from her. He didn't get angry at her for insisting that they meet in a public place, didn't object to Damon's presence; he just sat down and got down to business.

"Thank you for coming to see me," he told Reg in a low voice. She didn't feel the warmth that she usually did from him. He hadn't turned on the charm, so he seemed just like a normal man. An unusually handsome one, yes, but she didn't feel magically drawn toward him: no special tingles, no rose scent, no shivers.

"So, what exactly do you want to know that you couldn't have asked over the phone?" Reg asked. Was there really something that he needed to be face-to-face for? Other than trying again to seduce her and steal her powers?

"You and I are the only ones that I know of who are aware of the force at work here," Corvin said, leaning forward.

Reg reflexively held her breath, expecting the heady scent of roses to envelop her. She couldn't hold it forever, and when she released it and breathed in, the air was clear, filled only with the smells of the food cooking in the kitchen.

"Right," she said. "Why is that important? What does it mean?"

"There are other psychics in town who I would expect to have noticed it. Other witches and wizards have some level of sensitivity to the changing spiritual or magnetic forces in Black Sands. But so far, it's just you and me."

"So?"

He rubbed his jaw, fingers rasping over the short whiskers of his beard. "I think that if only you and I have felt it, that it must be something that connects the two of us. There is something that affects the two of us personally, that is unique to just you and me."

Reg shook her head, frowning. "Like what? I don't know what you mean."

"I'm not sure that I do either. I wanted to see what I could feel if we were together, to explore any connections that we have and to try to get a better picture of what it might be. I was hoping that you would meet with me in a private room where we would be more free to talk without distractions."

"No."

He sat back, shaking his head. "I'm not trying to ensorcel you, Reg. I'm trying to figure out what danger you are in."

"Me and you."

"What?"

"You said that you and I could both feel it, so if I am in danger, then you must be too. If it affects the two of us, won't it affect us the same way? If it wants to attack me, then doesn't it want to attack you too?"

Corvin contemplated her suggestion. Reg was impatient waiting for his answer, but leaned back to let him work through it and to decide whether she was right or wrong.

"I'm not sure I am in any direct danger," Corvin said slowly. "I think that Black Sands itself is under a pall and that you specifically are in danger. But I'm not sure that I am in any more danger than the rest of Black Sands."

"But something is going to happen. It isn't just me. When I... lose direct contact with... whatever it is... it's still here. It's still doing something that threatens..." Reg struggled to find the right words. She wasn't a scholar, hadn't ever done very well in school with her disrupted life, learning disabilities, and differences from the other children. But she wished for once that she could find the exact right words to express herself. She had an impulse to connect with Corvin, to establish a telepathic link into his head so she could tell him without words just what it was that she meant. She glanced aside at Damon, wondering whether it would be safe if he was sitting right there. She would never do it alone, but with magical security there, Damon could pull her back if Corvin tried to control her, couldn't he?

"Something that threatens the balance and the peace of the community," Corvin suggested.

It was as close as Reg figured they were going to be able to get using just words. She nodded. "It didn't come here because of me and it isn't staying here because of me. It has... purpose."

Corvin nodded. "Okay. But why is it that you and I are the only ones who can sense it?"

Reg reviewed the possibilities. As Corvin said, there were plenty of other psychics and witches she would have thought would be able to sense such a profound influence in their community. It was so strong to her that she felt that even non-practitioners should be able to feel the oppressive pall.

But what if it wasn't that much stronger than other influences in the community, it was just that Reg was extra sensitive to it? Why would Corvin also be able to feel it so strongly? He didn't ordinarily have strong psychic powers. He could feel shifts in the magical balance, but it wasn't his gift. She could remember the expression on his face when he had been in possession of her powers. How he had marveled at how strong the voices in his head were and he had experimented with exercising the powers that he'd taken from her. Powers that she had never really understood that she had.

"When you returned my powers, you said that you still retained something," Reg said slowly, "you compared it to the droplets of milk that stay in the carton when you pour it out."

Corvin's eyes were quick. He immediately caught on to her train of thought. "So maybe the reason that you and I can both sense it is that I retained something of your gifts."

Reg nodded. "Yes. Exactly."

He closed his eyes, and Reg could feel him exploring inside his head, trying to verify what she had suggested. She wondered whether his awareness of his own psyche was so strong because that was a natural gift or because he had grown up in the magical community, where his abilities were accepted and spoken of openly. Reg had been forced to deny her gifts and to stuff them down, so that she didn't know or understand them at all.

The minutes drew on. Reg glanced over at Damon. His eyes were on Corvin, alert for any changes.

"You have memories connected with this force," Corvin suggested, opening his eyes again.

Reg shifted uncomfortably. "I'm not sure if it's exactly this force, but… something like it."

"What happened?"

"Nothing happened. I… tried to run away from it. I hid from it. Moved from one family to another. Eventually… it was gone."

"It was just gone?"

"Yes."

Corvin took a sip of the ice water in front of him. He grimaced and raised his hand to motion to a waiter. He ordered a drink and raised a questioning eyebrow at Reg and Damon. "On me, of course. You need something stronger than water."

Reg ordered a glass of wine and Corvin argued for a moment with the waiter about the vintage. Damon waved off the offer of a drink. He was on duty and taking his role seriously.

"You do not remember correctly," Corvin challenged Reg.

Anger immediately lit up Reg's brain. "You think I'm lying?"

"No. As I said, I don't think you're remembering it properly. I think that like with much of your childhood, you've suppressed it."

"You don't know anything about my childhood," she snapped. And hoped that it was true.

"I knew about the imaginary friends, didn't I?"

"You guessed."

"And you suppressed. You weren't allowed to see spirits, so you had imaginary friends. And when you were too old for imaginary friends, you did your best to ignore them and block them out because you didn't want to go to the loony bin. And you made yourself forget about your imaginary friends, or at least the part about them being real people."

Reg gritted her teeth. "Yes. Fine. That much is true." Except that she hadn't blocked them to stay out of the loony bin, she'd blocked them to get back out. She knew that if she kept hearing them, she would never be released.

Corvin nodded. He took a sip of his scotch and set it back down. "You also had nightmares."

"Everybody has nightmares."

"Tell me about yours."

Reg hesitated. She didn't start with the nightmares she was currently having. She thought back to when she was little, when they had been so frighteningly real that she would wake the household up with her screams.

"All little kids have nightmares."

"Did you have the same or similar ones over and over again? Is there one that stands out more than the others?"

"I don't know. I would dream about... a shadow man. Someone who was there in the dark, when the lights went out. Waiting for me. Trying to find me."

"Did you see his face? Did you talk to him?"

"No. No, I just ran away. He was so scary. I'd wake up soaking wet."

"Did you get counseling?"

"I was always in counseling or therapy of one kind or another. They wanted to fix me. Make me normal like all of the other kids."

"What did they talk to you about?"

Reg shook her head. "I don't know. Shrink stuff."

"Like what?"

Reg eyed her glass. If she were going to hold herself to one glass of wine, she was going to have to ration it, not just to gulp the whole thing down like she wanted to do.

"Um… relaxation exercises. Thinking about good things. Not watching TV before bed. Asking me about what happened when I was really little. Just whatever they thought would help me not be afraid at night."

"What happened when you were really little?"

"I don't know." Reg anticipated his next question. "They said… it would help me overcome past trauma. Stuff that I couldn't even remember. Like… my mom dying."

"How did your mom die?"

"In an accident."

It was Damon who cocked his head at Reg's answer, his forehead creasing. Reg ground her teeth in irritation. Corvin might not have pursued it any further, but with Damon's easy-to-read face, Corvin knew in an instant that something did not pass muster.

"What? It wasn't an accident?" Corvin asked, looking from Reg to Damon and back again.

"Damon doesn't know anything about it," Reg snapped. "We just met."

"Damon is a diviner. He has a gift for recognizing the truth. Or lies."

Reg looked at Damon, scowling. "Why didn't you tell me that?"

"Would it have made any difference to anything?"

She tried to review the entire evening at once. How many times had she lied to him? And what about? Reg might not be a pathological liar, but she wasn't exactly dedicated to the truth, either. She was a good liar. She had to be. And most people couldn't tell.

"How did your mother die?" Corvin demanded.

"I don't remember."

Corvin looked at Damon.

"I'm not a lie detector," Damon said. "I'm here to keep Reg safe, not to be your human polygraph."

He drew the hood down farther, hiding his face in shadow. Too little too late.

"What do you remember?" Corvin pried, focusing his gaze on Reg once more.

"Why does this matter? What does any of this have to do with what's going on here?"

"That's what I want to find out. What does it have to do with what's going on in Black Sands now? How is it connected? You have the answer inside you somewhere."

"I don't," Reg protested. "I don't know what's going on or what it is that's out there. You're the one with the magical expertise."

"Then listen to me when I tell you something. The answer is in your head. This feeling and these nightmares are connected to your past. Maybe something to do with your mother, maybe not. But it's a good starting point."

"She was killed. I don't know how. I was too young to know anything. I didn't have any family, so they put me into foster care. But I was always trouble and no one would adopt me." She shook her head in irritation. "What does any of that matter?"

"What do you remember from the day she died?"

"Nothing. I don't remember anything. I was too young."

"What do you remember about the place you lived at the time? With your mother?"

"Nothing." Reg stopped and thought. She shook her head again. "No. nothing."

Corvin looked over at Damon, but he didn't need Damon's gift to tell that something was stirring in Reg's brain, keeping her from being sure of her answer. Every time she said she didn't remember anything about it, her brain did a little twist. A little tic that made her unsure of herself.

She had been too young to remember anything about her mother or about the place they had lived.

The voices in her head were growing more and more insistent, harder and harder to ignore. One of them, in particular, was louder than all the rest. Reg pressed her thumbs into her temples.

"What is it?" Corvin asked.

"Leave me alone. Just be quiet."

He frowned, looking at her. Reg pressed her temples harder.

"Shut up. Shut up. Shut up."

But Norma Jean's voice came through, her accent and cadence unmistakable. Reg had lost her own accent in all of the years moving from one family to another. But her mother's was still as clear as a bell.

"Regina, honey, listen to me. Don't push me out."

"No," Reg insisted. "Just go away. Shut up. Stop talking."

"You need to know what happened. You can remember. If you decide to remember, you can."

"I can't. I can't remember. I was just a baby at the time. That's all. Just a baby."

"Sweet child, you were more than just a baby. You were almost school age. Kindergarten, anyway. You would have been going to kindergarten at the big elementary school come fall."

"I don't have to listen to you."

"I know they didn't treat you right at the homes you went to after I died. I tried to help. Truly I did. But they didn't know how to take care of a traumatized little girl who had just seen her momma die. They didn't know how to care for you when you were taken away from everything you had ever known."

To say nothing of a child who could still hear her dead mother talking to her.

Reg felt a hand on her face and for a moment, thought that it was her mother's touch. It had been so many years since she had felt her mother's touch. Almost a lifetime.

"Hunter, back off," a man's voice snapped.

"Shh. I'm not hurting her." Reg recognized Corvin's purr.

She tried to sort out what was going on. But she was so consumed by Norma Jean's voice, she didn't know how to get back out of her own head.

"Corvin. Unhand her."

Reg felt the hand withdraw from her cheek and with it, the warmth and tenderness that she had been craving. Her mother's voice grew more strident. "You can't forget what happened to your mother. You know what they did to me."

Reg broke through violently, forcing her way past her mother's barriers and opening her eyes. The world swam in front of her. She reached out to Corvin to steady herself. She couldn't remember that he was dangerous, she only knew that he would feed her strength and he could help her to figure out what was going on in her head, why that locked box had been breached.

"Corvin." She could barely whisper his name.

"I'm here, Regina."

She held on to his arm, clutching tightly like everything else in the world might disappear and she would be left alone and stranded.

"You shouldn't trust him," Damon growled. "Why am I here if you're going to ignore what I tell you and he can just waltz in and do whatever he likes?"

Reg blinked, trying to focus on Damon. He seemed far away, on the other side of a dark room.

"Damon? What's going on?"

"Don't touch him. Don't let him touch you. He'll consume you."

Reg looked down at her hand, holding on to Corvin's strong arm for support. She dug her fingers into his arm, feeling the buzz of energy through his thick suit jacket. She took a few deep breaths and forced herself to let his arm go.

"What was that?"

"*Who* was that?" Corvin countered.

Reg breathed heavily like she had been running. She tried to stay in control of herself and not to open the door even a crack to let Norma Jean back in.

"Norma Jean."

"Your mother?"

Reg swallowed and nodded.

"You were communing with your mother?" Damon asked. "What did she say?"

"You couldn't hear her?"

"You're the only one who can hear her," Corvin advised.

"You could hear her," Reg insisted.

"No. I was trying. But your bulldog here wouldn't let me. Why don't you tell him to go home; then you and I can continue. Or we could go somewhere more private."

"He was trying to freaking mind meld with you." Damon's voice was hard. "I know what he can do, and so do you. I'm here to stop him."

"Yes," Reg agreed. But she wished that he had let Corvin complete the connection. She wanted him to see and feel it instead of her having to struggle to put it into words.

"Have a drink." Corvin nudged her wine glass toward her. "Quit trying to make it last all night. You need it."

What she needed was the energy he was feeding her, his hand held a few inches away from hers, hovering and radiating energy like a heat lamp.

"Have a drink and tell me what your mother wanted you to remember. Just get it all out, like ripping off a bandage."

Reg raised it to her lips with shaky fingers. The wine warmed her, but she would have preferred Corvin's touch. She remembered how it felt to be held by him, and she wanted to crawl into his arms where it was safe.

She had to settle instead for Damon, reaching out to grasp his hand and hold it tightly. No electricity. No warmth except for his normal body temperature.

"So?" Corvin prompted. "What happened?"

"They tortured and killed her." Reg's heart hurt like it had just happened. All of the years she had spent burying the memories and the pain, and it was as raw and fresh as if it had just happened.

"Who did? Did you see?"

"The man with the hair." Reg's voice was that of a little girl. She cleared her throat and tried to take over from the scared child inside her. "Long, black hair. In braids." Reg fingered her own braids. She looked at Corvin, the horror blooming up through her body, like ink spreading through clear water. "No, not braids. Dreadlocks. It was the witch doctor."

CHAPTER TEN

Damon wouldn't let Reg drive home, but insisted that she leave her car at the club and he would drive her. She could get her car at another time, or Corvin could have the club return it to her house.

"You can't drive in this state. You're too emotionally distraught."

She felt defensive. He hadn't said that she shouldn't feel what she did, but it still felt like a criticism. Like the foster parents and therapists she had dealt with over the years, he was telling her that she should be over it by now. Her mother had died decades before. It wasn't like she was still in mourning. She knew Damon didn't mean it that way, but she had been told too many times not to feel the grief. She had worked hard to wall that part of her life off and go on in a new direction. A fresh start. How many times had she been given a fresh start, and thought that maybe this time it would work? Maybe she would be able to go somewhere she could be at peace and start a productive life and live the same way as anyone else.

"I've been driving myself for years," Reg said crossly. "I know my way home. I'd be just fine driving myself."

"Let me do this favor for you. To make up for taking you out to bowling earlier, okay? This is my do-over."

"Some do-over," Reg grumbled. "I didn't want to go bowling and I don't want you to drive me home."

"You wanted me to provide personal protection. This is just part of the service."

Walking to his car, Reg hung on to his arm, still feeling shaky. She looked back toward the club. She couldn't see Corvin. He hadn't insisted on following them out. But she could still feel him and sense his restlessness and unease.

He hadn't known anything about the 'witch doctor' who had been working with Hawthorne-Rose when Reg had first moved to Black Sands and been caught up in the mysterious disappearance of Warren Blake. Reg had seen the black man with the dreadlocks and the round, white-rimmed eyes in Warren Blake's memories. He was one of the few players whose face she'd been able to see. She had thought that when Hawthorne-Rose had been caught and turned over to the authorities that they had busted up his smuggling ring and that Black Sands was safe once more. They had all thought so.

But something was going on. The Witch Doctor was once more operating in Black Sands. Reg didn't know if he was smuggling or doing something else. Why did she feel so unsettled? Was it just because he was close by and she associated him with the man who had killed her mother? Maybe seeing him in Warren Blake's memories had triggered new nightmares because he reminded Reg of her past. Perhaps the Witch Doctor wasn't operating in Black Sands at all, she was just having a delayed emotional reaction to a traumatic memory.

"Are you okay?" Damon rubbed Reg's hand, still clutching his arm, in an attempt to soothe her.

"I'm fine. Now I know what it was that was bugging me, so I'll probably sleep great tonight. I'm so exhausted, I'll just fall into bed, and I won't even dream."

She knew the nightmares were still there. She could feel them.

"Tell me the truth." Damon's voice was low and calm.

Of course. The diviner. He knew she was lying about being fine and about being able to escape the nightmares for once.

"I'm shaken up," Reg admitted. "I wasn't expecting… anything like this. I don't know what I was expecting, but it wasn't this."

"Do you really think that the man who killed your mother is in Black Sands?"

"No. The Witch Doctor just reminds me of him. Because of the dreadlocks. It was just an accidental association. The Witch Doctor probably isn't even here."

A strong, painful throb of her heart testified that it wasn't true. The Witch Doctor was there, and he was back at his evil business of smuggling magical objects and endangered animal organs used for spells.

But that was all. He didn't know or care about Reg. He wouldn't attack her. He didn't have evil plans to deal with her.

"You're hurting yourself," Damon said.

Reg loosened her grip on his arm, then realized that he'd said she was hurting herself, not him. She shook her head. "What do you mean, I'm hurting myself?"

"When you lie to yourself like that, you do damage to your soul. You cause a breach when your brain and your body know the truth and you choose to deny it or tell another story. Every time you lie to yourself, you are causing harm."

"I don't know what the truth is. I'm not lying to myself."

He looked at her for a minute, and Reg knew that he could still feel something from her. She didn't know how his gift worked and if he could tell what she was thinking and feeling if she didn't say anything, but he seemed to have a sense of it even when she was silent.

"I don't know how. I don't know the truth, so how can I lie to myself about it?"

"Maybe because you do know the truth."

Reg sighed in exasperation. Damon motioned to a big black pickup truck. "This is me." He gave a little shrug. "Sorry, it's not that easy for someone who is... smaller than me... to get into."

"I'm short, but at least I'm not wearing a dress today."

Damon nodded. "That might be awkward." He pressed the button on his key fob to unlock it, opened the door for her, and then looked like he was going to pick her up and put her in the seat. Reg held up her hand.

"I can actually manage by myself."

He stepped back a few inches, but was still hovering and acting like he might have to catch her if she fell. Reg stepped onto the running board, grabbed the inside of the door frame, and hauled herself up into the cab of the truck. She sat down and pretended to readjust an imaginary skirt.

"See?"

"Very ladylike," he approved. He shut the door and went around to the driver's side. He didn't have any trouble stepping up into the cab. He started the truck with a roar, then turned on the heat and pointed one of the blowers toward her. "I think you might be a little bit in shock. We'll get you warmed up a little."

Reg wanted to tell him to back off, she could take care of herself, but the warm air felt really good, so she held her tongue. They sat there in silence for a few minutes. He made no move to pull out.

She looked at him sideways. "Uh... do you need my address, or what?"

"I just thought... you might want to talk about it. I don't want you to feel like you have to invite me into your house to talk, so I thought if we talked in the truck for a few minutes... that might be more comfortable."

"I don't want to talk about it."

"You really didn't remember that your mother was tortured and killed?"

"If you can discern the truth, then don't you already know that?"

"Well... yes... but it seems so strange that you would be able to forget something like that. I would think that it would be burned into your memory, something that you could never forget."

"You don't know what it's like to have something like that happen to you. I couldn't deal with it." She shook her head. "I don't think I can deal with it now."

"How old were you?"

"She said I was going to go into kindergarten, so I guess I was four or five."

"And you were there when it happened?" he asked tentatively, obviously aware that he was treading on thin ice. "Did you... see...?"

"It's muddled." Reg held her head, pressing it between her hands. She didn't know whether to try to remember or to try to forget. If Damon was right, then forcing herself to forget about it might be damaging to her. Maybe that was what had triggered all of her psychic or psychological problems to start with. She had forced her brain to do things it wasn't supposed to do, and in doing so, had made a mess of things. "I don't know what I saw or didn't see."

"You remembered when Corvin asked you about the house. Can you remember the house?"

There were flashes. Reg had disjointed impressions of the walls, floor, and ceiling. The sparse furniture. She could see bits of herself, her own white legs and bare feet, her arms wrapped around her knees. Was she hiding? It would make sense that she was hiding somewhere they couldn't see her. If her mother were being tortured and murdered, then of course she would hide.

Her mother had probably put her there or told her where to hide so that she was out of sight before the intruders could see her. It seemed like she was somewhere cramped, a cupboard maybe. Peeking out to see what was going on.

Reg's nostrils flared as she had a sudden instant of clarity when all of the pictures gelled into one, and she could smell the damp under the sink and the sweetish smell of mice and the foreign musky odor of the man with the dreads and his companions. She could feel the same terror, as if she were there again, four years old, crying and screaming at them to stop.

But she couldn't have remained hidden if she was crying and screaming. They would have heard her and dragged her out. They wouldn't have left her behind, a witness to their violence. That part couldn't be true. Maybe it was like in her dreams, when she would scream and nothing would come out. She had cried and screamed, but it had been without a voice, so that she could stay hidden and they would be ignorant of her presence.

"It's okay. You're safe. It's okay, Reg."

Damon was rubbing her shoulder, trying to comfort her while tears ran down Reg's face.

"I'm sorry. I don't know what's wrong with me. I'm such a mess." She tried to wipe away the tears with her hands.

"No, it's okay. You need to let these emotions out. You shouldn't suppress them."

She opened her eyes and looked at him. He didn't seem disgusted by her display. He didn't look panicked like many men did when a woman broke down and they didn't know how to stop the waterworks. He just looked compassionate and understanding.

"I don't want to feel them." Reg sniffled and wiped at the corners of her eyes, trying to shut the tears off. "Why would anyone want to feel so scared and alone? Don't you understand what happened? They tortured and killed her right in front of me. Maybe she wasn't a good mom, but she was still my mother. She was doing all she could."

"I'm sure she was." He stroked her hair, pushing a few of the thin braids back over her ear. "What was she like?"

That question was a little easier to answer since Reg had still been in communication with her mother for years after she died. It wasn't like she had to rely on the memories of a four-year-old for that. But the way that Norma Jean had been in life and the way that she had been after death were not identical. Even though she stayed with Reg, she was no longer in charge of feeding and clothing her and making sure she was looked after when Norma Jean went out to party. She was no longer able to discipline Reg physically, but could only communicate with her using the words in her head. The lovey words that came to Reg's mind when Norma Jean talked to Reg after death were not the same words as she had used in life. In life, she had only been so mushy and loving when she was really happy or really smashed.

"She was… southern… she was… I don't know how old she was. When I look back now, I think she must have been pretty young. But of course, you don't know that when you're a little kid. Everyone is a grown up to a little kid. She must have had me as a teenager or early twenties, I think. She bragged about how pretty she was when she was alive, but I remember… she had a couple of missing teeth, and her hair was brittle, and she wore a lot of makeup."

"Was she an addict? A prostitute?"

"I don't know. Probably both. She can be so honey-sweet now, but back then… she wasn't very nice to me."

Damon extended his rubbing to Reg's neck and the top part of her back. She didn't mind his touch so much. Not like earlier when she'd felt like he was just trying to push her into a physical relationship. Now he was emotionally supportive and trying to help her work through what had happened to her as a little girl. He wasn't on the make.

"She probably had a pretty rough life too."

"Yeah. Probably."

"And this Witch Doctor? Was he someone she knew, or… did he just show up one day? Did they have a relationship, or did he happen upon her one day…"

Flashes of memory, watching the strange man and her mother, having to look through the legs of the chairs and table in the kitchen into the living room, where he crouched over her.

"No. Don't hurt my mommy!"

Damon pulled Reg closer to himself and squeezed her firmly. "It's okay. It's just a memory. It isn't happening now."

Reg wasn't so sure. The flashes were disorienting and she didn't know where she was. She wanted to stop them.

"I don't understand why they would hurt her. She didn't do anything to them. The scary man... he wanted to know..." Reg trailed off.

"What did he want to know?" Damon asked softly.

Reg pushed him away from her. She took a few deep breaths. It was getting too warm. The chill had left her and the truck seemed suffocatingly warm and close. She fumbled for the window controls and inched her window down a crack.

It wasn't any of Damon's business. He was prying into something that he had no business knowing, and she didn't want to share.

"I want to go home. I told you I don't want to talk about this."

"Okay. You don't want to talk about it."

"I want to go home. I can drive myself; you don't have to drive me."

"I'll still drive you. Just sit back and relax."

Reg let out her breath in an angry puff and leaned back against the seat, closing her eyes and pretending to rest.

CHAPTER ELEVEN

The truck came to an abrupt stop, throwing Reg unexpectedly against her seatbelt. She braced her hands against the dash, eyes suddenly wide open, and looked around in alarm.

"Sorry," Damon reached out and put his hand on her leg in a calming gesture. "Just a cat. Ran out in front of the truck."

Reg's heart was thumping a mile a minute. She took a deep breath, trying to fight the feeling of dread that knotted in her stomach, pulling tighter, stretching taut like something was going to snap.

"I didn't mean to startle you," Damon apologized again. "Are you okay?"

"It's not that. I'd rather you braked than ran over it. It's just…" her voice faded.

"The feeling again?"

"Yeah. Really strong here."

Damon glanced around as he released the brake and started to creep forward again. "Maybe it's just the location."

Reg blinked. "What do you mean?"

"The cemetery." Damon gestured to their right at a treed area Reg had taken for a park. "Maybe you're just getting unsettling feelings because of restless spirits."

She looked out the window, trying to see something through the trees, but it was dark, and the vegetation around the cemetery was thick. "I don't know. Maybe."

She had the impression that he thought she was being overdramatic about her feeling.

Sometimes being psychic sucked.

They went on without a word. Reg didn't close her eyes again, wanting to be alert for any more cats or any spiritual manifestations. She didn't want to be taken off-guard. Damon turned right so that they rounded one corner of the cemetery and were still traveling with it on their right. Reg frowned at the emergency lights flashing ahead of them. Damon continued to drive, hoping to be able to see what was going on and to get past to drop Reg at home. But there was a police barricade across the road, not letting anyone pass. Damon rolled down his window to talk to the police officer.

"Sorry, you'll have to detour around," a familiar voice advised. "This road is temporarily closed."

Reg leaned over, almost into Damon's lap, to see the figure standing outside the truck, not looking terribly enthused with her job directing traffic. "Detective Jessup."

"Oh, Reg. I didn't see you. I didn't know that you knew..." Jessup looked at Damon.

"We just met," Damon advised. "First date. So what's going on?" A flick of Damon's hand indicated the cemetery. They couldn't see much from where they were, but there were floodlights and people coming and going, clearly a crime scene.

"Sorry, I can't tell you anything," Jessup advised. "You'll have to go around."

"What happened? Was it a murder?" Reg strained to see what was going on and to get a psychic read on the location.

"Nothing so exciting. It's really not for public disclosure."

"If it's not a murder," Damon said slowly, thinking it through, "then it must be theft. Grave robbers?"

Jessup looked irritated. "I can't confirm or deny," she snapped.

Reg didn't need to be a diviner to see that Damon had guessed correctly. Reg tried again to see through the vegetation around the cemetery. Who would be stealing from the graves? Was it someone looking for valuables? Or something more gruesome, someone looking for organs or some grisly souvenir? She wouldn't have been surprised by seances or even by vandalism, teenagers trying to scare each other or being stupid. But grave robbers? She didn't think that kind of thing happened in modern times.

"Don't they have… cement vaults that they put the caskets into?" she asked. "I thought that graves were sort of… burglarproof nowadays."

Jessup shook her head. "If I could encourage you to be on your way, folks. It's late, and you don't want to be roaming the streets right now. Get home and get some rest." She spoke in a flat tone as if they didn't know each other. And maybe they never had. Reg had thought that Jessup was at least partway to becoming a friend, but if recent events and Jessup's tone were any indication, she had been mistaken.

Damon rolled his eyes. He raised the window and performed a three-point turn.

"What a crock. They think that there's some danger in revealing that there was a grave robber in the cemetery? Like if they tell the public that, there's going to be a panic? Over grave robbing? Nothing like taking themselves too seriously."

Reg was silent, thinking.

"You know Marta?" Damon asked.

"Uh, yeah. We're acquainted."

Damon laughed. "Okay, then. Maybe that's a sensitive area. I won't ask."

Reg hoped that he wouldn't pursue it. She turned her head away from him to watch out the window as he worked his way back to the cross street and detoured around the cemetery.

You don't want to be roaming the streets right now. Did Jessup know something about the Witch Doctor and the feeling of doom he carried with him? Could she feel it too? Reg knew that Jessup didn't have much in the way of magical gifts, and whatever she did have, she kept quiet. So maybe she wouldn't have told anyone if she too felt the spiritual disruption in Black Sands. She and Corvin and Jessup had been involved together on other cases. Maybe there was a psychic connection among all three of them.

It made sense that Corvin could feel it after having held Reg's powers and retained some portion of them, however minuscule. But it didn't make sense that Detective Marta Jessup, being practically normal, would be able to sense it.

So it wasn't that. Either Reg had misread her, or there was something more going on.

~

"Can I walk you to your door?" Damon asked.

Reg looked at the dark yard. She felt for any danger, but couldn't sense anything above the level of anxiety she was already feeling from the Witch Doctor. She hesitated, not wanting an awkward scene at the door with Damon, or to have to invite him in. She had already learned about the dangers of inviting warlocks into her home.

Another car whizzed up to the house, a low, red sports car. Reg frowned and watched Sarah get out of the passenger side, laughing. She said something to the driver, and he screeched his tires, leaving rubber on the road as he pulled away. Sarah looked at the big black truck and waved at Reg.

"Getting in a little late, aren't you, Reg?"

Reg shook her head and laughed. "I could say the same about you," she said, getting out of the car. She waved at Damon and hoped that he would take the hint and just leave, as Sarah's consort had done. She walked with Sarah up to her door.

"Did you have a nice night?" Sarah asked.

"Uh... no, not really."

"Oh, dear." Sarah's face fell. "What happened?"

Reg shook her head. "What didn't happen?"

Sarah unlocked her door and motioned for Reg to go ahead of her. "Come in and tell me all about it."

Damon was still parked at the curb. Reg turned and waved at him again and went in.

"Lights on," Sarah ordered, and the room magically lit up.

Reg looked around, marveling.

"I'll never get tired of home automation," Sarah said. "Do you know, if I did that a few hundred years ago, I would have been burned at the stake. But nowadays, everyone has the technology."

Reg was a little let down to realize that it was just technology and not a magic spell.

"I'll make tea," Sarah announced. "Let's go to the kitchen."

They went to the back of the house, and Sarah put the kettle on. She puttered around for a few minutes, finding a half-eaten bag of cookies in the cupboard and putting a few out on a plate and displaying a range of home-made tea blends to Reg for her to pick what she wanted.

"You got anything in there for evil witch doctors?" Reg asked.

"Witch doctors?" Sarah frowned. "Well, it depends on what kind of sorcery he is doing."

"How about nightmares?"

"Ah, let's go with this one, then." Sarah picked one of the packets out and handed it to Reg, along with a cup. In a couple of minutes, the kettle was boiling, and they both filled their cups. Reg raised hers and blew on it, hoping to cool it down enough to drink.

"Tell me all about it," Sarah commanded.

Reg considered how much she wanted to tell Sarah. An experienced witch, Sarah might have some suggestions for Reg. But on the other hand, Sarah already knew more about Reg's life than she was comfortable with, and she didn't exactly want to share her innermost feelings.

Instead, she told Sarah about the bowling. Sarah laughed about Reg's dislike of the rental shoes and awkwardness in trying to bowl for the almost-first time. She raised her eyebrows and waited for more when Reg told her about going home and trying to sleep. She knew that something else had happened. Reg hadn't been home in bed when Sarah had gotten home.

"So then Corvin called."

Sarah's lip curled in distaste. "I thought you had decided not to have anything else to do with him. He is shunned; you have the support of the magical community behind you. You told him no, of course?"

"Of course," Reg agreed.

Sarah nodded, satisfied.

"Only then, he kind of talked me into it."

"Why do you let him do that? You know how dangerous he is. But..." Sarah's brow wrinkled, "it wasn't Corvin you came home with."

"No. Corvin wanted to talk about this feeling, about this... dark force that we've both been feeling. He said to bring whoever I wanted to to make sure that I was safe from him. So I called Damon again."

"You don't think it was just a ruse to see you again?" Sarah suggested. "You know how obsessed he is with getting your powers back."

"No... I mean, I know that, but that wasn't why he wanted to get together. He didn't try anything."

Sarah raised her eyes doubtfully.

"Well, I mean, he didn't try to charm me. He did try to... link telepathically, but that was to help me and see what was going on, not to try to steal my powers."

"You didn't let him."

Reg shifted uncomfortably. "I didn't try to stop him. I thought it might help... it felt good... but Damon stopped him. He did what he was supposed to."

"A good thing. You're playing with fire, Regina. I don't want to see you get burned again. He's not going to give you your powers back like the first time. That was exceptional circumstances. You know that they don't do that. I've never seen it happen before and never expect to see it again."

"I know. But Corvin wasn't trying to take my powers. We were trying to figure out what it was disrupting the... spiritual atmosphere." Reg felt a little silly saying it aloud, but Sarah didn't seem to find it was odd.

"So did you succeed in finding anything out?"

Reg skipped over the stuff about talking to her mother and what she had remembered. "We figured out that it might be the Witch Doctor. You know, the guy with the dreadlocks that I saw in Warren's memories. I don't know his real name."

"Why would he still be hanging around Black Sands? Once the smuggling ring was broken up, he would go somewhere else, start over where he wasn't known."

"Well, the police couldn't identify him, so isn't it possible that he figured he was safe to keep working here? He just had to gather together enough people to start working again..."

"I'm not a police officer like Detective Jessup, so I can't tell you exactly how these criminals think, but usually when you hear about a bust like this going down... things go quiet for a few years. They don't just start back up again. They move to other places where it is safer."

"I don't know." Reg shrugged irritably. "Maybe there is something here that makes it special. But he *is* still here."

"How do you know that for sure?"

"I saw him. I know that's who it was."

"How do you know, though? You saw him with your natural eyes, or in a nightmare?"

"In..." Reg didn't want to have to explain about her memories of her mother and how she had made the connection to the witch doctor. Was he even the same man? She couldn't say for sure, but Corvin had said that it

NIGHT OF NINE TAILS

had to be the witch doctor. That was why they were both feeling the dark presence. "In a vision," she said finally.

"What kind of a vision? It could have been symbolic, couldn't it? You can't always interpret these things literally."

"I'm... I'm not sure, but Corvin is going to look into it further. He'll be able to figure it out."

Sarah shook her head. "Well, leave it to him, then. But I still think it's just a ruse."

"It isn't just a ruse that I've been having these feelings. That's real, and I was having them before he called me to tell me that he was too. Explain that."

"I can't, dear. But I think he's using what you are feeling to take advantage of you. This was the first step. He'll call you back to tell you about the developments, then maybe go on some wild goose chase with you to get you alone..."

"I won't go anywhere with him alone. I promise."

"You let me give you some wards. They are not one hundred percent effective alone, but combined with your own will and your powers... I want you to have all of the protections against him that you can. Saying that you won't go with him isn't enough, you know the influence he has on you once you're in his presence. He is very strongly attracted to you, and that makes his power over you that much more intoxicating."

Reg felt her face flush. "Okay. Sure. Another necklace or garlic in my pocket or whatever you think might help. I'll do whatever you say."

Sarah nodded, looking a little bit happier. "So is that it, the end of your night?"

Reg sighed and tried to decide whether to tell Sarah about the cemetery. Did it have anything to do with the rest of her night? Talking about the cemetery would end up just sounding paranoid and overly dramatic.

"What?" Sarah prompted. She took a sip of her tea. "What else?"

"Nothing, I guess. Just, I ran into Detective Jessup."

"Oh, what was Marta doing?"

"She was redirecting traffic around the cemetery. Because something was going on over there."

Sarah nodded, "Yes, I heard about that. Isn't it awful?"

Reg closed her mouth. "Uh... what? She wouldn't tell us what it was all about."

83

"There were graves desecrated, vandalism, people breaking headstones and opening vaults and all kinds of nonsense. Kids these days have no sense of right and wrong. I would never have done something like that in my day."

"And... they think it was teenagers?" Reg asked, baffled. She might have done some wild things when she was a teenager; she certainly hadn't been above breaking the law. But she couldn't imagine destroying a cemetery while out on a ramble.

"That's what they're saying. You know how kids are. No respect for a place like that. They're always hanging out there, having their little rendezvous, trying to scare each other with ghost stories. Getting the girls wound up, you know, so that they can... comfort them later."

Reg blinked. "I didn't know. I never heard about anything like that."

"Kids will do anything. The doctors say it's because their brains aren't fully developed yet, they don't mature fully until they are in their twenties. In my day, girls were getting married as teenagers. We didn't have to wait until we were twenty to develop the maturity of adults."

Reg opened her mouth to protest that getting married as a teen didn't mean a girl was any more mature than the ones who were hanging out at the cemetery knocking down tombstones. Then she closed her mouth. She was tired, and the conversation wouldn't go anywhere. Kids probably had been more mature in Sarah's day. They'd had a lot more responsibility a lot earlier. Their brains still might not have been fully developed, but society's expectations were a lot different.

"Anyway... that's all. We had to detour around the cemetery, and then we came home. Or, Damon dropped me off. He didn't come in. Obviously. You know that since you got home at the same time."

"Yes, I did, and I had a lovely time tonight."

"That's great." Reg forced a smile. She tried not to begrudge Sarah her nice evening. Not long ago, Sarah had been on her deathbed. Reg would not have been able to believe that she would soon be on her feet, bouncing around acting like she was thirty instead of... however old she really was. "You were out with a friend?"

"A group of us got together. I'm not really into dating one-on-one these days. I prefer a group just getting together to have fun. Not pairing off."

"That sounds nice."

"And you, my dear Reg, look like you have a headache and are badly in need of your bed. I shouldn't be keeping you up. Now, off you go. Do you need something for your head?"

Reg pressed her fingers into the center of her forehead where a deep, throbbing pain had settled. "Yes. No. I'll just go to bed. It's just because I'm tired. It will be better in the morning, I'm sure."

"Okay. Give me a call if you change your mind and need anything. I'll be up for a couple of hours yet."

Reg raised her eyebrows. She drained the rest of her tea and studied the leaves at the bottom of her cup. "You're not going to bed yet?"

"It's the witching hour. I have a lot to do."

"But you're up so early in the morning. How can you do that if you stay up for a couple more hours?"

"I don't need that much sleep anymore. I'll sleep when I'm dead. And in the afternoon, if I'm feeling fatigued. Nothing like a siesta to fill the tank for the rest of the day."

If Reg weren't already tired, Sarah's words would have done the job. She couldn't imagine keeping to the sort of schedule Sarah seemed to be on recently.

"Okay. Well, I'm going to bed. I'll see you tomorrow."

"Sweet dreams, Reg. I'm sure you'll sleep better now."

Reg wasn't so sure. She wasn't looking forward to more nightmares, or for the memories that would creep into her dreams. She rubbed her forehead for another minute. "Okay. Goodnight."

Sarah stood as Reg did. "You know…" she touched Reg on the arm, "if you're having that much trouble and don't want a potion, you could see a doctor. They might give you something to help you feel better."

Reg shook her head. "I've been there before and taken plenty of prescribed meds. This isn't… depression. It isn't normal anxiety. I know it's being caused by something going on in Black Sands. Like Corvin said."

Sarah shrugged. "Maybe so. We'll have to watch and see."

CHAPTER TWELVE

A s Reg had expected, she had a restless sleep and when she awoke was still feeling groggy and headachy and didn't want to face the day. She tried her best to ignore Starlight, but the cat insisted on waking her up and being fed. Reg dragged herself out to the kitchen to find him something acceptable, then after a detour to the bathroom to relieve herself and take a bunch of Tylenol, climbed back into bed.

She didn't usually go back to sleep once she was up, and her body didn't like it. But her brain was still too exhausted to deal with life. Maybe she was fighting the flu or another bug. Or perhaps it was the results of whatever had happened the night before when she had been at the club with Corvin. The memories of her mother and communicating with her had taken far more energy than a simple conversation should have, and she was pretty sure she'd ended up drinking more than one glass of wine—maybe more than two or three, which was her usual upper limit. Damon had been there to protect her from Corvin, not from overindulging.

Maybe she was just hung over. In which case, some more sleep and water would help.

After Starlight finished eating, he jumped up on the bed and pushed his face into hers, purring and rubbing against her, encouraging her to get up. Reg shoved him away from her. "Why don't you go to sleep now? You were up half the night too. You need a catnap."

Starlight returned to sit on her stomach. He began to wash.

"This is not exactly comfortable."

He stopped and looked at her, and then started over with his washing routine. Reg pushed him off.

"Go look out the window."

He actually did what she said for once, jumping up onto the windowsill and staring out into the yard. After staring and sniffing sufficiently, he turned toward her and yowled. Clearly, he wanted her to do something about the missing cat. Nicole, Reg remembered. She had told herself a couple of times to call one of the numbers on the Missing Cat flyer and let Nicole's owner know that Reg might have seen her in the garden. And then again, the previous night, when she had gone out. She wondered what kind of a cat Damon had seen over near the cemetery when he had stopped the truck so suddenly. It had been dark out; he probably wouldn't be able to tell her anything more than that it was a cat. All cats were black in the dark.

Starlight yowled again.

"Yeah, okay," Reg agreed. It was evident that she wasn't going to be able to get back to sleep again. Despite how groggy she felt, she was awake, and her body wasn't going to let her return to slumber. She sat up, putting the pillows behind her back, and grabbed her phone off of the side table. She had taken a picture of the flyer so that she wouldn't lose it, so flipping back and forth between the screens, she was able to tap the first phone number into the phone pad. There were three separate numbers, but they didn't say what they were for or what order to call them in. Home, work, and cell, maybe. But no indication as to which to try at what time of day.

"Hello?" The voice was soft and feminine. Reg didn't think that she had wakened the woman, but her voice had a bit of a breathless quality to it.

"Yes, I saw your Missing Cat flyer."

"Oh, yes. Have you seen my little Nicole anywhere?"

She had an accent that Reg tentatively identified as French. When she said 'Nicole,' it wasn't with a short I sound, but like a long E. *NEE-cole.*

"I might have. It's hard to tell, since she doesn't have any markings, and I didn't get that close."

"Where did you see this cat?"

Reg gave her address. "We saw a black cat around here a couple of times, but my landlord chased it away, so I don't know if it will come back here again. I've been watching, but…"

"Okay. I will come over that way and have a look around. See if she will come when I call her. I do not know why she does not come home."

"Well, they can't really protect themselves out there," Reg said. "It's better if you keep her as an indoor cat so that she doesn't get hurt... hit by a car or eaten by an alligator..."

"Cats need to roam," the woman said firmly. "They are not like dogs. They need to be out in nature like wild animals."

Reg looked over at Starlight, shaking her head. She had been so worried when he had run away. She had been sure that something was going to happen to him. She would never let him run wild. Maybe that was why the cat she had seen had looked like it had been outside for a long time.

"Well, thank you for calling," the woman said. "I will definitely come over and see if she is somewhere close by."

"I did see a black cat last night too, when I was driving away. So maybe..."

"There are so many around. Every time someone calls, I go and look and call, and it's somebody else's cat." She gave a little laugh. "I am calling the other black cats the Nicoys."

"Nicoys. Like decoys. That's so cute."

"And there are so many Nicoys! I think everybody in this town must buy black cats. I do not know why they are so popular."

Reg hesitated, wanting to point out that witches liked black cats as familiars, but she didn't know whether the woman was a practitioner. If she weren't, she would think that Reg was off her rocker.

"I... didn't catch your name."

"Oh! I am so sorry. How rude of me. My name is Francesca St. Martin. We are new here. I've only been here for a few weeks."

"We?"

"Me and Nicole. Just the two of us. I don't have anyone else. I thought that Black Sands seemed like such a nice, quaint little place to settle down. It is like a storybook, no?"

A fairy tale, maybe, complete with wicked witches who might eat small children. Or cats. Black Sands had its good points, and Reg didn't want to have to leave any time soon, but it had its detractors as well.

"Yes, like a book," she agreed. "I'm Reg Rawlins. You can stop in and say 'hi' if you come by here. Have a cup of tea and meet my cat, Starlight."

"Oh, you have a cat too! I should have known. The people who call me about the posters are mostly people who have cats."

"Yes. Starlight is quite taken with your Nicole, if it was Nicole who was by here and not one of the Nicoys. He keeps watching for her out the window and wanting me to go out and find her."

She waited to see what Francesca's reaction would be to this suggestion.

Francesca laughed. "Sometimes it seems almost like they could talk to us, does it not?"

So she didn't believe in any kind of communication between cats and humans. It didn't sound like she knew anything about the magical community in Black Sands. She was just a normal person, moving into what she thought was a quaint little town in Florida.

"Well, stop in if you are by. I'm pretty new in Black Sands too. I wouldn't mind meeting someone else new."

"Yes," Francesca agreed. "I will see you... this afternoon if I can."

"Okay. See you then."

CHAPTER THIRTEEN

S he took the rest of the morning easy, trying to recover her equilibrium and not to think about the things she had remembered about her mother and her death the night before. She had known that Norma Jean was dead, but it was a shock for Reg to remember that she had seen her mother murdered.

Had she been there to see it, or had Corvin just planted the idea in her head? She didn't like Sarah's suggestion that he was only pursuing the Witch Doctor angle because he wanted to get Reg somewhere that he could take advantage of her again. The last time, at the community dance, Reg had been rescued at the last moment by a fairy. She couldn't count on something like that happening again. She would get the wards from Sarah and learn everything she could about how to protect herself from him. But she needed his help to figure out what the Witch Doctor was up to in Black Sands.

She sat, staring at the crumbs of toast on her plate after she was finished eating. Could one read toast crumbs like they could read tea leaves?

Was it the Witch Doctor? Was he active again in Black Sands, so quickly after his smuggling ring had been shut down? And was he the man who had killed her mother, or was that only an association that Reg had made because of his black dreadlocks? It really couldn't be the same man. Not thousands of miles away and decades later. That defied belief.

She couldn't help closing her eyes to visualize the man who had stood over her mother. She didn't want to go back there, but she wanted to know that it wasn't the same man. It was just an unconscious association in Reg's memory.

His face resolved in Reg's brain. It became clear enough that she could hold it in her mind and look at it, turning it this way and that. He looked almost identical to the man she had seen in Warren's memories. And that meant it couldn't be the same person. If it had been the same person who had killed her mother, he would have been a much younger man at the time. He wouldn't look the same. She had contaminated the memory with the image of the present-day Witch Doctor. That happened with witnesses all the time. Show them a picture of someone a few times, and they would become convinced that was who they had seen. That was why they insisted on proper lineups and photo arrays.

The phone rang. Reg looked at the screen, not in the mood to talk to anyone. She wanted to sit and think and analyze the memories. She needed to explore them and decide what she wanted to do with them. Wall them off again? Deal with them, now that she was an adult with adult emotions and the ability to look at it dispassionately? How would it change her life if she processed the memories? Would it stay the same if she buried them again, or had remembering them once already changed her forever? She didn't know what to do about it.

The phone rang again, and Reg realized that even though she was staring at the phone, she hadn't really seen it and processed the name on the screen. Of course, it was the one person she really didn't want to talk to— and really did.

Corvin.

She took her time picking up the phone and deciding whether to answer the call. It would be easier if he just gave up or it went to voicemail. After a couple more rings, she touched the screen lightly.

"Corvin."

"Regina." His purr gave Reg the usual shiver of anticipation. How could her name sound so good on his lips when he was so bad for her?

"What do you want? I thought you were going to take a few days to look into what the Witch Doctor might be doing."

"I am looking into it, as I told you I would. I just wanted to make sure that you got home safely last night and had… a good sleep."

"Home safely, yes. A good sleep, no."

He chuckled. "I expect not. Did you get any?"

"I slept, but too many dreams and my mind was going in circles all the time. I can't understand… whether the man I saw was the Witch Doctor or just reminded me of him."

Corvin grunted in agreement. "It's difficult to wrap your mind around. What happened to you years ago and miles away… it seems so unlikely that it is related, and yet…"

"You don't think it is, do you? It wasn't the Witch Doctor that I saw when I was little. I'm just… superimposing his face over whoever it was that I saw. Someone who reminded me of him."

"It's possible, Reg, but I don't think so. You have been keeping those memories in a vault for so long… it isn't like you have touched them and contaminated them over the years with other ideas and faces. The memories that came out last night are pristine. They may not stay that way; you need to remember what you saw and heard. Write it down or draw a picture or whatever is your chosen way to record things."

"You think that it really was the Witch Doctor."

"I think… that seeing the Witch Doctor in Warren's memories helped to jar it loose. Seeing him again, after all of these years, made you go back and search your memories."

Reg argued, not wanting to hear that from him. She wanted to hear the opposite. That obviously it couldn't have been the same person. "He wouldn't still look the same. That means that I didn't really see him. I just took the way he looks now, and popped him into my memory, for some reason…"

"Do you think that's what happened?"

"Yes."

"Damon isn't still with you, is he?"

Reg was surprised at the suggestion. Was he jealous?

"No, of course not. He didn't come in."

"I just wondered what his face would look like when you said that."

"I'm telling the truth!" Reg insisted.

"You will say anything to protect yourself, won't you?"

"No!" It sounded just like the gobbledygook that had come out of her therapists' mouths over the years. And what her foster moms had said. Regina would say and do whatever it took to get what she wanted.

Foster parents insisted on full, uncompromising honesty, and Reg had done her best to convince them that she was truthful. That was pretty hard for a little girl who saw and talked with spirits. Those strictly honest foster parents had forced her to lie to satisfy their own consciences. Ironic.

"I want to help you, Reg. You aren't doing yourself any favors by lying to me about it. You and I know the truth. Are you ready to talk about what the Witch Doctor did to your mother? What it was he wanted?"

Reg had refused to go into any details the night before. She had been reeling with the realization that her mother had been murdered. Wasn't that enough revelation for the night? And for the next week. Or decade.

"I didn't see. I don't know what he wanted."

"You did see. You wouldn't be able to tell me that she was tortured if you hadn't seen anything of that. You would have just said that she was killed. Murdered, even. But you would not have said she was tortured. No one told you that as a little girl. You knew that because that was what you saw."

"I… can't."

"What did he want? I think that is more important than what it was he did. Why he did it. What did he want from her?"

"Who knows? He's this big, scary-looking dude. You think I listened to him? I was hiding. I wanted to hide from all of it."

"I believe that he was scary, that you were afraid of him. But I don't believe that you saw and heard nothing. You hid somewhere you could still see him. Where were you hiding?"

"I'm not sure. In a kitchen cupboard, I think. Under the sink."

"And he didn't look for you? He didn't know that you were there?"

Reg closed her eyes. She could see him searching through the apartment. Looking through her mother's closet, under the bed, in the broom closet in the kitchen. She couldn't see him opening the cupboard where she was hiding. Had it looked too small to hold a person? Had he not seen it? Why would he look in the other closets and not there?

"I think… he looked around, but he must not have known about me. Maybe he was looking for someone bigger. Older."

"Your father?" Corvin suggested.

"My father?" The idea was absurd. "I didn't even know who my father was. He didn't live with us. I don't know if my mother knew who he was."

"Did your mother have powers? Did she hide you?"

"I told you before that no one in my family had powers. Certainly not her."

"You might not have known. She might not have known. She might have suppressed them, like you. She might have been forced to act normal to survive. But that doesn't mean that she didn't have innate powers that even she didn't know about."

"No."

"Was she the one who hid you in the cupboard? Or did you hide yourself?"

Reg focused on the scenes she could see in her mind. A lot of it was still inaccessible. There were blanks. And what she could remember was not in the right order, but all a jumble of thoughts and feelings. Had she sneaked into the cupboard? Crawled in there, afraid of being discovered by the big scary dude with the dreads? Or had her mother pushed her in there, hiding her from sight when the Witch Doctor knocked on her door? Maybe that was something that happened with regularity, her mother wanting her out of the way whenever she had company.

Neither scenario rang true, and Reg didn't know what the other options were. Either she had gone there on her own or her mother had put her there.

"I don't know. I can't reach it."

"You need to try, Regina. We need to know what happened so we can see how it connects up with the present. If we know what he was doing back then, maybe it will help us to figure out what he is doing now."

Reg pushed the memories away, frustrated. "I can't do this," she snapped. "My head hurts and you're just making it more muddled. I don't want to do this."

"Fine." His voice was gritty. She supposed he was just as frustrated as she was. But he didn't have as much at stake. He wasn't the one that they were after. He wasn't the one with the memories. He was only concerned because he could feel the movements of the Witch Doctor. He wouldn't suffer more from the effects of a smuggling ring than anyone else in the town. There might be an increase in violent crime generally, making the streets less safe to walk on late at night. But Corvin was a big man, a powerful warlock, and he could increase his powers at will, as long as he had a source to feed on.

"Can you get power from other things too?" Reg asked.

Corvin seemed confused by the segue. "Can I... you know that I can. I can get something from magical artifacts and powerful objects. Not as much; it won't fill me up. But incrementally, yes."

"So if the Witch Doctor is starting up his business again, that might be good for you. He'll be bringing more magical artifacts into Black Sands, and that will make them available to you."

"Not unless I were to join him," Corvin pointed out dryly. "We're not exactly buddies."

Sarah said that the only reason Corvin was meeting with her and encouraging her to tell him about the Witch Doctor was to get her alone and steal her powers. But was it possible that he was looking for an opportunity to gain access to the Witch Doctor's artifacts as well? When they had busted the ring previously, he had only been given a few items as compensation for his help. The rest had gone… Reg wasn't sure where. Into the police evidence locker? If the Witch Doctor were back, maybe Corvin was hoping to get in on the action without police intervention this time.

"Reg?"

"Yeah, I'm still here."

"Can you reach out to him? Without alerting him to your presence?"

Reg shook her head at the suggestion. "It's not so easy with living people. I think… I would need to be closer to him, at least. I could reach out to Warren because he had already connected with me once. But the Witch Doctor… I don't have any way to reach him."

"You've been aware of his activities. You thought he was close to you in the parking lot, maybe even coming after you. So you have been connecting with him."

"No, it's not the same." Reg tried to explain the difference. "I haven't been connecting with his mind, just… feeling his influence. It isn't the same."

"I think it's close enough. Can you try? You've exercised some pretty sophisticated powers in the past."

"No. I don't want to. What if I get stuck? What if he knows I'm there? He could… he could bind me or something, couldn't he?"

She could tell by Corvin's silence that he was trying to form an answer that was not a lie, but would convince her to do what he asked.

"I'm not doing it, Corvin."

"Marta said that you did a call. You called Calliopia."

"Detective Jessup told you that?" Reg couldn't think of a way it would have come into casual conversation. And Jessup always acted like she didn't want anything to do with Corvin. Until she decided she needed him for something. Wasn't there any magical confidentiality? Some kind of rule that you didn't tell about the magic that other people were performing without their consent? Damon wouldn't even tell her what gifts he had; he considered it a personal matter. So what gave Jessup the right to share that kind of information about Reg?

"It came up in conversation," Corvin said casually.

"Did you talk to her this morning? Did she tell you anything else? Like maybe what happened at the cemetery last night?"

"No, not today. What happened at the cemetery?"

"I don't know. She wouldn't say."

"How do you know something happened at the cemetery?"

"When we went by there last night, it was blocked off and the police were detouring traffic around it. They were investigating something. Sarah said they've had trouble with vandalism. Teenagers, she thought."

"Hmm. If it was just some minor vandalism, I wouldn't have expected the police to be there late at night. They would leave it until the next business day. Did Sarah know something about it, or was she speculating?"

"It seemed like she knew. She said that headstones had been broken and... vaults opened. I don't know what else. I don't know how she found out, since Jessup wouldn't say anything about it."

"Marta's on probation. She's got to be pretty careful not to step out of line. But another cop might not have been so careful about it."

"I suppose. Well, you could call Sarah and see what she knows about it. I'm sure she'd be happy to tell you."

Corvin chuckled. "I wouldn't be so sure. You would think she would be grateful for my part in bringing her back from the brink of death, but she is remarkably stubborn. Keeps insinuating that I'm trying to do something underhanded. Can you imagine?"

"No," Reg said dryly, "really?"

"It would be different if I could see her face-to-face. But she seems to be keeping herself busy these days. I'll pop by The Crystal Bowl for supper tonight and see if I can have a chat with her."

CHAPTER FOURTEEN

Reg was surprised at how much time had passed when she looked at the face of her phone. She had talked with Corvin longer than she had thought, and the day was slipping away. She needed to eat. And make her bed. She was dressed, but she hadn't accomplished anything other than changing.

Starlight meowed from the other room.

And she had fed the cat. He would never let her forget to do that.

She wandered over to the fridge to see if there were something that appealed to her. With a knot in her stomach from the spiritual disruption in Black Sands, she didn't have much appetite.

There was a knock at the door, which made Reg jump and nearly drop the bowl in her hand. It hadn't been loud or violent, just unexpected. She picked up her phone and tiptoed over to the door to look out the peephole. It was a young woman, probably around her age. Reg opened the door and smiled at her, not sure what to expect. Had Sarah made another appointment for Reg that hadn't ended up in her appointment book? Or had it been there and she hadn't seen it?

"Hello," Reg greeted, giving a dramatic flip of her skirt. "I'm glad you came."

Even if it wasn't someone she should have expected, Reg figured she could get away with acting as if she knew the visitor. After all, she was a psychic. She could easily pretend that she had predicted the woman's arrival.

She was a pretty girl, slim, rose-cheeked, long, spiraling blond hair. She looked like a child's doll. One of the fancy ones that was supposed to represent the traditional dress in a particular country or place. Not that the woman was dressed in anything special. Just blue jeans and a blouse.

"I am Francesca," the woman said, holding out one slim, white hand. "But I guess you figured that out!"

Reg flipped through her mental contact list, trying to remember who Francesca was. There was a meow behind her, and she turned to look at Starlight, who was coming over to greet the new visitor as if he knew why she was there. Reg remembered in a flash. Nicole's owner. The woman looking for her missing cat.

"Yes, of course. Why don't you come in for some tea?"

Francesca gave her a smile full of even white teeth, and she entered the cottage. "What a sweet little house!" she commented, looking around. "I thought you said you had not been in Black Sands long, but you have made it very nice."

"Thank you. But I can't take the credit. It came furnished. All I had to do was unpack my clothes. It's my landlord who deserves the compliments."

"I see. You are fortunate to have found such a nice place, then. The house I am in…" she rolled her eyes. "Well, it is so old and dark. I looked around at other places, but I cannot afford much, and it was the best deal. I thought that once I painted and put up new curtains, it would be better, but so far… I cannot say it has done much."

"That's too bad." Reg wondered who had owned the house before Francesca. Maybe a dark witch or warlock who had left a spiritual impression on it? Or perhaps Francesca was also attuned to the oppressive atmosphere in Black Sands, only she attributed it to the house rather than the town. "You know… I know someone who might be able to do something about that, make it feel a bit better." Corvin blessed houses and removed old curses. If there were a magical residue in Francesca's house, maybe he could help with that.

"Oh? Is she a decorator?"

"He. No…" Reg wasn't sure what to say about it. Francesca so far hadn't given any indication that she knew about the existence of the magical community, and Reg didn't want to reveal anything she shouldn't or to make Francesca think she was a nut. "He is just good at… making spaces feel welcoming."

"Oh, like Feng Shui?"

"Yes, something like that."

Francesca shrugged. "I do not believe in stuff like that. I do not mean to bash anyone else's beliefs; there might be something to arranging your house in a way that makes you feel good, but all of the stuff about facing east or west, I cannot believe that."

"Sure." Reg nodded. So, magical or not? Did she not believe in any kind of spiritual energy, or just not in arranging objects according to a specific pattern?

Francesca sat down on one of the wicker chairs. Reg started the kettle heating again.

"And tell me about this little fellow," Francesca said, looking at Starlight, who was sitting up tall on his haunches and watching her intently. "He does look very wise, does he not?"

"He always looks like he knows better than I do." Reg laughed. "And sometimes I think he does. He saw Nicole out the window a few times, and he keeps sitting there looking for her now, yowling at me when she doesn't show up. I don't think he's too happy about Sarah chasing her out of the garden. If it is Nicole and not one of the Nicoys." Reg chuckled at the nickname.

"I hope it is her. I am getting quite worried, with her not coming back, and not being able to find her again. I hope that nothing has happened to her."

"There are a lot of dangers out there for an outside cat," Reg pointed out as she prepared the tray of tea things. "Cars and predators."

"Or people who might steal them," Francesca acknowledged, "use them for medical research." She gave a shudder. "I cannot bear to think of her in a cage in a lab somewhere. My poor Nicole."

"Well, hopefully, someone just thought she was cute and took her in. They wouldn't have any way of knowing that she had an owner when she's spending so much time outside and doesn't have any identification."

Francesca nodded. Reg took the tea tray over to the coffee table and set it down. She and Francesca were silent for a few minutes as they poured their tea. Francesca sipped hers while Reg was sure it was still too hot to drink.

"It is amazing how many black cats there are around here," Francesca said. "I am getting calls from all over Black Sands. But Nicole obviously cannot be all over town. I see these other cats, and they are too big to be Nicole, or they are the wrong shape, and they look at me with their cold, disdainful eyes. Nicole never looked at me like that. She is very friendly. She loves to cuddle and is a very nice cat. These other cats are just so... not Nicole."

Reg nodded. Maybe Francesca had psychic powers without realizing it. She could feel her own cat's affection for her and recognized that she didn't get the same feeling from other cats.

There was another knock on the door. Reg looked toward it in irritation. Francesca looked at the slim gold watch on her wrist. "You have other callers. I should be on my way."

"I don't have any appointments," Reg said, getting up to see who it was. She knew as she neared the door who it was going to be. She felt his presence like a pulsing heat on the other side of the door.

Reg opened the door a few inches to verify who it was and to talk to him without having to shout.

Corvin leaned toward her. "Invite me in," he said impatiently.

"I have company. And you're not coming in."

He tried to see who it was through the gap in the door. "Who? Damon again?"

"A client," Reg fibbed, not wanting to have to explain about the black cats. "What do you want?"

"We need to talk. How long will you be?"

There was a movement behind Reg. She glanced back and saw Francesca hovering behind her.

"I am just leaving," Francesca offered. "You go ahead and meet with your friend. I was just visiting."

Reg stepped aside, opening the door farther for Francesca to exit. Francesca looked curiously at Corvin but didn't stop to talk to him or seem unusually attracted to him. Corvin did, however, follow Francesca's progress with his eyes, swiveling to watch her walk across the yard toward the front of the property. Reg had to admit that Francesca was a very attractive woman and it would have been strange if Corvin had not shown some interest in her.

Corvin turned his eyes back to Reg. "A client?"

She shrugged. "Missing cat. You don't know her?"

"No. Haven't seen her before."

"She said she was new in town. I can't figure out if she knows about the magical community or not. I don't want to put my foot in my mouth or make her think that I'm loony toons. Isn't there some way to tell if someone is magical without actually asking her if she is a witch?"

He grimaced. "Not always. Especially if it is a fairly low level of powers. When someone has very strong gifts, I can feel it. But with someone like her… she might or might not be; I don't know."

"And with me?"

He gave a close-lipped smile and didn't answer aloud.

Reg took that to mean that he could sense her powers, and not just because he'd held them before. He'd shown interest in her from the start.

"So what do you want?"

"Invite me in."

"No. What's up? What are you doing here?"

"We need to talk."

"Not here."

"Regina," he growled impatiently.

"No. And don't give me any hurt-puppy look, either, because I'm not buying it. You know very well why you can't come in here. I'm not letting you charm me again."

"I'm not here for that. This is much bigger than your gifts."

"What is it, then?"

He stood there stubbornly. Reg folded her arms across her chest. "If you want to tell me about it, you can tell me about it. If you don't want to, then why don't you get off of my doorstep?"

"Not here. Not out in the open where we could be overheard. We don't know who might be out here listening."

"Then where? It's going to have to be around people who can overhear, because I'm not going to agree to be alone with you. You want me to call Damon, and we'll meet at your club again? Or head over to The Crystal Bowl?" After she said it, Reg realized that even that wouldn't be much of a protection. He had influenced her when she was around other people. She had to have someone who was there specifically to help her, not just bystanders who might not notice or know what to do. And she needed someone to make sure that she got home safely, without a warlock tagging along with her. When Corvin had stolen her powers, she'd thought that she was safe going out to eat with him, but by the end of the night, he had charmed her sufficiently that she had invited him in willingly. She'd thought that he was interested in her romantically; she hadn't realized that he was after her powers.

Corvin scowled at her suggestions. "We don't need anyone else around."

"I do. I'll call Damon."

"He's probably working."

"Then I guess you'll have to wait until he's not. Maybe you should get back to work and come back when it's a better time."

"This is important. This affects everyone in Black Sands. We can't just put it off for another time when it is more convenient."

"If it's that important, then you won't mind if we have company." Reg looked toward the big house. "Maybe I should get Sarah too. And I could bring Starlight along."

"You don't need to bring your damn cat!"

"I happen to know that he has the ability to interfere with your magic. If nothing else, he can bite your ankles."

She could feel Starlight behind her, keeping a close eye on what was going on, making sure that Corvin didn't enter. She should have had enough sense to listen to her cat the first time, but she hadn't; she'd locked him in the spare room, howling and crashing around when she wouldn't release him.

"I'm not charming you," Corvin said reasonably. "That much should be obvious. I'm not going to get distracted from my goal, and you're not going to be ensorcelled. So let's be grown adults here, and sit down and talk."

"Just because you're not charming me now, that doesn't mean that you won't. Even at the club last night, you still tried to get away with connecting with me, and that could have turned out very badly. I'm not going to risk it. You're too dangerous."

"I won't do anything."

"And you lie. So why would I trust you?"

"I don't lie."

Reg cocked her head at him. "What, you just shade the truth? I've heard you tell bald-faced lies. Don't tell me you don't."

He leaned against the doorframe. In his eyes was grudging respect. Reg hadn't broken down. She was being strong, and she wasn't going to let him talk her into anything. No compromises. He did things her way, or not at all.

"Call Damon, then. We can meet here. Call whoever you like to come and make sure you are safe, though I think he did a fine job last night. You are getting distracted from the importance of this case. It isn't just a matter of the Witch Doctor smuggling a few animal bones. That wouldn't be a big deal. This is far worse than that, and you know it, or you wouldn't be so disturbed by his aura. So call Damon. Call Sarah. Call Marta Jessup. Just don't delay."

Reg studied his face. She could hear the urgency in his voice as he tried to convince her that she needed to be concerned about it and act immediately. But she still wasn't sure. He had fooled her enough times before that she wasn't going to let it happen again.

"We're not going to meet here."

"Quit stalling."

"We're not. You're not coming into my house again. I don't know how all of the rules work about inviting you in and warding against you and all that, so I'm not even going to deal with it. You are not coming inside." She nodded toward the garden. "We can meet on the patio over there. Outside."

"I told you we can't meet outside." His eyes flashed around as if he thought someone were spying on him. "You don't know who might be eavesdropping. I can't secure an area like this."

"Where, then?"

"Maybe Sarah would agree…?" He nodded toward the big house.

"I don't know. Why don't you go over there and ask? Then you can let me know before I call Damon, so I'm not sending him all over town."

Corvin huffed impatiently and turned around, marching over to Sarah's back door. He rapped on it sharply, and Reg hoped that it didn't startle Sarah as much as Francesca's unexpected knock had surprised her. Reg closed her own door and turned to look at Starlight, worried that he would make a break for the outdoors now that Corvin wasn't blocking his path. Starlight paced back and forth, looking for an opportunity, then sat back when she wouldn't let him out. He stared at her with his blue and green eyes.

"Sorry," Reg said. "I know you want to go out looking for Nicole," she pronounced it as Francesca had, "but I don't want you going out and getting lost when all of this... spiritual unrest is going on. It's not fit out there for a domestic cat."

He stared at her crossly, tail switching back and forth.

Corvin returned a couple of minutes later. Reg opened the door partway.

"She won't let us have it in her house either," Corvin snapped. "What's with you women? I've been in your houses before. Especially Sarah's. You're shunning me now too?"

"If I was shunning you, then I wouldn't be talking to you now," Reg pointed out. "Where, then? You want to go to The Crystal Bowl? To some other meeting place? Back to your club?"

"The Crystal Bowl is close, that will have to do," Corvin said. "I'll go over and see if I can get a private room. You get Damon and meet me there."

"What if he is working and can't get off until later?"

"Impress upon him how important this is." Corvin met Reg's eyes, intense. "You both need to understand that I'm not joking around. This isn't just a prank. My coven may have shunned me, but they didn't take my powers away, and they are considerable. I'm not just a beginner. This is serious magic."

"You really think anyone is in danger? Other than me?"

"Yes, I do."

Reg sighed. "Okay."

"And so does Marta."

"She said that? I thought she was on probation and she wouldn't talk to anyone."

"I don't need her to explicitly tell me to know that she is concerned. I may not have your psychic powers, but I have some ability to read people. She is very worried."

"Okay. Should I call her too? I don't want to involve her in this, especially since..."

Corvin waited, but Reg decided not to finish.

"Since she's on probation?" Corvin suggested.

Reg nodded. "Yeah. That."

She could tell he knew that he had guessed wrong, but she wasn't about to tell him how she still felt about having been the prime suspect in the theft of Sarah's emerald. She was already going against her better judgment by agreeing to meet with Corvin again to find out what he had learned. She didn't need to attract the attention of the police force again too.

"I had them bring you your car back," Corvin said, nodding toward the front of the house. "Since you apparently rode back with Damon yesterday."

CHAPTER FIFTEEN

Damon was waiting for Reg in the parking lot of The Crystal Bowl, a restaurant that catered to the magical community, when she arrived. They both got out of their cars, and Damon approached Reg. He gave her a cursory hug around the shoulders and a peck on the temple. She pulled away slightly, not sure how she felt about the physical affection. They had only been on one date, and that hadn't even gone very well. But it was the second time that he had come at a moment's notice to help her out with Corvin, so maybe she did owe him something.

Reg shook her head in irritation. She didn't *owe* him anything. He might *think* that she owed him something in return for the favors that he had done for her, but she didn't owe him physical affection because he had agreed to sit in on a couple of meetings with her. If she owed him anything, it was cash payment for the hours that he had spent acting as her personal security officer.

Damon did not comment on her pulling away. Reg gratefully headed for the glass front doors of The Crystal Bowl.

"So, what is this all about?" Damon questioned.

"I don't know yet. Corvin is supposed to be telling me. I don't know whether he's really found anything more than he knew last night, or if it's just a bluff." She considered, thinking about the way he had been behaving. "If I had to guess, though, he does have something."

"Okay, well, let's see what it is."

They entered and looked around for Corvin. He wasn't in the main dining room or at the bar. Reg motioned to Bill, one of the bartenders that she knew. "Do you know where Corvin is? I thought he was supposed to be here."

"Got a private room. Just grab one of the waiters." Bill motioned to one of the nearby waiters and whistled to attract his attention. "Hey, take Miss Rawlins and her guest to the back. Room booked for Corvin Hunter."

The waiter looked at Reg, and then his eyes went to Damon. "I thought his coven wasn't supposed to have anything to do with him."

"I'm not in his coven," Damon corrected. "And I'm not sure who appointed you to the council. It's up to the coven to police him, not you."

The waiter turned a bit pink and didn't argue the point. Black Sands was not a big town, and Reg was always a little surprised when she found two people who didn't know each other. The waiter and Damon obviously didn't know each other well, or the waiter would have known Damon was not in Corvin's coven. It just seemed strange to Reg that in such a small place, everyone didn't know everyone else. She misjudged how people would run into each other everywhere they went.

They followed the waiter back to a hall with several unmarked doors. He knocked on one, then opened it to peer inside. "Yeah, this is the one." He motioned them in. Reg let Damon lead the way. Not that it mattered. Corvin wasn't going to do anything to her in the split second it took for her to walk into the room ahead of Damon.

The two warlocks nodded at each other and didn't exchange greetings. Corvin looked at Reg and motioned her to sit down. The waiter closed the door when he left.

The room was small and only dimly lit when the door was shut. Reg looked at the ceiling to see if the lights were burned out, but it seemed like they just weren't turned on. There was a small grouping of candles in the middle of the table. Reg leaned over to look at the flickering flames and saw that they were electric lights. Cheap dollar-store candle lights. She shook her head. Atmosphere. Window dressing.

She sat down in the chair opposite the one Corvin had indicated, and Damon sat in the other. She took pleasure in seeing Corvin grind his teeth over this little demonstration of her independence, but he didn't complain.

"Let's get down to business, then."

"Okay." Reg opened her arms. "Lay it on me."

"The activity at the cemetery wasn't just teenagers fooling around and desecrating graves."

"Did they… plunder them, then? Were they looking for valuables?"

Corvin shook his head. "No. It was a good lead. The police are doing their best to keep it quiet and out of public hearing. It wasn't just teenagers. They weren't stealing valuables from graves. They were stealing bodies."

Reg swallowed. She looked over at Damon to see what he thought about this. Was that something that happened regularly at Black Sands, and she was just naive? Maybe practitioners of black arts needed human body parts to produce their magic spells. Human hair or fingernails. Maybe even teeth. Reg didn't want to think of anything more graphic than that. She didn't need more nightmares.

She looked back at Corvin. "Why would they steal bodies?" she asked in as calm a voice as she could manage.

CHAPTER SIXTEEN

There was silence around the table for what seemed like a long time. Reg waited for Corvin to explain, or for Damon to jump in with questions or an explanation of his own. But Damon didn't seem to know what to do with this news any more than Reg did. So it wasn't something common.

"There are a few reasons that someone might want to steal human remains," Corvin said slowly. "None of them good, as you can well imagine."

"And that's why you said that Detective Jessup was worried. Because it isn't just vandalism or kids messing around. She knew that they were stealing bodies."

Corvin nodded.

Reg shifted in her seat. She looked around the room. Her eyes were more used to the dimness of the room, but she felt closed in. There was some kind of magic in the room that was making her itch. She looked toward the door.

"We are safe from being overheard here," Corvin said, misjudging her look.

"Yeah, I already figured that. But this room… can't we meet somewhere else? This is creepy."

"We could turn the light on," Damon pointed out the obvious, indicating the wall switch.

Reg nodded. "Yeah. Why don't you turn them on? I'm getting creeped out here."

Corvin shook his head. "It's easier for me to maintain the integrity of the room in the dark. It's going to take a lot more energy in bright light, and I need to be able to focus on you, not just on the room."

"Maintain the integrity of the room?" Reg lifted an eyebrow. Was he teasing her?

"If we want to be somewhere that we cannot be overheard, no matter who is trying to spy on us through magical means, then I need to cast a spell to seal the room from any eavesdroppers. Like I said to you earlier, I can't do that outside. I need an enclosed space. And it helps me if it is by candlelight, or at least not too bright. There is a reason most of us do magic at night rather than in the daylight. Moonlight or candlelight makes it a lot easier to focus and maintain the spell. With sunlight or bright overhead lights—I can't do that and carry on a conversation."

Reg looked over at Damon for confirmation. He was, at least, a warlock, and would know if it were just all crap Corvin was hoping she would swallow. Damon gave a nod. "Night is easier."

Reg shook her head. "We could have waited until tonight, then, and met somewhere else instead of this tiny room. It's claustrophobic."

"You're feeling the spell," Corvin said. "Not the closeness of the room."

"Why does it feel like that? If it's a protective spell, then shouldn't it feel warm and comforting? This feels… itchy and restless and irritating."

Corvin's smile was somewhat strained. "You're just going to have to put up with it, Regina, because I don't want to risk him overhearing us."

"Him? Who?" A second or two ticked by before Reg understood. "The Witch Doctor?" She looked around. "How would he be able to hear us here? Is he in the restaurant? I didn't feel him that close!" She half-rose out of her seat.

Corvin made a calming gesture with his hands, motioning her back to her chair. "No, he's not here. But his spies could be close by, and he has powerful magic, as you and I both felt. You know you can connect to people with your mind even when they are not in the same room. I don't know how far his remote capabilities are, but I don't want to take the chance that he can reach us. I don't want him to know that we know anything about him."

Reg sighed, letting as much air out of her lungs as she could in an effort to calm her breathing and slow her heart. As Corvin said, she was going to have to put up with the uncomfortably prickly feeling. She didn't want the Witch Doctor to be able to hear or see them remotely either. She closed her eyes and felt for the spell, trying to visualize it as a warm blanket around them instead of a force field. The itchiness eased a little. She rolled her shoulders and looked back at Corvin.

"So are you avoiding telling me exactly what he is doing for a reason? If you wanted me to come here and listen to you so badly, why don't you get on with it? Why does the Witch Doctor need bodies?"

Corvin's voice took on a professorial tone, like he was lecturing to a class. She knew that he did a lot of historical studies, and wondered if he lectured at some magical university about his topics. "In almost all cultures around the world, there are stories of the dead being reanimated through one method or another. Occasionally, such as in Christian resurrection, the resulting beings are seen as good, but in most cases, they are not. It is almost always believed to be the result of dark magic, creating malevolent beings that terrorize the living."

"Reanimated?" Reg repeated. She tried to wrap her mind around what he was saying. "Are you talking about… zombies?"

"They have many different names in many different cultures. That is… one of them."

"Zombies. The Witch Doctor is creating zombies. That's why he needs dead bodies."

"That is the only explanation I can find. Of course, other kinds of magic might use parts of the bodies, but he isn't taking parts. He is taking the whole bodies, and they are recently deceased. That tells me that he is… reanimating them."

Reg shook her head, feeling sick. "Zombies aren't real. Come on."

"If a myth persists across all cultures… you have to assume that it is real in some form. Maybe each culture gets it a little bit wrong, but myths that span the globe… they have at least a kernel of truth."

"And you want me to believe that zombies are one of those things. That they are real."

"I have studied this kind of magic in some detail. The mythos that I believe is the closest to the truth is the Viking draugr."

"A drow-ger? What is that?"

"The Vikings believed that any corpse could be reanimated into a draugr, a sort of a large, shapeshifting monster that has an animus toward the living. It usually takes a human form, which can grow to double its usual size. Unlike your shuffling TV zombie, it can look just like a regular human. One of the only ways to tell that it is a draugr is that it doesn't bleed. It can sometimes talk, quote poetry, or prophesy of the future. It can only be controlled by a powerful sorcerer."

"Like the Witch Doctor."

"Yes."

"I thought that zombies were created by... some drug that made people look like they were dead, and then controlled their minds so that they didn't have a will of their own." Reg tried to remember what she had seen about this on TV. "Like... pufferfish toxin...?"

"According to Wade Davis," Corvin said, rolling his eyes. "He claimed to have infiltrated a group of bokors in Haiti and learned all of the secrets of zombie conjuring. His claims were... sensational and widely-questioned. But what do you think everybody remembers? Pufferfish toxin." He sighed and shook his head.

Reg shrugged. "It sounds just as likely as what you're talking about. A powerful wizard that can raise the dead? That can't really happen."

"You're judging something that you know nothing about. What makes you an expert on the dead?"

Reg raised an eyebrow. "Well... talking to them."

"That's the spirit of the dead. I'm talking about the body of the dead. Two different things. The ghosts that you have talked to don't know anything about reanimation, because spirits are not reanimated. Bodies are. Have any of them told you any details about what has happened to their bodies after they died?"

Reg frowned. She shook her head. "No. Why would they talk about something like that? Once they've been separated from their bodies, they don't have any more sense of it. Except for Warren, but that was different. Because he wasn't dead, just bound."

"So how could they tell you about draugar? Most spirits wouldn't have any idea about them. You don't suddenly gain all knowledge about death just because you've experienced it. Do you know everything there is to know about what cold viruses look like and how they work in the body? And how many colds have you had? Experiencing something doesn't make you an expert in it. Even if one of your spirit friends had been turned into a living zombie by a bokor using puffer fish toxin, they wouldn't be able to tell you that was what had happened. Because they wouldn't have been aware of the fact of it."

Reg's brain was whirling. She looked aside at Damon for his take on the conversation, then looked back at Corvin again. "So how is a zombie made, then?"

"A draugr," he corrected. "I don't want you getting these creatures confused with the reanimated corpses you see in popular media. Thanks to *Night of the Living Dead*, everybody has a completely skewed idea of what a zombie is."

"Whatever. How is a draugr made?"

"I have studied the literature rather than the dark art itself, so I can't give you a detailed recipe or conjure. Whatever so-called experts might have said in popular media, you can't turn someone into a zombie just with drugs. You can keep a living person under your control, but you can't use a drugged person for your own means like you could use a draugr. Drugged people are not great at taking commands or fighting off attacks."

"Do you know for sure that the Witch Doctor is making draugrs? Couldn't he be using the bodies for something else? Or couldn't it be someone completely different stealing bodies?"

"Like medical students?" Corvin said dryly. "This isn't the dark ages. Could someone be using them for something else? Cannibalism or other bodily appetites? Ingredients needed for spell-casting? It's possible, but why would they need more than one or two bodies for such a venture? This was not a quiet operation. This wasn't one person sneaking into the graveyard at night to surreptitiously steal a body. You saw the police operation. They wouldn't have been out there for a simple disturbing the peace or suspicious behavior charge."

There had been a lot of police, Reg had to admit. And they had set up roadblocks and not allowed anyone close to the cemetery. Not just a simple case of vandalism. Something big and bad.

"How many bodies are missing?" Damon asked.

He had been quiet up until then, just serving in his role as Reg's protector. Reg had not expected him to take part in the conversation. She looked at him and then looked at Corvin for his answer.

"I don't have a handle on that yet," Corvin said. "But there were a number of them. My sources are not clear on how many. It is still under investigation, so maybe the police don't have a number either."

"They would know how many graves had been dug up," Reg protested.

"Not all graves contain bodies. Sometimes it is an empty casket or just a marker. Or there may be the remains of more than one person, which could also skew the numbers. The police have to investigate each one to find out how many bodies were taken. This just happened last night. They haven't had time yet to investigate fully. Or, they hadn't when I talked to my source."

"And that source wasn't Detective Jessup?" Reg challenged.

He looked at her and didn't answer.

Reg wasn't quite sure why she was so angry at the thought that Jessup would talk to Corvin but not her. Jessup and Corvin had a past. They had known each other for much longer than either had known Reg, who was a newcomer on the scene. Why would Jessup trust Reg with confidential information when she knew that Reg was a con?

"Did your source have a ballpark figure?" Damon asked.

Reg tried to suppress her irritation at him involving himself in the conversation. But she wasn't paying for him to be there. He had come as a friend, which she supposed entitled him to ask questions if he wanted to. But she didn't like to have a man speaking up for her, as if she couldn't ask questions on her own. She was more than capable of getting the facts out of Corvin. Just as capable as Damon. He might have a gift as a human polygraph, but he wasn't an expert interrogator.

"Somewhere between five and ten," Corvin said.

Reg's mind went into overdrive. Between five and ten of the zombie creatures, the Frankenstein's monsters that Corvin was talking about? Ten of them? She had imagined two or three, and that was horrific enough. But a larger number? She pictured them all walking down the street, dark shapes shuffling toward her out of the night—despite what Corvin had said, she still couldn't help thinking of them shuffling—and the feeling of horror and dread grew inside her, strangling her breathing.

CHAPTER SEVENTEEN

I have to get out of here." She rose to her feet. She didn't know where she was going, but she needed to get out of there. She didn't want to know anything else. She didn't want to hear any more horrors.

"Reg," Corvin was quickly on his feet as well, reaching out to grab her by the arm. "You need to stay here so we can talk. We can't talk about this openly outside this room."

"No." Reg jerked back, avoiding his touch. Damon was slower, but he was on his feet as well, edging closer to Reg to try to get between her and Corvin.

"Leave her be. If she wants to leave this room, she can."

"I'm not looking for your opinion on this matter. How is your experience in fighting draugar? You think you can do something about this plague? This is up to Reg and me. It's got nothing to do with you; you're just here as her guard dog."

Damon pushed past Reg at that, making her knock her hip hard into the table. The two warlocks were shoving each other, getting in each other's faces, acting like a couple of teenage boys in a schoolyard fight. Reg rubbed her hip and grabbed at Damon.

"Cut it out, both of you. Go to your own corners!"

They eventually broke apart. Reg grabbed Damon's arm and tried to direct him back to his seat. "Quit acting like a couple of twelve-year-olds. You think Bill wants a fist fight back here? Control yourselves."

They ended up on opposite sides of the table. Reg didn't know whether to make them sit down again. She really wanted to be out the door. She didn't want to stay there anymore, and she certainly didn't need to be schooling a couple of testosterone-driven adolescents when Black Sands was on the verge of a zombie apocalypse. The three of them stood there, eyeing each other, trying to formulate their next step.

"Reg, you need to stay here. We need to work out a plan."

"What kind of plan? What are you talking about?"

"We have to find a way to stop the Witch Doctor."

"You and me? Why? Can't you call in… Zombie Busters or something? There must be people a lot more qualified than I am…"

"Curiously, there are very few people who are equipped to fight draugar."

"Well, what makes it our job? What makes it mine? I don't care if you want to go fight the draugrs. But I'm not trained in zombie warfare. I have no idea how to deal with any of this."

"It is our job because we are the only two who are aware of what is going on. You and I can feel the Witch Doctor and no one else can. You have a connection with him, no matter how much you try to deny it. And that makes you uniquely qualified to fight him."

"Why?"

"Because you have insight into his mind that no one else has."

"I'm not getting inside his head."

Corvin huffed out his breath in frustration. "Can we please sit down and discuss this? Running away is not going to solve anything."

"I could leave Black Sands. That seems like the only logical thing to do at this point. If I want to stay safe, I should get as far as possible away from this lunatic. What the rest of you do is up to you. But like you say, I have a history with this guy." Reg didn't know if it was true or not, but she would use his own argument against him. "I know how dangerous he is. I'm not sticking around to face him down like some stupid woman in a horror movie."

"Please sit," Corvin repeated through gritted teeth.

Reg fought back against the urge to run. She could run after the meeting was over. She could hear Corvin out, agree with everything he said, and then bolt as soon as she was out of his sight. She didn't even have to go back to her cottage to pack; she could just get in her car and hit the road. There was Starlight, of course, but Sarah would make sure that he didn't starve. She could call and have Starlight taken back to the animal shelter.

But Reg hated to think of him back inside one of those little cages, depressed and thinking that she didn't care about him anymore. He had chosen her. Out of all of the people who had gone to the shelter and who had tried to engage with him and get him out of his grief for his previous owner, she was the only person that he had responded to. She was his choice as much as he was hers. More so.

So she'd have to go back to the cottage, but only for long enough to coax Starlight into the cat carrier. Then she was leaving. She would put Black Sands behind her and she would never have to worry about the Witch Doctor or warlocks like Corvin again. She could go to California. She hadn't explored the West Coast yet. She would be unknown there. She could take on a new name. She could leave all of the magic behind and go back to cold reading people and inventing stories. She was good at that. It had worked for her before she had arrived in Black Sands.

So she sat down. She would let Corvin say his piece. She would agree with everything he said. Then she would run.

Corvin smiled thinly and nodded, also sitting. Damon stayed on his feet for a few more seconds, letting Corvin know that he wasn't doing it just because Corvin had said to, but because he was there for Reg. Corvin paid him no attention.

"You and I are the only ones who even know that the Witch Doctor is back in operation," he told Reg, "So it's up to us to deal with him."

"Why not just tell Jessup where he is and have the cops deal with him? Why should we have to?"

"How are the police going to deal with him? Think about it, Regina. They have no idea what he is or how to deal with him. Someone like that isn't going to be caught by the police. You need someone who understands the paranormal and has some insight into his mind. If we sent the police, he would slip through their fingers. He'd be laughing. You've dealt with him before, remember?"

Reg fought back against the memories. She didn't want to remember anything about the Witch Doctor. She'd rather think that he wasn't the same man as she had seen torturing her mother. She didn't want to face that evil man. She had been a little girl, scared out of her mind. He had been so big and strong and horrible.

Reg was suddenly overcome by the sounds of her mother screaming. She swayed with vertigo and gripped the table, trying to stay in her seat when every muscle in her body was turning to jelly. Damon was there, his strong hands on her, trying to steady her. Corvin was there, the warmth of his energy flowing into her, but even in the state she was in, she could tell that it wasn't the same as usual. His energy seemed weak and slow, not flowing freely like it usually did.

"Just leave her alone," Damon snapped. "Don't you think you've done enough already? It's too much for her. And if you think she's going to be joining you hunting down this Witch Doctor and his draugrs, you'd better think again. She's not going to have anything to do with you."

"I'm trying to help her," Corvin argued, as he always did. He always had a way to justify himself, whether what he was doing was right or wrong.

"Stop. Give her a few minutes to recover on her own."

The warmth and energy faded. Reg felt like he had let go of the rope that was keeping her from drifting out to sea. She held on to Damon's arm but, while he was strong, none of that strength flowed into her. He couldn't hold her and anchor her like Corvin could.

"It's okay, Reg," Damon said quietly. "Just breathe. You're okay. Do you want me to get you some water? Something stronger?"

"No." Reg shook her head. If they left the room, it would mean breaking the spell that Corvin had woven to keep them from eavesdroppers. And she did not want the Witch Doctor to see her or feel her and to know how vulnerable she was. She didn't want to be that little girl anymore. And she didn't want to be her mother.

"You don't have to connect with his mind," Corvin conceded. "We can use what we know about him already to track him down and try to bring him down. But I need you. I can't do this on my own. You are the one who knows him."

"I don't know him. I've seen him in action, and that means I want to stay as far away from him as possible."

"I understand that. But we need to think about the other people in

Black Sands. What about your other friends here? There are people you care about. People you don't want to get hurt."

"What makes you think anyone in Black Sands is in danger? So he's smuggling. So he has these draugrs to… I don't know, to help him. Aren't they just slave labor? How does that put anyone else in Black Sands at risk?"

"Draugar are difficult to control when you only have one or two. I can't imagine someone controlling five or more. That means that the ones that he isn't in control of are free to roam around Black Sands doing whatever they want to. And what they want to do is terrorize and kill people. It isn't clear from the mythologies whether they consume people or not, but I think that's beside the point, don't you? Would you want one going after Sarah? After Damon? Anyone else here in Black Sands that you've gotten to know?"

"You, maybe," Reg muttered.

"Then I would think that you'd want to join up with me so that you could happen to push me toward one of them." The corner of Corvin's mouth quirked up in a sardonic smile.

"Exactly."

"I don't know why the Witch Doctor created so many. Maybe he is doing some experiment and needs to test it on several different subjects. But I hate to think about what kind of experiment he would be performing on draugar. What would he want them to do?"

"I don't care. Why don't you just tell people what he's up to and let them decide? They can leave if they don't want to face zombies. I don't know why anyone would choose to stay."

"Because most of the population, even the magical community, are not going to believe that what he's doing is possible. They're just going to roll their eyes and go on with their lives."

"Then that's their choice. Why do I have to put myself in danger for anyone who's too stupid to listen?"

Corvin was silent. Reg thought about Sarah, who had already told her that she didn't think there was anything to Reg's feelings of doom and the presence of the Witch Doctor. So was Reg willing to leave her behind to face the living dead? Reg pounded her forehead with her fist.

"Fine, okay! Tell me what you want from me. What's your plan?"

Corvin's expression was frozen. Reg looked at him, waiting. It slowly dawned on her that he didn't have a plan. He had no idea what to do. She looked over at Damon and then back at Corvin in disbelief.

"You don't know?"

Corvin cleared his throat. "Err..."

"You want me to hunt draugrs with you, and you don't even know what you're going to do when you find them?"

"I was hoping you and I could work through that and come up with a plan."

CHAPTER EIGHTEEN

Reg ran her fingers through her braids, massaging her scalp like she did when she woke up in the morning and was trying to get her brain running.

"I don't know anything about draugrs. How am I supposed to come up with something?"

"I probably know more about draugar than anyone other than the Witch Doctor, and you know all about the Witch Doctor. The two of us together should be able to come up with something. And the plural form is actually draugar, not draugrs—"

"I don't care! Do you think they're going to be correcting my grammar?"

Corvin fell silent, tucking his chin and looking down at the table.

"Tell me what you know about them," Reg snapped.

He licked his lips. "Distilling everything I know about them into a short conversation is not going to be easy."

"We're not getting any closer while you stall."

He nodded his acknowledgment. "As I said, there are myths in most cultures about undead or reanimated corpses. Zombies, draugar, vampires, barrow-wights, revenants; even the Asian cultures have jiang shi, ganshi, kyonshi, and ro-langs. There are remarkable similarities between all of them—"

"I'm sure."

Corvin heeded her impatient tone and moved on in his lecture. "The Vikings and other cultures started putting large stones over graves to prevent the dead from rising again. That is where our tradition of marking the graves with slabs of stone comes from, only now we stand them up instead of laying them over the body to keep it there."

"So that's what we need to do? Pin them down with something heavy?"

"Well, as it turned out, the Vikings found that the stones were not enough to prevent dead bodies from being raised as draugar. If men were able to move the stones onto the grave, they were able to remove them off again in the night. Or else the bodies were reanimated in the grave, and the draugar were big and strong enough to move them themselves."

"So, no stones."

"No." Corvin licked his lips again. He focused for a moment on the room, and Reg could feel the spell he had cast to guard against spies. She rubbed her arms, trying to rub away the itchy, uncomfortable goosebumps.

"So is there any way to defeat the draugrs?"

"The Vikings decided that the only way to prevent bodies from being reanimated was to burn them or bury them at sea."

"But we're not trying to stop bodies from being reanimated. They already have been, right?"

"The same principles apply. Bear with me. Remains have been discovered in Syria that show that stone age man had disinterred bodies that had previously been buried and crushed the skulls and separated them from the bodies. And of course, the Egyptians frequently destroyed the brains in their mummies during their burial rituals—"

"I thought they saved them. In jars."

"Not the brains. And the latest studies show that they—" Corvin stopped himself. He held up his hands. "Let's just say they were not preserved. No need to get any more graphic than that."

"Right. Zombies are bad enough."

"Suffice to say that in ancient mythologies as well as in the modern fairy tales we call TV, destroying or removing the brain or head is a sure-fire way to kill a draugr."

"So you suggest that we go out and find six to ten super-human giant zombies and cut off their heads."

"That's a bit of an oversimplification," Corvin grumbled.

Reg looked at Damon. "That's what I heard. Isn't that what you heard?"

Damon nodded.

Reg put her hands on the table and pushed herself to her feet. "Okay, I'm ready to leave. Is that everything?"

Corvin jumped up, his face flushing red with fury. Damon was also up in an instant, shoving past Reg and putting himself between them. Corvin swiped the electric candles off of the table, and they went pinging around the room, making it almost impossible to see.

"Do you think this is a joke?" Corvin roared. "Do you think this is just a fairy tale that I made up to entertain you? We are in danger. *You*, in particular, are in danger! Do you not understand that?"

Reg stood up. "Yes!" Her heart pounded in her throat, making it difficult for her to speak. "That's why I want to get out of town!"

"You can't just leave them here. Everybody else in Black Sands will then have to deal with them, with no idea what they are or how to handle them. The population could be decimated! These creatures are vicious and have no human feelings, none at all. They must be stopped before they can get a foothold."

Reg's hands were clenched into fists. "And what am I supposed to do about it? I am one person. Why does it have to have anything to do with me?"

"Because you can feel them."

"So can you."

"I can feel *him*. The Witch Doctor. I cannot feel the draugar."

Reg stared at Corvin. It was just one revelation after another. "You can't feel them?"

"You said that the feeling was growing and getting stronger. I haven't felt that. If the Witch Doctor is reanimating corpses, that would explain why your feeling is increasing. He is marshaling his forces. He will only continue to get stronger."

"How is he going to get any more bodies now? The police will be guarding the cemetery now, watching for him."

Corvin didn't answer. But he didn't need to.

The draugar could kill, and their victims could be reanimated.

~

Reg felt a sudden whoosh as if the door had opened. She looked toward it, startled, but it was still closed. She realized that the feeling wasn't air on her body, but feelings rushing into her, filling her back up with that dread that had been plaguing her—the Witch Doctor. For a few minutes, she had found some relief from it. Corvin must have blocked the influence of the Witch Doctor with his anti-spying magic, but then it all suddenly rushed back, and it was stronger than ever. Reg gasped and held her breath, trying to straighten her body and steel herself so it didn't crush her. Corvin and Damon were both looking at her, suddenly concerned.

"What just happened to your spell?" Reg gasped.

The angry flush left Corvin's face, leaving him pale and gray looking. He swore. "I was… distracted from it."

Reg pressed her fingers to her temples.

It was more than just the feeling of dread-filled expectation. Now that she knew what the Witch Doctor was doing, she could feel the individual forces. The draugrs he had created. Each was a little spot of darkness in Black Sands, like a miniature black hole. And they were only going to get bigger and stronger, drawing all of the light and goodness into themselves. The draugrs were strong. Picturing them in her mind, Reg saw their dark shapes as they moved around, following the instructions of the Witch Doctor.

"I can feel them."

"I know. I'm sorry. But I don't think I can repair the spell." Corvin moved around the room, gathering up the lights that were not broken and putting them in a group in the middle of the table again. "I shouldn't have lost my temper."

He might have said that he was sorry, and he was acting like his tantrum was over, but Reg could still feel the anger radiating off of him. If Damon could detect lies, then he undoubtedly knew it too. She glanced over at him, and he gave her a grim look. He knew, alright. He wanted to communicate to her that she should be on the alert and not let down her guard. Just because Corvin was pretending that his fit of pique had blown over, that didn't make it true. He was still seething beneath the surface, and it wouldn't take much to set him off again.

In her mind, Reg had a sudden vision of him raging. Not just the momentary loss of control that he'd just displayed, but a raging meltdown, destroying everything around him. She pretended to herself that she was safe from him as long as she had someone there to guard her and that the only danger came from his charming her again. But that wasn't the only danger. He was a powerful warlock, one of the most powerful in Black Sands, and if he lost it, he could do some real damage. He wasn't that soothing, warm, calming presence that he affected when he was solicitous of her. That was just one side of him. A thin veneer. One of the tricks that he had learned to do to gain women's trust.

Reg pushed the images away. Fearing him now would only make things worse. She needed to focus on the more imminent danger, which was the Witch Doctor and his undead minions.

"What do we do now?" Reg asked.

"Can you tell me where he is, what he's doing right now?"

Reg closed her eyes, focusing on the man with the dreadlocks. She hated to do it. She didn't want to see or feel him again. Every instinct screamed at her to run away, not to poke and prod and try to figure out what he was up to. She swallowed and breathed slowly in and out. She wished that Starlight were there. He was good at helping her to focus and acting as an antenna for her psychic powers. He helped her to feel calm and safe, which was not what she was feeling presently.

"I don't know the town well enough," she said, trying to pinpoint where he was. "It's... not that far from the other warehouse. The one that he trapped us in. Close to there..."

"Close to the waterfront," Corvin said. "Makes perfect sense if he's smuggling again. He needs somewhere to store his goods and access to the water so he can ship them out."

"Yeah." Standing there, opening herself up to feeling him, Reg could feel the motion of the ocean waves. The ocean was a deep well of power itself, and distracted her for a moment from the man. He stood on a dock, looking out at the waves, and she felt what he felt, the power of the water. The magnetism between the moon and the ocean, pulling out the tides. "He has... a connection with the natural world... a strong one..."

"I would think that he would need it if he's going to animate the dead. They don't have spirits of their own; each one is an extension of him. They can only operate independently to an extent. He needs to keep his thoughts on them regularly."

"He isn't right now. Right now, he's... resting. Gathering strength."

She opened her eyes and saw Corvin's nod of understanding. "Is he going to make more draugar, or is he done?"

"I don't know. How am I supposed to know what his intentions are?"

"You don't have to," he soothed her immediately. "I was only curious. Our job will be to stop him from making more and to destroy the ones he has already made. Then maybe we can drive him out of here if he doesn't have any more automatons to protect him."

"He's so strong," Reg protested. "How are we going to drive him out? He's much stronger than you or me."

"You are stronger than you know. And both of us together… and whoever else we can convince to help out…" Corvin's eyes went to Damon, but the other warlock did not jump in with an offer to help with hunting and slaying draugrs or the Witch Doctor. "We will gather together whatever powers we can. I can boost my powers… I still have some artifacts that I have not used."

And how else would he boost his powers? What if he didn't plan to use Reg, but only her powers? If he stripped them from her, then he could use them himself and focus them the way he wished. He wouldn't need Reg's help.

Corvin looked at her, his eyes narrow, as if he guessed what she was thinking. But he didn't tell her that she was wrong.

Reg felt a shift in the Witch Doctor's consciousness, and then what she had feared, happened. He felt her presence and reached out to touch her. Reg fought back against the intrusion, trying to wall herself off and to push him away.

When she had been a little girl, she had been able to, hadn't she? He had searched the apartment and never found her. He hadn't been able to feel her presence there or to hear her screams. She had been walled off from him as if sealed in an invisible box so that he didn't even know she was there.

Reg clutched at her heart, looking for extra strength, trying to channel all of her powers into making that wall around her so that he couldn't even tell she was there, but her efforts were feeble and she knew she wasn't succeeding. He knew she was there, and the curiosity he felt was palpable.

"Who are you and what are you doing here?"

And then worse.

"I remember you. I know who you are, little girl."

She swallowed back a scream. She clawed at the air, looking for something to hold on to. Damon and Corvin both closed in, asking questions and offering support, trying to get her back into her chair and to find out what was going on. Reg couldn't help crying out as the consciousness probed and pulsed, thick black laughter building up around her.

"I remember you, little girl. You are not going to escape me again."

"He sees me," she choked out to Corvin, trying to explain what was going on. "He knows!"

"He can't know who or where you are," Corvin soothed. His hands hovered above her, directing extra strength into her. He was trying to weave his spell again, to wrap that protective web around her, but he was too depleted from maintaining it for as long as he had. She didn't know whether he needed physical sustenance, or more ingredients or potions, but whatever he needed, he didn't have it in him. He couldn't protect her from the Witch Doctor.

Corvin's reassuring words were nonsense. Of course, if she could feel the Witch Doctor and tell Corvin where he was, he could do the same and know where Reg was. His powers were far greater than hers.

"You do not have a guardian this time," the Witch Doctor's thoughts came to her. "This time, you are all on your own."

A guardian. Reg grabbed hold of Corvin's arm and held it tightly, trying to draw the strength out of him faster than he was imparting it. She tried to find a way to use it, to build that wall up so that the Witch Doctor could no longer see her and threaten her.

Corvin's eyes were wide. He jerked back from her, breaking his connection, and abandoned his attempt to protect her. Reg looked at Damon.

"We've got to get out of here," she told him urgently. "Before he comes. I need to get out of here. Get out of town. I can't stay here now that he knows I'm here."

"He doesn't know you," Corvin protested.

But Reg already knew the truth. Corvin couldn't hear the Witch Doctor's words. He was trying to calm her with empty platitudes, acting like he knew what he was talking about when he had no idea at all. She looked at Damon insistently, widening her eyes. "Now!"

"Come on." Damon reached out to her and helped her to her feet and directed her to the door. As he reached for the door handle, Reg was terrified that when it opened, all of the evil would pour in on her and she would be lost. He jerked it open, but it did not open a pathway straight to hell as she had feared. He looked out into the hallway and nodded. "All clear. Let's get you out of here."

He went out of the door first. Reg followed close behind him. Corvin was behind her, slower, reluctant, not believing that she was in imminent danger and that she needed to get out of there to preserve her life.

Damon rounded the corner ahead of her and stopped. Reg ran directly into his back, her nose taking the impact and driving consciousness of the Witch Doctor out of her head with the burst of pain.

Another man was waiting in the hallway. He leaned against the wall casually, arms folded as if he'd been waiting there for them for some time. He gave Reg a broad smile.

"Hello, darling. Long time, no see."

CHAPTER NINETEEN

The man looked like some kind of circus performer. He had a black and white striped shirt and a large, curling mustache. He had long limbs and a casual manner. Reg stared at him. He was strangely familiar, and even in her state of panic, she searched her memory for how she might know him. It was a long time since she had seen him. She tried to remember his name, or at least what she had called him. Reg turned to look at Corvin.

"Is he… can you see him?"

She already knew the answer. Damon wouldn't have stopped so abruptly if he couldn't see the man. The man had to be real, corporeal, visible to the physical eye. He wasn't just a spiritual manifestation.

"I can see him," Corvin said, his voice low. He stared at the stranger, scrutinizing him.

"I'm disappointed, Regina," the smiling man said. "Is it so easy to forget me?"

"No… I… where did you come from?"

"I still check in on you now and then. This time, things seemed to be getting a little dicey, so I thought I should stop for a chat."

As he stood there, Reg felt a force enveloping her. Not like Corvin's spell, which had been uncomfortable and itchy, but like a soft, warm blanket. Something familiar and comforting. The Witch Doctor's voice was gone. The feeling of dread was swept away, like the air escaping a balloon. The familiar sensations and the release of the tension helped her to focus on the memories.

"Uncle Harrison?"

His grin grew even wider, and he nodded. "I knew you couldn't forget completely," he approved.

"You know this man? I thought you said you didn't have any magical relatives," Corvin accused.

"I don't. But I don't think he's a real uncle. Are you?" she appealed to Harrison. "It was so long ago."

"No, you're right," he agreed. "Just a friend of the family. A sort of a… godfather, if you like."

"How did you do that?" Reg looked around. She couldn't see any hint of his spell, no aura or shimmer in the air, just the warm feeling and the silence so that she could hear her own thoughts again and the Witch Doctor could not see her. Corvin had said how hard it was to cast his spell in an open area. He'd needed the small, dark room to keep their conversation private. Harrison seemed to be able to do it effortlessly.

"That? A little trick I learned a long time ago. You used to get anxious when I did it. I guess that as a child it was disconcerting because it would block out the other voices and you didn't know how to deal with that. But we had to practice so that you would not disrupt the spell if you were in danger."

"I don't understand."

He cocked his head, studying her. "How do you think I kept Destine from finding you that day?"

Reg swallowed. The day her mother had been killed. Destine had to be the Witch Doctor's name.

"*You* kept him from finding me?"

"Yes." He looked at her steadily. His eyes were clear and bright. She pictured herself hidden in the cupboard. Remembered how the scary man had searched through the apartment, but had not found her. She had screamed, and he had not heard her. If the Witch Doctor was the powerful force that she had just felt, then he should have been able to sense her in the apartment even if he couldn't see or hear her. So Harrison had blocked her thoughts and had used his magic to hide her.

"Yes. I am sorry that you had to go through what you did." His smile disappeared and he shook his head, eyes sad. "No child should have to go through such a traumatic experience. We did our best to keep you safe. To keep you alive and away from Destine."

"We? Who is we? And how did you know—and why would he want to find me? What was he looking for that day? Why did he… why did he do that to my mother?"

He continued to look at her. His eyes were warm and brown, and she felt like she had known him for a long, long time. "So many questions. I suppose there is no way you could know what was happening back then. We tried to stay out of your life and not to have any contact while you were growing up, to give you a chance at a normal life without Destine trying to find you. But you were so lonely, and no one in the mortal world could understand what you had gone through. So we had to help a little, here and there."

"Who exactly are you?" Corvin demanded. Reg looked at him, irritated. She was doing just fine talking to Harrison and she didn't need him butting in to her business. He was there only by chance. If she'd had a choice, he wouldn't be. She would be alone with Harrison and be able to ask all about everything she could remember and not remember. He could tell her all of the things that she didn't know. But she didn't want to share it with Corvin and Damon. She needed to talk to him in private.

"I am a friend," Harrison said simply. "You do not need to know anything else, warlock."

Reg examined Harrison closely. Was he a fairy? He didn't look like any of the fairies that she had seen. Nor was he a pixie. Too tall and long-limbed to be one of their kind. But the world was filled with all kind of folk that Reg had no idea of. By addressing Corvin as *warlock*, he gave the impression that he was not humankind.

"Can you get us out of here?" Reg asked. Standing in a hallway was not exactly the most comfortable or safe environment. Someone from the restaurant could walk in on them at any moment.

Harrison nodded. "Where would you like to go?"

Reg's mouth was dry. She held up her hands, having no desire to be magically transported somewhere else. "Let's just walk out of here normally, okay? As long as you can keep the protection in place, I mean."

"Of course." He gestured toward the door back to the main room of the restaurant, directing her to go ahead of him. Reg exited, followed by the two warlocks. While they did so, she was wondering where she did want to go. She didn't want to take everyone back to her cottage, even though she was pretty sure that Harrison could keep her safe from both the Witch Doctor and Corvin. But she didn't want Corvin entering her house, even under the protection of some other powerful being. The wards that had been set in place to protect her would be broken, and she would be vulnerable to him coming back at a later time if Sarah didn't have time to put them back in place. Reg didn't think she could create wards herself. She didn't know any real magic, just how to do a few mind tricks.

"You would like to talk here?" Harrison suggested, motioning to the restaurant, half-filled with witches and warlocks and others there for lunch or on breaks.

"No, we need privacy," Corvin advised. "We can't take the chance of anyone overhearing us."

"They can't overhear us while I am blocking them out," Harrison said in apparent amusement.

"You can protect a place as big as this?"

"I only need to protect us, not the whole room. That takes hardly any effort at all. We are not under active attack."

The three of them looked at each other, trying to guess whether the dining room would be safe. Eventually, Corvin nodded, just a slight twitch of his chin. Reg looked at Damon, who raised an eyebrow and shrugged, giving no opinion whether he thought it was safe or not.

"Well, okay then," Reg agreed. "Let's be seated and then we can talk."

She tried to catch the eye of one of the waiters to get a table, but Harrison just herded her toward an empty one in the corner and they all sat down. Reg slid into the booth first and Damon sat beside her. Corvin and Harrison sat on the other side. Reg looked around, still afraid that someone might overhear them. But no one was looking in their direction, not even the waiter who should be concerned with serving them.

"You were very young, and it is understandable that you would not remember much," Harrison said without preamble. "You were such a wee thing. It was our job to try to keep you safe, knowing that Destine would be interested in finding you, using you as leverage."

Reg frowned, trying to take it all in. The Witch Doctor would want to use her as leverage for what? Against her mother? So that her mother would give them whatever it was they wanted?

Somehow, that didn't seem likely. She could remember her mother's screams, her promises that she would tell if she only knew the answers they were looking for. She screamed and swore and insisted she would help them if she could. She would find out. She would do whatever they wanted her to.

"My mother…" she started awkwardly.

Harrison nodded. "Norma Jean. She couldn't protect you. And she did not understand what she was dealing with. We knew she would not be able to keep you safe if he came."

"She said… she would tell them if she knew…" Reg struggled for words. "She would have… she would have given me to him."

Harrison's smile dimmed again. He nodded. "You cannot judge her for that. Anyone would have broken under the torture. Even if she had loved you… she would still have given him what he wanted if she could. But he had not the magic to see you or free you from the protective spell."

"Even if she had loved me?" Reg repeated.

He shifted uncomfortably. "She was there for many years after she died. Do you remember?"

"She talked to me; I know that. I remember. And she's… she's talked to me a couple of times lately. Even though I don't want to hear from her."

"She tried to make up for the way she had been in life. Many spirits… they find themselves unable to depart or to find peace after they leave the mortal world. When they have regrets, it is very hard for them to rest."

Reg nodded slowly. She could remember very little about her mother or about life when her mother was still alive. But she knew that she did not associate her mother with a feeling of love and safety, no matter how sweetly Norma Jean talked. She associated her mother with fear and hunger and pain. Reg had only been four when her mother had died, but in those early years, she had not come to expect love and tenderness from the person who had borne her.

"She should go on anyway," she told Harrison. "She's never going to find any peace here. I don't have any intention of forgiving her."

Harrison shrugged. "The past is in the past, and no mortal can change it. You were in danger, and your mother was not able to protect you, so we did instead. Or we did our best. We were not as successful as I would have liked."

"What were you trying to do?"

He gazed off into empty air. "Simply trying to protect the innocent. Sometimes, innocent lives are threatened in the battles between the forces of the world."

"Why did the Witch Doctor want to find me?"

"Some entities are predators," Harrison offered obliquely. "And predators prey on those who are weaker."

Reg's eyes drifted over to Corvin. She had come to accept that he was a predator by nature, even if he said that he didn't want to hurt her. Even when he promised not to do anything to harm her, she had to assume that, given the opportunity, he would. Like the story that one of her teachers had taught about the scorpion getting a ride across the river on the back of a frog. The frog was worried about being stung but agreed to help when the scorpion pointed out that if he stung the frog, they would both die. Halfway across, the scorpion had stung the frog, and as they were both doomed to sink and drown, the frog demanded to know why the scorpion had stung.

"You knew my nature when you agreed," the scorpion had replied.

Even knowing stinging would result in his death, the scorpion had not been able to deny its nature.

And that was Corvin. He probably wouldn't do anything to her while she was helping him. He would probably wait until he had everything he needed from her, at least. But he was still a predator and, in the end, he would act on his instinct.

"This is all very well and good," Corvin said impatiently. "But we are not getting any nearer to the immediate question of the day, which is how we're are going to get the better of the Witch Doctor and his draugar. He is very powerful. Is it within your ability to defeat him?"

"He is one of my kind," Harrison said. "I am not permitted to harm him."

"Then this little rap session isn't likely to get us anywhere, is it? Reg has agreed to help me. If you are not going to help her, even though you claim to have her best interests in mind, then we're just wasting our time here."

Reg stared at Corvin coldly. "Since you're not getting anything out of this discussion, why don't you just leave?"

He looked back at her for a moment. She could still feel the anger bubbling under the surface, but she wasn't cowed by his anger. She had a new protector—one whose magic was stronger than Corvin's or Damon's. Corvin stood up.

"I will be in touch, Reg. I still expect you to help me."

He stalked away from her, whirling his coat dramatically as he made his exit. One of the waiters nearly walked into him, then took a step back, eyes widening at Corvin's demeanor. Reg watched him leave The Crystal Bowl.

"I never told him I would help him."

Laughter bubbled from Harrison. "Ah," he said, "but in the end, you will."

"Did you want to go?" Reg asked Damon. "I don't need you here with Corvin gone, so if you have something else to do, I won't keep you."

Damon looked at Harrison thoughtfully. "I get that you want to connect with this guy because he knows something about your past. But you don't really know who he is, so I would be careful if I was you."

"Certainly," Harrison agreed, "your friend is absolutely right."

Reg shrugged. "Harrison is not going to do anything in public. And if he did… I don't think you or I could do anything about it anyway. So… if you want to go, you can."

"Besides which, you don't want anyone to hear about your past."

There was no point in trying to lie to a diviner, so she didn't. "No. I don't."

"Okay. Call me later. I'd like to… do something less stressful one of these days. A real date. Where we both go home feeling good and don't have to battle any forces of darkness on the way."

Reg smiled. "Yeah. Sounds good to me. I'll call you."

Damon got up. He put his hand on her back for a moment in an intimate gesture. But unlike Corvin, no warmth and energy radiated from him. There was no electrical charge when they touched. His hand was just warm and strong and friendly. She closed her eyes for a moment and could see the two of them wandering along a beach somewhere, carefree, arms around each other, just feeling the sun and hearing the surf and picking up the occasional seashell to examine and throw back into the water. It was a pleasant daydream. She breathed out a little sigh.

"See you later."

He walked away. Harrison watched him go, then turned his attention back to Reg. "They are both attracted to you."

"No kidding."

"You know that the first is a magic drinker?"

"Yes. Would have been nice to know back when I first met him. We've had... some interesting times together."

Harrison's lips pressed together as he thought about that. "Most women would not stay around him if they knew what he could do. Women with powers, anyway. You have a lot to lose."

"He took my powers once. And then he chose to give them back. But having held them... he's kind of obsessed with me. Now there's all of this stuff with the draugrs, and I don't know what to do. He's talking about hunting them down and killing them, and I can't figure out why he would want to. I don't think he's altruistic."

"No. That kind will always be on the alert for chances to feed his hunger. Perhaps he thinks that he will be able to imbibe power from the draugar."

"Can he? Or is that impossible?"

"Who is to say what is impossible? Many things in this world are not known, even now."

"So you don't know."

He gave her a mischievous grin. "You must be psychic."

His words brought her back to the reality of the danger. She couldn't stay with Harrison forever. He couldn't protect her all of the time any more than he had been able to when she was a little girl. Sooner or later, she was going to have to face the Witch Doctor.

"What do you know about him? This Witch Doctor? You know his name."

"Destine. Samyr Destine. He is powerful. He has grown in his skill over many years. He is a formidable foe indeed."

"He remembers me. And wants me."

Harrison considered. He tapped the table like he was playing a musical instrument to music only he could hear. "I do not think he will come hunting you. I believe you are safe if you do not make contact with him."

"I didn't mean to. Corvin wanted to know where he was and what he was doing, and I thought I could find that out without him being aware of it."

"Anyone with experience will know when you are seeking them. It was not as bad as it could have been. You did not join with his mind. But you need to understand the danger in what you did."

"I do now. But it doesn't seem like I find these things out until after I do them. It would be nice if someone could tell me what not to do before I do it!"

"Ah, but how would you learn then? We must experience life, drink it in deeply. Yes, we will make mistakes. Maybe fatal ones. But is it better not to try?"

"Uh… well… I'm going to say yes. I'd rather not lose my powers, be consumed by a draugr or a prisoner of some Witch Doctor or other dark force. I'd rather not die trying."

Harrison gave a philosophical shrug. "To each her own."

CHAPTER TWENTY

Harrison was curiously difficult to get any information out of. He answered questions with questions of his own, answered vaguely or couched his replies in terms that she didn't understand. He was generally obstructive, leaving her with a feeling that she hadn't gotten any further ahead than she had been before he had appeared.

But the man could weave a protective spell.

Even though it was still afternoon, Reg was exhausted. Being in that little protective bubble, unable to feel the Witch Doctor and the dark foreboding that he brought Reg made her realize how tired she was. If she could stay in that protective spell, she would be able to sleep. Maybe for days.

"Time to get you home," Harrison observed. He rose and stood at her side, encouraging her to get to her feet. She must have been nodding off right there at the table, the first chance that she'd had to relax in days. In a few minutes, they were in her car, and without Reg asking or giving permission, Harrison was in the driver's seat. She didn't remember him asking her which car was hers or giving him her keys. He didn't ask for her address or directions.

Her cottage wasn't very far from The Crystal Bowl, so it only took a few minutes to get there. Harrison escorted her to the door of the cottage.

"Here we go. Let's get you settled in."

He still had her keys, which he inserted into the lock. He opened the door and motioned her in ahead of him.

He didn't seem to be constrained by Sarah's wards and didn't need to be invited in. He just walked in as if he owned the place. Reg wasn't upset about his being there, but she was a little concerned that Sarah's protective spells had so little effect.

Harrison shut and locked the door and took a look around, as if making sure there was no one else there. She half expected him to look under the beds for monsters and thought that he might have done that once or twice when she was young. Because there really could be monsters under her bed, or just to calm a child's imaginary fears?

Starlight must have been sitting in the windowsill again watching for Nicole. Reg heard him jump down. He came out of the bedroom at a trot, obviously sensing an unfamiliar presence.

He stopped and looked at Harrison, his ears pricked forward curiously. Reg watched him to see if he would hiss or growl at Harrison like he did at Corvin. Starlight and Corvin did not like each other.

Starlight didn't hiss at Harrison, but instead headed straight for him and rubbed against his legs. Harrison made a pleased noise and bent down to pick Starlight up. Reg was going to warn him about getting scratched, but before she could, Harrison had picked Starlight up and was holding him close.

"I didn't know you had a cat. What a wonderful surprise!"

"I guess you're a cat lover."

"Oh, yes. They are such interesting people."

Starlight was purring a loud, rumbly purr, and Harrison diligently scratched and rubbed all of his special cat places. Starlight was obviously in heaven with all of the attention. Reg shook her head slightly. They both seemed to have forgotten about her and were completely wrapped up in each other's company. There were waves of pleasurable feelings radiating off of Starlight. Reg laughed.

"Well. Glad you're having a good time. I'm going to bed."

"You should have something to eat," Harrison suggested, not looking up from Starlight. "You're going to sleep for a long time, and you need to have something to boost your blood sugar, so you feel better when you get up."

Reg raised an eyebrow. "I'm going to sleep for a long time?"

"Yes."

"Is that a promise or a prophecy?"

He finally looked at her instead of Starlight. "What's the difference?"

Reg conceded the point. She went to the fridge and checked through some unidentified fast food containers before finding something that looked appetizing and putting it in the microwave. Starlight didn't even abandon Harrison at the idea of food being warmed.

"You really do love cats," Reg repeated.

"Yes, I do. And Starlight is an exceptional cat. Very wise." He pressed his nose into the top of Starlight's velvety head, the same as Reg often did. She didn't think she had told him Starlight's name. He obviously had some pretty good psychic gifts himself to be able to pick that out of her brain without her saying anything aloud.

"Wise," Reg repeated. "What's he telling you? If he tells you that I don't feed him enough, he's lying. And about Nicole..."

Harrison stroked Starlight's fur. "He is rather concerned about Nicole," he agreed.

"I've been looking for her. And her owner came by the other day. Nicole will probably show up sooner or later; it's just that Sarah scared her away, back when she was sick."

"You haven't seen Nicole lately?"

"No. I've been watching. There have been a lot of other black cats around, but I don't think any of them have been Nicole. They don't look at me when I call her name."

He shrugged with one shoulder. "Cats are notorious for not responding to their human names."

"I suppose so. Maybe she doesn't like the name. But I don't think any of them have been her. I had... a different feeling about her than I have had for the other cats I have seen. It was... I don't know... warm and lonely. These other cats I feel... nothing."

"Hmm." Harrison nodded. "Well, hopefully, she will show up before long."

Reg thought he was speaking to Starlight rather than to her and didn't bother replying. The microwave beeped, and she took her chicken sandwich out and started to eat. It wasn't the best food reheated, but it was better than having to make something fresh herself. She didn't have the energy to pull anything together. She wasn't even sure if she could finish the sandwich before falling asleep. It was a good thing she was standing up. If she were sitting down, she would probably end up face-down on top of her sandwich.

Starlight made a few chirping meows, and Harrison put him down. Starlight approached Reg and rubbed against her legs. She looked down at him while she chewed her chicken.

"Took you long enough. You have deigned to acknowledge my presence now?"

Harrison chuckled. "He was just being polite by acknowledging my presence first," he advised. "I will get him something to eat now. When you are finished eating that, you will take yourself to bed."

"And what are you going to do? Are you going to stay here or are you going away?"

"I will make sure you get settled, and then I will leave. You do not need me here in your house while you are asleep."

"You're right about that. And you're not going to try to steal my powers from me?"

His mouth turned into a straight line. "Certainly not," he said haughtily. "We are not that kind!"

"I'm sorry," she realized that she had truly offended him. "It was only meant as a joke. I know that you're not going to do that. You're not like Corvin. Not in any way that I can see."

"No," he agreed. "Other than taking on a male form, we are nothing alike."

"Right. Sorry. It was only a joke."

His mouth released into a cheerful smile. "No harm done. Your human jokes are always so entertaining."

Reg wasn't sure whether he was being sarcastic or sincere. She only had a couple of bites left of her sandwich, so she started toward her room, chewing as she went. She didn't even care if she got crumbs in the bed; she just wanted to get there before she passed out.

Her bed was still unmade, rumpled from when she had gotten up that morning after a frustratingly restless night. Reg slid into her place between the sheets and pulled the bedclothes up over her, popping the last bite of sandwich into her mouth.

She was barely conscious of Harrison coming into the room to check on her.

"You'd better swallow that before you choke."

Reg swallowed. She felt her consciousness drifting away.

"I leave you in peace. Have your long sleep. Don't worry about anything else. The world will not end before tomorrow."

"Okay," Reg mumbled.

Starlight jumped up on the bed beside her. Harrison petted him. "Keep watch over her tonight. I will be close by, but I don't think she is in any danger now. The wards will keep Destine away for a while, as long as she does not reach out to him."

Starlight began to wash noisily. Harrison laughed and moved away from the bed.

And then Reg was asleep.

In the beginning, Reg slept soundly and sweetly, without the sense of doom hanging over her. But eventually, whether because her body started to catch up on sleep or because Harrison's influence began to fade, she started to toss and turn restlessly.

She dreamed about Francesca and the Witch Doctor, and somehow their stories became interwoven, and it was the Witch Doctor who had a black cat and Francesca who was a witch. She was definitely a witch. No pointy black hat, but her pretty blond hair was twisted into stringy masses, her nose was bigger, and she was stirring something steaming on the stove in a big black cauldron.

"My kitty, my precious kitty," the Witch Doctor crooned in Francesca's lilting accent. He picked up a black cat and cuddled and stroked it as Harrison had, lavishing it with attention.

There was a rock in the pit of Reg's stomach.

"He's a witch," she tried to tell Francesca. "The man with the dreads. He isn't a cat lover; he is a witch!"

"We are all witches, dear," Francesca replied, smiling cheerfully. "You have nothing to fear from witches."

"Nothing? Corvin said it would be the end of the world. He said that we have to kill them all or it will be the end of existence as we know it!"

"No," Francesca assured her. "Just the end of your existence, Regina."

The Witch Doctor put the black cat down on Reg's chest as she lay on the bed. "Just watch my little kitty for a while," he encouraged.

Reg stared into the face of the unfamiliar cat. It was not Nicole; she was quite sure of that. Its aura was very different from the feelings she got from Nicole. He was… menacing. Just like the Witch Doctor himself. Reg tried to remember what Harrison had called him. If she named him, she took away part of his power.

Destiny?

Was Reg's destiny somehow wrapped up in his? Reg wondered fleetingly if his name was Destiny to everyone, or just to her. Maybe Harrison, her guardian angel, was only there to protect Reg, and similarly, Destiny was put on the earth solely for the purpose of killing her. Two opposing forces. As long as they remained balanced, Reg survived, but as soon as Destiny overpowered Harrison, as Destiny must always do eventually, she would die. It would be the end of her time on earth.

The cat continued to stare down at her, his cat-breath in her face. He was much heavier than Starlight. His solidity was like that of a well-muscled man rather than the softness of a cat. And he seemed to be growing heavier with each breath. He weighed down on her, compressing her chest until she could barely breathe. She struggled, trying at last to push him off, but he wouldn't budge. He was like a rock. Like the tombstone that Corvin had spoken of, weighing down on her so heavily that she would never be able to rise.

There was a snarling cry, the rising notes of two cats facing each other, fighting over territory—a howl followed by snarls and screams.

And then Reg was awake. She breathed in the warm, sweet air in gasps. There were flashes of color in front of her eyes like she was on the edge of passing out, but she told herself that it was just her brain's reaction to the dream. She wasn't really smothering.

They said that if you died in your sleep, you died in real life. If the cat had stayed there any longer, would she have died?

Then there was a familiar furry, whiskered face nudging at her, Starlight's concern for her almost palpable. Reg tried to slow her gasps and convince herself that she was okay. She wasn't going to die because of a dream. People didn't die from dreams, no matter how scary they were.

It was just her brain's way of telling her that she'd had enough sleep and it was time to get up.

She petted Starlight, murmuring to him, telling him that she was going to be okay. There was nothing for him to worry about. She was just fine.

He started to purr, rubbing against her hand and then her face, lavishing her with love and attention, just as Harrison had given the cat attention a few hours earlier. Reg rubbed her eyes, even though she knew that she'd end up getting cat dander in them and would have bloodshot eyes the rest of the day.

She sat up and looked around.

It was still light out, so maybe she hadn't slept for as long as she thought she had. It seemed like it had been hours, but with the bedroom still brightly lit, it was probably only a couple. She looked at her phone. After eight o'clock. She frowned. It should have been starting to get dark.

Then she realized that it was eight in the morning, not eight at night. She had slept away the afternoon and the night, and it was morning again. She double-checked the date on her phone to make sure she hadn't slept for even longer, two days or a week. She felt like she had been asleep for a very long time.

But it had only been an afternoon and a night. Still a long sleep, especially after the problems she had been having recently.

Reg sat up and looked around. She looked toward the window.

"Were there cats fighting out there? I thought I heard a cat fight when I was dreaming."

Starlight rubbed against her, making little purring meows. He licked her hand, and Reg pulled back.

"Yuck! No licking! I don't slobber on you, do I?"

For once, it was easy to get out of bed. She didn't have to stumble like a zombie into the bathroom and splash water on her face to wake herself up. Starlight met her in the kitchen and Reg looked for something to eat and something to feed to Starlight. It was going to be a good morning. She felt rejuvenated and refreshed and ready to face whatever life had to offer.

Except for the Witch Doctor.

She didn't want to face the Witch Doctor.

CHAPTER TWENTY-ONE

S he knew Corvin was there before he banged on the door. She could feel the warmth of his presence as he approached the cottage. So she was already on her way over to the door when he knocked, a sharp, impatient rap.

Reg turned the bolts and opened the door a few inches to talk to him.

"Long time, no see," she told him.

"I tried to get ahold of you last night. Where have you been all this time? Out with your new best friend?" The rage had left, but there was still anger simmering below the surface. And maybe jealousy too? Did he even like her? Or was it jealousy at another magical man being in her life, worry that Harrison would remove her beyond Corvin's reach so that his dream of acquiring her powers would be dead?

"I was sleeping."

"I called you several times."

"I was sleeping," Reg repeated. She had looked at her call log and seen that he had called her several times. Damon had called too, and even Francesca. Francesca hadn't left a message, and Reg wondered idly why she would call. Maybe to say that she had found Nicole and Reg didn't have to watch for her anymore? That would be good news. Reg could use a little bit of good news.

Corvin's anger abated a little. "You weren't out with Uncle Harrison?"

"No. We talked for a bit, but he wasn't very forthcoming about anything I couldn't already remember. I came home—" she didn't tell him the part about Harrison coming home with her, "—and I went to sleep. I just got up. I really needed a good sleep."

"Well, now that you're nice and well-rested…"

"I never said that I would help you. You said that I had agreed to help. But I never did. That was a lie."

Corvin looked taken aback. "Regina, you know that you're the only person who can help me to bring down the Witch Doctor and his draugar."

"I don't know that. You've said that, but you have magical friends. Recruit some of them. Tell them the stories that you've been telling me. See if they'll help you. I'm sure they're a lot more powerful than I am. I'm just a psychic. I see and hear things in my head. That's all."

"You do a lot more than that. You've been showing psychokinesis, affecting things in the corporeal world with your mind. You were able to call Calliopia from halfway across the country. Those are more than *simple* psychic powers."

"Telekinesis is still a psychic power," she maintained. "It's not magic. And the call… that was just because Calliopia and I were joined. I couldn't have done it with anyone else. Now that our connection is severed, I wouldn't be able to do it again."

"Have you tried?"

"No, and I don't want to. It's very disconcerting, moving through space like that. I don't want to do it again."

"I still maintain that your powers are much greater than a simple psychic."

"That's all I am. And even that… I wonder about sometimes. So I'm good at reading people's faces and body language. I'm good at guessing and imagining things. That doesn't mean that I'm actually psychic. It's just… intuition. That's all it is."

"And seeking? And moving objects? Breaking glasses and lighting my cloak on fire? Those are all just imagination? Intuition?"

"You don't know that I was the one that did those things. It could have been someone else. Who would know the difference? I never intentionally did any of those things."

"And seeking?"

"I haven't been able to seek," Reg reminded him. "I wasn't able to find the knife or the emerald, remember? Sure, I've always been good at finding lost objects, but that's just logic and imagination. Thinking about where they should be and about where they could be. It's not magic and it's not going to have any effect against the Witch Doctor. I don't *want* to seek him!"

"You don't need to seek him to find him. You are already psychically connected to him, so all you have to do is feel that connection and tell me what he's doing. I'll… I'll do the rest."

"After yesterday? What happened when I felt for him yesterday? He talked to me and knew who I was. I am never going to do that again!"

Corvin studied her. Reg could feel him thinking things through. She hadn't been able to tell them what had happened the day before. She had been too panicked by his reaching back to her, and then in finding safety in Harrison; she had not had that conversation with Corvin or Damon. They didn't know what had happened in those dreadful few moments.

"The Witch Doctor spoke to you?"

"Yes! And he knows who I am and he wants to kill me. So why would I reach out to him again? That would be like shooting myself in the foot. Worse than that. Picking up a fully-loaded gun and holding it to my head. Why would I do that?"

Corvin ignored her histrionics. She could sense that was actually how he thought of them. *Histrionics.*

"What did he say to you? What do you mean, he knew who you were?"

Reg was impatient. He should have picked up at least some of those clues from her conversation with Harrison the day before. He'd been right there.

"Because he was the one who killed my mother. He knew about me then, and he knows who I am now. He recognized me."

"How could he do that? He's never seen you."

"He doesn't have to see me. He just has to… he recognizes my presence, my being, just like he would recognize my face. Probably better. He felt me and he knew who I was. So I don't want to have anything to do with him. I really don't. I don't want him to seek me out because I reached out to him. Someone else is going to have to defeat him. It's not going to be me."

She remembered Harrison's laughter the day before, and his comment that she would help Corvin eventually. She didn't want it to be true. She wasn't going to help him with anything.

"Regina. I'm not asking you to put your life in danger. Can I come in? We can look at a map. You can tell me where he is operating, where you can feel the draugar, and then I can formulate a plan…"

"You're not asking me to put my life in danger? How exactly are you planning on cutting off draugr heads without putting our lives in danger?"

"What I mean is… you don't have to face the Witch Doctor directly. And you don't have to reach out to him again if you don't want to. You can just give me a little detail about what you felt yesterday. Okay?"

"Not okay."

"Reg… let me in. Invite me for a cup of tea. We'll talk it through, and that's all you have to do. That's reasonable, isn't it?"

Reg could smell the scent of roses. She could feel the warmth and attraction radiating out from him, making her want to crawl into his arms and do whatever he said.

But she had been there once before, and having her powers stripped from her had been one of the most traumatic things that had ever happened to her. Up there even with seeing her mother tortured and killed. He had taken away something basic from her; he had stolen what made her Regina Rawlins and left her naked and vulnerable without them. Reg took a deep breath, even though she knew she was breathing in the rose-scented air and it went directly to her head. She focused the heat he was radiating into one sharp point and reflected it back at him, like focusing the sun through a magnifying glass into one hot spot of light strong enough to light a fire.

"Hey!" Corvin took a step back, not liking the taste of his own medicine. He pulled back on the charm enough that Reg could breathe without the dizzying intoxication. "What are you doing?"

"Quit trying to charm me."

"I wasn't."

"You told me that you don't lie. What exactly do you call that?"

"I was… it was an unconscious reflex. It's just part of who I am, Regina. I can't always control it. I want to come in. I want to discuss this with you, two grown adults on an equal basis. You don't have to tell me anything you don't want to. Yesterday you said the Witch Doctor was down at the wharf. Can you be any more specific? Can you tell what dock or building he is using? What ship or plane he is loading his goods onto? Just solid, practical stuff like that."

"You are not coming in."

"What danger is there in it if you can resist me?" There was a bitter edge to his voice. He hated it when she withstood him. When she had worn Sarah's ward, so he hadn't been able to be with her. When she had told him that she wouldn't dance with him unless he agreed not to ensorcel her. And when she used the heat of his charm as a weapon against him.

Reg couldn't help but feel some sense of accomplishment. Since she had first met Corvin, she had been attracted to him. She had been unable to resist his pull. But she was standing on her own two feet. It meant that she had power over him instead of the other way around.

"So much for not having anything more than intuition," Corvin growled.

"I still don't think it's a good idea for you to come in here. Besides, Starlight is here and you don't want to have to be in the same room as him, do you?"

"I'll put up with the animal if you will just hear me out."

"There's nothing else to say. To answer your questions… no, I'm not sure what dock or building he is in. Since you can feel him too, why don't you go down to the wharf and wander around until you can pinpoint it? Like a psychic game of warmer and colder. Then you'll know where he is, and you can sit there and watch his operations. Wouldn't that give you more information than some vague psychic mumbo-jumbo?"

"That's also more dangerous," he pointed out grumpily. "To watch him with my physical eyes, I have to expose myself."

Reg stared at him and waited for him to make the connection. That might be more dangerous to him, but it was less risky to her. Which was worse, for him to expose himself to the Witch Doctor's or one of his minion's sight, or for Reg to risk the Witch Doctor getting inside of her head and being able to control or kill her? It would be a lot worse for her if the Witch Doctor felt her than it would be for Corvin to walk past their operations on some dock somewhere.

"I suppose if that's all you can give me, that's what I'll have to do," he said grudgingly.

"I can't give you information I don't have. And I can't risk letting him inside my head. Harrison said that if I leave the Witch Doctor alone, he won't come after me. He has other things to do—his smuggling agenda or taking over the world or whatever it is he is hoping to accomplish. I'm just a little blip on his screen, and if I stay quiet, I'll be safe."

A crease appeared between Corvin's brows. "Did it ever occur to you that this Harrison could be working *with* the Witch Doctor? He makes an appearance immediately after you make contact with him? He tells you to stay away and not interfere? It sounds to me like he's trying to protect the Witch Doctor, not you."

Reg's jaw dropped. It was such a ridiculous idea she didn't even know where to start.

"Didn't you feel it?" she demanded. "His spell? He was *protecting* me. He was keeping the Witch Doctor out. You couldn't even feel that?"

"Or keeping you from reaching out to the Witch Doctor. It would be the same thing, wouldn't it? He puts a magical barrier there so that you can't feel the Witch Doctor. You feel like you are safe, but really, he's just suppressing your powers. You have the power to feel the Witch Doctor. That gives you a warning if he is near or if he is a danger to you. If dear old Uncle Harrison suppresses that power, then you are vulnerable. You don't know if the Witch Doctor can still feel you or not. You only know that *you* can't feel *him*."

Reg shook her head adamantly. "No. I know him. I trust him. He's not working with the Witch Doctor. That's ridiculous."

"How do you know him? You know him from back when the Witch Doctor was threatening your family. Why didn't he protect your mother? If he could protect you, why couldn't he protect her? Why did he let her die? Maybe he was working with the Witch Doctor back then. His job was to keep you out of the way so that the Witch Doctor could pursue his own nefarious plans."

"How was I going to do anything to stop him? I was four years old! I didn't have any powers to speak of. Sure, I could hear the ghosts, but that was all. I couldn't fight someone like the Witch Doctor. I couldn't have prevented him from doing anything."

"Why didn't he protect your mother?" Corvin pressed.

"Maybe he couldn't. Maybe he could only put a protective spell on me, not on both of us or the entire apartment. You don't know what powers he has or had then. You don't know what his limitations were." She felt the stirrings of anger against Corvin. She knew that Harrison was her friend. Her protector. He had always been there during her worse times.

She hated Corvin for the doubts that started to creep in. *Why* had

Harrison always been there during her worst times? Did the bad times come *because* he was there?

He hadn't been the one who had victimized her. She couldn't remember him ever doing anything that had caused her any harm. She could remember times when she had felt that protective blanket of power envelop her and protect her from the evil men and women who had wanted to hurt her or take advantage of her.

There had been other times when he hadn't been there. Plenty of times when she'd had to fight opposition all on her own. But the worst times, facing the strongest and most vile predators, Harrison had been there to help her.

Except with Corvin.

Where had Harrison been when Corvin had stolen her powers? Had it been such a small thing that he didn't think it mattered? Her gifts were weak when compared with Harrison's; maybe he felt that they were insignificant. Perhaps he thought that she was willingly giving them away, as Corvin had said she was.

She had agreed, after all. She had yielded to Corvin.

But she hadn't known what she was doing. She hadn't understood that she was letting him take something so precious from her.

So where had Harrison been then? Why hadn't he been there to guide and protect her?

"I know he's not working with the Witch Doctor," Reg said with certainty. "There's no way he is."

Corvin studied her for a long time, trying to read something in her face. Did he think that she was lying? Or that she didn't understand? He didn't try to probe into her mind, but he was too close. She could feel him trying to decide how far he could push it. She took a step back and closed the door a quarter of an inch.

"Reg!" He put up his hand to stop her.

"Don't try to mess with me, Corvin. I'm tired of your games."

"No games." He still held his hand up, but she couldn't detect any power or changes in his energy.

"What, then? I've answered your questions. I can't tell you any more specifics about the Witch Doctor. Harrison didn't tell me anything that might be helpful, but he wasn't blocking me. He's not working with the Witch Doctor."

"Someone is. I'm sure of it. If it's not him, then who? I don't believe he just recognized you from when you were four. That's a long time ago, and you've grown and matured and increased in your powers since then. People don't stay the same forever; they're always growing and changing."

"So… if you don't think he recognized me, then what?"

"I think someone we know is working with him. Someone who has been around here and knows that you've been feeling the changes in the spiritual structure of Black Sands."

"Well… that's pretty much everybody I've talked to."

"But you don't know a lot of people. Your circle of friends is still pretty small. So who could it be?" His eyes narrowed. "Personally, I favor Damon."

"Damon? You think he's working with the Witch Doctor? No." Reg shook her head, frowning. "No, he wouldn't do that. Besides… what powers does he have that the Witch Doctor would want?"

"It may not be powers; it may just be information. Keeping an eye on you, reporting back your activities. Letting him know your suspicions and your progress."

"Damon wouldn't do that."

"Did you ever feel the Witch Doctor before Damon came into the picture?"

"Yes."

Corvin waited, frowning, for her to think it through. Reg shook her head. "We just went on our first date this week."

"So you must have met before. That wasn't the first time you met him."

"No. He was at your hearing. He was one of the security guards there."

"Was he?" Corvin's voice was low and meditative. Reg wondered what he was thinking. There wasn't any way that Damon had anything to do with the Witch Doctor. There was no connection between the two of them.

"You still claim that you were not the one who lit my cloak on fire," Corvin said.

Reg blinked at the non sequitur. "Uh… no. I don't know how to do that. I've never lit anything on fire before."

"And Damon was there. He's sweet on you. Maybe he was the one."

"You're just paranoid. Why would he do that?"

"Because he liked you. Wanted to protect you. Wanted to punish me. Make me stop talking about you."

"I suppose." Reg shook her head. "But I really don't think it could have been him… does he have that ability? Wouldn't you know? He's been in the community a lot longer than I have been. He grew up here."

"Magical persons don't always reveal their powers. Sometimes they keep secrets. It's personal and private. He could have a power like that without anyone knowing."

"But when we were at the hearing, his hair started to smoke. It lit on fire, and he put it out. So it must have been someone else causing the fires."

He cocked his head at her. "Why? What does that prove?"

"If someone lit his hair on fire, well it wouldn't have been him, would it? He wouldn't have done it himself."

"Why not?"

"Because…" Reg fumbled. She couldn't find a reason. Because it was dangerous? Not if he was the one lighting the fire, managing it, and extinguishing it. Because it would draw attention to him? But it hadn't. Reg was the only one who had seen, while Corvin was taking the attention of the rest of the room. "I don't think it was him. What do you know about his powers? All I know is that he can discern the truth. And you're the one who told me that."

Corvin smiled a little. "He has another interesting ability. He is able to put visions into people's minds. Sometimes with such clarity that they think that something actually happened when it didn't."

"You think he's the one putting these feelings of dread into me?" Reg challenged. "You feel them too, so you know it's the Witch Doctor."

"I know that he is here and that he is disrupting the forces of the town. But you have had several experiences that I have not, feeling the force close by you, possibly even about to attack. That is the sort of thing I wouldn't put past Damon the Dreamer."

CHAPTER TWENTY-TWO

R eg thought about the vision that she'd had at the bowling alley about rolling the ball directly down the middle of the lane and getting a strike. That had given her the confidence to try again and to actually roll the ball down the middle and hit a couple of pins. Not a strike, but not a gutter ball. It had seemed very real at the time. And she remembered the vision that she'd had when he put his hand on her back the night before, of the two of them wandering on the beach.

Reg frowned. "Is that what was going on?"

Corvin nodded eagerly. "It is Damon, isn't it? You can see it now. He's been manipulating you."

"No… at least, not about the Witch Doctor and the Draugrs. But maybe some other things…"

"Are you sure? Are you really sure that he's not making you see these things?"

"Like what? Like Harrison? You saw him too. I didn't just see a vision of him."

"No, but these early memories, and feeling the draugar around you… he's been there. It could be him."

"Why would he want me to think there were draugrs? Wouldn't the Witch Doctor want to keep them a secret?"

Corvin's forehead creased. "Uh… maybe. I suppose it depends on whether he wants to terrorize people or whether he has another goal."

"I thought it was all about his smuggling business. Isn't he just using them for slave labor? Isn't that why witch doctors make zombies? I thought they were all about working sugar plantations."

"Traditionally, at least in Haiti. But draugar are used all over the world, not just in Haiti. He could be using them for some other dark purpose."

"You've been saying that everyone is in danger. Why would the Witch Doctor want Damon to warn anyone of that?"

Corvin's mouth was a straight line. "Maybe it's not Damon, then," he admitted. "But someone must have told him about you."

Reg didn't see it. She knew that the Witch Doctor had recognized her. Corvin was wrong about that.

"I don't think so. Now I've got some calls to make, so you should get on your way."

He looked at her phone as she took it out.

"Who do you have to call?" he asked suspiciously.

"Not that it is any of your business, but I was going to call this lady who lost her cat. I'm not sure why she called me again. Maybe she found it. Her."

"Cats," Corvin said with distaste. "She should be happy not to be burdened with it."

Reg glared at him. "Harrison loves cats."

"He *would*."

"You saw her here the other day," Reg reminded him. "You were here when she left."

He was still, thinking about it.

"I dreamt about her last night," Reg said. "Or this morning, whichever it was. She and the Witch Doctor were all mixed up. He was speaking with her accent."

"What kind of an accent?"

"I don't know for sure. French, I think. It sounds French. She says Nee-cole instead of Nih-cole."

"Could it be Creole?"

"I… don't know. What does Creole sound like?"

"It was a French pidgin. So it sounds something like French."

"Well then, yeah, I guess it could be." She shrugged. "Why?"

"She's white, so I wouldn't have taken her for Haitian. But of course there are white people living on and born in Haiti."

"Where the Witch Doctor is from?" He'd never explicitly said that the Witch Doctor was Haitian. But she assumed that he was. She didn't know of any other culture in the modern world that had the knowledge to make zombies.

"If she's from Haiti…" Corvin mused.

"You think she's the leak? She's the reason he knew who I was?"

"You talked to her before you reached out to the Witch Doctor. So she could have told him details about you."

"I suppose," Reg said reluctantly. Why was she so hesitant to accept that maybe the Witch Doctor hadn't really known her when she connected with him psychically, but had only been told about her? Wouldn't it be more comforting to believe that he was oblivious and her chance encounter with him when she was a child had not stuck in his memory? For some reason, though, it was not. And Reg didn't want Francesca to be involved in it.

But she didn't know Francesca or anything about her, other than the fact that she had a cat that she didn't appear to care for properly and she had only recently moved to Black Sands. Everything else was speculation.

"And then there's also…" Corvin trailed off.

"What?"

He shook his head. "I have to think about it. Read some of my research."

"So do you think… I shouldn't call her back?"

Corvin rubbed his chin, thinking about it. Finally, he shook his head. "No, I don't think you should. If there's any possibility that she's passing information on to the Witch Doctor, it's too risky. It's not like it was something important anyway, is it?"

"Just about her cat. That's the only thing I know about her." Reg raised an eyebrow. "That is important to some people, you know. Their cats are like their children."

He wrinkled his nose and shook his head. "People never cease to amaze me. Children are bad enough. Spoiling your pet because you don't have any children… you should celebrate the fact, not turn to zookeeping."

"Don't you have a familiar? Sarah doesn't like cats either, but she has a parrot."

"No, I have never seen the need for a familiar."

"Do you just not like animals?"

"I don't like cats. There's a difference."

"Cats are animals."

"Cats are just one kind of animal. Other animals are not so… offensive."

"Offensive?" Reg shook her head, smiling. "It's not like they smell. Now mice or guinea pigs… I don't have the super sensitive sense of smelling that my foster-sister has, but ugh—I hate the smell of rodents. And then there are dogs. They poop all over the place indiscriminately. At least cats are tidy."

"It isn't their cleanliness habits that offend me."

Reg raised an eyebrow, waiting for further explanation, but he didn't elaborate. Reg shrugged. "So, I guess you're going over to the wharf to dowse for the Witch Doctor or off to do your research."

"Yes…" He looked past her into the interior of her cottage for a moment before nodding. His shoulders relaxed, dipping down. "I will be back."

"Just call me," Reg urged. "There's no point in coming here to talk on the doorstep."

"But maybe next time, you'll invite me in."

"No. I won't," she said with certainty.

"Is your uncle coming back today?"

"My uncle? Oh, Harrison. I don't know. I don't understand who he is or what he's doing here… But he told me I would be safe if I stay out of the Witch Doctor's business, so… that's my plan. Stay out of the way."

"You think it's better to turn your back on this business and let the chips fall where they may?"

"Yes. If he is busy enough not to come after me, then why should I do anything to get his attention? I don't want to be targeted."

"I thought you were one of those people who put the common good ahead of herself. I guess I was mistaken."

Personal survival had always been more critical to Reg than the common good. Maybe that was what came from being hungry and endangered as a child. She had learned to look after herself when no one else did. The altruistic people were the ones who had been raised with safety and security and everything they needed. They didn't have a sense of mortal danger because their mortality had never been at stake.

"I put myself first," Reg told Corvin, shutting the door on him. "Just like you do."

He said her name, but nothing else, and he was soon gone without any cajoling. He did have other things to do, and he must have decided it was in his best interest to go and do them.

She was thinking about him and about what exactly he was hoping to get out of the Witch Doctor situation as she sat down to look at her phone and check her email. He had received some of the Witch Doctor's smuggled goods before, and she had to assume that that was what he was after again. Except for maybe more this time.

The phone rang when it was in Reg's hand and, not having expected the call, she startled violently and was distracted from what she had been doing. She looked at the screen, but the caller ID was blocked. She wondered if it were Francesca again, calling from one of her other numbers this time. Corvin had said it was best not to talk to her, but Reg thought she might be able to get information from Francesca. If Francesca were working with the Witch Doctor, which Reg doubted, despite her disturbing dream, then maybe Reg could find out what the Witch Doctor's plans and motivations were. She picked it up.

"Hello?"

"It's Detective Jessup, Reg."

"Oh, it's 'Reg' again instead of 'Miss Rawlins,' is it?" Reg asked, allowing the bite to enter her voice.

There was silence for a moment from Jessup. "Uh... do I do that?" she asked uncertainly. "Switch between the two?"

"Your cop persona calls me Miss Rawlins when I'm a suspect. I mean, I'm glad that I'm not anymore, but I'm not sure I'm ready for us to go back to Reg."

"Okay, then, Miss Rawlins," Jessup said in a stilted manner. "I'm sorry to disturb you..."

"What is it you want?"

"I would like to know... if you happen to know where Corvin Hunter is. I've tried to reach him a couple of times, but his phone must be turned off. I don't know if he's in contact with you, or whether you decided not to have anything to do with him. But I thought it was worth a try. In case he was hanging around your door."

"No. He was here earlier, but he's gone now."

"Do you happen to know where?"

"Not for sure." Reg wasn't sure she wanted to share any details with Jessup. Or whether Corvin would want her to. Since Corvin wasn't exactly working with the police on the case, they would undoubtedly not approve of him sneaking around the wharf trying to find out where the Witch Doctor was working in order to steal from him.

"Okay. I was hoping… I had something to discuss with him. Some… unusual reports."

"More draugrs?" Reg asked.

"Oh. Hunter told you about that, did he? I don't know if I believe in the whole thing, but we've had some strange things going on, and I hoped that he might have some insight."

"What kind of things? You may as well talk to me since he's not the one who can feel them. But I can."

"Can you? Could you come in so we could talk about it? I'm just not sure how to handle the situation, but if you could give me some direction…"

"Come in?" Reg repeated.

"Uh… to the police station. I know you're going to say no, but I could use your help."

"Then it will have to be somewhere else. Somewhere neutral. I am not going to the police station."

Jessup hummed and hawed uncertainly. Reg knew that she was delaying in hopes that Reg would just agree to come to the station. But Reg knew from experience that she didn't have to go to the police station if she wasn't under arrest. They could ask her for her thoughts on the draugrs and the Witch Doctor anywhere.

Maybe Jessup too wanted to secure a room against eavesdroppers, but then she could do just like Corvin and meet in a small room somewhere else. Maybe it was Corvin who had told Jessup to call Reg. If he couldn't get the information he wanted to out of Reg, maybe he thought Jessup could give it a try.

Reg didn't have any trouble waiting Jessup out. There was no benefit to her rushing in to make suggestions. She wasn't the one who wanted to consult with Jessup.

"I'm on probation," Jessup said. "I'm not really supposed to be out of the office interviewing subjects."

"Okay."

"So you'll come in?" Jessup asked, confused.

"No. If you can't interview me, then you can't interview me. Just tell them that I refused to come in."

"But Reg, it would really help me out if you could…"

"Uh-huh."

"Can't you help a friend out?"

"You've gone back to Reg again. And I don't remember you being willing to bend when I was a suspect and asking for your help."

"I helped you whenever I could," Jessup protested, "but my hands were tied. There is only so much that I can do."

"Yeah. That's too bad. I'll talk to you later, then. See you around…"

"Reg—"

Reg tapped the hang-up icon on the screen. She sat there, feeling self-satisfied for about ten seconds before the guilt hit. She probably shouldn't have been so rude to Jessup.

The phone rang again. It was, again, a blocked number. Reg considered. It hadn't been long enough for Jessup to go to her boss and get permission to leave the police station.

Reg answered the call. "Hello?"

"It's Detective Jessup."

"Oh, hi. I thought we were done."

"I can meet you somewhere. I'll get it approved. You want me to come there?"

"That depends."

"Depends on what?" Jessup asked with a sigh.

"Depends on whether you are coming over to talk or to make accusations. I'm not letting you in here to perform a search. I don't want my privacy invaded."

"I'm not coming to invade your privacy; I'm coming because you didn't want to meet at the police station. If you have somewhere else in mind, let me know now before my head explodes."

Reg couldn't help laughing. "Last time you were here, it was with a warrant," she reminded Jessup.

"Yes. I admit that. And you know I was required to pursue all leads. People were pointing at you and your cat, and I didn't have any choice but to follow up."

"So, no warrant this time?"

"No. Can I come over?"

"I suppose."

"Okay. I'll be maybe half an hour. Does that work for you?"

"Sure. I'll put on some tea."

"Thanks. I'll see you then."

CHAPTER TWENTY-THREE

R eg searched through the cupboards, thinking it would be nice to have something to go with the tea. She found half a bag of cookies, and when she tested them, they were still crisp and sweet, not stale, so she added some to the tea tray. When Jessup got there, everything was arranged, and the tea was steeping. Despite the knot in her stomach, Reg was feeling as calm and peaceful as she could at the prospect of talking to a police officer about zombies.

"This is nice," Jessup approved as she sat down and looked over the tea service. She stretched her legs out in front of her and massaged her neck and shoulders. "I'm just feeling so cooped up having to be at the police station all the time. When I'm not out directing traffic or paired with someone else on an investigation."

"They let you come over here without another officer?"

"I told them that I knew you and you wouldn't talk if there were someone else with me. They didn't like it, but I've been behaving myself, so they decided to throw me a bone."

Reg picked up her teacup and had a sip. She looked around for Starlight and saw him sleeping in a warm sunbeam.

"So what do you know about these draugrs?" Jessup asked.

"Well, it depends on what you want to know. Corvin is the one with the historical knowledge. I haven't spent my whole life studying zombie culture.

But he can't feel them. Corvin is sure that's what the Witch Doctor is doing with the bodies he disinterred, but he can't feel them himself."

"And you can."

"Yes. They don't feel good; I'll tell you that."

"I don't know if you've turned the TV on today, but we've had more trouble. Not with more body-snatching, but…" She let out a deep sigh. "We have some strange and suspicious deaths. And I think… it matches up with what Hunter was saying about draugrs."

The knot in Reg's stomach became tighter and heavier. Up until then, they had only been talking about the Witch Doctor using already-interred bodies. Corvin had said repeatedly that Black Sands was in danger, but Reg had hoped he was wrong and that they didn't have to worry about anything if they just left the Witch Doctor alone. But now the Witch Doctor had taken it a step further.

"What's happened?" she asked, not sure she wanted the details. Of course she didn't want the details. She just wanted to live in peace in her own happy little bubble and not have to worry about what a powerful magical being was doing in her town.

"They look like asphyxiation and crush injuries." Jessup seemed just as reluctant to give the details as Reg was to hear them. "There were four last night."

"And… did he turn them into draugrs too?"

Jessup gave Reg a puzzled look. "No. If he had, we wouldn't have found them, they would be missing. These victims were left behind after they were killed."

"Oh. Right."

"If he's planning on making them into draugrs, maybe he ran out of zombie powder. He'll have to steal them back from the morgue or the cemetery if he wants to use them."

"And you're sure that draugrs caused the deaths? Or the Witch Doctor?"

"They were killed at night, most of them in their own beds. But it is as if they were pinned down by something very heavy until they died. It just doesn't make any sense. They weren't strangled, and it wasn't a car accident or construction injury. They died in their beds while they slept. And that suggests something supernatural like the draugrs. If it wasn't, then I don't know what it was. Aliens from another planet, maybe." She rolled her eyes, signaling that she didn't really think it was aliens. Reg was relieved. She'd had to accept enough other inhuman races lately; she didn't want to believe that as well as the magical folk she struggled to accept now that she was also going to have to come to terms with extra-terrestrials.

"So what do you want from me?"

"If you can feel them… do you know where in town he is keeping them? Or how he is keeping so many of them under control? Corvin said there were half a dozen or more. I've never heard of a bokor who could control more than a couple at a time. He could put them to work like automatons, but after a while, they would decelerate… sort of fall out of orbit until they were started again. But he seems to be actively controlling all of them. I don't even know if that is possible."

Reg took a deep breath in and let it out again. "Okay. I can do this. As long as you're not asking me to tell you anything about the Witch Doctor. I'm not reaching out to him again."

"Oh…?" Jessup obviously hadn't heard from Corvin what had happened the night before. Reg just shook her head. She didn't have the time or energy to explain. Not if she were going to focus on the draugrs to try to give Jessup the information she needed.

"The Witch Doctor has been operating down at the docks. Corvin was going to head over there to see if he could figure out exactly which warehouse the Witch Doctor is operating out of or what ship or plane he is using."

She reached over and placed her crystal ball in front of her. It wasn't just a prop, even though that was what she had initially purchased it for. She had been able to see things in it quite clearly a couple of times. And even when she couldn't see anything in it, she found that it helped her to calm her brain to focus on something physical.

Jessup saw that she was preparing herself and was respectfully quiet. Starlight, stretched out in his patch of sunlight, lifted his head to look at Reg. She met his eyes. "Do you want to help?"

He rolled onto his feet and got up, stretched, and gave his head a shake so rapid it made his ears flap. He marched over to where Reg was sitting and assumed a regal posture in front of her chair.

"Do you want me to pick you up, or are you going to jump up here yourself, Your Highness?"

Starlight snorted and jumped up into her lap. He extended his claws just to remind her who was boss. He quickly settled in, tucking his feet under him, wrapping his tail around his body, and closing his eyes. Reg could feel the sharpening of her senses.

She gazed into the crystal ball. She didn't want to see them. She hated movies with rotting, peeling zombies. She didn't want to see the dead bodies. She just wanted to know where the draugrs were and what they were doing. Anything further would have to wait, until she was sure she wasn't going to attract the Witch Doctor by asking the universe to give her more information.

She could see Black Sands as if it were a map, stretched out in front of her. Hovering above the image were several small, dark clouds. Reg focused on them. They seemed to have a single heartbeat, throbbing a slow, steady rhythm as she watched, just barely discernible.

It was much more clear than her previous attempt. Reg did a quick scan of the black clouds. "There are nine of them."

"Can you tell me where they are?"

"They're not all in the same place." Reg studied the scene, trying to visualize where they all were. It was easier than a street map, more like a satellite picture, but she still had trouble placing everything and assigning place names to each. "Uh… most are along the waterfront, I guess, which is what we figured because that's where the Witch Doctor is operating." She thought about Corvin being over there. She squinted, wondering if she could tell where he was and bring him into focus, but she didn't want to release the vision of the draugrs to find out. "There are some… one over near the cemetery still. I don't know what he's doing. Keeping watch? Scouting out more bodies?" She let her eyes drift along the streets, trying to imagine driving down them to place them on her mental map of the community. "There are a couple…" She swallowed. "A couple that are pretty close to here."

"How close?" Jessup asked, her voice sounding far away. Reg shook her head. "Um… I guess they like dark, sheltered places while it's still daylight. There's a wooded area," she gestured toward the back of the cottage, "a few blocks that way."

"Centennial Park?"

"Yeah, maybe. I don't think I've ever been there. And there's one over this way," Reg made another gesture, focusing on the picture in her head. "I don't know what it's doing. Would it be inside a house?" She looked up away from the crystal ball, and the picture evaporated. "I never thought about them being in houses, just… you know… wandering through the streets."

"Corvin said that they can look just like regular people. They're not like the zombies on TV. So I guess they could come and go anywhere that people would normally go. Inside stores or other buildings. And if it was someone that no one knew had been turned into a draugr… then he could go back into his own house. No one would know, except that he'd be acting funny."

"And he wouldn't bleed. Corvin said they don't bleed either, that's how you can tell."

"We can't exactly go stabbing people wherever we go to make sure that they're human. We're going to need more than that to go on."

"Yeah."

"The one that's in a house… can you tell whose house? Can you tell me the address or what it looks like?"

Starlight's claws dug into Reg's leg. She winced and tried to detach him. "Come on. Nice kitty."

He snuggled and purred, so she let him stay on her lap and didn't push him off onto the floor. Reg stroked him, trying to absorb all of the comfortable, happy feelings that he exuded. He wanted her to feel good, not to continually have to feel the Witch Doctor's wicked aura.

"I can't do any more today," Reg apologized. Though she probably could have, she was willing to accept Starlight's warning and not look more closely. Did she really want to know which of her neighbors was now a zombie? How could she sleep at night if she knew that Old Mr. Kurtz down the street had been killed and was now inhabited by an evil presence, waiting to follow the instructions of the Witch Doctor?

Then again, how could she sleep not knowing who it was?

"Nine draugrs," Jessup said. "I do not like this at all."

"Did you like it before you knew there were nine?"

Jessup made a face at her. "No, smarty-pants. I didn't like it before I came here. But knowing the details… I like it even less. And Hunter is out looking for them? Or looking for the Witch Doctor?"

"I'm not sure, I think he's looking for the Witch Doctor and hoping to avoid the draugrs, but I can't figure out exactly why he's so interested in defeating the Witch Doctor. I would have thought he would just leave town. That's what I want to do. Get out of here and leave it all behind."

"For what it's worth, I'm glad you didn't. I really need every bit of information you can provide me with."

"You're welcome. I'm just not sure how much longer I'll be able to hold out. It's one thing if he's smuggling and doesn't bother anyone. But if he's killing or reanimating random people—or if he's trying to kill me—I'm not so good with that."

"I can understand that."

Reg petted Starlight and scratched his ears. "What about Corvin?" she asked him softly. "I think we should try to see him and what he's doing. Make sure he's not in danger."

Starlight dug his claws into her leg again and put his ears back. But he retracted his claws and waited, seeing what she was going to do. Reg looked over at Jessup. "I'm a little worried about Corvin being over there with the Witch Doctor and all of the draugrs around… I told him that if he wanted to find the Witch Doctor, he could go himself, but now I'm worried he's going to get himself in trouble."

"Well, he is not well-known for keeping himself out of trouble, unfortunately."

Reg nodded, thinking about the last couple of times that she and Corvin had walked right into a trap together, in too much of a hurry to remember to check for hazards. While she didn't like to compare herself to Corvin, she had to admit that they had impulsivity in common. Jump in first, figure out how to get back out of trouble later.

Reg burrowed her fingers into Starlight's short fur, closing her eyes to focus. "I just want to know where he is… and if he's okay. That's all."

She reached out with her mind, tentative because she didn't want to risk the Witch Doctor feeling her and following her back. Corvin wasn't exactly a friend. She wasn't sure why she didn't just leave him to his fate. But she couldn't.

She had been in his head before. He had held her powers. They had a strong connection, one that shouldn't be hard to reestablish. She didn't want to read his mind or communicate with him. She just wanted to see where he was.

She didn't see the overhead view again. Her fickle brain was determined not to make things too easy. She saw instead what she assumed was Corvin's viewpoint. A street, warehouses, gulls wheeling overhead. It was quiet other than the calls of the gulls and the lapping of the waves. Like he was the only person on the planet.

"He's outside," Reg said. "At least he's not a prisoner. I don't think there's anyone else around, so the Witch Doctor shouldn't know that he's there. He's not strong enough to reach out and connect with the Witch Doctor."

"Don't assume you know what his powers are," Jessup warned. "They can change as he takes strength… elsewhere."

Reg hadn't even thought of that. He hadn't taken her powers, so she just assumed that he hadn't taken anyone else's either. But that wasn't necessarily true. She nudged herself a little closer to his consciousness, curious about whether his powers had increased or had another gift added to them.

There was immediate resistance. He knew she was there. Or knew someone was there. She withdrew. He looked around. A glance back over his shoulder this time to make sure he wasn't being followed. Reg remained on the backward view, even though he had only spared a glance back. She searched the shadows and hiding places behind him. She strained to separate all of the shadows, to match them with the objects that were casting them. They seemed too thick and indistinguishable beside a dumpster, but she needed to get closer to see if there were anything there or not.

"I think there might be something…"

"What is it?" Jessup prompted after a minute of silence.

"I don't like it… he needs to pay attention. He needs to look again."

"Can you tell him to?"

"No, I…" It was difficult to communicate with a conscious person. Especially one like Corvin, who would have stronger defenses. If she did communicate with him, they would become even more inextricably linked, and she was discovering that magical links caused a lot of problems.

She worked on making out the shadows behind Corvin while he moved forward. Then one of the shadows finally separated and, for the first time, she saw the vaguely man-shaped form following him.

"Corvin!" Reg shouted a warning.

He whipped around, startled, and after a split-second of not understanding what he saw, he knew it was one of the draugrs. He ran. There were long rows of warehouses and other kinds of storage units with roads intersecting around them in a never-ending gridwork of streets. He put on a burst of speed, turning into one of the cross streets, and then as soon as he could, turning again. He didn't look behind him, so Reg had no way of knowing whether the draugr was in pursuit.

On TV, zombies could only shuffle, but Corvin had said that they weren't limited that way in real life. That meant that they should be able to move at least as quickly as a man, and had a good chance of catching up to Corvin. She wanted desperately for him to look back. He didn't, focusing on the road ahead and on making his way through a maze of streets. Reg was reminded of her move from one foster family to another, always with the feeling of dread behind her, until after many moves over several years, she had finally been able to settle into a foster home without the sense that he might find her at any moment.

How long had it taken? Much longer than it would take Corvin to lose the draugr. It was a much faster-paced game.

She encouraged him in her head, trying to hurry him ahead, to impress upon him that he needed to stay ahead of it. But he knew more about draugrs than she did. He knew what was at stake. He wouldn't want to be killed and turned into one of them.

If he were changed into a draugr, would she still be able to see through his eyes and communicate with whatever was in his head? Would he be gone from his body? A ghost? Or trapped in it forever?

"Regina!"

She was pulled suddenly out of Corvin's head by Jessup's cry. She was on the floor, Jessup feeling for a pulse and at the same time trying to raise a response from her. She didn't know what had happened to Starlight. Hopefully, he'd had the sense to jump free before she had fallen and she hadn't landed on top of him. She grasped Jessup's arm. "It's okay. I'm here."

"Sheesh!" Jessup sat back onto her heels. "Don't do that!"

"I didn't exactly mean to!"

"What did you see? Is Corvin okay?"

"One of them saw him. It was following him. He's running, trying to get away."

"Can you tell me where he is? I can send a car over there on a disturbance call."

"I... I'm not sure, and he won't be in exactly the same place for long, because he's running, trying to get away from it. He could be blocks away by the time a car gets there."

"I'm going to anyway. Can you give me some location? Two cross streets? A landmark?"

"Everything looks the same... uh... there was a number on a door. Sixteen-oh-two?"

Jessup frowned. It wasn't much to go on, but at least it was a start. She clicked the mic button on the radio mounted on her uniform and made a call. Reg was in a fog, having a hard time focusing on what was going on around her. Starlight came over and started to nose at her.

"Oh, there you are," Reg said in relief. "Are you okay? I'm sorry about that."

He didn't seem to be upset with her, rubbing against her and purring and snuffling at her face and neck, making sure that she was okay.

"I'm fine. It was just Corvin. I guess... I got carried away."

Jessup talked to her dispatcher for a while, then finally signed off. "Okay, I'd better get over there too, or I'm going to have a hard time explaining how I knew something was going on. Are you going to be okay?"

"Yeah. Really. Everything is okay."

"Everything? Corvin too?"

"I don't know... I'm okay."

"Let's at least get you up on the couch, okay? You can keep resting, but at least you won't be on the floor. Do you want me to see if Sarah is in and send her over?"

"No, I don't need anyone to baby me. Nothing to worry about."

Jessup helped Reg get to her knees and then up onto the couch.

"I don't need to lie down."

"Well, it's not going to hurt you. Just placate me and do it for a few minutes until you're not... dizzy or anything."

Reg let Jessup stretch her out on the couch, which was too short to accommodate her full height but, as Jessup said, it was better than being on the floor. Maybe she would have just a little nap while she got her strength back again. Communicating telepathically took a lot of energy. She was always surprised at how physically exhausted she was afterward.

"Okay. I'll call you in a few minutes to make sure you're okay and let you know what's going on. Have you got your phone? Can you get at it when it starts to ring?"

"Yeah. Right here." Reg patted the pocket of her skirt. Hopefully, the screen hadn't broken when she had fallen.

Jessup left quietly. Reg sat there, remembering how one of her foster families had investigated her "fits" to see if she had epilepsy, but, of course, the doctor had instead concluded that she was faking it for attention. That had gone over really well.

~

Reg was starting to doze off when her phone rang. She blinked sticky eyelids and fished her phone out of her pocket. It certainly hadn't taken long for Jessup to get to the scene and see what was happening. Or maybe time had passed faster than Reg had realized. Worse yet, maybe Jessup hadn't been able to find Corvin and was calling in the hopes of getting more details and tracking him down.

Or something might have happened to Corvin.

She was horrified by the idea that the draugr might have caught up to Corvin. It might have killed him. Maybe the Witch Doctor had even turned him into draugr number ten. How would Reg feel knowing that her enemy was permanently gone and he would never try to charm her again?

She didn't even glance at the ID on the face of the phone before answering it and putting it up to her face.

"Hello?"

"Reg!" It wasn't Jessup's voice, but Corvin's, harsh and out of breath.

"Corvin, are you okay?"

"How did you know that thing was coming after me? I thought I was a goner!"

"You're okay? You lost it?"

"Yes." He made a disgusted noise in the back of his throat. "You have no idea how big and dangerous those things are. How… disgusting!"

"You said they were just like normal people. That they weren't like the zombies on TV. It wasn't… rotting, was it?"

"Not visibly, no. But the stench…!"

"They smell?"

He swore and made a noise like he was snorting and blowing his nose at the same time. "You've never smelled anything so foul! Maybe not everyone can smell it, but I don't think anyone could think that that thing was anything but a rotting corpse."

"Yuck. I'm glad I couldn't smell it."

"Yes, you are," he agreed. He blew his nose again. "So are you coming here to help me? I don't really feel like running into another one of those creatures unaware. I need you with me so that I have some warning."

"No. I already told you I don't want to get close to the Witch Doctor."

"If he wasn't tipped off by you spotting one of the draugar and yelling at me telepathically, then I don't think he's going to know you're there just by proximity. As long as you keep it low-key and just tell me where the draugar are…"

"Corvin, I can't. Really."

"You're just going to spy on me telepathically? That's a little intrusive."

"I can't do that, either. I used up too much energy already. It's too hard to maintain at this distance and with your natural barriers."

"Reg, do you want me to get killed? Why bother warning me if you're going to back off again and refuse to be involved? You have to make a decision. Get off the fence; you can't stay balanced up there."

"I'm not hunting draugrs."

"Reg, just come!" he insisted angrily.

She was unnerved by his demand. Like a father who was at the end of his rope and tired of cajoling a recalcitrant child, he was serious now. She was to get over there and help him, or *else*.

Harrison had said that sooner or later, she would help Corvin. So why was she fighting fate? Corvin couldn't see the draugrs. Reg could. The logical conclusion was that it was her fate to help him, however afraid she was.

Reg pulled the phone away from her ear and stared at it for a minute, not sure what to do. She didn't have the words to argue with him. She couldn't keep resisting.

She hung up the call and closed her eyes, breathing slowly and trying to figure out what to do.

CHAPTER TWENTY-FOUR

R eg could see the police car lights flashing, so she pulled in behind them and parked her car. Jessup hadn't called her back yet, so Reg could only assume that they hadn't yet been able to sort the situation out. She climbed out of the car and looked at the little knot of people, trying to discern what was going on.

Jessup peeled away from the group and walked up to Reg, frowning.

"I thought you were going to stay at your house? What's going on?"

"Corvin called. I... I had to come."

"Hunter called you? Where is he? We haven't been able to find him or any sign of the... party who was stalking him."

"He's okay. He escaped. But he wanted me to come down to... I don't even know what I'm supposed to do. Be his early warning system, I guess."

"How about he stays away from here? Wouldn't that be safer? Leave it to the police to investigate."

"You know he's not going to do that. Why even bother suggesting it?"

Jessup gave a low chuckle. "You sound like an experienced mother."

"And Corvin is my child?" Reg wrinkled her nose and shook her head. "Heaven forbid."

"I wouldn't want to lay claim to him either."

"Besides which, you said he's... really old."

"I prefer to go with appearance rather than actual years. It just gets too complicated otherwise."

Reg's face warmed. This was not the conversation that she needed in the middle of a crisis. She was there to help Corvin stay alive, not to discuss whether their ages were compatible.

"I need to go find him."

"How are you going to do that? Did he tell you where he is? Are you going to use your powers?"

"I'm going to call him on the phone."

"Such secret superpowers."

Reg tried not to be pulled in by Jessup's sarcasm. She appreciated the dry humor and could easily be pulled into thinking that they were friends because they had an easy repartee. But it wasn't the same as being friends. Reg had learned the difference between friends and easy acquaintances over the years. Actual friends were few and far between. People like Erin. People who cared about her and wanted to share experiences. Not people who just wanted to use her for her powers, or as a scapegoat, or for some other use. Reg did not like being used.

She took out her phone and tapped the last number in the history to call Corvin back. He answered almost immediately. His voice was low and he was no longer out of breath.

"Hello?"

"I'm here. So, where are you?"

"You can't find me?"

"I don't want to exhaust my energy. Especially if you want me to keep you from draugrs. So tell me where you are."

Corvin was quiet for a few seconds, while Reg assumed he got his bearings and checked the nearest cross streets. Eventually, he gave her his coordinates.

"Hang on a sec," Reg told him. She repeated the streets to Jessup. "Where is that?"

Jessup looked around, orienting herself, then motioned. "Over there. Follow me."

"You just come with me," Reg suggested. "We don't want to attract attention."

"Then you can come in my car. Just leave yours here. It will be safe."

"No, I'm not going in a police car. Just get in my car or give me directions."

"Do you need to be so stubborn, Reg? I'd rather have access to my equipment."

"Get whatever you need out of your car and come in mine."

Jessup shook her head, frustrated, but she went to Reg's passenger door and got in. She didn't get anything out of her squad car. So much for needing her equipment. Reg got into the driver's seat.

"This way?" she pointed.

Jessup nodded. "Yeah. Head back down this aisle and turn right."

Reg twisted anxiously as they got closer to Corvin. He might have thought that he had lost the draugr, but Reg had a feeling that he hadn't. Or the draugr was on his trail a second time. Perhaps it had lost him for a few minutes, but it had been able to pick up his scent. Corvin probably smelled just as bad to the draugr as it smelled to him. Just following the stench, he would find Corvin again.

"Are you okay?" Jessup asked, noticing Reg's discomfort. She probably thought Reg needed to pee, the way she kept twisting around.

"I don't like being down here. Everything is... darker here. It's like walking through a forest at midnight."

"It looks just the same to me."

"It isn't the way it looks... it's the way it feels. I can feel how close the Witch Doctor is. The evil he is spreading. The draugrs... and one of them is really close. I don't know if we can find Corvin without tipping it off."

"Do you want me to call Hunter and warn him?"

"No. I don't want anything buzzing around the airwaves. Let's just keep quiet." Reg swallowed. "Keep your gun ready."

Jessup readjusted the gear in her heavy duty belt. "Can you kill them with guns? Do you need a silver bullet? Because I left my only silver bullet at home."

Reg didn't know if a simple gunshot was enough to kill a draugr, but at least it was a start, and hopefully, it would at least slow one down for a few minutes.

"I'm... not entirely sure. Aim for the head."

Reg slowed the car and crept along, her eyes open for any unusual shadows or an increase in the feelings of fear and anxiety. She didn't see anything, but she could certainly feel that it was close by. She remembered how it had been behind Corvin before, and he hadn't even known it was there because he only took quick looks behind him and didn't take the time to separate it out of the shadows or to watch it when he was on the move.

It was like a lightning strike to the heart. Like an explosion right beside her. Reg swerved and Jessup was forced to grab onto the door to keep herself upright.

"What the—"

"Look out!" Reg warned, hitting the gas and trying to avoid hitting the draugr. Why would she want to avoid hitting it? Didn't they want to kill it? A car could be a deadly weapon, one that the Vikings hadn't had on hand. If they had, maybe their draugr-killing instructions would have included running them down with a car. Reg corrected her steering to aim back toward the draugr instead of away from it.

Jessup held on to the door handle on one side and the parking brake on the other, taken off-guard by Reg's decision to go on the offensive. "Be careful! Watch out for the..."

Reg plowed straight into the draugr. There was a sickening thump and crunch as Reg plowed into it.

"Whoa!" Jessup exclaimed, reaching for the handle on her door to get out and see. "Hell, Reg, you just ran into—"

Reg grabbed her arm to keep her from opening the door. "It's one of the draugrs. Don't get out."

"It's a man—"

"Trust me; it's one of the draugrs. I know you don't believe it, but remember what Corvin said—they look just like regular people. You can't tell."

"Reg, you're barely functioning after your psychic contact. You don't know what's going on—"

"I know what's going on better than you do. Look, is it bleeding? Can't you smell it?"

As Corvin had said, the stench was something indescribable. Reg couldn't believe that anyone could not smell it.

"Smell what?" Jessup challenged. She again reached for the door handle. "I at least have to look, Reg. I can't just leave a body on the ground and not even take a look at it. I have a duty as a police officer—"

"You are doing your duty as a police officer. You're supposed to be protecting people. You can't do that if you're going to get out of the car every time we hit one of them. I don't know if I've killed it or just disabled it, so unless you're planning on cutting off its head or putting a bullet into its brains, stay put."

Jessup hesitated, her hand still on the handle, not sure whether to believe Reg or whether to think she was off her rocker.

"You need to listen," Reg insisted. "Do you see it bleeding?"

Jessup craned her neck this way and that, trying to get a good view of the fallen draugr. Her lips tightened. "I don't see any. But…"

"Then you know it's a draugr. Come on; we still have to find Corvin."

Jessup sighed. She let go of the door handle. "Okay, but we have to come back here after and make sure that…"

"That I didn't just kill an innocent bystander? Don't you trust me any more than that?"

Jessup didn't answer, which was in itself an answer. She stared out the window as Reg reversed the car and backed away from the draugr. She wiggled the steering wheel to try to dislodge the draugr from where it was caught on the bumper. Eventually, it fell away. Reg didn't feel the need to get a better look at it, but Jessup leaned into the window, looking down at it.

Reg continued down the road, scanning mentally for any more of them. One down, eight to go. Or one temporarily disabled, anyway. Reg wasn't sure how long it would actually stay out of business.

Jessup gave her directions and they eventually pulled into the road where Corvin was standing, trying to blend in with the dumpster and the detritus in the alley.

At the sight of the car, he approached the passenger side, then realized that Detective Jessup already occupied the front seat.

"What's going on?" he demanded, opening the back door. "Why is she here?"

"I'm here to find you and see if you're okay," Jessup snapped. "Since Reg was pretty wiped out after warning you. I don't know how you convinced her to come here when she's already too tired to do anything."

"I'm not too tired to do anything," Reg argued. "I did just run over the draugr that was on your trail again."

Corvin looked at her. "You killed it?"

"I don't know. I hit it. Left it back there."

"If it was a draugr," Jessup amended.

"Of course it was a draugr. I told you it was."

Jessup shrugged helplessly at Corvin, appealing to him. Corvin looked behind himself, making sure there wasn't another one following him, before addressing Jessup.

"Well, did you smell it?"

"I didn't smell anything. Reg said that it stank, but I didn't notice anything unusual."

"Did it bleed?"

"I didn't see any blood."

Reg nodded at Corvin. "Draugr," she said firmly.

"Okay. So you've taken care of the one that was following me. That's a good first step. Even if it isn't completely dead…"

"Aren't they all dead? That's the whole point, isn't it?"

"I meant dead as in… not a draugr or capable of being a draugr anymore."

"Then you should have said that."

"Are there any other ones close by?"

Reg took a deep breath, closing her eyes and feeling the atmosphere for the rest. "There are too many of them close by," she said. "Explain why we have to be here, right in the middle of everything?"

"Because this is where the Witch Doctor is operating and we want to be able to track him."

"There's no way we can beat him. He's too powerful."

Corvin gave a slight smile. "If we can find his warehouse, I can beat him."

"How?"

Corvin just shrugged, like he had a big surprise for her. Like it was her birthday and all of her friends were coming for a surprise party.

Reg had never actually had a surprise party. She'd had few enough birthday parties as a child, and of course, as an adult, she didn't bother to observe them. What exactly was the point in celebrating the day she had come into the world? Like that was such a great accomplishment? Sure, surviving another year was a good thing, but she could think of a lot of better things to celebrate in her life.

"Hunter," Jessup said seriously. "I hope you're not planning what I think you are."

He just gave her what Reg assumed was supposed to be an enigmatic smile. He looked around. "So? Are there any others close?"

"Yes."

Corvin climbed into the back seat. "Okay. Let me know where you see them. Is there a larger cluster? Somewhere they are gathering and working together?"

Reg was starting to get overwhelmed by the dark feeling. It was becoming less distinct, harder to separate into separate beings. They seemed to all be coalescing into one large dark force.

"I don't know if I can. This is… getting complicated."

"Just try," Corvin instructed. "You can do it. If you're getting low on energy, I can help you with that."

Reg knew that he could. But she worried about what else he might do if he knew she was too low on energy. It would be the perfect time to breach her defenses and to take instead of giving.

She inched the car forward, trying to drive to the area where the darkness was the densest. That meant more draugrs. As long as it didn't indicate the presence of the Witch Doctor. How was she going to separate the Witch Doctor's aura from the rest of the evil creatures?

A cat cut across in front of the car, making Reg jump and hit the brakes. Everyone was thrown forward. Corvin wasn't buckled in, and his face hit the back of Jessup's headrest with a thump. Reg glanced over at him. His lip had split and started to well up with blood.

"Sorry. There was a cat. I didn't want to hit it,"

Corvin was patting his pockets, looking for a tissue for his bleeding lip, and stopped suddenly. "A cat?"

"Yeah, sorry."

"Describe it."

Reg rolled her eyes. "Describe it? A black cat. That's all. Just like all of the other black cats in Black Sands. It seems like everyone has one these days."

"Was it a draugr?"

Reg frowned at him. He had hit his face pretty hard. Was he concussed?

"A *cat*," she said distinctly.

"A black cat. That thing that I said I had to look up… the Vikings believed that the draugrs were shapeshifters. As well as being able to grow in size to attack, they were also able to turn into *kattakyn*."

"Cats?" Reg demanded.

"I know. I never really thought anything of it. There are shapeshifters in many cultures, from werewolves to—"

"Shut up. Cats? Black cats?"

"Yes. And they could kill in their cat form, by sitting on your chest, and increasing in weight until—"

"Why didn't you tell me that?" Jessup interrupted, her lips white. "We've had several suspicious deaths, and they were all—"

"Asphyxiation?"

Reg felt again the sensation she'd had in her dream of the black cat sitting on her chest, getting heavier and heavier, until she wasn't able to breathe. It had been Starlight who had banished the draugr-cat, if it had really existed and not just been part of her wild dreams.

"Why didn't you tell me that?" Jessup demanded. "I've been running around trying to find out what was happening, and you knew all along—"

"I didn't know about any suspicious deaths. You didn't tell me."

"Asphyxiation and crush injuries. That certainly sounds like one of your cat draugrs sitting on someone's chest, doesn't it?"

"Yes. It does. Do you have names? Who are these people who were killed? If you don't give me the information, I don't know how I'm supposed to figure anything out."

Jessup pulled out her duty notebook and flipped through the pages.

She read the names out. Reg couldn't believe that Jessup would give Corvin the names without objection when she wouldn't tell Reg anything. What exactly was the relationship between the two of them? Was Corvin an official informant? She knew that he consulted with the police department, but she really didn't understand what he did for them.

Corvin considered. The names obviously didn't trigger immediate recognition for him. But his expression suggested he might be able to do something with them, given enough time. He looked at Reg, frowning.

"I don't know them," Reg said, putting up her hands defensively.

"I didn't think you did. I'm just trying to focus. I'm hoping that the two of us together can sort this out..."

"How?"

"If I could get just a little bit of your powers, not even enough for you to notice, I bet I can find a connection. You may think that you don't have much that would be useful, but you do."

"I can't control how much of my powers you take, and I don't think you could control it once you started. You'd suck me dry."

"What makes you think that? I returned your powers to you once before. What if I retake them, temporarily, on the promise that I'll return them, just as I did the first time…?"

"Who do you think you're kidding, Hunter?" Jessup asked in disbelief. "No one is going to lend you their powers voluntarily for just a little while. Reg knows that you wouldn't ever return her powers. After how hard you've been working to take them away from her?"

Corvin scowled at her. "If I promise to do a thing, I will. A promise is a promise. I'm a man of honor," he said pompously.

"With your track record? You are clearly not a man of honor. You would never return them."

Corvin's face suddenly lit up. "Check the ownership records of the warehouses around here," he said suddenly, switching tracks in an instant. "I'll bet that one of your draugr victims is the owner of the warehouse the Witch Doctor is using."

"Yes," Reg agreed, as it suddenly crystallized for her too. "The warehouse… the boat… everybody who had something to do with the Witch Doctor setting his business up here. That must be who he is killing. I couldn't figure out why he would be killing anyone without turning them into zombies. But that must be it."

"I'm sure he has plenty of people who he would like to kill," Jessup said. "All he has to do is tell his draugrs to kill them. I'll check the ownership records, see if there are any obvious connections. But the warehouse and boat could be rented rather than owned. He could be using a holding company. We can't just search every single company that owns something in the area."

"Where did the cat go?"

Reg pointed. "That way."

Corvin followed her finger to a building. "Did he go inside, or just in that area?"

"I didn't see. I was too busy making sure everyone was okay…" She indicated his lip as he dabbed at it with a white handkerchief. Seriously? Who carried fabric hankies?

"Can't you feel him?" Corvin suggested, still looking at the building in question.

"I can't separate them all right now. And with the cats... I've seen a lot of black cats lately, but I haven't had that dark sense from any of them. I would have noticed that."

"What have you felt? You said earlier that they didn't feel the same as the lost cat. Whatever her nonsense name was."

"Nicole."

"*Nicole*. She's a cat, not a soap opera character! What you felt from her was different from what you felt from the other black cats. That's why you didn't think they were her."

"Yeah. I don't know... I just felt emptiness when I saw them. It wasn't anything evil, just like... a shell."

"Well, that's a pretty good explanation of what they are. So maybe when they are in their feline form, they don't give off the same aura as when they are in human form."

Reg nodded slowly.

"Can you check the ownership of this building?" Corvin asked Jessup, indicating the one that the cat might have gone into.

"I guess that's how they get around without anyone noticing them," Reg mused. "I thought that if there were that many draugrs around town, it was weird that no one had noticed them. Unless they can become invisible. Or maybe if they just killed any witnesses. Could the people who were killed have just been people who happened to have seen them?"

Jessup shook her head as she dialed a number on her phone. "I doubt it. They weren't killed out on the street where they might have seen a draugr; they were killed in their beds. They didn't report any suspicious activity before they were killed."

"If they were killed in their beds... were the houses broken into?"

Jessup motioned for her to be quiet and spoke on the phone, giving the person who had answered her call the address of the warehouse.

Reg looked around restlessly. Her mind was going a mile a minute. "If this was the warehouse with all of the smuggled goods in it, couldn't you sense it? I thought you could feel the power of magical objects."

"He could be blocking it with a blocking spell similar to the one Harrison put around you. You can't tell if this is where the Witch Doctor's activities are centered?"

Reg moved around restlessly. She shifted the car into park and revved the engine, keyed up and unable to be still. She didn't want to reach out to the Witch Doctor. It was too dangerous. But she still wanted to do something, not just sit there waiting for more information. What difference did it make if they knew it was the Witch Doctor's warehouse? Were they going to attack him?

She wished that she had Starlight with her. Starlight had been a big bonus when they had fought the pixies, and she thought that if the draugrs could take cat form, he might be able to fight them too. He'd driven away the one who had come in her dream, hadn't he?

Jessup was nodding and ending her phone call. She tapped to hang it up. "They'll have to do a search," she said, "it's not exactly instant, because they have to match up the municipal address with a legal address and then if a corporation holds it, they'll have to see who is associated with that, and if it is rented, that will be another complication. But they'll call back when they know something."

"How did the draugrs get into the victims' houses?" Reg demanded. "Did they break down the doors when they were in their giant form?"

She really wanted to hear an affirmative answer, not wanting to know how close she had come to death herself.

Jessup didn't answer right away, considering carefully. It made Reg grind her teeth. If Jessup were going to be so reluctant to share information with her, then how was Reg supposed to help? What did she think Reg was going to do with the information about how the draugrs got into people's houses? How was she going to use that to her advantage? Take over the draugrs from the Witch Doctor and use them to break into houses and steal? Cat burglars? Did they really think she had that kind of ability?

Jessup glanced back at Corvin.

Corvin raised an eyebrow. "If you know, then spit it out, Marta. What are we supposed to do? Guess? Reg already did. Either they broke the doors down or they got in some other way. Which is it?"

"There was no sign of forced entry. No sign that anyone had broken into the houses or had picked a lock or entered through an unlocked door."

Reg looked at Jessup and then at Corvin.

"A locked-room murder?" Corvin asked. "Really? There must have been some sign of how they got in. Did they have keys? Charm the locks? Were the victims practitioners or not? Were there wards?"

Jessup shrugged. "It's under investigation, Hunter. I haven't had a lot of time to work with this, and the police force doesn't look for things like charms and wards. They work with physical evidence. All I can tell you is that they were locked room murders."

Reg sighed. "I know how they do it."

CHAPTER TWENTY-FIVE

They both looked at her. Reg couldn't help smiling at their shocked expressions. They had not expected any insight into the police work from Reg Rawlins. She was nice to have around if they needed someone with psychic powers, but they had not expected her to be able to help with the investigation.

"You know how they got in?" Jessup repeated.

"They were all killed while they were asleep?"

"Yes."

Reg looked at Corvin. "And you don't know? There isn't anything in the mythology about how they could get into a locked room?"

He looked baffled. Pressing the hankie against his lip, he wrinkled his forehead as he considered the possibilities. Reg was pleased that she was the only one who knew.

"The draugrs came into their dreams."

Corvin's face cleared. "Of course," he agreed. "I should have figured that out. The Vikings believed that the draugar could come into their dreams and that they could leave physical evidence of their presence. Sometimes they left objects behind to signify that they had been there. I don't remember ever reading that they could kill a person in their dreams, but it follows, doesn't it? It makes perfect sense."

Reg nodded.

"How did you know that?" Jessup asked, head cocked slightly.

"Because… one of them came to me last night."

Jessup and Corvin both gaped at her.

"One of them came to you?" Corvin echoed.

Reg nodded. "It was sitting on my chest, just like you said, getting heavier and heavier until I couldn't breathe." She thought about the mysterious deaths and how close she had come to being another statistic. "But then Starlight attacked it and scared it off."

"Are you sure?" Jessup shook her head, eyes wide in disbelief.

"Am I sure? Are you really going to ask me that? Do you think I could be mistaken about something like that?"

"No, I'm sorry. It's just an automatic reaction. I never thought… it never occurred to me that they could come after you like that. In your dreams? It's like something out of a horror movie."

"So is the rest of the stuff about reanimating corpses," Reg pointed out.

"I guess it is. It's just getting bigger and bigger… we need to recruit some more help, figure out how to get rid of these things. They're already killing at will. We need to figure something out."

"That's what I've been saying," Corvin agreed. "We can't just let them run rampant. We have a responsibility to try to defeat them."

Reg narrowed her eyes at him. "We're having a hard time believing that's really why you want to get involved here. Wouldn't it be safer to turn tail and run?"

"I may not normally be altruistic," he admitted, "but I do have friends in Black Sands, and I wouldn't want to leave them to the Witch Doctor and his draugar."

"So what are we going to do?" Jessup asked practically. "Are we going to get some help? Go in there and check things out? What's the plan?"

They both looked at Corvin. He smiled. "Can you get a search warrant? Or do we need to get in there without one?"

"We'll find out what the results of the ownership search are in the next few minutes. If it's one of the dead men, then I think we have enough to get a warrant."

"How is that going to help?" Reg demanded. "If you sent a bunch of policemen in there to search the place, aren't they just going to be killed? They're going up against draugrs, not illegal aliens."

"I want to get in there," Corvin reiterated. "If I can get in there, either

186

with a warrant or by some other method, then I can access the power of the smuggled items. That may give me enough strength to tackle a few of the draugar on my own."

"And then what? If you can't take on all nine of them and the Witch Doctor, then we're right back where we started."

"I can at least try. What's your suggestion?"

Reg didn't have one.

"What about the guy that Corvin was telling me about?" Jessup prompted.

"Damon?"

Corvin rolled his eyes. "No, not Damon. What kind of help would he be? She's talking about Harrison."

"Actually, Damon might be helpful…"

"Not Damon," Corvin repeated. "Do you know how to get ahold of Harrison? He has a vast store of power. I don't know what he is, but he could have what it takes to fight the Witch Doctor."

"He already said he wouldn't. He is prevented from killing someone of… his own kind, or something like that."

"He might change his mind if he thought you were in danger. He seems to be committed to protecting you. Can you call him?"

"I don't… have his number. I don't even know if he has a phone, he's sort of… I don't know… I don't think he's exactly… human."

"He's pretty obviously not human," Corvin agreed. "But that doesn't mean he can't use a phone." He sighed. "A lot of the more ancients won't have anything to do with technology. Can you just… reach out to him? You have some connection with him."

Reg wasn't sure why she hesitated. Harrison was a friend and protector. She wasn't afraid of him. But maybe she was afraid of calling him when she didn't need him, in case he might not be there the next time she did.

"Just try," Corvin coaxed. "What is it going to hurt?"

"Okay… but don't expect any help."

She closed her eyes and thought about Harrison, told him in her mind that she needed his help.

Rather than Harrison appearing, Reg was suddenly flooded with the memories of her mother and the Witch Doctor, while at the same time, Norma Jean's voice filled her head. Reg held her head with both hands, trying to steady herself and take back control of her brain. But instead, Norma Jean's voice just got more insistent, impossible to block out.

"Leave me alone!" Reg insisted.

"Listen to me," Norma Jean told her. "Tell him you know where Weston is."

"What?"

"Are you listening to me? Sam will want to know. You can stop him."

Reg pulled at her hair. "Get out of my head. I need Harrison. Not you!"

"Reg, are you okay?"

Reg waved off their concerned inquiries. She kept focused on an image of Harrison, his wide grin and mustache and his striped shirt, remembering how he had protected her from the Witch Doctor before.

She banged her head on the steering wheel in frustration. "Come on, Harrison, I need you!"

"Reg, maybe you shouldn't—" Jessup started, putting a hand on Reg's arm.

Reg shook herself free. "Don't touch me when I'm concentrating," she snapped.

"Okay, sorry, but I think…"

There was a knocking on the window. Reg startled, opened her eyes, and looked to see who it was.

Harrison, of course. He had on a royal purple silk shirt this time, but it was still unmistakably him. Reg rolled her window down.

"No need to beat yourself up," Harrison chided.

"Look, I know you said you couldn't do anything to harm the Witch Doctor, but is there something you can do to help us out? We can't go after the Wi—after Destine and nine draugrs by ourselves. We're not strong enough."

"You have the tools at hand."

"The tools? What are you talking about? What do we need? What are we supposed to do?"

"You need to use your brain, Reg, and your powers. You're right; I can't do anything to harm Destine. If you want to stop him and his draugar from devastating this town, then you need to do something, and it needs to be soon. He already grows stronger."

"What are we supposed to do? We can't fight him physically. If we go up against someone so powerful with just the three of us…" Reg gestured at herself and her friends. "I mean, I'm just a psychic. And Jessup…"

Jessup shook her head. Reg knew that she had some powers, but they were relatively minor. Reg had never asked her for details or what her background was.

"Then there is the spirit-eater," Harrison pointed out.

Reg glanced over at Corvin, still dabbing at his split lip. Yeah, he looked really powerful.

"That's not enough," Reg protested.

"Then you need to get more. Where is that nice boy who was with you the other day? The visionary."

"Damon?"

"We don't need Damon," Corvin growled.

"He's better than nothing. Shouldn't we have all of the power we can get on our side? And what about Sarah?"

"She won't have anything to contribute here," Corvin said, shaking his head. "She is not a warrior."

"Who, then? Who else can we get?"

"What about the charmer?" Harrison suggested.

"Who? Do you mean Corvin?"

He was the only one Reg knew who had special charms. But Harrison wasn't looking at Corvin, and Corvin shook his head, indicating that it wasn't him.

"The charmer," Harrison repeated. "The guardian of the other cat."

"Other cat…? Do you mean Nicole?"

"Nicole… that is a human name. I don't know."

"Starlight's lady friend."

Harrison smiled, his eyes dancing. "Yes, her. What about her guardian?"

"I don't know who her guardian is. Do you mean a guardian like you? I don't know anyone else like you."

"The human who cares for her."

"Francesca."

"You should call her. And Damon. Then you have a chance."

Reg looked at Jessup and Corvin for their reactions. They both seemed just as disconcerted by the suggestions as she was. She turned back to Harrison to ask him for further help, but he was gone again. Reg looked in front of and behind the car, hoping that he had just wandered off, but he was nowhere in sight.

"Thanks a lot, Harrison."

"Do you think those two will be of any help?" Corvin challenged.

"Well, I know that they can do more than I can by myself. What about you? Are you going to turn down Harrison's suggestions just because you don't know how they're going to work out? Didn't we ask for help? You're the one who said to call him."

"I was looking for power, not advice."

"Well, advice is what we got. So do we call them?"

"Go ahead. It's not likely to make anything worse. Though I warn you… I'm not protecting Damon if he gets himself into trouble. Ditto the cat lady."

"You don't even know the cat lady."

"I've seen her. And she's a lovely girl, but I don't trust her. Not if she's Haitian. If they're coming, it's to help us in the fight, not vice versa. I don't want to be pulled ten different directions. We're going to need to be focused when we get in there, and I can't do that if I have to protect anyone else."

"Fine. It's understood, you're only in there for your own purposes. Just like always."

Corvin pulled his hankie away from his lip, scowling at Reg. "Didn't I help you when Hawthorne-Rose was torturing you? And didn't I help you fight the pixies? I didn't have to do those things. I didn't do them for my own well-being. That was for you."

Reg's face got hot. She covered her cheek with her hand, not wanting him to see her flush. With the other hand, she took out her phone and found Damon's number.

CHAPTER TWENTY-SIX

Damon arrived before Francesca. Reg got out of the car to talk to him, looking back at Corvin anxiously as she did so. She hated to tell Damon that she was now working with Corvin. Again. Even though she kept saying that she needed to be protected from him. Damon looked into the car and saw Corvin sitting there.

"Again?"

"Uh… well, it's a long story."

"And do I take it you punched him in the face? Because that would make my day."

He had seen Corvin's split and swelling lip. Reg suppressed a smile at this.

"Actually, no, just hit the brakes too hard when he wasn't wearing a seatbelt."

"Well, at least that gives you plausible deniability," Damon approved. "So, what's going on? Why are we meeting here, out in the open, when I thought he was trying to avoid detection?"

"Yeah… well, we've been detected. The Witch Doctor tried to kill me last night, or this morning. And we're… trying to formulate a plan. We're just waiting for one more party, so maybe I could hold off on explaining until everyone is here."

Damon nodded. "Fine. We'll wait."

He leaned back against his car, arms folded, looking both casual and wary at the same time. Reg took a deep breath and let out a sigh.

"So what's this I hear about you being able to put visions into other people's heads?"

"What?" Damon's eyes went to Corvin again. "Did he tell you that?"

"Is it true?"

"Well, that is one of my talents, yes."

"So how many times have you done that to me?"

Damon shifted his stance, no longer looking quite so casual. He obviously sensed that Reg wasn't happy about being the target of his gifts any more than she was of Corvin's.

"You make it sound like it's some kind of assault. But it's not... it isn't like that at all. It's just... part of my way of communicating."

"Your way of communicating."

"Well, yes. How often have you had to describe something that is difficult to put into words? Wouldn't it be easier to just... put that image directly into someone else's mind?"

"Sure, but entering someone else's mind is against the rules. It's impolite. Right?"

"I'm not entering into your mind when I do it. No more than I am by talking to you. I'm just communicating in a different way."

"And how am I supposed to know whether I'm really experiencing something, or whether I am making it up or visualizing it, or whether you are putting it there? Why didn't you tell me you could do this?"

"It never really came up. It isn't something that's always conscious; it's often just... the natural way for me to communicate. It just comes out in visions instead of words."

"So you're saying it's like a speech impediment. A stammer."

He chuckled. "It isn't always something I can control. I do my best, but sometimes it does just kind of slip out."

"And when you put visions into my head while we were bowling? And that whole walk-on-the-beach vision the other day? Those were unintentional?"

"Uh..." Damon scratched his chin. "Well, not exactly."

"So you did intentionally put thoughts into my head."

"I suppose. But like I say... it's not like that. It isn't something I'm forcing onto you. We're just on the same wavelength, and I happen to..."

Reg frowned. "So do you have to be on the same wavelength to give someone a vision? You couldn't do it… by force? Say, against an opponent, someone you were fighting?"

Damon tilted his head toward Corvin. "Him?"

"No. Not Corvin. Worse than that."

"I could still do it. It would be more difficult if it was someone who wasn't… sharing a moment with me. But I could still do it if I had to. That would be… more of an assault, though. I wouldn't want to be censured for doing it."

"You're not in a coven, though. So you wouldn't be subject to discipline by them. And the non-magical police force wouldn't have anything to do with it. So how is a lone wolf censured? On a pillory in the public square?"

"There are methods for dealing with even lone wolves. I still have a job that I wouldn't want to lose. And I wouldn't want to be known in the community as someone who was breaking magical rules. People can be quite… hostile."

"I would imagine so."

Another car pulled up close. Reg watched Francesca climb out, her slim, graceful form attracting Damon's attention. Reg wondered what visions he might be putting into Francesca's head as she walked up to them. Corvin and Jessup got out of the car, and they formed themselves into a loose circle to discuss what was going on.

Reg looked around at everyone and waited for Corvin to begin the discussion. But Corvin looked at her and raised his eyebrows, inviting her to start. She didn't know whether that was because she was the only one there who knew everyone, or just because he didn't want to expose himself to criticism. Reg took a deep breath and looked down at her feet.

"So… here's what we're dealing with. A guy is operating out of this warehouse that we call the Witch Doctor. His name is…" She tried to dredge it up from her memory. "Uh… Samyr Destine—"

Francesca spit out what Reg could only assume was a Creole swear word or curse. Reg stopped talking and stared, not sure whether to go on or whether Francesca would explain further.

"I thought when I came here I would be leaving him behind!" Francesca said. "Are you saying he is here? Right here?" she pointed at the warehouse in front of them. "How could this be?"

"I—you know him?" Reg asked awkwardly.

"Yes, yes, of course, I know him. He is a very powerful bokor. He operated out of Haiti for a very long time, as long as one can remember. What is he doing here? I had hoped to escape his influence forever!"

"He's apparently smuggling magical artifacts. At least, that was what he was doing the last time we caught him. Or almost caught him," Jessup advised. "Just how familiar are you with him? You know him personally?"

"That is beside the point." Francesca waved this away with an angry gesture. "We need to get out of here—all of us. There is no way to fight his influence ourselves. We must leave here before we are all ensorcelled by him."

"We can fight him, and that's just what we're going to do," Corvin said calmly. "Between us, we have the tools to do it, isn't that what your friend Harrison said, Reg?"

Reg nodded.

"Harrison?" Francesca repeated. "Who is that?"

"He is… a friend of mine who knows the Witch Doctor."

"And where is he, when there is trouble? Why is he not here to fight?"

"He said that he is not allowed to harm the Witch Doctor."

"Then he is one of them?" Francesca shook her head. "You cannot trust their kind. This is just like them, to play their little games with the mortals and then to disappear when there is a real danger. They are never here when they are needed. Always they are gone." Her lips were tight, her movements jerky. Reg could feel her anger like electricity in the air.

"He said that we have all we need," Reg tried to keep her voice calm like Corvin's. It wasn't even her fight, so why was she getting involved?

But deep down, Reg knew that it *was* her fight more than it was any of theirs. She was the one who knew the Witch Doctor and had faced him before. She was the one the Witch Doctor knew and recognized.

"So what exactly is it that we have?" Damon questioned reasonably.

"Well, we have the police and a warrant so that we can get in," Corvin began, gesturing to Jessup. "Once we are inside, I should be able to access the powers of the magical objects that he is smuggling. That will give us a great deal of power, and gifts that we don't yet know of. We have Reg," he indicated her as if everybody didn't already know who she was. "She has powerful psychic gifts." He met her gaze. "Even stronger than she knows. She has a connection with the Witch Doctor and can pinpoint and communicate with him. She can lead us to where he is and keep him talking and distracted." He gave a little shrug. "Psychically, that is. Then we were advised to bring the two of you as well. Damon has the ability to detect lies and to give visions. I'm not sure how those powers will come into play, but they are apparently important. Unless there is some other gift that you have that you have been holding back and not telling anyone about?"

Damon shrugged and didn't suggest anything. "Lighting objects on fire, maybe?" Corvin suggested.

Damon looked at Reg, brows drawn down. "I'm not the one who can light fires."

Corvin went on. "And then we have Francesca, who Harrison referred to as a charmer."

She nodded.

"Again, I'm not sure what benefit there is to having a charmer with us, but it is apparently important. Harrison said that we were all needed to make this work. But he said that with all of us together, we have the tools needed to fight the Witch Doctor."

"And *win*?" Francesca demanded. "Because beings like him tend to miss the finer points—like that we could get killed in the process. It's all a joke to them, watching the mortals play games. Did he say that we could defeat the Witch Doctor? Or just that we could fight him?"

Corvin looked at Reg. She tried to remember his exact words, but couldn't be sure.

"He said that we could win," she said firmly. They needed as much confidence as they could get. Telling them that she didn't know for sure if they could defeat the Witch Doctor was not the way to go in with a winning attitude.

She saw the doubt flicker across Damon's face at her lie and hoped that no one else had.

"So is everyone ready?" Corvin asked. "Waiting will not prove efficacious in this fight. We need to go in, attack without warning, and have the advantage of surprise."

CHAPTER TWENTY-SEVEN

"Y ou, uh, might have forgotten to mention one thing," Reg said.

"What?" Corvin's tone was irritated. Here he was, ready to bust the doors down without even a plan, without even having briefed his companions appropriately. He must have really been champing at the bit to get his hands on the hoard of magical artifacts that the Witch Doctor was piling up in the warehouse.

"The draugrs."

"Oh." Corvin stopped, and looked at Damon and Francesca, making a face. "Yes. As well as the Witch Doctor, we will be facing his draugar as well."

Francesca rolled her eyes. "That might be an important thing to know. How long has he been raising draugar?"

"We don't know for sure. We've only been aware that was what he was doing for a few days, but it was probably some time before that."

"How many are there?"

Corvin looked over at Reg as if hoping she might have a different number this time.

"Nine," Reg said. "They're probably not all in there. They weren't all in one place last time I checked, but I'm too close right now to discern anything but the cloud around the Witch Doctor. So… hopefully less than nine that we have to deal with immediately."

"But once the fight starts, I'm sure they'll all be on their way," Corvin advised.

Francesca's face was white. Everyone else tried to look unconcerned, but they all knew that they were unlikely to win against that kind of a force, no matter what Harrison said.

"Nine draugar," Francesca said and muttered another curse under her breath. "You know how to pick them, don't you?"

Corvin gave an embarrassed shrug.

"And what form are they in? Human, giant, or kattakyn?"

"We don't know. At least one of them went inside in cat form, but I don't know if he stayed that way. Or what form the others are in. I assume if they are helping the Witch Doctor with physical labor, they must be in human or giant form."

"It will be important to get them into kattakyn form if possible."

Reg looked at Corvin and then back at Francesca. "And how are we supposed to do that? What makes them go into cat form?"

"When they feel the need to hide or take flight, they will shift to kattakyn," Francesca advised. "I will try to entice them as I can. But against so many... I don't know if I will be able to do it. Destine will do his best to keep them in giant form, as that is the most physically powerful. He must be distracted." Francesca pointed to each of Reg, Jessup, and Damon in turn. "That will be your job. Distract Destine in any way you can."

"Okay." That was at least something that Reg could wrap her mind around. "What kinds of things will distract him?"

"That is not my job. That is yours."

Helpful.

"So are we ready?" Corvin asked again.

"Who is going to open the door? Are we going to break it in? Pick the lock? Charm it?" Reg looked from Jessup to Corvin.

"I don't have a battering ram with me, so picking or charming it would be the best. Can you do that?" Jessup addressed this to Corvin.

"Not exactly my area of specialty."

Damon and Francesca didn't offer any suggestions.

"Oh, good grief." Reg pushed past Corvin and got back into her car.

"Regina!" Corvin protested, thinking she had decided to leave.

"Watch and learn," Reg advised.

She buckled her seatbelt, put the car into gear, and, aiming for one of the bay doors at the back of the warehouse, mashed the gas pedal. The car lurched forward, tires squealing for grip on the asphalt, and then headed straight for the door. Reg squinted her eyes almost-shut as she got closer, braced for impact, and drove straight in through the door.

It wasn't as bad as she had thought. Not like driving into a brick wall. The metal of the door burst open like a piece of paper, admitting her car with a long squeal.

Reg sat there for a moment to make sure that she was still in one piece. The airbag hadn't even deployed. She unbuckled her seatbelt and got out. The others ran in through the hole in the door, shouting to her and each other.

"Reg, what do you think you're doing?" Jessup demanded, grabbing her by the arm.

"I'm getting us inside. You forgot your battering ram."

"Well… you could have been hurt! And this definitely isn't something I am going to get commended for in a report!"

"I don't particularly care about your report at this point. I want to deal with this and hope that we survive."

Jessup made a face, but it was apparent she didn't have an argument. She kept her hand on her sidearm and looked around, waiting for the draugrs to burst in on them.

There was no clear leader in the group, everyone looking at everyone else for direction. Reg pointed to the loading dock a few steps up. "I assume we go that way."

There was nowhere else to go. They all advanced. There was nowhere to hide, nothing to shelter behind. Once they got into the warehouse proper, there would hopefully be pallets of crates to hide behind.

They variously climbed or jumped up to the loading dock platform and entered.

Corvin was drawn like a magnet to the nearest stack of boxes. They were not uniformly-sized packing crates like Reg had pictured, but various boxes, crates, and chests of every description.

Reg followed closed behind Corvin. "Can you feel them now?"

She didn't need to ask. His eyes were glazed. He reached out toward the nearest box and put his hands flat against the side. With an animal-like growl, he shoved it off of the stack, and it went crashing to the concrete floor. The wooden sides broke open and the artifacts spilled out.

Reg averted her eyes at first, half-expecting to see dismembered animal parts as she remembered the endangered species smuggling that was part of the Witch Doctor's business. But she looked back, and it just seemed like garage-sale items. Old urns and bowls and oddly-shaped sculptures. She reached over to pick up an urn to examine it, and Corvin shoved her roughly out of the way.

"Do not touch anything!" he snapped. "Some of them may be cursed, and you do not know how to counter such things!"

Reg flushed with embarrassment. Of course he was right. She didn't have any idea how to sense or fight any curses that might have been cast on the objects. She was, once again, rushing right into the thick of things without any idea of what she was up against.

At least Jessup was still right with her. Jessup was more cautious and liked to check for traps before rushing into danger.

Not that that meant they were safe. They were intentionally entering the Witch Doctor's domain, right at the heart of his enterprise.

Corvin was occupied with the treasures. Greedily touching each item, his face lit up in rapture. Reg swallowed and moved away from him, repulsed. She looked at the others. "Okay, so he's doing what he's supposed to be doing. Sucking up powers. How about the rest of us?"

"Distraction," Damon reminded her.

"Right."

They walked down one of the aisles. "Can you sense where he is?" Jessup asked Reg. "I assume you have some idea where we're going?"

Reg took a deep breath. She had been fighting against feeling for the Witch Doctor, knowing that as soon as she could contact him, he would see and feel her. And then she wouldn't be able to control anything else that happened. Harrison had already told her that he wasn't going to do anything that would harm the Witch Doctor, so it was up to her and her friends, hoping that their little bit of magic would be enough to fight the tremendous force of the Witch Doctor.

At least Francesca seemed to have some idea of what they were up against. But Reg wasn't sure that made her feel much better.

A shadowy figure loomed up ahead of them.

"Draugr," Reg warned, flicking a hand toward it. Definitely in giant form, he had to be nine or ten feet tall. The others looked at it and then at each other. "Distraction is my job," Reg reminded them. "Not casting spells."

She looked back for Corvin to see if he was joining them, newly empowered and willing to take on the Witch Doctor and his minions. But there was no sign of him.

"Go that way," Francesca instructed, motioning to an adjacent aisle. Reg turned, and Jessup and Damon with her, but Francesca was apparently not going with them. They were down another fighter; only the distraction squad was left.

It was time for Reg to do what she was there for. She closed her eyes and focused on the Witch Doctor. He wasn't far away. She was already in his shadow. She felt his attention turn to her, startled.

"It's the child again," he purred, "I'm so glad you have returned."

"I'm not a child any longer," Reg told him. Though she knew that the longer-lived races certainly considered her one with less than a century to her name. If the Witch Doctor was some kind of immortal, as Harrison and Francesca had implied, then she undoubtedly was a child to him.

"And you are here without your guardian. Making yourself a gift to me."

"No. I'm here to battle you."

His laugh was rich and deep. Reg could see him in her mind, just as he had been the day when her mother was killed. He had been looking for something. Reg didn't know what. He had employed torture as a means to get the information that he had wanted, but he didn't leave it at that. Even when he knew that her mother did not have what he was looking for, he had continued the torture until she had given up the ghost. He had reveled in it.

"You killed my mother."

The laugh continued. "Yes, I did, didn't I? A tasty morsel. Silly, weak humans. Why do you think you can stand up to a being as powerful as I? Your bravery is… inspiring, but misguided."

"Why did you do it? What were you looking for?"

Something niggled at the back of Reg's mind. What had Norma Jean said? Had she told the Witch Doctor something that night? Or had she told Reg, as a little child, something she was supposed to remember? She couldn't quite put her finger on it. She swore to herself.

"Why would I be looking for something?" the Witch Doctor asked.

"You were," Reg insisted. She was sure of that. He had not been there just to hurt her mother. Had he been looking for Reg herself? Reg had been hidden away by Harrison's protection spell, but she didn't think that she was what he had come for. She would have been another tasty morsel for him, but she was so insignificant.

"You think that with my powers I cannot find whatever I want?" the Witch Doctor bragged. "Your limited vision is laughable."

"I know where it is," Reg bluffed.

She felt an immediate shockwave back from the Witch Doctor. He was *still* looking for whatever he had been all of those years ago. Was that what he was filling the warehouse with? He was looking for some powerful object?

But she was wrong. It wasn't a thing. It was a *person*. Norma Jean had tried to tell Reg.

"I know where Weston is."

CHAPTER TWENTY-EIGHT

Immediately, it was as if all of the Witch Doctor's power coalesced around him, like an inverse explosion. Reg watched the darkness gather to form his human body in front of them, a tall black man with long, thick dreadlocks. His eyes burned with fire. Reg could feel her companions draw back, trying to pull her back with them. Jessup was firing her gun. Reg resisted, facing the evil man she had previously cowered before. This was her chance to get revenge for what he had done to her mother and for pursuing her for so many years as a child, from one home to another.

"Weston?" shouted the Witch Doctor. "Where is Weston?"

"What's the matter, Sam?" Reg asked impudently. "I thought you were all-powerful. I thought you knew everything. You could find whatever you were looking for."

He strode toward her, physically intimidating. But he wasn't close enough to touch her.

"You are an ignorant child. You have no idea of our ways! You do not know anything."

Reg imagined the protection spell that Harrison had put around her as a child and in the restaurant. It made his power seem farther away, providing a little comfort. She had the upper hand now. At least for a few minutes, he had to figure out whether she had the knowledge he desired before he could kill her.

He would undoubtedly torture her just as he had Norma Jean. Not that he needed any physical torture when he could reach into her mind and wrench out the information he needed.

Except he wouldn't find it there. She hadn't any idea who Weston was, much less where he was.

But she knew all she needed to; she had distracted him. He was no longer paying any attention to his draugrs or the tiny mortals invading his territory. He wanted to know what Reg knew. She split her attention between the Witch Doctor and her friends. It was easy, now that he was in front of her and she didn't have to worry about accidentally attracting his attention.

Corvin was still somewhere behind them, growing in power. She could feel him strengthening himself. And she could see the draugr individually now, those who weren't already at the warehouse homing in on it, obviously having been called to duty.

The Witch Doctor stalked around her, looking at her, pushing at her mind.

"You do not know anything. You are only mouthing words."

"That's what you say," Reg said with a shrug. She tried to build up the forces of her mind, to put a wall around her brain so that he couldn't dig into it and confirm what he already suspected. "Do you think that after all of these years I wouldn't have investigated it for myself? That I would accept what happened to my mother and not try to find out why? You have a very limited understanding of humans, don't you?"

He prowled back and forth, angry and restless.

"You thought that humans were not worth learning about. They were just vermin and couldn't affect anything you did. But we're not. We can be strong too. We can squeeze through the cracks like bugs and listen and learn and get more powerful."

She was teasing him, seeing how long she could keep him believing that she had the knowledge that he needed. Until Corvin was strong enough to strike, or at least to make an attempt. Long enough for Francesca to try her charms on the draugrs.

"Humans *are* bugs," the Witch Doctor hissed. "They are nothing more than little worms to be crushed. They have bodies and minds as weak as any animals. Put here on the earth just for our amusement. Put here to do with as we please, because they have no defenses, no way to fight back against us. They *never* have."

"Never?" Reg challenged. She reached for what mythologies she knew. If the fairy tales and the myths that Corvin had spoken of were true at their core, then she should be able to draw some inspiration from them. Humans fighting against immortals? She knew a few stories, but would it be enough?

She could feel Damon next to her again. She wasn't sure if he had moved closer again physically, or if he were nudging her mentally, trying to get her attention. She tried to open herself up to him to see what he wanted.

He was ready to help if there was anything he could do. Reg wasn't sure if she could tell him what she needed from him without addressing him directly. Had she been speaking with the Witch Doctor in her mind or aloud? Had the others been able to hear what they were saying? Or at least what Reg had been saying?

She was careful to speak out loud with her next words. "You are telling me that humans have never challenged immortals? They have fought them through the ages. Hercules, Perseus, Odysseus. They've all fought against monsters and immortals who were more impressive than you. They proved long ago that humans are more than capable of fighting any force that opposes them. Look at how we have spread over the earth now. We're not just a weak little tribe anymore."

She could see the images that Damon started to feed to the Witch Doctor based on her words. Rich pictures of the Greeks she had mentioned and their great battles. She could hear the roar of war and taste the tang of the sea. And the vast tapestry of humanity covering the earth, billions upon billions of human beings, living out their lives, oblivious to the immortals they had squeezed out.

"Stories written by the losers!" the Witch Doctor roared. "Pap! Children's fairy stories!"

"Haven't you ever heard that history is written by the victors?" Reg asked. "It isn't the losers who write the account of what happened; it is the winners. And you don't want to admit that the humans are the ones who beat the immortals. Where are the rest of you? You are living among us, pretending to be one of us so that you cannot be vanquished? You are the one who is hiding. It isn't the helpless little humans that cower and creep into the crevices to hide from your power. You are the one hiding from us."

"I have no reason to hide!"

"No? Then where are the gods and other immortals now? Is it just you? You're the only one who is left? You must be very lonely all by yourself."

He took another step toward her, pulling his hand back in a threat to hit her. "You think I can't kill you with a single blow? Will that be my lesson to the humans today? I can still crush you. I could crush you a thousand years ago, and I can still crush you today!"

Reg took a steadying breath, watching for his attack. She tried to strengthen the wall she had put around herself, but she knew it was pitifully weak compared to what someone like Harrison or even Corvin could construct. She had no idea how it was done. She was like a child building a house out of sticks.

"We are weak?" It was Corvin's voice that rang out behind them. Reg didn't turn to look at him, afraid to take her eyes off of the Witch Doctor and leave herself vulnerable to attack. "Do you think that I am weak now?"

The Witch Doctor recoiled. He attempted to gather his power into his physical form, but he had already done that, and there was nothing more to gather. He turned fractionally away from Reg, his eyes on Corvin.

Reg could feel Corvin approaching from behind her. He was strong, but was he strong enough? Had he left his feeding too early, driven by his sense of duty toward Reg and the others? She tried to weigh the two of them and to sense the balance between them, but it was impossible. Both were strong beyond her ability to comprehend.

"My hoard!" the Witch Doctor hissed. "You have no right to consume my hoard!"

"No right?" Corvin laughed. "Who is making up the rules now? That is what I was born for. That is what I have been seeking to do all my life. My lifespan may be short compared to yours, but I am in my prime. I will continue to drain every last bit of power from these magical trinkets, and I will leave nothing for you! Might makes right. I will be stronger than you. You will be the worm that I crush into the ground."

A tidal wave of visions came from Damon, so real that Reg couldn't sense what was true and what was imagined anymore. Corvin and the Witch Doctor in battle, hurling magical darts at each other, trying to overpower and crush each other. Corvin the victor, triumphing over evil.

The Witch Doctor fought back against the visions, pushing them away. He apparently knew where they came from and advanced on Damon, blasting him with a powerful blow that sent him crashing to the floor to lie there unmoving, unconscious or dead, disabled from feeding any more visions to the Witch Doctor or the rest of them.

"You are liars! Liars and thieves! These things are not yours to consume! You do not have the right to my treasures! And you!" He whirled around to face Reg again. "You are the weakest of all. You don't know where Weston is. Weston is gone the way of the earth decades ago. If he were not, he would have returned to protect his blood. Since he did not, he is either a coward, or he is gone from the earth! He is not here to protect you any longer. He was never there for you when you needed him. He is a coward and a weakling!" The Witch Doctor roared his imprecations and looked around him as if waiting for the building to fall around him or for some other opponent to attack. As if he were daring Weston, whoever he was, to appear and fight him.

But there was no appearance. Not from the mysterious Weston and not from Harrison. There was no one coming to their aid.

Corvin closed in. "Are you going to fight? Or are you going to hide? Fight or retreat, because those are your only two options. Do you dare to challenge me now, in my glory? You have failed. You have no more treasure. Your monsters have been defeated."

The Witch Doctor retreated a couple of steps and then held his ground. "You are mortal. You have not defeated me!"

"Only a mortal could defeat you," Corvin countered. "And here I am. It's time to face your fate."

And then Reg was caught in the middle of a chaos of spells. Unlike the picture that Damon had painted, it was an uncontrolled war of forces that buffeted Reg and forced her to the ground. She looked around for shelter and saw Jessup also on the concrete floor of the warehouse beside her. She grabbed Jessup's arm, and two of them slithered out of the aisle, trying to find some shelter between crates that clearly were not up to the task.

While the Witch Doctor and Corvin didn't appear to touch each other, there were crashes and explosions that felt like they would tumble the warehouse to the ground. Jessup shouted something to Reg, but she couldn't hear what it was. She put her ear right up to Jessup's mouth, straining to hear her over the war going on just inches away from them.

"Damon!" Jessup pointed toward the other warlock, on the floor a few feet away from them. He was gray and still. Reg's stomach turned, fearing it was already too late to protect him.

She nodded at Jessup, and the two of them dashed back out, each grabbed an arm, and with the adrenaline pumping hard through their veins, dragged him back to the sheltered space between boxes. Reg turned her attention back to the fight as Jessup bent over Damon, examining him.

Corvin was stronger than he ever had been, but was that really enough for him to defeat an immortal? How strong was the Witch Doctor? Did immortality mean limitless powers? Or was he still vulnerable to the powers of another?

CHAPTER TWENTY-NINE

Reg peeked out from her shelter to see how Corvin was faring, though she wasn't sure how she would be able to tell one way or the other. Whether she used her natural eyes or her psychic abilities, she didn't know what she would be able to see.

There were still crashes and shouts, and the air around them vibrated with magical activity. Corvin had his back to her so that she couldn't see his face, but he was glowing with power. Closing her eyes, she could feel him still drawing power from the artifacts in the boxes and crates around him.

He was walking toward the Witch Doctor one forced step at a time, as if he were fighting against a strong wind.

There was a subtle shift in the flow of power to Corvin. The flow from the magical objects slackened like there was a blockage, with Corvin sucking it toward him with increased force, but it was stuck, the suction power building to the point where it almost hurt her ears.

Corvin closed the remaining distance between himself and the Witch Doctor and reached toward him. Reg clenched her teeth and braced herself, remembering the electrical charge she felt when Corvin touched her, and the feeling of opposing magnetism she had felt when she had been in the pixies' shadowland and had tried to touch someone in the visible world. She expected to see one or both of them jolt with the pain of contact.

But there was no sudden shock when Corvin touched The Witch

Doctor. Instead, the stoppered feeling released, and rather than drawing power from the magical artifacts, Reg realized that Corvin had been trying to draw power from the Witch Doctor himself. Once in physical contact, he was successful. The Witch Doctor's head fell back and the magical power flowed from him to Corvin. The Witch Doctor was still on his feet, but it was clear he was utterly in Corvin's thrall. Jessup swore. Reg looked over at her and saw that she too was peeking out at Corvin and the Witch Doctor, her eyes wide and round.

Reg hesitated, unsure whether the fight was now over and it was safe to come out of her hiding place.

There was a starburst of energy from the Witch Doctor, and then he dropped from Corvin's grasp to the floor. The warehouse was eerily quiet for a few seconds. Reg scrambled out.

"You did it!" She was amazed. The human form of the Witch Doctor lay collapsed on the floor, unmoving. She could detect no energy or magical force from him. But then she realized she could still feel it, just not from the Witch Doctor.

"Regina." Corvin reached out his hand to her.

Reg didn't need Jessup's shout to warn her not to let Corvin touch her. She flinched back from him.

"I told you I could do it," Corvin gloated.

"He's not gone—" Reg warned, "—the draugrs!"

His gaze had been focused tightly on her, but at her words, he suddenly looked around, like a dog scenting the air, and realized she was right. He swore and started moving toward the area where the draugrs were gathering. Reg followed close behind him, though she wasn't sure how she was going to fight giant draugrs. She'd been told to distract the Witch Doctor, but now that that job was done—or seemed to be—what was she supposed to do? She glanced back at Jessup, who appeared to be torn between following them and tending to Damon.

"Stay with him!" Reg shouted back. Jessup had little magic; there wasn't any point in putting her in more danger. She would be in charge of cleaning up and explaining everything to the authorities once they were done.

If they succeeded.

"Why are they massing together?" Reg asked Corvin. "Shouldn't they be spreading out and looking for us?"

"Maybe they have something else in mind."

Reg didn't like the sound of that. She tried not to imagine what they might be gathering together for, but she couldn't help it. She imagined them consolidating their bodies into one huge draugr that could consume them all.

They slowed and crept along the side of the aisle, trying to approach without alerting the draugrs to their presence. Corvin peeked quickly around the corner then ducked back again. He looked at Reg, chuckled, and shook his head.

"What?"

"Have a look."

He and Reg switched places, and Reg took her quick peek. It was a moment before she could process what she had seen. The draugrs were gathering in their kattakyn form, a small group of midnight-black kittens. Reg hadn't been able to feel the Witch Doctor's aura in the cats before, but something had changed when he had sent his energy out, and she could now feel his malevolence even in the kattakyns.

And the thing that was attracting all of them to one place was not the opportunity to combine their powers into one giant, vengeful automaton, but the calls of the fair Francesca. She called to them coaxingly, reaching out her hands, encouraging them, speaking lovingly to them.

Reg bit her knuckle to keep from crying out when Francesca touched them, knowing how full of the Witch Doctor's evil they were and worried about the effect they would have on her. Francesca petted them, scratched their ears and chins, and let them rub against her. Reg saw Francesca counting them. She called one that was lurking in a corner, watching but not approaching. Her voice was a gentle, melodious purr, so attractive that even Reg felt like following the coaxing voice to its owner. Gradually, the last cat made its cautious way over to Francesca.

Her song changed perceptibly when they had all joined her. Her hands seemed to have purpose rather than just petting and scratching them. It was as if she were gradually wrapping a long, invisible thread around them, binding them to her. The malevolent force of the Witch Doctor started to diminish until Reg could no longer perceive it.

Reg rounded the corner cautiously. Francesca, crouched on the floor, looked up at her.

"It is quite safe," she assured.

"How did you do that? *What* did you do?"

Francesca raised her brows. "I am a charmer. I charmed them."

"And… is this permanent? They won't turn back into the other forms? The Witch Doctor can't re-form?"

She shrugged delicately. "It will last for at least a thousand years. Unless someone is to gather them together and unbind them." Francesca rose, one of the black cats in her arms, purring away like the most contented kitten. "We will need to find them new homes, of course. Preferably on different continents. That will make it less likely for the spell to be undone."

Corvin was coming up behind Reg. She turned, wary of him.

"You've been fed," she warned, "you shouldn't even care about my powers anymore."

He was still glowing, his cheeks fuller than they had been, eyes very bright. "I left room for dessert."

Reg laughed and shook her head. "No way. Stay away from me."

She could smell the roses and feel the same kind of magnetism that she had felt from Francesca when she was calling the kattakyns. A desire to cuddle up in his arms and be in his control. She tried to raise the wall of protection that she had used against the Witch Doctor. She was getting weak, and she was still only trying to imitate the feeling of Harrison's spell, but the pull toward Corvin slackened slightly.

"There are more artifacts here. You can't have used all of them yet."

"No. But human powers are always more satisfying than those that have been forced into an object."

"Stay away."

"Regina…"

"I mean it. I'll call Harrison."

His expression turned sulky. "And do you think he will be stronger than the Witch Doctor? I banished one, why not more?"

Francesca looked at Corvin and shook her head. "Your power is not without limits. I would not battle a second immortal in one day."

CHAPTER THIRTY

Reg hurried back to where Jessup was watching over Damon. "Is he okay? If he's dead because I asked him to come and help with this thing…"

Jessup shook her head. "It's not looking good, Reg. Where's Corvin? He might be able to help."

"He was supposed to be right behind me." Reg looked back over her shoulder. "Chatting up cat-girl, no doubt. Corvin!"

Corvin was not quick to saunter into sight. He looked at the other warlock on the floor and made his way over to them casually, looking unconcerned.

"Can you do something?" Jessup asked.

Corvin knelt next to Damon's prone body and held his hands over him. Reg had seen him do this before, both to help her and to help Sarah. He wouldn't be able to complain that he'd been depleted of too much energy this time. Not with the amount that he'd already absorbed and what was still available in the artifacts. Reg watched Damon's face for some sign of improvement. He was pale gray and lay so still that Reg would have doubted he had any life in him. Jessup kept her fingers on Damon's wrist.

Reg thought she saw some color coming back into Damon's face, but maybe it was just what she wanted to see. "You should call for help," she told Jessup. "There's no more Witch Doctor or draugrs, so it should be safe, right? Get some police to secure the place and bring an ambulance in?"

Jessup nodded, not looking at Reg. "I'd rather let Corvin do his thing… and then we need a story to explain this."

"A story that will satisfy the non-practitioners is not going to be easy." Reg rolled her eyes.

"You're telling me."

Damon stirred and opened his eyes. He stared up at them glassily.

"Hey." Reg pushed his hair back from his face, smiling. "How are you feeling?"

Damon groaned. "Not so good. What happened?"

"Well, you were crushed by an immortal," Corvin contributed cheerily. "Most people wouldn't survive that."

"Is he okay?" Jessup demanded.

"Lots of broken bones and internal bleeding. That's not easy to heal in a couple of minutes."

"But will he be okay?"

Corvin nodded, the corners of his mouth lifting. "Thanks to my enhanced powers, yes. Give him a few minutes to get his bearings. Being as good as dead, even for a few minutes, takes something out of a person."

Damon coughed and winced. "I'll be fine," he assured them.

Reg and Jessup continued to sit with Damon and tend to him, much to Corvin's disgust. As far as he was concerned, they should be lavishing their attention on him and giving Damon some space to recover and slink off back to his car.

In a few minutes, Damon was sitting up, leaning on one of the crates. Reg was glad to see more pink in his complexion. He had been gravely hurt, and they did owe Corvin thanks for that. And for his battle with the Witch Doctor. As annoying as it was to owe gratitude to someone so full of himself, he had been the only one who could have gathered enough strength to face the Witch Doctor in battle and even to be able to steal his powers, however much Corvin had managed to take from him.

"What happened?" Damon asked. "Did Corvin kill the Witch Doctor? Did he run away?"

"Corvin battled him until he gave up his mortal form," Jessup explained. "And then…?" She looked at Reg.

"He sent his… power… into the draugrs. I assume the idea was that he

213

could still control them and make them attack us. And then... he'd gather himself into one place again? I don't know."

"And Corvin killed the draugrs?" Damon shook his head, which made him look a little wobbly. "I thought you had to chop off their heads... Even Corvin couldn't chop off nine draugr heads, could he?"

Corvin was still standing close enough to hear them. "I could have," he argued, "if I'd had to."

"I thought that was the only way to defeat them for good."

"Francesca charmed them into cat form and called them to her, and then she performed some spell... I'm not sure exactly what, but she bound them. So now the Witch Doctor can't re-form and use his powers unless someone reunites all of the cats and unbinds them."

"Sounds like a plan," Damon breathed. "I guess your friend was right; you really did need all of us."

Damon and Corvin had both gallantly offered to escort Reg home, but she refused them both. She wasn't sure that Damon was fully recovered, and she should probably have accompanied him home to make sure that he got there safely. But she didn't offer, not wanting to insult his manhood.

And of course, she had refused Corvin because he was Corvin and she didn't want to have to defend herself against his charms and advances. As powerful as he had made himself, she didn't know how she was going to be able to resist him. She might have to leave town just to stay away from him. The little tricks she was learning to fend him off were helpful, but she feared they would be too weak to keep him away with his newly enhanced powers. Harrison had been able to walk past the wards that guarded her cottage without even a flicker; if Corvin had taken the same powers from the Witch Doctor, then how was Reg going to keep him out of her house?

Reg walked slowly down the path through the yard to her cottage, trying to comprehend all that had happened in the last few days. It seemed like the more she learned about magic in the world, the less she knew about anything. All that she had once believed to be true seemed like just a veneer placed over a chaotic world to make it seem sane and organized.

There was a movement in the garden. Reg froze. She reached out with her mind, trying to identify who or what it was before going any farther.

She saw a lithe, black shape, and realized it was one of the kattakyns. Her heart raced and she looked for some escape. Had she miscounted? Were there more draugrs than she had thought? Had the Witch Doctor been able to raise more of them in those final moments when they thought they had him bound forever?

The cat looked at her, head cocked, and Reg felt a familiar warmth. She breathed out in relief.

"Nicole," she said in a voice barely above a whisper. "Come here, Nicole. Do you want to come inside? Do you want to see Starlight?"

Nicole kept looking at her, not running away, but not getting any closer.

"Come on," Reg invited again. She tried to send Nicole thoughts of warmth and food and companionship. "It's safe now. You can come visit with Starlight, and I'll call Francesca."

Reg inched forward, trying to move so slowly that Nicole wouldn't even detect her movement. She would get to the cottage and open the door, and Nicole would be curious enough to enter. Reg could rest easy, knowing that Nicole was finally safe. And hopefully, Nicole would be the last black cat who crossed her path in Black Sands for a long time.

Reg unlocked the door and opened it slowly. "Starlight," she called in the same low, coaxing voice. "Nicole is here. Call her into the house. She'll come when she hears you."

There was an extended purr-meow from inside the cottage, similar to that of a mother cat calling her kitten, followed by a more musical yowl that made Reg's arm hairs stand on end. Nicole's ears perked up, pointing sharply toward the cottage. She eyed Reg, trying to judge her safety. Reg continued to send warming feelings toward Nicole, reminding her of all of the perks of living as an indoor cat. Nicole took a few tentative steps toward the door, then dashed inside, too quick for Reg to grab her.

Reg stepped in and pulled the door shut behind her. She turned on the lights and smiled as the two cats touched noses.

Reg had been sleeping, exhausted after a long day of fighting draugrs and an immortal, as well as the rest of the energy she had spent on connecting over distance with Corvin to make sure he was alright. She was glad that the destruction of Black Sands had been averted. With the malevolent feelings of dread and doom gone, she knew that she would sleep for a long time.

But she had only been asleep for a couple of hours when she found herself awake again. She lay in bed for a while, listening for any disturbance, reaching out her psychic powers for anything that might be wrong farther afield. But she didn't sense anything wrong. She had just awakened because...

It wasn't Starlight. For once, he wasn't pacing around restlessly and yowling at the window. Now that he had spent some time with Nicole and knew that she was well and safe, he had settled down again. He hadn't appreciated being separated from her again by Francesca, but he hadn't pouted for long, and he was sleeping beside her, a warm, soft pressure against her leg.

She didn't think it was Sarah's comings and goings. She was getting used to Sarah's more active nightlife now that she was well again.

It was something else. She kept reviewing the things that Harrison and the Witch Doctor had said to her. Reminders of the past and the things that had happened to her when she was just a little child. And Norma Jean, curiously quiet since Reg had faced the Witch Doctor. Was it possible for a ghost to be traumatized by the reminder of something that had happened in her past? Or had the stress of the encounter with the Witch Doctor damaged Reg's mind, silencing Norma Jeans' voice again?

Reg closed her eyes as if she were going back to sleep again, but she didn't know who she was trying to fool. Did she think that if she approached it obliquely, she could 'sneak up' on Norma Jean and avoid scaring her into silence?

"Norma Jean, are you still there?"

She didn't say it aloud. Even a whisper would have been too much. And she didn't really want an answer. It was better if Norma Jean *was* silenced. Maybe this was what she had wanted all along, vengeance on the entity that had tortured and killed her. Now that he had been banished, she could rest in peace.

But Reg could still feel Norma Jean stirring. She didn't answer, but she was still there, attached to Reg.

"Who is Weston?" Reg asked her.

There was no answer.

Reg rubbed her forehead, massaging the psychic third eye position on her forehead. It was throbbing and all of the muscles in her face and skull felt tense. She should be sleepy and relaxed and fall back asleep again, but she shifted restlessly, unable to get comfortable.

"Who is Weston? And where is he?"

Norma Jean was silent.

For those who fight the darkness every day

REG RAWLINS, PSYCHIC INVESTIGATOR 5

The Telepathy of Gardens

P. D. WORKMAN

To those whose voices are not heard

CHAPTER ONE

The kittens really were the cutest visitors Reg had ever had in the cottage. Nine pure-black little cats, they were almost impossible to tell apart. Yet they were each starting to show distinct personalities so that Reg could, in fact, tell one from the other. It was hard to believe that only days before, they had been draugrs, undead creatures raised by the Witch Doctor to do his bidding. Now, no one would guess that they had started their existence as zombies.

Francesca laughed as one little fellow chased her shoelace, so intent on it that Reg would have thought it really was a mouse or whatever kind of prey the cat imagined in his little kitty brain. "Come here, little kattakyn," blond-haired Francesca crooned in her Haitian Creole accent, "did you not hear Nicole tell you it was time to go bed? You are getting yourself all wound up instead of ready for sleep."

He continued to romp around her, pouncing on her shoelace and then darting back in retreat. Nearby, the kittens' surrogate mother, Nicole, patiently caught another of the kittens by the neck and wrestled it over to the pile where the others were washing or sleeping. They were too big for her to be bossing around, almost three-quarters her size, but she seemed determined that the little black cats were her own kittens and she would train them to obey her. She licked him and pressed him into place with the others, then approached the kitten that was playing with

Francesca, making low meows and purrs as she called to him. He continued to jump at Francesca's shoelace and then retreat as if it were a dangerous snake.

"You are never going to get this one settled down," Francesca warned.

But Nicole was undaunted. She put one long foreleg over the kitten's shoulders, pinning him down, and then dug her teeth into the scruff of his neck to drag him over to the other kittens. While they were acting sleepy and getting ready for their naps, the last kitten was having nothing to do with it. He pounced on the nearest tail, then bit it, rousing one of the others. Nicole again pinned him with a foreleg, and then lay atop him, licking him soundly, forcing him to be still as she gave him a bath. The kitten wriggled and turned his head, but she kept a firm hold on him, all the while licking persistently until his eyes started to shut into slits and they were both purring in unison.

Reg shook her head, her thin red braids swinging around her face. "Well, I never would have thought she could do it. That little guy has ADHD if any kitten ever did. Always distracted by the nearest movement."

"Or shoelace," Francesca laughed.

"Well, you have to admit, it did look pretty lively."

Francesca shook her head, her tinkling laugh filling the room.

Reg felt relaxed and comfortable. She liked the aura that Francesca brought with her. Despite the logistics of bringing ten cats over to the cottage for a visit, Francesca never seemed to be frazzled. Nicole and the kittens themselves also brought a calming, happy presence into the house, like the warmth of a fire. After all of the dread and fear that Reg had suffered as the Witch Doctor raised his draugr army, Reg needed the beneficial feelings they brought.

Starlight was the only one who didn't seem happy with the arrangements. It was understandable; the tuxedo cat with the mismatched eyes had been pining over Nicole since she had first appeared in the garden. Now that she was back inside and coming over for visits, she should have had plenty of time for him. But Nicole had been smitten with the kittens as soon as she had seen them and seemed oblivious to Starlight's advances.

"Don't you worry," Reg told Starlight, patting the seat of the upholstered couch beside her to invite him over. "The kittens will not be around forever. We need to find them all new homes. Then Nicole will have time for you."

He glared at her and washed his face, blaming her for the arrival of the furry interlopers.

It wasn't Reg's fault that the Witch Doctor had decided to make Black Sands his center of operations, nor that Francesca had charmed the draugrs into their kattakyn form and magically bound the Witch Doctor's life force that was dwelling within them. Reg hadn't wanted anything to do with the dark force from her past. She had been dragged into it by Corvin, much like the kittens being dragged by the scruff of their necks by Nicole.

It wasn't Reg's fault that she'd been recruited to protect Black Sands against zombies.

"We do need to find them new homes," Francesca agreed, watching the pile of black cats snoozing peacefully, Nicole on top of the pile looking very satisfied with herself. "It is vital that they are separated so that no one can unbind them. As long as they are kept apart from one another, Samyr Destine will not be able to re-form, and the world will be safe from him."

"Hard to believe that those little cats are all that separate Black Sands from the Witch Doctor's evil powers." Reg couldn't sense even a hint of the evil and dread that had accompanied the Witch Doctor. His force was completely suppressed by Francesca's spell. She and Corvin Hunter were the ones Black Sands owed their safety to. Without their powers, Reg and the others would easily have been killed, and the Witch Doctor would have gone on acquiring magical artifacts, gaining in strength, and raising more draugrs to do his bidding. Anyone who crossed his path or dared to stand up to him would be killed. It was a simple matter for a draugr to enter into its victim's dreams and to sit on his chest until he suffocated. Reg had only been spared that fate by Starlight's intervention. Reg wasn't sure how a real cat could fight off a dream cat that could kill despite not having real substance—but he had. The kattakyns were no longer dangerous, and it was easy to forget their origin, imagining instead that they were Nicole's natural kittens.

"How exactly are we going to find them homes all around the world?" Reg asked. "Is there some magical network that adopts cats?"

"These are very special cats," Nicole pointed out. "They will make good familiars. Even though the power of the bokor is bound, it is still there, and it will help to magnify the powers of the witch or warlock they are joined to."

"So is that a yes?"

"There is no magical network for cats," Francesca said, "but there are many people who will be happy to take one of these special cats. It is just a matter of finding the right homes. Not every cat is a good match for every practitioner."

Reg thought back to the day she had gone to the animal shelter and picked out Starlight. None of the other cats had responded to her the same way as Starlight. She knew that he was the cat she was supposed to have. The shelter worker's story of how Starlight had recently lost his old master and had not responded to anyone else who had approached him had sealed the deal. Reg needed a cat and he needed her. She hadn't anticipated just how compatible they would be. With the white star in the center of his forehead—his 'third eye,' as Sarah referred to it—his psychic powers were considerable. She was often surprised by how much he could boost her and enhance her psychic abilities when she needed a little extra help.

And he was furry and cute and lovely to cuddle up with when she was alone.

Starlight stopped washing and looked toward the window, his ears pricked forward.

"Someone out there?" Reg asked. Focusing her attention in the direction Starlight's ears pointed, she could sense Sarah Bishop, her landlord, along with someone else she wasn't familiar with. Sarah didn't seem to be headed toward Reg's door, so she wasn't bringing over a client or someone she wanted to introduce Reg to. Reg leaned over and pushed the curtain back an inch to see the two figures headed toward the garden. She only caught a glimpse of Sarah and the short man who was walking with her. Her seemingly middle-aged landlord was dressed in pink pants and a white shirt, with lots of pearls as accessories.

"Who is there?" Francesca asked.

"Sarah. Somebody else, maybe the new gardener."

"Good," Francesca approved. "That poor garden needs someone to take care of it."

Sarah had thrashed the garden with a broom when trying to shoo Nicole, then an unknown stray cat, out of the yard. The devastation caused by her impulsive act—the result of dementia caused by rapid aging—was

significant. When Sarah had regained her health, she had attempted to rehabilitate the battered garden herself, but it was too much for her.

"Do you think I should go out and say hello?" Reg ventured, unsure
what the proper etiquette was in a small town. She was only a tenant; Sarah
was in charge of the yard and its upkeep, so it really wasn't any of her
business.

Francesca shrugged. "You might introduce yourself. He is going to be
working in your yard; it could be awkward if you keep walking by without
saying anything."

"Okay. Makes sense," Reg agreed.

She got up and made her way to the garden back behind the house.
Sarah was standing with the man, pointing out this and that. Reg
wondered, looking at her newly-youthened face, whether she had also lost
some weight with her transformation.

The gardener was quite short, probably suffering from some form of
dwarfism. He was an old man with a wrinkled face and white beard. He had
on green coveralls and a red cap. Reg couldn't avoid feeling his pain as he
looked over the ruined garden.

Sarah turned, hearing Reg's approach. "Oh, Reg. Come and meet the
gardener who is going to get my poor little garden back into shape again."
She stretched her hand out in welcome and motioned toward the little man.
"This is Mr. Blumenthal."

"Forst," the gardener introduced himself gruffly, holding out a calloused,
stained hand.

Reg shook. He had a very strong grip—someone who had spent a lifetime working with his hands.

"I'm Reg Rawlins. I'm sorry this is such a mess." She gestured to the
garden. She wasn't taking responsibility for the damage, of course, just
acknowledging his pain at finding the plants in such poor condition. He
cared very deeply about his work.

Forst gave a single nod. He looked back at Sarah for further
instructions.

"Anyway," Sarah shrugged. "This is your area of expertise, so I don't have
to tell you what needs to be done. Let me know if you can't find something
you need. Come in for a cup of tea whenever you want one and have a
break."

Reg was a little surprised that she was inviting a stranger into her house, especially with all of the trouble that a magical intruder could cause. But maybe Sarah had known him for a long time. Or maybe she had special wards or knew something about his magic or lack of it. It wasn't Reg's place to object. But she wouldn't be inviting him into her cottage.

"Nice to meet you," Reg told Forst. "Thank you for helping Sarah to get this fixed up. I know she'll be much happier once it is looking better again."

He gave another nod and said nothing.

Sarah walked Reg back to the cottage door. "Let me know if you have any concerns," she said. "I don't want you to be disturbed by his work. If he is using a chainsaw during a seance… just let me know, and I'll take care of it."

"I'm sure it will be fine." As far as Reg could tell, there was no reason for Forst to be using any power tools. Sarah had beaten down the flowers and plants with a broom; it wasn't like Forst would need to cut down trees, and certainly not at midnight. He would be cleaning up the bits that were dead and maybe staking the plants that were bent over until they were strong enough to stand on their own again. But then, what did she know about gardening? The full extent of her plant-growing experience was planting beans for early school experiments. She'd never owned a houseplant, let alone tended a garden.

"He seems like a nice man," she told Sarah neutrally.

"They do tend to be very… laconic. Talk with each other, but not to outsiders."

"Outsiders?"

"Well, we aren't exactly his kind, are we?"

Reg came to a stop on her doorstep. "What exactly is his kind? Is he a fairy? A dwarf?"

Sarah laughed. "Fairies do have an affinity to nature and plants," she admitted, "but they are not likely to tend your garden for you. They are much too proud for that. They don't work for humans. And dwarves… you won't see them this near open waters. You're not likely to run into any dwarves outside the mountains, even in these modern times."

"Then what is he?"

"A gnome, dear." Sarah laughed again. "A garden gnome."

Reg had seen fake gnome statues in gardens, but she had no idea that they were really a thing. She shook her head at Sarah. "A garden gnome?"

"Of course. Who else would you get to rehabilitate a garden? A gnome will do it faster and with much better results than any other kind of expert. Those human landscapers that you can hire… well, they would take months to get my garden back to its natural glory. I would never hire a human to do a gnome's work."

"Of course not," Reg agreed dryly. "Who would do that?"

"Exactly," Sarah agreed. "Well, I shall leave you to your guest." A crease between her eyebrows, Sarah glanced at the living room window where Starlight was poking his head out between the curtains waiting for Reg's return. Reg wondered whether she could sense the other cats. Sarah would not have been happy to find so many cats in the cottage. She tolerated Starlight as Reg's familiar but had blanched at even the thought of a second cat around when Reg had started to look for Nicole.

Sarah had an African gray parrot and an affinity for birds, and she did not like cats.

Reg sat down again with Francesca. She looked at the cats all snoozing in a pile and picked up Starlight to give him some attention while she talked.

"So what do you need me for?" she asked Francesca. "It seems like you've got a pretty good handle on the market for the kattakyns. I don't know anything about giving cats away. I always wanted a cat as a kid, and I tried bringing abandoned kittens or stray cats home more than once, but that never worked out. Foster moms are usually overworked as it is, they don't need another mouth to feed or critter to look after. Even if I promised to take care of all of its needs, I could never convince anyone to let me have one. So I'm not sure how much help I would be to your case."

Francesca smiled, watching Reg pet Starlight, scratch his ears, and rub the white spot on his forehead. "It is not your marketing expertise that I am hoping for," she said with a lilt. "I am looking for someone who can help to match the kattakyns with the right owners. The ones who will suit them the best."

"Oh." Reg thought once more to her tour of the animal shelter, eventually finding Starlight there. She had found the cat that suited her the best or needed her the most, but was that a transferable skill? "I don't know. I've never done anything like that before."

"You are very good with the kittens," Francesca pointed out. "You can see their personalities. You can tell them apart."

"Well, yes, that's true. But they do have very distinct personalities; you've noticed that too, right?"

Francesca shook her head. She adjusted the lay of her sweater, looking uncomfortable. "No, I am afraid not... as much as I try, I only see nine little black cats. We want to be able to match them up with the practitioners who best suit them."

"Okay. Well, I guess I'll do my best."

"You want them to be happy in their new homes. We need them to stay put, not to roam around and find each other."

"Do you think that would happen? It wouldn't, would it? They would get lost, but they wouldn't be able to find each other. They wouldn't know where to go."

"They are bound together. They will eventually find each other. We want to keep that from happening for as long as possible. By placing them around the world, I hope to keep them apart for hundreds of years. The farther they are apart, the less chance there is of Samyr gathering enough power to reform himself."

Reg shuddered. "Okay, I'm in," she agreed.

CHAPTER TWO

Reg helped Francesca carry the cats to her car in a couple of boxes. Since they were half-grown rather than small kittens, they couldn't all be corralled in a shoebox. They scrabbled around in the large boxes, their claws slipping on the slick cardboard. A couple of them started meowing, protesting their situation. They put the boxes on the back seat of the car. Reg smiled at all of the inquisitive black furry faces looking back at her. She pushed a couple down when they tried to climb up out of the boxes and sent them calm, reassuring thoughts. Eventually, they all settled.

Francesca nodded and got into the driver's seat. "Thank you, Reg! I will be in touch when I have had a chance to talk to some of the potential buyers. Then we can sort out which one to send where."

"Okay. Sounds good. Drive slow."

"I do not want to have any accidents with this cargo," Francesca agreed, taking a look over her shoulder at them.

After Francesca's car pulled out, Reg became aware she was being watched. She looked around and saw a white compact car. Not a surprise, since the town was full of white compacts, but she knew by the feeling that started to grow and thicken around her precisely who it was.

Corvin extricated himself from the small car and approached her. His handsome face was sullen. "I've been waiting half the day for you to get rid of that woman and her cats."

"Oh?" Reg gave a careless shrug. That was another bonus of a houseful of cats—it kept Corvin at a distance. "I don't remember you calling or mentioning that you wanted to come over."

He looked like he had tasted something sour. "That would probably be because you've blocked me on your phone."

Reg smiled. "Yeah, that's probably it."

"But I still know where you live. All that means is that I have to come over here in person, which is not exactly a hardship. I would rather see you face to face."

That was a drawback of cutting off phone communications. Reg would have to rethink that. It wasn't like she could get a restraining order to keep him from hanging around her house. He wasn't doing anything to threaten or harm her. Reg also had no desire to stand before a judge and plead her case. She made it a policy to stay as far as possible from police and courtrooms.

Corvin's eyes roamed around. "Why don't we go for a walk?"

He knew, of course, that she wouldn't allow him in her house. Not with his track record. It was dangerous to invite any unknown warlock into the house. All that much worse, one like Corvin whose dangers were known.

"I'm not going for a walk with you. Spit out what it is you want because I'm going back to my house and you're not going to stop me."

"There's no need to be so vehement about it."

"There is every reason."

"I just wanted to talk. You know I don't have very many options of who to talk to right now."

"It's not my fault you are being shunned."

"Well…" He raised his brows. "It is sort of your fault."

"You're the one who attacked me. If you mean it's my fault because I testified against you, then fine. It's my fault you're being shunned."

He didn't look pleased that she had agreed with him. He was looking for a fight. Looking to engage with her. Reg couldn't afford to let him work his wiles on her. She looked at her phone to see what time it was.

"So, what did you want to talk about? Do you actually have a purpose here, or are you just hanging around because you're bored?"

He took a step closer to her, into her comfort zone. Reg took a step back and tried to raise her psychic defenses against him. Sooner or later, he would make his move. She needed to be ready for it. He wouldn't be able to resist trying to magic her.

"I didn't say I was bored," Corvin said, staring into her eyes, his manner confidential and intense.

"Well, good. Then I guess you have plenty to do and don't need to bother me."

"Regina," he crooned her name, correctly pronouncing it, Reh JEE nah, not like the Canadian city. "When are you going to stop this dance? Just admit that the two of us are fated. Stop fighting every word and every move. I don't want to hurt you. I want us to be friends."

"You want a lot more than friendship, and I'm not going to give it to you."

He shifted his feet, looking for a more comfortable position. But he wasn't going to her cottage, they weren't going for a walk, and he was too far away from his car to lean casually against it. He could only stand there, out in the open where everyone could see him, talking with Reg. Because that was all she was going to let him do. As handsome as the dark warlock was, and however enticing he could become when he exercised his charms, she couldn't give in.

Corvin leaned closer. "You realize that things could change very quickly."

She didn't like his proximity. Was he making a threat? Having gained so much more power in his fight with the Witch Doctor, who knew what he could do now. Or was he suggesting something else?

"What things could change?" she asked cautiously.

"The Council is considering commuting my sentence."

Reg felt like she had been punched in the gut. After all of the pain and suffering she had gone through, after having to face the humiliation of testifying against him, they were going to let him get off that quickly? They had said that they would shun him until he proved he could be a positive member of their society. His sentence was indefinite, and Reg had thought that meant it would be long, not short.

"How can they do that?" she asked breathlessly.

"Our encounter with the Witch Doctor proved that I am a valuable asset to the magical community. We saved countless lives and bound a dark force that could have done unimaginable harm."

"You didn't exactly do it for altruistic purposes."

"Who is to say?" he countered with a smug smile. "When I tell the story to the Council members, it certainly will be."

"The only reason you went into that warehouse was so that you could have access to the magical artifacts and consume their powers."

"Not the only reason."

"And to prove that you could defeat a powerful being. An immortal, or whatever he was."

Corvin's smile just grew. Reg shook her head, sickened by his attitude and the thought that the warlock council might reinstate him so quickly. It was beyond belief. How had he been punished for what he had tried to do to her? He had gone against all of the rules imposed on his kind and tried to steal her powers from her by force. If they reinstated him so quickly, it would be a sign that they didn't care what he did. He could go on doing whatever he liked; they didn't care a bit about his victims.

"Reg…" He cocked his head, looking at her like she had hurt him by not being excited about his news. He made a pouty face. "Don't be that way. I don't harbor ill will toward you. We can be friends. Forget the past, and look forward to the future."

"To a future where you can have whatever you want because you're the strongest? Where you can break all of the rules and no one cares about it one bit?"

"Obviously, people care, or they wouldn't have disciplined me to begin with. But I've learned my lesson. I won't let my appetites get away from me again." He blinked and smiled encouragingly. "You and I can get along. Our powers are synergistic. They go together so well, matching each other strength for strength. The two of us together could defeat any foe."

"Oh, that's your new line, is it? Now that you've got the power, you're ready to use it. And it's not to protect all of the innocent citizens of Black Sands anymore. Now it is to defeat all foes and get what you want."

"That isn't what I said. Think of how many people could benefit if you and I combined our powers. Think of all of those people that you would like to be able to help. The two of us together could do almost anything. Think about all of your lost and broken dreams. All of those things that you used to want that you've given up on. You could have them all."

Reg shook her head, trying to rid herself of his influence, like a fly buzzing in her ear. He didn't understand anything about her childhood and her lost and broken dreams. He thought that she had dreamed of money and power. But in reality, she had dreamed of a loving family, stability, enough to eat, and a future. She was doing well in Black Sands, but it was only a matter of time until that dream ended too. They would come for her and she would have to run again if she wanted to avoid incarceration. She would be on the skids once more, looking for a home and a stable income somewhere else where people had never heard her name.

"Reg." He reached out to touch her cheek. "You look so sad. You can have anything. Think about it. Whatever you want."

She could feel his warmth even before his fingers touched her skin. She swallowed and closed her eyes, wishing that she could swim into the warm, safe feeling that he promised. But she knew how she would feel if she surrendered to him. When he was done with her and had stripped away all of her gifts, she would be left an empty husk, with a hollow, echoing space in her head that used to be filled with voices. She would be more alone than she had ever been before. She pulled back from his touch, forcing herself to withdraw instead of leaning into him.

"Corvin…" She rarely addressed him by name, rarely told him anything about her past or how she was feeling. "You have no idea what it's like for me."

She opened her eyes and looked at him. Corvin frowned, wrinkle lines forming between his eyes. He pulled back his hand. "Then tell me. I know what it's like to hold those powers. I don't know how you could be unhappy with the richness of the powers in your possession." It was his turn to look at her longingly. He had untold powers after consuming many of the magical artifacts at the warehouse and the powers of the Witch Doctor himself. Anyone else would have been satisfied with that. But not Corvin. He had to have it all. He had to have Reg's powers too.

"How could you still be hungry?"

He shrugged and chuckled. "You know how you can spend a couple of hours eating at a buffet, until you're absolutely stuffed, and still want the dessert afterward?"

"And I'm your dessert?"

"Well, not you, but your powers."

"It's the same thing. I don't want to be consumed. You don't know what it feels like."

"Oh, but I do," Corvin reminded her. He had told them all at his hearing how his father, also a power-drinker like him, had consumed his powers multiple times. Because Corvin could gain power from other people and magical objects, then unlike most of the practitioners in existence, he could have his powers stripped away more than once. Reg looked away from him, embarrassed to remember his vulnerability.

"If you know what it's like, then how can you do it to someone else?" she demanded. "How can you do that, knowing how empty they will feel after you take their powers?"

"Because I need to do it to survive. Do you like the fact that animals are killed for your consumption? That to survive, you kill other living creatures?"

"Well... I don't like to think about it, no. But it isn't like I'm killing them myself. And if it weren't for the agricultural industry, I wouldn't eat them at all. It's just because... they are there. If I stopped eating animals, it wouldn't change anything in the industry."

"So if you won't stop killing other creatures to fill your appetites, then why would you criticize me for doing what comes naturally for me? I need to consume others' powers for my survival."

"I could decide to be vegetarian; then I wouldn't be eating animals. You could choose to just consume the powers from objects, not from people."

"Think of the pain you would be inflicting on the plants you ate. Is that any better than killing animals? You consume them alive!"

"Plants don't have feelings!" Reg rolled her eyes.

"Tell that to a nature guardian. Those who tend to the plants know better."

Reg shifted uncomfortably. She looked at him, squirming. "You don't need my powers right now. You don't need anyone's powers right now. You're still full from the buffet. With the amount that you filled up before the Witch Doctor gave up, you shouldn't need to feed again for about a century."

"You don't know anything about how long it will last," Corvin pointed out grumpily.

"I know that you're full right now."

"And did I say I was going to consume your powers? I suggested that the two of us could work together. That's all."

"And that you would still like dessert."

"A man always wants dessert."

"I'm going inside. I really don't want to talk about this anymore. I'm not about to become Bonnie to your Clyde, so you can forget about that. You're on your own."

He mouthed the words, Bonnie and Clyde, like he had no idea what she was talking about. The magical world could be so isolated from the real world. They just lived in their own little pockets, ignoring the rest of the world. Some of them didn't have any electronics. No phones. No TVs. Reg had no idea how they could survive without modern conveniences. It was a modern world.

"The answer is no, Corvin. I'm not teaming up with you. I wasn't happy about being forced to team up with you against the Witch Doctor. I'm done."

Corvin blew out his breath, frustrated. "You owe me. You just remember that. We are bonded together until you repay me your part of the covenant."

Reg swallowed. "You took my powers. The contract was fulfilled."

"I returned them to you. That means you still owe me. You agreed. You made a covenant. And until you fulfill it, we will be fated to cross paths."

"Ick. I'm going home. You can sit in your car and wait for me to come out again. Or you could go home and do whatever warlocky things are on your magical to-do list."

Reg pulled back, forcing herself to leave his circle of influence. The cooler air caressed her skin and she was able to take a full breath again. She had failed to notice just how much he had been stifling her.

She went back to her cottage, looking back once or twice to make sure that Corvin wasn't following her. He stayed out in front of the main house.

CHAPTER THREE

She was tired when she got back indoors. It had taken a lot of energy to fight the temptation to join Corvin. Even though he hadn't been magicking her the same way as he had in the past, he had still been doing something. Maybe he was trying out a new power. A way of influencing her with different methods from those he had used before. Who knew what powers he had acquired from the artifacts in the warehouse and the Witch Doctor?

Starlight meowed at Reg, scolding her for going away for so long. Or maybe he could smell Corvin's scent on her or sense that she had been talking to him. She hadn't actually been outside for that long. She stooped down and picked him up.

"I know, I know, Star. I didn't know he was coming over, and I didn't let him ensorcell me, so everything is fine."

He purred and rubbed the velvety top of his head against her chin. He reminded her that *he* was her cat. Not Nicole, and not the nine kattakyns. He was the one who had chosen her, and she was marked as his territory. She was his human.

"You're a silly cat, you know?" Reg said. "You think that you're the owner and I'm your pet when it's the other way around."

His disdainful gaze clearly communicated that she had it backward.

Reg was awake early the next morning, despite having been up for a midnight seance. For some reason, when the sun started to creep in through her window, she was wide awake. She made her morning coffee and gave Starlight some stew from the fridge to supplement his dry cat food, and was looking on her phone for a morning show that she had watched a few times before. Usually, she wasn't up early enough to see it. But it was easier for her to keep up on the news through televised programs than by reading articles.

As she stood next to the coffee pot, waiting for it to finish dripping, she heard crying. A man's voice, sobbing, "Oh, no, no, no…"

She looked at her phone at first, thinking that it was a pop-up commercial she had failed to dismiss. But it wasn't her phone. She hit the mute button on the morning show to silence their animated, chattering voices so she could hear where the sound was coming from. While it seemed much closer, she finally determined that it was coming from outside. She looked out her windows that faced the garden, but still couldn't see what was going on, so she went outside for a peek.

Forst, the garden gnome, was sitting on a big rock, his face in his hands, weeping loudly. Reg stood looking at him, unsure what to do. It was a private moment, and she was sure he wouldn't want to be interrupted or have to explain his sorrow to her. She should go back into the cottage and mind her own business.

But she couldn't get past his heartbroken sobs. She couldn't just leave him there to deal with whatever had made him so unhappy without at least offering a listening ear. What good was a psychic who wouldn't listen?

"Uh… Mr. Blumenthal…?"

He raised his head and looked at her. He started immediately to his feet as if she'd caught him doing something forbidden.

"Miss Rawlins!"

His blue eyes were watery and red, but his face was otherwise an unreadable mask. If she hadn't caught him crying, she wouldn't have been able to read his sorrow in the lines of his face. She took a couple of steps closer.

"I'm sorry. I didn't mean to startle you. It's just that… you sounded so sad. I wanted to make sure that everything is okay. Are you… all right?"

He rubbed at his nose with the back of his hand and reached into the pocket of his coveralls. He drew out a strange, curvy pipe like Reg had seen on Sherlock Holmes movie covers, and started to fiddle with it, filling it and lighting it without looking at her. His hands shook slightly, but otherwise, he betrayed no emotion.

But in her head, Reg again heard the sobs. "She's just a girl. What could she do?"

His lips hadn't moved and he continued to focus on his pipe, drawing in a long drag of smoke and then puffing it out in rings. Reg suddenly realized that she hadn't heard him with her natural ears, but had been hearing his thoughts. She looked away, embarrassed. It wasn't polite to listen in on other people's private thoughts. She hadn't meant to enter his head and wasn't sure how she had.

"I'll help you if there is anything I can do," she offered. She looked up at the pale blue sky. There were white clouds toward the horizon, but overhead it was just blue sky, a few birds far above them.

"A human does not help a gnome. But it is the humans we must deal with."

Reg waited. She made an offering gesture with her hands, not sure what else to say to him. He squinted at her, his blue eyes taking on a new expression.

"You hear my words?"

Reg nodded. "Yes. I'm sorry, I wasn't trying to read your thoughts. I don't know what happened. Maybe I'm extra-sensitive after the seance last night," she explained, aware that she was saying too much, providing information he didn't need.

"Humans cannot hear inside words."

"No. Not usually. But I'm a psychic. So I guess... I can. I'm sorry. I didn't mean to intrude."

He pulled the pipe away from his mouth, giving a sudden smile. His cheeks were red and his eyes brighter.

"Talking with humans is usually so hard."

She remembered his curtness when they had been introduced the day before. Maybe he hadn't been rude or abrupt, but just had problems forming words aloud.

"Do gnomes talk to each other... with their inside words?" she guessed.

He nodded vigorously. "That is our way," he agreed. "The outside words... are much harder."

"Well, you can talk to me with your inside words. I didn't mean to overhear you, but if there's something I can do to help, I would be happy to."

He puffed on his pipe again and considered. Reg realized she couldn't hear all of his private thoughts, only the words he wished to share, and was relieved. Maybe she hadn't been as rude as she had feared.

"It is my brother," he told her finally. "Fir, my twin."

"You have a twin?"

"All gnomen have a twin."

"Really? I didn't know that. That must be really... nice. You would always have someone to talk to, growing up. Someone who was always there for you." The loneliness of her childhood had been a far different story. Reg had moved from family to family, never with anyone who could understand her thoughts and feelings, who understood her past and could be empathetic toward her. She had longed for a sister she could share her thoughts with. There had been the occasional foster sister she had connected with, like Erin, but it had mostly been a lonely existence.

Forst nodded his head. "Gnomen twins rely on each other. We are closely bound."

That made sense to Reg. She'd always thought that twins must be the closest kind of relationship there was. In contact with each other from the time they were conceived, spending time together in the womb communing with each other and becoming familiar with each other's patterns and feelings.

"And something happened to your twin? What is it?"

The gnome was still holding his pipe in his right hand; his left clenched into a fist. Reg felt his distress heighten.

"He has been captured! Locked in a cage!"

"Oh, dear." Reg looked around, hoping that Sarah might be walking by. She didn't understand a lot of things about the magical world, and if some evil witch or other creature had kidnapped Forst's brother, Reg was going to need help from someone with much deeper knowledge and experience. "Captured by who? What happened?"

"The black coats took him away. They said he could not protect his patch any longer. That he was doing wrong and had to be punished." Forst's hand unclenched and reclenched. He tried to keep a hold on himself, but could not restrain another desperate sob.

"Who are these black coats? Are they witches? Something else? Where did they take him?"

"To the cage, the cage!" he wailed. "How can they lock up a free creature?"

Reg couldn't help walking closer to the gnome, and hesitated, not knowing if she could touch him, or if that would be considered inappropriate or an assault. He looked up at her, his eyes swimming with tears.

"What did they say he did wrong?" Reg prompted.

"They want to destroy his patch. They want to kill the plants. Humans always want to destroy everything! He did nothing but protect his own living."

Reg caught on the thoughts she could understand. "It was humans who took him? What kind of humans?"

"The black coats," he repeated. "They took him away and put him in a cage."

Understanding was dawning on Reg. "Do you mean police? Black shirts and pants, with badges and shields on them?" Reg gestured to her own chest and shoulder.

Forst nodded miserably.

"He was arrested? What did they say they were arresting him for?"

"For protecting his plants."

"What kind of plants?" Reg asked suspiciously. "Did he have... special plants? Like marijuana?"

"No," Forst's brow wrinkled. "No ditch weed. Not plants humans care about. They want to kill them."

"Why?"

"Building roads. Houses. Replacing everything with stone. Why do humans like stone so much? They must be part dwarf."

"Development." Reg finally understood. "Where is his property? Are they going to pay him for it?"

"Gold," Forst shook his head grumpily. "You cannot kill plants for gold. Gnomen need living things, not metal and rocks."

"I'm sorry," Reg shook her head. "Humans can be big bullies."

Forst tugged on her sleeve, looking up at her pleadingly. "You will talk to the black coats?" he begged. "You will get him out of the cage?"

Reg sighed.

CHAPTER FOUR

The last thing that Reg wanted to do was to talk to the police. Well, maybe the second last, the last being to be alone with Corvin Hunter. She didn't want to talk to them or to go to the police station or bail a gnome out of jail.

But she couldn't bear the abject misery on Forst's face. He didn't have a clue how the human justice system worked. He didn't know what to do and even if he did, his ability to speak—his outside words—were limited. He needed someone who knew what she was doing and could talk to the police to find out how to have his twin released.

She could call the main number for the police department, but she hoped to shortcut that by calling Detective Jessup, who could maybe smooth the way for her. Jessup could at least talk to the officers involved in the arrest, in case they were not part of the magical community. It didn't seem like very many in the police department knew about the magical community. Which must make some of the crime they dealt with in Black Sands seem very bizarre.

"Reg," Jessup greeted when she saw Reg's caller ID on the phone and picked up the call. She sounded pleased. It was back to 'Reg' instead of 'Miss Rawlins,' which she reverted to when Reg was a person of interest. "What can I do for you?"

This time she was interested in helping. Reg decided to use it to her best advantage.

"I have a friend with a problem."

"Sure. What's the problem?"

"His brother has been arrested; I'm not sure what for. Sounds like he got in the way of some developer who wants to appropriate his land. He's in jail, and…"

"And you want to know how to get him out."

"Yes. Maybe on bail, or maybe just to have the charges dropped. I doubt if he's really guilty of any lawbreaking."

"If he's been arrested, I have to assume that he did something. What's this guy's name?"

"Fir Blumenthal."

"Okay, hang on a second." Reg could hear her computer keys tapping away. "Ooh. Eco-terrorism?"

"Seriously? What the heck is eco-terrorism?"

"Looks like he is suspected of sabotaging a bunch of industrial equipment. Trespassing. He chained himself to a tree."

"He's just trying to protect his land."

"Doesn't work if it's not your own land. You know anything about the backstory?"

"Well… he's a gnome."

"Ah. We've run into this kind of thing before. They don't understand the way the modern world works. Private ownership of land and development and that kind of thing. They think that whatever land they squat on is theirs, and they'll buckle down and do whatever they can to keep other people from destroying 'their' land or removing them from it."

"Isn't there any treaty protecting them? Don't they have any of their own land? Any rights?"

"They've never been particularly interested in making agreements with humans or any other races. They just want to tend their gardens or forests and be left alone. Unfortunately… there's more and more encroachment on their land, and it's getting harder and harder for them to find virgin territory where they can stay for any amount of time."

"So what can you do? Can you get the charges dropped? Get him out on bail?"

"I can try talking to the powers that be around here. He probably hasn't given any explanation of why he was acting the way he was. They think he's just some eco-nut."

"And you can convince them otherwise?"

"I'll do my best. Are you going to come down here to get him?"

"Uh… I'd rather not. But if I have to."

"Could you? It helps to have some citizen saying that he's not a danger and he's not going to cause any more trouble. Because I doubt he'll defend himself. They aren't much for talking."

"Well, for outside talking."

There was a pause. "Outside talking?"

"That's what they call it—communicating out loud. Forst says it's really hard for them. But they're fine with inside talking."

"And what is inside talking?"

"Telepathy."

"Oh." Jessup laughed. "Trust you! The trouble is, they can't communicate telepathically with the rest of us. The cops aren't going to know how to communicate with him. He's not deaf or disabled. They can talk if forced to. So people assume that they're just hard to get along with."

"Can't you tell them he is disabled?"

"I'll try. It's not exactly true, but I can't very well tell them he's a gnome."

"What would you tell them if he could only speak using a voice synthesizer or picture board or sign language?"

"I wouldn't have any problem telling them that he was disabled then. Because it's true."

"Then how is this any different? He's not physically built for verbal communication. It doesn't matter if he can say a word here and there. He needs assistance. Accommodations."

"Well… yeah. So when you get down here, you can have a little chat with him in a private meeting room, and then you can advocate for him. I'm sure if you make a big stink about how his rights are being violated because of his disability, they'll be quick enough to let him go. No one wants that kind of publicity."

Reg took Jessup's advice and stormed into the police station, demanding that she be allowed to see her client, making plenty of noise about how they were brutalizing a homeless, disabled man, ripping him from his home and treating him like an animal, locking him up in a cage.

"Ma'am, ma'am," the desk clerk made motions for her to calm down. "Please, there's no need to yell. I don't know what has happened, but I'm sure we can work it out. Abusive language and behavior are not going to get you anywhere and will not be tolerated."

"You've locked him up! Don't you people have any sense? Aren't your officers given any disability training? But what was I expecting in a run-down little Podunk town like this? Of course you're going to act like commandos instead of knowing how we treat people in the twenty-first century."

"Who is it you are here to talk to us about?" the clerk asked, fingers hovering over the keyboard.

"Fir Blumenthal. Arrested yesterday afternoon. For daring to sit on his own property."

The woman brought the record up on her screen and scanned the information. "According to this, he was not sitting on his own property. He is not the registered owner, and the owner wanted him removed."

"Have you never heard of homelessness? Squatting? Just because someone doesn't have title, that doesn't mean they don't have rights! You can't just lock people up because they don't have a place to live! It's outrageous."

"I'm sure we can get this all sorted out. Do you have a place for Mr. Blumenthal to go? Someone who will vouch for him and put him up?"

"Now you're going to treat him like he's incompetent when you haven't even met him? Just because he has different communication needs than you, that doesn't make him less of a person. It doesn't mean he can't take care of himself. He has the same rights as anyone else. Do you require anyone else to prove that they'll be 'taken care of' when they are released?"

"I just meant... you said that he didn't have a home... I would be remiss if I didn't try to make sure that he was going to a safe situation and wasn't just going to be out on the street."

"Do you know how many homeless people there are out there? Are you telling me that the police are in the business of making sure that they all have safe homes to go to? That's not your job. You can't discriminate against him because he's indigent."

The clerk rolled her shoulders, frowning and trying to find some way to handle the situation without being ripped apart for being elitist or ableist. "Look, ma'am. I'm trying to help you here. This man was arrested for being a nuisance and a possible danger. We can't just let him go and pretend that nothing happened."

"Of course you can, you do it all the time. If there isn't enough evidence to build a case against Mr. Blumenthal, then you have to let him go. You can't just keep holding him because his brain doesn't work the same way as yours does. People who are considered to be a danger are released all the time. Suspected murderers, pedophiles, drug dealers. If you don't have enough to convict them, you have to let them go. End of story."

The clerk sighed, putting her hands flat on the desk in front of her and bowing her head in defeat. "Let me find someone who can help you with this."

Reg was shunted from one person to another, giving her spiel and attacking wherever possible, until someone agreed that she should be allowed to talk to her client. No one asked what kind of client he was. Probably no one dared, knowing she could go into a rant about how patients' rights were protected and they weren't allowed to ask anything that invaded his privacy or his relationship to a counselor or social worker or medical professional, whatever it was that Reg was pretending to be.

"Detective Jessup said that you were coming and that you would want to meet with Mr. Blumenthal," a tall, thin policeman advised Reg, acting like he had known what was going on all the time and hadn't been caught off-guard by Reg's invasion of the police department or Jessup's call advising that they should help her out. "If you'll just come this way…"

Reg followed the policeman. She couldn't help grinning when he wasn't looking at her. She'd never had so much fun in a police station, and she'd pulled some pretty bold scams in her time. She was enjoying the outraged mama bear act.

He offered her a seat on one of the plastic chairs, offered her coffee or water, and promised that Mr. Blumenthal would be brought in shortly. Reg sat down to relax, knowing that it could be another hour or more before they made it through all of the bureaucratic roadblocks and got him from the jail cell to the meeting room. She looked around the room, painted a flat green, with anti-drug posters, warnings about not smoking, and various other visual pollution.

CHAPTER FIVE

Eventually, Fir was brought into the meeting room. Reg could see at a glance that he had been poorly treated. Plenty of fodder for her outrage.

"Is this the way you treat all prisoners?" she demanded. "Or just the homeless and disabled ones?"

The tall police officer looked at her with apprehension. "I was not involved in his arrest. I don't know anything about the way that he's been treated."

"No?" Reg demanded. "You can't tell just by looking at him? His clothes are dirty and torn; he has a black eye and abrasions on his face—who knows about the rest of his body! Did the police beat him? Or did you just put him in with the general population where the other prisoners would abuse him? I will be calling the media, and this may just make the front page. Is that what you want to see? Mr. Blumenthal's battered face on the front page of the Black Sands paper? Maybe this is big enough it will make it to Miami, or even a national paper! This is outrageous."

"Ma'am, I think you need to calm down. Sit down and have a visit with your... friend. I'm sure you'll find that he's been treated with respect. If there have been any violations, we can address the specifics. Mr. Blumenthal has not had any complaints. He has not asked for a doctor or anything else."

She glared at him. "Mr. Blumenthal is nonverbal," she said acidly.

He swallowed, made a helpless gesture, and fled from the room, shutting the door behind him. Reg glanced around for surveillance equipment. There was no obvious camera or observation window. But that didn't mean that it was free of listening devices. She looked at Fir Blumenthal, sitting across the table from her, looking tiny and thoroughly baffled by what was going on. She leaned closer to him.

"Forst sent me," she said softly. "You can use your inside words and I will hear you."

His eyes widened. He looked very much like his brother. Of course, they were twins and the first gnomes she had ever encountered, so it was understandable that they would resemble each other. She didn't think they were identical twins, but Fir had the same white beard and round face as Forst. He had no cap, showing off a pale, gleaming scalp.

"You can hear us?"

"Yes. I can hear you. I came to help. Forst is very upset about you being arrested and wanted me to see what I could do about getting you out. I hope that my yelling doesn't bother you; it's just a way of getting the black coats to pay attention. They're not very good listeners."

"You can yell," Fir agreed, the corner of his mouth lifting in a small smile. "If that's what will free me from this cage."

Reg nodded. She looked at his injuries, the sadness that Forst had felt earlier washing over her. They had hurt the poor, defenseless little man just because he was different and vulnerable. He wanted to protect his plants from the developers who wanted to bulldoze them all away, and for that, they had hurt him and imprisoned him. "Tell me about what happened. Who hit you?"

Fir rubbed his abraded cheek, flinching slightly at his own touch. He touched his blackened, puffy eye tenderly. "Some of it from the black coats. The eyes and the worst pains, from the other humans in the cage." His large nostrils flared. "They call us animals, but animals do not behave that way. Only humans behave that way, attacking and imprisoning and causing harm."

"I know. We don't have a very good track record, do we?"

He again smiled, a little sunnier this time. "You are different. How did Forst know you could hear inside talk?"

"Well…" She didn't know if she should reveal that she had heard him weeping. Did the gnomes have a social code that men should not show

252

emotion? Or would he think it was normal and appropriate? "I heard him… talking to himself. So I knew. I didn't even realize at first that it was inside talk and not outside talk; it was so clear in my head."

"You will be able to get me out of here?"

"I think so. I have a friend who is going to try to help. She's here in the police station, though I don't know exactly where right now."

"You can talk to her too?"

"I can talk to her. Telepathically, you mean? No. I just talked to her on the phone earlier. I'll have to wait until she comes here or calls me back. She can't understand telepathy."

He nodded. He picked at the dirt under his nails. His hands were calloused from plenty of manual labor. She pictured him working in his garden, tending to his plants.

He smiled at her. "Yes. I miss my garden."

"Where is it? Who is the developer that wants to ruin it?"

Fir described the location, and Reg, picturing it, tried to place it on her mental map. He talked about the plants that grew there and what each one liked as if they were his children. He spoke of the small stream that watered them and the water birds that came to drink and to hunt for insects.

"That sounds lovely. I can understand why you don't want to leave it."

"I must get back there." His eyes swam with tears. "I must get home to my living things."

Reg nodded. She looked toward the door, but Jessup didn't immediately appear. "Tell me about what you did before they came to get you. They said that you vandalized their property and that you were trespassing after they told you to leave."

He described the things he had done to their vehicles and heavy equipment, and Reg suppressed a smile. She couldn't help cheering for the underdog, the little man fighting the big corporation. She delighted in the things he had done to show the company that he wasn't going to be walked all over.

"You understand that they say the property is not yours? That it belongs to someone else and they want to change it?"

"They want to kill it. They want to kill all of the plants and put in their stone highway and monstrosities. Any soil that is left, they will cover with their carpets of tame grass, and they won't even let that grow properly. They will plant trees and a few foreign flowers and then pat themselves on the back that they have made it look 'natural.' How could such a monstrosity be natural?"

"How much space is in your patch? How big is it?"

He shrugged. "A garden gnome does not need much. But we are being squeezed out of even the tiniest plots. They want it to be all stone and shelters that block out the light. They want nothing that is wild to be left."

Reg nodded, thinking about it. There was a tap on the door, and Jessup put in an appearance, poking her head in first to make sure that it was safe to enter.

"Come in." Reg motioned to one of the other plastic chairs. "Unless you've already figured out how to get Mr. Blumenthal out of here and we don't have to wait any longer."

"No such luck," Jessup said with a grimace. "But the gears are turning. It's in the works. Hopefully…"

"As you can see, Mr. Blumenthal—"

"Fir," the gnome inserted.

"Fir has not been treated well while in police custody. He's been beaten up by the police who arrested him and by the other inmates in custody. Why they would think it was okay to put a defenseless, disabled man into the general population, I have no idea."

"I've already talked to them about it. Although I didn't know the condition he was in. You, I mean," Jessup said, facing the gnome and addressing him directly.

"What kind of human is she?" Fir asked Reg, studying the Asian woman curiously. He had apparently not had a lot of interaction with humans of different races.

Reg answered Fir in her head instead of out loud. "I don't know for sure. It isn't polite to ask."

"She is not very ugly for a human."

Reg snickered and didn't pass this information on to Jessup.

"So how long do you think it is going to take? Maybe we can get Mr.— Fir some medical care? And some food? I would say clean clothes, but they might not have his size."

"And a pipe," Fir suggested. "They took my pipe."

"You can't smoke in here."

"We could take him to the doctor, but I think that just a first aid kit and

254

ice pack are probably all that's needed," Jessup said. "I don't know how gnomes feel about medical examination."

"What is medical examination?" Fir repeated to Reg.

"It's… looking at your body to see where you are hurt or sick so that you can be treated. So they can bandage you or give you what you need to mend properly."

He raised white eyebrows high. "We do not need human remedies. Gnomen know proper physic."

Jessup looked from Fir's face to Reg. "He doesn't want a doctor, does he?"

Reg shook her head in agreement. "Why don't you get a first aid kit, then? He'll get whatever kind of traditional healing he needs when we get him out of here."

Jessup was out of the room for just a few minutes, then returned with a small white plastic box of supplies and an ice pack from the freezer. "First, let's get these cuts cleaned up," she suggested, moving closer to Fir and leaning in to examine the injuries. She ripped open a pre-moistened pad and removed it from the foil wrap. "This might sting a bit, but if you just hold still—"

Fir jumped back when she moved it toward him. He grabbed it from her hand and brought it to his nose, sniffing. He made a face and threw it down on the table. "That is not a proper remedy," he accused.

"It's just to help to clean it up and keep it from getting infected," Reg explained. "Sometimes traditional remedies smell bad too, don't they?"

"I know what herbs smell like. That is not safe."

Reg shrugged at Jessup. "Okay. Maybe this wasn't such a good idea. I don't want to accidentally give him something that might do him harm." She turned back to Fir. "How about the ice pack? Just put it against your eye; it will help it to feel better."

He gingerly picked up the ice pack, examined it, squished it around in his hands, then carefully brought it up to his face. He relaxed, holding it there. "This is good," he approved.

"Good. And how about something to eat? Did you get breakfast? It's almost lunchtime now." She looked at her phone. The hours were speeding by. She hoped that Forst and Fir appreciated her efforts.

CHAPTER SIX

J essup did some checking around and managed to get a light lunch in for Fir. He picked up the sandwich and took a big bite out of it, then gagged and spat it back out on his plate. Reg gasped, shocked, and started forward.

"What is it? Are you okay?"

He opened the sandwich and looked inside. With an expression of revulsion, he pulled out the layers of processed meat, leaving just a tomato slice and some limp lettuce. "Gnomen do not eat creatures!"

"Oh, I'm sorry. I didn't know." Reg looked at Jessup. "Did you know?"

In spite of her complexion, Jessup had turned slightly pink. "I... might have heard gnomes were vegetarian," Jessup said, looking at the meat Fir had disposed of, "but I don't deal with gnomes very often. I didn't think of it. I'm sorry," she addressed Fir, "I didn't mean to give you something you don't eat."

He gave a curt nod and bit into the sandwich.

Reg looked over at Jessup. "So, any progress being made on getting him out of here?"

"I think it will work out. Someone should be here to tell us... hopefully, it won't be too much longer."

"And what about my plot?" Fir asked. "I am going back to my living."

"Uh… I don't know." Reg raised an eyebrow at Jessup. "He is going to go back to where he's been living. What's going to happen if he does that?"

"He'll probably be arrested again for trespassing. Or vagrancy. Whatever it takes to get him back off of it again so that they proceed with the development." She shrugged. "There's not much we can do about that. They have all of the appropriate permits, so it is going ahead, whether Mr. Blumenthal likes it or not."

Reg frowned. She shook her head. "There must be a way to stop it."

"Sometimes there are ways… but I don't think you're going to find any way to get them to stop at this point. All of that has to be addressed during the public hearings that happened long before this. Any objectors are expected to speak up and voice their opinions then."

"But Fir can't talk in a forum like that."

"That's the law. He could have taken an interpreter or someone to speak for him. But if he doesn't have any objection during those stages, he's missed the boat. It isn't like it is a historical site, or native land, or a graveyard. They are going to go ahead with development."

"What if… how about if there was a rare species discovered there? Some animal habitat… Then they would have to stop, wouldn't they?"

She'd heard of such things on TV. Maybe they could put some rare species there, or at least tell the authorities that they had seen one, which would give them the time to cook up something more permanent. The developers would have to take a few days at least to either confirm or refute the claim.

"Hmm." Jessup shrugged with one shoulder. "It's a possibility, I guess. But you can't go to the police with that. You'll have to find the proper authority. Department of the Environment maybe. And you'll have to do it quickly because they have probably started by now. I can't see them waiting around once Mr. Blumenthal was out of the way. They'd know that he might not be in jail for very long. If he really were an activist, he probably would have been out early this morning."

Reg's stomach knotted. She had hoped to get a jump on the developers, but Jessup was probably right. They had probably started bulldozing the moment Fir had been arrested. She pulled out her phone and looked at it. Finding the proper government agency could be complicated. She was sure to end up mired in the bureaucracy. Even government organizations that tried to be transparent and accessible usually ended up being so complicated that it was impossible for Joe Blow off the street to sort it out.

"Tell me about the plants and animals in your garden. Do you have anything rare? That there isn't much left of in the world?"

Fir considered the question. He put down his half-eaten sandwich and licked his fingers.

"Humans like to kill plants."

"Yes… but not the last of a species. They try not to wipe something off of the earth forever."

"There is the white glory. Humans call it beach clustervine. Very hard to find now. Not many places left that it can grow."

"Perfect. Beach clustervine." Reg considered her plan of attack. She looked over at Jessup. "You might want to go for a walk."

"What?"

"I think… you might not want to hear what I'm going to say. You should go for a walk, stretch your legs, see how things are coming along out there. Tell them that Mr. Blumenthal is ready to go home and is talking about calling… a lawyer or some advocacy group."

Jessup got slowly to her feet. "Just what do you have in mind?"

"Didn't I just tell you that you don't want to know? Why would you ask?"

The policewoman still hesitated. But after looking at Reg for another minute, she finally decided to go with what Reg had said and made herself scarce. She left the room. Fir watched Reg curiously, his eyes bright. He was eager to get home, but he was interested in what she was doing.

Reg did a quick internet search and called the local TV station. She bullied her way through the gatekeepers and, in a few minutes, was talking with Buzz Rockwell—his real name—who was the go-to news anchor for Black Sands news.

"It's a human-interest story," Reg said. "Big corporation versus the environment. But you need to get on it right away and get a camera crew going, or it's going to be too late to stop the destruction."

"What exactly do you have?" Buzz asked cautiously.

"A developer has had the police arrest the last of the squatters on their property and is ready to destroy one of the last places on earth where beach clustervine grows wild."

"What is that?"

"It's a plant. An endangered species. This is one of the only places in the world clustervine grows. If they raze it for a new highway and housing development, they are doing incalculable damage to the environment. Besides the fact that they are taking homes away from the indigent and using their size to commit injustices."

"Where is this? Can you meet me there? Show me the plant in question? We'll need proof before we start throwing accusations around."

"I'll get over there when I can, but right now, I'm trying to get this man out of jail. He's the only one who can show you where it is growing."

Reg described the best she could where Fir's patch was and emphasized again how they had nearly run him over with the bulldozer and would have the plant swept out of existence before anyone could stop them if Buzz delayed getting there.

After some more discussion, Buzz agreed to get his camera crew over there to see if he could stop the development. Reg would continue to work on freeing Fir and would join Buzz as soon as she could so that they could show him and the developers the location of the rare flowering vine.

Reg hung up, then looked over at Fir, wondering what he would think of her approach.

He gave her a bright smile. "You are very good at outside talking."

Reg laughed. "Yes, I've got a mouth on me. I'll admit that!"

"You will get me back to my patch?"

"Sooner or later. Hopefully, sooner."

On cue, the door was opened by a policeman Reg hadn't yet met. He was wearing a uniform that was slightly different from the others Reg had seen. No duty belt; he was not on the front lines fighting crime in Black Sands. He was an older, balding man, on the short side, but not nearly as short as Fir and Forst. He smiled reassuringly and sat in one of the empty seats.

"Hi, my name is Darcy. I'm sorry for all of the trouble that you've been through. I'm here to see that everything is straightened out."

Reg raised her brows. "I'll believe that when I see it."

"I want to thank you for advocating for Mr. Blumenthal. It is important that someone stand up for the… less fortunate in our society. For those who are not as able to speak for themselves."

Reg thought that was an insensitive thing to say in front of Fir, but she said nothing, sitting back with her eyebrows raised waiting for Darcy to explain what he was going to do for them. She didn't need any false praise. She didn't need cops pretending that they cared about what happened to Fir Blumenthal. If they had the kind of environment where all people were treated with respect and the presumption of innocence, they wouldn't be where they were, and Fir would not have a black eye.

"I'm sorry it has taken so long for us to mobilize and get into a position where we can help you. It doesn't usually take that long. Thank you for your patience."

Fir looked at Reg. "What does this human want?"

"He wants to make sure you don't sue him," Reg returned, speaking aloud so that Darcy could hear her. "He's just trying to cover his butt now."

"I can understand your perspective," Darcy admitted. "I hope that you will accept our apologies and understand that we have the greatest respect for the citizens of Black Sands and have no desire to see injustices done. Mr. Blumenthal was in an awkward position, and perhaps it could have been handled better. I'm just glad that we could figure this out right away and get on top of it now."

"So how are you on top of it? Are you ready to let him go?"

Darcy hesitated for a moment, maybe deciding just how much more smoke he should try to blow in Reg's direction. He rightly concluded that his approach wasn't getting anywhere with Reg. She'd been involved with too many police officers and in too many other sticky situations to believe anything that came out of his mouth.

"We believe that there has been a misunderstanding with Mr. Blumenthal," Darcy said slowly. "The officers at the scene were led to believe that he was a saboteur when perhaps he was only exercising his right to free speech… at any rate, we greatly regret that he suffered an injury while in the cell and that more action wasn't taken to facilitate communication… Maybe if he had asked for you when he was first arrested… if he had a card saying that he needed assistance or to call you in the event of an emergency…"

"So you're letting him go?" Reg demanded.

"Uh… yes. We will see to his immediate release. Again, if we had realized at the time…" Darcy trailed off, unable to give a full explanation. He shrugged dramatically. "I'm sorry for any distress…"

"Just get his possessions and get us signed out. He would like to be able to get back to his home before it is bulldozed into the ground."

Darcy tugged at his uniform collar. "Yes, of course. I hope that no permanent harm has been done…"

"Oh, you'll hear from us about that."

Darcy looked at her for another moment, his face pale and grave. Then he got up and retreated. Off to get Fir's possessions and get them on their way, she hoped.

Fir looked relieved. He nodded his head vigorously at Reg. "Yes, you are very good with outside words," he complimented her again. "You know how to talk to humans."

"Some humans. I'll drive you back to your plot, and talk to the TV guy and developers, and hopefully, that will mean a temporary stay to the development while they figure out what they have to do. They should be required to protect the habitat of the clustervine, but I don't know how much space they will have to leave around it, whether it's just the plant itself, or a wider area…"

"More than one plant," Fir advised. "A colony."

"Oh, good. That should give you more space, then. They'll have to protect the colony somehow."

"Humans protecting plants?" he asked skeptically and shook his head. As far as he was concerned, humans were in the business of harming plants, not saving them. A position that was usually true. Reg had to admit that while she enjoyed walking through a garden or hiking through a wilderness area, she never gave much thought to the plants themselves and who tended them or what their needs were.

Did plants have feelings? Did they know Fir cared for them? It had never occurred to her that they might have any level of sentience, but Fir's attitude toward them was more like a parent for a child than someone who just watered and fertilized plants.

"Of course plants have feeling," Fir said, a wrinkle in his brow.

Reg hadn't realized that she'd been so open with her thoughts. "I never knew that. What kind of feelings do they have?"

Fir's eyes rolled toward the ceiling as he considered. "They have likes and not. They know who cares for them. They can be hurt." He looked back at her again, checking to make sure she understood.

"That's amazing. I never knew that. I thought they were just… inanimate."

Fir shook his head like she was being foolish. "They are living things," he pointed out. "They are not dead."

CHAPTER SEVEN

J essup was the one who returned with Fir's possessions and had him make sure everything was there. She looked sideways at Reg. "So... did you get everything you needed?"

"Sure. We'll head over and have a little chat with the developers next. Then we'll see who's going to be bulldozing people's plants."

"Good luck. I hope everything works out. I don't like it when there are conflicts between the police department and the other races. I wish we had a better interface, but when most of the police officers are non-practitioners, it's impossible to make sure that they don't step on any toes. You can't exactly tutor them in the rights of other species."

"They can still do better than this. It's ridiculous that they would jail someone like Fir without making sure that his needs were met and he wasn't victimized. It's obvious he is vulnerable to people who are bigger and stronger than him and that he doesn't have the ability to ask for help."

Jessup shrugged uncomfortably. "Your perspective is different when you're a cop facing a potentially dangerous criminal. You see things differently."

Reg looked at Fir and couldn't believe that anyone would think he was dangerous. Yes, he had done some damage to industrial equipment, but he hadn't been causing anyone physical harm. He wasn't big enough to hurt anyone.

Fir made a mark where Jessup indicated on the release form, and Reg leaned closer to study it. "Is that… your name?"

Fir nodded. "It is the rune for my family. What we use for identifying our territory and property."

"Cool. I've never seen a mark like that before. Except maybe on some fantasy show on TV."

"TV?"

Reg cleared her throat. "Never mind. Let's go. I'll drive you home if you show me the way."

It had been a long day. Reg had not been planning to take so much time aiding a gnome in distress. But she felt good that she had. Fir had been so delighted to return to his garden plot and had immediately taken her to see the clustervine and several other favorite plants. She'd had a hard time disengaging from him, explaining that she had to go home to her own duties. He doffed his cap to her, bowing several times in thanks for all she had done. Buzz the TV anchor was in full swing with his camera crew, getting plenty of close-ups of the white flowers and the machinery operators as they mopped red faces and considered the little plants that threatened to derail their plans. Buzz thanked Reg for the tip. She advised him that Fir would not be doing an interview, but she was sure he would show Buzz around his little plot and show him all of the places that needed to be protected from the bulldozers of the eager developer.

"He doesn't speak," she warned for the third time, "so don't pressure him. It isn't because he's camera shy or obstinate; he just isn't very verbal."

"I understand. We can work with that. He won't be the first interviewee I've had who won't speak with the cameras on him."

"He won't speak with them off, either. Maybe a word or two, but don't expect a conversation, even off the record."

"I can handle it, Ms. Rawlins, I promise."

"Okay. Because he's going to tell me if you harass him. And I'm going to watch the coverage."

"We'll be very respectful. There's nothing to worry about. This is a great David versus Goliath story. We'll make the most of it."

"Good."

On her return home, Reg went around to Sarah's garden to see if Forst was still there. She didn't see him at first, but when she turned to go, saw a red cap out of the corner of her eye and turned back for a second look. She found him sitting on a tree stump, blending in so well with his surroundings that she thought at first she was seeing things.

"Is it well?" he asked immediately. "Did you get him out of the cage?"

"He is out of the cage and back home on his plot. We're fighting back against the humans who want to destroy his garden. Hopefully, that will work out, and he'll be able to keep some of it unspoiled."

"Oh, thank you!" He jumped up from his rock and ran to her, giving her a vigorous hug. "You are a gnomen champion! Much joy to the gnomen!"

"Well… thank you!" Reg tried to return the hug, bending down and patting him on the shoulder and back. "I'm glad I could help."

"This is wonderful news. Wonderful."

Reg nodded. "It is. And I… need to go back in now, and do my own work."

"Yes, yes. Tend to your living," he agreed. He made shooing motions for her to go back into the cottage. "Your cat has been watching us very carefully."

"He's probably wondering what you're up to. He's very curious."

Forst turned and surveyed the ruined garden, hands on hips. "There is much to do here. I must tend these plants."

Reg waved and headed back to the cottage. "See you later, then."

Back in the house, she made herself a cheese sandwich, thinking as she laid a slice of tomato on the cheese about the plant that had borne the fruit. Were plants happy to have their fruit picked? Did it hurt? Did they understand the animal's need for nourishment? Did they feel frustrated when humans kept taking their fruit? Or was she assigning them too much sentience? Fir hadn't sounded like they had a complex thought process, just feelings about the things around them. But Reg wondered how far that went.

She sent a little prayer of thanks in the direction of whatever tomato vine had supplied that part of her lunch, and sat down to eat it. Starlight rubbed against her legs, purring and seeking affection. She petted him with her toes, not wanting to get cat fur in her food. The phone rang. Reg put down her sandwich and dug her phone out of her pocket to answer it.

"Hello?"

"Regina! It is Francesca."

"Oh, hi. I saw you called earlier, but I was at the police station and had a lot to deal with."

"Oh—is everything all right?"

"Yes. Just helping someone out. What's going on?" The worried tone in Francesca's voice alerted her that all was not well. She hoped that her failure to answer Francesca's earlier call hadn't resulted in something terrible happening.

"It is the kattakyns. They are gone!"

"Gone?" Reg sat up straight, immediately alert. "What do you mean, they are gone? All of them? Where did they go? It isn't... someone who wants to get the Witch Doctor back, is it?"

"I do not think so. But I cannot feel him, so I do not know what is going on. All I know is, when I went to find the cats today, they were gone. Nicole is here, but the kittens have disappeared."

"Inside the house? Outside? You didn't let them all outside, did you?" Reg had been critical of Francesca letting Nicole run freely outside. She couldn't fathom that anyone would let nine kittens, especially ones bound to a dangerous Witch Doctor, to run free.

"No, they were in the house. I did not put them out. But I cannot find them. I have looked in all of the places that they normally play and sleep, but they are not there."

"Oh, dear. I hope nothing has happened to them. What if the binding spell didn't hold, and they all... got together and re-formed the Witch Doctor?"

"Can you not feel him?" Francesca asked.

"Oh... well, I could before." Reg took a moment to see if she could feel the Witch Doctor. She didn't feel the anxiety and dread that she had previously felt whenever he had been around. "I don't feel him. But what if he is blocking me because he knows that I can feel him? What if he's already back again and is being more careful this time?"

"I do not think that is the case. I am very sure of my spell. He could not have broken it again already. It will hold for hundreds of years."

"What if someone else severed it or broke it? What if he has an accomplice that we didn't know about?"

"You could come over here? Then you can see what you think. If you can feel him and if you think there was someone else here."

"I don't know if I can do all of that…" Reg sighed. She was exhausted after the trip to the police station and now she was expected to go out again and play Ghostbusters. "I guess I'll come over… but I don't know if I'll be able to feel anything. I'm pretty tired."

"I will wait for you. I will give you the address."

"Okay, yeah." Reg turned her phone to speaker mode and navigated to the maps app to input it.

CHAPTER EIGHT

I do not know what could have happened to them," Francesca said when she opened the door. She had worry lines across her forehead, unusual for the pretty blond who usually looked so carefree and had preached to Reg that cats needed to roam outside for their health.

"Well, let's look around, and I'll see if I can sense anything."

She walked into the house. Francesca had previously confided that she didn't like the feeling in her home, that it was too dark and she hadn't been able to make it feel any better. Reg thought again that Francesca should get Corvin to cast some of his magic there. He did house blessings. Now that she knew Francesca was a practitioner, she could talk about it openly, where before she could only hint at it.

Francesca was right. It did feel dark and cold, in spite of her efforts to decorate it to look light and airy, and having boosted the lighting. Reg closed her eyes and opened up her senses, seeing what she could feel.

Nicole walked into the room. Reg immediately felt waves of confusion. She opened her eyes and looked at Nicole. "Don't you know what happened to them either, Nicole?" She bent over to pet Nicole. After sniffing her hand, Nicole deigned to be petted. She rubbed Reg's legs and went to Francesca and back to Reg again.

"She must know something about it," Reg suggested. "She's been very interested in their care. She must have been keeping an eye on them, don't you think?"

Francesca nodded. She picked Nicole up.

"What about it, Nicole? Where are they?"

Nicole rubbed the top of her head against Francesca's chin. Reg focused on the cat, feeling discomfited.

"What is it?" Francesca asked, noticing Reg's expression. "Do you think you know something? Has someone been here? You cannot feel the Witch Doctor?"

"No, I still can't feel him. The thing is… I'm not getting any sadness from Nicole."

"Oh?"

"If the kittens are lost or ran away, then she should be sad, shouldn't she? She was acting like a mother cat toward them. She was bonding with them. So when they disappear, she should be sad."

"Yes. I would expect so. But you said that you are tired. Maybe this is just your tiredness."

Reg shook her head. "No. Something isn't right here."

She started looking around the room, checking the closet and under the furniture, trying to seek for lost objects as she had done so many times in the past. She had not been able to successfully seek since Sarah's emerald had disappeared, but she hoped that it would work anyway. The kittens were a significant presence. They should not be hard to find.

Francesca was quiet as Reg went into the kitchen, and into each of the bedrooms on the main floor. Reg looked everywhere she could think of that the kittens could be hiding.

"Is there an attic? A basement?"

"No basement," Francesca said, shaking her head. There were few basements built in Black Sands because of the high water table. "But there is an attic."

She went down the hallway and reached up for a cord in the ceiling where there was an access panel. Nicole, following her owner, nipped at her ankles, drawing a shriek of surprise and pain from Francesca.

"Ow! What are you doing, Nicole? Ouch, you do not bite me!"

She bent over, rubbing her ankles and scowling at the cat. Reg looked thoughtfully up at the attic access. Nicole, slinking away out of Francesca's reach, started to move toward Reg.

"No, you don't," she warned. "Don't bite me."

She grabbed the cord and pulled, causing a set of stairs to fold down into the hallway. Nicole folded back her ears and hissed. Francesca was shaking her head at Nicole's behavior. "What has gotten into you?"

Reg climbed the stairs. There was a light switch at the top of the stairs, and she flicked it on.

The attic was nearly empty. A few dusty boxes and some construction materials, but most of it was wide-open to Reg's gaze. And out from behind the boxes, she saw several sets of eyes in little black faces looking back at her.

"They're up here."

Francesca came up the stairs and looked. "There they are! The naughty kitties! How did they get up here? I didn't have the stairs pulled down at all."

Reg looked around for some clue. "Maybe they came up the ventilation ducts? Are there any vents that are not covered with a grill?"

"I do not think so… I guess we must look." Francesca climbed the stairs the rest of the way and went toward the kittens. "Back down you go!" she told them, shooing them with her hands toward the stairs. "Get out. Not allowed to be in the attic. Out you go!"

Reg went back down the stairs and saw Nicole waiting at the bottom, counting the kittens as they went by her. Nicole glared at Reg, waves of anger coming off of her. Reg stood there looking at her, trying to understand what was going on. Francesca finished shooing the kittens down from the attic and returned down the stairs after Reg.

"I think Nicole knows you're going to send the kittens to other homes."

Francesca shook her head. "How would she know that?"

"She's been around when we've discussed it. I didn't think she understood… but I guess she does."

"She is just acting like a mother cat. Moving her kittens around to keep them safe. It is instinct."

"I don't think so. I think she knows exactly what she's doing."

For a few days, things seemed almost normal. Corvin stayed away. There were no more appearances of the Witch Doctor or any other evil influences.

Reg had a few readings with clients, but nothing that taxed her too much or had weird results. She could almost convince herself that the strange events that had taken place in the time that she'd been in Black Sands had just been a dream or something she had imagined.

Reg saw Forst occasionally in the garden. Sometimes he was there, puttering around, tying up plants, talking to them, digging around them. At other times, he seemed to be absent, neglecting his duties, or maybe off to the store to pick up something he needed, or visiting Fir, who was enjoying the peace and quiet of his plot, undisturbed by the bulldozers that stood idle outside the perimeter that Florida Fish and Wildlife had set up to protect the rare ecosystem. It wasn't any of her business what Forst did. As long as Sarah was happy with the results, it didn't matter how much time he spent in the garden and how much he was absent from it.

She hadn't heard him crying again. But he did occasionally mutter to himself, looking out over the garden with his hands on his hips, trying to work through some knotty problem.

Starlight was sitting in the windowsill in the bedroom and started to meow, calling out to Reg in the voice that meant he wanted her attention for something. Reg set down her teacup and headed back to the bedroom to see what was going on. Was Nicole back in the garden again? Reg wouldn't be surprised if Francesca had let her out, considering her views on proper cat care. If Sarah caught Nicole in the garden again, Reg wasn't sure what she would do. She likewise didn't know how Forst would react to a cat in his territory. He wouldn't eat her, but not all of the magical beings Reg had met so far liked cats. In fact, few of them did.

She got to the window and scratched Starlight's ears. "What is it, Star? Is Nicole back?" She peered out the window, and her attention was caught, not by a black cat, but by Forst dancing around wildly. He whooped as he jumped up and down. "What's going on? Is it a spell?"

Starlight pressed his nose to the window, watching with great interest.

"Well... I guess I'll go find out what's going on. You don't think I'll be interrupting, do you? Will he be angry or embarrassed if I go out there?"

Starlight didn't give any sign that he understood or had an answer for her.

Reg went out to the garden, looking around the corner tentatively, worried that she might be interrupting something private. "Uh... Forst...?"

He looked at her and stopped dancing, but was still smiling broadly.

"What's going on?"

"I found it! I have been looking for days, and I finally found it!"

"What did you find?"

He brandished an object. "A key."

It was dark with corrosion. Too large for a modern house or car key. An old-fashioned key with an ornate handle. Reg raised her eyebrows, looking at it. "Well… I guess you did. Is that a good thing? Had you lost it?"

"Something was disturbing this garden. I could feel something… blocking the growth, casting a darkness over the plants, keeping it in the shadows. But I could not tell what it was or to find the offending object."

"And this is it? This was causing the problem?"

Forst nodded, his cheeks bright pink, looking immensely satisfied with himself.

"Can I see it?" Reg asked, drawn to the innocuous key, somehow the cause of Forst's difficulties rehabilitating the garden.

Forst looked at it for a moment, then handed it to Reg. "You can change cursed objects?" he asked.

"Is it really cursed?" Reg held the key in the palm of her hand, weighing it and studying it carefully. If didn't look cursed. She didn't feel a sense of evil from it as Forst did. It didn't burn her hand or buzz with energy. It just looked like an old key, buried there years before, allowed to rust in the damp ground.

Quite the contrary, she felt drawn toward it. She felt like it was hers, and that she needed to find the lock it belonged to. It was her fate to unlock that lock and take the treasure that it secured.

CHAPTER NINE

As much as Reg felt drawn to the key, it wasn't hers, and it wasn't up to her to decide what to do with it. She couldn't see Sarah wanting it, but she needed to at least check. She told Forst that she would take it to Sarah in the big house, and he nodded, unconcerned with what she did with it, as long as it wasn't disturbing the forces in the garden. He was happy to get rid of it.

Reg knocked on the back door and walked into the kitchen. "Sarah, are you home?"

"Upstairs," Sarah called back. Reg mounted the stairs and followed the sounds of movement to discover Sarah in her bedroom, tearing through drawers full of clothes, scattering them here and there as she looked for something.

"Spring cleaning?" Reg suggested.

"You wouldn't believe how many clothes I have in this house! I am looking for something…" she tossed a few more items around, "something a little younger. I don't feel like old fogey clothes, not since I woke up. I want brighter colors, trendier styles. What is popular again? I have years and years' worth of clothes; there must be something that will look sharp."

"I don't know," Reg admitted. She gravitated toward clothes that fit her medium/fortune-teller persona: the long flowing skirts, a headscarf around her box braids, breezy fabrics. They weren't fashionable or trendy. That wasn't the persona she was trying to project. "You could check some internet sites. Or go to a place where younger people hang around."

"I suppose so," Sarah agreed. She continued to plow through the drawers.

"Forst found something in the garden, and we were wondering about it."

"Oh? What did he find in the garden?"

Reg held up the key. "This. An old key."

Sarah peered at her. "Curious. I don't recognize it. I don't think it was ever mine. I've been here for a long time, so I'm not sure who else could have lost it here."

"Do you want it?"

"Want it? Why would I want it, dear?"

"It's your property. It was found in your garden. I would kind of like to have it, but I didn't want to claim it, in case it was something you wanted."

"If you like it, you can have it. I don't know why you would."

"Forst says that it was causing problems with your garden. The plants will grow better now that it has been taken out."

Sarah stopped and looked at it, picked it up from Reg's hand, examined it, and put it back down again. "Gnomes have different magic… I can't see or feel anything."

"I don't either. I actually really like it. It looks cool."

"It's filthy. Maybe it will look nice when you clean it and remove all of the corrosion, shine it up. But right now… I'm not sure what you see in it."

"Neither am I! But it's intriguing. I wonder what kind of lock it was meant to open."

Back in the cottage, Reg washed the dirt off of the key, then looked for metal polish in the cupboards. She couldn't find anything, so she tried an internet search instead, seeing what she could use to concoct her own metal polish. Maybe some steel wool to help to rub the corrosion off of the key.

The phone rang. Irritated, Reg answered the call. "Hello?"

"Miss Rawlins. This is Davyn Smithy. I don't know if you remember me…"

"Of course I do. You're the one who conducted Corvin's hearing."

"Yes, that's right."

"I don't think I need anything from you. I was not impressed with the way you handled that hearing. You weren't exactly on my side."

"I wasn't supposed to be on your side," Davyn pointed out. "I was supposed to be impartial."

"And I don't think you were. I think you were squarely on Corvin's side and did the best you could to get him off, even if it meant smearing my name."

"I'm sorry you saw it that way. That isn't the way it was intended."

"Huh. I think I was lucky that Corvin was disciplined at all, after the way you ran the hearing. At least the tribunal wasn't fooled."

"I was part of that tribunal. We did what we felt was right."

"What do you want, Dave?" Reg demanded bluntly.

He was silent for a moment, perhaps shocked by her attitude. "The fact is, we have been asked to review Corvin Hunter's case in light of recent events. Since his sentence was indefinite, we as a committee are required to review it on occasion to see if the requirements of the disciplinary action have been met…"

"You want to end his discipline. The shunning by the coven."

"We don't want to end his discipline. We are in a position where we need to consider what the appropriate action would be. Has he met the terms of the sentence, or do we need to continue?"

"You need to continue. Do you really think he's reformed? That he's somehow turned himself around in just this short time and is ready to be a contributing member of society again?"

"That is the question. It has been suggested that his defeat of the Witch Doctor was a service to the community and that this altruistic gesture demonstrated not just how much the community needs him, but also how he is willing to serve its needs…"

"It has been suggested? Do you mean that Corvin has suggested it? I can't see anyone else being fooled into thinking that he was doing something for anyone else. There was nothing altruistic about his actions."

"Since you were there, and since you have… experience with him and were the person who was most affected by his breaches of our code…"

"What?"

"I was hoping that you would be open to meeting together so that I could get your thoughts and feelings on his progress."

"You want my thoughts and feelings about his progress? He hasn't made any. He's just manipulating you."

"Could we meet?"

"My feelings aren't going to change."

"No, but I could get some more details. What happened with the Witch Doctor and the draugrs? I have one side of the story, but that is just one side, and there are going to be several views of what happened and what Corvin's motives were. I want to be able to go through some of your thoughts."

Ugh. Reg was not ready to meet with Davyn Smithy. As far as she was concerned, he was just a fanboy of Corvin's. He wasn't going to take her opinion seriously. He was going through the motions and would discharge Corvin's penalty once he finished his interviews.

"I'm not interested…"

"So you don't want any input into whether his punishment continues or not?"

"I've given my comments."

"Okay…" Davyn trailed off.

Reg's stomach rebelled, swishing around so that she thought she would be sick. "Oh, fine. But it had better be quick, and I'd better not hear anything out of your mouth that suggests that what he did was my fault."

"No, of course not."

As if that weren't what he had already suggested at Corvin's hearing. Now that they were in private, where there weren't other people to hear and be influenced by what he said, things would be different.

Reg looked over the profiles that Francesca had prepared on the people who were interested in adopting the draugr kittens. It was all very professionally done like they were job candidates. Headshots, biographies, background checks, everything pulled together into a concise portfolio for each individual. Reg looked away from the papers and watched the kittens playing and interacting with Nicole.

"Why don't you give me your impressions of each one," she suggested, "and I'll think about the kittens and which ones might fit with each person."

"I have written down everything you need to know," Francesca pointed out impatiently.

Reg wasn't about to say that she couldn't read that much information in the time they had arranged for, or that she didn't have the patience to work through that much text no matter how much time she had. She had learned that there was always a way to get around reading if she were creative enough.

"This is about intuition, not portfolios," she told Francesca. "You can have the best resume in the world and still be wrong for the job. You've been talking and emailing with these guys, so you have come to some conclusions already, even if you think you've kept an open mind. It's my job to dig into those impressions and match up the kattakyns' personalities, right?"

Francesca nodded reluctantly. She'd obviously put a lot of work into the profiles and didn't like to abandon them so easily. So Reg made a show of leafing through them, frowning as she studied the names and faces, and putting them into a new order. None of it mattered, it was a show to make Francesca feel like her work was appreciated and an essential part of the process. Reg sighed, squared all of the papers in one pile, and pointed to the one at the top of the pile.

"I'm interested in this guy. How did he come across to you?"

Francesca was eager to talk once Reg had validated the process. "Yes, I thought he was an excellent candidate too. He is in Egypt, and you know the history of Egypt and cats."

Reg didn't know much. She knew that they had worshiped cats and drawn them in hieroglyphs, so that must mean that they respected them. Or at least that they didn't eat them. She nodded thoughtfully.

"He is a respected warlock, leader of his coven. I have heard about him before, through several sources. Always good things."

"And he doesn't already have a familiar?"

"He did until recently. A very old cat, Massud, who passed away just recently."

"So, this wouldn't be his first cat."

"No. Exactly. He already knows how to care for a cat and has all of the equipment and food. No suggestion that he was ever abusive or negligent. Highly respected. And since Massud lived to an old age, he obviously is a good caregiver."

Reg watched the black kittens. "If he's had an old cat, how do you think he's going to manage a kitten? They're a lot more active and get into things."

Francesca considered this, biting her lip. "That's true," she agreed. "So maybe he's not such a good match…"

"He has to expect that any replacement for Massud is going to be a lot more energetic. But maybe we should match him with one of the quieter kittens. Not little Nico."

Francesca glanced over at them. "Which one is he?"

Reg was still amazed that Francesca couldn't tell the kittens apart. It was true that they were all black without any markings, but they were different sizes and body types, with widely varying personalities. Francesca was with them more than Reg was, she should have been able to see some of the differences.

"Over there…"

Francesca's head swiveled as she followed Reg's finger to the black kitten currently halfway up the drapes.

"Oh. Yes, I think you're right. Not Nico. Do you have one in mind, then?"

"I was thinking maybe Horace." Reg indicated the fatter kitten snoozing in the sun on one of the kitchen chairs, positioned in the sunbeam coming through the window.

"Horace." Francesca nodded. She typed something into her computer. "And what should I tell him about Horace?"

"He's quiet. Very intelligent. Likes to think things through. Good at solving problems." Reg waited while Francesca finished typing these thoughts out. "I think he'd be a good match for someone used to an older cat. I don't think he'll tear the house apart like a certain other kattakyn."

Nico, inching his way up the drapes, turned to look at Reg. He hesitated, trying to decide whether she was going to pursue him and pull him down from the curtain. When she didn't move or tell him to come down, he looked back up at this intended destination and kept going.

Reg took the profile for the Egyptian warlock and slid it to the bottom of her pile. "Okay, how about her?" Reg studied the Asian woman's face. "She looks very young." Of course, Reg had discovered a witch's looks didn't always reflect her age. Sarah, who appeared to be in her sixties, was supposed to be hundreds of years old, and Corvin, who Reg wouldn't have guessed to be that much older than she was, was decades older. She didn't know whether magic naturally kept him younger, or if he had some other long-lived race's blood in his veins, or whether he invoked some anti-aging spell. Sarah had a powerful emerald that kept her young and hearty. Reg would not have known that if not for the theft of the emerald. Once the emerald was no longer in Sarah's possession, the aging process had kicked in, and she had gotten very old and frail very quickly.

"She is young," Francesca agreed. "A fairly new practitioner, she comes from families that were not aware of their powers. She seems to have inherited the gene from both parents and is subsequently much stronger than they are. She has good reports from the mentors she has been working with so far. She has a natural affinity for cats, and they think that she would be able to stabilize and control her magic much more quickly with the aid of a cat."

"A stabilizing influence," Reg repeated.

"Yes."

So again, not Nico. Reg sensed that he was going to be hard to place. Just as Reg had been a challenge for Mrs. Bloom to find a long-term placement for, she was going to have to really search to find the right practitioner for Nico.

She closed her eyes and reached out mentally to the kittens. They needed one who would be responsive to a new practitioner's powers and requests. Not one who had his own ideas about what he should do or who would be distracted by a butterfly fluttering by.

She opened her eyes and studied them. A female had stopped playing and was looking at her, interested and responsive. Reg clicked her tongue. "Come here. Come on, Sally."

Sally moved immediately toward Reg, ears pricked up attentively. She padded up to Reg's side and stared up at her, waiting.

"Can you help me?" Reg asked. "I need a boost reaching a friend."

As Reg reached out mentally toward Sarah, for lack of a better plan, Sally stood up on her hind legs and put her front paws on Reg's leg. Reg could immediately feel the sharpening of her senses and an extension to her ability to reach out, like a pair of rabbit ears that helped to clear the picture on an ancient television set. She didn't actually need to get a message to Sarah or to know what she was doing, so after a few moments, she released her energy, and Sally dropped back down onto all fours.

"Sally," Reg told Francesca. "Definitely Sally."

CHAPTER TEN

Oddly enough, Davyn Smithy worked out of an insurance office. A bland, dreary sort of a place, thoroughly non-magical and uninteresting and as far as possible from the dramatic personality he tried to portray within the magical community. He met her wearing a white shirt with blue pinstripes, glasses with thin black rims, and dark slacks. Without his dramatic robes, he looked like an accountant instead of a warlock.

"Good to see you again, Miss Rawlins," he greeted with a polite smile, putting his hand out to shake hers. Reg did not shake. After an awkward moment, he lowered his hand, his neck flushing red around his collar. "I have a meeting room booked for us. Would you like coffee? Water?"

"Coffee. Just black."

He gestured. "This way."

Other people were bustling around the office. No one who took any note of Reg. No one who was expecting anything the least bit magical to happen while she was there. It was reassuring. She was sure there were still things Davyn could do to influence her, but if she kept up her guard, maybe everything would be fine. She would make sure he understood that under no circumstances should they believe what Corvin said about wanting what was best for the community.

They sat down, each with a cup of coffee.

"Let's get this straight right from the start," Reg said flatly. "There is nothing generous or altruistic about Corvin. He does what is best for him, not for anyone else. He'll portray himself in the best light possible, but don't believe it."

"I have known Corvin for a lot longer than you."

"So maybe you're not the best one to see him for what he is. He uses your relationship to pull the wool over your eyes. He laughs at you thinking that you are capable of making an unbiased judgment. Because if you saw him for the predator he is, you would know that he didn't go to that warehouse because he wanted to fight the draugrs and save the community. He went there because he wanted to suck the powers out of the artifacts that the Witch Doctor was smuggling, and eventually, even from the Witch Doctor himself. Do you have any idea how powerful he is now, after drinking all of that in? He's dangerous, and you're just going to turn him loose on the community."

"A decision has not been made. Don't assume that you know what will happen."

"You're telling me you believe what he is saying about saving the city from the Witch Doctor. So it's obvious which way you are going."

"You are jumping to conclusions."

Reg stared at him, meeting his eyes aggressively until he was forced to look away. "I wouldn't have survived this long if I hadn't been able to make snap judgments about what other people are thinking. You want him to be free in the community. You want to talk to him and to discuss business with him. You don't want to have to shun him."

Davyn sighed, looking down into his coffee cup. "All of that is true," he admitted. "But I am not going to make a decision without considering the opinions of everyone involved. I will rule against my own desires and preferences if that is what is best for the magical community."

Reg wondered whether that were true. Even if Corvin agreed to follow the rules of his coven, those rules were still biased against the women he preyed upon. Without any changes in the rules of how he was to conduct himself, women would continue to be victimized, their powers stripped away by him when they didn't understand what he could do. It had happened to Reg. It would happen to others. There was no doubt in her mind.

"So what's going to happen? If you decide that he did what he did because he was trying to protect everyone, then you'll decide that it is of benefit to the community for him to be a full part of it again. And then he'll be able to do what he wants to."

"He will still be expected to follow the rules of the coven and the laws of the land."

"He'll go back to doing what he's been doing all along."

"We don't have the ability to change his nature. The magical community strives to find a balance between allowing the races their own cultural norms and providing for their needs and preventing harm. Obviously, we cannot always protect everyone. We have to balance the rights of one people against the rights of another."

"In nature, there are predators and there are prey. That doesn't mean we let jackals roam the streets and steal children. Our laws make it illegal for people to kill, steal, and rape. *That's* how you protect people. Not by saying 'unless there's a good reason for it.'"

Davyn sat there silently. She didn't know if he was considering what she had said or just waiting for her to finish her tirade.

"I am not justifying anything Corvin has done," Davyn said finally. "But he is different than we are. We can't deny that."

"What are you going to do?"

"I don't know yet. That's why I'm talking with you, talking with other people who have been in contact with him while he has been shunned, visiting with him and talking to him about his plans and how he is going to contribute, and so on. I'll investigate fully, and then I'll make a recommendation to the council of the coven. And they will make a decision about whether to allow him back into full membership in the coven or not."

"You're going to ask him about his plans and expect him to tell you the truth? He'll tell you whatever you want to hear."

"I'm not that naive. I'll be watching for signs of deception. I'll be making my own observations about whether he is being open and honest."

"He won't be. I don't think you know the difference."

"The tribunal did rule against him after the hearing," Davyn pointed out. "I would think you would have some faith in the process after that."

Reg considered. Was it evidence that they were going to do the right thing and not be misled by Corvin's charm? "I'm more inclined to think that was a one-time thing," she admitted. "An anomaly."

"It wasn't. That's the way we work. We're not just spouting ideals and closing our eyes to reality. We understand what Corvin did and that it was wrong. We understand that he has victimized you more than once."

Reg nodded her agreement.

"And yet…" Davyn trailed off.

"What?"

"Even though he has repeatedly shown you his predatory nature, you continue to talk to him and to take on cases with him. You fought the Witch Doctor alongside him, in spite of your history."

"I can't help it if he shows up at my house or calls me on the phone. You know he can use his charms to involve people in things that they wouldn't choose to do otherwise."

"Why did you agree to fight the Witch Doctor?"

"I didn't." Reg's face flushed hot and she looked away from him. "I told him over and over again that I wouldn't. I told him he was on his own. To get someone else to help him."

"And yet, you still ended up in that warehouse with him."

"I had a vision… I saw the draugr that was stalking him and chasing him. I had to get over there to help him. He would have been killed if I hadn't intervened."

"And then you agreed to go after the Witch Doctor."

"It was the only thing left to do." Reg couldn't think of any other way to explain it. She wasn't sure herself how she had finally gotten embroiled in the fight. No matter how hard she fought it, she knew it was inevitable that she would get involved. Harrison had told her so.

Harrison.

Had his involvement been greater than she had thought? Had he pushed her into it, despite his protests that he couldn't do anything to harm another of his kind? He was the one who had told her she would fight the Witch Doctor. He had given her tips on what she needed to do to defeat him. And then he had disappeared. Was he the one who was responsible for Reg joining the fight? If so, what was his motive for wanting her to fight or to defeat the Witch Doctor?

Were they rivals? Enemies? Did they have a past? Old friends? Brothers? And what about the other immortal that Harrison had mentioned? Weston. It turned out that the Witch Doctor had been looking for Weston, even though he wouldn't admit it. And from his words to Reg… maybe Weston had some shared connection with her too. But she didn't like to think that it was true.

"Reg…?"

Reg focused her attention back on Davyn. "What?"

"You said that Corvin's reason for going into the warehouse was to consume the powers of the magical artifacts being stored there."

"Yeah. Exactly."

"How did you know that?"

"He'd said more than once that he needed to get into the warehouse. And when it got down to the fight, his role was to consume as much of the magic as he could so that he would be strong enough to face the Witch Doctor. That was his whole reason for getting into the building. It wasn't to kill the Witch Doctor, that was just a secondary goal. And he took magic from the Witch Doctor directly, too. Put his hands on him and just… sucked it out."

Reg remembered the feeling, being able to sense the flow of magic and sensing the shift when he started to pull directly from the Witch Doctor. It was terrible and frightening, like watching a lion take down a gazelle. Something she could hardly tear her eyes away from, no matter how awful it was.

Reg's fingers itched. She fidgeted. She slid her hand into the pocket of her skirt and touched the old key there. It was comforting in her hand. She pictured herself using it. Just what did it unlock? What kind of power or wealth would be hers if she could find the lock it would open?

"You don't think that Corvin would have fought the Witch Doctor just to protect the people of Black Sands. You think the only reason he faced him was to get the Witch Doctor's hoard and to take away his power."

Reg had been distracted by the touch of the key. She turned her eyes back to Davyn. "That's right. He wouldn't have done anything just to help a few insignificant people. He wanted power. That was the only reason he was there."

Davyn tapped a pen against the table, ticking away the time. His eyes were far away. How long had he known Corvin? Had they been boys together? Both were, Reg had been told, much older than they looked. Maybe not as old as centuries-old Sarah, but significantly older than their thirtyish bodies led her to believe. They might have been friends for decades, devoted to each other.

"Is there anything else?" Davyn asked eventually. "Are there other things

I should be aware of? Since you have been in contact with him and the rest of the coven has not, you may know of things that we have no idea of."

"He's still trying to steal my powers. Even after all he consumed at the warehouse, the massive amount of magic that he is holding now, he is still trying to steal mine."

Davyn rubbed the stubble of his beard. She had previously thought this was an affectation, that he wanted to appear wise before the others of his coven. But maybe it was just an unconscious gesture.

"Why would he still want your powers? He should be sated."

"Yeah, you would think so, wouldn't you? He compared me to dessert."

Davyn's lips twitched into a slight smile. "Dessert?"

"That even though he's full, he still wants... my powers too. For some reason, I guess they are sweeter to him."

"Because he has already held them once?"

"I guess. I don't understand it all. I don't understand my own powers, much less how it feels for him to hold them. And how he can hold so many other powers at the same time. It seems like... there should be a natural balance, a point at which he can't consume any more, or there is some... negative effect to consuming more. You know what I mean? With food, if you eat too much, you throw up."

Davyn shrugged. "I don't think any of us can understand it, only another one like him."

"Like his father?"

"I told you that warlocks like him are rare. We don't have others to ask. Others like him who would tell us what is fair punishment and what is not. How much he can control and how much is instinctual. Whether all warlocks of his nature would behave the same way, or whether that is just Corvin. We have the old texts, and have referred to them as much as possible, but they have always been feared. Others do their best to avoid them, not to document their histories."

"You can't just accept him back again. You can't say that after all that he's done, that a few weeks of shunning is punishment enough."

"But the verdict did not say how much he needed to be punished. It said that he had to be a contributing member of the community. And when he is performing a service like he did, even if it is the side effect of pursuing his own goals, that is a great benefit to the community, and those who didn't want him to be shunned in the first place are lobbying to have him reinstated."

"Don't they fear what he can do?"

"Of course… but as long as his target is someone else, it is easy for people to forget their fear. And even if he is being shunned, that does not protect anyone from him. The only thing that would protect everyone would be if he was bound. And that would be a lot more difficult."

"The Witch Doctor could be bound."

"Corvin has more power than the Witch Doctor. He is the only one who could overcome the Witch Doctor because he is the only one who can increase his powers that much. Who else is left?"

"Then why don't you banish him? Send him away. Tell him he's not welcome in the community."

"We can tell him that, of course, but we can't force him to leave." Davyn held her gaze until Reg was forced to look away.

CHAPTER ELEVEN

Reg did not feel very comforted as she left the insurance office. Davyn's words weighed down on her. Whether they allowed Corvin to be a full participant in the community or not was really an academic question. It provided him with society, but would have no effect on his powers. Even working together, the community might not be powerful enough to bind him or have any control over him.

If he chose to run rampant…

She walked slowly to her car, holding on to the old key. It was warm in her hand and drew her mind away from Corvin and the problem of not being able to control him. She couldn't help dreaming about what it might open. She had always been poor, on the edge of homelessness. Things had been going well for her since she had arrived at Black Sands, but she was still mindful that that could change in a moment. If Jessup decided to arrest her, or the people she served decided she was a scammer, or if they came after her for some crime, real or imagined, then she would once again be on her own, with nothing to her name but a cat with psychic powers, a car that barely ran, and whatever she could throw in a suitcase before she disappeared.

If the key unlocked a treasure, she would be rich. She could be wealthy enough never to have to worry about being out on the street again. She had seen the Witch Doctor's hoard, how he had gathered so much of magical value. There were other hoards like that. Kings and pharaohs had amassed untold wealth. And those treasures had not all been discovered. There were myths of secret treasures and lands that disappeared from the knowledge of men, but they could still be out there somewhere, if she had a way to find and access them. Like a magical key.

She had to let go of the key to start her car and drive home and, as she did, the problem of Corvin once again slid into her mind. Who could defeat him? Could Harrison? They said he was an immortal, like the Witch Doctor. She knew that his powers were far greater than anything Corvin had been able to wield before defeating the Witch Doctor. But now that he had the Witch Doctor's power, were they equals? Or was Harrison still stronger? What would happen if the two faced each other?

When Reg got into the yard, she was startled to see a dark shape on her doorstep. She stopped abruptly, looking at the cloaked figure.

"Hello?"

He turned around. Reg saw with relief that it was just Damon. Still, she wasn't expecting him and was a little unsettled to find him there. She didn't get any closer, but watched him warily, trying to analyze his body language and figure out why he was there without her.

"I just thought I'd drop by to see how you are doing," Damon offered. "It's been a little while and I haven't heard from you…"

"Yeah. I've just been busy with other things. I'm supposed to be helping Francesca with the kattakyns, and there's the gnome in the garden, and just… things." She didn't mention Corvin, knowing that Damon already didn't like or trust him, which was appropriate, but why aggravate him further? She hadn't needed Damon's protection against Corvin; she'd stood her ground quite well all by herself.

Damon smiled. "The gnome in the garden?"

"Well, yes… he's not exactly my responsibility, Sarah is the one who hired him, but since I'm the one he can communicate with telepathically, these things just keep falling on me."

"What things?"

"His brother was in jail, and I helped to get him out, and then he found the key, and I was trying to find out where it came from or what it opens…"

"An actual physical key. Did you have any luck?"

"Not yet, but I haven't had a chance to look around. Sarah didn't know where it came from, and she's lived here for a long time."

"Yes, she has. If the key predates her, it must be pretty old."

Reg walked closer to Damon, starting to relax after the surprise of his unexpected appearance. He wasn't going to do anything to harm her. He was a friend, and she'd previously used him as a bodyguard. He was safe.

He reached out tentatively, offering a hug in greeting. Reg wasn't a hugger by nature, so she was a little stiff, not knowing if she wanted to accept the hug

He kept it brief, probably sensing she found it awkward. "So where were you?"

"Uh—just now?"

"Yes. Where were you coming from?"

"Just… a thing."

"Work?"

Reg nodded. "Yeah. Meeting with a client."

Damon scowled. But it wasn't any of his business where she had been. She had momentarily forgotten he was a diviner and could tell when she was lying. Even a white lie or something unimportant like where she had been. Now he thought that she had something to hide. She just wanted to preserve her privacy. She didn't want to talk about Corvin and his possible reintegration into society.

"Were you with Hunter?" Damon asked suspiciously.

"No, I wasn't with Corvin." Reg rolled her eyes dramatically. "You know I don't associate with him."

"For someone who doesn't associate with him, you talk to him and meet with him an awful lot."

"That's over now. That was just over the Witch Doctor, and he's gone now, so there's no more reason for us to meet."

"Yeah? So you haven't seen him at all lately?"

"Sure, I've seen him, but that's different than… *seeing* him." Reg caught herself. "What am I doing justifying myself to you, anyway? Who I talk to is my own business."

"It's just that… I thought we could go out again, but if you're seeing Corvin Hunter, then…"

"No, I'm not seeing Corvin. I happen to talk to him now and then. He calls me. He shows up. What am I supposed to do about that?"

"You could tell him to get lost."

"Do you have any idea how many times I've told him to leave me alone? He keeps coming back. It doesn't matter what I say to him. It doesn't matter whether I light him on fire and testify against him before his coven," Reg pointed out. "You've seen. He keeps coming back. So what am I supposed to do?"

"Stop talking to him."

Reg shrugged impatiently. "The guy is being shunned. Who else is he going to talk to? He'll just keep showing up whether I talk to him or not. He hangs around waiting until everyone leaves. He shows up in my yard or on the street."

"Get a restraining order."

"You can't do that without any reason. He's not threatening me or being violent toward me. What am I supposed to do, tell the judge that I'm afraid he'll take away my powers? How do you think that's going to go over? I'll tell you—they'll lock me up. And I don't have any interest in going through that again. I know what I'm talking about. So why don't you believe I'd get rid of him if I could, and leave it alone?"

"You could go to his coven and ask them to take steps."

Reg thought back to her meeting with Davyn. "Trust me; they're not going to discipline him."

Damon studied her, then eventually nodded. "Okay. Fine. You weren't seeing him and you can't do anything about him coming around here. All the more reason for me to be around. I can send him on his way and make sure he doesn't bother you."

Reg rolled her eyes at Damon thinking he had the power to overcome Corvin anymore. "Like I said, he'll wait until you're gone. He's not stupid. You two really don't get along together, do you? Is that just now, because of me, or do you have a history?"

"We've never gotten along," Damon said brusquely. "Not many people do get along with his kind. It would be like having a tiger for a pet. You don't know if one day he's not going to turn on you. I'm sorry for sounding so…"

"Jealous?" Reg suggested.

"Yeah, I guess it could come across that way. But I'm not trying to be possessive or to assume a relationship that we don't have. I just want to protect you. I'm interested in you; I think we could have a good time together and enjoy each other's company. Maybe develop into something closer. But with him always hanging on the periphery... it makes me edgy. I don't know what to expect from him. Or from you."

"You know I don't want to get together with him; that's why I asked for your help before."

"That's also why I worry about you being off with him. He could still charm you. Catch you unaware, like before."

"I know what I'm doing now. Or at least, I know what he's trying to do, and I'm getting better at resisting him."

"I just hope... I don't want anything to happen to you."

Reg felt a warm flush. She appreciated both the sentiment and the warmth in his voice. She could see herself getting together with Damon. Their first date hadn't turned out so well, but he had a good heart. They'd nearly lost him in the fight with the Witch Doctor. He'd been badly hurt before Corvin had helped to heal him. But the two of them could find things in common. She and Damon could spend time with each other and enjoy each other's company. She closed her eyes for a moment and pictured the two of them taking in a movie, his arm around her shoulders, sharing a bag of popcorn, relaxed and happy...

"Stop it," she growled, opening her eyes, pushing the vision away from her as hard as she could.

"What?" Damon's brows lifted, but he was not very convincing. He knew exactly what she was talking about.

"Quit putting visions in my head. I don't want you forcing your ideas on me."

"I'm not forcing you. You're just thinking about the possibilities. There's not any coercion involved."

"I can come up with my own ideas. I don't need you putting them into my head."

"How is it any different than listening to spirits or communicating with your gnome? It's just a different mode of communication. I'm just painting a picture."

Reg couldn't put her finger on how it was any different from the way that Forst communicated with her. Damon's pictures were so rich that she wasn't always sure whether what she was seeing was really happening or not, and that was scary. At least with the gnome, it was still words, just on a different level—his inside words instead of his outside words.

"Just stop doing it… or tell me before you do it, or something. I don't like being fooled."

Damon frowned, but he didn't argue. He turned his back to her and reached into her mailbox. Reg tensed warily, not sure what he was doing. Was he putting some spell on it?

But he pulled a small envelope out instead. "I, er, left you a note," he said, his face getting pink. "I didn't know how long it was going to be before you were back."

Used to modern technology, Reg didn't know when the last time someone had sent her a handwritten note or letter was. She probably would never even have thought to look in the mailbox. Sarah received all of the postal mail at the big house and, rather than leaving it in Reg's mailbox, she always brought it in and left it sorted on the counter for her.

There was a card caught on the envelope of Damon's letter. He pulled them apart and looked at the card. His mouth twisted.

"Davyn Smithy. What was he doing here?"

Reg was confused. Why would Davyn have left a card in her mailbox when she was meeting with him at his office? It didn't make any sense.

Then she remembered what seemed like ages ago. She had refused to let him into the cottage or to take the card from him, worried that he might have laid a curse on it. So he had left it in her mailbox instead, and it had been there ever since.

"Uh… that's from a long time ago. When he was here to tell me about Corvin's hearing."

He examined it more closely and peeked into her mailbox to see if there was anything else incriminating. But being a diviner, he must know that she was telling the truth. He hesitated, not sure what to do with his note or with the business card.

"Just give them to me," Reg said, motioning impatiently.

"But I already talked to you, so I don't need to leave a note… and you don't need the card anymore."

"Give them to me."

Damon handed them to her. The envelope was stiff, not just a note on a piece of paper, but a card. Reg ripped the sealed envelope open. The front was a picture of a tuxedo cat sitting in a window beside some pink flowers in a vase. There was a brief note jotted inside that Reg would sort out later, when she could take the time to figure out the cursive writing.

She was floored that Damon would go to the effort not just to write her a note, but to get a card with a cat like Starlight on the front. He'd planned ahead; he hadn't just pulled a random piece of paper out of his pocket.

"Damon… this is really sweet. Thank you."

"I just wanted you to know that I was thinking about you. I hope everything has been okay since the big fight… I know it wasn't easy for you to face the Witch Doctor, and you were really strong."

"Well, nothing like you," Reg pointed out, embarrassed that she hadn't even asked after his health, let alone his mental and emotional state. The guy had basically been blown up and had nearly died. She could have at least checked in on him. "How are you doing now… everything healing okay?"

"I might not like Hunter, but he did a good job healing me. I haven't had any problems. You wouldn't know that anything had happened."

"Would you… like to come in?"

She hadn't been planning to invite him in. She knew it was a risky thing. If she allowed him into the cottage, then the wards that Sarah had set to protect Reg wouldn't work against him. But he wasn't planning to do anything that would harm her. He had just given her a mushy note.

CHAPTER TWELVE

D amon's face lit up. No need to study him to read his emotions. "Sure, if you're not busy."

"I don't know what kind of a mess things might be in here; I didn't pay much attention when I left earlier. And I do have to get back to business before too long. But there's no reason we can't visit for a few minutes."

She stood close to him to unlock the door and let him in, her heart racing with his proximity. But she didn't know if it was excitement or anxiety. She followed him into the cottage, reaching out to sense the atmosphere of the room to discern whether she had made a mistake by letting him in. But nothing felt any different. She didn't feel a spell breaking or darkness seeping into the room. It felt just the same as always.

"Have a seat." Reg gestured to the couch. She didn't normally entertain men there and it occurred to her that there wasn't anywhere that would be very comfortable for him to sit. She always found the wicker furniture to be bumpy and pokey, even if it was upholstered. Somehow she always ended up with something sticking into her. She didn't worry about it with her clients, because they were only there for a short session. She didn't want them to get too comfortable and stay on after she had finished with them. "Sorry…"

Damon sat down, easing into the wicker as if he were afraid it would

---

collapse right under him. It didn't break, sag, or creak, so he relaxed his posture.

"Something to drink?" Reg offered. "There's Jack Daniels."

"Sure, that sounds good. I thought you were more of a tea drinker."

"I guess I have been since I got here. You can't exactly drink whiskey all day with clients. But you can have tea; it doesn't hurt anything."

"Jack sounds just fine."

Reg went to pour it and wondered fleetingly if it were too early in the day to start drinking or to be getting friendly with Damon. She didn't want Sarah barging in and making a fuss. She didn't think she had any appointments with clients. Reg flipped the page in her appointment book to make sure and detoured to the front door to lock it before joining Damon. It wouldn't keep Sarah out. She did, after all, have a key, but they would at least have a warning that she was at the door.

She had a key.

Reg put the two glasses down on the coffee table and felt the pocket of her skirt. The old key was still there. Still tugging at her, telling her to find the lock and claim the treasure.

"What's that?" Damon asked, noticing her action.

"Oh…" Reg pulled the key and out displayed it. "Just an old key." She sat down on the couch a comfortable distance away from him.

He looked at it and raised his brows. "Not in very good shape, is it?"

"That's what happens when you bury it in the garden."

"Why would you do that?"

"I didn't. But somebody did."

"Why bother? It doesn't look like anything important."

"It's magical. I don't know what it opens, but I think it could be…" she trailed off, not wanting to speculate on a treasure. What if he wanted a stake or spread the news to others? She wanted whatever the key opened all to herself. "You're probably right. It's probably nothing. Whatever it unlocks probably doesn't even exist anymore. Someone lost the key, so they would have to rekey the lock, and now it's worthless. Someone just lost it in the dark some night."

"Could be," Damon agreed. "There are a lot of keys in the world, and a lot of them get lost."

Reg warmed it between her hands. "I think it looks cool. That's all.

You've probably seen tons of old keys in your life. They're probably all over the place here."

"I've seen my share," Damon agreed. "Every house in Black Sands probably has old chests and cupboards that took old style keys. And the keys get put in a drawer somewhere and forgotten about. People tend to collect them, thinking that they'll remember what a key was for or that it was important, and in the end just end up with a drawer full of orphan keys."

Reg sipped her drink. It felt good after the meeting with Davyn. She hadn't noticed how much tension she had been carrying in her shoulders since their meeting. The thought of them commuting Corvin's sentence was deplorable. She hated it. But she didn't have to think about it. She was having a pleasant visit with Damon. She didn't have to think about Corvin or Davyn or anyone else.

Damon also took a drink and gazed at her over the rim of the glass, contemplative. "So what does Reg Rawlins want out of life? Tell me about your hopes and dreams."

That was a tall order. Reg thought about what she could tell him.

But a voice whispered in her ear that she should not answer. Not her subconsciousness. An actual voice that she recognized. She closed her eyes so that Damon wouldn't see her rolling them, and she focused on building a wall around herself. A barrier between her and the irritating voice. It didn't work. She had blocked Norma Jean out for a long time, but since she had come to the surface when Corvin had held Reg's powers, Norma Jean popped up at the most inconvenient junctures. Reg focused on the present. Norma Jean belonged in the past. She was dead. She didn't need to follow Reg around, trying to look after her little girl. That hadn't worked before, and Reg couldn't see it working now.

"Those must be some dreams," Damon teased.

Reg opened her eyes again. "Oh... I don't know. What about you? What are your big dreams?"

"Well... I'd like to find a way to use my powers to make a full-time living. Right now, I do private security, but I really would like to use my talents full time. Not to have to resort to other ways to earn a living."

Reg nodded. "That sounds good."

"I admire you for starting up your own business and jumping in with both feet. There aren't a lot of people who can make good money using magical powers."

"It's not the first time I've done it… and it doesn't usually work out in the end. But maybe this time… things are quite a bit different this time."

"Because of Black Sands?"

"Yeah. I've never had contact with anyone with… real powers before. I didn't even know that's what I had. So to be somewhere like this… it's different."

"And the competition doesn't bother you? Knowing that there are other psychics out there who also have real powers?"

"It's been okay so far. People seem to stick with one practitioner for a while… so I get multiple jobs from one client… I guess sooner or later they'll decide they want to hear something else, and they'll seek out one of the other psychics or mediums."

"There's enough work to go around?"

"So far, so good. It helps that the rent is so reasonable, and Sarah is always getting me new clients. She's very hooked into the community."

Reg didn't express her fears to him. The fact that sooner or later, everything always went down the toilet. And then… where would she go next? That was why she needed the treasure.

"What did you do before you came to Black Sands? Were you doing readings there? Wherever you came from?"

Reg considered the question from several angles before answering. It was better not to answer him than it was to try to lie to him. She wanted to make sure that there was nothing he could use against her in her answer. Corvin had asked her about her past too, and then he had ended up investigating her behind her back, coming up with information that she had regretted him having. She didn't want to repeat the same mistakes.

"Yeah," she agreed. She'd already told him it wasn't the first time she had tried that gig, so by extension he already knew the answer to his question. "I've done readings different times, different places. Mostly just for enough change to get a meal, when I was down on the skids. And…" She decided to stop there. Nothing that would lead him back to Erin and Tennessee. Nothing that would give her away. "Like I say, I've tried it before."

"You didn't have any other practitioners in your family that you know of? Sometimes people don't even realize they have powers."

"It was just me and my mom, for the first few years. Then foster care. I didn't know anyone else in my family. My mom never said that there was anyone with powers. I think she would have said something if they had. If nothing else, she would have been trying to get something from them."

He raised an eyebrow. "Not very complimentary about your mother."

"There's not much I can say about her. She died when I was little. But what I remember… she wasn't the kind of mom on Hallmark commercials."

"Few of them are. But with the powers you have, you must have someone in your family. It doesn't usually come out of nowhere."

"No."

"You don't know anything about your father?"

Norma Jean was setting up a ruckus in Reg's head. She narrowed her eyes, trying to keep her focus on Damon rather than her mother's rampaging spirit. Was he fishing? Did he know something? She wasn't sure how much of her conversation with the Witch Doctor had been out loud and how much had been inside her head. Had the others heard? She was still trying to figure everything out herself. Hints dropped by the Witch Doctor, Harrison, and Norma Jean.

"No, nothing at all."

He clearly knew that was false. Reg cursed herself for not being able to lie to him convincingly. She was so used to changing the truth to suit her needs. Most people couldn't tell when she was lying. It was habitual, even though she knew that Damon would be able to recognize the truth when he heard it—or didn't.

"Look," she said, "this is none of your business. I don't want to talk about the past or my family. You don't know what it was like growing up the way I did. It's something I'd rather forget. We can… talk about your childhood or dreams. I don't like to."

He stretched his arm out behind her. He brushed the back of her hair, setting her thin red braids swaying. "You don't see a lot of redheads with cornrows."

His touch was comfortable. She didn't feel any anxiety over it. But on the other hand, she didn't feel the magnetism toward him that she felt toward Corvin, either. Was she going to compare everyone to Corvin now? She hated her magical attraction to him. Why did she have to react to his charms? Even when he wasn't there to magick her, she was still thinking about how amazing it felt to be with him. Would it never go away?

"Reg?"

She refocused on Damon. "Hmm?"

"Where did you get them done? It must have taken a long time."

"Oh, the braids. Yeah. Hours. But then I don't have to do much to take care of them." She fingered them, feeling down the tight bumps of one braid. "I'll have to get them redone before too long. I wonder if there is anyone here who does it."

"Bound to be someone. If not, you could go with dreadlocks like the Witch Doctor."

Reg shuddered. "I don't think I'm going to do that."

"You think the Witch Doctor was really the one who killed your mother? He wasn't just manipulating you to think that?"

"Well, I still remember the same things, so… yeah. I do. I wish I could remember more… and I wish I couldn't remember anything. It was better when I didn't remember any of it."

"Even though you didn't remember, it probably still affected you. Seeing something like that can cause a lot of psychological damage."

"It wasn't an easy childhood. I'm glad to be an adult now, independent. I was never really comfortable living in a family. Never fit in." She laughed. "How would I? Try fitting a traumatized kid with the ability to see ghosts into any home."

Damon smiled. "You're right. That would be pretty tough, unless everyone knew what they were getting."

Reg nodded. She looked away from him, trying to think of the best way to get back off the topic and to focus the conversation on him instead.

"And what about Harrison," Damon said slowly, "you don't think he's your father?"

"Harrison?" Reg shook her head; her forehead creased into worry lines that made it ache. "No, of course not. How could he be? These immortals, whatever they are, they wouldn't have anything to do with humans."

"I'm not so sure. There are plenty of stories about mortal women and immortal men."

"Mythology. That stuff isn't real."

"That's not what you said when we were fighting the Witch Doctor."

"I was trying to distract him. That was our job, remember? I didn't say I believed it. I was just trying to get a rise out of him."

"I see." His eyes were steady, burning into her. Seeing right through everything she tried to tell him. "So. Not Harrison. Then who?"

"No one. I told you. Some client or scummy boyfriend. Someone she'd never met before. A nobody. Street dirt."

"If you didn't get your powers through your mother's family, then you must have gotten them through your father's."

"Or they were just spontaneous. Or acquired some other way. I don't know. There are other ways, aren't there?"

"Yes, but they are very rare."

"So I'm a rare case."

"You certainly are," he agreed with a warm smile.

"Can we stop talking about my family? It's… depressing."

And she hoped that if they stopped talking about it, Norma Jean's voice in her head would stop screeching. She was getting a nasty headache.

She took another sip of her drink.

Reg heard Starlight jump down off the bed or the windowsill and, in a moment, he walked into sight and approached Reg. He sniffed in Damon's direction, watching the man suspiciously. Reg watched to see how Damon would react to Starlight. Corvin hated him. Harrison loved him. Reg thought that was a pretty good barometer of what kind of people they were. Damon smiled politely and reached his fingers down, holding them out for Starlight to smell. After ignoring his fingers for a few moments, Starlight decided to check them out. He sniffed Damon's hand thoroughly, then rubbed against it. Damon obligingly gave his ears and chin a few scratches, then sat back up.

"We always had cats around growing up."

"Were they familiars?"

"No, just house pets. They might have given my mother a little magical support; I don't know. She never said so. And they weren't treated like…" he searched for the words. "They weren't treated as equals. They were pets."

Reg nodded. Starlight wandered away to look at his dish. Altogether, the interaction between Damon and Starlight had been a non-event. So maybe that told her what she needed to know about him. He was just in the middle. Not great, not evil or dangerous, just a typical, everyday kind of guy. Other than the fact that he did have some magical powers. Reg was getting accustomed to the fact that everyone in Black Sands seemed to have something or other. She didn't ask what they were or what they could do, just trying to stay open-minded towards new people until she learned their quirks.

"Did you ever have a familiar? I thought it was pretty common, but I guess maybe not. Corvin doesn't like animals."

"That's probably because he is one. He doesn't like the competition." Damon snickered.

Reg wasn't sure how she felt about Corvin, but she didn't like making fun of him behind his back. She didn't join in Damon's laughter.

She had been moving the key from one hand to the other as they talked, absently fidgeting with it. She felt the now-familiar tug to unlock the treasure. She needed to know what it fit and she needed to open it. Was there an attic in the cottage? She didn't think so, but there were lots of rooms and, she was sure, an attic too in Sarah's house. Maybe Sarah wouldn't mind Reg going through the house to see if she could find the lock that the key belonged to and reunite them.

She could see herself fitting the key into the lock. Feel it turning in her hand, clicking into place just as it should with a satisfying click, and then the tumbler turning and revealing to her the priceless treasure within…

"Are you doing that?" she demanded.

Damon raised his eyebrows. "Doing what?"

"I told you not to put thoughts into my head. Were you just doing that with the key?"

He shook his head, looking baffled. If he were lying, she couldn't tell. It wasn't very fair that he could lie to her, but she couldn't lie to him. It should work both directions. "No. What do you mean? What about the key?"

"I just… never mind. I don't know what I'm thinking. I'm tired. I shouldn't be drinking."

He took the glass out of her hand and downed what remained in one gulp, then put it down on the coffee table with a grin. "There. Problem solved."

Reg stared at him in shock for a moment, then burst into laughter. He was right; one problem solved. And such an easy solution. She should put the key away too. If it were going to be that distracting for her, she should just let it go and forget about it for a while. She would search for the lock later. She didn't want to lose it, fiddling with it absently. Who knew where she might put it down in a moment of distraction.

But the key was warm in her hand and she didn't want to put it back in her pocket.

CHAPTER THIRTEEN

After Damon went home, Reg decided to focus on work. She got out her computer and worked on a marketing plan, wrote down the things she would need to do, who she should contact, what supplies she needed. But all the while, she was distracted by the key. The key would be better than a marketing plan. Because no matter how hard she worked on the marketing plan, there would always be more to do. She would never be able to forget about it and let the business run itself. That wasn't the way that it worked. But if she used the key to unlock the treasure, then she wouldn't have to worry about it again. She would be set for life. She would have all of the wealth she needed to live the way she wanted to.

That was way better than a marketing plan.

Reg decided to leave the computer alone and do something about finding the treasure. That would be much more productive.

She closed the lid of her laptop and went outside to the garden to look around. If the key had been found there, then why not the lock?

The garden was deserted. It was definitely looking better. She didn't usually see Forst working in it, but he obviously had been. A large portion of the plants had been beaten flat before and were now standing up on their own. A few were staked and tied, but most of them seemed to have sprung back up on their own. Birds were singing in the trees. It was very peaceful and calm.

"It is a happier place," Forst said.

Reg startled and looked around. He was standing just a few feet away from her, but she had failed to see him or to hear his approach.

"You scared me! Where did you come from?"

"Gnomen are like humans. The babies grow in the mother's womb. But Gnomen always have two kinder. And very rare to have more than one set."

"Uh… I didn't mean where do gnome babies come from. I mean, where were you just now? I didn't see you here and I didn't hear you come."

"I was in the soil."

Reg considered this, but she wasn't sure what he meant. Rather than look like a fool asking another fundamental question, she just shook it off. Forst was looking happy, his cheeks a glowing red. His overalls were grubby, but he looked like he'd been having a good time. Gardening certainly agreed with him.

"How is Fir? Is everything all right with him?"

Forst nodded vigorously. "He is still in his garden. No more black coats have taken him away. The living are protected, thanks to Reg Rawlins."

"Good. Glad to hear it." She didn't often do something just for others. She recognized that like Corvin, she wasn't altruistic. When she did a thing, it was because she expected to get something out of it. She liked to help others, but that was secondary to her goals. She had been on the streets enough to know that she had to take care of herself first. No one else was going to do that. But helping Fir hadn't been for her. It hadn't been done with any expectation that it would bring her something.

It had made Forst happy, and it was Forst who had found the key, so in a way, it had ended up benefiting her anyway. Life was strange sometimes.

She had the key in her pocket and wrapped her hand around it as she contemplated Forst.

"I'm looking for the lock for the key you found. Do you know anything about… where it is or what kind of a lock it would be?"

He shook his head. "The garden is happier without it. See how well it grows now. Even the birds sing more sweet."

"I thought that the lock might be somewhere close by." Reg looked around for inspiration. "A garden shed or a storage trunk. What do you think?"

"It was a key," Forst said with a shrug. "It opens something."

"Yes. I know. That's what I'm looking for. What do you think it unlocks?"

With his thumbs in his pockets and his belly sticking out, Forst shook his head. "Beware of what a dark key may unlock."

"A dark key?"

He patted his pockets for his pipe and lit it before answering. The smoke wafted lazily through the air. Reg raised her eyebrows, waiting for him to answer the question. "The key made the garden dark. The living plants did not want to grow strong while it was here. It was a dark key."

"But you don't know what it opens. You haven't seen one like that before, or seen anything around here that is locked that it might fit?"

He shook his head and puffed on the pipe. "I have seen no lock it might fit."

"And you don't know what kind of a lock it would be?"

He tapped on the side of the bowl. "It is an old key. It had been in the ground almost as long as you have been alive. Who would bury a key in this garden?"

"It's not that old, if it's only as old as me. There must be all kinds of houses around here that are a hundred years old or more. This looks much older than me."

"The key is older than you." His tone took on a note of impatience. "And it has been in the ground almost as long as you have been alive."

"Oh. But before that, it was somewhere else. It was lost thirty years ago."

"It was never lost."

"But it was lost in the garden," Reg pointed out. "Someone walking through here must have dropped it by accident and never found it."

"No. It was not lost."

Reg left Forst smoking, not sure what to make of this. She made a circuit around the garden, looking at the plants and flowers, but what she wanted to find was a treasure chest or storage shed she could fit the key into. She hadn't explored the back yard before; she usually just walked from the front where she parked her car, along the sidewalk, and into her cottage. She hadn't paid much attention to anything else in the yard.

There were trees, the garden, a birdbath with water in it, and a bench to sit on and take it all in.

But no storage shed. No trunk. Nothing that required a key.

When Reg awoke in the morning, she could feel Starlight sitting on the bed close to her leg. Normally, he was either looking out the window or poking at her face trying to wake her up. Maybe he was looking for some cuddle time. She reached out to pet him, but the form she touched was not a furry cat.

Her eyes flew open and she practically leapt out of her bed. It was not a cat sitting on the edge of the bed beside her, but a man. Before she had even had a chance to recognize him, her brain had already processed several possibilities. Corvin's powers had become great enough for him to break any of the simple wards that Sarah had placed there against him. She had allowed Damon in, and that meant that he was allowed to come back, recognized as a guest rather than an intruder. Or it was a burglar or some other stranger there to harm her.

Then as she clambered out of bed, her eyes caught up with her brain and she realized that it was Harrison.

The long-limbed, smiling man looked at her curiously.

As usual, he was dressed in a style that just missed looking like a modern Floridian. He had on a long-sleeved white shirt with puffy sleeves, like he was a pirate or an English lord of some bygone era. This was paired with long, narrow-legged gray pants with pinstripes. He did seem to like his stripes. He had an enormous, dramatic mustache, and while she stared at him, he twirled the ends, making sure that they were properly styled.

"You are... what are you doing in my house?" she demanded. "You scared the heck out of me. You can't just walk into other people's houses like that."

"I didn't walk in."

"Well, you can't apparate or whatever it was you did. You are supposed to call or knock and get permission before going into someone's house. And how is it you can just appear here? I thought Sarah put up wards against unwelcome intruders."

He shrugged. He got up from the bed and bent at the window to pick up Starlight, who immediately started purring. The traitor. He should have been supporting Reg by telling Harrison that he couldn't just appear in the cottage without warning.

Harrison walked with Starlight out toward the kitchen. Reg followed, not sure what else to do.

"I haven't seen you for a while. What have you been doing?" she asked him.

He put Starlight down and poked at the coffee machine as if trying to prod an animal into action. Reg walked over, added grounds, and pushed the button to start it working. Harrison's eyes lit up, and he smiled and nodded.

"Ingenious!"

"Yeah. Coffee machine. Pretty state-of-the-art. You haven't answered my questions. What are you doing here? Where have you been? I thought we would see you after the fight with the Witch Doctor. I thought you would appear, tell us what a good job we did… I don't know, knight us or something. It was really hard."

"You did very well," he confirmed with a nod. "Destine would have been difficult for anyone to fight, and for a group of mortals to be able to overcome him, that was impressive. You used your assets and accomplished something great."

But he said it without inflection, as if it didn't mean anything to him. What could mere mortals mean to someone like him? He must have had much more important things on his mind. Immortal things.

"What exactly is an immortal?" she asked, watching him as he watched the coffee machine pop and sputter. "Is it a god? An alien race? Where do you come from?"

Harrison glanced over at her. He looked down at Starlight as if he might have the answer to the question, then opened the fridge to find something to feed Starlight. As if Reg couldn't feed her own cat. But she knew how much Harrison loved cats and couldn't find fault with him for that.

"It is the best word we could find in your language," he said, "but it is rather inadequate. There is so much more to my kind than simply living longer than human memory. But it is the best we can do."

"Are you immortal? Un-killable?"

"Death is an interesting human concept." He found a bowl of spicy chicken Reg had brought home from The Crystal Bowl a few days previous. He started to shred it for Starlight.

"That might bother his stomach," Reg pointed out.

Harrison looked at Starlight, who stared at him, communicating something, then Harrison continued to shred the chicken. "Humans call it death, and yet they talk of life after death. They know that death is not the end of the spirit, that consciousness goes on somewhere else or in a new life, but they still believe it is permanent." He shrugged as if it were impossible to comprehend such convoluted logic.

Reg had to admit that despite her dedicated non-belief in any main-stream religion or the concept of heaven or reincarnation, she knew that spirits lived on after the death of the body. How else had Norma Jean continued to talk to Reg long after her death? And so many other spirits that Reg had communicated with over the years. The only other way to explain it would be to admit that she was insane and that the voices and visions were just a glitch in her brain, not something that was real and could be explained spiritually.

"And the immortals? How are they different from humans, other than having stronger magical powers?"

"Better fashion sense," Harrison deadpanned.

He bent down and put the chicken in Starlight's bowl. Starlight imme-diately charged in, chewing on the food noisily as if he hadn't been fed in a week. Reg shook her head. "I need to use the bathroom. Are you going to be here still when I get out?"

"I expect I will."

Reg wasn't sure what that meant, but it was probably as clear as Harrison was going to get. "And you understand the part about privacy and not walking in on people or apparating in the room when they are using the bathroom?"

He cast his eyes down like a child caught with his hand in the cookie jar. "I will not appear in the bathroom."

"Good."

She made quick use of the bathroom in spite of his assurance, not trusting that he would be true to his word. She splashed water on her face and inched the curtain back to peek out the window. It was still early, but it was, at least, light outside. He hadn't gotten her up in the middle of the night. But just how long had he been sitting on her bed before she had awakened?

She returned to the kitchen. The coffee maker was just finished filling the pot, so she poured a cup for herself and one for Harrison. She handed it to him, but he didn't take it.

306

"I don't drink coffee."

"Then why did you want to make coffee?" Reg demanded, exasperated.

"You drink coffee."

"You were just making it for me?"

"Yes."

"Oh." She sipped her coffee, a little mollified. "Well, thank you for thinking of me. Do you want to sit down?" she motioned to the wicker furniture.

He surveyed it for a moment, then nodded, and they both went over to sit. Starlight had finished eating his chicken and followed them over. Rather than joining Reg, he jumped up onto Harrison's lap, where he received plenty of scratches and snuggles. Reg shook her head at the black hairs collecting on Harrison's white pirate shirt.

"You have questions for me," Harrison said abruptly.

Reg tried to avoid rolling her eyes. "I have plenty of questions, but you never seem to answer any of them. You give some vague answer or change the subject."

"What do you want to know?"

Reg tried to prioritize her questions, suspecting that he would only answer one or two—if she were lucky.

"Who is—or was—Weston?"

He looked at her for a long moment, and she figured he regretted his offer to answer her questions. "Weston is an immortal."

"I figured that. Is he still…" She hesitated over her wording. Asking whether he was alive or dead would likely result in another philosophical discussion over the meaning of the words. "Is he still here, on the earth, like you are?"

"On the earth… not like me." Harrison considered, then nodded, looking satisfied with his answer.

It might have made perfect sense to him, but it didn't tell Reg any more than she already knew.

"He's on the earth right now."

"Yes." He looked as if he would qualify his answer, then shrugged. Reg analyzed his hesitation. Could Weston be on the earth but not on the earth? Maybe, like the pixies, he existed in more than one plane, so that it wasn't as easy to state what temporal space he occupied. If he even had a physical body. The Witch Doctor and Harrison seemed to be able to materialize at will, and she didn't know what happened to their bodies when they weren't visible. Did they occupy only one space? What happened to the matter that made up their bodies when they were not there?

"How is he not here like you?"

"He is… constrained. Not free to come and go."

"Okay…" That was interesting. "Why did the Witch Doctor want to know where he is? And what does he have to do with me or my mother?"

Harrison petted Starlight and looked down at his face. They seemed to be communicating at a telepathic level, but Reg couldn't hear whatever it was they were saying. She didn't like the isolation she felt at not being in on the conversation. It was strange to think that that was how other people felt all the time when she communicated with spirits or telepaths.

"Weston and Destine have been rivals for a very long time. This is not a bad thing in our kind. It creates balance. Keeps one entity from becoming too powerful."

"But you also said that you are prohibited from harming each other. The Witch Doctor definitely wanted to harm Weston. Even to destroy him."

Harrison shrugged. "Rules are broken… if we did not have the freedom to break them, they would not be rules. They would be…" he struggled to find the words, "impossibility. But it is not impossible for us to hurt our kind. That is why there must be a rule."

Reg tried to follow the logic but wasn't sure she did. "And my mother?"

"It is not against the rules to harm mortals."

Reg didn't like to hear that, but it wasn't what she meant. "I mean… how was she involved in all of this? She wasn't immortal."

"No," Harrison laughed, "certainly not." He looked down at Starlight and stopped laughing as if he had been reprimanded. "No. But she was a favorite. He gave her his blood."

Reg pictured some cannibalistic ritual and wrinkled her nose. "Gave her his blood? What does that mean? Did that… give her power?"

"No." Harrison met Reg's eyes, his golden brown irises glowing. "He gave her you."

CHAPTER FOURTEEN

E ven though Reg had half-expected this ever since the confrontation with the Witch Doctor, it still sent her reeling. She was suddenly lightheaded, bright spots appearing before her eyes. She didn't want to misunderstand Harrison's use of the English language. Things didn't always come out the way he intended them. She could be completely misunderstanding him. Maybe he meant that Weston had protected her at some point. That she had run away or been kidnapped, and he had brought her back. Or that he'd healed her from a potentially fatal illness.

He had given Reg to Norma Jean.

"He was a man," Norma Jean said in Reg's head. "Just a man like any other. He didn't seem that different."

But he had been, hadn't he?

"Do you mean… that he's my biological father?" Reg asked Harrison as calmly as she could.

Harrison scratched his head. "Biological… I am not sure. My kind… it is not the same as when humans meet. But without him, you were not. And with him, you were."

Reg groaned. She brought her feet up onto the chair, knees tight against her chest. "Don't tell me that! Then these… gifts that I have? They are from him?"

"They are… part of him." Harrison pondered. "We don't know when we create with a human, what will be the result. A child with great powers, or a child with little power at all. When a child is born, there is... a disruption in our order. We can sense it... That is how I knew of your existence and your need for protection."

"But why would you protect me? If Weston was my father, then wasn't it *his* responsibility?"

"He was... gathered in. There is a consequence to creation. He could not be there. But he left no clues to his chosen exile."

"So the Witch Doctor couldn't find him."

"Destine would have if he could. We are vulnerable when in that state. Destine hoped to remove him from this earth. The rest of us watched for him, but Destine was more... dedicated."

"And he thought Norma Jean would know where Weston went? That he would leave her a trail of breadcrumbs so she could find him again?"

"Breadcrumbs." His face lit up with a big smile. "What an apt word. For Weston to come back, he would need to be close to his loved one. But Destine was unable to find the trail. He was furious. And he has been searching still, waiting for some sign of Weston's return."

Reg shook her head. "And I walked right into him. What are the odds that I would move into the town he was operating out of?"

"Odds?"

"What are the chances that we would run into each other? I managed to lose him all those years ago in Maine. We should never have run into each other again. But then I decide to come to Black Sands because it sounded like a good place to run a con as a psychic. And things would never be the same again..."

"It is not chance," Harrison said slowly. "It was certainty. You and Destine were both drawn to this place."

"Why?"

He raised his eyebrows comically high. "Because Weston was here. He left his imprint on the place. It is very faint, so many years later, but not so faint that one of our kind cannot feel it."

"And me? Do you think I could sense him here too?"

Harrison nodded. "Why else would you come here? Traveling all across the country? Humans like to stay in one place, near their nesting place. They don't like to go long temporal distances. But you did not stay. You came here when you had no one to help take care of you, no job, no roots. Just… Weston's imprint."

"I don't know." Reg shook her head. "I know why I came here, and it wasn't just a feeling that I should. It was a decision based on logic. On trying to earn money to support myself."

"Humans can work anywhere. You did not have to come to this location to work."

"Well, no," Reg agreed. "I have worked in other places, and I move fairly often. But Black Sands seemed like a good place to land. I heard that there were more witches and psychics here than anywhere else in the country. So, of course, I came here."

Harrison nodded and petted Starlight with long, slow strokes.

"This is crazy. Everyone keeps asking me where I got my talents. And I thought… they were just something I developed to survive. Learning to cold read people. To avoid trouble. How to know when people were telling the truth, and whether they were a danger to me. I needed those things to survive. I didn't even know there was such a thing as a real psychic gift until I moved here. And even now, I don't understand it and half the time don't even believe it myself."

"We have observed that humans who go through hardship develop stronger gifts. Or humans with stronger gifts run into more problems. We don't know why this is. In some cultures, children are taken away from their families, are put through trials, in order to force the development of their inborn talents."

Reg remembered Calliopia's kidnapping and incarceration with the pixies. She remembered Calliopia's father talking about the ordeal she had been through. Reg had suspected at the time that he had been the one to put her through it, but she couldn't understand why he would do such a thing. Maybe it had been to force the development of her fairy gifts, to trick her into coming into her powers.

"That's cruel. I know what it's like to have to live without parents. No one should ever do that."

Harrison shrugged as if it were nothing. According to Francesca, immortals didn't have any feelings for humans, but saw them just as bugs or amusing toys, to play with and discard as they liked. Harrison had been helpful to Reg, and she had good feelings around him, but did he love her like the uncle he had once pretended to be? Did he care how she felt or how she turned out in life? Or was he part of the reason she had gone through so many difficulties, carefully nudging her gifts to blossom, like someone forcing flower bulbs?

Harrison's eyes roved around the room.

"Why are you really here?" Reg asked suspiciously. "You didn't come here because you thought I had questions you could answer. You haven't ever cared about my questions before. You always avoid answering them."

Harrison gave her a cheerful smile, a mask that covered up whatever his real motives were. He wasn't easy for her to read, especially since he could block her psychic powers. "Perhaps I wanted to see my old friend again," he offered, indicating Starlight. He kissed the top of the cat's head and cuddled him close to his face. Reg found it very uncomfortable to see him doting on a cat like a little child or crazy cat lady. It was nice that he liked cats, but he seemed to like them just a little too much.

"Do you want a cat? We have nine that we are trying to find new homes for."

He chuckled. "It would not be a good choice for me to provide a temporal home for another creature. Especially a kattakyn."

Reg watched him as he continued to lavish attention on Starlight. "Did you… know him in another life? Or when he was with another owner?" She had taken his 'old friend' as a tongue-in-cheek joke, but maybe it had been accurate. Perhaps he had known Starlight for longer than she thought. They had acted immediately comfortable and friendly with each other from the first time they met.

Harrison looked into Starlight's face for a moment. "He is a very old, wise soul."

"So you do know him?"

Reg picked up her coffee cup and sipped the cooling liquid. She really ought to have something to eat before all of the caffeine gave her the shakes. When she looked back at Harrison for his answer to her question, he was no longer there.

Reg spent what felt like hours on the phone with the people at the animal shelter, being passed from one person to another, trying to find out what they knew about Starlight's history and his previous owner. She would not have been at all surprised to learn that his previous owner had been named Harrison, or some other familiar name. Just how many people had lied to her about the cat's history? Did anyone at the shelter know that he was psychic? That he was an ancient soul? Reg didn't even know what that meant, but she felt embarrassed that she had always just treated him like a cat when he seemed to be something more, at least when Harrison talked about him. Corvin had once suggested that Starlight might be a reincarnate, a cat that had been a person in a previous life. But Reg didn't believe in reincarnation.

Just like she didn't believe in ghosts or magic. How far had that gotten her?

She remembered the worker at the shelter telling her that Starlight's previous owner had died, and that was why he had been so depressed and not responded to anyone until Reg's arrival. He had connected to her like he hadn't to anyone else. Was that something to do with Harrison? Maybe Reg had been predestined to go to Black Sands and maybe she was supposed to get a cat and be a psychic and whatever else Weston had declared.

She was angry whenever she thought of Weston. Why would he bring a child into the world when it was against their rules and she was bound to live a life of hardship and be on the outside, never belonging? What was the benefit to him? Was he playing with them like pieces on a chess board? Because of what he had done, Norma Jean had been tortured and killed. There had been so many negative consequences; Reg didn't understand why he would risk it. What was the good of bringing a child into such a world?

She put her phone down on the coffee table, watching Starlight, expecting him to start acting like a person or to be transformed into one in front of her eyes. But he acted just like he always did, finding a bright sunbeam and sitting with one hind leg splayed out while he washed. Her phone buzzed. She looked at the screen.

Corvin.

Not phoning her this time, but sending a text message.

How about dinner?

Reg looked at the time and texted him back. *Bit early, isn't it?*

She felt guilty as soon as she sent the text. Her answer should have been a resounding no. Or ignoring him. She shouldn't even consider the proposition. He was too dangerous.

But she wanted to ask him about Starlight and to see what he thought about Harrison's various claims. Was Harrison leading her on? Seeing what kind of imaginary story he could get her to believe?

Corvin was a historian. He would be able to tell her about the immortals, what the rumors and myths were. And he could tell her why he didn't like Starlight, and why Starlight didn't like him. Was the enmity between them more than just that of someone who didn't like cats?

Corvin's return text buzzed. *Early or late, whatever time you like.*

She shouldn't even be able to receive a text from him. Hadn't she blocked him from her phone? He must have either changed his number or somehow magicked her phone to change the settings. Maybe that last time he had been there, waiting on the street for her. He'd said that he knew she had blocked him, something that she didn't think he should be able to tell from his end.

Where? She texted back. *Somewhere with people.*

It hadn't stopped him the last time. He had just charmed her into wanting to go somewhere they could be alone. He had convinced her to do things she swore she would not do. But she was stronger now. She had learned how to block him. Most of the time. She was feeling stronger and more sure of herself. And if she had the magic of an immortal, then she should be able to do anything she set her mind on, shouldn't she?

She was half-expecting him to suggest The Crystal Bowl, since that was where they had met more often than not. He obviously liked it there. And then there was the fancy place that he had taken her the night that he did manage to steal her powers. She wouldn't want to go back there, though the food had been fantastic. With the way that he had charmed her, she probably would have thought that dirt tasted good.

Harbor Port of Call?

Reg hadn't been there before. It would, she assumed, be a seafood menu. Which was okay with her.

Okay. Send me address.

I'll pick you up, Corvin texted back.

Reg considered. It would mean he would be coming back to the cottage with her. Would she be able to keep him out?

She was feeling reckless. She was angry at Weston, the Witch Doctor, and even Harrison, feeling betrayed by these immortals who played with human lives. They had affected the course of her life. If she would even have had a life without them in the first place. If Corvin had all of the Witch

Doctor's powers, then she wouldn't be able to withstand him anyway, so what was the point of planning every move? If she lost her powers, then maybe she would live a normal life. Maybe she would be able to be a normal person who didn't have to face all of the hardships that had dogged her for her whole life.

Fine. Seven o'clock?

He texted her back a smiley face. Reg was slightly disconcerted. She was used to most of the witches and warlocks she knew eschewing technology, at least to some extent, living as if they had been born a couple of centuries before. She wouldn't even have predicted that Corvin knew how to make a smiley.

She put her phone back down and sat down.

Her heart was pumping hard as if she'd been running. Starlight had been snoozing on the couch next to her. He raised his head and looked at her reproachfully, as if he knew what she had just done. Reg rubbed her nose. "It was going to happen sooner or later anyway," she told him irritably. "I just don't feel like fighting anymore."

She had the rest of the afternoon and early evening to feel guilty and unsettled, but at the same time, pumped up and excited. She felt like she was doing something proactive instead of just sitting around waiting for magical forces to control her life. She had made at least one decision for herself.

She had no idea how formal the Harbor Port of Call was. She assumed that if it were very formal, Corvin would have told her. She could ask Sarah, but that would mean telling her that she had a date with the warlock she was not supposed to be going out with. It was almost certain to end in disaster.

One of her skirts should do just fine. If it wasn't fancy enough, Corvin could deal with it. They could go to The Crystal Bowl instead.

When seven o'clock finally rolled around, Reg was ready to go. Far from deciding to jam out on Corvin after all, she was eager to get on with it. It was perhaps the stupidest thing she had ever knowingly done in her life, but she felt there was no other way to move forward. She was looking at her phone to check the time when the text from Corvin came in.

I'm here. Coming around to your door and assuming you don't have plans to shoot me.

Reg grinned. That wasn't a bad idea—one way to get rid of him once and for all. Though with the powers he had acquired from the Witch Doctor, she wasn't sure a bullet would be enough to kill him. His ability to heal Damon had been impressive. If he could bring the same powers to bear on his own injuries, it was going to take a lot more than a bullet to kill him.

Come at your own risk, she texted back.

In a couple of minutes, she heard his footsteps on the path and got up. When he reached her door, she opened it. She was all ready to go. She didn't invite him in, but stepped out and pulled the door shut behind her.

Corvin looked down at her, his dark eyes gleaming. "I wasn't expecting this."

"I know. I... wasn't either. But I had to get out and I... want to do something. Not just sit around waiting for something to happen to me."

"That's fine with me."

He touched her arm to escort her to the front of the big house, and Reg thrilled at the buzz like an electrical shock that ran all the way up her arm in a shiver. Corvin smiled. "You are indeed reckless tonight."

Reg nodded. Corvin walked with her out to his car. The big black one, not the little white compact she usually saw him in. Dates dictated the bigger car. He opened and held the door for her. The paint on the vehicle was glistening, looking like it had been hand-detailed, and the interior was freshly shampooed and vacuumed, in pristine condition. Reg slid into her seat and Corvin shut the door gently.

"Have you been to the Port of Call before?" he asked after getting into the driver's seat.

"No. I wasn't sure what kind of a place to expect." Reg appraised Corvin's dress. Dark slacks and black silk shirt with a cloak over the top. "I'm not underdressed?"

He shook his head and pulled the car out into the street. "No, you're just right. As usual."

Reg rolled her eyes at the comment.

"I take it you didn't talk to Sarah about it."

"No, certainly not. I didn't need a lecture."

"Well, I'm delighted you changed your mind. Can I ask... why? I know you said that you wanted to do something; I'm just wondering if something happened to prompt that."

"We'll talk about it over supper. I want to pick your brain."

"That seems only fair."

Reg watched out the window, not wanting to look at him. Since capturing the draugrs, she had not seen any more black cats roaming around Black Sands, but she still kept her eyes open, just in case. Maybe the Witch Doctor had created more and Reg hadn't detected them all. Or perhaps he had an apprentice who knew how to do it. Or he could still operate on some level since the kattakyns were still all together.

CHAPTER FIFTEEN

T he Harbor Port of Call was a large white house, lots of square corners
and windows, the warm light glowing from inside like a fire. Reg
stayed put as she was told while Corvin walked around the car to her door
and opened it for her. Old style manners. But she wasn't fooled. She knew
they were just a veneer over the predatory creature underneath. He dressed
up well, but a wolf in sheep's clothing was still a wolf. He escorted her up to
the door of the restaurant, and inside the hostess quickly found his reserva-
tion and escorted them to a table.

"Is this all right?" Corvin asked, giving Reg the opportunity to approve
of or reject it.

It wasn't a private room where they would be all by themselves, but in a
busy part of the restaurant, near the bar, where there would be plenty of
people coming and going. Witnesses if he tried anything. A good distraction
if she wanted to people-watch instead of visiting. He wasn't going to try
anything until it was time to go. He would be charming, but not use his
magical charms. Maybe just a little to soften her up, but the real attack
wouldn't come until later.

"Yes, this is fine."

The hostess nodded, informed them that the waiter would be coming
for their drink order in a moment, and left them alone. Reg picked one of
the chairs and sat down so that she could see people coming and going from

the bar. And she could also see one of the TVs that hung behind the bar, currently showing a baseball game.

"I assume the thing to get here is the seafood?" Reg questioned, flicking open her menu and looking at the pictures.

"Of course. Very fresh. Swimming until moments before it hits your plate."

Reg felt revulsion at his words. She liked fish and seafood, but she didn't like his cold reference to them being alive. She preferred to ignore the reality that she was eating another creature. Especially after Corvin's talk about how his drinking a person's powers was no different from her eating meat. There was a difference. Wasn't there?

She looked at the salads. Maybe something lighter. She thought about Forst and Fir and their gardens. They loved living things so much. Gnomes were vegetarian. She could anticipate their joy over eating something they had grown themselves. Something they had nurtured from a seed.

"What are you thinking about?" Corvin gazed across the table at her, his mouth curling up slightly.

"Oh… Sarah's garden gnome. I never knew they were a real thing."

"She has a gnome?"

"Well, it's not hers. He's not, I mean. He's working for her, but she doesn't own him. He's helping her with the damage that she did to the garden when she was… not well."

"They are a very ancient race," Corvin said, nodding. "Very… natural. Earthy. Anchored."

"They have…" Reg struggled to find the right words. "They don't seem to have the same prejudices about emotions that humans do. Most of the other races that I've dealt with are quite reserved; they don't show you what they're feeling. But the gnomes are… emotional. Happy or sad, they let you see it. It's very… freeing."

"You feel the need to wear a mask?"

"Doesn't everyone?"

"Some more than others."

"I guess that growing up, I was always told to suck it up. If you have a problem, you deal with it the best you can. You don't complain or tell anyone how hurt or scared you are. Nobody wants to have to deal with your problems."

"That must make it very difficult to ask anyone for help as an adult."

"Yeah. Sure does. Especially since grown-ups are supposed to be able to handle their own problems. You're supposed to be able to do everything for yourself. Make those tough decisions. Be successful. People who can't take care of themselves are… sort of a lower caste. If you're homeless or disabled or mentally ill… then you're vulnerable."

Corvin nodded. "You've had to be very tough. You've been forced to be hard, to be stubborn."

"To look out for myself." Reg remembered what Harrison had said about her gifts causing her hardships, or the hardships bringing out her gifts. Her mouth twisted into a scowl, though she tried to hide it behind the glass of water that the hostess had poured for her. She looked around for the waiter. They should have been able to place their drink orders already.

"Did something happen today?" Corvin asked. "You said we were going to talk about it."

"Harrison." Reg caught the eye of one of the waiters and gestured him over. Corvin waited for her to provide more information, but she was more interested in getting a drink. They each placed their orders, Corvin taking care this time not to offend her by ordering on her behalf, and the smiling waiter promised to be back with them in short order.

Reg sat back, waiting. She wanted something that would help to numb the feelings and calm her anxiety. She really shouldn't have broken down and agreed to see Corvin. But with his increased powers, she figured he could do pretty much whatever he wanted to, whether she let him or not.

"Harrison is back?" Corvin prompted.

"Yeah. Showed up at the cottage. I wasn't expecting him. Freaked me out to have him appear there!"

"I would imagine so. You think you're safe, not that you're going to have to defend yourself against intruders in your own home. It's locked up tight, you have protective wards; you should be allowed to have your own private space. Not to have another race sticking their noses in where they aren't wanted."

"So… how much do you know about them?"

"Them?"

"The immortals. Do you have some other name for them? Can you tell me about their history and… I don't know… explain to me how it all works."

Corvin considered this. He sipped his drink. "Well… lots of rumors and stories, but not so much that is known for certain. There have always been stories about gods, demigods, and other beings with unusual mental, psychic, or spiritual abilities walking the earth. Think of the myths of Buddha, Jesus, and whole pantheons of gods visiting the earth. What are they? Have they always been here? Are they dying out?" He shrugged. "There are more questions than answers."

"That's not at all helpful. You must know something about them... their interactions with humans. Their powers, their rules..."

"I don't think there are a lot of rules, to tell the truth. They seem to do pretty much what they want."

"Harrison said that they weren't allowed to hurt each other."

"But throughout history, we have stories that say that they did. There are a lot of stories of wars, battles, and jealousies between them. There may be rules against it, but I don't think that stops them."

"That's kind of what he said," Reg agreed. "Just like enacting laws doesn't keep people from breaking them. But what about punishments? Are there consequences for breaking the rules? Or can they interfere with humans however they like, and no one cares?"

"Most of the rules are about their interaction with each other, not with humans. I think humans are pretty... inconsequential to them. We are fragile, short-lived creatures. There are too many of us. We're more like cockroaches to them then than cousins."

"Except we don't procreate with cockroaches."

Corvin's brows went up. "No. That's true. There have been punishments and consequences... immortals bound or banished... efforts to curtail their powers by cutting them into pieces so that they can't re-form. But on the whole... the stories make them seem more like petty children than all-powerful beings."

Reg looked away, thinking about that. Corvin's words resonated with her. Harrison was childlike in many ways. And if there were no consequences for them, why would they be any different? They could afford to do whatever they liked.

She watched a couple of women at the bar. They were stunningly beautiful. One was blond, but it seemed like something had reacted with her bleach, because it had a greenish tint to it. When she moved and her skin caught the light, it too seemed slightly green and iridescent. Was she a fairy? Reg had never seen fairies in such a casual setting. They didn't associate with humans in that way, and whatever interactions they had with each other were out of sight. Reg imagined they were stiff and formal even in private, as she had seen them in public.

The other woman was a brunette, with hair in long, loose curls that fell around her face and shoulders. She had a white sheath dress with a neckline that plunged so far Reg could hardly pull her eyes away.

The waiter returned to take their dinner orders. Reg pointed to a picture, answered his questions about how she wanted the fish steaks prepared and what sides she wanted. Corvin placed his order, long and detailed. The waiter collected their menus and left them alone once more. Reg looked back at Corvin, sighing.

"You must know more," she said. "You took the Witch Doctor's powers. So you know a lot more about what they can do. Maybe you got some memories or instincts from him too. What did you learn?"

Corvin tapped his glass with his fingernail, considering. He gave her a warm smile, and Reg felt her attention sliding away as she started to admire his facial features, the warmth around him, the memories of that one night coming back and tempting her to spend another with him. She looked away and carefully built a wall to keep his charms out. She told herself that she couldn't feel them. He was just a man like any other, and she was trying to have a conversation with him. He was distracting her for a reason.

"Quit that and answer my question. I'm not going to forget what I asked."

He looked at her for a moment, waiting for his magic to overcome her, then dropped his gaze.

"There are problems with imbibing so much power," he admitted. "I don't have the same clarity of purpose and ability to control it. Like trying to carry too much at a time, it gets heavy and unwieldy. Or when you have eaten a big meal, and instead of feeling pleasant and satiated, it just hurts, and you want it out again."

"Really." She studied him, reading his face for the truth. Was it just another of his lines, trying to make her feel sorry for him so that he would yield to him? "So you want to give up some of your powers?"

He smiled at her. "You want some?"

On the one hand, it made her curious. Could she take on someone else's powers like he had taken on hers if he offered them to her? She remembered how it had been when he'd fed his own back into her. Could he do that with any of the powers he held? Not just her own?

But she also knew that the moment he put his hands on her or pulled her in for a kiss, she would be in his control. She wouldn't be able to stop him from taking her powers instead of giving her his.

"No. That doesn't sound like a good idea."

He nodded his understanding. "It is hard to sort through what I have and to figure out how to use them and put them to the best use. It's easier in times of emotion. When I was angry and fighting him, that's when instinct took over, and I just did what came naturally."

"Is that what it's like for them? Are they more powerful or capable when they are angry?"

"Perhaps. I'm not sure. History would suggest that they can be very powerful and cruel when in a temper. They can do things that they would come to regret later."

They people-watched in silence, considering the conversation but not speaking. Reg was fascinated by the two women at the bar. All of the men who entered their orbit seemed to be entranced by them. Not just interested in a couple of beautiful faces and bodies, but under a spell, like Corvin held over women.

"Who are they?" Reg asked, noticing that Corvin was watching them as well. He seemed to be far enough away not to be taken in by them, but he was still interested. "Do you know them?"

"I don't know them, no… They don't usually hunt here."

Reg swallowed. "Hunt? Are they… like you, then?"

"No." He shook his head but took no offense at her words. "Not like me. They don't want powers; they want flesh."

"Ick. Really? I assume you're not just talking about… the seafood."

"No. If they try to take anyone from here, the management will stop them, have them ejected. But if they lay in wait outside… they might drag some poor soul away without being caught."

"How can you sit there and let it go on? Shouldn't we do something?"

"Do what?"

"You're the one with powers. Why don't you… tell them to get out of here and not come back. Why don't you magick them into leaving and make it so they are distracted if they ever think of coming here again. You can't just let them…"

"They haven't done anything. It isn't against any law for them to sit in a restaurant. No one can do anything unless they try to drag someone out. And even then... it's hard to do anything but tell them they're breaking the treaty and have to return to the water."

"What are they, then? Some kind of water fairies? What are those water spirits called, naiads?"

"No, they are not naiads, although the naiads would probably act similarly if they were able to go far from their springs and slews."

"What, then?"

"You can't guess?" he challenged.

Reg looked back at them again. She had always enjoyed learning about mythology, but she had a hard time wrapping her mind around the fairy tales and myths becoming real in Black Sands. It was one thing to read a children's story for enjoyment, but quite another to be confronted with monsters and immortals in real life.

"No, just tell me. What are they?"

"The green one is a mermaid. The brunette is a siren."

Reg immediately craned her neck to see the green woman's feet. She was wearing high heeled pumps, a brilliant jade green, but had feet just like any other woman.

"They don't have flippers out of the water," Corvin told her with a grin. "And actually, having them even in water is pretty rare. A recessive gene mutation. Of course, those are the ones sailors could recognize readily, so those are the ones who got all of the attention in literature and art."

"She's a mermaid?"

"You don't think so?"

"Well... I guess so. I just didn't know." She looked at the brunette. "I don't remember much about sirens. They have a powerful song that can distract sailors and make them jump into the ocean."

Corvin nodded. "Yes. Two beautiful races with all the wiles necessary to capture a man."

"But aren't there male mermaids and sirens? Mermen and... I don't know. Guy sirens."

"In some cases, yes; but they are not the hunters. It is the women who... bring home the bacon... so to speak."

"Ugh." Reg grimaced. Was he expecting her to eat? All of the talk about predators and flesh was getting to her. She wasn't sure she'd even be able to look at the fish when the waiter brought it to her. She should have done as she had planned and gone with a salad.

She averted her eyes and shook her head. No more watching the two women. She couldn't bear to watch them tempt some man out of the restaurant and then to try to drag him into the ocean.

When she'd been read fairy tales as a child, she'd always thought how amazing the magical world sounded. So many treasures, magic that turned people beautiful or made them fall in love, talking animals, fairy princesses. Of course, there were also children being lured into the forest to be eaten by a witch or some ferocious beast.

Reg had always told herself that she couldn't be tricked like that. She would always leave a trail back home, and if any old hag tried to hurt her, Reg would punch her straight in the nose and run like hell.

CHAPTER SIXTEEN

Despite her misgivings, Reg's stomach rumbled when the waiter set her dinner plate in front of her. She inhaled the fragrant steam and sighed. "This is the best. I don't think I could ever be vegetarian."

Corvin eyed her. She knew what he was thinking, but he kept the comment to himself. She didn't need him to remind her that she was confirming what he had told her before. That it was in his nature to consume the powers of others just as much as it was in her nature to eat the fish that was on the plate in front of her. Changing that about him would have been trying to change what he was. And no one could change what he was. It was built into his genetic code. If genes were how magical nature was passed from father to son.

They ate in silence for a few minutes, each appreciating their meals. Corvin took a drink.

"So what did you learn from Harrison? Did he tell you anything, or was it all just more questions?"

Reg sighed. "He answered some things. But they were things I didn't want to know. The things that I want to understand, he doesn't answer or says he doesn't know, which is stupid, because he's supposed to be all-knowing and all-powerful, isn't he?"

Corvin cut a neat bite out of his scallops. "I think you're confusing immortals with the Christian god. The Greeks and other cultures with a pantheon of gods never claimed that they were all-knowing or all-powerful. Sometimes they were remarkably short-sighted. They just claimed that they couldn't be killed, or if they could, it was only temporary."

"So Harrison doesn't know everything."

"Obviously not."

"Just like the Witch Doctor didn't know where to find Weston."

Corvin looked up at that. He laid down his fork for a moment. "And who, may I ask, is Weston?"

"You don't know him?"

"How would I know him?"

"I thought if there were stories about all of these immortals, you would already know who he was. There aren't any stories about him?"

"I don't know. They are often known by many different names. They might have different names and different roles in one culture. And then when you add in multiple cultures, there are even more. I would have to know more about his nature and the things he has done. Then I might be able to figure out his other names."

"I don't know much about him. I know that he's… not exactly hiding from the Witch Doctor, but hidden. He broke the rules and so he was bound. Or bound himself. Somehow there was a consequence, and he was hidden from the others."

"Who wanted to do what to him?"

"He and Harrison are friends, I think. But the Witch Doctor is an enemy, and he hoped to destroy Weston while he was still… in hibernation or whatever kind of state he was in. But the Witch Doctor couldn't find him, and Weston didn't manage to get out of this prison he's in. Harrison and the Witch Doctor thought that he would be near Norma Jean so that she could let him out. But he wasn't. Or if he was, they couldn't find him. That's why… the Witch Doctor killed her. Or why he tortured her, anyway. I think he killed her just because he could."

Corvin nodded, scratching his whiskered chin. "That's all very interesting… so he's been banished or bound… but they expected him to build a back door, or to be able to escape from it by now. Maybe years ago."

Reg nodded.

"And why were you and Harrison talking about Weston? Why didn't you want to know about him? Or was it just unimportant information and you wanted something that affected you."

Reg looked down at her plate and toyed with the next bite of fish, wondering how much she wanted to reveal to Corvin. If he knew enough, he might be willing to help and might have some relevant information. But she didn't like to share anything about her personal life, and particularly about the immortal who now appeared to be her father.

"It seems like his fate is tied up with mine," she hedged.

That wasn't a lie. And if he thought about it, then it was apparent that Weston's existence had affected Reg and the course of her life. Things would have been very different for her if she had grown up with her biological mother.

"And... what? Do you need to find him? Do you have a mission? Harrison thinks that when Weston comes back, it will affect you somehow?"

"I don't know. So... can I change the topic? I don't know much more about Weston, but I had another question."

"Okay... what is it?"

Reg furrowed her brow, thinking about what she wanted and what he might know. "I have questions about cats. Particularly about Starlight."

"I don't know anything about cats."

"Of course you do. You know about everything. At least some things about everything."

He smiled tolerantly. "You think that buttering me up will get me to answer your questions?"

"Of course. You have a big ego. You won't be able to help yourself."

"Wanna bet?"

Reg looked at him, waiting. She didn't look away. Eventually, he broke.

"What exactly do you want to know about cats, and Starlight in particular?"

"You said once that maybe Starlight was a reincarnate. That he had been a human in a previous life."

"I don't remember that. I was probably joking."

"Does that mean that cats *can't* be reincarnated humans?"

"No. Of course he could be."

"How would we be able to tell?"

"Sometimes there are clues in a person's or animal's behavior as to who they were in a previous life. If that soul was very strong."

"I'm pretty sure that Starlight was someone Harrison used to know in a past life."

"It's not out of the realm of possibility. As an immortal, Harrison has likely been around for a very long time."

Reg's brain jumped ahead and she discarded her planned question to address that. "How long have immortals been around? Are there… new immortals and old ones? Where do new ones come from?"

"I don't claim to know much about immortal physiology or reproduction. I imagine they are created in much the same way as humans."

"I don't think so. Harrison was pretty ambiguous about… conception."

Corvin's eyes twinkled. "You brought it up with him?"

"In Greek mythology, the gods weren't all conceived and born like humans, were they? Didn't Athena… spring full-grown from Zeus's head?"

"Yes. And there were also cases of demigods or creatures being born from the sea or other non-human, non-god parents," Corvin admitted.

"So maybe it isn't exactly like with humans. Maybe they can create offspring as they like. Or through various means."

"Maybe."

"So their progeny might not have their DNA. Or their powers."

"I thought we were talking about cats."

"We—oh yeah. I got sidetracked." Reg shook her head. If she pursued the subject of children of the immortals, Corvin was bound to start wondering why. "So… cats as reincarnated humans. Do you think Starlight really could have been a human in a previous life?"

"Sure he could. But why does it matter? In this life, he's a cat."

"Harrison said that he was a very ancient, wise soul."

"Great. So you have a very ancient, wise soul in the body of a cat. He still acts like a cat. He still is a cat. What has changed?"

"Well… I don't know. Do you think *he* could be Weston?"

"Immortals don't die, let alone get reincarnated as cats."

"But if the Witch Doctor could be turned into nine kittens, then why couldn't Weston be a cat too?"

"Well, that's not precisely what happened. The Witch Doctor's power and presence was sent into the draugr kattakyns, and so—"

"So now he's nine kittens," Reg said flatly.

"Well, okay. Now he's nine kittens."

"So why couldn't Weston be one cat? Maybe someone turned him into a cat. Maybe he turned himself into a cat or put his soul into a cat."

"What makes you think that Weston is Starlight?"

"Well… the way that he responded to me at the animal shelter, when he didn't respond to anyone else. He picked me out more than I picked him. Maybe that's because I'm his… our fates are intertwined. Maybe he somehow planned this, that I would meet him in his next life as a cat, and then… I don't know. I have no idea what would happen next."

"You would pet him and feed him and change his litter box for him."

Reg wrinkled her nose. "Corvin!"

"He's a cat. Like I said, if he is Weston, then what changes?"

"I don't know. Maybe he… can communicate with me. Tell me about what happened in his past life. Why he did what he did."

"Which was…?"

Reg wasn't about to reveal any of that. "Break the rules. Become bound. And then… I don't know. If I knew, I wouldn't have to ask him."

"Right." Corvin took a few more bites of his meal. "This is quite a metaphysical discussion for the Port of Call."

"Would it be better somewhere else?"

"At your cottage," he said promptly. "You could even involve Starlight in the conversation if you like. You could take him home a piece of fish and tell him that you wouldn't give it to him until he told you all about his previous life."

"How would he tell me?"

"I assume… telepathically. Since he can't hold a pencil or speak."

"But he doesn't communicate telepathically. I mean, he communicates psychically sometimes, but not in words and sentences. Just in… feelings… nudges."

"Then how do you expect him to tell you about his previous life, whether it was as Weston or someone else?"

Reg sighed. "I don't know. It was just an idea."

"Harrison is the one who can answer your questions, not Starlight."

"And he won't. Or he doesn't. He pretends that he does, giving me some vague or impossible answer, and then smiles like he just gave me the wisdom of the ages. It's frustrating."

"Maybe you and I could put our heads together and come up with something. After all, I do have the powers of an immortal. Maybe I can… compel him."

"I don't think they can compel each other to do anything, do you?"

"No," he admitted, "probably not. But it would still be fun to try."

"By putting our heads together, do you mean putting all of my power into your head?"

"Now, there is an entrancing idea."

"No. Forget it. I came out to dinner with you to keep you company, not to give you my powers."

He motioned to the waiter for another drink. "Don't you find it… cumbersome? Don't those powers weigh down on you at times? It is a big responsibility, and using them takes so much energy out of you…"

His words were soothing and persuasive. Reg caught herself thinking about what it would be like to be a normal human without any psychic powers. How nice it would be to have her brain to herself and not have to worry about all of the other voices.

She pushed back against the idea, scowling at Corvin. "I know what it's like to have them taken away, and it didn't feel good. It didn't feel freeing or nice at all. It was horrible."

For a brief moment, his brows pushed down and the corners of his mouth fell as if he too were remembering what it was like to be drained of powers and be left with nothing but hollowness inside. He quickly masked the expression and looked away from Reg. The waiter brought Corvin a refill and he sipped it, looking over at the bar to see how the ladies were faring.

Reg didn't want to look, but felt compelled. She turned her head and saw that there was a sailor or fisherman with them, his movements drunk and sloppy, leaning on the bar and practically crawling into the siren's lap. He was drooling slightly, his eyes wide and gaze fixed.

"Uh-oh," Reg said.

"Looks like they've got one on the hook," Corvin observed. He lifted his chin and caught the eye of the bartender farther down the bar. The bartender nodded that he was aware of the situation. Corvin looked back at Reg.

"I would normally want to linger over coffee. But I think we might want to leave before things get ugly."

They had both made short work of their meals. And he was right; she didn't like to rush out, but she also didn't want to see what happened to the man or to the mermaid and siren. It wasn't going to be pretty.

"Yeah. I think we should."

"We can stop in for coffee or a drink somewhere else."

Reg nodded her agreement. Corvin raised a hand to signal one of the waiters. Things were suddenly very busy, but the waiter came over, eyebrows raised.

"Your bill?" he suggested.

Corvin inclined his head. "Please."

"Everybody wants to clear out of here all of a sudden," the young man observed. He glanced over his shoulder toward the bar, sweat glistening on his forehead.

"Why don't you call the police?" Reg demanded. "Say that they're being disruptive or acting suspiciously."

"I'm just a waiter, ma'am, I'm not in charge here."

"Nothing the police could do," Corvin advised. "They would come here, see a couple of lovely women, and probably kick the sailor out. They wouldn't understand what is going on."

"Why isn't there a magical police force? This is ridiculous. Everybody knows what's happening; why do they act like ostriches, sticking their heads in the sand?"

"You know, I don't think ostriches actually do that."

Reg glowered at him.

The waiter tapped their order into a hand-held credit card terminal and handed it to Corvin. He glanced at it, punched a few buttons and, in a moment, the waiter was handing him a receipt. They got up and made their way toward the door, along with several other couples who were looking pale and anxious.

"There is no magical police force because it would never work," Corvin explained, as they hit the cool night air and walked toward the car. "It's been tried in several different forms. Humans are the most interested in such things, but you can't have a group of humans administering justice for a dozen different races. It doesn't work. What you end up with isn't just racial prejudice, but war. We have treaties that are supposed to give each race the autonomy they need to follow their cultural norms and physical needs.

Allow us to live side-by-side without interfering with each other's rights and freedoms any more than necessary."

"And that includes letting a sailor be dragged out of a restaurant by a mermaid and a siren? To be killed and eaten?"

"No. I told you, they will take action once the ladies reach that point. They'll do their best to see to the safety of that man. But until they attempt to take him, they haven't done anything wrong."

Reg got into the car when he opened the door for her. She sat with her lips pressed tightly shut, not saying all of the things that she wanted to. They needed to overhaul their entire system. How could there not be a way to stop the mermaid and the siren from doing what they were?

"Look," Corvin said after he got in and started the engine. "Even if all of the parties involved were human, what would you suggest doing? The police can't arrest someone they think is a serial killer without some evidence. They can't just take a call from a little old lady who thinks that her neighbor is up to no good and go out and arrest him. They can investigate, but they need evidence of wrongdoing before they can take any action. You can't arrest someone because you think they looked at a child the wrong way. You need to wait until he takes some action to kidnap or harm the child. You can't arrest someone you think is going to drink too much and get into their car until they actually get behind the wheel. We can't do anything about the mermaid and the siren until they do something that crosses the boundaries. And those boundaries have become very strictly defined over the past centuries."

"People take matters into their own hands all the time. Vigilantes. Cops who think they know better. Why isn't there anyone in there who dares to do what is right?"

"They are doing what is right. None of us like it, but you can't do anything about what people are thinking. You can't just start killing every mermaid who shows up in a bar, or go out hunting and killing every mermaid within a hundred-mile radius to ensure that they don't encroach on the land. Those things have been done in the past, and it doesn't make us safer. It just increases the violence between our societies. More people will get killed in a war with the mermaids than are killed by their hunting."

"That's ridiculous."

"I didn't see you walking up to them and challenging them to a battle."

"I don't mean that. I mean… telling them to leave. You can tell someone to move on. Homeless people get kicked out of stores and restaurants all the time. Owners have the right to refuse them service."

"And do you think that a mermaid is just going to agree to leave? They are a bloody race, Reg. A bloody, violent race. Don't get caught up by all of the Disney sweetness. They make movies about cuddly lions and bears, too. Does that make them good pets for your children?"

CHAPTER SEVENTEEN

Reg brooded silently as they drove to a small coffee house and sat down. When she had her coffee in front of her, Reg couldn't hold it inside any longer.

"You know what? I hate this place. I regret that I ever came here. I thought that I was coming to a nice little town with a higher-than-normal population of confidence scams relating to magic. I didn't expect to find... real magic, predatory magical races, and dangers out of a fairy tale. I just wanted to live a nice quiet life and be able to make a good living for once."

"And instead, you find pixies and draugar and mermaids," Corvin finished.

"Exactly. All of these things, when you read about them in children's books, they are so much fun. You think that living in a fairy world would be... magical—beautiful happily-ever-after endings for everyone. But fairies aren't cute little sparkly creatures flying around your head and granting wishes. They're..."

"Haughty and self-absorbed and rarely care to have any interaction with humans."

"Yeah." Reg thought about Lord Bernier and knew that she was being unfair. He hadn't had to step in to save her from Corvin or to appear at his hearing to testify against him. That had been his choice, and even if he did think of her as a child, he had done what was right when nobody had asked him to. And she remembered how the pixie Karol Blackmoor had been so intent on getting her sister back, on reversing the spell that had turned Calliopia into a fairy so that she could return to her pixie family. The other races had good qualities too, even if they were not kindly disposed toward humans. "I don't know what to think. It's so different from what I expected. And from what I would have expected if I had known that there was real magic and real fairies and everything. I want it to be normal, or to be... non-violent, with everyone living together harmoniously."

"Have you ever been in a family where everyone got along together without any arguing or fighting?" Corvin challenged.

Reg laughed. "No! Not even close."

"And they were all human—or at least, I assume they were. If humans cannot even get along with each other without conflict, how do you expect humans and other races to live together without running into some problems?"

"I don't know. Disney again, I guess. In the movies, you have good and bad, but the dividing lines are obvious. The humans are always going to be on the side of good, except for one or two bad apples. And the fairies are good. You might have trolls or mischievous elves, but they can always be defeated by the good guys in a single battle. You know who the bad guys are because they wear black and are accompanied by ominous music and evil laughter."

"Well, that would all make real life pretty interesting. But in real life, you don't have one race that is good and one that is bad. They each have their good points and bad. Things that conflict with each other's societies. You have to make compromises and rules if you are going to live side-by-side as peacefully as possible."

Reg nodded. She was beginning to see that he was right. They had developed their interspecies laws and treaties over many years, coming to the best compromises and set of rules that they could.

But she didn't have to like it.

"And the bad guys aren't always wearing black," Corvin pointed out with a smile.

Reg was reminded that he was dressed all in black, as he usually was.

At least Disney got that part right.

She took a long sip of her coffee. She probably shouldn't be drinking coffee so late in the day, but she was becoming resigned to the fact that she wouldn't get to sleep until two or three in the morning anyway, so there was no need to curtail her caffeine intake just because it was early evening.

"And then there are immortals," she said bitterly, "who apparently don't need to follow any rules about interacting with humans, other than not having babies with them."

Corvin's brows went up.

The bells over the coffee shop jangled and Reg let herself be distracted, glancing over to see who had come in. Someone safe or another magical race that was going to cause conflict? A human sitting down to visit with family or friends or to read a book? Or a troll intent on raising havoc?

Or worse yet… it was Damon.

Damon saw Reg a moment after she saw him. He wasn't pleased. Reg felt herself flush. How many times had she told him that she didn't want anything to do with Corvin and she wasn't going to get involved with him? And yet, there she was, sitting with him in an intimate little after-dinner conversation. As if they were best friends and she didn't have a care in the world. As if he couldn't consume her powers, leaving her an empty husk.

Corvin took in Reg's reaction and turned in his seat to see who had just come in. His mouth tightened and, for a moment, she was sure that he was going to accuse her of inviting Damon to join her.

Damon was by himself. He hesitated for a moment, looking at Reg and Corvin, then went up to the counter to place his order. Reg looked for something to say to Corvin to hide the fact that they were both waiting to see what Damon was going to do. She couldn't manage to pick up the thread of the conversation again. After Damon got his large cup of coffee, he walked over to their table.

"Reg, good to see you. I didn't know you were going to be here."

"Uh… neither did I. We just…" She didn't want to describe the scene at the Port of Call or to tell him that she and Corvin had not just gone out for coffee, but for dinner too.

"Just coincidence," Corvin said smoothly. "We hadn't particularly made plans to be here."

"You just met up by accident, then? Ran into each other?"

He was looking at Reg, not Corvin. Reg didn't answer. If she lied, he would know it.

"How about you?" Corvin asked. "Just out to top off the gas? Not meeting anyone?"

Reg felt the subtle jab. Corvin was there with Reg, who Damon had been dating, and Damon was there all alone.

"I was guarding at the Conjurecraft Conference all day. Surprised I didn't see you there." Damon allowed a couple of beats to pass. "Oh, right. You don't currently hold membership in any coven."

Ouch. Reg could see Corvin grinding his teeth and could feel the anger rising off of him. Damon shouldn't be provoking him like that, but Corvin *had* started it. The trouble was, if Corvin blew, who knew what kind of harm he could do to Damon. He had already observed that his magic was easier to manage when he was angry.

Reg looked from one to the other anxiously. Had she escaped the violence at the Port of Call only to have to witness a war between the two warlocks? She cleared her throat and addressed them in a voice that pretended to be much more confident than it was.

"Put the wands away, boys. I can talk to who I want to. I don't belong to either one of you."

Neither of them was willing to back down first. Reg raised her eyebrows and gave them both a stern look. She wished that she could manage 'the look' that foster moms had always given her. That one that would make even the most stubborn and recalcitrant teen back down and drop his eyes.

It was Damon who broke first. He looked away from Reg.

"I know I don't own you," he agreed. "It isn't that. I'm just concerned about you. We both know how dangerous Hunter can be…"

"It's my choice who I associate with and whether I ask for your help or not. And I didn't."

"I don't get it. You're willing to become his thrall? You give up?"

"I haven't given up. But I'm tired of running away. I don't like running."

Damon eyed Corvin, who sat back with a smirk that indicated he had won the contest and Reg had chosen him.

"You think you're so slick?" Damon demanded. He threw a card down on the table in front of Corvin. "She's seeing Davyn Smithy too. Did you know that?"

Corvin's eyes dropped to the business card and he frowned. He looked back at Reg. She was not about to explain to him why she had met with Davyn. Just thinking about the meeting made her feel sick, especially when she remembered how hard she had pushed back, insisting that they needed to do something to protect people from Corvin, and there she was sitting across from him as if her words had meant nothing at all.

Corvin and Damon obviously interpreted her guilty look to mean something else. Both of them were now angry not just at each other, but at her.

"Look," she said, "I can meet with who I want about what I want. It's none of your business. I don't have a relationship with Davyn Smithy. I could, if I wanted to, though, and neither of you would have any say in it."

Neither of them had to like it either. Clearly, they didn't. That was fine with Reg. If they were both going to be so jealous and act like teenage boys, then maybe she needed to find someone who was more mature and able to have a trusting relationship with her. She shook her head.

"I'm going to get a cab home. This is ridiculous."

"So you didn't just run into each other here," Damon said triumphantly.

"I didn't say we did. Back off, Damon. If you're going to keep showing up and accusing me of having relationships with other people, then I've had it. Enough is enough. I'm done with you. I'm done with both of you."

She stood up. Luckily, her path was unimpeded; she didn't need Corvin or Damon to move out of the way for her. She walked away from them, feeling grimly satisfied with herself. She didn't have to choose between them. She didn't have to date either one of them. If they thought that fighting over her was going to get her worked up, they were wrong. The rivalry didn't excite her.

She assumed that once she had walked away from them, there would be no point in their continuing the conversation. Damon would pick up his coffee and walk out. Corvin would finish his or leave it on the table, and with a shrug, get back into his big black car and go home. Or maybe back to the Port of Call to see how things had ended up there.

There was a long moment of silence, as she assumed they both watched her walk away and decided that pursuit wasn't going to bring her back. But then Corvin let out an incoherent shout of anger, and Reg whirled around to protect herself from attack.

Corvin swept the little table out of his way so that there was only empty space between him and Damon. Damon was looking at him, but not defending himself, not acting like there was any danger in his standing there.

Whatever Corvin was seeing enraged him. He clawed at the air in front of him, making grunts of protest and tried to shove something invisible out of the way. Reg blinked. Damon was feeding a vision into Corvin's head, but Reg didn't know what it was. She couldn't see it herself, even when she strained for a glimpse. Damon kept her blocked out.

Corvin fought more frantically. Damon grinned, thoroughly enjoying himself as he watched Corvin fight the empty air in front of him. Reg tried to signal to him to stop. Nothing good could come of enraging Corvin. Especially not with the increase in his powers.

Then Corvin apparently broke through the vision, and he knew exactly what had happened and where the images had come from. He launched himself at Damon and, even though Reg was several steps away, she flinched and backed away as far as she could. There were a few other customers in the shop watching with wide-eyed interest. The baristas ducked behind the counter and then peeked over it to keep an eye on the action. Reg didn't know if anyone was calling the police yet, but it wouldn't be long before the thought occurred to someone.

But she was more concerned about what damage Corvin could do to Damon than anything else. She watched them anxiously. If it was just a physical fight, she didn't need to worry. But if Corvin unleashed his magic on his opponent, there could be dire consequences.

"Corvin. Corvin!"

She had to yell to make herself heard over their scuffling, growls, and curses. Corvin looked across the room at Reg, scowling. Like he couldn't understand what she would be objecting to.

"Just stop," Reg urged. "Come on; this is stupid."

"He is an untrained young pup who ought to learn to have some respect for his elders!" Corvin snapped.

Damon laughed. "I should have respect for you? For someone who has no powers of his own and only steals them from others? You are the lowest kind of witch. A bottom feeder."

Corvin swept his hand toward Damon, and Reg saw in a fraction of an instant that he wasn't just waving him away. She could see the energy gather around Corvin's hand, and she was immediately there, holding him back.

But not physically. She hadn't actually moved from her spot. She stopped him without moving a muscle.

Corvin looked across the room at her again, furious at her holding him back. She could feel him struggling to break free of her psychic hold, going rapidly through his new powers and gifts to find one that would combat her hold on him. It wouldn't be long before he succeeded.

Damon had ducked, also sensing the magical energy that Corvin had been about to throw in his direction. The Witch Doctor had nearly killed Damon. Maybe Corvin would have gotten the job done.

When Damon realized that something had stopped Corvin and was holding him back, he looked around, eyes wide. He realized that it was Reg's doing and laughed again.

"Looks like you've got your hands full with this one," he mocked Corvin. "She's no damsel in distress. Good luck with that!"

"Just get out of here, Damon," Reg urged. "I don't know how long I can do this."

Damon took his time getting to the door. He looked back one last time before exiting, smirking at Corvin. Then he was gone.

CHAPTER EIGHTEEN

When Damon was gone, Reg looked at Corvin uncertainly. She wasn't sure what would happen when she released him from her hold. Her upbringing had trained her to run when there was trouble, and she prepared to do that. But before she could let go of him, she felt Corvin's effort slacken, and he stopped fighting her. Reg released her hold and watched him warily, measuring the distance to the door. Unfortunately, he had a car and she didn't. But she could get through narrow alleys and jump fences. There were ways to lose a car if she had enough lead time.

"What a little weasel," Corvin said, shaking his head.

Reg still didn't move. Around them, people were starting to talk again, still watching covertly. The baristas were popping up behind the counter.

"We should probably go," Reg suggested.

"Shall we try for restaurant number three?"

"Please, no."

Corvin chuckled. He lifted the table he had knocked down and put it back in place. He arranged the chairs around it. There was coffee all over the floor from their spilled drinks, but Reg's and Corvin's mugs had not broken. They probably saw a lot of rough handling throughout the day and they were very sturdy. Corvin went up to the counter and pulled several bills out of his wallet, handing them to the nearest employee.

"Sorry about that. And the mess."

The employee took the money, nodding wordlessly. Corvin touched Reg lightly on the back, sending an electrical shock straight up her spine, and they walked out to his car. He silently opened and held her door for her and then got into the driver's seat.

"Well," he said eventually, when they had almost reached Reg's house. "That was an eventful evening."

"It was. I guess… I learned a lot." She closed her eyes, thinking about Damon, who she was sure would not be knocking on her door again. And Corvin, who would now expect to be invited into the cottage, but she couldn't take that risk. She'd done enough risky things for one evening and, while she had been able to hold Corvin back, she wasn't sure how much longer her power would last. Then she wouldn't be able to prevent him from charming her. "What a night."

"I'm sorry it ended on such a sour note." Corvin looked over at Reg, his expression sheepish. "I don't generally… act that way. I know I have a temper, but I usually control it better."

"You probably don't usually have someone feeding images directly into your brain, either. What exactly did he show you?"

"Despite what he did, I should still have kept it under control. What is he? Just an untrained young pup trying out his powers and showing off for a girl. I've been around longer than his parents. You would think that my experience would give me some control."

She had seen him so angry before. But not violent. When he fought the Witch Doctor, he had been powerful and focused, but not out of control. Reg held her hands together in her lap to stop them from vibrating. The whole thing had shaken her up far more than she would like to admit. She wanted to think that she was tough and unflappable, that she could deal with anything. But a physical threat still sent her into a tailspin, flashing back to the violence she had seen or experienced as a child.

Corvin pulled in front of Sarah's house. He looked at her. "Are you all right?"

"I'll be fine. Watch an old movie before bed to relax. Have some tea." Or some whiskey. That might help her to sleep better.

"I know that we're not… an item, Regina… but I can't help feeling possessive. Not just because you're attractive and I like you, but also because of your gifts. I can't help feeling like they should be mine. They were mine, once."

"You held them for a little while, but they were not yours. You took them away from me. You didn't own them and you still don't."

"I paid for them. I compensated you."

"We had a nice evening. That's all. That doesn't mean I owe you anything, especially my powers. So get over it."

He frowned deeply, but he didn't try to argue the point. Maybe he was starting to come around.

Or maybe he was just tired from the fight.

"Can I walk you to your door?"

Reg took a deep breath and let it out. "No magic and you're not coming inside."

"Deal."

She looked over at him, frowning, wondering whether she could trust anything he said. Not that she'd ever been able to. Eventually, she nodded. "Okay. You control yourself."

He didn't touch her as he escorted her down the sidewalk to the cottage, maybe sensing that she would object.

At the door, he hovered close, looking down at her, and she felt his warmth. That feeling of contentment and attraction that she felt whenever he walked into a room. She'd been able to ignore it most of the rest of the night, especially when violence had been threatened, but now that they were at her door, and it was dark, and she was coming down from the adrenaline rush, she was especially vulnerable.

"You should go home now," she told him.

"I will. You sure you'll be okay tonight?"

"You're not coming in."

"I'm sorry for the way things ended up. I shouldn't have lost my temper so badly."

"Yeah. It would have been nice if the two of you could have behaved like mature adults instead of children."

She hadn't seen him move any closer, yet she was sure he had. She could feel his breath on her and the cloying scent of roses was coming off his skin. "No. You said you wouldn't use any magic."

"I can't help my body's autonomic responses. I'm not doing anything to you."

"You can control it. You've said so before."

"Not everything. Some things… a man can't help feeling…"

She pushed him back mentally. It was an effort, after the eventful evening. She tried to build a psychic wall around herself. She could barely find the strength. She tried harder, remembering the feeling of Harrison's protective spell around her. Corvin pushed closer, almost pinning Reg to the door. She fumbled for the doorknob.

"Back off, Corvin. Give me some air."

"Regina…"

She gave one final mental shove. He stepped back, but in a moment had recovered his balance and was back. He took the key from her and tried to fit it into the lock, then looked at it, holding it up in front of his face, frowning.

"What key is this? Where is your house key?" He handed it back.

Reg patted at her pockets, then shoved her hand into her purse and stirred it around, feeling for the ring of keys and listening for the tell-tale clink, keeping her eyes on him. Corvin pulled the purse from her and looked inside.

"What a rat's nest. Here they are." He fished the keys out and fit the house key to the doorknob lock. He pushed it open behind her. Reg stumbled in. It was a relief to get far enough away from him that his breath wasn't right in her face. She felt behind her, moving like she was blind and had never seen the room before. She needed to get in far enough to close the door and then she could relax.

Corvin stepped through the doorway.

Reg gasped in shock. She took another step back. "I didn't invite you in!"

He just smiled.

Reg swore, looking around, trying to figure out a way to defend herself. She didn't carry a weapon or keep one in the cottage. She didn't even have a pocketknife or broken bottle. But she did have a kitchen! Reg moved toward it, keeping her eyes on Corvin, keeping plenty of space between them. The room was already filling with the floral scent, getting more and more stifling. Reg fought back against her natural reaction, telling herself that it was a skunk. It was unpleasant. She didn't want to smell it, and it didn't make her feel good.

She wasn't attracted to Corvin; she didn't have to surrender to him.

"Calm down, Regina," he said softly. "I'm not going to hurt you. Forget about all of that. You and I can be friends. We can sit down and have a chat. I want to make sure that you're all right. You're very pale. It wouldn't be responsible for me to leave you here by yourself without making sure you are okay."

Reg's feet touched the tile of the kitchen. She was close. She darted a glance to the side to measure the distance to the knife drawer, the angle of access, planning in her head how she would move and which knife she would pull.

As much as she abhorred the violence of the evening, she would do whatever she had to to protect herself. She wasn't going to give way to him this time. She was stronger. She had her replica of Harrison's protection spell.

Harrison!

Reg thought of him there in the living room, sitting on the couch, his long legs out, Starlight in his lap. He had been there not twenty-four hours before. She should have asked him for his help in more practical matters. How to protect herself. How to cast simple spells. Instead of having meta-physical discussions about immortals.

"I think it's time for you to leave."

Corvin whirled around and looked at Harrison sitting on the couch, his long legs stretched out in front of him. He had on his striped shirt this time, looking like a mime, an escaped prisoner, or the juggler at a circus. He smiled at Corvin and twisted the ends of his large mustache.

"What are you doing here?" Corvin demanded. "No one was here; we were alone." Frustration had entered his voice. Reg couldn't help smiling at Corvin's tone of betrayal.

"Reg wanted me," Harrison said with a shrug. "Something about a protective spell?"

"Yes," Reg agreed. "I needed your help. I don't know how to cast a spell. I'm not magical, just psychic."

"Pish. You have powers. It doesn't matter what you call them."

They both looked at Corvin.

"It's time for you to go," Reg told him. "You don't need to worry about taking care of me. I have someone here to keep me company now."

Corvin's face contorted with anger. He looked back and forth between them, looking for some way to still get what he wanted. He had been so close; having his prize snatched away right under his nose sent him into a paroxysm of fury.

"Why don't you tell *him* to go?" he demanded, pointing at Harrison. "He is the one who used magic to get in here, who bypassed all of your wards and intruded on your privacy. He should be the one you are kicking out, not me."

"I needed him because you wouldn't listen to me. If you'd behaved yourself like you promised, I wouldn't have needed him."

His hands clenched into fists and he shook his head.

"This is unbelievable! I gave you a nice evening. I protected you from having to see what went down at the Port of Call. I defended your honor. And this is how you repay me? By treating me like a criminal? Implying that I did something wrong? I haven't done anything to harm you."

"You would still take my powers if you had half a chance. Admit it; you can't even think about anything else right now. You want it so badly you can taste it."

"Have I attacked you? You can't accuse me of doing anything just because you can sense my emotions. A person can feel one way and still make a decision the other way."

"Maybe so. But tonight you don't have to be tempted anymore. We're both tired. Maybe that's made your willpower weaken. Just go home."

He rubbed his face and chin. He did look fatigued. Maybe with everything that had happened, his hunger had gotten the better of him when it wouldn't have otherwise. He hesitated, turning partway toward the door.

"This doesn't mean anything. If coming in here to check on you was a mistake, it's just one small mistake. I didn't do anything to you. You know that. You don't know what would have happened next."

"I'm not going to make any decisions about you tonight," Reg said. "Just let me sleep on it."

Until the appearance of Damon, they had been having an enjoyable night. Corvin had behaved himself reasonably well and Reg had been able to resist him until she had gotten too tired. Maybe they could be friends, as long as neither of them got too tired or let their guard down. Corvin started to walk toward the door. Starlight darted out from under one of the wicker chairs and nipped at his calves. Corvin let out a shout and whirled around, trying to swipe at the cat or to kick him.

"That cat! If he's going to attack me like that, he's going to get hurt!"

"Poor Corvin," Reg said in fake sympathy. "Being attacked by the nasty kitty! If you do anything to hurt Starlight, you can forget about us ever being friends. I mean it. I will never talk to you again."

Corvin glared at Starlight, who had taken refuge behind the kitchen island. Starlight peered around the corner, the emotions emanating from him just as strong as the ones coming from Corvin. He was definitely not having warm fuzzy thoughts about the warlock.

Corvin scowled. He turned and stalked out without another word, slamming the door behind him.

CHAPTER NINETEEN

Reg looked at Harrison. "Thank you for coming."

"I didn't have anything better to do."

"Well… good. I don't mean to call on you whenever something bad happens, but I didn't know what else to do."

"You were upset after we talked."

"Yeah, I was."

"That's why you went with the spirit-eater?" He shook his head slowly. "I will never understand human emotions."

"I'm not sure I can explain it myself. I wanted to… prove that I could take care of myself and that I could make my own decisions. It wasn't all just… fate and immortals."

"You made your own choice."

"I knew it wasn't a smart one at the time. But I didn't care."

"Are all humans as confusing as you?"

"Maybe not. I'm kind of… nonconforming."

He nodded. He made a sort of a purring sound and Starlight came running from behind the counter and jumped into his lap. Harrison petted him.

"You need to learn to protect yourself against the warlock if you are going to allow him in your home."

"I didn't invite him in. I don't know how he was able to get past the wards. He hasn't been able to before. Do you think he's that much stronger now?"

Harrison raised an eyebrow. "He is much stronger. But he does not yet have control of his powers. Much like you."

Reg shook off the criticism. "Then how did he get past all of the wards?"

He looked slowly around the room. "He did not break them. Therefore, you let him in."

"Those can't be the only two ways for him to get in, because I didn't let him in. I didn't invite him. I didn't allow him. He just… followed me in."

"Maybe you do not remember properly," Harrison suggested kindly.

"It just happened five minutes ago! I haven't forgotten!"

"Humans have very faulty memories. Maybe you were drinking tonight? Or something else happened that might have altered your memories?"

"No! I had a couple of drinks, but not enough to cause any problems with my memory! I know exactly what happened."

He scratched Starlight's ears and bent down to whisper something to the cat. He looked back at Reg. "Tell me what happened, then."

Reg started her narration with when they were still in the car when she had explicitly told Corvin that he would not be coming into the house. Harrison did not seem to find this significant. Reg went on and described his helping her to unlock the door when she had been so shaky.

Harrison nodded. "You see?"

"What?"

"You gave him your key, and he unlocked and opened the door."

"Well… not exactly, but…"

"When you give someone a key, you are giving them permission to enter."

"But… I told him he couldn't come in. I told him I didn't want him in. Doesn't that mean that I didn't invite him in? Yes, he helped me to find my keys and get the door open, but that doesn't mean that I gave him permission to come into my house."

Harrison steepled his hands together, looking at her. Obviously, that was precisely what it did mean.

"No," Reg protested.

"I am not in charge of human magic," Harrison said. "I did not set the wards or set the conditions of their operation. Your witch friend did that.

The wards will only function against those who you do not permit to enter. You permitted the warlock to enter by giving him your keys."

"He took them out of my bag. I didn't exactly give them to him."

"He opened the door with your key. That makes him an invited guest."

"And what if… someone stole my purse and used my key to let themselves into the house. The wards would not work?"

"No. They would not."

Reg stared at him in disbelief.

"A key has potent magic," Harrison explained. "You must always guard your keys well. Anyone who can use it has your authority."

"But… what kind of magic is that? That's stupid!"

"It is ancient magic. For as long as there have been powers, there have been keys."

Reg's head hurt. Maybe she'd had more to drink than she thought. Or maybe it was just everything that had happened. She was tired and confused. Holding off Corvin during the evening and the final struggle against him had been exhausting.

"Fine. Then I guess I invited him in. The invitation doesn't stand, though, does it? Now that he's gone, and he doesn't have my keys, he can't get back in?"

"Correct."

"Okay. Why does it all have to be so complicated? And why can't anyone tell me the rules to start with, instead of everything being a secret and having to figure it all out on my own through trial and error?"

"It is not complicated. It is very simple. You lack knowledge."

Reg growled at that. "I'm going to bed. You do not need to come and tuck me in. And Starlight has been fed, no matter what he might tell you."

Harrison looked at Starlight's face, and Reg knew that he was going to feed Starlight despite her words. Reg put her hand on the counter to steady herself. She looked at the doorway to her bedroom, then back at Harrison.

"Do you have anything else to tell me? If you do, you'd better do it now."

"Have a good sleep, Regina."

She rubbed her eyes. "In the morning, will you show me how to do a proper protection spell against Corvin?"

"If I am here."

"Will you be?"

"We will know when it is tomorrow."

~

Reg tossed and turned restlessly. At first, she thought it was because Harrison was there, but later Starlight came in to watch out the window and afterward snuggled with her, so she knew that Harrison must be gone. He definitely preferred Harrison when he was there. Unless Harrison had sent Starlight to watch over Reg as she slept, he must have gone home—or wherever it was that immortals went. Mount Olympus? Hades? She wondered what kind of a place Harrison lived in.

When he disappeared, was he anywhere? Or everywhere? She suspected that he would tell her that she was again conflating the immortals with the Christian god. The immortals were not everywhere. But could they be? Were they somewhere, or were they nowhere or scattered across the universe?

She rolled over, scratched Starlight's ears, and closed her eyes, trying to find that sweet spot so she could find sleep. She had gone to bed too early. She'd been keeping later nights recently, and getting up in the morning was becoming difficult.

"Just go to sleep," she muttered to herself. "You're tired. You want to have the strength to do things tomorrow, especially if Harrison will show you how to do a protection spell. You need to get some rest."

It didn't work. But then, it never did, so she wasn't exactly expecting it to.

Eventually, her brain started to wander from one thing to another, and she knew she was close to sleep. It made illogical leaps and switched from one line of thought to another, and she strove just to let it wander so that eventually she could find the way to dreamland.

And then she was dreaming, and she wasn't happy about it.

"Wake up!" a voice told her, and even though she tried to open her eyes and to look around, it was like her lids were stuck together with superglue. She ignored it and decided to stay asleep.

"Reg, it's not safe. You need to listen to me. Regina!" The voice reached a screech, and Reg found herself pulling away in fear, knowing that physical punishment would follow continued disobedience. But how was she supposed to get the sleep she needed if she let the dream wake her up?

"Are you listening?" The voice was definitely Norma Jean's. "The door. You need to make sure it is locked."

"The door is locked," Reg mumbled, her words thick.

She had locked it after Corvin had gone, hadn't she? It wasn't like he was going to be coming back there anyway. He would go away and sulk and try to come up with another tactic to get what he wanted.

She was safe.

Besides, Harrison was there. He wasn't going to let anyone hurt her. He was her guardian.

"You cannot trust them," Norma Jean's screechy voice lowered to a whisper. "You can't trust any of them. They don't tell the truth."

"Men?"

"Men, angels, immortals, they are all the same. You cannot know what is in their minds. Their lips are lies. All lies."

"When you got pregnant, did you know that Weston was your baby's father? Did you know that he was magical? An immortal?"

"Who knows what they really are? They come in cover of darkness, and they do not let you know who they are behind the mask. All men are like this."

Reg groaned. "Oh, just let me go to sleep, mother. I'm not getting tangled up with any men, so you don't need to worry about that."

"Check the lock. Make sure the door is locked."

Eventually, Norma Jean's shrieks and threats woke Reg up completely. She lay there in bed, waiting for sleep to come back, but the dream kept returning to her and she knew she couldn't get back to sleep until she got up and checked the door.

"The lock, the lock, the lock…" echoed in her head, repeated over and over again in a litany.

Starlight looked up and made a little noise as Reg got out of bed. Hardly able to keep her eyes open, Reg stumbled across the cottage to the front door. Harrison had, she noted, thought to turn off the lights before he had disappeared to wherever it was he went. She got to the door and checked the locks. Both the handle and the deadbolt were in the locked position.

Reg shook her head.

"Crazy ghost. You'd better let me go to sleep now."

In the morning, she eventually wiped the vestiges of her restless dreams away and got out of bed. Starlight wasn't in the room any longer, and she hoped that might mean that Harrison was on hand and she could get some lessons from him on protecting herself. She had not done too poorly in constructing protective spells since he had first protected her from the Witch Doctor, imitating his spell the best she could, but she didn't know how to make it stronger and wasn't sure she was going about it the right way at all.

When she walked out to the kitchen and looked around, it was apparent that he had not returned. Starlight was standing by the fridge and looked up at her imperiously.

"Well, good morning to you too, your highness. Thank you for letting me sleep in."

He stretched his muscles without changing position, making a little shiver run through him from ears to tail. He waited, drilling into her with his eyes.

"If no one else can tell me who you are or where you came from, maybe you can. Are you Weston?"

He blinked. She didn't get the feeling that he was. He was a cat, and it was silly of her to think that he could be an immortal, especially not the immortal who was her father or had created her.

"No? Were you owned by an immortal? How does Harrison know you?"

No response. Maybe Starlight didn't want to communicate before break-fast. It wasn't like she couldn't figure out what he wanted as he sat by the fridge door waiting for her. Maybe after breakfast, he would find a way to communicate more to her about his past. She had been able to get information from him before, just little bits of ideas, like his name. He was the one who had chosen Starlight, not she. She would probably have ended up naming him something lame like "Tux" or "Whiskers."

Reg added some dry kibble to his bowl, and while he had been eating the pricey brand that she had started to buy, he didn't show any interest in it when she was there to get him something better out of the fridge.

"No spicy chicken today," Reg told him. She opened the fridge, having to push him out of the way with her foot to avoid hitting him. It wasn't like he didn't know where he needed to sit for her to open the fridge unimpeded. He seemed to block it deliberately.

Reg looked inside. There was half a pizza, and she had no idea where it had come from. Harrison didn't drink coffee; did he eat pizza? Did immortals need to eat food? Or could they eat it for enjoyment? She remembered something about a special drink on Mount Olympus. And they had definitely had parties with lots of wine and food. Maybe they could eat if they chose but didn't need to. Maybe Harrison didn't like coffee, but had the same need for physical nourishment as she did. She opened the lid of the pizza.

Meat lover's. Definitely not the gnome, then.

Would immortals be vegetarian? She decided not. If they didn't care what happened to humans and didn't have any rules against hurting them, then she doubted they would have any regulations about hurting non-human animals either. Was it Artemis who was the goddess of the hunt and had led the gods to kill some special kind of deer? Reg shook her head. She pulled out a couple of pieces of pizza for her breakfast and looked in the various bowls in the fridge for something for Starlight's. Spicy Italian sausage would not be a good choice for Starlight, and she had heard that they didn't digest cow's milk very well. That probably applied to cheese as well. She found some roast beef that Sarah had left on Sunday and turned around to put it on the cutting board.

She just about fainted with the shock of seeing Harrison on the other side of the island, helping himself to her pizza.

That answered the question of whether immortals could eat, then.

"Can't you warn me before you appear like that?" she demanded.

"How could I tell you I am here before I am here?" Harrison took a big bite out of the slice of pizza. Reg put a couple more slices on a plate and then into the microwave. She cut up the roast beef for Starlight while she waited for the pizza to warm. When she took it out of the microwave, she could see Harrison's nostrils quivering.

"Do you want yours warmed up too?"

He nodded and pushed his slices toward her. Reg obliged.

"Did you come back to help me with my protection spell?"

"Perhaps."

"I really could use some instruction. I can do a little bit… but I don't know if I'm doing it right."

"If you are able to stop the spirit-eater, you are doing it right."

"Well, that's good. Then I just need to learn how to strengthen it. Or do it when I'm tired."

She waited for the microwave, not wanting to start eating before Harrison had his pizza back. When it beeped, she pulled the plate out and handed it to him. "Now be careful. That will be hot. Don't burn yourself."

Harrison nodded at this wise advice and stood there, staring down at the food.

"We could sit down," Reg offered awkwardly. She rarely sat down at the table to eat, usually standing at the island or sitting down in the living room. But she could act like a civilized person and eat at the table.

But they never got that far.

CHAPTER TWENTY

Reg's phone started to ring. She looked down at it.

"Oh, it's Francesca. You remember, the charmer, who helped with the draugrs."

Harrison nodded. "I remember her," he agreed. He stared at her phone. "You'd better answer it."

Reg was going to put it off and call Francesca later, but she was struck by the urgency in Harrison's tone. She swiped the phone and answered the call.

"Hi, Francesca."

"Reg? They are gone again! I do not know how they can disappear like this. I know that Nicole doesn't want me to give the kittens away, but that's what we have to do. You and I understand that, why can't she?"

"Maybe because she's a cat. All she has are instincts that tell her to mother the kittens. She probably can't figure out why you would want to take them away."

"If she is smart enough to understand that I want to take them away, she ought to be smart enough to figure out why."

"I think you're just upset. Why don't I come over after we have break-fast, and then—"

Reg didn't even get a chance to finish her sentence. She was still talking into her phone when she was suddenly in Francesca's living room, face-to-face with her. Reg blinked and looked around, not sure what had just happened.

Harrison was a couple of feet away from her and Starlight was there to, bent over like he was still eating from his dish. He put his ears back and looked around.

"What?" Reg shook her head at Harrison. "Did you do that? You can't just transport people across space without warning them!"

Harrison twirled the ends of his mustache. "I may have helped a little," he said, "but mostly it was the passageway."

"What passageway?"

His raised his brows. "The passageway between your homes." He took in their blank expressions. "You might call it... a wormhole?"

"A wormhole. Like on Star Trek? Are you kidding me?"

"A wormhole is real," he said, somewhat petulantly.

"A wormhole is not real. It's a made-up thing in science fiction movies. You can't tell me that they are real."

He scratched his ear and looked at Francesca, who was still holding her phone to her ear and looking at them in shock. Reg shrugged dramatically.

"I'm sorry. Don't ask me. I didn't tell him to transport us. It just happened. I don't know what this nonsense about a wormhole is; I haven't heard anything about it before."

"Not to worry," Francesca said politely. "You are here now, and that means we don't have to wait."

"Right. Do you have any idea where they went? Did you check the attic?"

"I did look this time, in case they got up there again. And I looked for a vent or a hole in the wall that they could have climbed, but I could not find anything. I do not know how they got up there, and I do not know where they went this time."

"Cats can squeeze into some pretty tight places. The kattakyns may not be real kittens, but they are small enough they could get through a pretty small hole."

Francesca shrugged. "You see if you can find any very small holes that they could get through. Can you sense where they are?"

Reg closed her eyes, thinking about it and feeling for Nicole. Last time, Nicole had tried to confuse her to keep her from finding them. This time, Nicole must have gone wherever the kittens had. Reg rubbed her fingers together to get Starlight's attention. He approached her, rubbing against her legs and purring, giving her extra psychic energy to extend the search. Then he drew away from her, sniffing along the ground. Reg watched him.

"Do you know where they are? Can you smell them?"

He continued to move away from her, intent on some scent, and Reg decided it was worth it to go with him and see if he had any luck. They got to a closed door in the kitchen. Reg raised her eyebrows at Francesca.

"A basement?"

"I told you I do not have a basement."

"Then where does that door go?"

Francesca looked at it. "I do not know."

"You don't know where the door goes? You live here. Is it a broom closet?" She reached out and turned the door handle, but the door did not open.

Francesca made a noise that was half-laughing, nearly a sob. "I have never seen that door before," she said. "There was just… a blank panel there."

"Well, now there is a door. It seems like it's stuck."

"Pull harder," Francesca suggested. She reached out and took the door handle in Reg's place. "Just… pull…" She gave it a yank, but it didn't budge. Reg turned around and looked at Harrison. "Can you open this door?"

He looked at it for a moment, then shrugged. He made a flicking gesture, and it shuddered, then opened on its own.

"Uh… thanks. That's a good trick."

Reg pulled the door open the rest of the way. The air smelled moist. There were wooden stairs that descended into the darkness. Reg felt the wall for a light switch, but couldn't find one. She tried to peer into the darkness above her, and moved her hand around, searching for a pull-string, but she couldn't find any way to turn on a light.

"How could they be down here?" Francesca demanded. "How could they get through that door? They cannot open normal doors. They cannot open a door that is stuck or magically sealed."

"I don't know… but something is down there, and we are going to go see what it is."

"You should not tread into darkness without a light," Harrison contributed.

"I've got a light." Reg turned on the flashlight app on her phone and held it in front of her. "Am I going by myself or is someone coming with me?"

Reg descended the stairs slowly, shining her phone light ahead of her on each one to make sure she wasn't stepping into a dark abyss. The stairs felt spongy beneath her feet, each giving way slightly as she stepped on them. Francesca followed a step or two behind her, grumbling as she went. The kattakyns couldn't be down there. They shouldn't just walk into it without knowing what they were going into. But how were they supposed to know what was down there without looking?

"Are you down here, kitties?" Reg called softly. "Nicole? Kittens? I'm coming down."

The staircase was longer than she expected, more than the thirteen or fourteen steps that she would expect for a typical basement. And they didn't have basements in Florida. So why was there one in Francesca's house? Reg pushed away the anxiety she felt about going underground. She had been able to go underground when they entered the pixie realm; it shouldn't be hard to walk into someone's basement. Even if it were just a dirt floor, what was she going to find that would be so terrible? Skeletons? Rats? If the cats had retreated to the basement, then she wouldn't have to worry about rats. And she was quite sure she wasn't going to find any skeletons. That kind of thing didn't happen in real life.

Ghosts?

There certainly might be ghosts, but that would be nothing new for Reg. They couldn't do anything to scare her. No more than Norma Jean could. She was the scariest spirit that Reg could remember.

Finally, Reg's feet hit the floor. It was concrete rather than packed earth. Everything was damp, as she had expected. She shone the phone light around the large room. It didn't penetrate far into the darkness, but there wasn't much to see. The room was almost entirely empty.

"Nicole!" Francesca saw the cat's shining eyes in the darkness and moved past Reg. "You are a naughty kitty! You quit trying to hide the kittens! I don't know how you got down here, but you just stop it! It scares me when I cannot find you!"

Francesca moved into the room and shooed the cats toward the stairs. Reg felt their disappointment at being found and resignation at going back upstairs to the main part of the house. Francesca had said before that cats needed to roam outside, and Reg was sure that in this case, Francesca was right. The cats would have gone outside if they could have. They didn't want to be cooped up in the house. They wanted to get away before Francesca could split them up.

Starlight meowed. Reg looked at him, startled. She hadn't realized that he had followed her down the stairs. He was looking at her, his ears standing up in attention, whiskers bristling with curiosity. Reg looked around. She was surprised that he hadn't gone upstairs with Nicole. He always loved being around Nicole. But he seemed to be more interested in the basement this time. Maybe there had been rats, and he could still smell them. All Reg could smell was dampness.

She walked around the room, shining her light along the wall and into each dark corner. The basement was undeveloped. Reg had expected some dusty old preserves lining a few old storage shelves. Unlike some of the homes she had lived in farther north, there was no furnace in the basement. Under the stairs, there was another closed door—a little storage closet. Probably filled with old brooms and spiders.

Reg grasped the handle and tried to turn it, but unlike the hidden door at the top of the stairs, the handle did not turn. It was locked. Reg looked around for the others. Francesca was shooing the cats up the stairs. Harrison hadn't followed them down. It was just Reg and Starlight. She tried the door once more, but it didn't budge.

"Well, I guess that's it," Reg told Starlight.

He looked at her. He sniffed along the bottom of the door and then pawed at it. He clearly wanted her to open it, but Reg could not comply. She tried to imagine the inner workings of the lock to see if she could persuade it to unlock. Since being locked up in the warehouse with Corvin and Warren and the others, she had been attempting to manipulate locks with her mind. It hadn't worked in the warehouse because there had been a spell on the locks. But she had been able to open some of the locks she had tried at home.

The lock to the closet resisted her efforts and she wasn't able to get it open. She walked back up the stairs, Starlight trailing behind her. When they reached the kitchen, he sat down and started washing. Reg imagined that if she had to walk through the basement barefoot, she would have wanted to clean her feet off too. They were probably caked with dust and cobwebs.

Francesca was trying to count up the cats to make sure that all ten were there. Harrison had either disappeared or was in another part of the house. Reg wasn't sure how she was going to get back home. Maybe a cab.

"Do you have a key to the closet down there?" she asked Francesca.

"What closet?"

"There is one under the stairs."

"I did not see a closet," Francesca said dismissively.

"Well, you didn't go through the whole basement. It was under the stairs; you had to go around and under…"

"I do not have a key for any door."

"What about the door to the house? Maybe it would fit? Or maybe there were some keys left here by the previous owner, on a peg or in a junk drawer?"

Francesca hesitated, then nodded. She opened the drawer closest to the back door. She picked through it, taking out a few random keys on rings. Sometimes there were two or three keys on one ring, sometimes just one. There were a few that were obviously for padlocks, too small for a door lock. Reg looked through the remaining keys.

"It could be any of these."

She went to the basement door and again went down the stairs carefully, using her phone as a flashlight. She went around the stairs to the little cubby underneath, and stopped, staring at a blank wall. "What the…"

She felt along it, looking for a panel or crack. There had been a door. A doorknob with a lock. But there was no longer any sign of it.

"What's going on here?"

She closed her eyes and tried to picture it in her mind. She knew where it had been. She drew the lines out in her mind, glowing bright lines around the crack in the door. A bright door handle. She reached out and grasped it. She could feel the knob in her hand. It was warm and rough. But it was still locked. She opened her eyes and could see nothing but the faint afterimage of the light. She was still holding on to the doorknob, but it wasn't there. She felt for the keyhole and, keeping track of it with one hand, brought the first of the orphaned keys out and tried to fit it into the hole. It didn't go in. She went methodically through each one of them, but couldn't force any of them into the hole. They were all wrong.

Or she couldn't fit them into the keyhole because there actually wasn't a doorknob with a keyhole there.

Reg went through each key again. She could feel the cutaway of the keyhole, but she couldn't fit any of the keys into it.

Finally, she turned and went back up the stairs.

"You see?" Francesca said immediately. "There is no door down there."

"There is a door, but it's gone invisible again. I could still feel the door handle, but I can't fit any of the keys into it."

Francesca lifted one eyebrow in disbelief. She probably thought Reg was making up those details to cover up the fact that there was, in fact, no door in the basement. Reg put her hands on her hips.

"There is a door!"

"I did not see a door. Perhaps you are right… but perhaps you are not."

"Just because you can't see a thing, that doesn't mean it doesn't exist."

"That is true," Francesca admitted. "But it is not usually the case with a door."

"You never saw this door before." Reg pointed at the door leading to the basement. "So why don't you believe there's another door you can't see?"

"I can see this one. I just never noticed it before," Francesca said, revising her previous recollection. Reg had seen that reaction before. When something was impossible to believe, the person simply made up an explanation that they could believe. They replaced the memory, and then the world made sense again. Reg didn't like to think of how many times she might have done that herself. There had been a lot of things in her previous life that hadn't made any sense. How many memories had she replaced in order to keep her sanity?

Francesca closed the basement door. As she did so, it disappeared into the paneling. Reg stepped forward, trying to grab the door handle and open it again. "You can't do that! Don't shut it!"

But she was protesting far too late. Francesca had already closed it, and they were both left to stare at the blank panel. "You see," Francesca pointed out. "It's just because it blends in so well."

"It's gone!" Reg felt for the door handle, but couldn't find it.

"The cats are back, so everything is fine," Francesca pointed out. She wasn't going to be deterred by missing doors. Her only concern was with the cats, and now that they had been found again, she could forget about any inconvenient wormholes or disappearing doorways. Reg looked around, wanting to ask Harrison whether there was any relationship between the doors and the wormhole. Maybe they had come in through the door, and that was why it had become visible. Or maybe it had been Harrison's presence, or he had worked some magic to make it appear so that they could find the kittens. He loved cats, after all; it followed that he would do whatever was necessary to make sure they were found and kept safe.

He wasn't in the kitchen. Reg went into the living room and found him sitting on the floor, the cats surrounding him and crawling over him. He was giggling like a toddler. Starlight and Nicole were nearby, rubbing against and grooming each other and watching the strange man play with the kittens.

"Harrison."

It took a couple of times before Reg was able to get his attention. Harrison looked up. "Oh, Regina. Did you find what you were looking for?"

He was playing with the cats, so obviously he knew she had found them. Reg shook her head, brushing away the question. "Can you help with the door? It has disappeared again."

"You must open it to see it," Harrison advised.

Reg stared at him, willing him to say something sane. She had to open it to see it? She had opened it, but she had been able to see it before that. She could not open it if she couldn't see it. He was getting it backward.

"I've tried. I can't see it. I can't feel it. I want to get back to the basement. There is another door down there. A closet. I want to see what's in it." That didn't fully express what she was feeling. "I *need* to see what's in it."

"The door does not belong to you."

"No. I know that. It's Francesca's. But she didn't do anything to make it appear or disappear."

Except to close it. Maybe she was more than a charmer. Maybe she had some pretty sophisticated magic that allowed her to manipulate those doors and to hide them when necessary. She had some secret to hide and didn't want Reg to see it.

"It is not Francesca's door either."

"It's in her house."

"It is not her door."

Reg shook her head. "Okay. Then how do I get it to appear again?"

"You need all of the keys."

"I have the keys." Reg held up the keys from the drawer in the kitchen.

"Humans are so charmingly literal."

Reg blew out her breath in frustration. "Tell me what I need to do to see the door again. And I might need you to open it like you did last time. Then I want to be able to see the one downstairs too. And to unlock it so I can see what is in the closet."

"You got it right the first time. Use your tools, Regina. You have been given everything you need." Harrison held a kitten on either side of his face, cooing at them and making silly faces.

Reg didn't know how she was supposed to take him seriously when he behaved like a fool.

She had been given everything she needed. What had been different when she'd walked up to the door the first time?

She had been following Starlight. He had led her to each of the doors.

"Starlight. I need you. Let's go look at the doors again."

Starlight was busy with his lady friend and did not even flick a whisker in Reg's direction.

"Come on, Star. Don't you want to see what's in the closet? You were trying to get in there. Let's go see."

He still didn't pay her any attention. Usually, when Reg needed help with a psychic project, he was quick to come when called. It was the only time he did. But he was too distracted by Nicole to pay her any mind. Nicole was, once again, throwing up barriers in Reg's way. Why did she care whether Reg opened the closet or not? She had been down there with the kittens, so she had, in effect, led Reg to the closet.

Reg marched over to where Starlight and Nicole were grooming and picked Starlight up.

He gave a startled squawk and tried to twist around to right himself. Reg let him turn himself right-side up, but wouldn't let him go. He kicked with his strong back legs, giving her a long scratch down one arm.

"Ouch! Stop it!"

Starlight stopped kicking. He looked at Reg reproachfully.

"Don't look at me like that; you hurt me! And you're not listening to me. You're my familiar. You're supposed to help me at least when I ask you to help with a job like this. Even if you don't pay any attention to me the rest of the time."

He was still in her arms. Reg walked with him into the kitchen and stood in front of the blank panel where the door had been. And there it was, just as it had been before. Reg rolled her eyes. "This is getting ridiculous. Doors shouldn't appear and disappear. So why do I need you to see the door?"

Reg knew that the first time, turning the handle hadn't worked. Harrison's magic had been required to make it open. But Reg had some of those powers herself. If her father was Weston, who knew what powers she had inherited from him?

She focused on the doorknob, feeling inside it. The doorknob itself wasn't locked. The door had just stuck. Magically sealed. Until someone who knew the right magic could open it.

She mentally ran her attention all the way around the door, making sure that it was free of the frame.

Open.

As when they had asked Harrison to help with the door, it simply creaked open.

"There, you see?" Reg asked Starlight. "Just a little bit of the right kind of attention, and it opens all by itself."

Reg put Starlight down at the top of the stairs. "Now, are you going to go down with me and see if we can get the door open?"

He stood there, sniffing the air from the basement. He looked up at her.

"Are we going to do this? Harrison said that we have what we need to open the door. I don't know why I need you, but apparently, I do. So let's go down together and see what's in that closet."

Whatever was in the closet, it didn't belong to Francesca. Not unless her ignorance of the basement and the closet was an act, and Reg was pretty good at discerning when someone was lying. She didn't think that Francesca had anything to do with the appearing and disappearing doors. Or at least, not intentionally. Whatever was behind that door, it was Reg's.

Starlight started to descend the stairs, placing his paws carefully on each step. Reg took his lead and was also careful not to trip or to stay on any one stair for too long. Who knew how rotten they were?

They walked around the stairs again to the place where the closet door had been the first time.

And there it was. Reg didn't need her psychic powers to see it or to remember where it was. She again tried the random keys in the keyhole, even though she knew none of them had fit before. Maybe they would now that the door was visible. It was, at least, easier to try them.

Again, none of the keys fit. Starlight prowled along the bottom of the door, sniffing it and scratching at it.

"I'm doing the best I can," Reg told him.

He sat back and looked at her as if waiting for her to get herself together and figure it out. Reg raised her eyebrows. "What? Exactly what do you expect me to do about it? I need the key. Without the key, I can't get in."

Harrison had told her that she had the key and that she could unlock it. So why couldn't she?

CHAPTER TWENTY-ONE

I t was as if she had been resisting putting the puzzle together until then. She knew very well what the answer was, but she hadn't been able to make the connection. She reached into her skirt pocket and drew out the key that Forst had found in the garden. *She had a key.* She had been trying to find the lock for it so that they could claim her treasure. Now she was presented with a lock without a key, and she hadn't made the connection.

"Do you think this is it?" Reg asked Starlight. She held the key up. "Is it that simple? The key was in the cottage garden; there is a wormhole from the cottage to here. There is a locked closet here."

On the one hand, she was disappointed. She had been hoping for a treasure chest, sarcophagus, or some other proper receptacle for a treasure. But a basement under-stairs cubby? What treasure was she going to find there?

There was no reason it couldn't hide a trove of gold bars, jewels, or some other priceless treasure. But it seemed highly unlikely. Probably it was nothing but dust and spiders. And a broom. Maybe she could ride the broom home if Harrison didn't want to transport her again or the wormhole had mysteriously closed.

Reg held the key in the palm of her hand for a few more seconds. It was warm, and the familiar tug was stronger than ever. It wanted to be reunited with the lock. That was its purpose.

She reoriented the key and slid it into the lock. Unlike the other keys, which didn't even fit into the slot, let alone turn the tumblers, it fit neatly into place. Reg held her breath. She looked at Starlight, then twisted the key.

There was no explosion or magical spell. Reg turned the handle. It was now unlocked. She pulled the closet door open.

The magical phenomenon she had expected when she had turned the key blasted into the basement. Light seared Reg's eyeballs after the darkness of the basement. It exploded out of the closet and lit up the room like midday. She couldn't look into the closet; it was far too bright.

"What is it?" she asked aloud.

"It's about time," a male voice boomed.

The light coalesced into a single form but was still too bright to look at.

The basement disappeared, and Reg and Starlight were, once again, in the living room with Harrison, Nicole, and the kittens. But this time, there was another man too.

He was tall like Harrison, but fuller in the chest, a huskier build. He didn't have a mustache and looked vaguely like the lumberjack in a TV commercial—handsome, rugged, and glowing from inside.

CHAPTER TWENTY-TWO

He looked around at each of them, his eyes bright and intelligent. His eyes pinned Reg down. "It is you?" he asked. "You are the child?"

Reg looked at him uncertainly. She diverted her gaze to Harrison, looking for help.

"She is the child," Harrison agreed. "We expected you to be near the woman."

The man ignored the comment. He looked at Starlight. Then his eyes moved to the kittens and he started to laugh.

It was a deep belly laugh that shook his whole body and brought tears to the corners of his eyes.

"Destine, Destine! What have you done?"

Reg smiled a little. He obviously recognized his old enemy, even without a proper physical form and with his consciousness divided through the nine kattakyns. She tried to get his attention again.

"Are you... Weston?"

His lips curled upward. "Of course. Who were you expecting?"

"I don't know that I was expecting a who... I was expecting more of a what."

"A hidden treasure?" he suggested. He laughed heartily. "What treasure could be better than releasing me from my prison?"

Reg was still trying to wrap her mind around what had happened. "So all of this was intentional? Planned? Me moving here and finding the key? Starlight and Nicole? The wormhole from the cottage to this house?"

Weston shrugged. "Human intelligence is limited," he told her condescendingly. "You are not expected to understand how it works."

"Well… thanks for that, but I think I can actually sort it out." Even though the magnitude of what he had done was beyond her grasp. How could he have known where she would go, who she would develop friendships with, how the key would fall into her possession and eventually lead her to find and unlock the hidden doors?

Weston watched the kittens, chortling again, but quietly this time.

Starlight picked his way over to Weston delicately, as if tiptoeing through water. He sat at Weston's feet and drew himself up tall.

"Ah, my old friend," Weston said. He made a noise in the back of his throat, then bent over to pick Starlight up. Starlight rubbed against the bottom of Weston's chin, purring.

Reg watched the interaction between Weston and Starlight with a certain amount of jealousy. What was the deal with the immortals and cats, and Starlight in particular? Was he indeed the reincarnation of another immortal or a human whom Harrison and Weston had known in a past life? Or was he that long-lived? Cats weren't supposed to live for more than fifteen or twenty years. How could someone who had been banished or bound for thirty years or more know him?

And more than that, why wasn't Weston paying Reg any attention? If she was his long-lost daughter, shouldn't he be happy to see her? Maybe a hug or a declaration of love? If not for her, then maybe a word for Norma Jean, the lover he had lost? It was as if she were some tool that, once used, he was now ready to discard.

"If you're Weston, then does that mean you're my father?" she demanded.

Weston looked at her as if surprised to hear her speak. "How long has it been?" he asked Harrison. "In human years?"

"Longer than one would expect, maybe, but less than a century."

"Thirty years," Reg answered. "I am thirty years old. And if you left when I was four, it has been twenty-six years."

"Four what?" Weston asked with a frown of concentration. "Four orbits? You were not so much. Still in the woman's belly."

"You left with Norma Jean pregnant with me? You never even saw me after I was born?"

She could hear Norma Jean's agreement in her head. He had left her, abandoned her pregnant and alone, without any resources. Just like a man.

"Waiting four years, the others would surely have found me and dealt with me. Destine especially." Weston chuckled, looking at the kittens. "He used to be a threat."

"I know. We had to face him."

"You?"

"Me and my friends. Humans. Since the immortals would not help us out."

"Brought so low by humans. *Oh, Destine!*"

"Aren't you listening to me?" Reg said. "You abandoned Norma Jean. You abandoned me. I didn't live an easy life. Destine killed Norma Jean! Tortured her to death when she couldn't tell him where you were. And me and my friends had to confront him and defeat him. Humans facing a powerful immortal. Don't you have anything to say about that?"

He stared at her blankly for a few seconds in silence. Then he shrugged. "You did well," he said eventually. "You must have strong gifts."

"I don't know what gifts I have, how strong they are. I have been trying to understand what they were and where they came from. I don't know how… what I have."

Weston petted Starlight thoughtfully. He eventually put the cat down, giving him one last scratch behind the ears.

"Continue to guide her. We will talk."

And then he was gone. No poof of smoke or other drama, he was just there one instant, and then he was not. Reg looked around the room. She didn't know whether his words had been directed at Starlight or Harrison. She had no idea where he had gone. She looked at Harrison, confused, looking for his direction.

"What was that all about? Where did he go?"

Harrison pursed his lips, looking at her. "Are you sure it was such a good idea to release him?"

CHAPTER TWENTY-THREE

Reg looked at Harrison, her mouth dropping open in disbelief. "Do you think that I released him on purpose? I had no idea that was what was in the closet. I thought... maybe there was something valuable there. I didn't know it was Weston! Did *you* know?"

He shrugged. "That was the most likely outcome."

"Why didn't you tell me?"

"I assumed you knew."

"How would I know?"

Harrison's brows lowered slightly as he thought about it. "This is where the breadcrumbs led," he said slowly. "Didn't you know they would lead to him?"

Reg dug the sharp knuckles of her fist into her forehead, trying to fend off the headache starting between her eyes. "I didn't know! Why didn't you say something to me? If you had told me, then I would have been able to make an informed choice!"

"I told you that you came here because of him. That you could feel his imprint here. I told you that the path led from your house to this. I told you that you had the keys to open the door." He shook his head. "I did tell you, Reg."

"You need to... not assume that I know what you mean. You need to tell me clearly, like we're talking right now. Tell me 'Weston is probably in the closet and if you use the key to open it, you will release him.'"

Harrison scratched an eyebrow, then nodded. He curled his mustache around his index fingers and released the ends again. "Weston is probably in the closet—" he started out.

"It's too late now; I already let him out!"

"Well, yes."

"You were supposed to tell me that before I let him out."

"To be fair, you didn't tell me that until after."

Reg growled in frustration. Harrison scratched the back of his neck. "There is a problem."

"What?"

"When Weston was previously free... his power was balanced by Destine's."

"Yeah?"

"But now..." Harrison fluttered his fingers at the cats. "Destine's power has been divided. And most of it consumed by your spirit-eater."

"He's not *my* spirit-eater."

Harrison shrugged, his expression doubtful. "But he is."

"He took most of the Witch Doctor's powers," Reg attempted to move on from the argument about whether Corvin was hers or not. "All except what the Witch Doctor was able to retain when he went into the draugrs. So what does that mean? Corvin needs to fight Weston?"

"They do not need to fight... as long as their powers are balanced."

"Okay... what then? What does he need to do?"

"Perhaps, as you said, we should tell him directly."

"Yeah, we probably—"

Reg blinked at Corvin, standing in front of her. He stared back at her. He had a stick razor in his hand, held close to his face as he leaned forward. There was shaving cream layered thickly over his face like a banana cream pie.

Corvin straightened up and looked around the room. His eyes took in Reg, Harrison, and the cats. Looking through the doorway, Reg could still see Francesca in the kitchen. She clearly did not want anything to do with the drama Reg and Harrison were in the midst of.

"Regina..." Corvin greeted. "Nice to see you again..."

"I'm sorry. It wasn't my idea. He just... poofed you here."

"I see."

"Your power is great," Harrison observed. "But you do not yet have it under control. You struggle to master it."

Corvin darted a look at Harrison, then shook his head at Reg, his eyes indicating his confusion.

"It's… it's about Weston," Reg said.

"Do we now know exactly who Weston is?"

"Um… I guess he was my father. An immortal. He was bound. And now… he is free again."

"Regina released him," Harrison contributed helpfully.

"Uh… yeah. I guess I did. But it wasn't intentional. It would have helped if someone had given me all of the information. If someone knew how to give a straight answer to a question."

"Someone did not," Harrison agreed with a sober nod of agreement.

Corvin's eyebrows were up as he tried to take all of this in and get caught up on what was going on. "Okay, then. You've released an immortal from his exile. I assume that's going to be a problem."

"His power is no longer opposed," Harrison explained. "When he was last loose, he was counterbalanced by Destine. But since your defeat of Destine…"

"He is no longer in the equation," Corvin contributed.

Harrison was nodding.

"But wait a minute," Reg interrupted. "If the Witch Doctor was the evil force, and he counterbalanced Weston, then Weston is the good guy, and if the Witch Doctor is not opposing him, that is a good thing, not a bad thing. He can… do good without worrying about being stopped by the Witch Doctor. Isn't that right?"

"Mmm…" Harrison pursed his lips and shook his head slowly. "No, that is not right."

Reg sighed in exasperation. "Why not? Doesn't that make sense?"

"It is not a matter of good and bad," Corvin said. "I think that rather, it is an issue of having absolute power. You've heard the expression that power corrupts, and absolute power corrupts absolutely."

"You're afraid he is going to take over the world?" Reg put the question to Harrison. "Is that what you're talking about?"

Harrison looked down at her. "Humans do have strange ideas of their importance in the universe."

"Explain to me what he is going to do, then."

Harrison stared at her for a moment, then looked at Corvin. "In some cases, words do not suffice," he said helplessly. "We will go to him."

Before Reg could protest or could prepare herself, the room changed around them. Instead of being in Francesca's living room, they were in a tiny, foul-smelling apartment. Little more than a flop house, it was covered with filth, the walls spattered and stained with unidentifiable matter, garbage on the floor, and the smell of rats permeating the air.

"Where are we?" Corvin asked softly.

There was a hard knot of iron in Reg's stomach. "I think... I don't know. Please get us out of here," she begged.

Corvin gave her an odd look. Reg pressed her knuckle into her teeth. She did not want to be there. It wasn't fair of Harrison to bring her there. Or for Weston to be there. He had run away. He had not stayed around to see her born or to protect her or Norma Jean. He had disappeared and had not been a part of either of their lives.

But now Norma Jean sat on one of the chairs, giggling and talking animatedly. The person that she was talking to was Weston. He leaned over her attentively, a big smile on his face, treating her as if she were a princess.

Norma Jean was missing teeth, and what she still had were rotting. Her hair was brittle and falling out. She was not the lovely lady she claimed to have been when she left her home as a teenager to start a life on her own. The streets had seen to her quick decline and the loss of her youth, beauty, and health. Reg didn't understand why Weston was treating her as if she still had those things. Maybe in his eyes, she was something different. Perhaps he could see her the way that she had been.

"This is wrong," Reg said anxiously. She could no longer hear Norma Jean's voice in her head. Norma Jean had been a resident there for so long that Reg wasn't sure what to do without her there. Had Norma Jean been returned to life? Was that what Weston had done?

"Her name is Regina," Norma Jean was saying to Weston, not inside Regina's head, but outside of it. "She is just a little thing. You have to meet her."

"No," Regina protested. "No, this isn't right. Norma Jean is dead. This isn't happening."

"I don't know if this really is happening," Corvin cautioned. "It might just be a vision..."

"She is really there. She isn't inside of me anymore. She's alive. That can't be. Did we go back in time?" Regina looked around the room, trying to remember the place she had lived before going into foster care. She had been so young. She looked around, shaking her head, trying to match it to the imprint in her brain.

"Where is she?" Norma Jean asked, her voice growing more strident. "Are you hiding again, you silly girl? She's always squeezing into the smallest spaces, hiding away like a mouse."

Weston straightened up. He walked confidently across the apartment to the kitchenette. There wasn't a separate kitchen, no separate food preparation or eating area. More like a hotel room, just a few cupboards and a counter for a hot plate. Reg hugged herself tightly.

"No," she protested, "no, no, no!"

Weston opened one of the lower cupboard doors. Regina saw the pale, dirty little red-haired girl pressed into the corner. The child covered her face as if that would keep Weston from seeing her. Weston reached down and wrapped his long fingers around her body, picking her up. She was a tiny waif of a thing; it took no effort for him to lift her.

"Stop. You need to stop him! This isn't right. This isn't the way it happened."

"If you don't change things, this is the way it happened," Harrison said.

"That doesn't make any sense! This isn't what happened. You protected me. You made it so that the Witch Doctor couldn't find me."

"The Witch Doctor is no longer here," Harrison explained. "That means that Weston could come. He could see you and affect the course of your life."

"No! He wasn't here. He abandoned us." Reg was frantic. They had to stop Weston from changing everything.

"Isn't this what you want?" Corvin asked as he scraped the shaving cream from his face into the sink. "Don't you want him to protect you and your mother?"

Reg pressed her fingers to her temples. How many times over the years had she dreamed of being rescued by her father or by anyone? She had longed for someone to appear in her life and whisk her away to safety. She even prayed for her mother to be returned to life so that she could go back to a stable home and not have to be shuffled from place to place in foster care. Now, if she were to believe Harrison, that could all change. The past could be changed. Weston could rescue them and she could have what she'd always wished for.

But what would that mean?

If Reg stayed with Norma Jean instead of going into foster care, would Reg still be the same person? Would she be wiping out her entire existence? And would staying with Norma Jean be better than foster care? She'd had to deal with a lot of disruption and abuse in foster care, but she knew Norma Jean was just as abusive. Reg would live in abject poverty, moving from flophouse to shelter to sleeping rough on the street. There had been good foster homes, parents who had tried their best to give her what she needed and help her to heal the wounds of the past, even if Reg had always proven to be too difficult a case and had not been able to stay anywhere long-term. There had been therapists and specialists and even hospitalization. Staying with Norma Jean would have meant losing all of those supports.

Staying with Norma Jean would not have been an idyllic life. Norma Jean had just been her first, most traumatic loss, the one from which she had always been trying to recover.

CHAPTER TWENTY-FOUR

"Mommy," Reg whispered, her throat tight, realizing she was going to have to lose Norma Jean again, and this time it would be her own choice.

She grasped Corvin's arm, drawing strength from him. "We have to stop this. He can't be allowed to change everything."

At first, he tried to pull out of her grasp, then he let her hang on to him. "I don't know how you do that," he muttered.

"What?" Reg was focused on Weston, not Corvin, trying to figure out how best to deter him.

"Draw on my powers."

"If we work together, we can defeat him, can't we?" Reg asked desperately. She looked at Harrison. "Tell me we can."

Harrison shrugged. He looked interested, but not overly concerned.

"That's why you brought us here. You said that Corvin could balance out his power."

"If he can *control* his powers," Harrison said, doubt in his tone.

Reg tightened her grip on Corvin's arm, seeking the warmth and energy he held, drawing on it. "Weston! Put the girl down! You need to leave them alone."

Her voice didn't come out nearly as authoritatively as she wanted it to, but it was the best she could do, with her throat constricted and her knees shaking. Weston didn't even look at her, still talking to Norma Jean and tickling the little girl under the chin like a cat.

"Weston!"

He turned and looked at her, then glanced over at Harrison and raised his eyebrows. "There is no need to bring so many people to this family reunion. It is just my dear one and me and the child."

"You can't have her. You aren't allowed to do this. That's why you were bound."

"I have served my exile and been released. You cannot punish me a second time." He gave a little laugh. "You could not punish me anyway."

"We have the power of the Witch Doctor—of Destine!" Reg told him shakily. "You can't just do whatever you want without consequence."

"Indeed." Weston studied Corvin move closely, taking a step toward them. "How could this spirit-drinker best Samyr Destine? Unless it was his time. Did he grow careless? Or had he run his course?" he mused, not directing the question at any of them.

"Let the little girl go," Corvin commanded, his voice sounding much more commanding than Reg's. "You are not allowed to be here."

"I am not allowed? I am immortal; I go where I like. There is nothing to stop me from being here."

"You are not supposed to have contact with the woman or the child. You broke the rules. I am here to stop you."

Corvin was bluffing pretty well, considering how little he knew. But he probably had a little more background knowledge on the immortals than he would disclose. He had pretended only to have a general understanding of them, but he seemed to be up-to-date on the rules on not having children with the mortals. Or had Reg told him that?

Her head was hurting like it was going to split right down the middle. If she were anywhere else, she would have lain down to go to sleep. Her brain was shutting down with the pain and the confusion over what she was supposed to do and how she could possibly influence what had happened in her past. Or maybe it was just a side effect of traveling through time.

Maybe she was having a stroke, and none of it was happening after all. It was just a very vivid dream caused by the damage spreading through her brain. She would be seeing the light at the end of a tunnel soon and meeting all of her loved ones who had gone on before.

Or maybe Norma Jean was the only one she would ever meet. The only one she had ever loved, in spite of the way Norma Jean had treated her.

"*I am,*" Weston said thunderously. "You have no control over me. The others have no control over me. I have paid the price and I can now choose my own path without retribution."

"No!" Reg insisted. She lunged at Weston, letting go of Corvin, her source of strength. "Not if I have anything to say about it!"

Weston was startled by her attack, merely buffeting her with the back of his arm to keep her away from him, not casting any spell or using his immortal powers. Reg immediately renewed her attack. She needed to stop him. To get the child away from him and prevent him from changing everything. The child could not stay with Norma Jean. Weston could not protect the two of them. The results would be disastrous. She grabbed ahold of Weston this time, not letting him simply smack her back again. She grabbed his fingers and bent them back, attempting to pry the little girl away from him.

"Let her go! Her fate isn't yours to choose. You already made your decision; you can't go back and change it now. She has to grow up like I did."

The little girl was cowering away from Reg. She hid her face against the strange man in an attempt to escape the scary, screaming, wild-eyed woman. She was starting to sob, but held back, trying to keep them from seeing her tears. How many times had she been punished for crying?

Weston attempted to shove Reg back again, but she threw up the wall around herself so that he couldn't touch her. She yelled, an incoherent war-cry. She was the protector of this child. She had to keep him from messing everything up. If he did what he planned, he would only hurt her more. Reg drew on the powers that Corvin held. They were no longer touching physically, but she had left a path open to him, and when she directed her thoughts back to him, there was an immediate connection. They worked together in sync as if they had practiced this scene a thousand times. Each knew what the other was going to do the instant before it happened.

Reg tried to force the child from Weston's arms. To begin with, he only resisted physically. Perhaps his powers were rusty after all of his time in the closet. Or maybe he didn't believe that she could hold any power that would challenge him.

But as he struggled with her, he started to put up a magical resistance as well. Reg had to work harder and harder to keep her hands on the little girl and to even stand in front of the immortal. He tried to hit or push her, but the wall that she had put up protected her from physical harm. He started attacking her psychic forces, the power that she was drawing from Corvin.

She felt him stirring inside her mind and tried to fight back and push him out. How could it be so easy for him to get behind her defenses? He stirred up old memories.

Reg, cuddling in Norma Jean's arms as her mother rocked her, sitting in a rocking chair in a hospital or shelter somewhere, not in the dirty little apartment. Little Reg was warm and felt protected. She didn't understand the words of the song that her mother sang to her as she relaxed and tried to find a peaceful sleep without dreams. She didn't have any idea, as the Reg of older years did, that rather than a lullaby, it was a drinking song, normally raucous and rowdy.

Then she felt Harrison's warm protection spell as she hid in the cupboard, but then the terror of watching her mother being tortured.

And then the horrible sense of being alone in the world, ricocheting from one place to another as they searched for a home that could manage her, promising that she would have a forever family who would take care of her and keep her safe forever if she would just be good—knowing that she never could be.

Reg could barely hold on to consciousness, faltering in her attempts to fight back against Weston. He picked and chose the memories that would weaken her, that would best convince her to leave the child with him and Norma Jean. Together, they could be the perfect little family. He could protect her from every negative force in the world. He could keep her safe at all times. He could be the loving father she'd never had. He would see to it that she had food to eat and was warm and safely tucked into bed each night.

"Regina!" Corvin tried to shake her from her stupor. "Reg, fight! Don't let him get to you. You don't *want* him to protect you. He never will, anyway. You know what these immortals are like. They have great ideas, how they're going to change the world and make it a better place, and instead, they end up destroying civilizations or leading countries into war and then wandering off when they get bored with it. He wouldn't have stayed with you. He would have taken off after the next shiny new idea."

It was true. Reg renewed her attempts to fight against him and against the memories he endeavored to drown her with. She could not let him lull her into a sense of security. Those warm fuzzy feelings weren't true. He hadn't been there her whole life, and even if he intended to protect the child, he would never follow through. He would always be chasing after a new woman, idea, or treasure. The immortals were fickle.

Even Harrison, her trusty, helpful Uncle Harrison, who had promised he would always be there to help and protect her had disappeared more times than she could count. Had he stayed near her to ensure that the Witch Doctor could never harm her? On the contrary, time after time, he had left her alone, making her vulnerable.

And when he had known that she was getting close to opening the closet and releasing Weston from his imprisonment, he hadn't warned her. He'd just stood by and let it happen.

"You get out of my head and out of my life forever!" Reg shouted so loudly it hurt. "She is not yours!"

"She *is* mine," Weston argued, sounding angry and dangerous for the first time. "She is my blood! I gave her to Norma Jean. She will always be mine."

"No. You gave that up when you abandoned her. You cannot have her!"

"Her power is my power," Weston's voice was low and gravelly. "Your power is my power. You have nothing you can use against me because I am the source!"

Reg was shaken, but she continued to fight back against him. She didn't just have her own gifts to draw on. She was also using Corvin's. And his came from the Witch Doctor, not from Weston. Destine held the power that had counterbalanced Weston for years. Maybe for epochs. They could continue to fight him all day long; Weston couldn't get the upper hand. There was a balance of forces.

Reg held him off, but she couldn't make any progress.

Maybe she could go no farther. Her power combined with Corvin's was not enough to get the upper hand. Reg stared at the little girl. She had to do it for her younger self. She had to do it to protect the little girl from all that would happen to her if Weston succeeded in changing the course of her life.

That little girl was her, and that little girl had the powers that Reg would eventually wield. It didn't make any sense that together they could hold any more than Reg did by herself, but nothing was working the way she thought it should after years of watching Star Trek.

"Look at me, Reg," she said softly, trying to meet her eyes and to smile at her encouragingly. "I know what to do. You can help me. You can help me to protect you."

The little girl looked away, frightened. Reg swallowed. The little girl had never been told she could do anything. How could Reg explain to her what powers she had? Powers that she wouldn't understand for years. Reg was still trying to wrap her mind around them.

Reg's hands were still on the little girl, trying to pull her away from Weston. She relaxed her grip to make sure it didn't hurt. To convey a sense of concern to the girl so she wouldn't be scared. She reached out with her mind and attempted to touch the little girl's inner self. It wasn't truly an invasion of her mind if it was into her own head.

There was a blast of brilliance like she had never experienced before. The little girl's mind was so bright and alive with light and color it just about knocked Reg over. She let out her breath in a puff like she'd been punched in the stomach.

"Whoa!"

The little version of herself looked back with guileless innocence. She cocked her head to the side slightly, trying to figure out who Reg was and what she was doing. Reg couldn't explain, but she tried to show her how to push back against Weston, how to resist him and to build a wall around herself, Reg, and Corvin. She drew on Corvin's strength and funneled it toward the little girl. Corvin sensed what she was doing, and after an initial tug of resistance, he did the best he could to help. But Reg could feel his reluctance. He had battled with an immortal before, and when he had done that, he had been able to pull powers from him. He was hungering again, tugging here and there like a dog on a leash, drawn toward the powers Weston wielded.

"Don't," Reg told him. "Last time, you had just filled up with power from the artifacts. It's different this time."

Corvin spoke through gritted teeth. "I can. I am strong enough."

"Harrison said you don't have control yet."

"He's wrong. I can do this. I did it before without his help."

Reg was losing her grip on the little girl's mind and had to refocus her attention. "Come on, honey. You can do this. You're strong. Wow, all of that power inside of you, you're like a magical princess!"

The little girl's face lit up at this suggestion and, in spite of the dirt on her face and the hollowness of her cheeks, she glowed, exuding light, her power flow amping up noticeably.

Weston's physical grip on the little girl slackened. Reg was able to tug her out of his hands. She held the waif against her body, the desire to protect her welling up even more strongly inside her. She wanted to hold this little girl and protect her from all of the trouble that was going to come to her. But she wasn't going to be there for her.

Or she was, but not with the knowledge and power that she would gain later in life. The little girl could rely only on what was inside her as a four-year-old. Reg kissed her cheek and tried to pump her up as much as she could inside her mind. She told her how brave and strong she was and that she was beautiful and smart no matter what anyone else told her. And there would be people there for her. Uncle Harrison sometimes, and social workers and doctors and foster parents who really did care and wanted to do the best for her. The bad times would only be temporary. She would be able to get through them.

The girl clung to her neck. Reg turned her attention back to Weston and built a spell against him.

"You can't have her. She is not yours; she is her own person. You stay away from her."

"She is my blood!"

"It doesn't matter. That doesn't mean you possess her. Humans are independent. You leave her alone."

"I can make her great. I can build her powers, teach her how to use her gifts and talents properly. By the time she is grown, she will be a sorceress beyond description. Think of having that kind of power. Think of how different your life would be."

It was a temptation, as Weston knew it would be. She had always struggled for control. She hadn't cared so much about having power over other people as just having the right to make her own choices and not have her life run by all of the adults.

But that was what had made her the person she was.

"No. That's not what she needs."

"Of course she does. It's what you always wanted. Do you think I can't see that?"

In wrestling with him, however much she had tried to build a wall with him, she had allowed some glimpses into her mind. But wanting a thing and knowing what was right for her was not the same. She had to give the little girl the same life as she'd had if she were going to survive. Or as close to it as she could manage under the circumstances, strange as they were.

"No. You leave her alone."

CHAPTER TWENTY-FIVE

Weston was gone.

The room was quiet. They could hear sounds outside of it; music, shouting, the sound of traffic; but inside it was quiet as they all looked at each other.

"Is that it?" Reg asked. "That isn't it." She didn't need Harrison to answer. She already knew. Weston may have given up on that particular battle, but he would be back. None of them could know whether it would be an hour, a day, or a millennium, but sooner or later, he would be back causing more trouble than ever. Reg just hoped that they would have a break. After the stand-off, she really needed a good nap.

Reg looked at Corvin and realized she was still drawing on his powers. She hurriedly broke from him, and he staggered in place for an instant, his face a waxen gray.

"Sorry. Are you okay?"

"For someone who has been so vehement about me stealing powers, you are remarkably quick to use mine."

"Uh…" Reg wasn't sure what to say. "I wasn't… I didn't even think about that."

"At least *I* get permission."

"Well, sort of," she pointed out, "some of the time. It isn't like you can claim to have been that diligent about it. At least, not with me. I guess… I just didn't think about it. I thought that since you came, you were on-board with what we were doing."

"I didn't exactly come of my own free choice."

Reg looked at Harrison. "Did you bring him against his will?"

Harrison made a brushing-away gesture with his hand. "Humans have such weak wills; it is hard to say."

"Harrison. Really. Did you bring him here without asking?"

"I told you what I was doing."

"But… that's not the same as asking."

"I think it's close enough," he assured her.

Reg gave one bark of laughter and shook her head. She looked back at Corvin. "Immortals! I'm sorry. Will you be okay?"

"I just need a few minutes of recovery time. I'm not used to expending energy so quickly."

"Yeah. Okay. Next time I'll try to remember to ask."

"I'm hoping there won't be a next time." Corvin wiped a dab of shaving cream off of his ear.

Reg turned her attention to the others. Norma Jean was staring at her, eyes glassy with shock. She had been happy when Weston had been flirting with her and paying her compliments, but the battle and Weston's vanishing act had been too weird for her.

She had that look that Reg had seen in the eyes of others when they couldn't believe what they had seen Reg do. Withdrawal, a blank aspect, and then, eventually, revision of those memories, rewriting them into something that made sense. Probably some version of Reg playing a prank on them.

Reg felt a kinship with Loki, the Norse god who was always referred to as a trickster. She hated being painted as the naughty girl who was always trying to trick people and pull something over on the adults who were her caregivers.

Then Reg looked at herself. The little girl who would grow up to be her, or some version of her. Being so young, she would be a lot more resilient than Norma Jean. She would probably believe what she had seen for years to come, until she was old enough to realize that it was impossible and must have just been something that she had come up with in her overactive imagination.

"Are you okay?" Reg asked.

The little girl nodded. Reg wet a thumb and rubbed away a smudge of dirt on the girl's pale cheek. She tried to clean away another and found that it was not dirt, but a bruise. Reg stroked her hair instead, smoothing down the tangled red locks and hoping to soothe away the trauma of what she had just experienced.

"Everything is going to be okay. I don't think he'll come back here again. And Uncle Harrison will keep an eye on you. Won't you, Harrison?"

Harrison nodded cheerfully. He was holding Starlight and petting him. Reg frowned. She didn't think he'd been holding the cat a moment before. Had he disappeared, transporting back to Francesca's house in the future, and then back again, all in the blink of an eye? Or had Starlight once lived there, right in little Reg's own building, and she had never known it? It was all too confusing for Reg to sort out.

The little girl's eyes sparkled when she saw the cat. "Oh, a kitty! Can I pat your kitty?"

She wriggled to get away from Reg. Reg put her down gently, and she hurried over to Harrison. Harrison obligingly stooped down to let her pet Starlight, and when the little girl showed that she could be gentle and pet him nicely, he sat down on the dirty carpet and released Starlight, letting him explore the room and wind his way around the little girl's legs. She was in transports of delight, petting the cat and talking to him like a baby, then growing more serious and talking to him as if he were having an actual conversation with her.

Reg noticed that Starlight didn't beg for food like he normally would have; maybe he knew that even if there were a few crumbs of food in the apartment, there wasn't anything to spare for him.

"Look, Mommy!" The little girl tried to get her mother's attention. "Look, Unca Harrison broughted a kitty! Can I keep him? He's so nice!"

Norma Jean focused on the cat and shook her head. "You know you can't have a cat, Regina. How many times do I have to tell you?"

"But this one is so nice. I take care'f him. He would catch mice!"

"I said no, Reg! Don't argue with Mommy!"

The little girl shrank back and fell silent. She sat on the floor, petting Starlight when he rubbed against her and pulling him into her lap to cuddle him. Her face was sad and resigned.

Reg watched the cat and the little girl interact. Maybe that was how she and Starlight had recognized each other when Reg had gone to the shelter looking for a cat.

Except that wasn't the way that things had happened in Reg's past. Not in her timeline. But it would be in the revised thread of time.

She shook her head, deciding not to try to understand it.

Harrison must have had a little more understanding of humans than he pretended. He didn't return everyone to Francesca's house, but Reg found herself in her own cottage with just Starlight and Harrison. She bent down and picked Starlight up, holding his warm, soft fur against her face and trying to see Harrison's blurred form through teary eyes.

"Will she be okay?" she asked.

Harrison's laugh rumbled deep in his chest. "You're here," he pointed out. "And you got your tuxedo cat and cottage near the ocean."

It took a few moments for Reg to realize that the little girl had grown up to be her, and wasn't a scared, lonely child anymore. What had happened decades ago was part of the misty past, something she could barely remember anymore.

"That's… just weird."

Harrison smiled. "I think you turned out okay, Regina."

"So nothing changed? It all happened the way I remember?"

"That depends what you remember."

"Harrison…" Reg rubbed at the pain in her forehead. Too much psychic work in one day. The spot that Sarah referred to as her third eye was pulsing with pain and no matter whether it was day or night, she was going to climb into bed, pull the covers over her eyes, and sleep for at least eight hours.

"Go sleep it off," he agreed, reaching out to take Starlight from her arms. "Temporal travel is always hard on human bodies. At least you didn't throw up."

"Weston is gone, right? He's not going to be back tomorrow trying to take over the world?"

"He's not gone. But he knows there are opposing forces and he won't be too quick to interfere in humans' affairs again. It's easier to seek satisfaction on other planes."

"And you don't have to worry about those things? What do you do if there are no humans to oppose him? Why couldn't you be the one to challenge him?"

"It is against the rules for me to harm one of my own kind."

"But Corvin and I didn't harm him. Why couldn't you do what we could?"

"It's not my world." Harrison shrugged. He twisted the ends of his mustache. "You will sleep well."

As usual, she didn't know whether it was a command or a prediction. And she didn't care.

"You going to come in, Star?"

Starlight made a soft purr-meow and Reg nodded. "Okay. See you in a bit."

CHAPTER TWENTY-SIX

There was a knock at her door. Reg sipped her tea, then got up to see who it was. She wasn't expecting any appointments until after dark.

She couldn't see anyone through the peephole and, after hesitating for a moment, opened the door anyway to see if UPS had left a package on the doorstep. Forst and Fir stood there together, below the level of the peephole. Reg smiled, genuinely happy to see them.

"Hi! I didn't know you were coming. How is everything?" She wasn't sure whether she should invite them in for tea. Inviting pixies in was a bad thing, but what about gnomes? She didn't think they would do anything mischievous.

"We brought you a living thing," Fir said, displaying a small green plant in a pot. He held it reverently with both hands and looked down at it with a smile. "Every home should have a living."

Reg held her hands out to receive it from him. "I do have Starlight, he's a living thing, but you're right; I don't have a plant."

"They help to keep the air clean and make you happy."

Both gnomes smiled at her, showing that they were happy. Their cheeks were round and rosy in spite of the many wrinkles from working in the sun.

"Thank you so much." Reg studied the plant. "It isn't the endangered one, is it? They wouldn't let you dig up the, uh, cluster…"

"Clustervine. No. It is not the clustervine. That is still safe on my plot, thanks to Reg Rawlins."

Reg smiled. "Good. And where should I put this little fellow? Does he like to be right by the window?"

"North facing. Diffuse light." Fir poked his head in Reg's door to look around. He pointed to one of the side tables in Reg's living room area. "It would like that space."

"I'll put it there, then. I've never had a plant before, so I don't know if I have a green thumb. How much water do I give it?"

"Once every week or two, enough to keep the dirt moist when you push your finger into it. Not enough to drown it."

"Okay. I hope I can manage that." She knew how much they loved plants and how much it would hurt Fir if he knew she neglected his gift. Maybe Sarah would help her to keep an eye on it too, just to make sure she didn't forget about it for a month at a time.

"And don't let the cat eat it," Forst warned. "Sometimes, cats eat things they shouldn't."

Fir nodded solemnly.

Reg hadn't wanted to go to Davyn's office again, but she was also not prepared to invite him to her house. Even though she was getting better at building a wall of protection around herself, she was by no means an expert. Corvin had still been able to trick her into giving him admission and she hadn't had the strength to fight back. That stung, and she didn't want to provide Davyn with an opportunity for an attack either. He was the leader of his coven and, while Reg didn't know all of what that entailed, she figured that meant that he was a pretty powerful warlock, despite appearances. Just because he hadn't done anything to threaten her in previous meetings, that didn't mean she could trust him. He was a close friend of Corvin's and didn't seem to understand the way the modern world worked.

So, she had only agreed to meet with him again if they did so in a public place, and it could not be The Crystal Bowl or anywhere she might run into someone she knew. Davyn suggested the dining room in a nearby hotel. They could have a meal, they'd be around other people, but not likely anyone she knew. It would mostly be frequented by out-of-town guests, which would be ideal for their purposes.

That had been her reasoning, anyway.

"The Council has made a decision not to readmit Corvin to the coven quite yet," Davyn informed Reg when their meals came and they had exhausted the usual small talk. "I wanted to let you know this personally and to reassure you that we are not just taking his word that he has mended his ways. We will continue to watch him and to evaluate his actions to decide whether he can be... a safe and productive member of our society."

Reg pushed food around on her plate. She had been hungry, and the delicious smells of the chicken stir fry had smelled good when the waiter put it down in front of her, but talking about Corvin and his behavior or his potential return to full membership of the coven made her forget how hungry she had been.

"Well, that's good," she said slowly. "I'm glad you weren't fooled by him."

"It has come to our attention, however, that you have been seen with him again in... possibly compromising circumstances. I am concerned about these reports."

"Why?"

"It is my duty to be aware of what Corvin is doing in the community... something like a probation officer. And his continued relationship with you is concerning. I'm also a little confused about why you are seeing him socially when you are so adamant about him not being returned to our society. It seemed like a conflict."

Reg searched for a coherent argument. She didn't really have any excuse for agreeing to see Corvin after all the conflict they had experienced already. Her choice had, once again, resulted in her being put in a dangerous situation with him. Saying that she had been testing him to see if he would resist his impulses seemed like the best story, but it didn't exactly put her in a good light. If she was afraid of Corvin and objected to what he had done in the past, then why put herself in that position again, even as a test?

She pushed a piece of chicken around and eventually put it into her mouth and chewed slowly. Davyn waited for her response.

"I just... I don't know. He wears me down. He uses his charms, and I forget how dangerous he is... I just want to be able to do what I want and still be safe."

She took a sip of her wine.

"I guess I want to believe that he has reformed or that I am strong enough to resist him. But instead… each time the results are the same. We start the evening with my rules firmly in place… but by the end of it, he has the upper hand again, and all my arguments and protests and the barriers that I have tried to build up are gone."

"It's a dangerous game. Why don't you simply avoid him?"

"I try. But he says that we're bonded together. Whatever decisions I make… our futures are still intertwined."

Davyn looked troubled by this. He nodded slowly and took a few bites of his dinner. They sat in silence, each considering the matter.

"Do you think that if you moved, he would follow you?"

"Why should I have to move?" Reg snapped.

"You don't. I'm asking you what you think would happen. You're a fortune teller, aren't you? Why don't you give me a prediction of the future? If you chose to move, would he follow you? Or would that break the connection between you?"

Reg sighed. She thought about it. What if she decided it was time to move on? Not back north, but maybe across the country to California or Nevada. If she put enough miles between them, that would be the end of it, wouldn't it? That would be the end of the conflict and any potential relationship with Corvin.

A vision started to fill her mind. She felt a strong hand in hers, imagined his breath in her ear and his husky voice coming to her in the night. But it wasn't Corvin. How could it be? She could never have a romantic relationship with him without risking the loss of her powers. She could only have that kind of relationship with a warlock who couldn't take her powers. An equal like Davyn or—

Reg swore and looked around. She knew exactly who could put a vision like that into her head. And once she was looking for him, she spotted Damon across the room, watching her, his face flushed with jealousy.

Davyn turned, following her gaze. "An admirer?" he asked lightly.

Reg shook her head. "This is getting ridiculous. I can have dinner with anyone I like!"

"Of course you can," Davyn agreed. "If he can't understand that, maybe you should tell him to leave you alone."

Which was precisely what Reg had done. But he was back, still trying to fill her head with his visions, twisting what she wanted to suit himself.

"Where is a magical restraining order when you need it?"

Under the weight of both of their gazes, Damon eventually caved and walked out of the room. Reg didn't see him again when she left.

She was sure it was only a coincidence that he had seen her there. He was acting as a security guard at some conference being held at the hotel. He had said so the other day.

It had just been a coincidence that he had seen her there with Davyn.

Reg had agreed to go with Francesca as she shipped Sally and Horace to their new owners in China and Egypt. Each carried one crate with an unhappy black kattakyn inside, leaving the house with Nicole's mournful cries ringing in their ears. It was heartbreaking to have to separate them, but they both knew it was necessary to keep the Witch Doctor from re-forming any time in the near future. And Francesca could not keep ten cats, even if they hadn't been the Witch Doctor's draugrs.

"Do you think the kittens knew about Weston being detained in your house?" Reg asked, hoping to distract them both from the unhappy felines. She was a little irritated with Francesca for hiding in the kitchen when Reg had accidentally released Weston. But then again, Francesca had experience with one immortal and Reg could understand her not wanting to get involved with another. "Is that why they went to the basement? If they are still the Witch Doctor at some level, they must have sensed that their old rival was there."

"I do not know," Francesca admitted. "It was very strange to have them disappearing in the house, when there was no way to get into the attic or the basement. There was strange magic going on in the house."

"Maybe it was the wormhole. Maybe that's how they kept getting into inaccessible rooms."

Francesca nodded in agreement. "Probably."

"They haven't disappeared again since then?"

She shook her head, lips pressed together. "No. But I also performed some cleansing rituals... did you notice the house seems brighter and more cheerful now? I think that immortal of yours must have been what was causing it to be so gloomy."

"He's not *my* immortal."

If one of the immortals was hers, it was Harrison. He was the one who had tried to protect her and had been there through the hard times. Then again, Weston was her father, and he *had* tried to go back to change the course of Reg's life, but neither of them was really *her* immortal. They had their own minds and wills.

"Well, anyway, I'm glad your house is feeling better now. I guess you'll be happy when it's just you and Nicole again and things have settled down."

"Yes, of course." Francesca sighed. "It will seem very empty with only one cat."

"Maybe you could get a plant too. I hear they are good company."

Francesca looked at her with pursed lips, puzzled by her comment. She shrugged. "Perhaps."

"It's a big house. You could get more than one plant."

Francesca didn't offer any response to this. They carried the cat crates into the small airport. Reg expected to just check them in with the luggage and leave them there, but after registering with the private airline counter, they were instructed to wait with the crates until the pilot was ready to take possession of them.

When the pilot showed up, Reg was surprised to see a young man she already knew. She hurried forward to shake his hand. "Warren Blake! How are you doing?"

His face was much fuller than the last time she had seen him, quite gaunt from being in a magical coma in a nursing home. He looked much more alive and happy than he had before.

"Reg Rawlins!" He pumped her hand, brown eyes alight. "We should have you over to dinner one day! Ling would love to see you."

"Yes, we should get together," Reg agreed. It was nice to see him looking so well and happy after all that he had been through. "I guess you're flying our cats today."

"To the international airport in Miami," Warren agreed. "Not all the way to their destinations." He looked into the crates and wiggled his finger through the bars to engage with the cats. They just huddled there, looking miserable. Warren checked the big stickers on each of the crates with their destination information. "Wow. World travelers. Well, don't you worry, I'll get them safely to Miami, and the airline is very good with these special deliveries."

Francesca was teary-eyed but seemed happy that Horace and Sally were going with someone Reg knew and trusted. Reg didn't tell him that the last time she had dealt with Warren, it had been after a plane crash. What were the chances that Warren would have a second crash? He was probably the safest pilot they could choose. He couldn't be unlucky enough to crash a second time.

They both said their teary goodbyes to the kittens and left them with Warren.

~

Reg's phone started ringing as she got to the door of her cottage. She fumbled with her key and hurried to put down her grocery bags and dig out the phone, not wanting to answer it on the doorstep.

It was an unknown number—a Maine area code. Reg hesitated before answering. Had someone from her old life tracked her down?

It wouldn't be the police. They wouldn't bother to call her. They'd contact the police department and work with them to get Reg into custody. And it had been a long time since she had operated in Maine, anyway. No one there would still be looking for her.

It was probably just a telemarketer. If they could operate out of India, then why not out of Maine? She swiped the screen to answer and brought the phone up to her ear.

"Hello?"

"Is this Reg Rawlins?" The voice, its tone, accent, and cadence were startlingly familiar. Reg shook off the feeling of deja vu, frowning.

"Who is this?"

"You probably don't remember me, but I knew you a long time ago when you were just a little girl." There was a hitch, a hesitation. "My name is Norma Jean."

Reg kept the phone at her ear, her mind spinning. Her legs folded under her and she sat down in the middle of the kitchen floor.

"Norma Jean?" she whispered. Norma Jean was alive. But hadn't she been killed by the Witch Doctor?

Not, it dawned on her slowly, in the new timeline. She and Corvin had banished the Witch Doctor. Weston had returned to his lover and child in the past where they were well and safe. Reg and Corvin had been able to persuade him to leave, but in a timeline where there was no Witch Doctor in corporeal form to hurt Norma Jean.

"They took you away from me when you were just a little mite," Norma Jean explained. "They said I couldn't take proper care of you and they put you into foster care. I didn't get clean for a long time after that, and when I did, they said my rights had been terminated. I couldn't get you back."

Reg swallowed, not sure what to say.

"I've been looking for you for a long time, honey," Norma Jean went on. "I'd like to come and see you."

DELUSIONS OF THE PAST

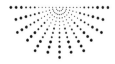

REG RAWLINS, PSYCHIC INVESTIGATOR #6

To those in search of their heritage

CHAPTER ONE

R eg didn't recognize her right away. She looked at the woman who stood on the doorstep of the cottage and raised her eyebrows questioningly, wondering who she was and what she was there for. She didn't have a lanyard with ID to identify her as a canvasser for any charity or a utility repair person. She wasn't someone that Reg recognized from the area. She might be a client that Sarah, Reg's landlord, had lined up or someone who had seen Reg's advertising and decided to drop by instead of making an appointment as requested in all of her posters.

Reg cocked her head and was about to ask the woman who she was when she suddenly realized. The woman looked a lot different now. Clean and tidy, her shoulder-length brunette hair smooth and silky, her face enhanced by a little makeup and not covered with sores and pockmarks. She'd had her teeth done. Maybe a full set of dentures or implants. She bore little resemblance to the mother that Reg remembered.

"Norma Jean," Reg said, heart sinking.

Norma Jean smiled brilliantly, showing off the perfect teeth. "Oh, my baby. It's been so long since I saw you!"

She fell upon Reg, embracing her, trying to pull her in close for one of those warm Hallmark moments. Reg pulled back, pushing her away, trying to get her personal space back. "Don't do that! Don't touch me."

Norma Jean's eyebrows went up, and the corners of her mouth went down. She gave Reg a kicked-puppy-dog look, all hurt and offended.

Reg held her hands up in front of her in a 'stop' signal. "You can't just go around hugging people. You're not my mother. Not anymore."

"I am your mother and will never stop being your mother, no matter what you say or do." The slight southern cadence and accent were the same as Reg remembered. That woman had lived in her head for decades, from the time she had died when Reg was four, until... Reg shook her head to try to rid it of the feeling of vertigo she felt whenever considering the timeline and the changes that Weston had caused when he went back to see her mother.

Norma Jean had died when Reg was four. But not in the timeline Reg now inhabited. Whatever Weston had done had changed essential parts of Reg's past. Norma Jean had not died. Her spirit had not attached itself to Reg, her guilt making her a constant companion, always telling Reg what to do and attempting to undo the harm she had done while she had been alive.

Reg just stared at Norma Jean, trying to comprehend it all.

"Well, aren't you going to invite me in?" Norma Jean queried, giving a flirty little pout, acting the role she had made up. Why had she suddenly shown up in Black Sands, Florida? Reg had made it clear that she didn't want to see Norma Jean. Either Norma Jean was thicker than Reg believed, or she had wholly disregarded what her daughter had said, deciding to fly in from Maine regardless.

"Fine, come in," Reg said finally, glancing around the yard to make sure Norma Jean was the only one there. She wasn't sure who else she was looking for. Weston or a more current boyfriend? There was no way for her to prevent the powerful immortal from entering even if she tried.

She opened the door wide enough for Norma Jean and stepped back.

Norma Jean gave a smile and came in, acting like the queen of Black Sands. She looked around Reg's little cottage, chin lifted, smile set firmly in place. Reg went to the kitchen to put on a kettle for tea, an action that had become habitual since she had moved to Black Sands and started seeing clients for psychic readings. A cup of tea always went over well with someone who was about to take a foray into the unknown. And Reg could read the tea leaves in the bottom of the cup if they were so inclined. Reg would go with whatever psychic reading method they preferred.

"This is real nice," Norma Jean told her.

"Yeah." Reg wasn't in much of a mood for conversation. It was just a cottage in the back yard of Sarah's big house, but it was better than anything else Reg had ever had on her own. Clean and neat and furnished in Sarah's breezy Florida style. Certainly better than anything that Reg had ever lived in while she was still with Norma Jean, a series of flophouses, shelters, and cold nights on the street.

She watched the kettle intently, hoping that it would take all day to boil.

Norma Jean wandered around, looking at the decorations and furnishings. She touched the leaves of the plant that Fir had given to Reg when he told her that she needed living things in her environment. It did perk the place up a bit, giving the cottage a more homey feeling. Fir said that plants had feelings, and maybe Reg was sensing the warm feelings of the houseplant itself. Or perhaps it just looked good on the little side table.

Eventually, Norma Jean settled on the wicker couch and waited for Reg to make the tea and bring it over on the tray. She helped herself to one of the cups, and they both gave their attention to their tea, Reg studiously ignoring Norma Jean, until it was no longer possible, because Norma Jean was talking, forcing Reg to acknowledge her existence.

"They took you away from me when you were still real little." She took a tentative sip of the tea but didn't look like she enjoyed it. Reg couldn't remember Norma Jean ever drinking tea. She would probably have preferred the Jack Daniels in Reg's corner cupboard. "I didn't have any say in it. I would have kept you if I could."

Norma Jean had been destitute and addicted, completely unable to care for a child. The times that she had ignored Reg had been the best. Better to be ignored than abused. It was a wonder that it had taken child services four years to apprehend her.

"You couldn't be a mother."

"No… I guess I couldn't," Norma Jean admitted. "I needed to take care of myself and deal with my own problems before I could be responsible for someone else."

Taking care of herself was all Norm Jean had ever done, self-serving and focused on her own gratification. How long had it taken for her to get straight after Reg had been removed? Ten years? Twenty?

Reg played with one of the red box-braids that hung down next to her face. It had taken Norma Jean twenty-five years to make contact with her daughter again. How much of that time had she been clean and sober?

"I'm sorry that you had to grow up in foster care. I would have gotten you back if I could have. But they wouldn't even talk about letting you come back unless I cleaned up my act. And..." Norma Jean wavered, "after I was off the drugs, I decided it was probably best if you stayed there. I needed to figure things out... learn how to support myself. I recognized that I didn't have what I needed to take care of a kid."

"Good for you."

"I've been looking for you. Once you were old enough to look after yourself, I kind of looked around... tried to find out where you might be... but I couldn't find you. They wouldn't give me any information, of course; those government agencies act like they're so superior and won't tell you a thing. I thought... that maybe you might be looking for me too. Once you aged out of the system, then you could go wherever you wanted to and you could look for me."

Reg shook her head. Of course she had never searched for Norma Jean. She had known exactly where Norma Jean was. Dead and lurking in a corner of Reg's brain. She had tried to banish the voice, not to go back there. Her life with Norma Jean had never been a happy place. She hadn't liked the instability of foster care, but she had rarely wished she was back with Norma Jean again. "They told me you were dead," she told Norma Jean flatly.

"What? Why would they do that? They knew I wasn't dead!"

"Well, that's what I thought."

Norma Jean shook her head angrily. "I should sue them! I cannot believe that they would lie to you like that. We could have been reunited years ago."

Reg sipped her tea, not answering. She wouldn't have wanted to have reunited with Norma Jean.

Or would she? In the timeline where Norma Jean had not been killed, had Reg yearned to be back together with her again? If she'd known that Norma Jean was alive, would Reg have gone back to her once she was sixteen or eighteen and had a mind of her own? At least there would have been someone in her life who was a constant, even if Norma Jean wasn't able to provide the care of a parent. It would have been better than being out on the streets, as Reg had been several times since her graduation from foster care.

There was a soft thud, and Reg turned her head to watch Starlight come out of the bedroom to see who was visiting.

Norma Jean looked at the tuxedo cat with the mismatched eyes and white spot on his forehead, her eyebrows drawing down in puzzlement. Starlight went to Reg's side and, after surveying Norma Jean for a moment, jumped up into Reg's lap. Reg put down her tea and petted him, stroking the longer fur down his back and scratching his ears and chin. Norma Jean shook her head.

"Where have I seen that cat before?"

Reg knew very well where she had seen the cat, but thought it interesting that Starlight would seem more familiar to Norma Jean than her own daughter. Did she not remember the woman who had been with the cat? Or had her drug-addled brain lost that detail or morphed it into something else?

"Maybe you saw a cat that looked like him," Reg said. "This is Starlight."

"You always wanted a cat. I don't know how many times you dragged some stray in and tried to convince me that you would take care of it."

"Did I?" Reg didn't remember that. But she didn't remember a lot of specific experiences from when she'd been with Norma Jean. She had, after all, only been four. A lot of people didn't remember anything before they were five, not just traumatized kids taken into custody after a parent was murdered. Maybe Norma Jean remembered only that one time when little Reg had met Starlight and hugged and cuddled him and asked if she could keep him. Maybe that had become 'dragging home random strays and asking to keep them.' Parents did that sometimes. Blew one little incident up into something the child 'always' did.

Reg put her face against the top of Starlight's head and breathed into his fur. It was always very calming to hold Starlight. He gave out good vibes. He had chosen Reg when she went to the animal shelter, rather than her choosing him, and she was glad that he had.

"So, tell me all about your life." Norma Jean leaned forward. "I want to know everything. When you were little, where you've been, and what you've done. If you have a boyfriend. What you're doing all the way in Black Sands."

Reg disliked sharing information about her past. She particularly didn't want to give Norma Jean any ammunition. Who knew how she might use it.

"Nothing to tell. This is just where I moved. Now I try to make a living... doing personal consulting."

"Personal consulting," Norma Jean tasted the words. "What exactly is that? What kind of consulting?"

"Life planning. Making decisions about the future. I help people to... look ahead in their lives. Or sometimes, to take a look back at the past and make their peace so that they can move forward again."

"That sounds very interesting." Norma Jean was impressed. "How do you get all of your business? You must make good money to live in a place like this."

Reg cleared her throat. "It isn't as much as you might think. My landlord helps me get some work; she's really... tuned into the community. I advertise, mostly locally, put posters up on community bulletin boards or places they might frequent. It's picking up steadily."

She always worried about how long it would last, and wished that she'd discovered a treasure like gold or jewels instead of Weston. Why couldn't it have been gold?

"Maybe you could help me. I'm always so confused about where to go with my life... I guess I don't have very much direction. I don't have any big talents. You must have gotten an education, to be able to do that kind of life planning for people."

"All self-educated. I didn't have any money to go to college. Nowhere to live. No one to cosign a loan. I didn't do great in school, so there were no grants or scholarships."

"Yeah. That's the trouble with foster care. I've heard it's really hard."

She'd heard it. Too bad she hadn't lived it. She might not be so sanguine about it.

"What about you? What are *you* doing?" Reg turned the question back on Norma Jean. She had enough money to buy a plane ticket across the country. She looked well-fed and focused. Not gaunt and wretched and scattered, unable to conceive of how to make it from one day to the next.

"I do a little of this and a little of that… just whatever I can pick up. That's why I said I should have you give me one of those consultations."

"You pick up what kind of work? Cleaning? Cooking? Outdoor work? Hooking?"

Norma gave a shocked laugh. "Oh, not that! Yes, sometimes cleaning or outdoor stuff like mowing lawns. Some retail stores. Just… positions that don't require any experience. I don't have much on my resume. Employers don't think much of that."

The same kind of jobs as Reg had hopscotched between until she had happened onto the psychic gig. That had worked well enough that she'd been able to give up the back-breaking, footsore work.

Reg got to her feet and put Starlight down. She moved around restlessly. She didn't like having Norma Jean there. It made her anxious. She was too anxious and restless to sit in one place and chat as if they were old friends.

She went to the window and looked out into the yard. The grass was all neatly trimmed around the paving stones that made up the pathway. She couldn't see the main garden from that side of the cottage, but she could see well-maintained bushes, trees, and lawn. It had looked nice before, and since Sarah had hired Forst as a gardener, everything was looking lush and bright and happy. He had done an excellent job.

A movement in the corner of her eye caught Reg's attention, and she turned her head to look at it, but as soon as she did so, it was gone. She watched for a moment to see if it came back. Maybe a bird or the wind blowing a tree. She waited for the movement to repeat itself but she didn't see it again.

"What are you looking at?" Norma Jean inquired.

"Nothing. I'm just looking." Reg moved away from the window again. "So, how long are you here? What are your plans? I use the second bedroom as my office, so there is nowhere here for you to stay overnight."

"Oh, I would never impose on you," Norma Jean assured, her voice earnest and smooth. Reg didn't believe it for a minute. Norma Jean had been hoping for an invitation, or failing receipt of an invitation, to be able to talk her way into staying in Reg's cottage while she was in town. Reg hoped that she couldn't find anywhere to sleep and had to go back home right away.

Reg drifted into the kitchen and cleared a few dirty dishes away. Norma Jean watched and didn't offer to help. Not that there were enough dishes for her to help with. By the time she got to the kitchen, Reg would have been done.

There was a quick tap at the door, then the handle turned and Sarah bustled in. "Good morning, Reg. Isn't it a lovely day out there today? Oh." Her eyes settled on Norma Jean. "I didn't know that you had company."

Reg didn't have quite what it took to say 'she was just leaving' to get Norma Jean out of the way. "This is... Norma Jean." Reg swallowed and tried to think of how much information to share. "My mother."

Sarah looked stunned. She put a hand over her heart. "Your mother? But I thought your mother—"

Reg waited for Sarah to say "was dead," but she trailed off, not finishing the thought.

"Apparently not. That's what they told me, back when I was little, but I guess it was just a lie."

"Well, this is quite a shock." Sarah landed heavily in the chair that Reg had recently vacated. "That's amazing news. How... wonderful for you." Sarah smiled at Norma Jean, turned her head and looked at Reg, and the smile on her face faltered.

"I was so excited to be able to track Reg down," Norma Jean gushed. "And you must be her friend...?"

"Sarah." Sarah stuck out her hand to Norma Jean and shook vigorously. "Yes, I'm Reg's friend and her landlord."

"Oh, so this is your place."

Sarah nodded. "Well, I own it, but it's Reg's for as long as she wants to live here. I needed someone stable to take it for me. Reg has been a lifesaver for me."

Did Norma Jean know she was being lied to? Reg didn't do anything for Sarah but pay a minimal rent for the cottage. Sarah came and went, keeping everything clean and tidy, feeding Starlight when he insisted he was hungry, lining up clients for Reg, delivering her mail and flyers, and telling her about the community events coming up. She was like... a mother to Reg.

Maybe Norma Jean sensed this. Her mouth was a straight line, lips pressed together. She didn't like this interloper in Reg's life.

But to Reg, Norma Jean was the interloper. Who did she think she was, showing up on Reg's doorstep without any warning and expecting to be invited in and even being allowed to stay with her for... however long Norma Jean was planning to stay? Reg bit her lip, worrying about that.

Norma Jean hadn't said anything to indicate that she had ties back home. She might be planning to move to Black Sands permanently. A choice that would make things very difficult for Reg.

"It's very nice to meet you," Sarah told Norma Jean pleasantly. "I'm sure Reg will have the best time while you are here."

Norma Jean gave a broad smile, which to Reg looked utterly fake. She nodded vigorously. "Oh, yes, we are going to have the best time, aren't we honey?"

Reg didn't try to match Norma Jean's smile. The answer was no; they were not going to have the best time. Reg looked around, trying to figure out some way of getting out of the situation. She looked back at Sarah, wondering whether she could see the panic in Reg's eyes.

"Did you… need something, Sarah?"

"Well…"

"Did you need me to do something for you? Norma Jean can go, I'm free if there's something that you wanted…"

"No, no. It's not that. It's just that I needed to do some maintenance here. I know I haven't given you the proper forty-eight hours' notice, so I really shouldn't spring it on you like this, but I was going to see whether you were going to… be out for part of the day. and then if you are, I could come back then to work on it."

"Oh." Reg looked around. "Well, you gotta do what you gotta do. Norma Jean, we're going to have to vacate, so…"

"Are you going to go out to lunch?" Sarah suggested. "You could take her to The Crystal Bowl. Maybe go out shopping for a while or go for a walk in the park. Then by the time you are done, I'm sure I'd be mostly finished here."

"Oh, yes, let's!" Norma Jean jumped in. "That sounds like fun."

Reg glared at Sarah. "I don't think that I can fit that into my schedule today."

"You can make time for your mother who you haven't seen in years," Norma Jean pouted. "It's my treat. I don't know the restaurants in the area, so you'll have to tell me what's good, but I'll take you out and we'll have a nice time."

"Go," Sarah encouraged, making a motion to shoo Reg out of the room. "You go on. Have a good time. I need the space to work."

Reg shook her head. "What about Starlight?" she grumbled. "Do you need me to lock him up? What are you going to be working on?"

Sarah looked at the cat. She was not a cat person and would probably prefer that he weren't underfoot, but she was always good about it and didn't make a fuss. "Oh, no. He'll be fine. I'll only have the door open for a few minutes, and I'll keep an eye on him to make sure he can't get out."

"And he won't be in your way? You know how he has to get right in the middle of whatever you're working on."

"He won't bother me. The two of you go ahead, go have a nice lunch together."

Reg fetched her purse, moving slowly, still trying to think of an excuse to get out of it. She could tell Norma Jean that she had somewhere else to go. A competing appointment. But Norma Jean was going to know that something was up. And she would keep persisting until she got her own way. At least if they were going to lunch together, there was a natural break point where they could each say their goodbyes and go their separate directions. She only had to put up with Norma Jean for an hour or two.

That sounded like a very long time.

CHAPTER TWO

When Reg got back from lunch, it was quite late. She had intentionally given Sarah a couple of extra hours to finish whatever she was working on at the cottage. Norma Jean had pouted and whined about Reg having to take care of other matters, but she couldn't have expected to have all of Reg's time. Reg was running a business. Norma Jean had grudgingly accepted this, and though she had tried to get Reg to let her stay at the cottage, Reg had been firm about that. She didn't have a second bed and Norma Jean wasn't sharing Reg's.

"When are you going back north? There isn't really anything for you to do here."

"What do you mean, there isn't anything for me to do? I am here to see my daughter. I want to know all about you. Really get to know you. We've lost so many years."

"Norma Jean…" Reg held up her hand in protest. "I told you not to come here. I think I've been pretty nice to let you into my house and to go out to lunch with you, but you have to understand, you're not a part of my life. And you're not going to be."

"You can't *not* be my daughter. I gave birth to you and nothing is going to change that."

Reg wasn't sure that either of those statements was true. The more she discovered about the magical world, the less confident she was of anything. Maybe Norma Jean had given birth to her in the usual way, or maybe Weston, being an immortal, had somehow created Reg in a different way. And just because something had always been one way, that didn't mean that it couldn't change. Norma Jean had been dead for almost Reg's whole life, and now she wasn't. If that could change, anything could.

There were lights when she approached the cottage. Reg was surprised that Sarah would have left them on. She should have finished earlier in the day when it was not dark, and wouldn't have thought to leave the lights on for her. Reg hung back from the cottage, looking things over, hesitating about what she should do.

She was being silly. What did she think? That there was someone else in her cottage? That someone had broken in? Or that Norma Jean had arrived back ahead of her, refusing to listen to Reg's refusal to let her stay for the night? If Norma Jean was there, Reg was going to call the police. She'd had enough of her mother's nonsense and wanted to make it clear that she was not welcome there. She could go back north and do whatever she wanted to, as long as it was far away from Reg.

A shadow passed across the window. Not Starlight. Definitely a person.

Reg heard the faint tinkle of bells, which didn't seem like they came from inside the house. Maybe a neighbor had recently installed new wind chimes. Reg couldn't remember hearing them before then.

Was it Norma Jean? Or another intruder? Should she call the police? She didn't want to have any more dealings with the police in Black Sands and didn't need to attract any attention to herself.

Reg crept up to the window and tried to peek inside without exposing herself. If it was just Norma Jean, there was nothing to be afraid of. But if it was some other person or shadowy creature, she wasn't about to go barging in and get herself eaten or cursed.

She watched for the intruder, waiting for them to cross back across the window again. She was at a bad angle and couldn't see inside very well. She could go around to a window with a better view of the interior, but then she would have to contend with the horizontal blinds.

The intruder came closer to the window and, straining her neck for a better angle, Reg finally relaxed. It was just Sarah. Still there after so long? The maintenance must not have gone the way she had hoped.

Reg went to the door and hesitated, wondering if she should knock before entering so that she wouldn't startle Sarah. But knocking on her own door? That didn't seem right. Reg opened the door, jingling her keys, and went in.

She stopped, stock still, her mouth open, as she looked around at the changes to the cottage.

～

"Holy cow! What happened here?"

Sarah beamed at Reg. "Do you like it?"

Reg didn't know where to look first. There was what she was pretty sure was holly, with shiny green leaves and red berries, and another plant with white berries. There were strings of twinkle lights and a wide assortment of candles flickering in jars around the room. There was an evergreen tree in a bucket and wreaths, pinecones, and garlands everywhere. It seemed like every surface was covered with some new decoration.

"Is this for Christmas? It looks like a department store blew up in here!"

"For Yule," Sarah corrected. "Isn't it lovely? I love decorating for solstice."

"Yule," Reg repeated, looking around. "I thought Yule was Christmas? Yuletide greetings and all of that. Isn't that right?"

"Christians may think that Yule and Christmas are the same things because they borrowed so many of the symbols and traditions from Yule, but they are not the same thing. This is for our holy day. Little Jesus couldn't have been born in December. Not if sheep were lambing in the fields."

"Uh… oh. Okay. I don't know much about the origins of either of them. I mean I've been forced to watch or read the Christmas story enough times, with all of the different foster families who wanted to educate me as to what Christmas was really about, but I never really saw the connection between a baby being born and Christmas and all of the rest—gifts and Santa Claus and…" She looked around, "…this."

"That's because there is no connection. It is a bunch of traditions cobbled together in an effort to keep the pagan converts happy hundreds of years ago. Christmas today is a chaotic mishmash of Christian legend and pagan symbolism and Coca Cola and Clement Clarke Moore. Hallmark and commercialism. Nothing like Yule." She folded her arms and looked around at the decorations adorning every surface with a contented smile. "I love the simple symbolism and stories of Yule. They have barely changed during the time that Christianity was trying to get a foothold and build its empire. Still the same symbols and rituals that have always been part of the season."

Reg indicated the garlands of twinkle lights. "Nothing has changed?"

"Well, if you want to bring modern technology into it. It is a little easier to string lights than it is to try to fill the house with candles. Most of these..." Sarah indicated one of the many candles flickering around the room, "are actually electric." She reached into one jar and pulled the fake candle out, not burning herself. "I get them at the dollar store by the case."

Reg laughed. "Well, you wouldn't want to burn the house down."

"Yule is a time of light, so I always try to provide lots of extra inspiration. You do want a few real candles to practice meditation and healing, but most of them can just be electric."

Reg picked up another of the fake candles and looked at it. She put it back down. "Healing?"

"Fire is a powerful element. It can hurt and do devastating damage, but it can also heal."

"I'll have to take your word on that one."

"If you want to learn about it, I am more than happy to share."

"Yeah... why don't you tell me about the rest? Are you telling me that the Christmas tree is really a Yule tree?"

"Yes, it is," Sarah laughed. "Evergreen trees and branches were a symbol of life for long before the Christians borrowed them. They stay green all winter with the promise of reawakening in the spring. How could that not be a powerful symbol in any pagan culture?"

"Well, I guess." Reg looked around. "Not that anything turns brown in December here. It's sort of funny to be somewhere green all year long."

"It is paradise," Sarah agreed. "I have had enough of cold nights, snow, mud, and miserable weather. Florida is the perfect place."

"As long as there are no hurricanes," Reg suggested.

"Well." Sarah shrugged, conceding the point. "I'd still rather be warm all year. My old bones do not like the cold."

Reg supposed that if Sarah were hundreds of years old, as she claimed, she was entitled to complain about aching bones.

"When is Yule? Is it the same day as Christmas?"

"It is winter solstice. December twenty-first. But it is traditionally held for twelve days, so—"

"The twelve days of Christmas?"

"You didn't ever wonder where that came from?"

"Uh… no."

Reg had always had more pressing concerns around Christmas time. Was she living in a home where she was expected to give gifts? That could be a problem, especially if it was supposed to be paid for out of her own money, something she rarely had.

Was she going to be staying with her foster family for Christmas, or would they be visiting extended family and she would be required to go to respite care for the holiday, where the parents would know nothing about her?

Would she be forced to sing? To perform? To sit through mind-numbing hours of preaching? Or would it be a family that didn't celebrate Christmas and was sneered at by the kids at school and other people in the neighborhood? Many years, she had wished that she could just skip Christmas. She had never once been tempted to research Christmas traditions and to find out where they had come from.

"I'll tell you more about it later, then. We have plenty of time. I wanted to get the decorations up early to get plenty of usage out of them. I'm not one to put them up the day before Yule and take them down again the day after."

"Sure, that makes sense. You may as well enjoy it all."

Sarah clearly did, or she wouldn't have been decorating the cottage as well as her own house. Reg assumed that it was not a Yule tradition to decorate other people's homes.

"Are you going to decorate the tree?"

"You and I can do that over the next few days. I'm afraid I'm out of energy today. The well has run dry."

"Okay." Reg might have fun decorating a tree. But she couldn't make any assumptions as to what they would be putting on it. She was pretty sure that round Christmas baubles and an angel on top of the tree would not be part of the prescribed decorations. "Well, thank you for all of this. It's lovely.

I didn't expect anything. I thought when I came home, and the lights were on that… it might have been burgled."

Sarah laughed heartily. "No, just an old lady who doesn't know when to stop. I'm going to get something to eat and hit the sack. I will not be out partying tonight."

CHAPTER THREE

W here is Starlight?" Reg looked around.

Usually, Starlight wanted to be right in the middle of it if strange things were going on in the house. He seemed to think that everything was done for his sake and he needed to supervise and ensure that it was done correctly. Even if Starlight hadn't been interested in the decorating being done, he should at least have come out when he heard Reg's voice. He always greeted her and wanted to be fed, even if there was plenty of food in his dish. "Did you end up having to shut him up after all?"

Sarah looked around. "He was over by the tree, last I saw."

Reg walked to the corner, looking for the cat. Starlight was, in fact, underneath the tree, and he didn't look happy. When Reg bent down for a look, his eyes were as round as saucers. When she extended her hand to touch him, he put back his ears and hissed. Reg jerked back, surprised.

"Whoa. What's got into you?"

"Cats don't like change," Sarah said, as if it were a well-known fact. "He's probably just disgruntled by the decorations."

"He's never behaved like that toward me before."

"Give him some space. I'm sure he'll be just fine. It will wear off, and he'll be back to his usual self again."

"I hope so." Reg watched him analytically. "You'd better be on your best behavior tomorrow, since Nicole and the kattakyns are coming by for a visit."

Sarah cleared her throat loudly. "Reg, about that…"

Reg looked away from Starlight, hearing the sternness in Sarah's voice. "What is it?" Her stomach clenched like it used to when she was in school and would be called before a teacher or principal to explain something she had done wrong or to get a dressing-down.

"Having all of those cats in here… I don't like it. We didn't discuss cats before you moved in here, so I conceded the point about Starlight. But you know my stance on cats now… and I don't like all of those mischievous creatures running around here."

"They'll be fully supervised and they won't be outside the house. We've been very careful not to let them damage anything."

"Even so…" Sarah eyed one of the chairs, and Reg wondered how she could possibly know that Nico had been clawing it the last time they were over to visit. There wasn't any visible damage. "I would much rather you took Starlight over to Francesca's house after this. I'm sure she would be much happier with that anyway. It can't be easy to bring all of those kittens over here at once, especially as they are getting bigger."

Reg couldn't argue that fact. But Francesca liked to get them out of her house for a few hours. Reg had a talent for settling them down and helping them to work through their problems. Francesca wanted them properly socialized and prepared to go to their new homes as they identified suitable matches.

"I'll have to talk to Francesca about it."

"I don't want them here. They get hair and dander everywhere, even if they don't claw the furniture. And I worry about them attracting other cats into the garden. I don't want those filthy beasts using it as a toilet."

"I don't think that's going to happen…"

"But that was why Nicole came here in the first place. Because of Starlight sitting in the window. I don't want more cats coming around here, Reg. Really."

Reg sighed. She was getting a great deal on the rent and everything else that Sarah did for her. Sarah didn't really ask for much in return. "Okay. I'll talk to her in the morning."

∽

Starlight wouldn't come out from under the Yule tree when it was time for bed. Reg had been enjoying the lights and candles and the peace she felt being surrounded by the other decorations, but it was strange not having Starlight to cuddle with during the evening. And he always bugged her for food when she started making preparations to go to bed. He knew it was his last chance for hours and, poor starving creature that he was, he couldn't go that long without fresh food and water. She stood in the kitchen, putting her dishes into the dishwasher and watching the Yule tree, waiting for Starlight to come out.

"Are you just going to sulk under that tree all night?"

He didn't answer or come out.

"I know cats don't like change, but this is a little ridiculous, don't you think? There's nothing here that's going to harm you. And after Christmas —Yule—it will all be going away again. It's just for the month. You can deal with it."

He still didn't leave the shelter of the tree. Reg shook her head, feeling foolish about trying to reason with a cat. If he wanted to hide under the tree, what harm was there in that? Maybe he was pretending he was in a forest, like a kid playing in a tree fort. Or perhaps he was just sulking and letting her know how displeased he was with the changes. Or it might have been something to do with Sarah. Reg always suspected that Starlight understood far more than he should, and maybe he was displeased that Sarah had put her foot down about Nicole and the kittens coming over to visit. He always had a soft spot where Nicole was concerned. Reg would be glad when they had found appropriate magical homes for all of the kittens and it could be just Nicole again. It wouldn't be so hard to smuggle only one cat into the cottage without Sarah knowing about it.

"Okay, I'm going to bed," she tried once more. "Last call."

He didn't come darting back out to show her that even though he was still mad at her, he was hungry too and she'd better keep up with her duties. Reg gave a shrug and didn't touch his bowls. If he wasn't going to insist that she change the food and water, then why make more work for herself? It wasn't like he would starve overnight even if he decided he didn't want them.

In the morning, Reg was used to being awakened several times by Starlight before she finally conceded to start her day. She was up late nights with seances and readings, so she slept quite late in the morning, and Starlight took offense to this and thought she should rise early. But she'd slept through. She looked at the windowsill, where he liked to sit and watch the birds in the garden. It was empty; he wasn't there. Reg rubbed her eyes. The bed was cold; he wasn't sleeping curled up against her. He wasn't on the bed at all. After the months of being harassed by a furry feline when she wanted to sleep longer, it was very disconcerting.

Reg got up and used the bathroom and rinsed out her mouth. She pulled her braids back behind her shoulders, looking at herself in the mirror, then walked into the kitchen.

She saw the tip of Starlight's tail behind the kitchen island and was relieved.

"You finally decided to come out of the tree?"

His tail didn't twitch. Reg rounded the island and gasped.

CHAPTER FOUR

Starlight was laying on his side, unmoving. He was so still, she couldn't even see him breathing, and she reached out and touched him, sure he was going to be cold and stiff. Tears were already running down her cheeks, and she was breathing with her mouth wide open, trying to stifle sobs and get enough oxygen.

"Starlight? What happened? What's wrong?"

He was still warm and soft. She put her hand over his throat and chest and could feel shallow respirations. She looked all over his body, what was visible, for any sign of an injury. What had happened? He had been just fine the night before. Had he been up on the counter and fallen the wrong way? Had he gotten sick in the night? It didn't make any sense. He'd been in perfectly good health.

The only change in his behavior had been in hiding under the Yule tree the night before. Animals, cats in particular, often isolated themselves in dark corners when they were very sick. That was what one of the videos on cat care on YouTube had said. If your cat started hiding in dark corners, he might be seriously ill, and a trip to the vet was strongly recommended.

Starlight had never been sick since she had bought him. He'd complained, but he'd never been sick. Reg gathered him up in her arms, crooning to him. There was no response to her words or the fact that she was manhandling him. Reg held him close and kissed the top of his head.

"Come on, Star. Don't be sick. Don't let this happen."

She closed her eyes and tried to feel his spirit, his consciousness. But she couldn't sense him. Only an aura of sickness and destruction, something left behind by someone else. It was so strong that it made her feel sick. She focused on building a wall around Starlight like she had done before to protect herself from Corvin. If there was some menacing force that had resulted in Starlight's unconscious state, then she needed to protect him from further harm. Another hour or two in that malevolent environment and she wouldn't be able to get him back.

She wrapped layer after layer of protection around her furry friend until she was so exhausted she could do nothing more for him. Then she wrapped him in a soft, clean bath towel and took him out to the car to transport him to the vet.

The veterinary assistant who hustled Reg into one of the examining rooms with Starlight stood beside her with a clipboard as the vet examined her comatose familiar.

"Do you have any idea what he might have eaten?"

"He didn't eat anything unusual. Just his usual food. Maybe some leftovers."

Reg knew very well that Starlight had eaten leftovers; he always begged for human food and only ate a little of the food that was scientifically engineered to suit an active cat's nutritional needs. She racked her brain, trying to remember what he might have had in the previous twenty-four-hour period.

"He usually begs for food when I'm going to bed and he didn't do that last night. He was just hiding under the tree and wouldn't come out."

"Under the tree? He was outside?"

"No, no. He's an inside cat. He's only been out once. He was hiding under the Christmas tree." She hesitated, wondering if she should correct herself to say Yule tree, but they might have no idea what that was, and they did know what a Christmas tree was.

"I see. Do you have other Christmas decorations out? Anything that might be harmful to a cat? Plants?"

"My landlord decorated. I... I have a plant that someone gave me, and he said not to let Starlight eat it, but he's never shown an interest in it. He doesn't eat plants."

"You never know when they might get it into their heads to eat something they shouldn't. You should be careful not to have toxic plants in the environment. What kind of houseplant was this?"

"I… don't know. I guess I could find out."

"It might be important." The veterinary assistant scribbled notes on the clipboard. "That's the only plant?"

"Aside from the Christmas decorations, yes."

"What Christmas decorations do you have?"

"Well, I guess they're not actually for Christmas, they're for Yule. That's what my landlord celebrates. I don't know what they all were."

The woman holding the clipboard raised her eyebrows, waiting for more information. Reg looked down at Starlight, still unmoving as the vet poked and prodded and made his examination. She swallowed hard and pictured her living room after Sarah had decorated it.

"Lots of evergreen boughs and wreaths, with pinecones. Uh… I think holly. And something with white berries."

"Probably mistletoe. White berries are almost always poisonous. And so is the holly, by the way."

"If he ate one of those or the other plant, you can still do something, can't you? How bad is it?"

The veterinary assistant didn't answer. The vet stroked Starlight and grimaced at Reg. "Our little friend isn't in very good shape. You need to be prepared that he might not make it. I'm not sure what he got into. We'll do some blood tests, stomach contents, see if we can figure out if he ate something. We'll give him fluids and do what we can to clean him out. But…" he shrugged apologetically, "the damage may have already been done."

Tears ran down Reg's face. She wiped at them with her hand. "I wouldn't have left him with all of those plants if I had known… I thought… he's never tried to eat anything like that; I don't see why he would now."

"There are other household items that can be toxic to pets as well. Antifreeze, for example. We sometimes see cases where pets were intentionally poisoned. You don't have a boyfriend or neighbor who doesn't like him, do you?"

Reg thought about Sarah's complaint just the night before, not about

Starlight, but about the other cats and not wanting them around. She shook her head slowly. "No, I don't think anyone would have hurt him intentionally. I live alone. It's not like he does anything to bother anyone."

"Well, we'll do what we can for him. But he's in pretty bad shape."

Reg gave Starlight one final pat and ear scratch, her throat aching and tears streaming down her face in earnest.

Reg returned to her house in a fog, unsure of what to do next or how to deal with the crisis. She couldn't just go on as usual and hope that Starlight recovered, but what could she possibly do about it? It was too late to take action after he'd been poisoned. She felt like just climbing under the covers and going back to sleep, but she tried to coach herself into facing the problem and not hiding from it. She was a grown-up. She needed to act like one. The loss of her familiar would be devastating, but animals did die, and people too, and she had managed to carry on before. Her loss of Starlight, if he didn't manage to pull through, couldn't possibly be more catastrophic than the loss of her mother when she was four and the dark years that followed. She still had a house to live in, clients who would want to see her, and friends who would be sympathetic. If worse came to worst, she could get another cat.

Reg sobbed as she drove. "I don't want another cat! I need Starlight! He's not just a cat; he's a… he's really important to me." Her voice broke and she coughed and sputtered, trying to see properly through her tear-filled eyes. She probably should not be on the road. She wasn't exactly in any shape to be driving. But what else was she going to do? She needed to get home. She could pull over to the side of the road and try to get her composure back, but chances were that if she did, she would completely break down and wouldn't be able to go anywhere.

So she kept going.

When she finally reached the house, she parked the car and walked in. The Yuletide wonderland gleamed around her. All kinds of festive greens and lights. And she didn't want any of them. She found a storage box in the closet and started to throw all of the greenery into it. The doctor had not said that the evergreen boughs were a problem, but she didn't want to take any chances. If Starlight came back home, she wanted it to look just like it always had, and not to have anything around that could harm him.

Just what kind of a pet owner was she? She figured that watching a few videos on YouTube on caring for pet cats made her an expert? She hadn't had any idea that the plants could be a problem. He'd never eaten plants before. She had thought that all she needed to do was feed Starlight and clean his litter box. Take him to the vet when he needed his shots. He was an indoor cat, so he wouldn't be in any dangerous situations.

So she had thought. And she had almost lost him. Might still lose him.

Sarah came in while Reg was dashing around the room, pulling down all of the decorations. What about the lights? Could he strangle on the strings? Burn his whiskers on the real candles; or worse, knock them over and light the house on fire? Reg didn't even see Sarah until she spoke.

"Uh, Reg…?"

Reg whirled around and looked at her. She looked down at the box full of decorations, thrown haphazardly together without any regard as to whether it was something important to Sarah or not. She froze for a moment, not sure what to say. Sarah's eyes were hurt. She thought that Reg was taking down all of the decorations because she didn't like them or had something against Yule or against Sarah herself.

Reg put down the box and swallowed.

"Starlight is sick. He might have been poisoned by this stuff."

Sarah's eye went wide with shock. "What? What happened?"

"When I got up this morning…" Even though Reg had been crying all morning, the tears came again, and she could barely talk around the lump in her throat, "he was lying on the floor in the kitchen. I thought he was dead."

"Oh, my dear!" Sarah moved toward her, holding out her arms. Reg was not usually a physically affectionate person, but she fell into Sarah's embrace, sobbing loudly.

"He's unconscious. The vet doesn't know if he's going to make it or not. They're not sure what he ate, but they said that all of this stuff is poisonous."

"Oh, Reg! I would never have brought it over if I had realized that! I didn't intend to hurt him."

"He might die. I'm so scared he's going to die."

"We'll find a way to save him. What did the vet say? Does he need surgery? Dialysis? What are they going to do?"

Reg couldn't remember any of the details. "They're going to try to get the poison out of his system. But he says… the damage is already done, and he doesn't know whether Starlight will make it or not." Reg gasped for breath and wept into Sarah's shoulder. "What am I going to do? I miss him so much! I don't know if I can do… all of the psychic stuff without him. He was always there if I needed him to give me a boost. And having someone around the cottage, so I wasn't all by myself. It just won't be the same. I don't know if I could ever live with another cat."

Sarah rubbed her back. "Don't get ahead of yourself. You don't know yet that he isn't going to make it and you'll have to get a replacement. You don't know the future. Just live for today. Think about what you can do today."

"I can't do anything. He's at the vet's… I had to leave him there… I don't know if I'm ever going to see him again."

"You will. You will," Sarah assured her. "Oh, Reg, I'm sure it can't be as bad as all of that. Starlight is a young, strong cat. He'll fight it. He'll recover."

Reg shook her head. "I don't know that, and neither do you. We don't even know how old he is. Harrison said that he was a very old friend. I don't want to lose him. I can't lose him, Sarah."

Sarah moved Reg over to the couch to sit down, holding her tightly to keep her from collapsing.

"What's going on?"

Sarah looked toward the door she had left open in her haste to help. Reg didn't look up. She knew that voice. She had ignored it for so many years it was practically second nature.

"Oh, it's your mother," Sarah said, looking awkward. She shifted her position, not sure whether to get up and offer Norma Jean her seat or not. Reg grabbed onto her and kept her from getting up. She did not want to be hugged and comforted by her mother. Sarah had never been anything but good to her. Unlike Norma Jean, who had failed on every level.

"Reg's cat is sick," Sarah explained when Reg didn't rush to give Norma Jean an explanation for what was going on. "She had to leave him at the vet, and she's very worried about him."

"What's wrong with it?"

Reg did raise her head then and looked into her mother's eyes. Cold, empty eyes. This was the same mother who had refused to let her have a cat when she was a little girl. The same mother who looked at Starlight suspiciously when she had come into the cottage, commenting about how familiar he had seemed. She couldn't have done anything to Starlight, could she? Reg didn't remember leaving her alone there. She couldn't have poisoned Starlight without Reg seeing something.

"He was poisoned," Reg told Norma Jean evenly, watching her face carefully for even the slightest change in expression. She was good at reading people. Really good at it. Scary good.

Norma Jean looked away immediately. She patted her hair and scratched her nose, keeping her gaze averted from Reg's. "Who would poison your cat? Did you let it outside? Maybe it ate something it wasn't supposed to."

Reg looked at the box, nearly filled with the Yule decorations. "No, he didn't go outside. And I don't know whether it was something he got into and didn't know would harm him, or if someone gave him something intentionally. If someone did poison him on purpose... all I can say is, they'd better get out of town before I find out."

Norma Jean still didn't look at her. Reg wondered if that was her answer. Well, she was serious. If Reg found out someone had intentionally harmed her familiar, they had better disappear at the first available opportunity. She wasn't going to go easy on them.

"I didn't do anything to hurt your cat," Norma Jean said sullenly. She looked at Sarah, clearly hoping she would leave. She thought it was her place to be there to comfort Reg.

But Norma Jean was wrong. Reg didn't want her there. "I can't entertain right now. And I don't think I'll be able to in the near future. So why don't you just go back home?"

Sarah made a little noise. "Reg!"

"I didn't ask her to come here, and I don't want anything from her. She can go back home and do... whatever it is she does now."

"But she is your mother," Sarah murmured, looking at Reg searchingly.

"She is not my mother. Giving birth to me does not qualify her as my mother."

Sarah didn't have anything to say to that.

Norma Jean drew herself up, raising her chin and standing very straight. "Fine. If you don't want me here, I will leave. I'll be back when you are feeling better and are ready to be civil to me."

Reg wiped her nose. "That's not going to be for a very long time."

CHAPTER FIVE

Sarah stayed with Reg for quite a while, not speaking, but rubbing her back and keeping her company and trying to make her feel better. Eventually, Sarah stood up and continued with the work of collecting all of the plants that could have hurt Starlight and putting them into the box. Reg sat with her elbows on her knees and her face in her hands and tried to keep herself calm.

It had felt good to explode at Norma Jean. To lash out at someone, whether she deserved it or not. And she did deserve everything Reg had said. It was all true. Norma Jean was not the kind of person she would want taking care of a child. Reg wiped her eyes and watched Sarah. She indicated the potted plant on the side table.

"Take that too. Fir said not to let Starlight eat it, so I guess that means that it could hurt him too. I shouldn't have accepted it in the first place, but he was so nice, and he wanted to give me something for helping him get out of jail and get his garden space back." Reg sniffled. "What kind of a useless pet owner doesn't do any research to find out how to cat-proof her house? I didn't know that any of these things were poisonous. He's never eaten anything like that before. He just wants me to feed him my food. I didn't think he'd eat anything that would hurt him."

"He is a remarkably intelligent animal," Sarah agreed. "And he obviously has some knowledge or instinct for the properties of herbs, or he wouldn't have brought you the yarrow when you were hurt. I find it very strange that he would eat anything harmful."

"Yeah. I hadn't thought about that." Reg got up and went to the kitchen. She picked up the dishtowel and dried her face, then tossed it into the hallway so that she would remember to put it into the laundry. "Does that mean that someone intentionally poisoned him? If it couldn't have been an accident…"

"It still might have been. You never know what cats will do. You don't even know what people are going to do. They still make mistakes and do stupid things. How are we supposed to figure out animals' behaviors when we don't even understand human behavior?"

Reg was still sniffling, though she was trying to stop. She felt wrung out, empty of any more tears.

"I guess you'll want me to take the tree too," Sarah suggested, looking up at it.

Reg wondered how Sarah had gotten it in there in the first place. She must have had some help. Maybe Forst, though he was so small he might not have been much help with such a large tree. Sarah looked at her watch.

"I'll have to come back for it. Is it okay if I do that tomorrow? Starlight isn't home right now, so there isn't any more danger in leaving it one more day…"

"Yes. That's fine," Reg agreed. "Are you going out tonight?" Sarah had been seeing a lot of younger men lately. At her age, practically all of the men in the community were significantly younger, but the men that she had been dating looked it, too.

"I am." Sarah looked at her watch again and picked up the box, now heavy with the ornaments, garlands, and wreaths. "He will be here to pick me up any minute, so I need to go freshen up. Will you be okay, Reg? I can call him and tell him I need to cancel tonight. If you need someone here with you…"

"No, you go ahead. I think I'm going to put on a movie and fall asleep in front of the TV."

"That's not a very healthy way to sleep. You won't get the rest you need sitting in front of the TV."

"It will be more than I'll get lying down and trying not to think and worry about things. I need something to occupy my brain without having to think about it. I'll binge-watch some rom-com. You go out and have a nice time." Reg shook her head at the incongruity of telling the older woman to have a nice date. She forced a smile and a lift in her voice. "Don't stay out too late and don't let him get fresh with you."

Sarah laughed merrily, carting the box of decorations toward the door. "Oh, I don't know about that, Reg. Didn't you say you wanted me to have a nice time?"

Reg chuckled and watched Sarah go. She shut the door and shot the bolt. She didn't want any more visitors. Especially not Norma Jean.

A few minutes later, she saw Sarah walk past her kitchen window, which Reg could see from her living room. She was changed, all dolled up for the dance or wherever it was she was going on her date. Reg wished she knew what kind of practical magic that was. She would love to be able to look beautiful and polished within two minutes. A few minutes later, she felt Sarah's presence fade, and knew she had been picked up for her date. Reg was left completely alone to spend all night worrying about Starlight.

The night was drawing on and, despite Reg's determination to watch mindless pap on TV until she fell asleep, her plan wasn't working. She was so tired she could cry. But she couldn't go to sleep. She surfed channels, looking for something to occupy her attention, but she wasn't getting very far. She had a cup of Sarah's sleepy tea in hopes that it might help but was still feeling just as restless and empty as ever. She needed her cat. She needed his furry cuddles and his peaceful aura and the way he had of looking at her as if he had human intelligence—or greater than human intelligence—and could understand when she was trying to sort something out.

The tea hadn't worked, so Reg got up one more time and poured herself a slug of Jack Daniels to see if that would work. Just one; she wouldn't allow herself any more than that. It would take the edge off just enough to settle down and sleep without her cat.

She'd slept her whole life without a cat? How could that have changed so completely in the few months she had lived in Black Sands?

She sat down with the Jack and watched the TV while she sipped it, trying to stretch it out and make it last since she knew she would not be going back for another. She was all cried out. Her eyes felt as dry as a desert, and she had a headache and congested sinuses. She had called all of her appointments and advised them that she wouldn't be able to do a reading that night because she wasn't feeling well. She was sure they could hear her congestion, and no one complained about it. There were no emergencies; everyone just rescheduled. Reg wondered when she would be able to do them. What if Starlight never recovered? She couldn't exactly tell them she couldn't do any more psychic readings because her cat had died. People would expect her to recover and move on, to get back down to business.

Reg fiddled with her phone, bored with everything on TV. Maybe she could be distracted by a game. Or maybe she could call someone and talk until she got tired enough to fall asleep. She flipped through screens, looking at the icons, checking in on a couple of social networks to see if anything was going on.

Eventually, she ended up on her contact list and stared at the list of Black Sands friends.

Sarah was on a date, so she was out. She would probably not be back until quite late. Detective Jessup was being too much of a cop and Reg was still kind of irritated with her. So she was a maybe. There was Francesca but, although another devoted cat owner might seem like the perfect conversational companion, Reg had previously lectured Francesca on how she needed to keep Nicole indoors where it was safe, and she hated to admit that Starlight had been harmed while inside the house. Besides, if Francesca was too sympathetic, she might set off the water-works again, and Reg didn't want to take the chance of crying anymore. She'd cried quite enough. But she needed someone who could take her mind off of Starlight, lying in a cage at the vet's office, the life slowly draining out of him, because Reg had been too ignorant to take care of him properly. Starlight had done his best to take care of her, and she had let him down.

Damon? She wasn't sure where their relationship was going to go after their last encounter. Damon had been horribly jealous since their one failed date, and she wasn't sure she was up to dealing with him. He was a nice guy, attractive, fun to be with if he weren't trying to convince her that she wanted to go bowling. But he could also read her and tell when she was lying, and he could put visions in her head, and she did not like people messing around inside her head. Even though she had told him not to, he continued to do it, telling her that he couldn't help himself, it was just the way that he naturally communicated.

No, probably not Damon. She didn't have the energy to try to sort out his emotions as well as her own.

There was always Corvin. The warlock that she knew she should not talk to or see, but was inevitably drawn toward. He was too dangerous. His powers had grown immensely and, despite all that Reg was learning about her powers and ability to resist his charms, he was still stronger than she was and, in her exhausted state, she wouldn't be able to build the psychic barricade that she needed to keep him from charming her and stealing her powers. He had done it once before when she was naive and had no idea what he could do to her, and she wasn't going to let it happen again, no matter how hard he continued to push.

But that didn't mean she couldn't talk to him on the phone, did it?

She wouldn't let him come over. She wouldn't go out for a late meal or drink. She would just chat with him on the phone. See how he was doing, and let him distract her from her anxiety. He couldn't do anything if he weren't in the same room with her.

Just a conversation. That wouldn't be so bad. He would be sympathetic, but only superficially. He didn't like cats. Starlight, in particular, was a thorn in his side. They did not like each other and always had words if Reg allowed Corvin into the cottage or took Starlight out with them on a case.

Hardly even thinking about what she was doing, Reg tapped Corvin's name and watched the screen as the call started to ring through.

She heard him answer, far away and tinny, and she lifted the phone to her ear.

"Hi."

"Reg." His voice was warm and full, like an embrace. "How unexpected. How are you doing?"

"I'm... having a tough night. Just needed... to talk."

"Sure, of course. What's going on? Some sort of metaphysical conflict?"

"No... very physical. It's Starlight. He's sick."

He grunted. "Sorry to hear that. Are you going to take him to the vet?"

"He's already there. I'm all alone." Not something that she should have revealed to him, but he would have guessed it anyway. "I just needed to hear someone else's voice. In the time that I've lived here, I was only ever alone here that first night. Then I got Starlight at the shelter, and... he's been with me since."

"Do you want me to come over? Keep you company?"

"No. Don't come here; I won't let you in."

"Come on, Reg. I could help. I could make you feel better."

"You making me feel better always ends up with my powers being in peril. I don't think so."

"That's not true. You know I have helped you in the past. Given you strength when you needed it. Given you companionship. Helped you with some of your tricky cases. Don't make it sound like I am just a predator."

"You *are* a predator."

"Yes, but not *just* a predator."

Reg couldn't help but laugh at this. His tone was half humorous and half peeved. He knew what he was, but he didn't like to be classified as an animal. He wanted everyone to recognize what a powerful and intelligent warlock he was. He wanted them to forget the rest of it, how he could seduce and steal powers. He had been strong enough to overcome the Witch Doctor, sucking most of his powers right out of him. If he could do that, he could do pretty much whatever he wanted, whether the Council and the community allowed it or not. They were fooling themselves if they thought their silly rules would have any effect on him.

"So if I can't come over there to provide you comfort, what can I do?" Corvin asked in a husky voice.

"Just talk to me. I need someone to take my mind off of things."

"I could do that so much better face to face."

"Not going to happen."

"Okay," he conceded. "So what does the cat have? Some feline flu?"

"No… the vet thinks that he ate something poisonous. I don't know what; he was going to do some testing to figure out what it was, but I haven't heard anything back from him. It could have been the plant that Fir gave to me, or it could be the Yule plants that Sarah decorated the cottage with. Or the vet's assistant said that it could be something else around the house, or that someone might have done it intentionally. I just can't believe that someone would try to kill him."

Corvin was silent for a few seconds too long. Reg had to wonder if he were looking for a diplomatic way to say that *he* could understand someone trying to kill the annoying beast. He would have done it if he thought he could get away with it.

"Has there been someone in the cottage?" he asked. "He hasn't been outside, has he?"

"No. He's just been at home. So it would have to be something here."

"Then who…?"

Who could have had the opportunity to poison him? If it was intentional, then how had the perpetrator done it?

"Well… Sarah was there, of course, and all of the poisonous plants were hers. I don't think that she intentionally made him sick, but she could have. Or she could have fed him something else. She was there alone with him for hours, and she can come and go as she pleases when I'm not there. She had every opportunity."

"But you don't think it was her."

Sarah had insisted that she wouldn't have brought the Yule plants into the house if she had known that they were harmful to cats. She had seemed sincerely sympathetic. She might not like cats, but Reg couldn't see her trying to kill one. At least, not while she was in her right mind, and she had seemed perfectly sane the day before.

"No. I don't think that it was. She seemed… really sorry that it had happened. It's just that she was talking about cats earlier, and how she didn't want any extra cats around the house or yard. She said that Starlight was okay, but not any other cats."

"And you wonder if she changed her mind and decided that she might not want him around either."

"Wouldn't she tell me that, though? Give me a chance to find a new home for him?"

"If she knows how attached you are to that animal, she would have a pretty good idea that if she gave you an ultimatum, you would be looking for a new place to live. And I think that she likes having you there, even if she does have to put up with Starlight."

"Yeah."

"And no one else has been around the house?"

"Well… of course there has been. I have clients in and out, doing readings. I had three or four people here last night. But none of them would have any reason to hurt Starlight. He wasn't in anyone's way, and none of them were people that I know very well. I can't see anyone having a grudge against him or me."

"Well, then, I'm not sure who else could have poisoned him intentionally. It must have been an accident."

"I guess so." Reg should have felt better about that conclusion, but she didn't. She still had the nagging feeling that someone had done it on purpose. Maybe she just didn't want to take the responsibility herself. Because if someone else hadn't done it, then that meant she had poisoned her own cat, and she couldn't bear to think of him at the vet's office, dying all alone.

"But, you wanted to be distracted from this, not to talk about it," Corvin reminded himself. "So why don't you tell me what else is new. Have you had any interesting clients recently? Any exciting readings? Read any good books lately?"

He probably knew her well enough to know that she didn't read books. She hadn't read a single book since she had left school, and had probably not read a full one even when she was in school. She had done everything she could to avoid books. She liked to watch the movies instead, but the teachers knew the differences between the books and the movies and always caught her. Reg didn't know why reading was so important. There were so many other ways to learn and communicate. Multimedia was the way to go. Face-to-face interviews or teleconferencing. Live broadcasts. Books were antiquated. But then, so was Corvin.

"No good books," she told him. "And there's nothing on TV. I don't want to say too much about my clients; I like to think that we have a sort of confidentiality between us, like with a doctor or a priest. They tell me some pretty personal stuff, and it wouldn't be right for me to break their trust and share it with someone else."

"You're not making this easy. How about Sarah? What's she up to?"

She was about to ask him why he didn't talk to Sarah himself. But she already knew why. Because his coven was shunning him and, even though Sarah was in a different coven, they were shunning him as well. He didn't have any contact with anyone who was in the established covens in Black Sands. Only people like Reg, who was not associated with any organization. Lone wolves like Damon. But Damon and Corvin were not friends.

"Sarah... well, she's out on a date."

"Again?"

"Always. She's always out with someone these days. You'd think she was a teenager again."

"With the amount of energy she has now, she might as well be. She doesn't have a steady guy?"

"No, I don't think so. Always someone new over there. She's just having a good time, doesn't want any commitments right now."

"That would just slow her down."

"Exactly. If she has to stick to one guy, settle down, get married, she's going to be bored."

Reg stretched and turned her head back and forth, trying to release the tension in her neck and shoulders. It was no wonder she couldn't settle down when her body was so knotted up. She gazed out the window into the dark yard. Lights were twinkling, and she tried to focus on them. Twinkle lights at Sarah's house? Lightning bugs? She couldn't seem to focus on them. As soon as she tried, they vanished and appeared somewhere else.

CHAPTER SIX

E arth to Reg?"
"Hmm?" Reg brought her attention back to the phone. "Sorry. There are lights outside, and I was trying to figure out…"

"Lights? What kind of lights?"

"I don't know. I was trying to figure that out, but whenever I try to focus on one…"

"Maybe I should come over and check it out."

"You get points for persistence, that's for sure."

Corvin chuckled. She could imagine the smug smile on his face. He was just so darn handsome. Even when she was just thinking of him, she felt flushed.

Unless he was closer than she thought. It wouldn't be the first time that he showed up when she thought he was too far away to be a danger to her. She tried again to make out the lights. Was he out there? Was he the one who was causing them? They didn't look like anything man-made. She had heard of foxfire lights in the swamp, but she didn't think they could be anywhere else, like in her yard.

"What are you doing tonight?" Reg asked, hoping for reassurance.

"I have been out collecting some plants and am just preparing them now. Chopping, drying, freezing, the method of preparation depends on what plant it is and what they are being used for."

"What do you do with them?"

"A wide variety of things. Some are used in potions; some are burned during rituals. Some are used in healing poultices. It all depends. There are many beneficial plants and herbs in this area."

"What did you find tonight?"

Corvin listed off several plants that Reg had never heard of. He could be making it all up, and she would have no idea. But she didn't feel like he was trying to deceive her. She usually had some sense if he was lying to her. It wasn't like he was usually subtle. If Corvin had something on his mind, she usually knew about it pretty quickly.

Even so, she tried to see him. She had been able to before, when he was in danger. This time, she could be the one in danger, so it should come to her easily. She tried to envision him preparing his leaves, roots, and berries. Was he in his kitchen, or did he have a special potions room in his house? Damon had once referred to Corvin's house as his lair. Was it some dark, underground laboratory? Or was that just figurative, and he lived in a bright, modern home with white cupboards and gleaming marble countertops?

She had never been to his house, of course. That would be putting herself in unnecessary danger. He could do whatever he wanted if he were on his own property instead of Reg's, which was protected with Sarah's wards.

He was still going on, giving a lecture about what plants he was working with. He taught classes sometimes, and Reg didn't have a hard time imagining him lecturing at the front of a class. He had no trouble pontificating on his pet topics. Usually history and politics in the magical community, but apparently herblore was right up there on his list too.

The vision came to her gradually, not all at once. She stared into her crystal ball, trying to remain focused. It wasn't easy without the magnifying influence of Starlight and with the effects of grief, exhaustion, and Jack Daniels on her brain.

She could see him in his kitchen. Just a regular kitchen, not an underground lab or a stone temple with a sacrificial altar. And he was doing just what he said he was, chopping up his various herbs, which were laid out in piles on his counters. There were bowls and jars and all kinds of other culinary equipment. Like some grandma on jam-making day. She enjoyed watching him remotely when he couldn't see her or know that she was watching him. Her heart sped, and she felt that warm flush again.

His cheeks, ordinarily clean-shaven, leaving just a neat goatee around his mouth, were dark with whiskers, all stubbly and rough. He was wearing a black cloak and had the window open, the cool night air washing through the kitchen. His dark eyes were intent on what he was doing, his hair just a little too long in the back, making him look like a knight in a medieval castle. Or in the crusades. Or something.

His phone was on the counter in front of him, on speaker phone so that he could chat with her while he continued his preparations. He paused in his lecture.

"You still there, Reg?"

"Mmm. Yes, I'm still here."

"You sound tired. Do you want to go to bed?"

"I want to, but I can't. That's why I called you."

"I could help with that."

"I'm sure you could." She remembered the one night they had been together, before she knew what it was she was agreeing to, what it was he could do to her. The physical intimacy had been amazing. She felt an electrical buzz whenever she touched Corvin, and to be that close and intimate had been incredible. Her body thrummed with heat just thinking about it.

But she wasn't about to let that happen again. Not when the price was the loss of her powers. Waking up in the morning with all of the voices gone and a silent, flat world around her instead of the chatter she was used to had been devastating. She never wanted to feel that lost and alone and powerless again. And that was why she could never yield to him again.

"You are helping," she told him. "Especially droning on about your plants. That could put anyone to sleep."

"You know me. Always happy to oblige."

Reg's eyes wandered to the lights again. Sarah must have put a couple of strings of lights out there, and Reg just hadn't noticed them earlier. Or maybe she had invoked some twinkle-light spell to make it look more festive.

"What are you doing for Christmas?" she asked Corvin. "I mean… whatever it's called…" Her mind was getting too fuzzy to remember what it was Sarah was celebrating.

"Winter solstice? Well, I'm sure you know that it's a day of celebration and renewal. Normally, I would join my coven for some rituals. This year…" he sighed, "I guess I'm on my own."

Because of Reg, he had been shunned from his coven. She hadn't thought about him missing out on special holidays like that. She felt a little bad that he would have to miss the celebrations. It was like being sent away for Christmas. Reg knew what that was like.

But he wasn't shunned because of Reg. It was because of what he had done. Because he had broken the rules, even after he had repeatedly promised not to harm her. He'd resorted to more than just trickery to get her in his thrall. He had broken the established rules of the community. Rules that were utterly inadequate to protect the women in the community whose powers he desired. He'd broken his promises to her and his promises to abide by the rules of the community.

She hadn't even been the one to bring charges against him. She was so embarrassed by the whole thing that she would have preferred to fade into the woodwork and not bring attention to herself. The hearing in front of the tribunal had been humiliating.

"How about you?" Corvin prompted. "Your first solstice in Black Sands. You must have something special planned."

"Well, no, I don't, actually. I didn't even know about this Yule thing until yesterday. I just thought… everybody celebrated Christmas. I mean, not in a religious way, just… exchanging presents, enjoying the season. Celebrating something."

"And we do. It just happens to precede Christmas. Even the Christians think that Christmas has become too commercialized. Too much about buying the best presents or getting the best deals, making a turkey dinner that will put everyone into a food coma, and racing from one end of the state to the other visiting all of their family and friends without the opportunity to really enjoy each other's company. Yule or solstice is much simpler and quieter. Much more about our connection with nature than about elaborate gifts or meals."

"I don't know. I guess I'll do something. I can buy some pre-cooked turkey for me and…" Reg suddenly remembered, and her words trickled off. There was no Starlight. Not unless he miraculously recovered. She was going to be alone for Christmas or solstice. All by herself. Like she had been for so many other Christmases past.

"Have hope, Regina," Corvin murmured.

Her eyes welled with tears again, as she had known they would if she were subjected to too much sympathy and understanding. Corvin's voice was kind, and she wished that he were there and she could cuddle up against him and take his warmth and strength for herself. He would tuck her into bed and…

Reg gave herself a sharp mental 'stop!' not allowing the images to go any further. She wasn't looking for comfort from Corvin. He was supposed to be the distraction, the one person who wouldn't make her feel worse about Starlight.

"How can I?" Reg wiped her eyes. She had thought that they would be dry for a week after the amount she had cried already. "The vet didn't think he had much chance. He's the expert. How could I have been so stupid? I would never have done anything to hurt Starlight intentionally. How could I not have even looked up what things around the house could hurt him? Are they like dogs? Could chocolate poison them? I don't even know! I didn't even look it up!"

"But you didn't give him chocolate. You didn't give him anything that would harm him. He got into something he wasn't supposed to. It wasn't something you fed him. You take excellent care of him, that's obvious to anyone who sees the two of you together."

Seeing Corvin in her crystal, she saw his nostrils flare, his mouth twist into a sneer, and he shook his head. He did not like Starlight. But he didn't allow that dislike to creep into his voice.

"I know you don't like him," Reg said, "but…"

He glanced over at the phone. "I didn't do anything to harm him. I haven't been around your house in days."

445

CHAPTER SEVEN

R eg focused sharply on Corvin's words. Why did he get defensive
when she hadn't accused him of anything? Was it a case of protesting
too much because he was guilty? She reviewed the last few days in her mind.
Was there any time he could have come by the cottage without her knowing
it? Even if he had, there was no way he could have had access to Starlight.
Starlight was inside the house, and Corvin was still prevented from entering
by the wards Sarah had placed.

Unless Corvin had grown powerful enough to overcome Sarah's spells.

There was no telling how strong he was. Harrison had said that Corvin
was not yet in control of his new powers. As Corvin grew more skilled and
comfortable with those new gifts, he would be able to do many things that
he hadn't been able to before. Opening locked doors and getting past
protective wards did not seem like much of a stretch.

"You haven't been around here," she repeated.

"No, I haven't. Just because I don't like the beast, that doesn't mean I
would do anything to hurt him. You don't go poisoning everyone you don't
like, do you?"

Reg allowed herself a smile at that. If she did, there would be a long trail
of bodies behind her. "No. I haven't poisoned anyone recently."

She saw his lips curl up at her words. He chopped a root into fine dices.
"Do you need someone to go with you to the vet tomorrow?"

Reg felt a warm rush of gratitude at his question. "Actually, yeah. That would be really good. I don't really want to go by myself, and coming home today… I had a real tough time and probably shouldn't have been driving."

"What time do you want to go over?"

"I'll have to check their hours. Probably late morning."

"Sure. I'll make some time for it. You can call me when you know what time for sure and I'll drive you over."

"Thanks. That would be a really big help."

"You know I'm always happy to help you, Regina."

At some point, Reg finally did fall asleep in front of the TV. She was restless, waking up several times in the night and staring at the TV, which was tuned to a shopping channel with a too-excited host talking about the latest technology in ladies' tights. It was enough to put anyone to sleep.

Morning dawned and, with the light streaming in the window, she was unable to go back to sleep. She could go to her room and lie down in bed, pulling the covers up over her head, but she wasn't going to be able to sleep in there either, thinking about Starlight and how he wasn't sitting in the window and wasn't going to be trying to wake her up to feed him breakfast.

So she got up and made a cup of coffee and stood sipping the piping hot liquid and considering whether there was anything that appealed to her in the fridge. There wasn't. She deeply missed the little fur-ball winding himself around her legs. It ached like a hole in her chest. How could she go on without him?

Reg was on tenterhooks waiting for Corvin to confirm that he was on the way, and then for him to get there. She sensed as soon as he pulled in front of Sarah's house and she left the cottage without waiting for his call or text to indicate that he was there. Or for him to show up at her door. She didn't need him coming in to get her.

As soon as she slid into the seat beside him in the car, she was enveloped in a warmth that wasn't coming from the car's heater or the sun beating down on her. It was a warmth that reached right inside her and helped her to feel calm and prepared for what was ahead. Reg eyed Corvin appreciatively. She wondered if he understood how much it meant to her to feel strong facing the return trip to the vet's office.

Corvin smiled and nodded at her. "Reg. All set?"

"I guess I am. Let's go."

While he was driving, he rested his hand on her leg. She would normally have found this too intimate a gesture and shaken him off, but she could feel the flow of strength from him.

It was what she needed. But on the other hand, she had to be careful not to let down her guard. The moment she did, he would ensorcel her and she would easily slide into his power in the fragile state she was in. She said nothing, watching out the window and gathering her thoughts the best she could.

She was scared to death that the vet would tell her that Starlight had passed away in the night. The receptionist had Reg and Corvin sit down, and Reg watched the other people with their sick or hurt pets, her heart aching. She needed to hold Starlight again and to know that he would be well.

Eventually, the vet called them in. There were a couple of chairs snugged up against the examining table in the tiny room, and Reg and Corvin sat down. Reg waited in trepidation as the vet looked through Starlight's charts on his clipboard as if he didn't know what the cat's status was. Surely he had seen Starlight already that morning and had reviewed any of the tests that had come in overnight.

Eventually, the vet looked back at their faces. He shook his head slowly, expression serious. "I wish I had better news for you. I did warn you that he was in serious condition, but sometimes animals can surprise us and bounce back much earlier than we would have predicted. Unfortunately, such was not the case here. Starlight is hanging on, which is the only good news that I have for you. He is a fighter. He hasn't yet succumbed to the poison, whatever it was."

"You still don't know?" Reg asked. "I thought you would have identified it by now."

"Real life isn't like you see on TV. You can't just pop a sample in the machine, and have it spit out the poison and how to treat it. We can test for the top few poisons, but we have to know something about what to look for if it isn't one of the usual suspects. I can't just put a leaf in a machine and have it tell me that he was poisoned by a lily. We don't have that kind of ability here."

"But you do think it's a leaf? A plant?"

"He had several leaves in his stomach. But they are too masticated to tell what they are. It doesn't appear that it was anything in the lily family, or holly, or mistletoe. But that still leaves a wide variety of options." The doctor tapped the end of his pen on the clipboard. "I haven't seen a case like this before. The properties of this plant are… strange to me. With poisoning, we expect to see vomiting, diarrhea, maybe seizures. A recognizable constellation of symptoms. But he is quite… he doesn't have many symptoms, other than being unconscious and having a very slow heartbeat and respiration."

"Something is depressing his system," Corvin offered. The doctor looked at him, frowning.

"Yes."

"But you don't know what it is. Could it be… could he have also gotten into someone's medication? A Valium or something else that affects the respiratory system?"

The doctor raised his eyebrows at Reg, asking the question silently.

"No," Reg said immediately. She didn't take tranquilizers. She didn't take anything that would make her sleepy. And no more psychiatric meds. They never helped, and always had annoying side effects. "I don't have anything like that around the house. No prescriptions. No illegal drugs." She shot a glance at Corvin to express her displeasure at being accused in front of the doctor of taking something that would have harmed Starlight.

"What about Tylenol? An herbal tea?"

"It's not Tylenol," the vet said, shaking his head. "A tea… it could be, depending on what it had in it and what its properties were. Do you know what is in your teas?"

"He didn't drink my tea," Reg protested. She couldn't give him any explanation. Starlight was, she supposed, just as likely to have licked the remains of her sleepy tea or some other concoction out of her teacup as he was of chewing on Fir's plant or a Yule decoration. Just because she didn't think it was likely, that wasn't proof.

"I don't know." The vet sighed. "I guess we're just going to have to watch and wait and hope that he recovers."

"You think his symptoms are unusual," Corvin said, giving Reg a meaningful look.

"Yes, they are unusual. Not wildly bizarre, but not what I would have expected."

"And you need to identify the poison before you can treat for it."

"I'll keep doing what I am, trying to get on top of it and turn him around. But right now, he is not responding to treatment."

"That's unusual," Corvin said, again emphasizing the word.

Reg tried to figure out what he was getting at.

"Is there any way we could see him before we go?" Corvin asked.

"He's settled in a bed; I don't like to move him. Best if he stays put where he is."

"We'd really like to see him before we go. We don't know if it might be the last opportunity we have."

Reg swallowed a sob, trying to keep her composure. The doctor was hesitant, then nodded.

"Let me check on things. I'll see whether it is easier to bring him in here or to take you into the kennels. We don't usually allow owners back there."

He left the room. Reg looked at Corvin. "What's all that about? I don't understand what you're trying to do. Why would you care about seeing him? You don't even like him."

"The fact that the symptoms are unusual doesn't bring anything to mind? It doesn't mean anything to you?"

Reg shook her head. What had she missed? What was she supposed to understand?

"If they are that unusual, maybe it's because it wasn't just a natural poisoning," Corvin pointed out.

"Which means what?"

"Maybe it was part of a spell. Maybe there is a magical component, and that's why he is not responding to medical treatment."

Reg inhaled sharply and held her breath. "Yeah... maybe."

"That's why I want to see him. I might not be able to tell anything looking at him or being near him, but I can try. And you and I can both see whether there is anything we can do to help him."

"Okay." Reg breathed out slowly. She couldn't think of anything that she would be able to do to help Starlight, but if Corvin thought there was something he could do... She'd seen him work before, helping Sarah when she had been so close to death. He was able to give strength when he wanted to and maybe, if there was some spell for him to counteract, there was some hope for her kitty.

CHAPTER EIGHT

I t was some time before the vet's assistant came to the examination room and nodded to Reg and Corvin, her eyes gentle and sympathetic. "We've got kitty settled in another room for you. Come this way."

She led them through the back door of the examining room, the one that the vet used, which led to the rooms that were off-limits to customers. They walked past laboratory benches and a bank of cages with sick, sad-looking animals resting in them. One dog on the bottom row barked and growled as they went past, but all the rest were quiet. Much too quiet.

The veterinary assistant smiled again and gestured to a door. "This way."

Reg entered first, with Corvin behind her. Starlight lay on a towel on the examining table, completely still and unaware of their presence. Reg felt the tears flood her cheeks again. How could she bear it? How could she keep seeing him and saying goodbye, knowing that it might be the last time that she would ever see him alive? He seemed to be even farther away from him than he had been before, getting smaller and more faded, his body just a shell that used to hold the bold, vivacious spirit of her companion. Corvin put a hand on Reg's shoulder. Electricity jolted her. The warmth of his hand seeped down into her shoulder and, without any effort, she was suddenly on a different plane. She couldn't explain it any other way. It was like when she had been banished to the pixies' unseen world. She was still in the same place that she had been physically, but everything had changed.

"Reg?" Corvin murmured, his hand tightening slightly.

Reg waited for the vet's assistant to leave the room, pulling the door closed behind her. She turned and looked at Corvin.

"What happened?" he asked.

"I thought it was you. Wasn't it?"

"No... I don't think so. Though it's hard for me to tell. You do things to me that no one else can."

She ignored his claim, which was probably intended to make her feel sorry for him. She looked at Starlight on the examining table. There was a halo of light around him. His aura or his spirit. She led Corvin a couple of steps closer to the table. He released his comforting grip on her shoulder, and Reg took his hand in hers, not wanting to break the connection they had made. She looked at Starlight, then closed her eyes.

"Show it to me," she breathed. "I don't know what I'm supposed to be seeing here. What do I look for?"

She didn't know whether she was talking to Corvin, or just making a plea to the universe in general.

"I'm not sure if you and I are seeing the same thing. I see light around him, do you?"

"Yeah. All around him. What am I supposed to do?"

"Let's look for any changes in the light. Places where it is dimmer or more diffuse."

Reg studied Starlight, turning the picture over in her mind, manipulating it and trying to come to a conclusion. "I think... around his head and eyes, it's darker. And inside... I can't really see inside. I think... He's bleeding in there. But how could I know that?"

"Don't question it. Just accept it. If you think he's bleeding inside, then we should probably stop that. Do you know how to do it?"

Reg shook her head. "I don't know anything about any of this."

Corvin worked his hand out of Reg's grip, and positioned both hands over Starlight, as if warming himself by a log in the fire. But Reg had seen him do that before, healing and providing strength to the subject. He'd done it to Sarah and Damon, and he'd done it to Reg on occasion as well. But what about cats? Was it all the same for cats? Or did he have to have an affinity for them in order to heal them?

Corvin stayed in that position for a long time, then shook his head. "I'm not feeling anything. I don't think it's having any efficacy."

"You can't heal him?" Reg's voice choked up.

"I don't think so. I've given him as much strength as I can, but that's all I can do. I can't initiate the healing process."

"Is it because he's a cat? Or because it's magic? Or something else? I don't know what to do."

"You can try it yourself. He knows you and his body may respond differently to you. Just pet him and talk to him, like you normally would. I know I'm not doing that, but most subjects prefer I don't actually touch. The cat knows your touch. Try to give him more strength and to make him whole."

"I don't know how to do that." But Reg petted him anyway—long, soothing strokes, followed by cuddles and ear scratches and loving words whispered into his ears. She focused on that warm transfer of strength that she had felt from Corvin. If she could take it from him, she could give it too.

She rested, her hands still on Starlight. She breathed in and out and tried to relax her whole body and brain. If she were going to heal him, it was going to take a lot of energy, and she wasn't sure whether it would 'take.'

"You protected him before," Corvin said, talking while she rested.

Reg was surprised. "Well... I tried when I found him, and he was so sick. I wanted to stop him from getting any worse. But I don't think it did anything. It was already too late at that point; he'd already taken—or been given—whatever made him sick by then."

"I think it has helped. I think that's probably the only reason he's still with us."

"You think so?" Reg felt a little heartened by this. She hadn't known what she was doing, she had just gone on instinct, but maybe it had helped.

"I do," Corvin agreed. "And I think he recognizes that you are here, trying to help him."

"I don't... feel his presence at all," Reg confessed. "I don't think he's conscious."

"No, I don't mean that... but I think he still knows that you are here, deep down inside. Whether it's a coherent thought or not."

Reg shook her head. She remembered Harrison's comment when she had asked him whether Weston was still alive. That humans had funny ideas about life and death that he couldn't comprehend. As an immortal, he didn't have to deal with death and the unknowns that came after. Not if he really was immortal, and not just long-lived. Reg wasn't sure whether the immortals even understood the difference. Humans talk about death, but then life after death, and reincarnation, and so many other opposing theories, Harrison wasn't sure what they meant by death.

"He's not dead, is he? Is he out of his body? Is that why I can't feel him?"

"No, he's still here. I'm sure we wouldn't be able to see the light if he wasn't."

"Yeah?"

Corvin nodded. Reg took a couple more deep breaths and then tried again, trying to locate the bleeding that she could see in her mind and to tell the body to heal itself. In spite of the bleeding, there was not a lot of pain. Reg hoped that much was true. She explored his stomach, which is where she thought the poison must have come from, and explored for damage that radiated out from it. She'd seen pictures of neurons, little dark blobs with spidery legs stretching out from them, and thought that was the best visual description for what she could feel. Multiple spots of damage, with branching blood vessels or nerves radiating out. Reg focused on each one in turn, hoping that she could do something to heal them and make them whole again.

It was a long time before the vet entered the examining room. Reg opened her eyes and looked at him, exhausted from her work, unsure what to do next.

"Miss Rawlins, we really should be getting Starlight back on his IV and settled in his room. I don't think it is doing either of you any good to spend so much time with him. He needs his rest, and frankly, you look like you do too."

Reg nodded. The vet looked relieved that she had agreed. He looked at Corvin to see if he had any objection, but Corvin said nothing.

"We'll do our best for him," the vet promised, "Keep praying; that's all you can do at this point. And if you can figure out what plant he might have eaten... do let me know."

"Should I... bring you samples of the plants that were in my house? Other than holly or mistletoe?"

He nodded. "That might be helpful."

"And your tea," Corvin suggested.

"It wasn't my tea."

"You can't know that."

"If you have the ingredients list for any tea or other substance that you think he might have consumed," the vet said. "Don't bother to bring me the tea leaves, I won't be able to identify them any better than I can what was in his stomach. Whole plants, I might be able to identify from their appearance, but not dried and crushed leaves."

"I don't have the ingredients… I'll have to talk to Sarah. She's the one who makes the tea."

And Reg had also given her Fir's plant. Reg hoped she hadn't destroyed it.

She prepared to leave, petting Starlight one last time. "He's bleeding," Reg told the vet.

The vet stared at her, then looked over at Starlight. He made a quick physical examination and shook his head. "He looks just the same. There's no blood."

"But he's bleeding inside." Reg put her hand over the location. "Right here."

"How could you know that?"

"I… I'm a psychic. It's what I do."

He refrained from rolling his eyes, but Reg was sure he'd heard this line before. He couldn't practice in a town like Black Sands without running into practitioners who had no qualms telling him that they were witches, psychics, or some other kind of magical practitioner.

"I see."

"Please check. If you can stop the bleeding… I don't know. Maybe he'll survive."

The vet nodded. He palpitated Starlight's stomach gently. "We'll do some imaging. See whether I can see any bleeding. I don't believe in this stuff… but I've seen it be right often enough that I know I'd better not discount it."

CHAPTER NINE

Reg was quiet as she and Corvin walked out of the vet's office and back to Corvin's car. It was a good thing that he had driven her, because she wasn't sure how she would have gotten home otherwise. She was too much of a mess to be responsible for driving herself. What was she going to do? Had their visit done any good? It just reinforced in her mind how precarious Starlight's health was. Even with all that she and Corvin had done to try to give him strength and healing, she wasn't sure it would do him any good or prolong his life more than a day or two. Even if the vet could figure out what he had eaten and stop the bleeding, she wasn't sure that would help. Especially if there were magic involved. The vet was clearly not a magical practitioner, so he wouldn't be able to reverse the effects of any spell. They would need someone skilled in healing arts. The only person she knew who had such skills was Corvin, and he hadn't been able to heal Starlight.

Maybe he didn't want to. Maybe he would rather have Starlight out of the way. He might have only been putting on a show for her.

But if he had put a curse on Starlight, then why would he bother telling her that? It would make more sense for him just to let the curse and poison run their course without telling Reg anything about it.

Reg caught a movement out of the corner of her eye and turned her head to see what it was. She couldn't see anything that would account for the movement she had seen. But she had seen something; a shadow, a surreptitious movement. Something that she couldn't quite identify.

Corvin noticed her look. He raised his eyebrows. "What?"

"I… saw something."

"What?"

"I don't know. I thought there was someone there. But there isn't."

Corvin stared in the direction she was looking. "I don't see anything."

"No… I don't know either."

"Just a trick of the light," Corvin said with a shrug. "Maybe a shadow or a bird."

"But it was…" Reg tried to think of the words to explain that it had seemed like a person. She hadn't seen it well enough to be able to say more than that, to describe it in terms of height, build, or gender, but she had seen something there that was not a shadow or a bird. "I don't know."

"You're distraught. Let's get you home."

Reg fumed silently at his dismissal. She wasn't seeing things due to grief. Being upset didn't make her have hallucinations.

But even as she thought that, she had to wonder. She had been treated in the past for seeing and hearing things that weren't there. Since she had come to Black Sands, she had come to believe that the psychiatric disturbances in the past were not mental illness, but a manifestation of her psychic abilities. She saw and heard spirits. She could see things that other people couldn't, hear them and feel them as clearly as she could see Corvin standing next to her. She'd been able to see the pixies when they had turned invisible. Not well, but their shadowy shapes. There was no reason for Corvin to suggest that just because he didn't see something, it wasn't there.

"Maybe it was a spirit," she said as she got into his car.

Corvin looked at her, confused for a moment before he caught up to her line of thought. "I suppose it could be," he admitted. "Do you have a spirit attached to you these days?"

"I always have spirits attached to me." He knew that from when he had held her powers. For Reg, it had never been difficult to see or hear the spirits around her. The challenge had been to filter out the voices so that she could listen to them one at a time or be able to think her own thoughts without the other voices crowding in.

"Is this one that you know? Is it trying to communicate something to you?"

Reg settled herself in the seat and looked back to where she had seen the movement. She reached out psychically, trying to isolate it and figure out who it was and what they wanted from her. But the presence shifted and withdrew. It seemed not to want to communicate with her. Reg shook her head.

"I don't think it wants to be seen. I don't know."

He looked at her, waiting for more, but Reg didn't have anything. She didn't know what to tell him about the movement she had seen. It had been too quick, just out of her sight, and now that she was looking for it, she couldn't see it. A lot of good psychic vision did in a case like that. She didn't know what the shadow wanted, if it even wanted anything from her. Perhaps it had just been watching her by chance and hadn't expected to be seen. Then it had withdrawn when she tried to reach out because it didn't want anything from her.

Reg sighed and pressed her fingers to her temples. "I can't deal with this right now."

"You don't have to. You saw something. You turned your head and it wasn't there. That kind of thing happens all the time. If whatever it was isn't trying to communicate with you, then ignore it. I'll get you home, and you can rest and relax."

"How can I relax when Starlight is in there..." She couldn't bring herself to say the word *dying*. Putting it into words was just too much.

"We've done everything we can for the cat. Now, we'll have to wait, and hope that the vet is able to do something for him."

"But you know he's not going to be able to. Not if it was because of a spell or curse. He can't treat for that. And sitting around at home waiting for something to happen isn't going to help. I can't just sit around waiting. We need to figure out who did this to him and why they did. If we can figure that out, maybe we can find out how to make him better."

Corvin started the engine. He pointed the nose of the car toward home. For a few minutes, he just drove in silence. "Of course I'll help you however I can," he promised. "But I'm not sure it will make any difference. You might make yourself crazy, trying to do something that you have no control over. What help will that be to him? It's better if you just... focus on other things and let nature take its course."

"You think I should let him die?" Reg's voice came out in an indignant squeak. She couldn't believe that he would even suggest such a thing.

"That's not exactly what I said. We've done everything we can for him. He's in the best hands. At this point, you turn it over to… fate. We can't fight against what is intended to happen."

"I sure as heck can!"

He shrugged. "You can… but you may be risking your own sanity. There is only so much that we can do. If you keep fighting after the struggle is over, you are harming yourself."

Reg pressed her lips together. There was no point in arguing it with him. It wasn't his cat that was in peril. He couldn't know how it felt. She would fight to her last breath to save Starlight. She wasn't going to stop just because someone else thought she should.

Reg stared out the window at the passing scenery without seeing any of it. She tried to make a list in her head. Her foster sister, Erin, was always a great one for making lists. Even as a young teenager, Reg could remember Erin sitting down and pulling out a notepad and balancing it on her scraped knees. "We just need to make a list…"

It had always made Erin feel better to have a plan, and Reg had been jealous of that. She wanted to feel better too. But her plans always remained tangled up in her head and things generally spun out of control. Maybe making a list would help Reg to keep a logical sequence in her head, but it had never come easily to her.

Reg needed to talk to Sarah to get the plant from Fir and the ingredients to the tea, and to find out what other plants had been in her house other than holly and mistletoe that could have poisoned a cat. She should ask whether Sarah had seen anything unusual around the yard or the cottage too. There had been a lot of odd feelings or occurrences over the past few days, and Reg didn't know how to explain them. Maybe Sarah could.

What about an animal healer? There were all kinds of gifted people in the magical community. There had to be someone skilled in healing cats. Witches and warlocks had to have somewhere to go when one of their familiars fell ill. Somewhere other than to a vet who didn't know the first thing about magical curses or healing.

Who would want to poison her cat? If there had also been a magical curse involved, then it wasn't just a random neighbor, it had to be someone who was a practitioner and who, for some reason, didn't want Starlight around. Was it to clear the way to get to Reg unimpeded? Or was it to prevent her from using his psychic powers to boost her own?

All of Reg's meditations were dashed from her head when they pulled up to the house.

CHAPTER TEN

Reg saw a white car in front of the house and knew immediately who was sitting there waiting for her. She swore and hit the dashboard with the heel of her hand. It smarted, but she was angry, so she didn't care. Corvin looked at her, eyebrows raised, wondering what was wrong.

"Norma Jean," Reg snapped. She pointed to the car. "Sitting right there."

"Norma Jean?" Corvin's tone was incredulous. "When did this happen? How?"

He had held Reg's powers, heard Norma Jean's spirit in his head. He knew that the Witch Doctor had tortured and killed her. In the other timeline.

"She's alive," Reg stated the obvious. "When Harrison went back, he must have prevented the Witch Doctor from killing her. So now she's here, wanting to be all buddy-buddy. I do not need this today!"

"But if she didn't die, then what does that mean to you? Did she raise you? And why would we be able to remember the way the timeline unfolded before?"

"Child Services took me away from her. Because she was a terrible parent. So no, all that stuff is still the same. Fate, I guess. It was going to happen to me whether she lived or died."

"But we shouldn't be able to remember what happened before. That creates a paradox. We should only be able to remember our own timeline."

"Don't bother me with theoretical nonsense. A bunch of scientists speculate on the results of time travel. They don't know. They haven't done it!"

Corvin's eyes widened at her outburst. He nodded. "Of course." He looked toward the car. "Would you like me to get rid of her?"

Reg settled back in her seat. "Yeah, do you think you could?"

"Sure. When I go talk to her, you get out and go to the cottage. I'll distract her and get her to come with me."

Reg hesitated. "How will you do that?"

He smiled, and she could smell roses and feel his power sweep over her, an overwhelming attraction to someone she knew very well was a danger to her. She braced herself against the door and the dashboard.

"Stop that! You can't charm her."

"Why not?"

"Because…" Reg tried to marshal her thoughts, already foggy from his magic. It wasn't like Norma Jean had powers Corvin could steal. He would just be tempting her, enticing her away from Reg. What was wrong with that? There would be no harm done.

"I just… I guess I'm just worried. You won't… you can't…"

"I'll just take her for coffee." He shrugged. "Surely you can't object to that?"

"Well… no… I guess not."

Corvin raised a brow at Reg and waited for her to confirm that she was really okay with it. Reg sighed and shook her head. "Why not. There isn't any harm in it, is there? If you're just going to take her to coffee?"

Corvin opened his door and got out. Reg watched him approach Norma Jean's car and, once she figured he had blocked Reg from Norma Jean's view, she got out of the car and headed toward the back yard. But she couldn't help stopping to take a quick look at how things were progressing. Corvin was leaning on the car, radiating charm. Reg could feel the heady mix of magic and pheromones even from where she stood. There was no way that Norma Jean would be able to resist him.

She still felt guilty about letting Corvin do that. She kept repeating to herself that there was nothing wrong with it, he was just helping Reg out by chatting up Norma Jean; but she had spent a lot of time and energy denouncing his use of magic to seduce Reg in multiple attempts to take her powers again. And he wouldn't be giving them back a second time. That had been a one-time deal, to save her from torture.

There was a movement behind Corvin's car. Reg turned her head to see who had arrived. But there was no one there. There was only empty street behind his car, when she was sure someone had been there just a fraction of a second earlier.

"I am losing my mind!"

She said it aloud, trying to jolt her brain into working properly. Why was she suddenly hallucinating everywhere she went? Was she having a breakdown because of Starlight? The stress was too much for her, and she was going to have a complete nervous breakdown because she couldn't handle it?

"There's nothing there. Quit worrying about everything and go home. Make something to eat. Have a nap." Reg muttered to herself as she walked the path back to her house.

She took a look over her shoulder to make sure that no one was lurking nearby as she fit her key into the lock and let herself in. She hadn't managed to convince herself that there hadn't been anything there. But whatever it was hadn't followed her to her door. She wasn't letting it in by unlocking her door and letting it trail in behind her. Keys were powerful, Harrison had told her. They held their own special kind of magic.

She closed the door behind her and locked it. But only the handle, not the bolt or the chain. Sarah could still come in if she wanted to. Reg was used to Sarah looking in and checking to make sure that Reg had everything she needed. She frequently brought nourishing food or invitations to community events, intent on keeping Reg healthy and happy.

But how could she be, without Starlight?

Reg wandered around the empty house, feeling Starlight's absence keenly.

"You need to eat something, Reg." Sarah clucked over her, tidying up the cottage and checking out Reg's fridge to see what she could heat up. "You're not doing yourself or Starlight any favors by not eating. You need to keep up your strength."

"I can't eat anything right now," Reg objected. "I'm not feeling well. I'm not just... avoiding eating because I'm sad. I really can't."

"Surely you could get something down. I can even go out and get you something. What about..." Sarah considered what might appeal to Reg. "Ice cream?"

That gave Reg pause. She hesitated. "Uh... maybe. I don't know."

"What's your favorite kind of ice cream?"

"I'm not picky. I'll eat anything."

"Any kind? You don't have a favorite? Rocky Road? Chunky Monkey? Mint chocolate chip?"

"No. Any kind is good for me."

She had always had a bit of a sweet tooth for ice cream. She didn't think Sarah was going to be able to introduce her to any new flavors that she hadn't tried yet.

"That's what we'll do, then."

"Can you get me that list of tea ingredients first?" Reg had already told her about how the vet was trying to figure out what Starlight had eaten, and needed to see the plant and know the ingredients to any teas Reg had had out the day before Starlight had gotten sick.

"Of course, dear." Sarah looked at her watch. "But the vet will be closed soon. It will have to wait until tomorrow."

Reg hated to wait one more day. Why didn't the vet have extended emergency hours for patients like Starlight? He needed to provide better service than that.

"He needs to figure out what's going on, and I'm just sitting around here, doing nothing."

"You've been recovering. You can't be expected to be bouncing around here like usual when your cat is in the hospital."

Reg didn't think that she bounced around normally. She wasn't a bouncy person.

"That doesn't help Starlight."

"Being calm and finding your center will always help, even if you can't see how."

Reg rolled her eyes, but Sarah didn't catch her doing it.

"Has there been... anything unusual going on lately?" Reg thought about the half-glimpses she had been catching over the last few days.

"What do you mean?" Sarah got down on the floor to pull some miscellaneous objects out from under the TV entertainment stand. Probably things that Starlight had hidden away. He was often batting little bits of paper or plastic milk bottle caps around the cottage, chasing them and pretending that they were mice or some other kind of prey, until they rolled underneath the fridge or a piece of furniture where he couldn't get them back out.

"I mean… I keep seeing or hearing things. Just for an instant. And then they are gone when I look more closely."

"I'm sure it is nothing. The unseen world is all around us. Things slip through the veil from time to time. It is almost solstice, and the boundaries separating worlds become thin."

"So… that happens all the time?"

Sarah shrugged. "I would imagine it happens to some people more than others. You are psychic and very sensitive, so it would not surprise me that you see more than most people do. I wouldn't think it was anything to worry about if it isn't accompanied by… a feeling of menace or darkness."

"Like I had with the Witch Doctor."

"Exactly. When he was working his magic here, you knew something was going on. Little shifts in the veil and chance glimpses of the other side… that doesn't sound like anything worrisome."

"I guess not," Reg agreed. Sitting on the wicker couch, she drew her knees up to her chest and watched Sarah, too tired and sad to move, but also too keyed up to eat or sleep. "You don't think anyone is following me, then?"

"Do you think someone is following you?"

"Well, I saw something before Corvin and I got into the car, and then after we got here. Was that just a coincidence? Or was it the same… person or force each time?"

Sarah shook her head. "I can't understand why you would be spending time with that warlock. You know how dangerous he is and how much he desires your gifts. If it was me, I wouldn't have anything to do with him."

"But you do. You don't avoid him. You've asked for his help, had dinner with him, why can't I?"

Sarah pursed her lips. She shuffled through Reg's mail and flyers on the kitchen island. "It's different for me. An old woman, it's harder for him to tempt me than it is for someone like you, simmering in a stew of hormones.

I'm past the age when I can be influenced by a little charm and a handsome face."

"Oh, sure you are! I've seen how you react when he influences you. Why is it different for you? Do you think that it's just because he wants my gifts so badly? I don't get why he wants them more than anyone else's. I know he compared them to having dessert, that they are particularly sweet to him, but… I don't know. I think he's obsessed. Over the top. One day, he'll probably go off on some other woman and forget all about me."

"Not any time soon. Was that your mother I saw him with earlier?"

"Uh…" Reg cleared her throat and tried to think of a way to deny it. She looked at the face of her phone to see what time it was. She had expected to hear from one of them hours ago. Corvin saying that he'd just left and giving her an update on whether Norma Jean was still trying to connect with her daughter in a meaningful way. Or Norma Jean knocking on her door again, telling her what a nice break she'd just had with the very handsome warlock. But there had been silence from both of them. No calls, no knocks on the door. She wanted to call Corvin to find out what had happened, but she didn't want to know.

And she did.

"Yeah… Corvin was running interference for me, so I didn't have to talk to her. It's nothing. Just… a favor."

"Just like him going with you this morning?"

"We just went to the vet," Reg protested. It wasn't like she had gone to a restaurant with him, out dancing, or to something more daring. "He was just there to help me get through seeing Starlight again and to see if there was anything he could help with. He was really nice about it."

"You know what he wants, and it's not a casual relationship."

"I think we can still be friends. I know he's made wrong choices in the past, but I think he's really trying. Would you ever have thought before that he'd suggest driving me to the vet's? Mr. Chivalry he is not."

"Exactly. He will do whatever it takes to worm his way into your life. Today you're going to the vet with him, and tomorrow you're inviting him home." Sarah gave her a sideways look. "Don't think that I don't know you brought him back here that night."

"What night?" Reg's heart was beating fast and she knew she couldn't hide her reaction from Sarah for long. She was going to have to come up with a cover story double-quick, something that made sense.

"You know very well what night. I thought I was going to have to come over here and break things up with a baseball bat before Harrison showed up."

Harrison.

He had saved Reg from her own stupidity that night, for sure. Reg wouldn't make that same mistake again, letting Corvin take the keys from her to let her into the house. Give him the keys, and you give him permission, Harrison had told her. She had thought she was being careful, but she still didn't know all the rules to the game.

"I, uh, didn't know that you saw him here," Reg said, squirming in embarrassment.

"I see a lot more than you think I do. These old eyes still don't miss much."

CHAPTER ELEVEN

S arah did see a lot more than Reg would have liked. It was too bad she'd seen Norma Jean with Corvin earlier. Sarah sounded quite sure that there was something more going on than just Corvin doing a favor for Reg. And maybe there was. Reg had been watching the clock all afternoon. She didn't like Norma Jean, but she hadn't intended to put her in harm's way, either. Maybe letting Corvin take her out for coffee had been a stupid idea. It had been a spur of the moment decision. One she probably should have stopped to think about.

"But your mother doesn't have any powers, does she?" Sarah asked.

"No."

"So he can't take them from her. The most he could do is… show her a good time."

"He wouldn't do that."

"Why not?"

"She's old. I mean, maybe not old, old, but she isn't in her prime. She looks nice enough now that she's had all of that work done, but she's not a young woman anymore. Corvin is…" Reg trailed off. She had no idea how old Corvin was. Like with Sarah, Reg had been told that he was older than he looked. Decades older than Reg. So he was closer in age to Norma Jean than to Reg. Maybe he had been interested in Norma Jean, and not just taking a hit for Reg. "Oh, I don't know. I don't know how you all do it, remembering how old everyone is and making appropriate matches. I don't understand the way any of this works."

"It's just like the rest of the world, dear. If you are interested in someone or find them attractive, then see if they have similar feelings. You don't have to be the same age… or even the same species." Sarah shrugged. "Our community is much more understanding about differences than the rest of the world."

"I suppose that's why it doesn't make a lot of sense to me. I think of the old mythology stories, and it sounds like anything goes. But you still have some social structure, and rules about how the different races interact with each other, and what Corvin is allowed to do with his powers. There are *some* rules."

"Just like anywhere," Sarah agreed.

Except that Reg wasn't sure she knew what all the rules were or what would happen if she violated them.

~

It was a long night.

Reg devoured a bucket of buttered pecan ice cream, scraping the bottom with her spoon and licking around the top edge for as far as her tongue could reach.

She considered calling Corvin several times, but couldn't bring herself to do so and show herself to be concerned about Norma Jean's welfare. Norma Jean was an abusive monster and Reg didn't want to admit to caring what happened to her. She went to bed, but couldn't sleep. She sat in front of the TV, but that didn't work either. She looked at her phone and considered calling Detective Jessup or Damon. But what would she tell them? That she was worried about her missing mother, who she hadn't cared about until then? Or that she was worried about her sick cat? They would think she was just a crazy cat lady. She especially didn't know about Damon. Several times she tapped his name and then stared at his headshot, finger hovering over the phone icon, trying to muster up the courage to call him.

And talk about what? What exactly was she going to tell him? The last time she had spoken to him, she had been angry about the jealousy between him and Corvin. The two warlocks had fought, and Reg was done with that scene. She didn't want to continue to encourage their jealousy by seeing them both, even as friends.

So she and Damon had to be finished.

If Corvin had decided he wasn't interested in pursuing her anymore, then she could see Damon. But not calling Reg back after his coffee date with Norma Jean did not mean that Corvin had given up on her. It just meant that he didn't see the need to call her after a casual cup of coffee. Like Reg had told Sarah, he was doing her a favor. Just something casual. It didn't mean anything.

Reg looked at Francesca's icon too, but by that time it was so late, she was worried that anyone she called would be asleep, and she didn't have the kind of relationship with Francesca where they could call each other at all hours. Reg had no idea what time the woman went to bed, but she seemed like a very normal, business-oriented woman, and that meant she probably kept regular hours and was in bed by midnight.

Reg wandered to the window in the bedroom, sitting on the low windowsill where Starlight often perched, watching the garden. There were fireflies out again. Having seen them once before, she knew that they were nothing to worry about. Just little bugs with a "flare" for fashion. She watched them spark on and off and breathed in the cool, salty air that blew in through the screen.

Starlight should have been home enjoying the sights and smells and sounds. He should have been there with her.

The sleepless nights eventually caught up with her, and she woke up on the floor under the window, where she had apparently either passed out or had lain down, unable to make it a few feet to her bed. Her cheek was wet with drool and there was a crack in the corner of her mouth that send out darts of pain whenever she opened her mouth or moved it the wrong way. Reg rolled over and eyed the bed, trying to decide if she had the energy to climb into bed and go back to sleep where it was more comfortable. Her bones and joints ached from lying on the floor.

She managed to prop herself against the wall and waited for her body to wake up. She needed to use the bathroom, so she wasn't going to be getting back to sleep until she had taken care of that necessity. Afterward…

maybe she would slide under the covers and try to sleep for a few more hours.

Once she managed to get to her feet and visit the bathroom, though, she knew there would be no getting back to sleep. Her head throbbed, her mouth felt like something had died inside it, and her stomach had a tight knot. She couldn't identify whether it was illness or too much ice cream or just dread of the coming day.

Her brain started to click through the things she would have to take care of, just as if she were Erin making a list. She had to get the plant and the information from Sarah to take to the vet. She should visit Starlight again and see whether there was any improvement. Only this time, she was going to have to go alone, since Corvin hadn't checked back in with her.

She wasn't sure how she was going to face it alone.

Eventually, Reg made it to the kitchen and, after deciding that her stomach could not handle any food or coffee, she found herself calling Detective Jessup. She just couldn't get through the day without someone's help, and Jessup seemed like the best option. She probably wouldn't be able to drop everything to rush to Reg's side. She would be on shift and have duties to attend to. But Reg called her anyway.

Jessup answered after just a couple of rings. "Reg? Hey, how are you?"

Reg let the words hang in the air at first, not sure what to say to that. How was she? She didn't even know how to begin.

"I'm… hey… I'm wondering if you're working today, or if you could…"

"No, I'm off." Marta Jessup's voice was curious. "What is it? Is something wrong?"

"Yeah. It's Starlight. He's pretty sick. I don't know what to do. I didn't know who to call."

"Well, didn't you take him to the vet? You should find out what's wrong with him."

"I did. Yeah. I did that. He's been at the vet for a couple of days now. I need to go over to see him today, take the vet some information… see if Starlight is doing any better. If he's still… okay. You know."

"The vet doesn't know what's wrong with him?"

"He was poisoned."

Jessup gasped. "Poisoned? Are you sure? Who would do that?"

"I wish I knew. Somebody… I think he might be cursed too. It might have been a magical potion. It's something really bad."

"I'll come over. You must be feeling awful. I'm so sorry. I'll come right away, okay?"

Reg found herself nodding. "Yes," she agreed with relief, hot tears prickling her eyes, "that would be good."

"I'll be right over."

Reg hung up. She stood for a long time at the island in the kitchen, absorbing the silence of the house.

She needed Starlight. She needed him to come home so that she could be whole again. She hadn't understood before she had brought him home how important he would become in her life and how much he would help her with her psychic vision. He seemed like the missing piece in her brain, the one that made her almost normal. He stopped her mind from jumping haphazardly from one thing to another and helped her to focus. She imagined that was how everyone felt, all of the normal people who didn't have ADHD and learning disorders and who couldn't hear voices or see things from another plane.

All her life, they had been trying to find the drugs to tame her brain, when what she needed was a cat. Not just any cat. She needed Starlight, with the white spot between his eyes that Sarah called his third eye, the old soul who happened to inhabit the body of a cat. She had been looking for him for her whole life.

Or at least, since she had been four.

Reg looked out the living room window to see if Jessup was there yet. How long would she take to get there? Had she been at home or with someone else? Would she use her lights and siren to get there faster? That was probably against department policy. Reg went to the door and unlocked it. She opened it and stared out into the yard. It was lush and green despite being December. Since Forst had started working for Sarah, it was practically vibrating with life, and Reg imagined that when he walked into it—or appeared in it, since he always seemed to come out of nowhere—that his living plants greeted him excitedly, like a spaniel rushing to see its master at the end of the day.

She sat down on one of the deck chairs near the door, which she hardly ever used. She closed her eyes, feeling the nature around her and, without realizing she was going to, fell asleep again.

CHAPTER TWELVE

R eg. Hey Reg, I'm here. Are you okay?"
     Reg woke up groggily and, even though she could only have
been asleep for a few minutes, she felt like it had been hours. Like she had
been sitting there waiting for Jessup all day. She gave an involuntary start
and immediately looked at her wrist, where she had never worn a wrist-
watch, then looked for her phone to check the time. She was sure it must be
late in the day. Afternoon or evening. She had missed her chance to get to
the vet and give him the information that he needed to take care of Starlight
properly.

Jessup put her hand on Reg's arm. "It's okay. What's wrong?"

"What time is it? How could it be so late?"

"It isn't late. Relax."

Reg couldn't find her phone.

"Your door is open," Jessup pointed out. "Do you want to go back in?"

Reg looked at it and couldn't remember why she had left it open. Had
she been waiting for someone? Had someone gone into her house while she
was asleep? She couldn't just leave it wide open for anyone to walk in. What
if Corvin had shown up for a visit while she was asleep there? He could walk
right in. Or could he? Would the wards keep him out if she left the door
open? If she didn't give him the key, would he still be prevented from
entering?

Reg rubbed her eyes, trying to clear her brain and think straight. "Is Corvin here?"

"Corvin? I don't think so." Jessup poked her head in the door and looked around. "Hello? Anyone here?" There was no answer. Jessup shook her head. "No, I don't think so. Was Hunter supposed to be coming over?"

"No. I don't think so. But I haven't heard from him since yesterday when he took Norma Jean out for coffee. I don't know what happened to him."

"What happened to him? Why, have you tried to get him? Has he disappeared?"

"No… I don't… I don't think so. But he hasn't called me back. I thought he would call me once he was finished coffee to let me know that she might be on her way back again." Reg pressed her temples, trying to get her train of thought back on the rails. "That was a really weird nap. I feel all addled."

"You're probably just short on sleep and I woke you in the middle of a REM cycle. You'll feel better in a few minutes. Should we go inside and get some coffee?"

"Yes."

"Now, exactly what happened?" Jessup asked as they both stared at the coffee maker, waiting for the coffee to finish brewing.

"I don't know. He's been out all night. I was worried that…"

"Hunter can take care of himself."

"No, I mean… Norma Jean… he was with her. I am kind of worried—I don't need to worry about her either, I know, but… I can't help it. I know what he did to me, and I said it was okay for him to take her out. Was that the wrong thing to do?"

"Isn't Norma Jean your mother?"

"Yes."

"I thought she was dead."

"Long story. She's not."

"Sounds like a rather short story to me. So Corvin decided to take her out?" Jessup's lip curled. "Why would he do that?"

"It was a favor to me. I couldn't face her after being at the vet's and dealing with this stuff with Starlight, so he said he would take her out to coffee and take her off my hands. Only… I don't know what happened after that. I thought he'd let me know when he was done, but he didn't call me."

"That doesn't necessarily mean he's been out with her since then. Did you call him? He has probably just been working on other things and didn't think he needed to report back to you. Did he say he would call you after?"

"No."

"Well, there you go. He just didn't realize you'd be waiting for his call."

"Then where's Norma Jean?"

"Is *she* missing?"

"I… don't know. I thought that she'd turn around and come back here after she was finished with him. I thought I'd just get a little bit of time to myself; I didn't think she'd be gone all afternoon and all night."

"Do you want to see her?"

"No."

Jessup rolled her eyes. "Then why does it matter that she didn't show up here? Maybe Corvin did you another favor and managed to talk her out of coming back to see you. So you could have a longer break from her. Why don't you want to see her?"

"Because she's an awful person."

"Okay…" Jessup cocked her head and waited for more, but Reg didn't feel like detailing any of the ways that Norma Jean had been negligent or abusive all of those years ago, or what it was like having Norma Jean in her head for all of those years, always telling her what to do.

Reg stared at the coffee maker. The coffee was dribbling into the pot, almost done. Then she'd be able to have a cup of coffee, and her brain would come into focus, and she'd be able to have a sensible conversation with Jessup instead of making Jessup look at her like she was half crazy.

They both watched it in silence for the last few drops. Then Reg grabbed it off the hot plate and poured a couple of mugs. They drifted over to the seating area in the living room and settled themselves.

"So Corvin and Norma Jean are missing, only they're not actually missing. You don't want to report them missing, and you don't want to see them, you just want to know what happened when they got together yesterday?"

Reg thought this through. It all sounded right. "Yeah," she said with relief. "I think you nailed it."

"Okay. Great. Well, why don't you give Corvin a call then? Assuming that he is the least objectionable party to call."

"Yeah, I guess so."

Reg's phone had been on the counter in the kitchen when she stepped back inside. She looked at it uncertainly, then back at Jessup. "I actually don't want to talk to him. I guess… I'll just wait until I hear from him."

"Okay, then. Feel better?"

Reg sipped the piping hot coffee, knowing that she was going to regret scalding herself later. She couldn't wait for it to cool; she needed the shot of caffeine right away if she were going to be able to think straight and carry on a sensible conversation. It hurt when it hit her stomach. She wondered if she had an ulcer. It really hurt. Reg put the coffee mug down, feeling out of sorts. Betrayed by the coffee that was supposed to make everything better, and instead just lit her stomach on fire.

"Are you okay?"

"Yeah. I'm fine." Reg brushed the inquiry away. "I'm wondering about Sarah."

Jessup sighed. "What about Sarah?"

"She's been gone all night. Why is everybody staying out all night? They don't usually do that."

"How do you know Sarah's been gone all night?"

Reg didn't answer. She wasn't sure what she should respond. She knew that Sarah wasn't back at the big house yet, she could sense Sarah's comings and goings if she paid close attention. Sometimes even when she wasn't trying to tell, she knew. But she also wasn't sure why it mattered that Sarah wasn't home. It didn't mean there was anything wrong. Sarah and Corvin and Norma Jean were all free to come and go as they liked without reporting to Reg. She had never wanted to hear about their comings and goings before.

"Are you worried about Sarah?" Jessup pressed.

Jessup was more likely to care about Sarah's absence than anyone else's. Sarah was an older woman, and she and Jessup seemed to be pretty good friends. They all felt more responsible for Sarah. She had nearly died once, and they liked to keep track and make sure she was okay. It was what you did in a community.

"No. Not really. It's just… unsettling. It feels like everybody was gone to a party except me."

Jessup chuckled. "Well, maybe they did. There might have been some sort of Yule ceremony going on. It's early yet, but sometimes there are Yule mixers or Yule craft days, to get everything ready before Yule. It's nice to have a community where everyone is celebrating. For a lot of witches and warlocks around the world, it's a bit isolating, celebrating Yule when everyone else is getting ready for Christmas. They'll participate in Christmas stuff, but it's not quite the same." Jessup took a sip of her coffee.

"So you think she was probably just out at some craft club? All night long?"

"Not handicrafts. Witchcraft. And yeah, a lot of them go overnight, or everyone crashes somewhere after instead of going home."

"Oh." Reg thought about that. Was Sarah just off at some witching ceremony with her coven? She tried to remember if Sarah had been alone when she left. Reg had just jumped to the conclusion that she was out on a date, but maybe that was because Sarah always seemed to be on a date lately.

CHAPTER THIRTEEN

B ut Norma Jean and Corvin wouldn't have been at any Yule celebration or ritual," Reg said suddenly, raising his eyes to Jessup's, feeling a scowl crease her forehead.

"No, that's right," Jessup agreed, sounding surprised. "I guess I forgot about him being shunned. He wouldn't be able to participate in any community rituals this year. That will be weird."

"And Norma Jean doesn't have any powers."

"Doesn't she?" Jessup cocked her head. "I thought that was who you got your powers from."

"No. Not from her." Reg didn't explain any further. For that, she would have to tell Jessup all about Weston, and it was much too long a story to be trying to tell Jessup now. It would have to wait. Since Reg had called Jessup, she supposed that meant they were friends again, and she would end up telling Jessup all about it some other time, when she wasn't worrying about Starlight. When Starlight was healed and back together with Reg again.

If that were ever going to happen.

Tears sprang to Reg's eyes, and she tried to hide them by taking another drink of the coffee, which again caused further shots of pain radiating out from her stomach. She wasn't going to be able to drink any more of it. She would have to take an antacid and hope that would settle her stomach down.

"Not feeling very well?" Jessup sympathized.

"No. Everything is wonky."

"Sorry about that. When did you want to go over to see Starlight? You said you had some stuff to take to the vet?"

"Yes, I need to get him the plant and the ingredients to the tea that Sarah gave me." It wasn't until then that Reg realized that she still hadn't gotten that information from Sarah. Sarah had promised it to her, but then she had been gone all night and hadn't returned to the house. "I need to… maybe she left it in the big house. I'll have to go over and check."

"Do you want me to come with you?"

Reg eyed Jessup. In spite of Jessup's helpful tone, Reg couldn't help feeling like Jessup was worried about Reg doing something if she went to the big house on her own. Even though Reg hadn't been the one to steal Sarah's emerald, she felt like there was still a cloud of suspicion over her head. Jessup knew something of Reg's past and maybe knew that she had previously been accused of theft. Reg couldn't very well say that it was unfair, since she had, in fact, walked off with certain possessions of value in the past to survive through rough times. She was untrained and barely had a high school education, so she needed to take her opportunities where she could. She had honed her ability to con and steal, sharpened them the best that she could. If that was the only way she could survive, that was what she was going to do.

"I don't need you to come to the house with me," Reg said firmly.

Let Jessup stew about what other mischief Reg might get into at Sarah's house. If she was going to be a suspicious person, then she deserved the anxiety that would go along with it when Reg refused to cooperate. Reg *wasn't* going over to steal anything from Sarah. If she did, it would mean having to run before she was discovered, and she had a good gig in Black Sands.

Sarah was worth far more to her as a landlord and friend than she was as a mark.

Reg left Jessup in her cottage while she went to Sarah's big house. Jessup couldn't do anything about it unless she admitted that she thought Reg was going over there to steal while Sarah was gone. She had offered to help, and Reg had declined.

She hoped that she would find the plant and a list of ingredients on Sarah's table, where she had left them intending to take them to Reg in the morning. But when she entered through Sarah's back door, she was disappointed. The box of Yule decorations was near the back door, but there was no sign of a list of ingredients. Reg dug through the box to find the plant from Fir. It was looking a little worse for wear after being thrown into the box with everything else.

"Sorry," Reg apologized to the little plant. It wasn't the plant's fault that Starlight had been poisoned. If Starlight had eaten some of its leaves, that was on Reg, not the plant. She felt guilty for not taking care of it the way Fir would have wanted.

She set it on the table while she looked for a list of ingredients. There was nothing left out for her. Reg started looking through cupboards. She found a supply of handcrafted teas in one cabinet. Each jar had a label indicating what kind of tea it was, but none of them listed what herbs were included. Reg scowled and shook her head. "Come on, Sarah… how hard is it to list the ingredients?"

Maybe the ingredients varied from one batch to the next. Did Sarah even know what the exact ingredients of the tea were? She had said she would give Reg a list, but maybe she couldn't.

Reg finished her inventory of the cupboards without any luck. They were bursting at the seams with various culinary and medicinal herbs, but she couldn't find a recipe book or box.

"Where did you put it, then? On a computer?"

At first, she thought that Sarah probably didn't even have a computer, but then she remembered Sarah talking about ordering herbs on Amazon and selling items on Etsy. So she must have a computer somewhere in the house.

"Okay, where is your office…?"

She hesitated for an instant before resuming her search. Going into Sarah's kitchen while she was gone was one thing. It wasn't really an intrusion. In a community like Black Sands, walking in someone's front or back door was not unusual or unexpected. It was small-town hospitality. But going through the rest of the house was not so usual. If Sarah returned home while Reg was searching her house, could Reg explain or justify herself? Would Sarah be upset? Would she, like Jessup, think that Reg had let herself into the house just to help herself to any valuables that caught her eye?

Maybe it didn't matter what anybody thought. Reg wasn't there to lift anything, and Sarah wasn't going to charge her. Reg was there for Starlight. What anyone else thought was irrelevant.

Having made her decision, she left the kitchen quickly to look for Sarah's computer. When she found it, she was going to have to figure out how to get past the password, but she had a few tricks up her sleeve. She closed her eyes partway, focusing on the computer, trying to let it guide her to her destination. It was a big house, and she didn't want to have to check every room or take the chance of Frostling, Sarah's African gray parrot, attacking her.

It should have come as no surprise to Reg that Sarah's house was decked out in the finest of the Yuletide season. Twinkle lights and green boughs everywhere. Reg followed her instincts and went up the stairs to check out the bedrooms in that part of the house. Sarah probably had an office next to her bedroom, or had a computer in her bedroom, though Reg didn't remember seeing one there when Sarah was sick. But she had only had eyes for Sarah at the time, worried as she was about her friend. Reg walked down the hall, trying to remember which room housed the emerald necklace that was guarded by Frostling. She did not want to open that door. She'd been attacked by the bird once, and she didn't want to experience it again.

"Just the computer," she murmured. "I just need to take a peek at the computer to find the recipes for the teas, and then I'll be out of here. No one will be any the wiser."

She hadn't been prevented from entering by any of Sarah's wards, as she would have been if she had entered for sinister purposes. Sarah's magic obviously recognized that she was not there to steal anything or to harm Sarah in any way.

Why hadn't Sarah returned home? Was it just a Yuletide celebration, as Jessup had suggested? Jessup would have a pretty good idea if there were anyone in town targeting older women. But that didn't mean that nothing could happen to Sarah.

She'd be in trouble for going into Sarah's house if anything actually had happened to her. But then, so would Jessup, for letting Reg go inside unsupervised. So maybe Jessup would think it wise to stay quiet.

Reg opened the door she thought was Sarah's bedroom, and was rewarded with the familiar furnishings. First guess. She looked around the room but didn't see a computer or laptop anywhere in evidence. What about a tablet? That could be tucked away in a bedside table or bookshelf, much less visible.

Reg decided to check the other rooms quickly, and then to return for a more thorough search if it didn't turn up in one of the other nearby rooms.

She ducked into the next room and found it to contain clothing — racks and racks of every imaginable kind of outfit. Whatever Sarah needed, she had it on hand. It was no wonder she had been able to dress Reg up for the dance Reg had attended with her. Reg had been to boutique stores that had half the amount of merchandise on the racks.

But Sarah's computer wasn't going to be in her dressing room. Reg went on.

Reg tried the next door and found a spacious bathroom, white marble sparkling in the morning sun. Not a smudge or fingerprint on anything. Reg kept going. At the end of the hall was a large, unoccupied bedroom that she thought must function as the guest bedroom. She started on the doors at the other side of the hall, the pain in her stomach growing as she knew she was running out of options. Maybe Sarah had kept her computer closer to the kitchen so she could record recipes close at hand. Or maybe it was a tablet, and Reg had overlooked it in her quick scan for a desktop or laptop computer. Sarah wouldn't just rely on her phone, would she? Her older eyes would need the larger screen for anything detailed.

She probably should have stopped and called Sarah when what she wanted wasn't just in the kitchen waiting for her. Checking the cupboards for a list of ingredients or recipe book was one thing, but checking the rest of the house for a computer she could hack into and search for the recipe? Sarah probably didn't even keep the recipes on a computer. She had probably memorized them.

Reg stood in the hallway for a minute, frustrated with herself and unsure what she should do next. Go back downstairs and out to her cottage without checking the rest of the house? When she might have found what she needed in one of the last rooms?

Keep going even when she had decided it was a violation and she shouldn't be there?

She couldn't just stop what she was doing. She needed to know whether the information was there. She needed to figure out how to help Starlight.

She decided to open the last few doors, and if the computer weren't obvious, she would go back to the cottage. She'd call Sarah to see if she could tell Reg the ingredients. If not, she at least had the plant to take to the vet.

Holding her roiling stomach, Reg peeked into the last few rooms. Another guest bedroom, this one with an ensuite, another room full to bursting with clothing. And directly across the hall from Sarah's bedroom, her craft room.

Not a craft room like Reg would have thought of a year ago, before she knew that there were real practitioners of the magic arts living in Black Sands.

The craft room was full of items of every description. Jars and jars of herbs, roots, mushrooms and other fungi, and jars that Reg decided held pickles which she didn't want to look at any more closely. There were candles, pots, salvers, tweezers, tongs, measuring spoons and cups, and bunches of dried flowers tied together. There were pieces of clothing hung on pegs. Cloaks and hats and gloves and whatever else Sarah needed to perform her magic spells. And there was a computer.

Reg held her breath, looking at it and wondering if she dared enter the craft room. There would probably be additional wards there to keep it safe and she might be prevented from entering the room. Or something bad might happen to her once she did. There was no telling. She'd twice been trapped by spells when entering a room without permission, and it probably wasn't a good idea to be stuck there when there was no one to help her to get back out again. Though at least Jessup was close by and would know something was up if Reg didn't return.

CHAPTER FOURTEEN

Jessup raised her brows when Reg returned to the cottage carrying the little plant. "Find everything you needed?"

"No. But I'm going to have to wait until she gets back. If she has the recipe I need written down somewhere, it is probably on her computer." Reg shrugged. "I checked for a recipe book or box in her kitchen, but there wasn't anything, so I thought I'd better leave it at that. At least I can take this to the vet."

"Do you think he'll know what it is? Think that it will help?"

"I don't know. If there was a spell involved, then… it might not make any difference. He can try as much doctoring stuff as he likes, but Starlight isn't going to get better if there isn't some way to counter the curse."

"Corvin went over there with you?"

"Yeah."

"And he couldn't do anything? Didn't he try to reverse the spell and heal Starlight?"

"He did his best. Or what appeared to be his best, anyway. And I tried to talk to Starlight and do something for him. I don't know what else to try right now. Do you know any magical vets? Is there such a thing?"

"I don't know. I think most people take their pets to the regular vet. And supplement with spells and charms at home, when they can. I don't know if there is anyone experienced in removing curses from cats."

"There has to be someone in a community like this…"

"You would think so," Jessup agreed. "You might want to ask around. I don't know anyone, but that doesn't mean that there isn't. Just that you need to ask someone better qualified. I've never had a pet, so I don't know…"

"He's not just a pet," Reg snapped. "You keep saying that."

"Well… okay. He's not just a pet. But he is still a pet too. I know that he helps you with some of the psychic stuff, but how much of it is him and how much of it is you? Are you sure you're not just… assigning him some power that he doesn't have? Like a placebo effect? You think that he gives you a signal boost, so you're able to do more?"

"No," Reg said flatly. She quickly discounted the idea. She knew that Starlight often knew things before she did. That he had herblore, since he had brought her the yarrow when she needed it to treat the festering wound in her hand. He had fought pixies beside her. There was no way that he was just a cute cat who gave her more confidence in herself.

Jessup nodded. "Did you want to go to the vet right away, then?"

"Do you mind going over with me? I know it isn't any fun, but… I could use the support."

"Of course! Why do you think I came over here? Besides, I'm off today. If I didn't help you, I'd have to stay home and do things like clean the toilet, which I would rather not do."

Reg smiled. One of the problems of being independent and living in a house was that there was suddenly a whole list of things to do to keep the house clean and take care of her possessions. Sarah did a lot of them without Reg ever asking, and Reg was still trying to navigate her way through being an adult and taking care of all of the things that a responsible adult was supposed to do. She was used to living in hotels, flophouses, shelters, or on the street, and then she didn't have to do anything but get her next meal or wash up at a sink. Living in a house where she had to keep up appearances was a whole different ball game. She was happy that Jessup didn't seem to think much of the chores she had to do either. Better to visit a sick cat with a friend than to have to stay home and scrub toilets.

"Thanks. Do you mind driving?"

"You bet." Jessup headed toward the door. "Do you need anything else? Did you want to put that coffee in a 'to go' cup?"

"No." Reg wrinkled her nose. "I think there's something wrong with it. It's really bothering my stomach."

Jessup frowned down at her empty mug. "It seemed okay to me."

They walked out to the car together. Reg took a look around, watching for any of those little peeks through the veil that Sarah had referred to. *Was* she being watched? Was it just a glimpse of another plane and they weren't even aware of her?

Again, there was a shadow just outside her field of vision, which disappeared when she turned her head and tried to pinpoint it.

"Did you try calling Sarah?" Jessup asked. "She's usually an early riser, so I don't think you need to worry about getting her out of bed at this hour."

Reg looked at her phone, but already knew it was past eight. Sarah had probably been awake for several hours, even if she was up until the wee hours of the morning.

That was another reason she was starting to worry. If Sarah had been up for a few hours, then why hadn't she returned home? Why hadn't she given Reg the information she needed by the time the vet's office opened? It was so unusual for her to be away from her home at night, Reg didn't know what to think of it. It was worrying.

"I don't know. Do you think I should? I didn't want to interfere with her life, to act like I was monitoring the hours she was out like I was her mother. She's a grown woman; she can certainly keep whatever hours she likes."

"At this point, I don't think you need to worry that you're hanging over her. You don't even have to say that you know she's been out. You can say that you were wondering if she had the recipe that you needed before you head over to the vet."

Reg nodded slowly. She sat down in the car and selected Sarah's number. As it started to ring, she looked around, trying to spot the shadow again. It seemed to be following her, too interested in her comings and goings to be a coincidence. She trusted her instinct when it came to being time to get out of a situation, and she had the uncomfortable feeling that she was going to have to leave Black Sands. What if it wasn't something supernatural on her tail, but a federal agent with a warrant? What if they were watching her to see what her scam was this time, just waiting for the right time to swoop in and make a bust?

Sarah's voicemail kicked in. A pleasant, grandmotherly voice telling her to leave a message and she would call back. Reg chewed on her lip and tried to decide whether to leave a message or not. She rushed at the last minute, wanting to get her message in before the voicemail timed out.

"Sarah, it's just Reg. Looking for those ingredients, you know? For the vet? I picked up the plant, but I couldn't see the recipe anywhere. Would you let me know if you have it? Thanks. Call me. Please."

Jessup nodded her approval. Reg had a sneaking suspicion that it had been a test to see if Reg were telling the truth. Now she was satisfied that Reg's story was consistent. Although Reg could have dialed anyone she wanted to on the phone and left that message. Or called no one at all. She was good at misdirection.

Reg slid her feet into the car and pulled her door shut. Jessup started the engine and made sure she knew where she was going.

"And... you're sure Starlight was intentionally poisoned?" she asked tentatively.

"I don't know. The vet said there are a lot of household things that could have poisoned him accidentally, but if there is a spell involved too, that means that it wasn't just an accidental poisoning. He didn't just chew on this plant," Reg looked down at the potted green plant in her lap, "or get into something else that he shouldn't have. That means it was intentional, and I can't understand anyone doing that! How could they poison an innocent creature? And not just poison him, but curse him so that he couldn't get better?" Reg sniffled, trying to hold back the tears. She shook her head impatiently at her own emotion and lack of control. "I have to figure out who did it so that we can figure out how to counter it."

Jessup watched the road ahead of her, thinking about it. "You haven't reported it to the police?"

"What could the police do? Would they take the poisoning of a cat seriously? It would go on the back burner. No one would care about it. They wouldn't go out and question anyone; they'd just wait for me to provide evidence as to who it was. Right?"

"Yes, probably. But if you had some evidence, they might go out and talk to people. They might be able to make some progress on it. And if there was magic involved, you really might want to do that. Magic means that it was intentional and targeted."

"But if there is magic involved, then the police can't handle it because so few of them are practitioners. They'll roll their eyes at any of the magical stuff."

"But you can't expect them to do anything about it if you don't tell them."

"No. I'm not expecting them to do anything." Reg glanced over at Jessup. "I called you as a friend, not as a police detective. Can't you just be a friend for once and forget about your job? You said it was your day off."

Jessup's lips pressed tightly shut, thinning out into a straight line. "Yes. I didn't realize I was doing anything wrong."

"You're not. It's just... this isn't an official investigation. I don't know what to do, but inviting the police into it and trying to justify myself to them isn't even on the list."

"Right." Jessup was silent for a couple of minutes as she drove. "Do you mind if I ask... non-official questions about it?"

Reg rolled her eyes. Even when she asked Jessup not to be a police detective, she still couldn't help herself.

Jessup took her silence for consent and proceeded. "What benefit would it be to anyone to poison and curse Starlight? Who would want him out of the way?"

"I don't know. I've been thinking about it. But I don't think that anyone would do that. I mean... I know some people don't like him or don't like cats in general, but would they hurt him just because of that? That takes... a certain kind of person."

"But you can't always tell by talking to someone if they are that kind of person. Psychopaths are usually very charming, very friendly and good at getting people to trust them." Jessup opened her mouth, then closed it, not saying what she had been about to.

"I know plenty about psychopaths," Reg said dryly.

She didn't care whether Jessup thought she was one or not. Reg herself had given up on trying to figure out if there were something wrong with her brain, or whether it was just a combination of her supposedly psychic gifts and the traumatic events that she had been through as a child. It wasn't that she didn't care about anyone else. But she had been hurt and had to protect herself and to lie, cheat, and steal to survive. She had to put herself first, no matter how it might endanger anyone else. If she didn't take care of herself, no one else would. If that made her a psychopath, then she would wear it like a badge of honor. And if not, she had still dealt with enough people in her life who were evil and showed one face to the public and another to their victims. She knew how charming they could be.

"Who were you thinking of?" Jessup asked. "Who did you think of who doesn't like Starlight or want him around?"

Reg stared out the window at the street ahead of them. "Corvin, of course. He hates Starlight and won't even call him by name. Starlight hates him and hisses at him and yowls and gets angry if I let him into the house."

"If you let him into the house? Why would you do that?"

"Sometimes it has been accidental…" Reg squirmed uncomfortably.

"But you don't think that Hunter did anything to him, because…"

"For one thing, I don't think he's had the opportunity. Starlight has only been in the house. Corvin hasn't been, not in the last few days, when Starlight was poisoned. So how could he have done it? No opportunity."

"Are you sure he doesn't have the ability to get into the house? You said that he has been in there by accident."

"I don't know. I don't understand all of the details of how wards work and when they don't work and if Corvin is powerful enough to break them."

"So he is still a *maybe*."

"But he went over to the vet's with me and tried to heal Starlight."

"And you know he could very well have done that just to mislead you and make you think that he was sincere about helping and didn't have anything to do with him getting poisoned and cursed in the first place."

Reg let out her breath. "Yeah."

"So he's on the list. Who else?"

"Sarah doesn't like cats. She puts up with Starlight, and she talks to him and feeds him when she comes over. She was there putting up all of the Yule decorations when he got sick. There were a lot of things that were poisonous to cats. Holly and mistletoe, I don't know what else. I packed it all up, but not until after Starlight was poisoned."

"And you think she dislikes cats enough to have poisoned him?"

"No, I don't. But like you said, you can't always tell. People lie to you. Pretend that they care and are kind and loving when they aren't. Do I think Sarah is that kind of person? No, but that's just what I would think of a very successful psychopath. I don't think she would poison him just because she doesn't like cats. But she *has* been complaining about the other cats coming over to visit and is kind of paranoid about them being around the house or in the garden. She thinks that too many cats in the cottage will attract more cats, like when Nicole first came to see Starlight when he would watch her out the window. Even though he was an inside cat, he still attracted a cat who was allowed to roam. Sarah was worried about being overrun by them and of them catching birds. And she does like birds."

"Yes, she does. Okay. So Sarah is on the list. She had lots of opportunity and some motive. And she hasn't given you the list of ingredients in the tea that you want for the vet."

"Yeah. But I think she still will. I don't think she's intentionally holding that back. We wouldn't have any way of knowing if she gave us the wrong information. If she did poison him intentionally, she wouldn't tell us what she used. I don't think he was poisoned by the tea. That was Corvin's idea, and I don't think it's what happened."

"You think he's trying to cover up how he gave Starlight poison?"

Reg considered. "Maybe," she admitted reluctantly.

"Corvin and Sarah. Who else?"

Reg thought about it. There weren't a lot of people in her life who had reason to dislike the cat. Most people liked him or even loved him. "There are the fairies and the pixies. They don't like cats."

"No. But would they come to your house to poison him? Why would they do that?"

"I *don't* think they would. But you're asking for a list of possible suspects, and the fairies and pixies have to be on it. The pixies don't like cats and they don't like me because I took Calliopia away from them. And then Ruan left to be with her too. They could get up to the house through the sewers, and then... I don't know how they could get into the house, but they are tricky. Maybe they could find a way. Or they could cast a spell on him from outside when he was sitting by the window."

"Okay. I suppose. And the fairies? They have helped and protected you. I don't think they would do anything against your cat."

"I don't think so. I haven't done anything to hurt them. It's just that... some things I have seen lately made me think that maybe they are around lately, in the garden, watching the cottage. And if they are... maybe they didn't like Starlight being there or thought he was a danger to them. I don't know. They've said that they won't hurt me because I'm protected by Calliopia's blood. But that wouldn't stop them from hurting my cat, would it?."

"Right." Jessup pulled into the vet's parking lot but made no move to get out. "So the fairies are a possibility... but probably not as likely as the other suspects."

"Yeah."

"Anyone else?"

Reg was silent for a minute, thinking before she brought up the one that had been bothering her. "My mother."

"Norma Jean? Why would she want to hurt him?"

"I don't know, exactly. But she's the kind of person who lashes out and hurts people. She might apologize afterward or say it was just because she was high or drunk or tired, but that doesn't stop her hurting people. She might actually enjoy it."

"What was she like when she came to see you? Why did she come here?"

"Apparently, because she's turned over a new leaf. She's all cleaned up and wants to reconnect with me. But I don't believe people can change that much."

"It's been a lot of years."

"Yeah. But she was in my head for a lot of years too, and she didn't change then. She would act sweet as honey one minute and then be cursing and threatening the next. If I didn't listen to her, she'd be screaming and ranting. That kind of person doesn't change to permanently sweet. She can pretend, but she can't do it forever."

"And would she have any reason to hurt Starlight? She didn't even know that you had a cat before she came here, so it isn't like he did something to hurt her."

"He's very smart. The way he reacts to people... it's a good guide for what kind of people they are. He's intuitive that way. And he didn't like her. She certainly didn't like him. And she had met him before, even if she didn't know he was my cat."

"How would she have met him before?"

"When we..." Reg realized that Jessup didn't know any of what had transpired with Weston and Harrison and tried to think of the best way to explain it briefly. If she didn't, they'd be sitting in the vet's parking lot all day while Jessup tried to get caught up. "Let's just say... we kind of went back in time and saw her. Back to when I was four and she was still alive. So she saw me then and saw Starlight. And the little me, the four-year-old Reg, she wanted to keep Starlight. So maybe Norma Jean was jealous of him. Maybe he came to represent all of the things that her child demanded. I don't know. But she knew him, and she recognized him when she came to see me. She was... suspicious of him. Didn't know what to think of him."

"And do you think she could have poisoned him? You said she doesn't have any powers, so she couldn't have been the one who cursed him."

"No, but Weston could have."

"Who is Weston?"

"He's… an immortal like the Witch Doctor."

"And he knows Norma Jean?"

"Yeah. They were… very close. I thought that he had gone away and didn't have anything else to do with her after we went back in time, but I don't *know* that. He's an immortal. He could have done anything, right? He could have poofed himself into the cottage, poisoned Starlight, cursed him, and gotten away, and no one would be any wiser. I saw the way that he flirted with Norma Jean, even when she was a drug addict on the skids. He would do anything for her."

"Okay. So Norma Jean and Weston in concert. Is that everyone?"

Reg thought about it. "Yeah… I think so. But… there's been someone following me, too. I don't know who, and I don't know what powers they do or don't have. But someone has been… showing up at the edges of my vision and then disappearing…"

"Like a pixie?"

"Like that, but I don't think that's what it is. I thought it was bigger, like a human, but I've only caught glimpses out of the corners of my eyes. Sarah said that the veils between the worlds are thin around solstice. She thinks I'm just getting accidental glimpses through those veils. But I don't think so. The pattern seems too deliberate."

"What is the pattern?"

"It's whenever I leave the house. Whenever I go out or come back."

"Is it following us now?" Jessup squeaked, immediately turning her head back and forth to scan for something that couldn't be seen.

"Yeah. I saw the shadow again before we left the house. I don't know if it has a vehicle or some kind of teleportation. But I saw it here before when I was here with Corvin and at the house a few times. It obviously wants to know where I'm going."

"That's a bit creepy. You should file a restraining order—"

"Against who? Or what? I can't go to a judge and say that I saw a dark shadow out of the corner of my eye, and I want him to make it stop following me."

Jessup nodded. "No… I suppose not."

"I can't do anything about it. I keep watching for it and trying to figure out who or what it is. It hasn't tried to attack me."

"You lead an exciting life, Reg Rawlins."

"I kind of wish I didn't."

Jessup opened her door, and Reg followed suit. She led the way into the vet's reception area and approached the receptionist to explain why they were there. The young woman recognized her and nodded a friendly greeting. She didn't rush in to tell Reg that Starlight was alive or dead. She just gestured toward the chairs. "If you want to sit down for a few minutes, I'll see when the doctor will be able to see you."

CHAPTER FIFTEEN

R eg sat in the waiting area and was again drawn to look at the sad animals of everyone who was waiting in the chairs. She hoped that they were all just regular checkups or deworming, not anything serious. Not people who were going to have to have their animals put down. No one who'd had a pet poisoned as Reg had. It was too much sadness.

She didn't know how anyone could work in a veterinary hospital or anywhere else where there were sick and injured animals or children on a regular basis. It would have taken too much out of her. Being a psychic was bad enough. She didn't like having to talk to people who had just lost family members or who had significant trials in their future. But most of the time, she made people happy by giving them a chance to talk to their loved ones who had gone on before, or she could find something in their future, no matter how small, that she could pick out to help cheer them up about their futures. She liked giving good news and reconnecting loved ones who really wanted to talk to each other. Or finding lost items or making her clients happy in other ways.

She supposed that being a vet would have happy moments as well. Animals healed and made well, new babies, new pets who made their owners happy. It wouldn't all be sad. But she thought that too much of it would be. She couldn't handle that. It would be like being a cancer doctor for little kids.

She shifted in her seat, unable to get comfortable. She wanted the vet or his assistant to come out and tell her how Starlight was, so she didn't have to sit there wondering if he had died and they were trying to clear a room in order to tell her. She reached out mentally, trying to make contact with him. She hadn't been able to since she had found him unconscious, but that didn't keep her from hoping. When she couldn't sense him, it didn't answer her question as to whether he was okay or had passed.

Jessup eyed her and flipped through some magazines and coffee table books in front of them, showing Reg cute pictures and asking her questions about what kinds of animals she would like to own and what she would never have. Reg tried to focus and engage, knowing that Jessup was trying to help.

"I have a foster sister, and her half-sister has a lizard," she commented, looking at the picture of a snake lovingly wrapped around its owner's arms and shoulders. "It freaks her out. My foster sister, I mean. Erin. She doesn't like lizards. She has a cat and a rabbit."

"Yeah? Do they get along with each other?"

"Yeah, they do. It's kind of cool. But they get jealous of each other when they both want her attention. Her boyfriend has a dog, and the cat doesn't like the dog, but the rabbit is okay with him. And the dog is okay with the cat. But he puffs up into a big furball and hisses when he sees the dog."

She was babbling. Jessup didn't care about Erin's animals. Neither did Reg.

Finally, the veterinary assistant came out looking for Reg and directed her and Jessup to one of the exam rooms. "The vet will be right with you."

Reg licked her lips in preparation for asking whether Starlight was okay or not, but she couldn't get the words out. She ended up just going into the tiny exam room with Jessup. There wasn't enough room to pace, but she felt too crowded sitting down, the seats too low for her to look over the examination table. She stood up, thumbs in her pockets, trying to look casual, but Jessup had to know that it was driving her up the wall. The potted plant sat in the middle of the examining table, incongruous.

It was only a couple of minutes before the vet came in, rubbing his hands with an alcohol gel that cut the air sharply with its scent. Reg didn't offer to shake hands with him, wondering what animal he had just been handling and what procedure he had performed.

"Oh, is this something we need to identify?" he asked, hovering over the plant.

"I just had it for a little while before Starlight got sick. The guy who gave it to me said not to let him eat it. And I didn't think he would. I don't know if he did. I never saw him near it, and I don't see any bite marks on it…" She trailed off and shrugged.

The vet inspected the plant, pushing the leaves around, looking at the soil, sniffing it. "I don't recognize the species. I'll have to get to work on the computer and see if we can identify what it is. It may not have anything to do with Starlight's illness, but we can at least check it out."

"Is he… okay?"

He nodded. "I would say… he's doing a little better today. Not enough that I can say he is definitely on the road to recovery, and I don't think he's going to be waking up today, but… a little stronger. You were right about the bleeding, and we were able to stop it. Pulse and blood pressure are up a little bit. That's good news. If we can keep him going in the right direction, there is some hope for recovery."

Reg let out her pent-up breath and felt the tears immediately flood from her eyes again. She rolled her eyes up to the ceiling and tried to convince herself to stop crying, but it was such a relief to have Starlight show even a tiny bit of improvement, she couldn't help herself.

Jessup got up from her chair and gave Reg an awkward hug. "Hey, Reg. It's okay. He's doing better. This is good news."

"I know. These are happy tears." Reg had never understood happy tears before. She'd had parents or teachers tear up when they were happy or relieved about something, but had never understood what it meant. She'd never experienced the kind of good emotion that was strong enough to cause tears. She sniffled and tried to stop the flood without success.

Jessup rubbed her back. Reg squirmed away from her, not comfortable with the contact. It had been better when Corvin had gone with her. She always felt good in his proximity. And when he touched her. She got goose-bumps just thinking about it.

"Can I see Starlight? It doesn't have to be for a long time, but I think it helps him."

The vet nodded. "My assistant will be bringing him in a moment. She's just getting him ready right now." The vet moved the potted plant to the counter. "I hope this gives us some clues as to what we can do to speed his recovery. Right now, I'm afraid all we can do is palliative care and hope that he continues to recover on his own."

"If he does… that would be good."

"Yes," he chuckled. "I would take that."

The veterinary assistant brought Starlight in, snugly wrapped in a towel and cuddled in her arms like a baby. "Here's your mommy," she crooned to him, even though he was still not conscious. She put him down on the table and unwrapped the towel, readjusting him so that he looked like he was in a natural position. Reg moved forward as soon as she could and started to pet him and whisper to him, rubbing his head and scratching his ears and chin. The vet and his assistant withdrew so that she could have some time with him. Reg stroked him and held her hands against his body, again trying to fill him with her strength and to build up the protections she had wound around him when she had first found him unconscious before bringing him to the vet.

"You can do it. You can get stronger. We'll find a way to counter this magic and the poison and to make you better again. I promise. You'll be able to come home again and have some tuna fish and sit in the window and watch the lights outside. I'll make sure there's never anything around the house that can make you sick again. I'll do everything I can to protect you so that no one can hurt you. They won't ever be able to hurt you again."

She knew, of course, that she was making promises she couldn't follow through on. Just like a parent who promised her child she would always be there. Or the cops on TV who promised that they would find the person who had been kidnapped or find the killer of the person who had been murdered. Reg always scoffed at those scenes, at the ridiculousness of the thought that a policeman would ever feel compelled to make promises like that. They would never make a promise they couldn't keep and, obviously, they couldn't keep a promise to bring a criminal to justice. Plenty of crimes went unsolved for years, decades. Look at Jack the Ripper. Had the police on his case promised that they would bring the killer to justice? If so, they had failed miserably. It wasn't something that they could follow through on.

But the words welled up from her heart, and she promised Starlight over and over again that he was going to be okay, even though she had no way of helping him or knowing if he would even last another day. The doctor said that he was getting better, but he still looked the same, and Reg still couldn't reach him when she tried to reach out and touch his mind. He was deeply unconscious.

After a while, she didn't have any more strength to spare. She could barely stay on her feet. She withdrew from him and leaned against the wall, tears streaming down her face again. Tears of frustration this time that there was nothing more she could do for him.

"Are you okay?" Jessup asked solicitously.

Reg shook her head and didn't answer. The vet's assistant returned and wrapped Starlight back up like a burrito. "We'll take good care of him, momma. We're doing everything we can for him."

"I know."

She disappeared through the other door of the room, into the inner rooms, where in the distance a dog was whining and whining and wouldn't stop.

"Let's go." Jessup escorted her out of the room with a supporting arm around her shoulders. "It'll be okay, Reg. They're taking good care of him."

"I know." Reg sniffled and sobbed and tried to catch her breath. "But they can't do anything as long as the curse is still on him. Even if they counteract the poison, they can't do anything about the magic."

"Maybe there is someone who can. We'll find out. We'll figure out what to do."

CHAPTER SIXTEEN

I'm glad I came with you," Jessup said, taking Reg back to the car. "This would have been really tough for you to do on your own. Are you going to be okay at home? Do you want me to stay with you for a while?"

"I don't know." Reg slumped into her seat, exhausted. "I just don't know."

"Okay. Well, see how you feel. I'll understand if you do. And like I said, I'm okay with not cleaning my toilet today."

Reg smiled and closed her eyes, not wanting to engage. She needed to rest for a few minutes, not to have to have a conversation.

Jessup accepted this and drove her back home without any questions about who might be suspects in the poisoning and cursing. When they got home, Reg sat still for a minute, not getting out. She looked toward the house and could feel that Sarah was home at last.

Jessup looked at her. "Do you see it? The shadow that you were talking about earlier? Did it follow us again?"

Reg continued to look at the house. As soon as she turned her head, the shadow, if it were there, would disappear. She just stared at the house, monitoring the edges of her vision, before turning and looking around. "No, I didn't see anything this time. Maybe it's given up."

"Maybe." Jessup didn't look convinced.

"Sarah is at home."

Jessup looked at the house. "How can you tell that?"

"I just can."

"Well, at least that's one missing person you don't have to report."

"I'm going to the cottage. I don't think I can deal with anyone else."

Jessup hesitated. "Does that mean you don't want me to come in, or do you mean you don't want to talk to Sarah?"

"I don't know…" Reg took a deep breath and tried to sort out her emotions. "You can come in. But I might want to go to sleep. And if I do…"

"It's fine. I'll just let you sleep."

"Okay."

Reg pushed herself out of the car and shuffled back to the cottage. They were barely in the door when Sarah's back door opened and she walked briskly to Reg's door.

"Oh, Reg, you're back. I'm sorry I was so late getting back. I did mean to have everything ready for you this morning." She took in Reg's appearance. "Is it too late, then? Is… did something happen?"

"He's still hanging on," Reg assured her. "Maybe a little better. I'm just… I tried to build him up as much as I could, but this healing thing is not something I've ever tried before. It takes a lot of energy."

Sarah nodded. "Yes, of course it does. I don't know if I would waste my effort—" she cut herself off and changed direction. "I have those ingredients here." She patted her pockets and found a piece of paper, which she handed over. Reg looked down at the scribbled list and nodded. As she had told Jessup, she didn't think that the tea had poisoned Starlight and, if it had, Sarah wasn't likely to tell her what had hurt him anyway.

"Sarah, what about your emerald?" Jessup suggested.

They both looked at her.

"What about my emerald…?" Sarah repeated, eyebrows raised.

"I mean, it is very powerful. Couldn't you use it to heal Starlight?"

"No."

Reg and Jessup looked at her, waiting for further explanation. Sarah just shook her head.

"No. That's not what it is for."

Reg wasn't sure if she meant it wasn't for anyone but Sarah, that it wasn't for healing someone from poisoning or cursing, or if it wasn't for animals.

But whichever it was, it was clear she didn't intend to use the powerful crystal for Starlight's benefit.

"Okay," Jessup muttered. "I guess that's not what it is for. What about some other potion or charm? Is there anything you have that might help him? Anything you can think of that might help him to get better faster?"

"I am not a cat healer. You'll have to find someone who knows about cat physiology and what is beneficial to them. It isn't something that I can help with."

"Do you know anyone…?"

"Why would I? I haven't ever had a cat."

Reg was getting irritated with Sarah's unhelpful responses. "You don't really care whether Starlight gets better, do you? You would rather he didn't, so that there isn't a cat over here and you don't have to have one on your property."

"I think I have been very kind to allow Starlight to stay here. I wouldn't want anything to happen to him. But I don't have the skills or the resources to help you."

Reg shook her head. "Fine. I'm going to go lie down."

Reg awoke to knocking on her door. She rubbed her eyes and looked around, disoriented. She tried to remember what day it was and why she was sleeping in the middle of the day, and slowly, the events of the past few days seeped into her consciousness. The pain in her stomach increased as her muscles tightened. She rolled over and sat up slowly, giving her body time to adjust being in an upright position, then wandered out to the door. It wouldn't be Sarah; she would just walk right in. And Jessup would either have stayed while Reg slept or would have gone home and wouldn't be back looking for her again. She would call.

Reg looked out the peephole and saw Damon. She opened the door, considering.

"Hey." Damon looked a little uncomfortable. They hadn't been dating. Reg had told him to take a hike after he and Corvin had a big jealous fight over her. In public. Crashing tables, splashing coffee, it had been a scene, and Reg hadn't appreciated it. Then he'd shown up again later when she was meeting with Davyn about Corvin's sentence. He'd again showed his jealous side, and Reg wasn't going to put up with him being jealous every time she spoke with another man. Big red flag. "I was checking in on you. I heard about Starlight and wanted to make sure you were okay."

Reg stared at him. "You heard about Starlight. From who?"

"Uh… I don't know… it was, I think it was Bill over at the Crystal Bowl."

"How did he know?"

Damon raised his brows. "I didn't ask him how he knew. I guess he heard it from someone else. Bartenders know everything, you know. They hear all of the rumors going around."

"I didn't tell him about it. The only people that knew were Corvin and Sarah."

"Then I guess one of them has been over to the Crystal Bowl." Damon shrugged. "Was it supposed to be a secret?"

"Well, no, I guess not. But it is kind of personal."

He shifted his stance, angling toward the door. "So are you okay? Could I come in?"

"I don't know. I don't like to invite men in here, since Corvin, you know."

"You don't seem to have a problem hanging around with him, and he's the one who is a predator. I don't know why you would have a problem being with me."

Reg grimaced. He was right. When she looked at it from a logical perspective. But her emotions and her attraction toward Corvin were not logical. She couldn't control that. Damon was a nice guy, and he was probably more compatible with her since he wasn't going to steal her powers if they got too close. But she had a hard time getting to know him. The fact that he could tell when she was lying and could put thoughts into her head made her suspicious of him.

"I guess… come in for a few minutes. But it's not a date, and I don't want you putting visions into my mind."

She moved back from the door to let him in. He stepped over the threshold before answering her. "I'll do my best, but have you ever had someone tell you not to think of a thing? I don't know what you're thinking of right now, but what would you think of the minute I tell you not to think about elephants?"

Of course, Reg hadn't been thinking of elephants, but now she was. "I don't know what that proves."

"Just that telling me not to communicate using the part of my brain that shares visions is counterproductive. The more I try to avoid using it, the more it is triggered. I don't understand what your objection is. It's just the way I communicate. It's part of my language."

"I don't like the way that your visions pop into my brain and affect the way I'm thinking. I don't know when I've imagined something, and when it's you. It's unsettling."

He shrugged. "I'll do my best, but I don't have perfect control."

She suspected that he had a lot more than he pretended to. She could control what she said or didn't say out loud; it didn't have to be the same as what she was thinking in her head. So he should be able to control whether he shared a vision or just kept it in his head. If it were just like speaking. And of course, she could be completely wrong.

But right or wrong, she didn't like it, and she would kick him out the minute she thought he was putting thoughts or visions into her head.

She motioned Damon to the couch and he sat down. He had a lot of physical similarities to Corvin; the dark hair and eyes, short beard, and dark hair. But he was nothing like Corvin. She didn't feel the same warmth and attraction when she was near him. She liked him well enough as a person as long as he behaved himself, but she didn't feel the desire to curl up in his arms as she did with Corvin. She got him a tumbler of Jack without asking what he wanted, and the same for herself. It wasn't a 'tea' day.

"So how are you feeling?" Damon prompted. "It must have been a pretty big shock, finding Starlight… sick like that."

"It was awful. And I don't think I've recovered. If he doesn't get better, I don't know what I'm going to do. I never realized how important he would become to me. I thought I was just getting a prop for my business, and he's ended up being so much more. I can't imagine carrying on without him."

"You could get another cat. And even though you don't think so, you would probably get just as attached to a new one just as fast."

"No. Starlight is special. Another cat wouldn't be the same."

"You might be surprised."

Reg hated people who always thought they knew more than she did or what was right for her. She knew a lot more about cats than she used to. She had not just been around Starlight, but also around Nicole and the kittens.

She had discovered that they all had different personalities and gifts. People talked about cats as if they all had the same personalities and behaviors, but they were so wrong. Each of the cats and kittens was as different from the others as humans were. They might not have language and communicate the same way as humans, but that didn't mean they weren't really personalities.

She sipped her drink. It felt good going down, but as soon as it hit her stomach, it burned, and Reg's stomach reacted so violently that she almost brought it right back up. She put her glass down. Coffee and whiskey were both out of the question. She needed real food in her stomach, and maybe milk or water. She was going to have to take care of herself, or she would wind up in the hospital herself.

"Reg?" Damon asked, a note of alarm in his voice.

"I'm not feeling very well. I should probably go back to bed."

"You're so pale. What can I get you?" He stood up and went into the kitchen. He looked around, opening cupboards and the fridge. "I could make you some tea. When was the last time you ate? Do you want some toast?" He poked through the takeout containers in the fridge. "Leftover pizza?"

"Maybe... toast. I don't think I could keep anything else down. And maybe some Pepto from the bathroom."

He put a slice of toast in the toaster and depressed the handle. He disappeared into the back hallway for a few minutes—a little longer, Reg thought, than he needed to in order to find the pink medicine—and then he was back, shaking the bottle and reading the dosing instructions.

"I should probably have the toast before the medicine."

Damon nodded. "Whichever you want. It should only take a couple of minutes. Are you sure there isn't anything else you want?" There was a crease between his brows. "You don't seem to have any herbs."

"I'm really not into herbs and remedies. Sarah is the one who knows all that stuff; I don't. Pepto Bismol works for me."

He put the bottle and a tablespoon down on the coffee table for her. "You should see someone if it lasts too long. Is it just a bug, or...?"

"Just worried about Starlight, I guess. I haven't been able to eat very much."

"Sarah could probably prepare you a calming remedy. Something that would help you to be less stressed about it."

"Probably," Reg agreed. That didn't mean she was going to do it.

The toast popped a minute later, and Damon looked in the fridge again. "Do you want butter? Jam?"

"Nothing, just dry toast. Really, I'm not even sure if I'll be able to handle that."

He put it on a plate and took it over to her. He sat back down and watched Reg take an experimental bite. Reg chewed the dry toast and swallowed, then waited to see how it would feel. It didn't bother her stomach too much, so she sat there nibbling at it while Damon looked around the house and searched for a safe topic.

"I gather… you don't know how Starlight got sick?"

Reg turned her eyes to his face, studying his expression carefully to see how much he knew. She hadn't seen him around, but that didn't mean that he hadn't been around without her seeing him. With his black cloak on and the cover of night, he could go pretty much wherever he wanted without anyone knowing about it.

"He was poisoned. And cursed."

Damon portrayed shock. "Really? Who would do that?"

"I don't know." She continued to stare at him. "I have a few suspects."

"It takes a pretty bad sort to poison a pet. You think you know who did it?"

"I said I have suspects. And Starlight is not a pet. He's my familiar. He's a…" she wanted to say 'real person,' but wasn't sure how that would go over. He seemed like one to her, but Damon would think she was crazy. He wouldn't understand what Starlight meant to her.

"Well, I hope you find out who did it. Is he going to be okay? You caught it in time?"

"I don't know. The vet said he was doing better today, a tiny bit better, but I don't know… It's pretty serious. We don't know if he'll recover."

Damon shook his head. "Shocking. I'm so sorry to hear that."

He took another sip of his whiskey. Reg tried to figure out a way to get rid of him quickly.

Later, when she was alone again, she thought about Damon and wondered whether he had been closer than she thought. She hadn't seen him, but he might have been around without her being aware of it. What if he was the one who had been following her? She didn't know the extent of his powers, but she suspected that with his ability to project visions, he could cloak himself, making her think she was looking at an empty street when he was standing right there.

Maybe she had been catching glimpses of him, and he had been hiding himself with his powers whenever she turned toward him. It was odd that he should know about Starlight being sick when it wasn't common knowledge in the community. It wasn't like she'd posted it on her social networks. She'd told a couple of people, and yet word had apparently made its way back to Bill at the Crystal Bowl and Damon. If Damon was telling the truth. Reg knew Bill, but she couldn't imagine him talking to Damon about her personal life. Why would either of them be interested in Starlight?

CHAPTER SEVENTEEN

When it started to get dark, Reg took a walk in the garden. She was feeling restless and she wanted to look around. Were the things she had seen and heard in the yard at night indicative of fairies? If so, why were they there? Were they guarding her? Investigating her? Just there by chance?

Or was she seeing and hearing things that weren't actually there? Maybe she was ill. Perhaps all of the strange happenings were just indicators that she was slowly losing her mind.

The night air was crisp and pleasant. Even in the dark, the garden was pretty and had a feeling of calm. Reg sat down on a large decorative rock and closed her eyes, listening to the breeze blowing through the trees and smelling the salty tang of the ocean it carried. It was such a beautiful, peaceful place.

And then she heard it. A sound that reminded her of the tinkling of bells and of childish laughter. Like the trees were whispering secrets to each other and laughing at their own jokes. There were flickering lights, but she couldn't see the fireflies themselves, just the lights, which didn't seem to move the way that bugs did. Maybe it was some other phenomenon. Not the northern lights so far south. What other natural phenomenon produced light? Ball lightning. In children's movies, pixies lit up like little lights, but they were nothing like the real-life pixies she had encountered, dirty and vicious and cold.

The whispering noises swept past her, as if a group of invisible people had passed.

Reg got up, trying to follow the noise but, as soon as she moved, it was gone. She walked toward the front of the house. She could go for a walk. Or go talk to Sarah. She felt like she needed to do something to help solve the problem of who had poisoned Starlight, but she couldn't think of anything that would actually help. She took off down the street at a brisk pace, and in a few minutes found herself turning and heading toward the Crystal Bowl. Usually, she drove there, but it wasn't far; it didn't actually take much more time to walk there than it would take to drive. And she got the exercise she felt like her body needed, sluggish after so much sleep and sitting around. She pushed open the doors of the Crystal Bowl and walked into the babble of voices. No one turned to look at her. She headed up to the bar, even though she knew she couldn't have anything to drink. Whatever she got would just hurt her stomach.

Bill was not on duty, so that wrecked the idea of asking him where he had heard about Starlight and if he had been the one to tell Damon about it. She didn't trust Damon's explanation.

One of the other bartenders, a tall thin man called Taco, shuffled down the bar to her.

"Evening, Reg. What can I get you?"

"I can't really drink anything."

He raised an eyebrow.

"My stomach. I'm not feeling well."

"Oh," he nodded. "Milk or water? Ginger ale? Ginger is good for sick stomachs."

"Okay, I'll give it a try."

He poured her a glass and set it on a napkin in front of her.

"Has Damon been in here today?"

"Damon? I only just started my shift, but I don't usually see him around here."

"He said that he heard about my cat here."

"Your cat?"

"Starlight. About him being sick."

Taco shook his head, bemused. "I don't know. I haven't heard anything. What's wrong with him? Is it contagious? Rabies?" His mouth quirked into a grin, questioning why it would be news that her cat was sick.

"No. He was poisoned and cursed."

The grin disappeared. "Oh. I'm sorry. Why would anyone do that?"

"That's the question. Who would want to hurt my cat? Why would anyone do that? Was it to hurt me? Did he... offend someone? I mean, what does a cat do that he deserves to be killed for?"

"Is it that serious?"

"Yes."

"I guess... I couldn't know that without knowing more about the cat. People talk about trapping or poisoning animals that dig in their gardens or get into the garbage. No one likes to have to clean that crap up."

"No, he's an inside cat. He's not getting in anyone's gardens."

"Well, then, who else would he bother? Someone who came over to your house who didn't like him? A roommate?"

Reg shook her head again. She sipped the ginger ale and looked around the crowd at the Crystal Bowl. It was usually fairly busy. They did good business. "How about Corvin? Have you seen him around?" She couldn't help it that her mind kept going back to him. The way he hated Starlight. The way Starlight hissed and acted toward him, as if they had been mortal enemies in a previous life. Had they? Corvin had suggested that Starlight might be a human reincarnated as a cat. Harrison had said he was an old friend. Maybe they were right. Maybe Starlight knew things about Corvin. Maybe Corvin had something to cover up by killing Starlight; it wasn't just that he didn't like Starlight being around when he tried to get in to see Reg.

"Saw him here last night with a woman. Stranger I didn't know."

"Norma Jean."

"Could have been," he nodded slowly. "We weren't introduced, but they were around most of the night. That sounds right."

"She's my mother. Biological mother, anyway." Though who knew how much of Norma Jean's DNA Reg actually had. Harrison had been very vague about how an immortal like Weston and a human woman would create a child, so she wasn't sure the process was the same as two humans having a baby and the baby inheriting both of their genes. Maybe Reg was a new creature, who did not share in the genetic heritage of either of them. She didn't look much like either one of them. Though who was to say whether Weston always took the same form, or whether he could take whatever form he pleased.

"Your mother?" Taco raised his eyebrows, surprised. "I had no idea."

"I hadn't seen her since I was four. It wasn't like she was in my life."

"Corvin was behaving… very strangely, for him."

"Oh?" Reg leaned in closer to Taco, hoping for more details. He moved farther away from her to serve up a couple of refills, then moved back to her again.

"He was acting as if… the roles were reversed," Taco said slowly. He frowned, trying to decide whether there was a better way to describe what he was talking about.

"What do you mean, the roles?"

"Well Corvin is the one who is always charming the women. He can have a very powerful effect on them." Taco gave an apologetic shrug, doubtless knowing Reg's history with Corvin.

"Yeah, I'm aware of that."

"But this time, he was the one who was acting… a little loopy."

"Corvin?"

"Yeah, I know. They were sitting together, and usually, it's the women who are falling all over themselves, pulled in by his charms. Even the ones that he isn't trying to charm; the ones without powers or who are older. They are still attracted to him, it's natural. But this woman—your mother—she was the one charming him."

"No."

He shrugged, holding his hands palms up. "I don't know how else to describe it."

"She doesn't have any powers."

Taco cocked his head. "Yes, she does."

"No. She doesn't. She's just a regular human. No special gifts."

"Then we're not talking about the same woman."

"Maybe not," Reg agreed, relieved to find an explanation. "He wouldn't have been here that late with Norma Jean. He took her out for coffee earlier in the day. He must have been here with someone else."

Taco nodded, accepting this as the explanation. "It must have been someone else. I'd like to know who she was, though. It was quite something to see the tables turned."

"I'd like to see that too," Reg admitted. "Let him see what it's like, for once."

She felt immediately guilty for even thinking it. She wanted Corvin to have a taste of his own medicine? After all she had said and done to try to make him and the other warlocks understand what the women who were his victims went through? If she didn't want it for the women, then she didn't want it for him either. It would be reprehensible to wish that on anyone. No one deserved to be treated like prey and to have their willpower taken away from them by magical means.

She covered her mouth to hide her frown, then rubbed her forehead. She was still having trouble focusing on anything but Starlight's immediate condition. She worried that any time, her phone would ring and it would be the vet calling to tell her that he hadn't made it.

"Well, if you see him…" Reg started, then stopped. If Taco saw Corvin, then what? Did Reg really want to pass a message on to him? 'Let me know if you're okay' or 'Call me and let me know how it went with Norma Jean' or, worse yet, 'tell me what you thought of her.' Ugh. Why did relationships have to be so complicated? Her relationship with Corvin was difficult enough without adding in her relationship with Norma Jean and then mixing them up with each other. Whether it had been Norma Jean that Corvin had been with the night before or not, what right did she have to ask Corvin to look after her? She should have been doing her best to keep them apart, not complicating things by letting them talk to each other. The stories that they might have shared over coffee…

"Yeah?" Taco's brows went up, waiting.

"I don't know. Nothing, I guess. I'll see him when I see him. I'm sure we'll run into each other again, that's never been a problem before."

Taco nodded. He moved away from her, polishing the bar counter with a white towel. Reg sipped a little more of the ginger ale, but it didn't seem to be doing much for her stomach. She should probably go home and go back to bed. Maybe she'd be feeling better by morning.

But she was used to being up late and, since she'd already had a nap, her body was wound up, and she wasn't ready to go back to bed so soon.

She left a tip for Taco with what remained of her drink and headed back out. There were a few stores to browse along the street that the Crystal Bowl was on. She would do a little window shopping and see where it led her. Maybe she'd even stop at the grocery store and pick up something healthy to eat. Like a bag of chips. Chips were vegetables.

She continued walking up the street, looking in the windows of the shops that were still open. Most were closed and dark. If she wanted to buy anything, she would have to start earlier in the day. The stores in Black

Sands didn't stay open late, despite the large magical community, which she would have thought would have preferred shopping at night over shopping during the daylight hours. Maybe there was another area of town where the stores stayed open late, but you had to be a local to know about it.

She crossed the street and walked back the direction she had come, down the other side. She saw a drunk slumped in one of the benches along the street, and looked back at the other side, deciding whether to cross back over and avoid the drunk. It wasn't like he was being belligerent, though, he was sleeping. He wasn't going to harass her. She decided to keep walking and pretend she didn't see him, like everyone else was doing.

Until she was a few feet away from him and felt the familiar stirrings inside her. She looked back at the drunk, frowning. He hadn't shaved. His clothing was rumpled and stank of sweat. The hood of his cloak was up over his head and obscuring most of his face. But she knew the warm feeling she had as she got closer to him, it was unmistakable.

"Corvin?"

She said it too quietly. He didn't even stir. Reg got close to try to get a good look at his face. She hooked one finger around the edge of his hood to pull it away from his face for a better view. It *was* Corvin. A Corvin who had clearly had too much and maybe hadn't even gone home since his date with the mysterious woman the night before. Reg poked him a little gingerly.

What did she think? That she was going to catch something from him? Intoxication or a hangover was not contagious. She wasn't going to catch any cooties. She gripped his arm and shook hard. She could feel the buzzing electricity of their contact, just as she always did. Even with him unconscious. That just proved that it wasn't something he had full control over.

"Corvin! Wake up! Corvin!"

It took determined shaking and shouting in his face before he finally began to stir. People walking by were glaring at Reg. Why? It wasn't her fault that he was drunk. No one else had taken it upon themselves to intervene. She was doing what any responsible citizen of the community should do and making sure he was okay.

Corvin's head tipped back, wobbling back and forth. He looked at her through slitted eyelids, not opening them any farther than he had to. "Regina."

"Hey. What's going on? You can't sit here passed out on Main Street. Some cop is going to roust you. What are you doing here?"

He stared at her, not responding.

"Come on. Corvin. What are you doing here?"

"Is she gone?"

"Who?"

"Your mother." His words were thick and slurred. "Norma Jean." He gave a smile and a small shake of his head. "The incomparable Norma Jean."

Reg laughed in disbelief. "Good grief. Don't tell me you're falling for her scam. She's a con artist, Corvin. She was one long before me. Where do you think I learned all the tricks of the trade?"

"She's… such a lovely woman."

"No. She's not. What are you talking about? Everything you see is fake. The hair, the teeth, the body. You should have seen her when she was a junkie. You *did* see her when she was a junkie. So how can you look at her and fall for the image she's trying to project now? She's just trying to lure you in. The only reason she ever cared for a man was when she wanted something from one of them."

Corvin grasped Reg's wrist. The skin-to-skin contact gave her a much stronger jolt of electricity than just touching his arm, with a layer of cloth between them. Reg gasped and tried to steady herself. But he pulled her over so that she fell into the seat next to him on the bench.

"She's gone?" Corvin asked. "Where did she go? Tell me—tell me she didn't go back home."

"Oh, I highly doubt it. But I haven't heard from her. Why don't you tell me what happened yesterday? I can't believe the shape you're in." He was usually so classy. So elegant. Rakish, but well-groomed and always aware of his presentation. "What happened when you took her for coffee?"

"We came here." Corvin looked around to orient himself. "To the Crystal Bowl." He finally focused on the restaurant and bar across the street and nodded to it. "Had some coffee."

"Yes. And then what? Taco said you were there with another woman later. That you were acting…" Reg tried to think of the appropriate word. *Loopy*, Taco had said. *Besotted* would be impolite. "You were… attracted to her."

"Of course I was," he agreed, leaning toward her. His breath smelled awful. How long had he been sitting on that bench? Since the Crystal Bowl had closed? Had he gone home? Gone to Norma Jean's hotel? She shook her head. No, he'd been with another woman after Norma Jean. The powerful, charming woman. "I think I love her, Reg. She's not like any woman I've ever met before."

Reg recoiled. "Norma Jean? Tell me you're not in love with Norma Jean. You couldn't be."

He smiled dreamily. "Norma Jean," he said slowly, drawing it out. "The beautiful and charming Norma Jean."

"No. Not beautiful and charming. You know what she's like under all of that fakery, Corvin. You remember. She's a snake. She was horrible. She's only pretending to be interested in you. She isn't really."

"I love her," Corvin declared to the world.

"Oh, man. I think we'd better get you home. Is your car around here?"

Corvin didn't look for it. Reg looked up and down the street and found his little white compact. Usually, when he went out on a date, he used the big black car.

"There it is. Do you have your keys?"

He patted at his pockets, expression bland, not looking as though he understood what he was looking for. Reg took it upon herself to check through his pockets and was glad to find his keys in the loose outer pocket of his cloak rather than having to fish them out of his pants pocket. "Come on, big guy. I can't carry you, so you're going to have to get there under your own power. Up on your feet."

She poked him and pushed him from behind and, eventually, he got the idea and was on his feet. Reg watched him, making sure he was going to be able to walk. He didn't seem too unstable, so she got beside him and took his arm, encouraging him gently toward the car. Corvin tried to go to the driver's side, and she pulled him harder to the right, forcing him to go around the passenger side and get in there. He looked around the interior of the car, clearly confused. When she slid into the driver's seat, he was looking around for something that he might have lost.

"Seatbelt on," Reg advised, and reached around him to pull it out and lock it into place. "What are you looking for?"

"Someone has taken the steering wheel," he pointed out.

"Oh. Yes, it looks like they did."

CHAPTER EIGHTEEN

Reg wasn't sure where she should take Corvin. She didn't want to take him back to the cottage. It could all be a ruse to make her think he was unable to take advantage of her, and that would quickly change once he was in her door. He was that kind of person. He'd faked illness or fatigue before and almost drawn her in. She shouldn't be fooled by a little bit of wobbling and slurred words. She'd never been to his house and didn't know if it would be any better to take him there. She would still be alone with him, and he would not have to deal with any warding spells at his own house. He could have all kinds of spells that could bind her. He could have his own little dungeon.

She looked around for inspiration. There was a flutter in her peripheral vision, and she turned to catch it, but could not. Again, she was too slow to catch whoever it was following her. Now whoever it was knew that she and Corvin were together.

Was it Damon? He had been jealous of Corvin. He seemed to know things that he shouldn't have known. He could have been the one who had followed her to the vet's office, and that was how he knew Starlight was sick. Not because anyone at the Crystal Bowl had told him so.

Reg dug her phone out of her pocket and tapped through the recent calls until she came to the number she was looking for. She hadn't input him into her contacts, but she had taken a call from him. There was no answer. Reg waited for the call to go to voicemail, trying to figure out what she was going to say. It wasn't exactly her responsibility to take care of Corvin when he was on a bender. But she wasn't sure who else would want to be involved.

"Uh, hello?"

Reg collected her thoughts. "Yeah. It's Reg Rawlins. This is Davyn, right?"

"What can I do for you, Miss Rawlins?"

He sounded a little too formal, which made her wonder about asking for the favor she had been planning on. She hesitated. "Well... I sort of have a problem. I was hoping you could help, since Corvin is in your coven..."

"Corvin is being shunned."

"Yes, but... He's still a member of your coven, right, and don't you have... any responsibility to help him when he needs it?"

"No, I don't. In fact, I am prohibited from helping. What seems to be the problem?"

"He's... kind of in bad shape. I need somewhere to take him, but I can't take him back to my place. I don't want to be alone with him. So I thought... you could help. I could bring him to your place, and he could sleep it off there and make sure everything is okay. Couldn't you?"

"No, I can't. I can't have anything to do with him. What kind of example would I be setting to the rest of the coven when I, as their leader, cannot follow the ruling that was made by the tribunal? I must obey the decision of the council, no matter what I might want to do personally."

"Then who can help me? I don't know enough people in town that I could take this to."

"You would have to pick someone outside of the coven. There are not a lot of practitioners who will have anything to do with him while he is being shunned. Most will heed the ruling of the council even if they are not part of the coven. That is one of the reasons that shunning is such a harsh punishment. It is very isolating."

"And you can't do anything, even if he is in danger."

"What kind of danger is he in? It sounds like you have everything under control."

"I don't. I'm confused and I don't know what's happened to him. I've never seen him like this before. And I don't have anywhere I can take him. What am I supposed to do?"

"Why don't you take him back to the Crystal Bowl? Or to a coffee shop? Sit him down, give him a few cups of coffee, I'm sure he'll be fine."

Reg looked in her rear-view mirror at the Crystal Bowl. She didn't want to take him somewhere quite that public. Rumors would be flying all over town in an instant. She didn't need that and neither did Corvin. Whatever had happened, he deserved a little privacy while he recovered and got his head back on straight. Reg shook her head. *In love with Norma Jean?* He had to be out of his mind. There was no way he could be falling for Norma Jean.

"I guess… I'll try a coffee shop. But I don't know how late they'll be open. Won't they be closing before too long? Then what am I supposed to do?"

"I've given you my advice, Miss Rawlins. If you can't find a coffee shop that is open… you could try the medical center. Or the jail. Call it in as drunk in public, and the police will take care of him for you."

"But I'm not sure he's just drunk." If he had been drinking the night before, that was way too long for him to still be intoxicated. He could have been drinking the whole time, but he didn't smell like alcohol in spite of his unsteadiness and slurring. He acted… loopy, just like Taco had said. Maybe he had been drugged. Or ensorcelled. Taco had said that the woman he had been with the night before had powers and that she had charmed him. She might have taken his wallet, or something else of value, and then left him there, still in an enchanted state. "He might have had a spell cast on him. He's acting weird. I don't want to turn him over to the police, and if I take him to the hospital, they're not going to know what to do with him any more than the vet knows what to do with my cat!"

"That's the best I can come up with. If you want something else… you'll have to come up with it on your own. Or call someone else. I shouldn't even be giving you advice on dealing with someone who has been shunned. I shouldn't even be acknowledging his existence."

"That's pretty hard when you're supposed to be keeping an eye on him and deciding when he is worthy of being readmitted to the coven," Reg snapped.

"You're right, of course. I have to maintain a level of distance and decorum yet still be aware of what he is doing, and that is not a simple matter."

"Well, you're doing a great job of it." Reg pulled the phone away from her ear and tapped the red button. She missed the days of being able to slam the phone receiver down with a loud crash. That was a satisfying way to end an angry phone call. Tapping a touch screen didn't even come close.

"Where are we going?" Corvin asked.

"Coffee, I guess. We'll try to get as much in you as possible and hope you're just drunk. How much did you have to drink?"

"I haven't had anything to drink." He leaned toward her in the manner of drunks all over the world declaring their soberness. "I—am—not —drunk."

"Then what are you?"

His head raised, he gazed toward the stars. "I am in love."

Reg sighed and shook her head. "Did she roll you?" She reached over to pat his breast pockets, hoping that he kept his wallet there rather than in his back pocket. There was a solid rectangular lump. She reached inside his cloak to find the pocket and pulled the wallet out. Everything appeared to be in order. Credit cards, identification, and cash. No empty slots. Nothing was obviously missing. And he'd had his keys. So what had the mysterious woman been up to if she hadn't been after his wallet or keys?

"What did you do last night?"

"We had coffee. And we talked. And we had supper. And we talked. And she was so delightful. And then we came outside, and we sat and looked at the stars… and then…" Corvin shook his head. "Did I fall asleep? Maybe I fell asleep."

"What did she want?"

"She didn't want anything. Just to be together."

Reg snorted. Norma Jean wasn't sweet to anyone for no reason at all. When she had been an addict, she had used men for drugs or money. Now that she was clean, or appeared to be clean, what did she want? She was probably still after money. Norma Jean figured Corvin was a rich mark— and Reg suspected from the way that he wined and dined her that he prob- ably was—and she wanted his money.

But she hadn't taken his wallet or his watch, so she was after more than just pocket change. She was looking for a bigger score. Marry him and get access to it that way? Or convince him to be her sugar daddy? Reg's head hurt with how tight her facial muscles were as she thought through the possibilities.

Then there was the question of why Norma Jean had come looking for Reg in the first place. Did she think that since Reg was in Florida, she had money? Or she wanted to see what kind of a scam Reg was running to either get in on it or to blackmail her?

Reg didn't believe for a minute that she just wanted to see her long-lost baby girl.

"Well, let's see if we can get you sobered up."

The best suggestion that Davyn had been able to offer was a coffee shop, and Reg decided that would have to do. There had to be a few in Black Sands that would be open all night. She wouldn't pick the one that she and Corvin had gone to after the Harbor Port of Call. He and Damon had busted things up there when Damon had happened to show up and caught Reg with Corvin. Reg didn't want to show her face there again.

As she drove, she told her phone to find a coffee shop nearby, and it directed her through a few winding streets to The Witches' Brew. Reg rolled her eyes at the name. Maybe just a little too cute. There was a lit 'open' sign and people inside. And hopefully if it catered to the needs of witches, it would be open late.

CHAPTER NINETEEN

"Get out. We're going in for coffee," Reg told Corvin in a stern voice.

He looked around vaguely for a moment before moving to release his seatbelt and get out of the car. She was glad to see that he was awake enough to get out of the car and head toward the door of the coffee shop under his own power. Maybe once he'd had a coffee or two, he'd be back to normal.

"A couple of black coffees to stay, and keep them coming," she told the barista, and steered Corvin to a table. Once he was sitting down, she went back to the counter to pay. The barista, an aging blonde in a long white dress and apron, peered over at Corvin.

"Is he okay?"

"I'm sure he'll be fine when he's had a bit of caffeine."

"Is that Corvin Hunter?"

Reg nodded. She expected that Corvin would be pretty well-known in any of the magical establishments in Black Sands. "Yeah, and if I hear rumors being spread around about this, I'll know where they came from."

The woman's lips tightened. "I would never spread rumors about the clientele."

"Good. Then you don't need to ask any more questions."

The barista poured a couple of black coffees without further comment. Reg took them to the table where Corvin was sitting and put one in front of him. "Drink up. I want to know more about what happened with Norma Jean."

He smiled and picked up the coffee. He had a sip and put it back down. "Is she really your mother?"

Reg shrugged. "As far as I know. Don't know why she would have been raising me otherwise. No reason for her to claim me as hers when she disliked having me around so much."

"It's no wonder I am so attracted to you with a mother like that." He smiled, showing teeth.

"You think she's pretty, huh? Should be, after all of the work she's had done. You think those teeth are hers? She probably lost all of her own to meth use."

"It's too bad you can't see how special she is."

"Oh, she's special, alright. You think it was pleasant having a mother like that?" Reg shook her head. "What's with you and Weston being attracted to her? Even when she was an addict, he was doting on her. Are you men blind?"

"We can see what she's really like. Beyond the surface."

"I know what she's like underneath that veneer. Trust me; she's no princess."

Corvin shook his head, bemused. He had another sip of coffee. He was still looking—for lack of a better word—lovestruck.

"Who else were you with last night? After Norma Jean."

"No one. Just my lady, Norma Jean…"

"Focus here, Corvin. After you had coffee with Norma Jean, you were seen at The Crystal Bowl with another woman. Someone with powers."

"Sweet Norma Jean."

"No, not Norma Jean. She doesn't have any powers. This other woman must have addled you. She's changed your memories."

"You really should give her another chance, Regina. She's a lovely woman."

"No. She's not. I know that better than anyone else. She can't be trusted. Any time she's making eyes at you, you can bet that her real focus is on your wallet. She doesn't care about me or you. Only about herself."

Corvin swirled his coffee in the mug, splashing a little over the edge onto the table. "Oops! Better be more careful. Pay attention."

"Yeah. You'd better. Or you're going to end up in real trouble. Now, look at me." She tried to hold his gaze. If she could connect with him mentally, it would be a lot easier to sort out his confusion and keep his mind on track. "Corvin. Look at me." He met her gaze, but his mind was still meandering, his eyes sliding away to look around the coffee shop as if he'd never been in such a place before. At the rate he was going, he might burst into song at any moment. She touched his arm, careful to keep the fabric of his cloak between her hand and his arm, to at least dampen the electricity that flowed between them whenever they touched. His eyes went back to hers, and she tried to hold his focus. "Let's think this through. Norma Jean doesn't have any powers, right?"

"She is the loveliest creature—"

"No, she's not. But that's beside the point. She doesn't have any powers."

"Yes, she does."

"No." Reg shook her head impatiently. "She doesn't. She doesn't have any powers."

"You don't know the first thing about your mother. Your own mother."

Reg swallowed. Her mouth was suddenly dry. She took a sip of the hot coffee and kept focused on him. "I know her better than you do, and she does not have powers." She tightened her grip on his arm. "Come on, Corvin. Wake up and remember."

The physical contact seemed to galvanize him. The silly, sloppy manner dissolved. His gaze grew sharper. "Regina."

"Yeah."

He blinked at her. "Regina... you really don't know what she is?"

"She's a woman. A junkie. Or a recovering junkie. That's all. She isn't anything special. Nothing magical."

"She is part siren."

"Siren?" Reg remembered the brunette she had seen at the Port of Call with Corvin, a predator working in tandem with a mermaid to seduce and capture a man at the bar. The woman had been beautiful. She hadn't looked inhuman. So how would one even know who was a siren? They presumably would only be near the water because, as Reg remembered it, the sirens lived near the ocean. So it had made sense for one of them to be at the Port of Call, right on the shore. But how else could one tell a siren from a regular human woman? Corvin had clearly not been dragged to a watery grave. Was there some other giveaway? "How could she be a siren? She doesn't even like water. She doesn't have any powers. She isn't… she just isn't anything else. You're mistaken."

"Part siren," Corvin emphasized, "not full-blooded. Or you probably wouldn't be here. And she's on the hunt."

"She's not a siren."

"Saying it doesn't change the facts."

Reg stared at him, shaking her head. But she remembered the way that Weston had hung over Norma Jean, talking and flirting like she was a beauty, even when she'd been a dirty, sickly junkie. Was that why? Could an immortal be affected by a siren? "Is that why… Weston was so smitten with her? Why you're acting all loopy and lovestruck?"

Corvin rubbed his bristly jaw, looking embarrassed. "I… don't recall everything that I might have said or done… you might want to take it with a grain of salt."

"Are you in love with her?"

Corvin cleared his throat uncomfortably. "In love with her…? That sounds so juvenile. It doesn't really express what I feel when I think of her." His eyes slid away from hers, but not because he was distracted this time, because he didn't want her to read the emotion there. Reg waited. "She's a very attractive woman. And she has… sirens have ways of pulling men in. Entrapping them."

"So you realize that she was… ensorcelling you?" She hated the word but didn't know what else to say. She didn't believe that Norma Jean could be a siren, even a half-blooded one. Norma Jean was just a regular person who had become addicted to drugs and made wrong choices. A woman who was hard and cruel, it was true, but because of what she had gone through in her life, not because she was some mythical predatory creature.

Corvin rolled his eyes up toward the ceiling. He took a long drink of his coffee, not answering. It was mostly drained when he put it down, and Reg motioned to the barista for a refill.

"She was very charming," Corvin said finally. "I can't say I've ever been magicked by a siren before, so I don't know exactly how to describe it. I suppose that it is her powers that attract me to her. But what I feel isn't any less real because of that."

"Exactly." Reg answered too quickly, then her face flared with a violent blush. She had been thinking of the way that she responded to Corvin's charms, and he had described it accurately. Even though she knew it was magic and not her own feelings, she couldn't help feeling that way, and it wasn't fake, it was really what she felt.

It was her turn to look away and pretend to drink her coffee as she waited for the flush and the awkward moment to fade.

"How could she be a siren? A part siren, I mean. She's really... hunting men to drown in the ocean?"

Corvin gave a little shudder. Not something dramatic that he was just putting on, but an actual physical reaction to Reg's words. Of course he didn't want her to drag him back into the ocean to drown. He knew that she had charmed him and was powerful enough to affect his behavior.

"The world's siren population is pretty small. You'll note that when Odysseus talks about them, he only talks about one. They tend to be very competitive and need a wide-ranging hunting ground. That means that they will kill each other if they become too overcrowded. I don't know Norma Jean's ancestry or how much siren blood she has. One of the ways that they preserve their territory is that... they tend to kill their own young. So for a siren's progeny to survive, they generally need to be raised away from other sirens."

"You mean like me being raised in foster care, instead of staying with Norma Jean." Reg pictured Norma Jean as one of those species that ate or killed their own young. Like an enormous spider or rat. It was her turn to suppress a shudder.

Corvin nodded. "I don't know. Maybe Norma Jean doesn't have enough siren blood in her to be concerned about her having that instinct. But maybe... it might explain why she treated you the way you say she did."

"You think she would have eventually killed me if I had been left with her?" Reg tried to swallow the lump rising in her throat. "I guess she probably would have."

Corvin shrugged and sighed. He rubbed his eyes as if he were still waking up after a long sleep. Had he been passed out on that bench all day, in a stupor after Norma Jean had ensorcelled him?

"This is a bit much to be laying on you. I'm still trying to comprehend it myself. It was like I could see myself falling for her, but I couldn't stop. Right now, I can think about it logically, tell myself that I wasn't attracted to her because of who she was or any real emotional response... I can think that, but I still want to see her again. I still don't feel like I could ever be complete without her."

"So what about your powers?" Reg asked curiously. "Do your charms work on her? Can you get her to fall for you, so that you're both making the other person fall in love with you?"

Corvin's forehead wrinkled. He rubbed his temples, looking at her. "I have... no idea."

"Well, you must have tried to charm her yesterday when you realized she had powers. Didn't you try to take them from her?"

"By the time I realized she had powers, she had already magicked me. I was helpless to do anything but what she wanted."

Reg raised one eyebrow. "And what did she want?"

"I don't know... I'm at a loss. She apparently left me behind, which makes no sense for a siren. Maybe she doesn't have enough siren blood to have the instinct to drag me into the sea. Maybe she's like an animal raised by humans, so it has no idea how to hunt on its own. Once she had me, she didn't know what to do with me."

"Maybe." Reg felt a little bit better about that. As much as she feared and despised Norma Jean, she didn't like to think that her own mother was that kind of predator. And that Reg might have that blood running in her veins. "So do you think... they were too weak for her to have passed it on to me. These... siren instincts?"

"Inheritance is a weird thing, and when you're talking about powers and gifts, it can be even more unpredictable than other human traits. Throw in some questions about your parentage, and I don't think we can predict what you have or haven't inherited from her."

"You said that must be why you were attracted to me."

Corvin looked like he'd been forced to swallow a pair of dirty socks. "Forget I said that. I wasn't myself. In fact, I'm still not myself." He gave his head a shake. "I feel like I need a week to shake this off. Then maybe I'll be able to think straight and make a reasonable judgment."

"But I want to know. Do you think that I inherited something from her? I don't have her looks. Or Weston's, for that matter. I'm just... my own person. Do you think that I inherited any of her powers? Or her instincts?"

"You should look to your past for that. Do you have a long history of luring men to their deaths? Or luring them and then leaving them passed out on a park bench somewhere?"

"Corvin, be serious."

"I am." He looked away from her. "Or, I'm trying to be, anyway, but

I'm not expressing myself very well. What have your past relationships been like? Do you pull men in and then not know what to do with them once you've got them? Or have impulses to do… inappropriate things?"

"Like drowning them?"

"Perhaps. Even if it's just a fleeting thought. Or… do you like to sing and think you have a particularly entrancing voice? What about children? Do you want to have children? Or is the thought repellent to you?"

"This is ridiculous. You're just making this stuff up. You and Norma Jean got together for coffee, and then you thought, 'why not see what kind of a con we could pull on Reg? Why don't we see if we could get her to believe this bizarre story?' So ha-ha, you got me. You had me going for a while there. You're an excellent actor. You deserve an award."

Reg faked clapping for him. She was angry and frustrated. She didn't know how to respond to Corvin's revelations. But what made the most sense to her was that it was all just a joke. They were gaslighting her. Trying to get back at her for being so impatient with her mother and for constantly spurning Corvin. They wanted to turn the tables and make her see how it felt.

"Reg… I wouldn't do that."

"Sure, you would. You do everything else you can to get me alone, to try to take my powers from me. This was pretty elaborate, but look where you are. You didn't get back to my house, but I nearly took you there. And as it is, you're the only magical one here, as far as I can tell."

Reg glanced around at the other occupants of the coffee shop. Business was slow. Besides the barista, there were only a few other people talking or nursing coffees on their own.

"So if you wanted to, you could start charming me right here, and by the time the night is over, who knows how far you could get with me. Now that you've got my attention and got me alone, you're free to do what you want. And Norma Jean… Norma Jean gets back at me for not being there when I was little. Maybe she thinks it's my fault I was taken away, so she wants to get back at me. Nice job. Really nice work."

CHAPTER TWENTY

C orvin stared at her.

Reg looked away, her face hot again. Why was she attacking? Because she felt like she had to defend herself? Because she thought that he was saying she was a predator, when all along, he had been the predatory one?

She had been getting better at protecting herself against him. She had been practicing building up that psychic wall between them to prevent him from charming her, learning how to reflect the heat back at him as a weapon. She had thought that she was learning to control her gifts and that Harrison had been helping her to understand how to use them properly. But had it been her heritage from Norma Jean all along? Was she becoming her mother? She was horrified at the thought. She never wanted to be like her mother in any way.

"Reg, I'm sorry for all of this," Corvin said slowly. "I let things get out of hand. I didn't realize, when I took your mother out for coffee, what it was I was facing. I thought, like you, that she was just a regular human without any powers. I had no way of knowing, before she turned her wiles on me, what she really was."

"It's not your fault," Reg muttered.

"Maybe not... or maybe I should have looked before I leaped. I've gotten used to the idea of being able to work my charms on whoever I like.

There are those who can resist, or who do not have a natural attraction toward me, but I've never had someone charm me. I was too sure of myself."

"None of us knew she had any powers. Well... I didn't. None of us mortals knew. I guess Weston knew since she lured him too. Can a siren lure an immortal? Is a siren mortal?"

"Having seen her with him, I would guess the answer is yes. She can. Or at least that immortal in particular. Maybe that should have been a clue. but I missed it."

"Do you think Harrison knew? He must have—don't they know everything?"

"You're mixing up immortal and omniscient again. Just because they are long-lived, that doesn't mean they know everything. They clearly keep secrets from each other, or the other immortals would have known where you-know-who was, even when he hid himself."

Reg blinked. "Are we not saying his name now?"

"I prefer not to conjure him up if I can help it. If he's gone away... I prefer to keep it that way. I don't want to be calling him back by invoking his name."

"Okay. What about the other you-know-who? He's not a danger to us, is he? He helps me out."

"I don't know. They are fickle beings. Just because he's helped you out a couple of times, that doesn't mean he will every time. It doesn't mean that his interests won't sometimes be against you."

Reg rolled her eyes. She took a deep breath. "Do you think H knew that Norma Jean was a siren?"

"I expect so. He seemed to be pretty familiar with her."

"But she wasn't interested in him, so he didn't have to worry about being taken in by her charms?"

"I don't know. Do we have proof that he wasn't?"

"That he wasn't...?"

"That H wasn't taken in by Norma Jean's charms. He took an interest in protecting you from the other immortals. Was that just because he liked cute little redheads? Or was he charmed by Norma Jean too?"

Reg rubbed her eyes. Her head was whirling. She tried to remember everything that had happened in the past, but she didn't have enough information to answer all of the questions that sprang to mind. She kept her hands over her eyes, elbows on the table.

"Are you okay?" Corvin asked.

"I guess. Do you know where Norma Jean went after she left you alone? She didn't come back to my house. I thought that as soon as she was done with you, she would come back to see me. She obviously wanted to talk to me again."

"Yes, that's what she said. I'm afraid I don't know what happened next... I don't remember anything past dinner."

"Then where is she? It's been twenty-four hours."

"Maybe she got distracted. Went hunting somewhere else."

"One can hope."

"But she'll come back," Corvin said wistfully, "Won't she?"

Reg sighed. "I'm sure she will."

"Do you mind driving me home?" Corvin asked, massaging his temples again. "I'm afraid I may still be... somewhat impaired."

"Do you promise not to try to charm me when we get there?" Reg countered.

"Regina... I don't think I could even begin to charm you right now," he said, his voice sounding as tired as she'd ever heard him.

"Yeah, I've heard that before. 'I need just a little bit of strength from you, Regina, I'm feeling so tired.'"

"I'm not trying to fool you. I'm being completely open and honest."

"I'm not buying it. But I'm warning you now, you try anything, and I'll invoke whatever names I have to to get you off of me. I'm not dealing with any of your nonsense tonight. I've got too much else on my mind."

"After my recent experience, I can totally relate to that," Corvin declared.

Reg snorted. "Sure, you do. At least she didn't suck all of your powers out and leave you an empty husk, never able to get any back again."

"Well... no."

"So don't tell me you understand what it's like."

"Okay."

Reg studied him suspiciously, not believing that he wasn't going to plead his case or to try to get away with charming her again. He said he couldn't help it, so what good were promises to the contrary? If he couldn't control it, then he couldn't promise to stop it.

"You ready to go home now, then?"

Corvin nodded. "Yes. I think I need to head to bed. You wouldn't think so, since I've been asleep for…" he trailed off and looked at her, eyebrows raised.

"A good twenty-four hours, it looks like," Reg supplied.

"Twenty-four hours. Good heavens. I feel like I've been dancing the Tarantella the whole time."

Reg got up, and the two of them walked together back to the car. Corvin got in and buckled up, and put his head back, sighing.

"It's going to be a while before I dare show my face at The Crystal Bowl again."

Reg looked at him, something tickling the back of her brain. She couldn't figure out quite what it was. Corvin opened his eyes again in a minute and looked at her.

"Reg? Waiting for something?"

"I'm trying to remember…"

"What?"

"What you just said, made me remember something… or almost remember something, and I can't quite grasp it…"

Corvin nodded his understanding. "I've been there. But right now, I can't remember much of anything. I hope I didn't do anything too stupid while I was with that woman. I would never have guessed that I would be so easy to enthrall."

"Welcome to the club."

"Well then… shall we head home?"

"Yeah, I guess so…"

Reg turned the key to start the engine. She put the car in gear.

"I don't know where your house is, so you're going to have to give me directions. Or at least the address, if you can't keep your eyes open."

"Sure." He gave her the address, and Reg entered it into her phone to get directions to his house. Her mind started to replay the conversation with Davyn about taking Corvin home or back to her own house.

Or take him back to The Crystal Bowl.

Reg hit the brake.

"Wait a minute!"

Corvin looked at her sourly. He really was tired and wanted to get home. She would have felt bad for him, but she was too close to figuring it out.

"Back to The Crystal Bowl," Reg said.

"I… don't want to go back to The Crystal Bowl."

"Because that's where you were. But how did he know that?"

"Who?"

"Davyn. How did he know that you had been at The Crystal Bowl?"

"I don't know what you're talking about."

"I called him. Because I didn't know where to take you or what to do with you."

Corvin blinked. He shook his head. "Why would you call Davyn?"

"You were in pretty bad shape. I thought maybe he could help out."

"He couldn't help. He's the head of my coven. If he did that, he'd get booted. He has to be an example of good behavior. Following the rule that the council imposes. I was shunned. He couldn't disobey that."

"Yeah, that's pretty much what he said. I think he still could have helped you. Why listen to a bureaucracy when someone is really in danger?"

"Clearly I wasn't in that much danger."

"No, but you could have been. He didn't know that. He didn't know what had happened to you, what kind of spell you had cast on you. You could be in a magical coma like Starlight. I know how powerful magic spells can be."

"Yes… you do. How is the cat? Any improvement?"

"A little. I tried to give him more strength again, but I don't know if it helped. I wish you had been there to help again."

"I would have preferred that to being magicked by a siren."

"At least she was only a part-siren, or you could have been in much worse trouble."

"Yes."

"So why wouldn't Davyn at least ask more questions to find out if you were really in any danger? And how did he know that you had been at The Crystal Bowl?"

"Maybe he was there when I was there with Norma Jean."

"Did you see him?"

"Not that I recall. But things are a little fuzzy around the edges as far as last night is concerned."

"Even if he was there when you were, how would he know twenty-four hours later that you were still just across the street? He didn't ask where you were. Why would he assume that you were close to The Crystal Bowl? That you had never really left there?"

Corvin pursed his lips, then shook his head. "I don't know. Maybe you're not remembering the conversation correctly. Maybe you did tell him where I was and try to tell him what kind of condition I was in. Or he might have understood more than you think. He might have been there when I was at The Crystal Bowl with Norma Jean, so he knew what kind of shape I would be in later."

"If he knew that you were eating supper with a siren, wouldn't he have been a little more concerned? Because chances were, you wouldn't be asleep on a park bench. You would be in your new digs under the ocean."

"Well... yes... but..."

He was usually more coherent than that. The magic must have really affected him. Reg felt bad about pushing the matter when he was clearly not in shape to be discussing it, but she pressed forward anyway.

"Somebody has been watching me. Following me. I couldn't figure out who it was, because he's never there when I turn and look. I thought maybe it was Damon, but it must have been Davyn. He followed us to the vet and back. He's been watching my house. He knew that you were at The Crystal Bowl. Because he was watching us."

Corvin's dark eyes showed that he was taking it in. "Davyn has been following us. Which of us?"

"Well, me for sure. You've been with me some of the time. I don't know whether he's been following you too or just me."

Corvin shook his head in disgust.

"Why is he doing that?" Reg demanded. "Don't tell me that he's jealous like Damon is? Honestly, I don't know what's wrong with all of you warlocks. I'm not the only game in town."

"Maybe you're the only part-siren."

Reg scowled and opened her mouth to retort.

"I'm only joking," Corvin assured her.

"Then why do you think he's following me? I'm getting tired of this."

"Because of me."

"Why? Because he's jealous?"

"No. Because one of his charges is to determine when I have served my sentence. Until he decides that I can be a productive member of the community. How is he supposed to know that without keeping an eye on me or at least checking in from time to time?"

"He's going to keep following you until he decides that you can be read-mitted to the coven? But that could be…"

"It could be a long time. Or, if he decides that I am still breaking the rules of the coven, he could make the opposite decision. He could decide to bring me back before the tribunal for further judgment. They could bind me."

"But they wouldn't. I know, I've talked to Davyn about it a few times. They hate even having you shunned. They don't want to bind you."

"Reg… you don't understand the way that a community like this works. I know that in the real world out there, people get away with breaking the law all the time. They don't think that it's really a big issue. They'll let you off with a slap on the wrists, look the other way if they don't think you are really harming anyone else. But that's not the way it works here in Black Sands."

Reg cocked her head, considering this. She didn't think anything was any different in Black Sands. She had been pleased that they had at least decided to discipline Corvin for his misdeeds, but she didn't think that any of them were that concerned with making sure that he really complied with all of the rules of the coven or the community.

Corvin shook his head. "You don't understand, Reg. Here, with so many different magical folk in one place, we have to follow the rules strictly, or there end up being problems between the races. That can lead to a massacre or an all-out war. If a certain race thinks that they're not getting the protection they need, or not getting what they have been promised, they won't follow the rules anymore. We've worked very hard to get these treaties in place and to come up with rules that everyone can abide by. If you get one person who refuses to follow the rules, then…"

Reg shook her head. "Then what? All they did was shun you. You've tried to take my powers against the rules time after time, and nothing happens to you."

"I have obeyed the rules of the community… mostly. It was just that one time that I lost control. And I have been disciplined for that. If Davyn suspects that I am breaking other rules, or that I am going to break the rules, then he would be within his rights to bring me before the council again. And if he has proof that I'm doing something I'm not supposed to, then they will bind me this time."

Reg stared at Corvin, her eyes wide, trying to see as many details of his expression as she could in the darkness of the car. She tried to read how much he was telling her the truth and how much he was bluffing. She needed Damon there to tell her. Corvin was a very convincing liar.

"But you're not breaking the rules. So you don't have anything to worry about."

He nodded. His pupils were widely dilated to pull in as much of the dim light as they could. They made him look like a cat out hunting.

Reg felt a shift in him. The change from victim to predator once more. He was looking at her, trying to decide just how vulnerable she was and if he dared to make another attempt at taking her powers.

"Corvin."

"He can't be here all the time," Corvin said softly. "And he can't do anything to stop me if he's not here. He can't take me before the council if he doesn't know what happened."

"You're not thinking straight. You're still being affected by Norma Jean's magic."

"Do you think so?" He reached out and ran the back of one finger down her cheek.

Reg couldn't help shivering with pleasure, goosebumps popping up all over her skin. She knew that he was the predator now and she needed to fight back against him, but she couldn't convince herself to do it. She needed to raise the psychic walls again, build a fortress around herself to protect herself from him. But something was wrong. She couldn't seem to find the place in her brain that would do that. She couldn't remember the steps to go through. It was like she had forgotten how to ride a bike. Or even how to get onto one.

"You can't do this," she said firmly. "You were just telling me, they won't let you get away with it again. You can't break the rules again, or you will be bound."

"If they don't know, they can't do anything about it," he breathed, leaning closer to her.

"They will know. Do you think they won't know what's happened when I tell them you took my powers away? Do you think they won't be able to tell the difference?"

"It will be too late," Corvin reminded her. "They can bind me, but they can't force me to give back what I have taken. Once I have what I want, no one can take it away from me. I can only give it back voluntarily. And I won't be doing that again."

"No, Corvin!"

"And if they can't find you, they won't even know what happened. Reg Rawlins has run away before." He licked his lips. "They'll think you've just left town."

His hand slipped down to her shoulder. She knew that she had to push him away and get out of the car. The only way she could protect herself was to run, since her powers seemed suddenly to have abandoned her. But she was paralyzed. She couldn't move. She couldn't fight back against him. The words froze in her mouth, and she wasn't sure she was even protesting aloud anymore, or whether she was just saying the words in her mind, trying to communicate them to him telepathically.

What had come over him? Why was he suddenly so reckless and apparently ready to simply rip her powers from her by force, without even pretending to follow the ridiculous rules that the community had enacted?

"Corvin… stop…"

Tears sprang to her eyes. She could hear screaming in her head. She knew what was going to happen, and so did they. She had been left without the voices once before, completely alone and bereft, and she couldn't handle it again. She didn't know how to stop him, but she couldn't just sit there, frozen, and let him do it.

But she was prevented from moving.

His hand was on her shoulder, not holding her down, but controlling her powers, already starting to drain the energy from her. He put his other hand on her, pulling her closer. She fought against him, but it was all in her mind. Her body did not fight back. She couldn't reach her powers.

He was going to succeed this time. She was going to lose her powers again, and this time nothing would persuade him to give them back to her. Reg closed her eyes. She didn't want to see it happen.

CHAPTER TWENTY-ONE

The door opened, and Reg nearly fell out of the car. Her eyes flew open, and she tried to figure out what was going on. A strong hand grabbed her and pulled her out, away from Corvin. When they broke physical contact, she felt both relieved and sorry at the same time. While she knew what he was capable of, her body wanted that contact with him so badly, it was maddening.

"Get out of here!" a voice ordered.

But Reg didn't run. She stood there blinking, trying to get control of her faculties again and to figure out what was going on. The dark, cloaked shape moved quickly around to Corvin's side, before he could get himself untangled from the seatbelt and get out of the car. The two forms collided as he got out, and Corvin was pushed back against the vehicle with a loud thump. He swore and protested, but Reg's mysterious rescuer didn't let him go. The two struggled until Corvin was leaning back against the car, puffing, unable to fight any longer. The stranger's hood came down, and it wasn't a stranger. It was Davyn.

Reg knew it. She *knew* he had been the one following them.

"What are you doing here?" Corvin growled. "You have no right to interfere!"

Davyn shook his head in disbelief. "No right? It's my responsibility to stop you. If I didn't, I would be just as responsible as you for the consequences."

"She was mine!"

Davyn leaned in, studying Corvin's face. "What is wrong with you?"

Corvin pounded his fists against the car in incoherent rage. "She was mine; you have no right to take her."

Davyn held Corvin's head still by pinning his jaw. He stared into Corvin's face.

"What happened?" he asked Reg.

"I don't know. We were talking. Everything was pretty normal, once he had some coffee and I got him to focus. And then everything just… shifted."

"What does that mean?"

"He was talking about how he had to follow the rules of the community. He had to do what you said, or you would bind him. I had just realized that you were the one watching us. Following us. Or me."

He glanced over at her and didn't deny it. How could he, when he had just rushed in to save the day?

"And then?"

"He was looking at me… and I knew he was going to try it again. He said it didn't matter; no one would find out. He said that… I would disappear so I wouldn't be able to tell anyone what he had done." She swallowed. He had never said that before. He had never threatened physical violence against her. He had always insisted that it was a two-way exchange, and had pretended that it was what was best for both of them. Even though he was feeding himself, he still pretended to care how she felt. Reg's throat was tight and hot again. She didn't want to cry in front of Davyn, but it was all so overwhelming.

"Sit down," Davyn advised. He clearly couldn't move from where he was and give Corvin any latitude to move. "On the curb here. Just get off your feet for a minute, I don't want you passing out. You've had a shock."

Reg wobbled over to the curb and lowered herself to the ground. It felt good to get off of her jelly-like legs.

"He wasn't acting like himself," Davyn said.

"No. I mean… he was, for a little while there. When I first woke him up, he was so loopy and silly. Saying how much he loved her. And then when I—"

"Loved her? Loved who?" Davyn demanded.

"Norma Jean. My mother. That's who he was with yesterday. She magicked him. Charmed him, like he does to me. Then she left him there behind, even though sirens usually drag their prey into the ocean—"

"Sirens? What are you talking about?"

"He said she's a siren. Or part-siren. Corvin thought maybe her instinct just wasn't strong enough to know what to do once she had him. So she left him there. And he was really dopey when I woke him up."

She waited for more questions and demands. Davyn just looked at her. Reg went on. "So I gave him coffee, and I… I connected with him, and he went back to normal…"

"What do you mean, you connected with him?"

"I touched his arm and made him look me in the eye… and then he went back to normal. We talked about what had happened, and he told me about her, what she was, and what had happened. He was tired, so I was going to take him home. Then I realized that you were the one following me. And we were talking about that, and how he had to follow the rules, and then he just changed."

"And it was like he was someone else."

Reg frowned. "Well… he was, and he wasn't. Usually, I can fight back when he starts to charm me. I've been working at it, and I'm getting better at protecting myself. But it was like I was paralyzed today. I couldn't do anything, physically or mentally. I was just… trapped like a…"

"Was there anything different about the way he was behaving? Different from when he is usually trying to charm you?"

It all came to Reg in a flood, all of the images at once. She tried to sort them out, to compare Corvin's usual stalking behavior to what had happened in the car. "Yeah… it was. There were no roses. Usually, I can smell roses when he starts charming me, so I have some warning, and I can still talk to him and fight back. But this time, it was like he was using different powers altogether. He was touching me and I couldn't move or do anything."

"And when I caught him, he didn't use magic to fight me," Davyn said. "Since he fed on the Witch Doctor, his powers are exponentially greater than mine, so why didn't he blast me away? He could crush me if he wanted to."

"But he didn't," Reg said softly.

"Like he was a different person."

They looked at each other, trying to understand what it all meant. Or maybe Davyn already understood what it meant and Reg was the only one who was too slow to understand the importance of these words. They were both silent for a few minutes. Corvin continued to look at Davyn with animosity, but he didn't use his powers to break Davyn's hold on him. He remained trapped, held against the car by physical force.

"Can you come over here?" Davyn asked Reg. "Are you feeling well enough to stand up?"

"I'm okay." Reg got slowly to her feet, though, making sure that she was steady enough to approach him. She went to Davyn's side and looked at Corvin, trying to comprehend what it was she was seeing.

"It's not him," Davyn said. "Is it?"

Reg looked into Corvin's eyes and still saw the predator there. Not like the Corvin she knew, always warm and inviting and promising her that she would be compensated for her sacrifice. That dark temptation was gone, replaced by something that was wholly predatory. Something that wanted to consume and destroy her, not to give her pleasure in return for her valuable powers. Looking at him, she didn't even think he cared about the powers, just about destroying her. Corvin had never wanted that. He'd hungered for what she had, but he hadn't wanted to hurt her.

"No." Reg shook her head and swallowed. Her eyes were hot with tears, and she didn't even know why. "No... who is he?"

She knew it was Corvin, yet it was not Corvin. She had been talking to him just minutes earlier, and he had been wholly himself, talking to her naturally just like he always did. And then something else had sprung up and taken over.

"You don't know?" Davyn asked.

"No."

"You said that you connected with him in the coffee shop, and then he was acting like himself instead of intoxicated. Can you do that again?"

Reg wasn't sure it was a good idea. She didn't want to connect with this monster, whoever he was. She knew that the physical form was Corvin. That hadn't changed. He wasn't a doppelgänger, because he had been Corvin only minutes before. But she wasn't sure she could connect with the old Corvin if he were still there under the malevolent entity on the surface. She was afraid.

"You can do it. Try."

Reg looked into the wide, black pools of Corvin's pupils. Though afraid to hold his gaze, she did her best anyway. She reached out and touched his arm. Tentatively. Not his bare skin, but with a layer of clothing between them so that the electricity wouldn't overwhelm her. She felt the familiar buzz and tried to communicate with him psychically. She had been able to many times before. Once they were connected, they could exchange more than words. It was a kind of communication she hadn't experienced outside of the spirit world.

"Corvin." She said his name, trying to reach down under the surface of the pool and pull him back up. He was still in there somewhere. She just needed to make the connection. The being on the surface struggled, trying to fight back against her and break the hold. Just like she had tried to break away from him, but had been unable to use her powers. She tightened her grip on Corvin's arm. "Corvin, come back. Talk to me."

"No," the being growled. He writhed under her grip, trying to pull away from both her and Davyn. "You may not!" He struggled more, muscles writhing in their grips. "He is mine!"

"He's not yours," Davyn said firmly. "Release him."

"You cannot do this!"

Reg pushed harder mentally. She knew Corvin. She could find him despite what the being possessing him tried to do. Corvin was still in there, just suppressed.

Corvin's body howled, his head pulled out of Davyn's grip and thrashed back and forth as it tried to free itself. Then he suddenly relaxed. Reg didn't release her hold on him. It could just be a trick, a final attempt to get away from her.

Corvin blinked. He looked at her from the depths, then gradually rose to the surface.

"Reg...?"

"Hey. You're back."

He swallowed and looked around. He seemed disoriented by what he saw. Himself, pinned against the car by Davyn. Reg holding on to his arm, leaning toward him, inside his mind trying to figure out what had just happened.

"Where... was I?"

"I don't know. Something else took over."

Corvin blinked some more, like she was shining a bright light in his eyes. Reg tried to mediate her connection with him, soften it a bit, so it wasn't so overwhelming. It was not polite to invade someone's mind.

Corvin looked at Davyn. "Something else?"

"Have you been playing with sirens?" Davyn asked, humor coming into his voice for the first time. Reg hadn't seen Corvin and Davyn interact before. She had wondered what kind of a relationship they had outside the courtroom, but she had never seen it. There was clearly some history of brotherhood and teasing between them.

"Uh… one siren," Corvin admitted. He thought about that. "Is that what happened? She took over my mind?"

Davyn nodded slowly. "That would be my guess. When she left you there, asleep, she didn't leave you. She was just waiting for the right opportunity."

"That's why she didn't come back?" Reg relaxed her hold on Corvin's arm. Still keeping contact with him, but not so strong. "She didn't come back because she was… inside Corvin? Just waiting for me to come looking for him?"

"She knew about your connection," Davyn said. "She must have known something about your history with each other. That you would gravitate toward each other. She knew that he could charm you, so she used that to her advantage."

"But it wasn't the same. I didn't smell roses and I couldn't fight back the way I usually can because… it was her magic instead of Corvin's."

Davyn nodded his agreement. Corvin looked at the two of them, making the mental connections gradually. Reg could feel how tired and confused he was. Norma Jean had used his body and his mind, and he was depleted. She released her hold on his arm to make sure that she wasn't pulling strength from him.

"Reg."

Reg nodded.

"I'm sorry… I didn't…"

"I know. I get it. It wasn't you."

"I never intended to let her possess me. I didn't know that she was. I've never… experienced anything like that before."

"It's okay."

They were all quiet for a few moments, considering the chain of events.

"Where is she now?" Reg asked. "Is she still inside of Corvin? How could she possess him when she has her own body?"

Davyn raised his eyebrows and didn't propose an answer. Reg looked at Corvin. "Do you know?"

"I didn't know sirens had that power… I told you there are only a few around the world; they haven't been well-studied. She has mixed blood; maybe she is more than just human and siren. Or maybe she had help." He met Reg's eyes. "Someone like W."

"Yeah."

"Who is W?" Davyn asked, trying to follow the conversation.

"He's her lover… an immortal."

"How incredible… I've never heard of a siren taking a lover. I mean, clearly they procreate, but they almost always drown their prey."

"She couldn't drown an immortal."

"No. Of course not. It makes logical sense, but I've never heard of such a thing."

Reg persisted with her question, which still had not been answered.

"But is she still in there, or is she gone?"

"And if she is gone, can she return at will?" Davyn added his own question.

"I don't know," Corvin admitted. "I think… I think she's gone, but would I be able to tell…?"

Davyn withdrew gradually, releasing Corvin. They both watched him to see what his reaction would be.

"I'm not going to attack you," Corvin said after a minute.

Davyn shrugged. "Had to make sure." He looked at Reg. "You should be getting back home. I'd like to know that you are safely ensconced in your own domicile."

"Really?" Reg raised her brows. "Domicile?"

"You are safest if you are at home. And take my advice and do not let Corvin or your mother in if they come calling."

"Well, I wouldn't, of course. But I don't know if that will stop them. I can't stay in my house forever."

"No… of course not," Davyn agreed, "But at least while we're figuring this out. It's the best I can do."

"Are you going to take him home, then?" Reg nodded toward Corvin.

Davyn hesitated. He scratched his bearded chin, and Reg knew that he was not trying to decide, he was trying to figure out how best to tell her 'no.'

"Why not? What other solution is there? You want to leave him here in his car to sleep it off? That didn't work so well the first time. Who knows if he'll wake up on his own? Maybe he'll end up unconscious like Starlight, with no way to wake him up."

"But how would taking him home prevent that?" Davyn countered. "I admit I don't have a good solution to suggest, but what else are we going to do? I can't have anything to do with him. I shouldn't even be here talking to the two of you. But I also have a duty to the public, and I had to balance those two duties."

"You're still not going to talk to Corvin? How exactly do you plan to sort this out?"

Davyn looked at Corvin, then dropped his eyes. "I will have to investigate independently. I can't have direct contact and communication with him." He gave an apologetic shrug, aimed in Corvin's direction.

Corvin looked too tired even to care. He looked at his car. "I can probably drive home."

"No, you can't," Reg insisted. "There's no way. You'll end up crashing and killing yourself or someone else. You're exhausted."

"I can't ask you to drive me. And I can't ask Davyn to drive me. I'm pretty much up the creek if I can't drive myself."

"I can drive you. It's not far, right? I can't abandon you like this, even if he can." She glared at Davyn.

"What if *she* comes back out? Without Davyn there, what are you going to do?"

"Well, now I know how to fight her," Reg said, pretending confidence she didn't feel. "I know that I just need to connect with you. As long as we stay connected, she can't come."

"How are you going to stay connected?" Davyn challenged. "You'll be driving. You'll be focused on that."

"How much attention do I need for driving? It's pretty much all automatic. I can't keep eye contact with him, but I can touch him. If we're physically in contact, it's easier."

Davyn shook his head. "This is too dangerous. I can't allow it."

"Allow it? Since when are you in charge of me? I'm not in your coven."

Corvin smirked. Even as tired as he was, he could enjoy Reg's rebellion against Davyn's attempts to control her. Reg wasn't going to do what anyone told her. Especially not a warlock who refused to cooperate with her even when she asked nicely. Davyn made a calming motion with his hands, maybe realizing that he had pushed it too far.

"Reg. Surely you can see the folly in this. You need to go home where it is safe. You have wards there against malevolent forces. Out here, and in Corvin's car, you are at the mercy of evil forces. You can't protect yourself against them."

"Now that I know who it is and what to do about it, I can," Reg insisted. She motioned to the car. "Get in," she told Corvin. She started to walk around to the other side of the car to drive. "And unless you're going to help out, I'll be seeing you around," she told Davyn. She didn't expect him to jump in and change his mind. He was too stubborn, too much a rule enforcer. Reg, on the other hand, was not. "And you know what? I'm tired of seeing a shadow sneaking around following me here and there and every-where. I don't know exactly how you do it, but stop. If you want to follow me, you stay visible. And I'd prefer that you not follow me. I don't like being stalked."

"I wasn't stalking you. I was trying to keep you safe." Davyn shifted his stance uncomfortably. "I am responsible for the members of my coven, even when they are under discipline. If Corvin were to hurt you again, then I would be held partially responsible. Knowing that he could be a danger to you, and yet you are still seeing him socially... I can't just ignore that. If I don't keep track of him or you... the only option is to bind him."

"Well, I've told you to take a hike, so you can report that. I don't want you following me. I can take care of myself."

Reg got into the driver's seat and pulled the door shut with a slam. She couldn't believe that Davyn would refuse to talk to Corvin, but still follow them around, monitoring whether he was keeping the rules of the commu-nity. She couldn't deal with him. If he wasn't willing to actually help her, then he was just one more person in her way.

"Okay, you'd better give me directions."

CHAPTER TWENTY-TWO

They were both anxious in the car, neither knowing for sure what was going to happen. Even though Reg had told Davyn that she knew what to do if Norma Jean put in another appearance, she wasn't so sure. Corvin did his best. He kept a hand on her leg, keeping a physical connection to her as she had suggested. He gave her his address and then directed her, but his voice was sleepy, and he was drifting in an out. Reg was afraid of getting lost, or that the intruder would reassert herself when Corvin fell asleep, breaking his psychic connection with Reg. She nudged him.

"Stay awake. Come on. It's not much farther, right?"

"No." He yawned. "Nearly there."

"Do you think that Davyn will stay away? Now that I've told him to?"

Not that she cared what his answer was. She just wanted to keep him engaged so that he wouldn't fall back asleep. They needed to work together as a team if she were going to keep her mother's spirit away from them.

"I wouldn't count on it," Corvin admitted.

"Did you know that he could do that? Turn invisible?"

"No. We don't all share our powers with each other. Sometimes you know someone's biggest gift, especially if you've known each other for a long time because it can be hard to control them when you're a little kid. You go to school with someone, or you've known their family for a few generations, and you know what their gifts are or what gifts run in their family. But invisibility… no, I never knew that Davyn could do that. He's apparently pretty proficient at it, too."

"So he could be sneaking around, spying on the warlocks in his coven all the time."

"Why would he want to do that? Being part of a community like this doesn't mean policing everyone. That's not the purpose of a coven. He doesn't want to have to enforce discipline. What reason would there be for him to creep around and watch people invisibly?"

"I dunno. I'd take invisibility. I'd like to be able to see what other people were saying and doing when I wasn't around. See what they really think."

"You think that people are talking about you behind your back?"

"Of course they are. Don't you?"

Corvin squeezed her leg. He looked up the street and motioned with his unoccupied hand. "Just up there, at the end of the road."

Reg looked at the dark, forbidding houses. It was getting late, so she supposed it made sense that all of the non-magical practitioners were off to bed. But it made the neighborhood feel empty and lonely.

"Thank you," Corvin said. He shifted his hand, but didn't remove it from her leg. "I appreciate you doing this, especially knowing the danger."

"What should I do with your car?"

He rubbed at the corner of his eye. "I suppose… drive it to your house. Tomorrow, I'll either find someone to drive over with me and pick it up, or I'll take a bus and a walk to your house."

"Are you sure?"

"You can't leave it here. Then you wouldn't have a safe way to get home. I don't know if the buses are still running right now, and for sure they're not the safest place to be at night all by yourself. It would be one thing if you were out with a group of friends, but alone like this… I'd like to know that you are safe. I don't want to be worrying over whether you can make it home or not."

"Okay." Reg was happy to take his car. She didn't want to have to catch a bus or call a cab either. He could sort it out the next day when it was safe to do so. "Thanks. Um… I'll let you know when I get home. So you don't worry." She looked at the keys and unclipped the ring that held what appeared to be his house key. "You'll need that."

"Yes. Thank you." He lifted his hand slowly from her leg to take the key, and they both did their best to maintain the psychic connection between them. It was a strangely intimate dance, him slowly withdrawing and getting out of the car, both of them remaining connected so that the predator could not reassert herself. Corvin shut the car door and Reg immediately locked it. She let out a breath. They had made it safely. He couldn't reach her. She could go home and go to bed and not worry about being attacked.

Corvin walked up to his door, and she watched him in. He turned to wave just before shutting the door.

Once Reg got home, she would be safe and could go to sleep and forget the crazy magical world around her.

Reg breathed a sigh of relief when she reached home. She sat in Corvin's car in front of the big house for a few minutes, just breathing and looking around and feeling for any disturbing presence. She hadn't seen any shadow of Davyn, but that didn't mean he wasn't around. She wasn't going to discount the possibility. She could take care of herself, but if Davyn wanted to make sure she got home safely, why should that bother her?

She eventually got out of the car and walked to the cottage in the back. The blooms in the garden were giving off a heady scent, making her think of Corvin again. Reg couldn't help feeling a little bit sorry for him. She had lived with Norma Jean in her head for a long time. She knew what that was like. It probably wasn't the same for him. He couldn't hear her voice like Reg had been able to. But Reg hadn't had to deal with her body being taken over by Norma Jean, either. She'd only been a constant voice in Reg's head. It would have been a lot worse if she'd had to fight for control over her own body.

Reg pulled her phone out of her pocket and tapped a quick message to Corvin that she had reached home safely. The garden was quiet and peaceful, cool in the evening, and she breathed in the smell of the flowers and tried to relax her body.

If she could just know that Starlight was going to be okay, she would be happy and at peace. Until then, she was waiting for him to recover, always waiting and worrying.

Reg sighed and walked the rest of the way up to her door and let herself in. As she stepped over the threshold and pushed the door shut behind her, she heard and felt it thump against something. She turned to see what was blocking it from closing. A woman stood there in the breach, holding it open. Reg lunged, trying to slam the door shut. If she could shut it and close the deadbolt, she would be safe.

But Norma Jean wasn't about to let that happen. She put all of her weight into shoving it open so that she could enter the house.

"Reg? What's wrong, honey? I just came over for a visit."

"You can't come in!" Reg barked. "There are wards against you here. You can't come in!"

Even as she said it, Norma Jean floated into the room as if there were no barriers. Reg cursed under her breath. What was the point in having the wards there? They never seemed to protect her. It seemed like there was always some rule that she didn't know about. Some loophole that everyone else could exploit.

"What are you doing here? You shouldn't be here!"

Norma Jean just gave a puzzled smile, as if she couldn't figure out what Reg had to be upset about. "I came to see you," she said innocently. "Don't you want to see your own mother? We've lost so much time, Regina. Don't you think it's time to start recovering it? Why don't we have a little visit? We could stay up and watch scary movies. Make some popcorn. You're not tired, are you? It isn't the witching hour yet," she said in a teasing tone.

"I *am* tired," Reg said desperately, hoping that Norma Jean would listen to her. "I need to get to bed. It's been a long, tough day."

"Why don't you tell me about it, and I'll make you some tea. That will help you to get to sleep."

"No, really, I'm just going to fall into bed. We can talk about it later. Why don't you give me a call in the morning and we'll set something up?"

Norma Jean's smile was fixed and unwavering. "I can at least see my daughter off to bed. Do you know how long it's been since I was able to tuck my baby girl in?"

Her honeyed tone set Reg's skin creeping. She had looked at this same being in Corvin's eyes just an hour earlier. She'd seen the hate there. Now Norma Jean was behaving as if nothing had happened. She was using her sweetest manner to suck Reg in, to make her think that she was sincere in her wish to spend some time and mend fences with Reg. They were the same eyes, yet there was no hint of the malice that had lurked there earlier.

"I'll make some tea," Norma Jean repeated. She glided toward the kitchen. Reg stared at her. She sure as hell wasn't going to drink anything her mother made for her. She sat down on the couch and watched Norma Jean like a hawk, but didn't see her put anything into the drink. Reg was experienced with sleight of hand. She should have been able to see it, but Norma Jean moved slowly and smoothly, and her hands were in view all the time. Reg still couldn't see her put anything into the cup but the tea that Sarah had prepared for her and the boiling water.

"There. That will help you get to sleep much better," Norma Jean assured her. "It certainly is nice of that woman to take such good care of you. She isn't your mother, but she is so very nice to you."

"She's been a good friend," Reg said. "Just a friend. She's not trying to mother me and usurp your place." Reg didn't want Norma Jean going after Sarah next. Sarah was an experienced old witch and could, Reg was sure, protect herself, but it was better if she didn't have to, if Reg could head off Norma Jean before she even began an attack.

Norma Jean smiled. "That's nice, dear." She set everything out on the tea tray and carried it over to the living room, where she set it down on the coffee table. "There you go. Let's have a nice soothing cup of tea together."

Reg picked up one of the cups before Norma Jean could decide which one to give to her. She sat with it in her hands, staring down into the tea leaves. What was in her future? A quick but painful death from poison? A long and lingering one? Having to listen for hours to made-up stories of Norma Jean's past? Reg put the cup to her lips and pretended to drink.

"Where were you earlier?" she asked Norma Jean carefully. "I thought I'd see you downtown. Didn't you go there with Corvin?"

"Corvin?" Norma Jean's eyebrows went up. "Oh, such a nice man. But that was yesterday, sweetie—not today. I haven't seen him today. I was looking for you."

"Oh. Sorry I missed you."

Norma Jean beamed at her and sipped her tea. Reg couldn't tell if she was really drinking it or not, but she appeared to be. Maybe there was no poison. Maybe Norma Jean just planned to use a spell on her. Like she had on Corvin.

"Do you remember him from when I was little? He came to visit us once."

Norma Jean's brows drew down in a frown of concentration. "How could that be? No, I don't remember ever meeting him before."

"He had a cat with him. One like Starlight."

The small frown turned into a scowl. "I remember that cat," she spat. "Why did he come?"

"He came to help. The cat and Corvin were both there to help." Reg didn't mention her own presence there, as an adult as well as the child who belonged in the timeline. That would raise too many questions.

"I didn't need any help."

"You knew some dangerous people back then. People that could have hurt me. Or you."

Norma Jean took a thoughtful sip of her tea. "Do you remember much about that? You were just real little. I didn't think you could remember anything."

"I remember some stuff."

Norma Jean's thumb stroked the handle of the teacup. "I don't think it was that bad. I don't remember a lot of it, but I don't think social services should have taken you away. They're always doing that. You hear about it in the news. They take kids away for no reason at all, and then it takes the family forever to get them back, if ever."

"You were drinking, doping, and hooking."

"But that didn't hurt you. Addicts can still be good moms. Housewives get addicted to meth and their husbands and children never even know it. They shouldn't be able to take kids away just because of that."

Reg stared at her. Did Norma Jean truly not remember what kind of a mother she had been and what kind of life they had led? Was she telling herself stories and rewriting history, or was she just trying to fool Reg?

She didn't want to trigger the rage she had seen in Corvin's eyes earlier, but she also didn't want to let Norma Jean get away with the fiction. "You weren't a high-class mother with a pill addiction. You were mainlining." The image of her mother shooting up was burned into her brain, something she could never forget.

Norma Jean shrugged as if there were no difference. Reg kept her mouth closed. They sat and drank in silence. Or Norma Jean drank, and Reg pretended, hoping that wetting her lips would not be enough to poison her.

"I'm getting really tired," Reg said finally. "We'll have to put this on pause and get together again later."

Norma Jean faked a yawn and looked at her watch. "I suppose so. I thought a young person like you would want to stay up late."

"I have things to do in the morning, and it's been a long day." Reg stood up. Norma Jean stayed sitting there for a moment longer, then grudgingly got to her feet.

"I had to find a hotel. It's a nasty place, I would much rather have stayed with you."

"No, I don't have the space. I'm sure you'll be much happier there."

Reg shuddered to think of what might have happened if she had allowed Norma Jean to stay with her, forced to share the same bed or sleep on the floor. If Corvin was right about sirens needing a lot of territory and killing each other for it, Norma Jean probably would have killed her in her sleep.

She walked Norma Jean to the door and saw her out. Norma Jean eyed her before she stepped out the door, moving her body at an angle as if she intended to give Reg a hug goodbye. Reg shifted away to try to avoid any physical contact. Eventually, Norma Jean nodded and walked out of the cottage.

"We'll get together tomorrow," she suggested. "Maybe for lunch."

Reg nodded her agreement, though she didn't intend to go anywhere with Norma Jean. She would try to avoid any further contact.

CHAPTER TWENTY-THREE

R eg had typed a text to Corvin almost before she finished shutting and locking the door. She sent it out with an accompanying swoosh sound and moved over to the window to see if Norma Jean were really leaving. She strained to see her mother walking down the path away from the cottage, but eventually was satisfied that she had left and wasn't lurking around just waiting for her first opportunity to return and attack Reg. She looked down at her phone, expecting an immediate reply from Corvin. But there wasn't one.

She tapped her foot and looked down at it, willing Corvin to message her back. She even closed her eyes and tried to reach out to him mentally to prod him along, but she was too exhausted after the day's events to raise the mental faculties. She went to the kitchen to check the fridge for something real to eat. And a trip to the cupboard to fetch a glass of Jack Daniels to replace the sleepy tea that Norma Jean had prepared. She looked at the tea, wondering if she could call Jessup and convince her to send it to the police lab for testing. Maybe they could find out what was in it. Maybe that would help her to save Starlight.

She would ask in the morning. Jessup would either be asleep or on duty, and neither one would bode well for Reg getting a favor if she interrupted her with a call. Reg looked down at the phone. Still no reply. She reached down to change the water in Starlight's bowl and had to stop herself. Starlight wasn't there.

She wanted to talk to someone about Norma Jean. Starlight was a good listener, even if he didn't contribute a lot of fresh content to a conversation.

Reg tossed her phone down on the counter, more roughly than she should have. It wouldn't help anything to break the phone. But she was frustrated and wanted to do something to show it.

There was some fried chicken in the fridge. Reg didn't remember when she had gotten it, but it still smelled good, so she put it in the microwave to heat.

No messages came in while she was waiting for the chicken to heat up.

When the microwave beeped, Reg pulled the too-hot dish out, and then left it on the counter, turning around to pick up her phone. She couldn't wait any longer. She dialed through to Corvin. If he wasn't going to answer her text, he'd have to answer a call.

It rang through to his voicemail. Reg hung up and tried again.

And a third time.

Finally, the call was answered. Corvin's slurry voice. "Reg? What is it?"

"She was here!"

"What?"

"Norma Jean was here. In my house!"

There was a silence while he considered that. "Well… why did you let her in?"

"I didn't! I tried to shut the door and she forced it open. And then she just walked in. I thought the wards were for my protection and were supposed to keep that from happening! Is there some loophole? Some exception for sirens or people who are related to me? I'm getting really frustrated with all of these exceptions!"

"If she walked in, then you must have invited her. Are you sure you didn't do anything that might have been construed as an invitation?"

"No. I didn't ask her in. I didn't open the door to her. I didn't give her a key. I tried to shut her out. I told her she wasn't welcome. And she still just walked in."

Corvin cleared his throat. Reg pictured him rubbing eyes sticky with sleep and trying to concentrate on what she was saying. It wasn't fair of her to put him on the spot like that. The poor man had been asleep, after the rather traumatic experience of having his brain and body ripped out of his power.

"The… has she been to your house before?"

"Yes, one time. But just because she's been here once before, that doesn't give her the permission to come back in again later, does it? Because that would be crazy."

"No. But she may have left something personal behind. Something that she would have to come back to retrieve later. In that case, she might have been able to break the wards."

Reg swore. She looked around the cottage, trying to see anything that was out of place. What had Norma Jean left behind?

"Are you okay?" Corvin asked.

"She gave me tea. I don't know if it was poisoned or not. I didn't drink it."

"Good girl."

"Do you think that's why she's here in Black Sands? To kill me?"

"It's a distinct possibility."

"Why? It doesn't make any sense. I haven't been hunting in the same waters. I'm halfway across the country from her. Why would she have to come here to kill me?"

"Sirens are very—"

"Competitive. Yeah, that's what you told me. Does she need half the world for herself? When she's not even a full-blooded siren?"

"I don't know. Sirens have not been studied very much. We know very little about how they live and socialize with each other and work out their territories and differences."

Reg sighed in exasperation.

"Go to bed," Corvin advised. "I need some sleep."

Both the drink and the chicken were still on the counter when Reg got up the next morning.

CHAPTER TWENTY-FOUR

I'm sure you must have fairies in your garden," Reg told Sarah the next morning. "I keep seeing things there every night—little lights and movement. I hear voices or bells or birds singing when they shouldn't be up. Maybe it's not fairies; maybe there is something else that I don't know about. But I was looking online, and those are things that it says you see if you have fairies."

Sarah smiled. "Google isn't the best tool for diagnosing illnesses or paranormal happenings in your garden."

Reg walked with her around the cottage to the back garden, and they looked around. Sarah had a big travel mug of tea and was wearing garden clogs. Reg had put on some flip-flops in order to join her in her survey of the garden, which was literally blooming under Forst's care.

"It's so beautiful," Reg said. "I can see why the fairies would want to come here."

But she was going by what she had found online, and those articles were talking about the little flying fairies. The fairies that Reg had met in real life liked plants and gardens and surrounded themselves with living things even inside their homes, but they were tall, pale, remote people, not little flying fairies like Tinkerbell. She couldn't imagine Lord Bernier or Calliopia's parents flitting through Sarah's garden to have a look at her plants. Even though Sarah's garden was spectacular, they would more than likely knock on the door and ask permission to have a look at it—excessively formal—than to flit in and make themselves at home. She didn't think they could turn themselves into the diminutive creatures that she'd seen on TV and the web.

"I don't know what you have been seeing, but I don't think we have been having visitations from fairies," Sarah told her.

Reg sighed. She'd liked the idea. She looked around for Forst. He was often camouflaged in the garden; she wouldn't even see him until he decided to speak to her. They waited for a few minutes before he showed up, pushing a wheelbarrow full of supplies. It was so laden down; Reg wasn't sure if she would have been able to push it herself.

Forst's face broke into a wreath of happy wrinkles when he saw her there. He put the wheelbarrow handles down and hurried over to her. "We are so pleased to have a visit from Reg Rawlins today!"

Reg's cheeks burned at his effusive greeting. Sarah might not be able to hear it, but she could certainly see the expression on his face and his eagerness to take her hands in his. Reg smiled, looking to the side in her embarrassment.

"Hi, Forst. It's so nice to see you again," she said aloud so that Sarah would be able to hear at least her half of the conversation.

Forst turned to Sarah with greater reserve. He bowed to her, doffing his red cap. He didn't say anything to her in his 'inside words,' knowing that, like most of the rest of the humans, she wasn't able to hear them. Sarah knew it was difficult for him to use his outside words, which was one reason she had stopped in at the cottage to see if Reg was available.

"Everything is looking so beautiful," she told him. "It is the most beautiful garden in the neighborhood. Everyone says so."

He smiled and nodded.

"I would like to add more wild herbs and magical plants," Sarah said. "I've always wanted a crafting garden, but I don't have the green thumb that you do. It's been the most I could do to keep a respectable-looking vegetable garden."

"What would the lady like in her crafting garden?"

Reg relayed the question to Sarah. Sarah had a notepad in her apron pocket, and she pulled it out to list off some of the plants she had thought of. When she had read it, Forst took it out of her hand. He looked at the list and looked around the garden, nodding and scratching his white-bearded chin. He pulled off his cap, rubbed his head, and put it back on again. He looked down at the list.

"I will get started on this," he agreed. "I will need to prepare the right location. Then I will find some good plants to start with. It might take a while to get it established. They are different plants; not all will like the same soil."

When Reg had repeated this to Sarah, she nodded. "You know much better than I do where they should be planted and whether they will compete with each other or be beneficial to each other. The list is only a starting point. You will need to decide how they will like it here and whether they will live together."

Forst smiled and nodded, happy that Sarah understood this.

Reg thought about Norma Jean and the idea that she thought Reg was competing with her, even though she lived so far away. When Norma Jean had visited, she hadn't expressed any animosity. And her behavior ensorcelling Corvin and then leaving him behind suggested that she might be acting instinctually without even knowing why. Maybe her negative feelings toward Reg, whatever they were, were unconscious as well.

"Do fairies like herbs?" she asked, not wanting to drop the previous topic. Now that Forst was there, maybe he could give her some clue as to what she had been seeing.

"Fairy folk? Certainly." Forst agreed. "Fairies like all natural plants."

"Maybe they'll come here to look at them. Or to ask for samples."

"Cuttings?" Forst suggested.

"Cuttings."

"Fairy folk do not come into the town," Forest said with a head shake. "Very rare. Only for important business. There are too many autos and houses, not enough living green."

"I thought maybe some of them have been in the yard and the garden. I thought I might have seen some."

"In Miss Sarah's garden?" Forst shook his head, chuckling, "They would not kommen here."

Reg tried to hide her disappointment. "I was sure... what do you think I saw, then?"

Still chuckling, Forst asked her what she had seen. Reg described it the best she could, and also tried to send him mental images of what she had seen and heard over the past few days. Forst's eyes lit up. "Not fairy folk," he told her. "Elves!"

"Elves?" Reg repeated aloud.

Sarah looked surprised. "Really? Elves in my garden?"

Forst nodded emphatically. "Elves. It is almost solstice. That is when they move house. Set up somewhere new."

"They're not setting up house in my garden, are they?" Sarah asked in alarm.

"No," Forst looked around, shaking his head. He walked through the garden, looking up into trees and down under bushes and around other plants that Reg was not familiar with. He shook his head again. "They come through here, mayhap. But not set up house here. You are on their way. They stop to refresh and frolic here."

Reg laughed, pleased. "What are they like? Are they little like on TV? Or are they big like the fairies? Can I see them, or can humans only see the lights? They're like little fireflies out here, swirling around."

"Elven folk take different forms. They may come through here as little people or lights. But they can also appear tall. Taller than me."

Not that Forst was particularly tall. But that meant they could be human height or tiny little lights. Reg was thrilled at the idea. And she was the one who had discovered them there. Of course, if Starlight had been around, he would have been the one watching them out the window. He would yowl at her to come see, and she would...

There was a soft touch on her arm. Reg focused on Forst's face. He was looking back at her with concern. "Reg Rawlins is not happy. What is wrong, fair maiden?"

Reg tried to shrug it off. She was sure he had probably already heard her woes. "It's just... my cat, that's all."

Forst turned and looked at the cottage, at the window where Starlight usually perched to watch him and the birds and whatever else appeared in his yard. Where he would have watched the elves frolicking. "Where is the cat? What has happened?"

"He's sick. Didn't anyone tell you?"

Forst shook his head. Reg looked at Sarah. Sarah might have at least mentioned it to Forst. But maybe she hadn't cared, hadn't thought that it was anything of importance.

Sarah shook her head. "I didn't think there was anything he could do, so why involve him?"

"No… no reason why you would." Reg gave a sad shake of her head. There wasn't anything anyone could do.

"Sick with what?" Forst prodded.

"He was poisoned… and magicked. He is unconscious." Reg didn't know whether Forst would know the word or what it meant. "Asleep. Near to death."

"Oh!" Forst took off his cap and wiped his brow. He wrung the hat with his hands, looking distressed. "Oh! You should have told me! How long? What physik has he had?" Forst shook his head. "These humans do not know good physik!"

"They've done everything they can. He's been at the doctor. I took him the plant, in case Starlight had eaten any of that. And there were all of the plants around for solstice. I didn't know that they could be poisonous to cats… But apparently… it looks like he was poisoned intentionally, he didn't just eat something without knowing it would hurt him."

"I must see him. Will you bring him here?"

"I don't think I can bring him here. Could you go with me? To the vet?"

"What is the vet?"

"A doctor for animals. Veterinarian. He is good at taking care of sick animals, but he doesn't know exactly what is wrong with Starlight, and he's not a practitioner. He doesn't know about the spell or how to counter it."

"Why would you take him to such a place?" Forst asked in alarm. "We must go to him. He cannot be left there, all alone, without an experienced physician."

Reg nodded. "Okay. Yes. If you want to come, and think you can do something for him, then please do. We can go over there…" she looked at the time on her phone screen. "They open in half an hour."

"We must go." Forst looked at Sarah. "The garden will have to wait for a few hours."

Reg translated for him and explained that Forst thought he might be able to do something for Starlight.

"Well, of course you must go see him," Sarah said. "The garden won't miss you."

Forst blinked at her, looking hurt.

"I mean, of course it will miss you," Sarah amended quickly. "But it will be fine until you get back."

"Yes," Forst agreed out loud, and gave a nod.

CHAPTER TWENTY-FIVE

R eg hurried back into the house to get her purse and grab a granola bar for breakfast, and then was out to the front to drive with Forst over to the vet's. Then she realized she'd left her keys in the cottage, and went back to get them, lock up properly, and unlock the car. Forst climbed into the passenger seat beside her, and Reg wondered if she should be using a booster seat to keep him safe. She didn't have one and it would probably be rude to ask, so she just kept her mouth shut about it. Forst watched out the window with great interest as they drove. Reg looked over at him.

"You don't drive much?"

"No. Gnomen don't drive."

"You probably could. It isn't very hard."

He looked at his short legs. "Must reach the brakes."

"Well, yes. But they can make extensions for the pedals. Or they can put in hand controls, so you don't need pedals."

He shook his head at the silliness of this idea. Reg shrugged. She didn't care whether he drove or not. It was only a suggestion.

"Do you think you will be able to help Starlight?"

"Cats are not the same as plants," he said slowly. "They are not as easy to make well. But I can try."

"Yeah. I sure hope there's something you can do. I don't know what I'll do without him if he doesn't make it."

"Do not think that way. We will see what is the matter and help him."

"Okay."

Reg looked in her rearview mirror for any tailing vehicles. She couldn't see Davyn anywhere. But then, he was difficult to see when she was looking for him. It was easier when she wasn't looking and just caught the movement out of the corner of her eye. She wondered what his other powers were. He was the leader of his coven, so he obviously had some ability to talk to people and get things done. He didn't seem to get bogged down in the bureaucracy; it came pretty naturally to him. He could turn invisible to follow her around. What else was he hiding? Corvin hadn't known about that power, but he must know about other gifts that Davyn had. He wouldn't be a leader of the warlock coven if he didn't have some power he could show his people, would he?

She looked back at the road and wished she could get to the vet without having to wait for all of the traffic lights. That would be a nice power to have. The ability to change traffic lights to what you wanted them to be.

It seemed like it took forever to get to the vet's office but, of course, it hadn't. She was just in such a hurry to see what Forst could do for her cat. He seemed quite confident in being able to do something for him.

Reg nodded at the receptionist. What did the woman think about her coming to the vet with someone different every day? That she was popular and had a lot of friends? Or that she was a flake and kept bringing all of these weirdos by because she couldn't bear to see her cat alone?

"Can we see him?" Reg asked, not sure what else to say.

"If you'll just have a seat, I'll have someone get him ready."

Reg breathed a sigh of relief. He wasn't dead, then. She wouldn't have said that to Reg if Starlight were dead.

She and Forst sat on the waiting room chairs. Forst's feet didn't reach the floor, and he watched his feet, swinging them back and forth. Eventually, the vet's assistant invited Reg to follow her. Forst jumped down behind her, and they walked in a line to the small examination room where they had brought Starlight. Forst stood up on one of the visitor chairs to be tall enough to look at Starlight. He ran his hands over the cat, shaking his head and making noises expressing his distress. Reg stood beside him, waiting for his verdict.

"Can you do something for him? Do you think you can help?"

"Poor beast," Forst said inside her head. "Poor, poor beast."

"Can you do something?"

The vet arrived. He looked at Forst with a slight frown, and Reg was afraid he was going to tell Forst not to climb on the furniture or that he wasn't allowed to touch Starlight, but he didn't. He just gave a bemused look and then focused on Reg.

"Still not much change," he said soberly. "But he hasn't declined, either, so that's good. I wish I could give you more hope, but…"

"Forst might be able to do something," Reg said, motioning to him.

The vet raised an eyebrow. He probably knew all of the vets in a hundred-mile radius and knew that Forst was not certified.

"The plant," Forst said aloud, in his curt way.

Reg looked at him. "What? I left the plant here so that they could test it," she said tentatively.

"We haven't been able to identify it, exactly," the vet offered. "I think we have the family narrowed down, but it is a very unusual—"

"Why did you not give it to him?" Forst asked Reg, using his inside words again.

"I thought you said it was poisonous. You said to make sure that he didn't eat it."

Forst shook his head impatiently. "No, he should not eat it. But if he has been poisoned, it is a remedy."

"The plant is a poison and a remedy?" Reg asked incredulously.

The vet looked at her, obviously thinking that she was off her head.

"Can you bring the plant here?" Reg asked him. "Forst thinks that we can use it to help Starlight."

"Alright… but I have to tell you… I can't in good conscience recommend you using a plant that we can't even identify, much less know the properties of."

"I don't care. Forst knows."

He nodded and left the examination room. He probably figured they couldn't make things any worse. Starlight would eventually die if they were not able to reverse the damage that had already been done.

CHAPTER TWENTY-SIX

The vet brought the plant into the examination room. His assistant stood behind him, straining to see past him to what was going on. She wanted to see the show too, if there was going to be one. They probably didn't think that Forst could do anything about Starlight's condition, but Reg had hope. He was very confident, and she had seen some extraordinary things in the time she'd been in Black Sands. A gnome curing a cat would not be the weirdest thing.

Forst reached across the examining table to take the plant from the vet. He placed it before him very gently. He touched various leaves and bent down to examine them and to whisper to the plant. Even though Reg could hear his inside words, she couldn't make out what he was saying to the plant. The words were not meant for her. He pulled off a couple of brown leaves and examined the bent stems and the moisture of the soil. Reg felt a pang of guilt over neglecting the little plant. They had just thrown it into a box with all of the Yule decorations and then had left it at the vet's office without giving him any instructions on its care, thinking that it was the culprit in Starlight's poisoning. She hadn't cared how the plant was treated once she gave it to the vet. But plants were important to Forst. He could understand them and treated them like his children.

The vet watched this process without comment. He didn't roll his eyes, and he didn't sigh and leave, saying that he had better things to do.

Forst picked a couple of green leaves from the plant. He pinched them between his fingers and rolled them around, releasing a pungent smell into the air. He held it under Starlight's nose and, after a minute, he peeled back Starlight's lip and mushed the ball of crushed leaves into his cheek. He massaged Starlight's jowls and throat, and Reg imagined the healing juices from the leaves running down Starlight's throat a drop at a time.

Forst petted Starlight in long strokes, watching his face and waiting for a reaction. Reg shifted restlessly. Should they see a reaction right away? Would it take a day or two before they saw any change?

There was a low growling noise from Starlight.

Reg gasped and bent in closer. "Starlight?" She petted him, her eyes filling with tears. "Star, I'm right here."

Forst didn't try to stop her from touching Starlight. Reg scratched Starlight's ears tentatively, unsure whether he was waking up, or still deep beneath the surface.

"Is he okay?" she asked Forst. "Is he waking up? What should I do?"

"He is your beast," Forst said as if she should know what to do by virtue of that fact.

Reg wiped away a tear with the back of her wrist. The vet was edging closer.

"May I…?"

Reg nodded and withdrew to give him some space. Forst didn't move. He was still watching Starlight intently, one hand on his side. The vet did his best to work around Forst. He listened to Starlight's heart with his stethoscope, moving it from one place to another. He peeled back Starlight's eyelids to look at his eyes and Reg saw the big pupils shrink rapidly when exposed to the light of the room. She put her hand on Starlight, stopping the doctor.

"He should rest. I don't think we should be poking and prodding him."

The vet withdrew. "There is an improvement," he admitted. "I don't know what that plant is, but…"

"It is healing," Forst said. "But it will not cure all of his trouble. We need to take him home. Continue to work on him there."

"I wouldn't recommend it. Here, we can monitor his vital signs, keep giving him IV fluids, make sure that he's getting all of the care that he needs. If you take him away from here, he could go into shock, and be gone by the time you could get him back." He looked at Reg, making sure she understood these points.

Reg looked at Forst. He was the one who knew what to do and had finally given Starlight a treatment that was helping, not the vet. The vet could be as cautious as he liked, but that hadn't helped Starlight so far. He had kept Starlight alive, but that was all he had been able to do.

"If Forst says we need to take him home, then that's what we'll do," she said firmly. "There isn't anything else you can do for him, is there?"

"No. That's true."

Reg nodded at Forst. "We'll take him home."

The transfer was nerve-racking. Reg kept hearing the doctor's dire warnings and was worried that the minute they got away from the vet's office, Starlight would go into seizures and be dead by the time they could get either home or back to the vet. But unless that happened, taking him home was the right thing to do. Even if he died when they got there. He should be in his home, the surroundings that were familiar to him and the people he loved. Reg swallowed a lump in her throat and again checked on Starlight, making sure that he was comfortably wrapped in the towel the vet's assistant had swaddled him in and that he looked as comfortable as possible. Forst held Starlight cradled in his arms for the journey home, the little plant nestled in a jumbo cup holder so it wouldn't tip over. Forst checked both assiduously on the way home, and all arrived back at the house safely.

"He is doing well," Forst promised, when Reg leaned over again to see how Starlight was.

"Is he going to wake up?"

"He will. We will get him inside where he will be comfortable."

Reg wanted to take Starlight from Forst, but she refrained and let him carry her furry familiar to the cottage in the back, while she juggled her keys and purse and the potted plant. Sarah was watching for them and met them in the back yard, looking over Starlight and making sympathetic noises.

"Oh, the poor thing. You think you can do something for him, Forst?"

Forst nodded and followed Reg as she unlocked the door and entered. He looked around. "Does he have a bed?"

"He sleeps on mine." Reg motioned toward the bedroom. He took

Starlight in and laid him down. He loosened the towel and spread it out and stroked Starlight's body and limbs gently.

"More of the plant, I think."

Reg had put it on the island in the kitchen as she walked by it. She trotted back out to get it and brought it to Forst's side. He again crushed a couple of leaves, whispering to the plant, and held them under Starlight's nose. The cat snorted and sneezed, but didn't wake up.

"What else can I do?" Reg asked. "Is there anything I can do?"

Forst scratched Starlight's ears, watching him. "You are his companion. Can you speak to him? Strengthen his soul?"

Reg knelt by the bed. She wasn't sure she could do exactly what Forst intended, but she would do like she had the previous couple of days. It had seemed to help a little bit. With the plant remedy in his system, maybe it would have a more significant effect. She stroked him gently, then held her hands over him and closed her eyes. When she reached out for his consciousness, it was closer. She hadn't been able to feel him in all of the time that he'd been at the vet's, but with Forst's treatment and in the comfort of his own home, she could now feel Starlight closer to the surface. Not yet awake and conscious, but sleeping beneath the surface. She tried to strengthen all of the defenses she had erected around him to protect him from the harmful magic, wishing that she were more experienced and understood better what she was doing.

"Come on, Star. I miss you so much. You need to get better."

She stayed with him for a long time but eventually had to withdraw and give herself some time to recover. Forst watched her with quick, intelligent eyes. He put his gnarled hand on her shoulder and squeezed it comfortingly. "This is a very strong curse. We have need of help."

She sighed. "I don't know who to ask. Corvin has tried. I've asked others for help, but…" Reg glanced at Sarah and trailed off. "No one seems to know anyone who can heal something like this. You are the first one who has been able to do anything."

"You need to rest and regenerate." Forst directed his gaze at Sarah. "Food and tea," he told her aloud.

"Oh. Yes, of course," Sarah agreed. "What would you like?" she asked as she headed toward the kitchen.

Forst bent over to listen to Starlight's breathing and to scratch him under the chin. He put the crushed leaves on the bed close to Starlight's nose and straightened up. "I must go back to the garden. I will return."

Reg watched him leave the room. Sarah returned, looking confused. "Is the food for you or him? Gnomes can be so difficult to understand!"

"Me, I guess," Reg murmured, petting Starlight again and resting her head on the bed.

"Okay. I'll get you something. You skipped your breakfast, didn't you?"

Reg thought about the granola bar she had intended to eat. She hadn't even had her morning coffee. It was no wonder she was feeling so tired. Sarah went back to the kitchen. Outside the bedroom window, Reg could hear Forst in the garden, his voice sonorous and slow as he sang to the plants.

CHAPTER TWENTY-SEVEN

R eg wasn't even aware of what Sarah made her to eat. She watched and
listened to Starlight as he lay there, sometimes growling or purring,
but mostly just quiet. She wondered if she should crush a couple more
leaves and try to bring him out of his deep sleep, but decided she'd better
leave that to Forst. He knew the properties of the plant and she did not. She
had not even known that they had the remedy to help him on hand.

Partway through the afternoon, she lay down on the bed next to
Starlight, her body curved in a protective crescent around his and, closing
her eyes, had a nap, listening to the drone of Forst working outside in the
garden. Sarah brought her more tea around suppertime, which Reg
consumed, but she couldn't get any solid food down. As twilight fell
outside, she heard Forst gather his tools, and then he returned to the
bedroom in the little cottage. Reg moved to get up, and he motioned her
back.

"No, no. Stay there beside him."

He bent over Starlight, laying his ear on the cat's side. He lifted his head
back up and rubbed the white star on Starlight's forehead.

"Come on, little friend. It is time to wake up."

Reg's eyes welled up with tears. She'd hoped that Forst would be able to
rouse Starlight from his deep sleep, but it would seem that he was running

out of things to try. He was able to treat the poisoning, but the magic was too strong.

At the sound of bells, Reg lifted her head and looked toward the window. "There, do you hear that?"

Sarah, standing in the doorway, looked at her blankly, but Forst cocked his head, and a smile grew across his face. "Elven folk!" he exclaimed, delighted. He went over to the window and pressed his face against the screen, looking out. He called out to them in a language Reg did not understand. The bells stopped. Reg shook her head. He'd scared them away, like a dog running into a flock of birds to play. But after a moment, there were more bells in reply, up and down the scale. Forst banged on the screen and pried at it, attempting to get it out. Frustrated, he looked at Reg. "Invite them in!"

"What? You want me to ask them in? But Starlight...?" She looked toward the window. "I don't even know their language."

"Call them. Call them!"

Reg scrambled to get off of the bed and went over to the window. She could see the twinkling lights in the garden, but no human shapes. "Come in," she called, though she had no idea whether they would understand her, or what the proper protocol for inviting elves was. She might insult them with her bumbling words. "Please come inside!"

The lights twinkled out. Reg let out her breath in frustration. Why was she forever bungling everything? She heard Norma Jean's voice in her head. Not a spirit this time, but a memory.

You are such a stupid girl. You are so weak and stupid!

She tried to control the sob that came to her throat. She couldn't cry in front of Sarah and Forst, who would wonder why she was being so emotional over not being able to call the elves inside. She rubbed her eyes with her palms and turned away from the window to face them.

They were no longer alone.

CHAPTER TWENTY-EIGHT

Reg felt like her eyes were going to pop right out of her head as she looked around the crowded room. The elves had, apparently, responded to her invitation. They stood around the room, shadowy figures, men, women, and children. They had pointed ears and were dressed in muted greens and grays. Many had bundles on their backs. They examined her with the same curiosity as she felt in looking at them, something foreign that she had only ever dreamed existed. She had been watching them and listening to them for the previous few days, but she had never thought to find them standing around her bedroom looking back at her.

"Uh… hi!" she squeaked.

There was probably some long ceremony for properly greeting them. She was, after all, meeting real live elves for the first time. But she couldn't think of what to say, and Forst didn't provide her with the words. Sarah's eyes were just as wide as Reg's felt, and she was secretly glad that Sarah, who had lived for hundreds of years, was also seeing elves for the first time. It was possible she had seen them before, but it obviously wasn't very often, not if Reg were to judge by her expression of amazement.

"She is so strange!" one of the children exclaimed, his eyes shining. "Look at her ears! And her flaming hair!"

The other elves seemed to share this opinion. Reg blushed at being the object of their scrutiny. She fumbled for something to say to them.

"I've been hearing you the last few days. And seeing your lights in the garden. I didn't know… Forst was the one who said you were elves…" She indicated the gnome.

Several of the eyes turned to Forst, and they looked at each other and nodded. Forst smiled broadly at the elves.

Reg's eyes fell back to Starlight on the bed. She had, for a few seconds, forgotten his plight in her excitement about the elves. She went back to the bed and patted him and leaned in close to him. "I guess… maybe we shouldn't all be in here, where we might disturb Starlight."

One of the children, a girl who looked about six years old, stepped forward and spoke to Reg shyly. "Can I pet him?"

Reg hesitated. She didn't know if Starlight would like being petted by a stranger. Or would he even know the difference? She didn't like to turn the little girl down, remembering herself at four, so enthralled with Starlight, holding him close and loving him, like she hadn't loved anything else in her short, wretched existence.

"I… I suppose," she said. "Be very gentle; he is sick."

The little girl elf stepped closer and stroked Starlight's fur gently. Reg didn't think he would mind that. The elf petting him caused static electricity shocks, and the little girl laughed. Reg didn't think that the air was dry enough for static electricity, but she couldn't deny what she saw with her own eyes. One of the other elves came forward and touched Starlight tentatively and, before long, they were all crowding in close for a chance to touch him, and the tiny sparks transformed into something else, little elf-lights floating around the room and glowing through Starlight's fur. Reg watched in amazement. She looked over at Forst, and he gave a slight nod, saying nothing, but the smile on his face confirming that this was not unexpected and that it was not harmful to Starlight, but might be helpful.

"He has been very sick," the little girl told the other elves authoritatively. "He has a spell on him. Can you feel it? It's very bad. It was dreadful of the woman who put it on him."

The other elves murmured to her. Reg watched, hoping to see Starlight awaken, healed by the elven magic. Forst had said that they needed help. Was that what he had meant? Had he just been waiting all day for the dark, so that the elves would come and he could enlist their help?

CHAPTER TWENTY-NINE

Y ou shouldn't be here!"

Reg jumped at the male voice that sounded from nearby.

"She's not answering her phone. I want to make sure she's okay." That voice she knew. Corvin.

"If you weren't invited, you shouldn't be here. You're supposed to stay away from her."

"The coven can shun me, but they can't dictate who I am allowed to associate with. If I don't exist as far as the coven is concerned, then they have no interest in where I am or who I talk to."

"If you want to be reinstated, you need to leave Reg Rawlins alone." It had to be Davyn. She didn't know his voice as well as Corvin's, but he was the only one who would be putting conditions of reinstatement on Corvin.

Reg exchanged glances with Sarah. *Warlocks.*

The looked back toward the window, where the voices were coming in. It wasn't until then that she realized the elves were gone. She stood up straight and looked around, panicking. Where had they gone? She had been counting on them to counter the spell binding Starlight. At the sound of the two men arguing, they had disappeared.

"No, come back," she pleaded aloud, looking around. She hoped to see the little lights or some shadow that indicated they were still there. "Please, come back!"

Forst shook his head gravely.

Reg broke down. "No! No, no." Tears streamed down her cheeks. Were they ever going to run dry? She sobbed, sitting next to Starlight. She stroked his silky fur, searching for some sign that the elves had done their job and he was going to wake up. "Star... come on, buddy."

"Reg," Sarah said in a low voice.

"They didn't lift the curse," Reg wept. "Why can't anyone do it?"

"I think you'd better deal with those two before any harm is done."

Reg focused again on Corvin's and Davyn's voices. Why did she have to deal with the two battling warlocks? If they wanted to fight, why not let them have at it? But she could imagine the damage they might do to the garden if they got into a fight, either physical or magical, and that would hurt both Sarah and Forst. She sighed and pushed herself up off the bed. She leaned into the window. "Can't you guys knock it off? You're making things worse!"

They were both silent for a minute.

"Reg?" Corvin finally asked.

"Well, who do you think lives here? What are you even doing here?"

"Making sure you're alright."

"Well, I was until you showed up."

Corvin approached the window. "What's going on? What's wrong?"

"The elves were here and they were trying to reverse the spell on Starlight, and the two of you bozos scared them off. What do you think you're doing here?"

He didn't say again that he was just there to make sure she was okay. He probably figured she wasn't accepting that as an answer.

"Why are you lurking around back there? If you wanted to talk to me, why didn't you come to the door and ring the doorbell?"

"I already knew you weren't answering your phone; I figured I would have the same problem with you answering the door. I thought that if I just came around here, where your bedroom is, I could peek in and see whether you were asleep, or whether... you needed something."

Reg was silent. That was all she needed, Corvin sneaking around behind her house, peeking in the window to watch her sleep. That wasn't creepy at all. Especially when she still wasn't sure what all of his expanded powers were. She was still waiting for the day when he would just snap and decide that if he wanted in, he was going to go in, and that would be that.

"Your last message about your mother being here was disturbing," Corvin said. "I didn't know if she would be back here. I don't know if I could stop her from…"

"From ensorcelling you? Possessing you?"

He didn't answer, and it was getting too dark for her to see anything but his shadow out there. She couldn't see his body language and facial expression, and she needed to if she were going to judge whether he was telling the truth or not. He was a good liar, but not that good.

"Go around to the door like a normal person," she told him.

It was a moment before Corvin decided she wasn't just suggesting future behavior, but that she wanted him to go to the door now. He gave a nod and headed back around the house to the door.

Davyn took it upon himself to accompany Corvin to Reg's doorstep as well, which suited Reg just fine. Corvin would have to behave himself, or Davyn would have him before the council again and they would put a stricter consequence in place. Reg didn't want to think about that part. She didn't want him to be bound, but if that were the only way for her to keep her powers, she would have to deal with it.

She opened the door and let them in without a word. Davyn entered, but Corvin stayed on the doorstep.

"Are you inviting me in?" he asked.

Reg nodded and made an impatient motion for him to enter. Sarah had followed her out of the bedroom and objected.

"You're not going to allow him in your house! Reg, there could be consequences!"

"You're too late," Corvin told her, smirking. He stepped over the threshold.

"Do not let him leave anything here," Sarah warned Reg. "You watch him like a hawk."

"That's what I'm here for," Davyn put in. And he did look particularly hawk-like as he gazed at Corvin. Davyn didn't look at all happy with this development. Reg understood why, but as she had told Davyn before, her fate and Corvin's were bound together. Whatever Reg did to try to avoid him, she was always drawn back to him for one thing or another. Whatever she did, he was always right there.

"So," Corvin looked around at the assembled company, "Norma Jean is not here?"

"No. I was supposed to meet her today for lunch, but... I guess I slept through that. It's been a rough day." She sighed. "A rough week."

"How is Starlight?"

"Come and see." She set off toward the bedroom.

"He's here?" Corvin asked in surprise.

How else did he think the elves were going to heal the cat? Was that something that they could do remotely? Reg's spirits lifted a little. Maybe they could continue to work at the spell even though they had vanished from sight. If they were only invisible, or if they were still nearby, maybe they could still help.

Corvin, Davyn, and Sarah followed Reg back into the bedroom. She sat down on the bed beside Starlight and petted him again, wishing she could sense a change in his condition. His fur was still static-charged and gave off a crackle as she ran her hand over it. Corvin shuffled a little closer, with both Sarah and Davyn sticking close to his sides, making sure he didn't try anything.

Corvin looked at Forst and cocked an eyebrow in Reg's direction in question.

"He's been helping too," Reg explained. "He was able to counteract the poison. But the spell... That's another story."

"May I?" Corvin asked, motioning to him.

Reg nodded and moved to the side to let him reach Starlight. He raised his hands over the cat and held them there.

"Cat scan," he quipped to Reg.

She wasn't amused.

She could feel the heat start to come off of Corvin and knew that he was trying to give Starlight more energy to see if that would help. Maybe if he were strong enough, he'd be able to break the spell himself. Reg waited, but there was no detectable change in Starlight's condition.

"Come on, Starlight," she begged. "Come back to me."

After a few minutes, Corvin withdrew. "Sorry," he shook his head. "Not much I can do. I'm not sure what else to try. You've been working at it."

Reg nodded.

"I can tell. But we're not there yet. He's stronger, and having the poison cleared from his system is a big help. But I don't know what else to try."

Reg nodded.

Davyn spoke. "Have you tried a fire caster?"

Reg blinked at him. "A fire caster. I don't even know what that is."

Corvin shook his head. "I didn't think that would be of any help. Is this a spell a fire caster could help with?"

Davyn nodded slowly. "It may be. Do you know who cast the spell?"

Corvin and Reg exchanged glances. "We have some ideas, but no, we don't know for sure."

Davyn folded his arms so that the voluminous sleeves of his cloak hid them. "Do you want me to try?"

"Are you a fire caster?"

"Yes." Davyn looked sideways at Reg. "And from your activity at the tribunal, I suspect that you might have the gift as well, though it is undeveloped at this point."

"I wasn't the one who kept lighting things on fire."

"Lighting *me* on fire, you mean," Corvin corrected.

Reg tried to suppress a smile. As painful as the trial had been, that part had, at least, been satisfying. She let out a sigh. "I don't know anything about fire casting. If I did have anything to do with that... and I'm not saying that I did... then I don't know how to do it again, or how to manage it. I wouldn't want to... light Starlight on fire."

"No," Davyn agreed. "That would not be a good use of your power. How about you step back as far as you can. I wouldn't want you to light up in sympathy. Not when you can't control it."

Reg looked at him to see whether he was serious and decided he was. She backed up from Starlight until she was against the wall. She didn't want to be so far away from him but, as she had said, she didn't want to light Starlight on fire either. Davyn stepped closer to the bed. Corvin decided to step back as well and positioned himself just to Reg's left. Reg glanced at him to make sure he wasn't going to try anything, then watched Davyn.

Davyn unfolded his arms and rubbed his hands together briskly like he was cold and trying to warm himself up. Then he held his hands away from himself, positioned as if he were holding out an invisible basketball. Reg waited for something to happen and, at first, she couldn't see it. Then she managed to see the light that was starting to glow in the space between Davyn's hands. It flickered and grew slowly, until it became a ball of flame, suspended in the air between his hands, not quite touching them. Reg took a step forward for a better look. Corvin put out his hand to stop her and motion her back. Reg was attracted to the fire and wanted a better look. Corvin put his hand on her shoulder and pushed her back to the wall.

"Don't get closer."

"But I want—"

"Your magic wants to join him. But it's not a good idea. Not when you don't know anything about how to handle it yet."

A tightness started to grow in Reg's chest. She breathed in and out slowly, trying to disperse it, but it continued to grow tighter and to get hotter and hotter.

"Just watch Davyn," Corvin tried to redirect her attention. He must have been able to see something in her expression. How much she wanted to light a fire. To see it getting bigger and bigger and burning out of control. She looked up to the ceiling, trying to suppress the hard knot of anxiety in her chest. She had known a few firebugs growing up in foster care. She had lit more than one fire herself, and she knew what it felt like, that feeling of power and that hunger to destroy.

She tried to do as Corvin said and focus on Davyn. The ball of fire cupped between his hands, he started to roll and manipulate it, looking like a baker working with a ball of dough. He bent closer to Starlight, held it over him. Pushed it down until it was almost touching Starlight.

Reg opened her mouth to warn him that it was too close, that he was going to burn Starlight. Then Davyn gave a sudden push like he was dribbling the imaginary basketball, and the ball of light disappeared.

Reg jumped forward, too fast this time for Corvin to stop her. She was at Davyn's side in an instant. "Where did it go? What did you do?"

She couldn't see the fire but, once again, Starlight seemed to be glowing with light. As if Davyn had taken up where the elves had left off. So maybe he was doing something helpful. He motioned Reg back but didn't touch her or answer her question. Reg stared at Starlight, hoping to see a change. His feet started to twitch.

"Is that it? Is it working?"

He jerked and danced like he was having a dream of chasing mice. Reg wanted to reach down and pat him, to calm him down and wake him up. But Davyn kept her back.

"Let it work," he whispered. "You mustn't touch him or interfere."

"Is it working?"

He nodded.

Reg's knees went weak with relief. Maybe there was hope. Maybe Davyn had been the answer all along.

"Can we do anything else? Can I help somehow? Does he need anything?"

Davyn raised his eyes from the cat and looked around. "Do you have any candles?"

"No... I... we had some, but when he got sick, I was thinking about things that could be dangerous to have with a cat around, and I thought candles would be too much of a hazard, so we took them all down again..."

"They are just at the big house," Sarah pointed out. "I'll go get them."

Reg didn't offer to go and help. She watched Starlight, hoping that at any minute he would open his eyes and see her there watching over him and know that everything was going to be okay. He would see that she had helped him and protected him, that she hadn't just sat around waiting for him to wake up.

CHAPTER THIRTY

S arah returned with the candles and went out to the kitchen to find a
box of matches in the drawer. Davyn gave Reg a mischievous smile and
started to take candles out of the box, tapping the wick of each one to light
it. He began to place them around the room. Reg was longing to light a fire
herself after witnessing Davyn's power, and she tried to do the same as he
had, tapping the wick to get a candle to light. She shook her head when
they didn't immediately light up as Davyn's had. He shrugged.

"Keep trying."

Corvin watched Reg for a moment. "Why don't you just use your
mind?" he suggested. "At the hearing, you didn't touch me; you just lit fires
from across the room."

Reg looked down at the candle she held in her hand and focused on the
wick, telling it that she wanted it to light. Nothing happened. She was
getting more and more frustrated, but nothing seemed to be working. She
looked down at the box of decorations, wondering if maybe there were
something wrong with the candle she had taken out of the box. There was a
'whoomp' sound, and the entire box was suddenly engulfed in flames.
Corvin and Forst jumped back. In the doorway, Sarah gave a little shriek.
Davyn looked at the box and looked at Reg. Unhurried, he walked over to
the box and gathered the fire together into a ball and scooped it up in his
hands. Everyone watched in horror, but he wasn't burned, and he wasn't

alarmed by the accidental inferno. He held the ball of light between his hands and approached Reg. He held it out toward her.

Reg stared at the small, controlled fire, and wasn't sure what to do.

"Just take it," Davyn said calmly. "Don't think about it."

Reg reached out both of her hands and swallowed. She put her hands beside his and inched them together until she could feel the warmth of the fire licking against them. But it didn't hurt. She slowly backed away from Davyn, holding it between her hands.

"This is weird."

He chuckled. "You need to learn control. Don't just send your fire out like that. Use your hands. Keep it small and controlled. When you have mastered that, you can move on to sending your fire out."

"What do I do now?"

He bent over the charred cardboard box and selected a candle. They were all somewhat melted after Reg ignited the box. He held out the single candle. "Hold the fire in one hand. Touch the wick with your index finger on the other."

Reg reached out her right index finger, cradling the fire in her left hand, and tentatively prodded the wick. It took a moment, but then it lit.

"I did it!" Reg said excitedly. "I really did it."

The fire in her left hand flared up. Davyn winced. "Stay calm. Fire is very emotional. If you get excited or angry, you will feed it, and if you are not careful, you will lose control again. Just stay calm and controlled."

"Okay." Reg took a few calming breaths, and the fire got smaller again. "Can I do another one?"

He handed them to her one at a time, passing them to Corvin once they were lit so that he could place them around the room. No one else wanted to get close to Reg while she was handling the fire. They all hung back.

In a few minutes, they had all of the candles lit, and every flat surface in Reg's bedroom flickered and glowed with the small flames. Reg looked down at the ball of fire still in her hand. "Now, what do I do with this?"

He took each of her hands in one of his and brought them close together until they were palm to palm, and the fire slowly flickered out. He opened her hands again and waited, watching to see if it would flare up again, then nodded and released her hands. "Your first lesson in fire casting."

"That was amazing."

"I'm glad you enjoyed it."

Reg looked back at Starlight on the bed. He was no longer twitching. She didn't know if that was good or bad. He was still glowing. "Is he okay?"

"We need to let him rest and let the fire work. It is a very strong curse… I don't know how long it will take, and if we'll need more help."

"It seems like everyone has already tried, and no one can counter it."

"It's very strong. What kind of a sorcerer cast such a spell?"

Reg looked over at Corvin.

CHAPTER THIRTY-ONE

Y oo-hoo, anyone home?"

Reg looked toward the open bedroom door at the sound of the call. She had obviously left the front door unlocked after letting Corvin and Davyn in. Or Norma Jean had used her powers to unlock it. Reg still hadn't been able to determine how she was able to get past the wards in the house, but it was a little late to be worrying about it now.

Norma Jean walked through the cottage to the bedroom and looked in the doorway.

"Well, here everyone is." She looked around at all of the candles and visitors. "Exactly what kind of party is this? Are you having a seance?"

Reg tried to figure out what to say. She couldn't think of anything. Norma Jean shook her head.

"It's a pretty good scam, getting all of these people to believe in something that doesn't exist. You can't really talk to spirits."

Reg had been able to talk to Norma Jean when she had been dead, in the other timeline. She had spoken to plenty of spirits ever since she was a little girl. She studied Norma Jean's smiling face, trying to figure out whether she knew this and was hiding the fact, or whether she didn't believe that Reg could communicate with ghosts. Had she understood that was what Reg had been doing as a little girl when she talked to her imaginary friends?

Did Norma Jean understand that she herself had powers, or was it all accidental?

"And Corvin is here," Norma Jean purred, sidling toward him. "I wondered where you had gotten to, handsome."

"He was right where you left him," Reg snapped.

"What? Right where I left him where? What are you talking about?"

"You ensorcelled him and then left him on the street in a stupor."

Norma Jean's eyebrows went way up and she laughed. "I did what? Even if I could, sweetie, why would I do such a thing? That's ridiculous."

"You did. I don't know why. It doesn't make any sense. Maybe you wanted him to meet up with me and to take my powers. Is that what you were thinking?"

Norma Jean looked from person to person, her eyes narrow and calculating. She must know something. She might not know everything, but she knew what Reg was talking about and she was trying to figure out what everyone else in the room knew or guessed. She slid an arm around Corvin, and he made no move to stop her. The way he looked down at her was... it was very similar to the way that Weston had looked at her when Reg had gone back in time. He was clearly smitten with her, whether she was actively charming him or not. She snuggled up close to him and looked at Reg with fiery, watchful eyes.

Was that it, then? Was she jealous of Reg? She wanted Corvin and thought that he was Reg's boyfriend? She could have him if that were the case.

"Have at it," Reg said, making a motion toward Corvin. "Go ahead. I don't care."

Norma Jean frowned at this. Davyn gave Reg a warning look. Reg bit the inside of her cheek. She had forgotten that a siren's natural reaction was to drown the men she caught. She might have abandoned Corvin the last time, but the next time... she could drown him for real. And Reg had just told her to go for it.

"I didn't mean..." Reg shook her head. She didn't know whether that was Norma Jean's intention or whether she would be putting the thought in her head. That wouldn't be a good idea. She rubbed her head. It was starting to throb. She needed to be at the top of her game, but with how little sleep she'd had and the constant worry about Starlight, it was difficult to think things through clearly. She decided to switch tracks. Distraction was the best course of action. "I'm sorry I missed you for lunch today. Things got crazy. You know that my cat has been sick..."

Reg looked over at Starlight, hoping for some change in his condition. He did look a little different. Like he was sleeping instead of nearly dead. Reg couldn't think of what was different or how to quantify it, but he looked... fluffier. The glowing fire was dissipating, but he looked healthier. Maybe they were making progress. Maybe Davyn's fire had done the trick. And if Reg could learn how to cast fire, she would be able to do something herself the next time instead of being so helpless.

But there wasn't going to be a next time. She wasn't going to let it happen again. Once Starlight was better, she was going to protect him and make sure that nothing happened to him.

"Oh, you brought him home," Norma Jean observed. "How is he doing? He doesn't look too well."

"No thanks to you," Sarah snapped. "Are you the one who poisoned him?"

Reg's jaw dropped. She hadn't been expecting anything like that from Sarah. Sarah didn't even like cats and hadn't seemed very upset about Starlight's condition. She was usually sweet and Reg hadn't expected her to accuse Norma Jean straight out of being his attacker.

"Uh..." No words came out of Reg's mouth.

Norma Jean looked at Sarah, her mouth pinched into a sour, bitter expression. "What are you doing here? I thought your house was the big one over there," she gestured in the direction of the main house. "Why is it that I always find you over here? You're not Regina's family. You're just her landlord."

"I may be, but I look after her better than you ever did. What kind of mother are you?"

Norma Jean looked at the others in the room, not liking being accused in front of the strangers. "What I did or didn't do when I had Regina is none of your business. You're not her family. You're not a cop. And what happened was a long time ago. I've already paid the price for my mistakes."

"How have you paid?" Reg demanded, the words coming out of her mouth without planning. As far as she knew, Norma Jean had never suffered anything for what she had done to Reg. Reg had been the one to suffer from the abuse. She had been the one who had been hurt and neglected and who had been taken away from everything she knew and passed from one home to another as she tried to deal with her traumatic beginning. Maybe in this timeline, Norma Jean hadn't been tortured to death in front of Reg's four-year-old eyes, but in the timeline Reg remembered she had been, and that had been a terrible thing to live with.

Norma Jean's eyes reflected the flames around her, making her look like a demon. "Do you know what it's like to be addicted? To have your only child torn from your arms? You don't know what I went through. I was in recovery for years, and all the time, I was missing my daughter and knew that I didn't have any chance of getting her back. Can you even imagine what that's like?"

Reg shook her head in amazement. Norma Jean's self-pity was unbelievable. She acted as if she were a victim rather than the perpetrator of the abuse.

"What about me?" she demanded. "I'm the one you hurt! Do you even remember what you did to me?"

Norma Jean pressed her face into Corvin's shoulder, closing her eyes. "I know I did things I shouldn't have when I was under the influence. But that wasn't me. That was the drugs and booze. That isn't the kind of person that I am. I'm not a bad person."

"When you harm a child, an innocent child, that makes you a bad person. You can give all the excuses you like, but you did that, and I remember it."

"Until you have children of your own, you can't judge me. You don't know what it's like. An innocent child? You were never an innocent child. Right from the time you were a baby, you were manipulative. Had to have your own way. Get everything you wanted. You think I was the only one who hit? You hit and kicked me, bit and scratched. You imagine trying to take care of a little monster like that. You imagine what it's like to have to nurse a... a snake. You never wanted a mother. You just wanted someone who would fulfill your every demand."

The room was silent. Sarah, Davyn, and Forst looked from Norma Jean to Reg with wide eyes. Corvin was staring adoringly down at Norma Jean. Reg bit her lip and tried to control her rage. She didn't want everyone looking at her as if she were a monster. If they believed what Norma Jean was saying... Did they understand that Norma Jean was lying and just trying to throw the blame back on someone else? Surely they didn't believe that Reg had been a monster from birth, intentionally hurting her own mother and being manipulative and demanding.

Reg had seen her four-year-old self when she had gone back with Harrison. That child had not been mean or devilish. She had been sweet, scared, longing for attention and comfort. She'd had incredibly strong psychic powers that it had taken her mother and foster families and doctors years to beat down and stamp out.

Maybe that was how all sirens saw their offspring. They were competitors in a limited environment, rather than children to be nurtured. If they wanted to live, they had to run away or escape somehow, to survive on their own or in some other family where no one knew what they were.

The candles in the room flared. Davyn turned his head to catch Reg's eye. It probably wasn't the best idea to be in a room full of candles while she tried to control her fury at the woman who had given her such a difficult start to life. Reg tried to tamp it down, but could feel the fire building in her chest again.

Starlight stirred, turning his head to the side and curling together a little on his side—a natural movement for a sleeping cat. Reg's anger at Norma Jean was immediately forgotten. She dropped onto her knees on the floor, putting her face right up to the cat. She put her hand on his body, and he twitched and breathed. He felt normal like he was just sleeping. He still didn't wake up, though. Reg whispered to him as if she were the only one in the room with him, instead of all of the others being crowded into her bedroom.

"Starlight. Hey, Star, are you feeling better? How's it going? Are you going to wake up?" She rubbed his side and scratched his ears. He tucked his head in more tightly and flicked his ears, not waking up.

"What's wrong with him?" Norma Jean asked. All of the accusation and bitterness was gone from her voice; it was back to being honey sweet, as if she were concerned about her daughter and her pet. Reg felt like she was sitting on the swinging pendulum of Norma Jean's emotion, off balance and having to shift and adjust to each fresh swing.

"Don't you know?" Reg asked.

Norma Jean released her hold on Corvin. She brushed her fingers across his bearded chin, then stepped toward Reg, looking down at the cat.

"How would I know what was wrong with him? I'm not a vet."

"When you were here before, you did something to him." Reg turned her head to look into Norma Jean's guileless eyes. There was no knowledge in them of what had happened to Starlight, no hint of the jealousy or anger. Did she not remember what she had done from one minute to the next? Forgetting about charming Corvin and leaving him on the street. Forgetting that she had harmed Starlight. Forgetting how she had treated Reg as a child, pretending that she had been wronged by social services and everyone else who had dealt with her at the time.

Had the drugs damaged her brain and caused holes in her memory? Was it something to do with her siren nature warring with her human nature or whatever other species she was a part of? Or was it denial?

Or just lies.

"Why would I do something to your cat?"

"Because you don't like him. He makes you think of... something you don't like to remember. You think that he's done something to you. I don't know what. But something about him bothers you."

Norma Jean gazed at Starlight for a few long moments. Her nose wrinkled and her lip lifted in a sneer. "He's not so special. You'd be better off getting a different cat. Or a dog. Maybe you should get something else. Cats are useful for getting rid of mice and other vermin, but they aren't real companions. Having kitty litter in the house is so stinky and messy."

"Cats are very tidy," Reg insisted. "And I don't want a different cat or a dog. I want him. He is special. I need him back."

Norma Jean reached out her hand. Reg panicked, not knowing whether she should let her mother touch Starlight or not. Would she make it worse? Kill him? Or did she really not remember? If she had cast the spell that was keeping him unconscious, then she could remove it. But Reg didn't know what to expect. Did Norma Jean intend to help or harm him?

"What are you doing?" She touched Norma Jean's hand, stopping her before she could touch Starlight. It wasn't forceful or violent, just the barest touch, like a butterfly.

CHAPTER THIRTY-TWO

There was a burst of light from Norma Jean's eyes. Reg found herself suddenly paralyzed. She was frozen in Norma Jean's gaze. Was that what Corvin had felt? Or had he felt the same type of warm, satisfying charm from Norma Jean as Reg felt from Corvin? Reg first tried to struggle physically, but there was no way she could move a muscle. Norma Jean pulled her arm away from Reg's touch, and proceeded to lay a single finger on Starlight's head, right on the star marking on his head.

Reg couldn't move physically, but that wasn't her only option. She tried immediately to block Norma Jean's magic and make a safe cushion of space around herself. She tried to extend it around Starlight to keep him safe from Norma Jean's spell.

She could feel the barriers she had built around Starlight on her previous visits to him at the vet's office. She could feel the strength that Corvin had given him and the heat of Davyn's fire casting. She could even feel the elves, the little pockets of energy, the tinkling bells.

Norma Jean was frowning. She looked at Reg in consternation. "What have you done?"

Still frozen, Reg tested out her voice and found that it still worked. "I've done everything I could to protect him and heal him. Please don't hurt him any more. Please."

Norma Jean stood there, touching Starlight, a scowl on her face. "You don't want this animal. You don't know what he is."

Reg was startled by this claim. She had wondered about Starlight's history. Who was his previous owner? What was his history before he had come into her life? Or in a past life, even before he had been born as Starlight.

"I might not know much about his life before," she said slowly, "but I know what he's like. What kind of a—" she caught herself before she said 'person he was.' But she couldn't bring herself just to call him a cat. She remembered how Harrison had cuddled with Starlight, called him an old friend. Harrison was the one person who knew what Starlight was and could counter whatever Norma Jean had to say about him. Harrison was an immortal, the one force that might be able to counter Norma Jean's spell over Starlight.

Harrison. Reg reached out to him in her mind. *Please come.*

She looked around the room, but he didn't appear with his usual aplomb. Reg was a little disconcerted. She had thought that he would always come when called.

Norma Jean was looking at Reg with cold, hard eyes. "What are you doing?"

"I was just... I just..." Reg looked around at the others, looking for help. With so many magical practitioners in the room, was there no one who could stand up to Norma Jean and counter her powers? Sarah looked like she didn't know what was going on and Forst like he wanted to run from the room. Corvin's eyes were still misty and lovelorn. Reg looked at Davyn. It was down to her and Davyn, but she hadn't worked with him before and knew nothing about his powers except that he could become invisible and was a fire caster.

"You can't call to one of them while I am in the room," Norma Jean said coldly. "You can't do anything here without my permission. You should say 'please, Mommy,' like when you were a child. Because that is all you are. You cannot usurp me."

"I'm not trying to usurp you. I just want my cat back. I want him to be healed. If you can make him better, then I don't need anyone else. You could do it for me."

"Why would I do that?"

"To show me how powerful you are. No one else has been able to heal him. You could show me that you're more powerful than any of them."

Norma Jean's eyes sparkled at this. The candles were dancing and throwing weird lights and shadows into her face. Reg could see that her suggestion had struck a chord. Norma Jean liked the idea of showing Reg how powerful she was. Even though she had already done that by cursing Starlight with a spell that no one else could overcome, by charming the charmer, and by being able to come and go as she pleased despite any wards against her.

Norma Jean tapped Starlight's white spot. He stirred and opened his eyes.

"Hey, Star." Reg found herself released and able to pet him. "Hey, buddy, how are you feeling?"

He stretched and yawned widely, then shook his head, his ears making the flapping sound that always made Reg laugh. She could feel his consciousness gradually growing as he blinked and looked around the room at all of the people and candles. He gave a snort and sneezed on Reg's arm. She didn't even care.

"Thank you. Oh, thank you so much," Reg breathed, looking at Norma Jean. "You don't know how much I missed him."

Standing tall, Norma Jean looked down at her. "Imagine how much I missed you."

Reg swallowed. She didn't believe it, but had to admit the possibility that Norma Jean might have felt something when Reg was taken away. Maybe she did have some motherly feelings toward Reg, deep, deep down.

Norma Jean turned and headed toward the bedroom door. She hooked a finger through one of Corvin's belt loops and pulled him with her. Corvin gave no resistance, following her lead.

"Wait, no! You can't take him," Reg protested.

Norma Jean arched an eyebrow. "You said that I could have him."

"I said that you could... you could charm him. I didn't say you could take him away."

Norma Jean rolled her eyes. "If I can control his mind, I can have him."

"No. You can't. It's... it's against the rules." Reg looked at Sarah and Davyn for their guidance. She wasn't actually sure what the rule was on the point. She had only ever seen one siren and talked to Corvin about what the rules were. She knew that Norma Jean was not allowed to take him down to the ocean. They were allowed to stop her if she tried. But with the strength of Norma Jean's powers, Reg was worried about what would happen if they tried to force the issue instead of reasoning with her. She had already disabled their most powerful member. Davyn watched her with wide, bright eyes and Reg suspected it wouldn't take much for her to draw him in as well.

"You cannot take him from here under your power," Sarah agreed. "He can only leave with you by his own choice."

Norma Jean gave Corvin another tug toward the door. "He is willing."

"You have him under your thrall. You must release him to make his own choice without your influence."

Reg remembered what it was like to be under Corvin's control. So foggy and deeply under his influence that she couldn't make a decision that would keep her safe. It was an intoxicating state to be in. Corvin would need more than just a brief release from her charms to return to his own mind and make a reasoned choice.

"Just leave him," she said. "You don't really want him anyway. You already got bored with him yesterday."

Norma Jean considered this, looking at Corvin. "He is a nice specimen."

Reg cleared her throat, trying not to laugh. "Yes… he is that."

"I think I will keep him."

She continued out of the bedroom with Corvin beside her. Reg swore and hurried after them. She didn't want it to come down to a knock-down, drag-out fight. Norma Jean was too powerful; she could paralyze Reg with a look. The only one that might be able to fight her—besides Corvin, who was already under her control, was—

Reg found Norma Jean in the living room, her finger still through Corvin's belt loop, standing frozen, looking at the man stretched out on the couch.

"Harrison!" Reg couldn't believe that he was there. She had called him, and he hadn't shown up. Or he had, but hadn't even bothered to go to the bedroom to help her out. He lounged on the couch, long legs stretched out in front of him, feet resting on the coffee table. He was dressed with his usual flamboyance, his outfit just missing looking human. The purple, long-sleeved shirt looked like something out of a Broadway musical rather than something a man would wear on a casual night out.

"Regina. So nice to see you and your mother again."

"Where were you? I wanted you and you weren't there!"

"Sometimes, humans don't know what they want. They think they want one thing when they are perfectly fine with another. You didn't really need me, did you?"

"Yes, I did!"

"Why?"

"To heal Starlight! You're the only one who is strong enough to reverse the spell—"

"That is clearly not true."

Harrison was looking past Reg, where Starlight was following her on rather wobbly legs. Reg stopped and picked him up.

"Well, Norma Jean could, obviously, because she's the one who cursed him in the first place."

"And she has reversed the curse. So there is no harm done."

"You need to tell her that she can't take Corvin away from here. She has him under her spell, and she could do him harm. She's part... she's part siren."

"Yes."

"You knew that?"

He gave a little shrug.

"Why didn't you tell me that part? Why do you always leave out the most important points?"

"I don't think that is true."

"What else do you know about her? What else is she? Human or immortal? Or something else? Where does she get these other powers?"

"She is a mixture of origins, like most humans. Like you yourself."

"Don't even get me started on myself, I'm still trying to figure out how *that* happened. Why can't you ever give me a straight answer?"

"I give you the best answer I can. I cannot help it if you are too human to understand the answers."

"What are you doing here?" Norma Jean asked, staring at Harrison. She gave no acknowledgment that they had been talking about her.

"Hello, Norma Jean."

"What are you doing here?" she repeated. She released her hold on Corvin and walked over to Harrison, towering over him like a mother who had just caught the child who had stolen the cookies intended for the church bazaar.

"It's nice to see you too," Harrison said politely.

"You aren't supposed to be here."

"Indeed."

He didn't look offended by her accusations. They didn't seem to faze him a bit.

"You were there." Norma Jean said, staring at him. She turned and pointed to Starlight in Reg's arms. "And he was there. And him," she indicated Corvin, still standing there like a lovestruck zombie. She looked at them all again. "Why were you all there?"

Reg wondered again why, if Norma Jean could remember them going back in time to visit her, that she didn't remember Reg as well. She seemed totally oblivious to the fact that she had been visited not just by the men, but by the adult version of her own daughter. Shouldn't she be more surprised that her grown daughter had been there too? Occupying the same time and space as her four-year-old child? All of the scientists and Star Trek writers had said that such a thing was impossible. It would cause a temporal paradox that would cause a rift in the universe. But apparently, it wasn't even worth remembering.

"We were there to help you," Harrison said. "To prevent further damage from being done."

"Damage? What are you talking about? Damage to what? To me? To my child?" She gestured to Reg. "Are you the ones who called Social Services and had her taken away from me? I always *thought* it was you."

"Called who?"

"You are the ones who called Social Services and reported me. You told them lies about me hurting Reg and had her taken away from me. Admit it!"

Harrison shook his head. "I would not contact more humans than absolutely necessary."

He was very good at avoiding a direct answer.

"And now you're here. Why? To send me back?"

Reg tried to wrap her mind around that. To send her back where? Back to Maine? Back to the point in time when Reg was four? Back to the siren's island, which should have been her real home?

Harrison's smile made Reg uneasy. "You don't need me to send you back," he told Norma Jean. "You can go back by yourself. Voluntarily. There is no need to involve anyone else, is there?"

Norma Jean's expression was fierce. She bared her teeth at Harrison like a snarling animal. "I didn't escape torture and death just to be forced back there by you! You have no authority over my life! I am a free creature!"

"Then what is your decision?" Harrison asked pleasantly.

She didn't move or answer. Harrison pulled his feet down from the coffee table and arose. Now Norma Jean had to look up at him. She held her ground and didn't back down. Harrison reached out and touched her arm.

"I am a free creature!" Norma Jean repeated, jerking her arm away from him.

"Then make your free decision. Choose to be free, not to be constrained by these humans and their rules. Go back where you belong and live a free life."

Norma Jean indicated Reg. "She is my daughter!" She didn't say it tenderly. It was more of an accusation.

"She is."

"She cannot be allowed to be here. We cannot both be here."

"Then what is your choice?"

She looked around the room. Her eyes stopped on Reg, holding Starlight in her arms. Reg tightened her grip, afraid that Norma Jean was going to strike Starlight with another curse. She had just gotten him back. She couldn't let him be hurt again.

Starlight's fur crackled with electricity. She could feel his strength, his growing consciousness. Starlight always helped her to focus her attention and her psychic powers. He magnified her gifts, or her control over her gifts. Reg took a deep breath and gathered as much of his focusing power as she could.

"Don't hurt him again. Don't hurt me again. I'm not doing anything to hurt you. I'm not competing with you, if that's what you think. I haven't done anything to disturb your… hunting grounds. And I won't. You go ahead and… do whatever it is you do. As long as it isn't hurting me or my friends." Reg reached out and grasped Corvin's arm, pulling him back toward her. "Just leave us alone, and quit these games about being a sweet mother and wanting to get to know me. Because you don't want to. We both know that."

Norma Jean scowled. She looked as if she were trying to decide whether to strike Reg down for being so impertinent. Was that the way for a daughter to talk to her mother? Reg had no idea how a siren daughter talked to her mother. Apparently, it was normally a battle to the death, but Reg preferred to talk things out. Her social workers, doctors, teachers, and foster parents had always taught her to use words to sort out problems. It was less messy. At least, there was less visible damage.

"This one is yours," Norma Jean said finally, indicating Corvin. "You claim him."

Reg nodded, hoping that wasn't going to spark a magical battle.

"You choose not to claim your heritage."

Reg nodded again. "I don't want to be a siren. That's not my thing."

"You claim these waters." Norma Jean motioned in the direction of the ocean. "This is your territory."

Reg hesitated. That seemed like a bad idea. She looked at Harrison, trying to get some clue from him as to what the right answer was. If she claimed a territorial right, would Norma Jean fight her on it? Or would Norma Jean accept Reg's claim and move out of her territory to establish her own? Harrison watched with interest but gave no clue as to the right answer. He was interested in human affairs, but they seemed to provide him entertainment rather than him being concerned with the impact on the humans involved.

She buried her nose in the short, soft fur at the top of Starlight's head, breathing in his clean cat smell and searching for inspiration.

"This is where I live," she said slowly. "I'm not going to be moving somewhere else, not in the near future."

Norma Jean's eyes were sharp. Her mouth was a thin line, drawing down at the corners. Reg's body was tense, prepared for attack. The memory of Norma Jean's anger were there, stored in her body, even if she didn't remember every separate episode. Her body knew to be ready.

"I'm not going to be hunting here," Reg said. "I just want to live in peace."

"You are what you are. It is in your nature. Sooner or later… you will."

Reg swallowed. "I'm not interested in that kind of life. I just want to live in this cottage in peace, with my cat, running my psychic consulting business. That's my nature. I don't have any interest in hunting."

"These southeastern waters shall be yours," Norma Jean declared. "If you venture north…"

"I won't. If I have to travel… do I have to call you ahead of time? Let you know that I am going on a trip?"

Norma Jean scowled. "Don't hunt in my territory. If you do, you will live to regret it." Her chin lifted slightly. "If you live."

Reg squeezed Starlight a little more tightly, making him squirm and start to kick his hind feet in protest. She relaxed her arms.

"Fine," she agreed. "It's a deal, then."

The wind suddenly picked up, blowing a cold blast of air through the open windows of the house, filling the room with the salty tang of the sea. Reg shivered, goosebumps popping up on her skin. Starlight rubbed his head against the bottom of her chin. Reg cuddled him and kissed the top of his head.

Norma Jean gave Harrison one more look of spite, and then without a word to her daughter, swept out the front door and was gone. Reg heard bells tinkling in the distance.

She gave a sigh and looked at Harrison. "Any more surprises?"

He cocked an eyebrow. "I am constantly surprised by humans."

"No, I mean are there any more surprises for me? Finding out that my father was an immortal and my mother part siren? Time traveling? What else?"

"There are always more surprises," he assured her with a beatific smile.

Reg shook her head. She shook Corvin's arm to try to wake him from his trance. He turned his eyes to her, foggy and shifting back and forth drunkenly.

"Regina? What are you doing here?"

"This is my house."

He looked around, puzzled. "Then what am I doing here?"

CHAPTER THIRTY-THREE

S tarlight's recovery called for celebration and, with winter solstice upon them, Reg decided on a loosely-organized Yuletide dinner with everyone who had been involved in his treatment.

Corvin was there, invited once more and in full possession of his faculties. Forst looked like a miniature Santa Claus with his white beard, round face, and red cap. Reg invited his twin Fir as well, thinking that it wasn't right for her to have one of them and not the other there for Yule. Jessup and Sarah had helped to pull everything together, helping Reg with the decorations—none of them toxic to cats—and the Yule feast.

Reg didn't know Davyn very well, but he had been a big part of Starlight's recovery, and he helped Reg to light candles and the Yule log, making sure that the surfaces Starlight might jump up on were clear of candles to prevent him from singeing his whiskers or starting a fire. Reg hadn't been sure whether Davyn or Sarah would come, knowing that Corvin was an invited guest, but they could apparently join in the celebrations as long as they didn't acknowledge Corvin's presence.

Reg caught Forst outside, standing on a ladder in order to reach the eaves, where he hung a couple of wind chimes that tinkled in the breeze.

"Mayhap the elven folk won't come by this way again," he said, face pink, "but the bells will tell them thank you."

"Oh, that's great. Thank you!"

"It is a great honor to be visited by elves."

"It was good of them to try to help, too."

Forst nodded his agreement.

Even the vet and his staff had been invited for the first part of the celebration, partaking in appetizers and drinks and enjoying the good feelings of the season. Everyone was delighted to see the guest of honor well again and treated Starlight like a king.

Reg sat with her feet under her and her hands wrapped around a warm mug of mulled cider. "It's hard to believe that it all really happened," she said to Corvin. "When I see Starlight and everything else back to normal, it feels like it was all just a dream. And a bizarre one, at that."

"For me, a lot of it was a dream."

Reg chuckled. "I guess so. Are you feeling stable again? Got your footing?"

He shrugged. "I'm not sure I will ever entirely recover. I still feel… longing for her. I can't believe that she abandoned me. Even though I realize that if she had followed through on her promises, I would be dead now."

"For what it's worth, I'm glad you're not."

"Thank you," Corvin said dryly, having a sip of the Yule wassail. "That's nice to hear."

Reg caught a movement out of the corner of her eye and turned her head to see what it was. She was half expecting it to disappear again. Instead, she smiled to see Harrison in full holiday regalia, dressed in red silk with white fur trimming from head to foot. Reg tried not to laugh at the ridiculous figure he cut. He seemed completely at ease with his costume.

"Seasonal greetings," he told Reg.

"Thank you. And you too, Uncle Harrison. I'm glad you could make it."

"Would I miss my god-daughter's seasonal Christmas Yuletide solstice celebration?"

"I guess not. You didn't have any other plans?"

"I always have other plans." He offered it as if it were a compliment, and Reg supposed that if he chose her party over whatever his other plans were, it was.

"Oh. Well, thank you for making the time."

"Making time," Harrison mused.

"It's just an expression."

"Indeed. What is your wish?"

"My wish?"

"Is there not…" he made a twirling motion with his finger to indicate all of the Yule trimmings and company, "…a wish made for this observance?"

"Well… I don't know if there usually is or not." No one else had mentioned making a wish to Reg. But she wasn't going to turn down the opportunity to let the universe know what she was hoping for. If there was one thing that living in Black Sands had taught her, it was that the unexpected could happen, no matter how unlikely. "I wish… for safety for Starlight. And wealth. I could use a little extra money, just to make sure I have something to fall back on."

Reg had not noticed Fir kneeling down to talk to Starlight. He rose to his feet and intoned a warning.

"Be careful of thy wishes. You never know which ones will be granted."

Did you enjoy this book? Reviews and recommendations are vital to making a book successful.

Please leave a review at your favorite book store or review site and share it with your friends.

Don't miss the following bonus material:
Sign up for mailing list to get a free ebook
Read a sneak preview chapter
Other books by P.D. Workman
Learn more about the author

Sign up for my mailing list at pdworkman.com and get Gluten-Free Murder for free!

PREVIEW OF FAIRY BLADE UNMADE

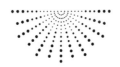

CHAPTER ONE

Reg looked around the cottage for some sign of the small black cat. Starlight, her own cat, a tuxedo with mismatched eyes and a star in the third-eye position on his forehead, gazed at her, radiating irritation and displeasure. Reg looked down at the bowl Nico had knocked to the floor, scattering popcorn everywhere.

"What happened?" she asked Starlight.

He stared back at her. What did she think had happened? Did she think that *he* had somehow been involved in the incident?

Reg shook her head. "I know *you* didn't do it. But did he mean to? Or did he just—was it just an accident?"

Starlight's gaze didn't shift, nor did the emotions hanging around him like a dense cloud.

"Where did he go?"

Starlight broke her gaze and looked around. He stopped, ears pointing at the couch. Reg walked over to it, then got down to her knees to look underneath.

Nico, all black with blazing yellow eyes, crouched under the couch and, when she got down to his level, hissed at her, putting his ears back.

"I didn't threaten you, why are you hissing at me?"

He hissed again, just to make sure she understood what would happen if she reached under the couch and tried to pull him out. Reg already knew; the scenario had been repeated enough times. She had scratches all up and down both arms from previous attempts to pull him out of a hiding place, down from the drapes, or out of some situation he had gotten himself into. He was not a cat who appreciated any interference or help.

Starlight had spoiled Reg. She hadn't ever had another pet, not even a goldfish. Despite his quirks, Starlight had been a pretty easy animal to deal with. He might like to get her out of bed too early, make demands about the kind of food he wanted, and bite her ankles if he didn't like what she was doing but, dealing with Nico now, she understood what an easy cat Starlight had been. She'd had no idea how antagonistic a cat could be.

"Why did you knock down the popcorn?"

He stared at her. His aura was red, as it often was. She had trouble sorting out what he was feeling. Confusion? Anger? Fear? She sometimes had the feeling that Nico's emotions were much the same as Reg's had been when she'd been a child in foster care. Hypervigilant, always afraid of what was going to happen next, unable to trust adults no matter how nice they might seem on the outside. Because all adults betrayed her sooner or later. If they didn't do something to hurt her, they were disappointed in her behavior, or they told her social worker that she needed more therapy. Or medication. Or hospitalization. Even the nicest foster parents were still trying to force her into a different mold, an unnatural fit. Reg had been the typical square peg people tried to jam into a round hole.

Was that what she was doing with Nico, expecting him to be like Starlight? Was she expecting his behavior and personality to be like a cat who was much older and had grown up in a different set of circumstances and had a different personality or needs from Nico's?

Before the arrival of the nine kattakyns, the magical black cats that the Witch Doctor had sent his self into, Reg had assumed that all cats were the same. People talked about them as if their natures were all the same. But she had found the nine identical black cats were not identical at all. They all had completely different personalities, some of them sleepy and some of them energetic, with different affinities for magical or psychic gifts, preferring different activities and social contact even when Nicole (pronounced NEE-cole in her owner Francesca's charming creole), the cat who had adopted them all as her own kittens, expected them to do the same thing—taking a nap, play hunting, or eating.

Nico was particularly distractible, always off doing something different from the rest of the cats. Chasing Reg's shoelaces when it was time to sleep or hunting for mice when there was food in his bowl. Then, of course, he would want to eat in the middle of the night and was very vocal and insistent that he be fed immediately.

Francesca was Nicole's owner and had taken on the job of taking care of the kittens. But Nico was getting to be too much for her and Reg had agreed to take him for a few days to see if she could do something with him. She had been pretty sure it was just a matter of persistence and paying attention to catch him being good, but he was wearing her down too. She was no longer sure that she was going to be able to do anything with him.

Detective Marta Jessup came back from the bathroom. She looked at the popcorn all over the floor and at Reg, on her knees in front of the couch. "What happened?"

"Well, that's just what I was asking him, but he isn't in much of a mood to discuss it."

"You know he's a cat, right?" Jessup inquired.

"I know. But that's no excuse."

"Do you want me to pop some more?"

"I don't know. You can check in the cupboard to see if there is any left, but I don't think there is."

Jessup shook her head. She went to the kitchen and looked through the cupboards.

"You see?" Reg said to the cat. "You ruined our girls' night. We were going to do popcorn and a movie, but how do you do that without the popcorn?"

"We could have something else," Jessup suggested as her search petered out. "There's a bottle of wine and some pretzels."

Reg grimaced. Who knew how long they had been in the cupboard. Wine might improve with age, but that was when the bottles were properly stored in a cool cellar, on their sides and turned regularly, or whatever you were supposed to do with wine. Not when you just shoved it into a warm cupboard in Florida and hoped for the best. And the pretzels might have been there from the time she had moved in. She couldn't remember buying any. Sarah, her landlord, lived in the big house at the front of the lot. She might have purchased them, but usually, the stuff that Sarah bought for her was nutritious. Sarah tried to get Reg to eat properly instead of just snarfing down convenience foods whenever it was... convenient. But Sarah might have bought pretzels for herself and then decided she didn't want them, so she had gifted them to Reg.

"How about in the fridge? I think there might be ice cream in there."

Jessup opened the freezer door and pushed a few unidentified packages around.

"Yes, there is ice cream," she agreed, pulling out a couple of small tubs. Reg was of the opinion that if she bought the small, expensive containers, she wouldn't eat as much and wouldn't put on weight, but she had already noticed her skirts starting to get tight. She gave herself the excuse that she had been too skinny before, living hand-to-mouth and barely keeping herself off the streets, but she had a suspicion that if she were to weigh herself, she had put on a bit more weight than she hoped.

"Why don't you get the popcorn cleaned up, and I'll dish up the ice cream," Jessup suggested.

Reg sighed and got back to her feet. There was no point in dragging Nico out from under the couch. He would scratch her, and she wouldn't be able to explain to him what he had done that was wrong. He would growl and yowl and try to squirm out of her grip and, eventually, she would just let him go. He would slink off to pout in some corner. Or back under the couch.

She got out the broom and dustpan and started to sweep up the popcorn.

Starlight, who had an irrational fear of brooms and dusters, immediately bolted, running to hide in the bedroom.

Then again, Reg didn't know much of Starlight's history. His pathological fear of brooms might be totally logical. Maybe a previous owner had hit him with one. Or maybe witnessing Sarah beating down the garden with a broom as she tried to chase Nicole out of the yard had traumatized him.

Who was to say what a cat thought or why they did the things they did?

When Reg was finished cleaning up the popcorn, Jessup presented her with a large bowl of ice cream, several scoops of different flavors, complete with a spoon. Reg sat down on the wicker couch and sighed in satisfaction.

She regretted the loss of the popcorn, but she couldn't deny the comfort of a bowl of ice cream.

Jessup sat down beside her, and they turned on the TV.

CHAPTER TWO

While Reg was trying to train Nico to be a good kitty, Davyn was training her.

As Reg had grown up, any sign of psychic or magical gifts that Reg might have shown had been quickly beaten down. People didn't like unexplained things and, when something didn't make sense, they would alter their memories to a more logical explanation. The things that Reg heard in her head were easy to pass off as a wild imagination in the early years or psychosis as she got older and should have been leaving her imaginary friends behind. Reg being able to find lost items was easily explained; not that she had a gift for finding lost objects, but that she was the one who had stolen them in the first place.

When they saw something that wasn't easily explained, like glass breaking without anyone touching it, their memories were revised. The window hadn't just broken spontaneously, but Reg had thrown something or hit it with something. Other things that happened when she was upset were easily explained as violence originating with her temper tantrums and uncontrolled anger issues. A child obviously couldn't break things or fight someone without touching them, so she *had* touched them. And that was what everybody remembered.

Since she had arrived at Black Sands, things had been different. Instead of people denying what was going on and telling Reg that it was just her imagination, they told her that the voices in her head were the spirits of people who had passed on and that things breaking or falling down when she was angry were not just bizarre coincidences, but telekinesis. She had thought that the reason she was so good at fortune-telling was that she could cold-read people really well, but the witches and warlocks that she had met in Black Sands told her that she had actual psychic gifts.

While they had encouraged Reg to use her gifts, no one had ever trained her in any of them. They had given her bits of advice or told her that she could do things she didn't think she could, but the idea of someone training her to control and develop her innate gifts was new.

Davyn, the leader of one of the warlock covens in Black Sands, happened to be a fire caster—among other gifts—and having seen in Reg the signs that she shared this gift, he had taken her under his wing to teach her to use the gift without putting herself or others in danger.

"You don't want to be practicing fire casting without any instruction," he had told her. "That's just going to lead to injuries. Either to you or those around you. Or maybe you just burn down the cottage."

Remembering the way that the box of Yule candles had burst into flame when she had tried to send out her fire, Reg had been quick to agree. She didn't want anything like that happening without an experienced fire caster there to help her.

"You can teach me how? Is that… something that is done? Do I need to sign a contract with you or pay a retainer…?"

"Younger practitioners are traditionally mentored by those who are more experienced," Davyn assured her. "You don't have to sign in blood or mortgage your soul."

Reg had been a little worried about something along those lines, so she nodded in relief, laughing it off. "Okay, good. But I'm not exactly that young. I mean, I'm adult, I'm not a kid."

"You are younger than me."

Reg found it difficult to assess the age of the magical practitioners around her. They all seemed to possess a youthfulness that belied their actual age. She would think that someone was fifty, only to find out that they were centuries old. She didn't think that Davyn was centuries old… but she believed that he was older than he looked, which was maybe his late thirties or early forties, like Corvin. Of course, Corvin too looked younger than his age, though she wasn't sure how old he really was. It was disconcerting.

"Besides," Davyn went on, "mentoring doesn't have anything to do with your chronological age, but with how long you have been using your gifts, or how much training you've had."

"Which is none."

He gave a grave nod. "A situation that needs to be remedied, especially with a fire caster. I'm surprised you haven't had any serious accidents in the past."

Reg nodded, frowning.

"Maybe you have, but you just haven't told me about them," Davyn suggested.

"No. I mean… not that I can remember. When I was in foster care, there were a few kids who were firebugs."

He raised his eyebrows. "Firebugs?"

"Kids who light fires. They would do it whenever they were feeling stressed or overwhelmed. Like kids who cut themselves. It's a safety release valve; helps them to feel better."

"I see."

"Not because they were fire casters; just because it made them feel in control, and to put on a show for people. They liked the attention. Seeing how much they could do without getting caught."

"You seem to be very well-versed in the situation."

"Well, yeah. You get to be if you live in the same house with one of these kids. You have to be aware of where they are at all times and what they are doing. You can't assume that just because things are quiet, you are safe. A fire can cause a lot of damage or injury before people discover it."

"Yes, it can."

"So I had to know about them. Why they did it and what to watch for. So I could help and get an adult if anything happened."

Davyn held his hands a foot or so apart, and slowly conjured a ball of fire between them. Reg watched it intently, feeling it call to her gift. She wanted to hold it and control it, to add to it.

"Are you sure that the other kids in your house were firebugs?"

"What?" She turned her attention to Davyn's face with difficulty, having a hard time prying her eyes away from the fire.

"Are you sure that it was one of the other children who was a firebug, and not you?"

Reg blinked at him. "Of course I'm sure."

"Were you ever around when they lit a fire?"

"No. Not there in the same room."

"So you never saw one of them light a fire."

"No. But why would they do it while I was there? They would hide it from me."

"Did they admit to lighting the fires?"

"No." But that was a ridiculous idea. Any kid would deny it. They didn't want to get in trouble.

"Then how can you be sure that they did it?"

"Because they were firebugs."

"Maybe you were the firebug. But you didn't light fires in the room you were in, because that would get you in trouble. So you sent it out farther away from you. And someone else took the blame."

"No…"

He squeezed the fireball into a smaller space, compressing it between his hands. Reg reached out to take it from him, eager to handle it herself.

"You went your whole life without lighting a fire?" he challenged.

"Of course I've lit fires. But just… the conventional way."

"And you never got in trouble for it? Or had one get out of control?" Davyn passed the fireball to her slowly, his movements small and deliberate.

Reg held the fire between her hands, feeling the warmth radiating from it. Not dangerously hot. She didn't fear that she was going to burn. It just felt… friendly and healing. Like sitting next to a fireplace on a chilly day. Or roasting marshmallows over a campfire. That warm, safe, welcoming feeling.

"Reg?"

Reg tried to focus on Davyn again. He had asked her a question, but she wasn't sure what it was. "Sorry, what was that?"

"You've never lit a fire that got out of control?"

The burning that came to Reg's cheeks didn't have anything to do with the fire in her hands. "Well…"

Davyn chuckled. "Yeah, that's what I thought. Maybe more than once?"

"I'm just… really good at lighting fires. If you wanted someone who could light a campfire at a youth camp or in a furnace that kept going out… I would be the one to call."

"Because you're really good at lighting fires."

"Yeah."

"Even with damp wood? Even when others had tried and hadn't been able to get it going?"

"Yes."

"And every now and then, maybe it's gotten a little bit larger than you intended it to?"

"Yeah, maybe. But… I was just a kid. Kids don't know…"

"I think you did know. You might have wanted to control it and keep it small, but you also wanted to burn. You wanted the fire to get bigger and bigger, and to consume all of your problems…"

The ball of fire in Reg's hands flared. She tried to keep her focus on it, to make sure that it stayed small and in control. Davyn's hands hovered around hers, not touching her, but shadowing her position and taking back some of the control over the fireball.

"Don't," Reg protested, "I can do it."

"One step at a time. You need to learn to keep your focus."

"How am I supposed to do that when you're talking about fires getting out of control?"

"I want you to feel the difference between when you have the fire under control, and when you let go."

"I didn't let go."

"You were close. You were losing control."

Reg made the ball smaller, trying to show him that she was still fully in control. The fireball quieted, letting her take back her control. Just like that. She could control it. It only took a little more focus. And Davyn not talking about how many other fires she had lost control of before.

It wasn't possible that the firebugs she had known in foster care hadn't really been firebugs. They had a history.

Didn't they?

It wasn't like her foster mothers had ever sat her down and told her about their history of fire setting. There had been discussions about staying safe and monitoring what was going on in the home, about everybody playing a part in keeping the family safe. But talking about the history of another foster child would have been a breach of confidentiality.

"Stay focused. I want you to put your hands together."

Reg inched her hands closer together. The fireball stayed steady, glowing between her hands.

"All the way together."

Reg wasn't sure what would happen if she did that. Was it possible that she would get burned? Would Davyn tell her to do something that would be dangerous to her? She cast a sideways glance at him. "All the way?"

"Press them together, palm to palm."

Reg was anxious about pressing her hands into the flame, but she had seen Davyn press the fireball into Starlight when he was sick and needed healing. It hadn't hurt him. She took a deep breath and pressed her hands closer and closer together. Eventually, the flames were licking at her hands, but it just felt like the warm tickle she got when she passed her finger quickly through a flame. She had loved that trick when she was a kid, scaring the others by passing her finger right through a fire. Was that something all kids did, or just those with an affinity for fire casting?

She looked at Davyn. He nodded. She kept moving her hands closer to each other until the palms were pressed against each other, the flames disappearing. She didn't know whether she had smothered the fire, or if it was still there, inside her hands. She looked at Davyn for his next instruction.

"Good," Davyn approved. He didn't tell her to do anything else.

Reg parted her hands slightly to see if the ball of fire was still there, between her hands. Her hands glowed a little, but the flame was gone.

"You can safely take the flame within yourself, if you are properly focused," Davyn advised.

"What if I'm not focused?"

"Then it might be a little hot."

Reg grinned. It wasn't really funny, but she couldn't help smiling at his dry tone.

When the training session with Davyn was over, Reg saw him to the door. In the beginning, she hadn't been sure whether to allow him into the cottage. She'd had bad experiences with Corvin, another warlock, and was leery of inviting any others into her home. Nobody had warned her to stay away from Davyn as they had about Corvin, but what if there was some reason they wouldn't tell her he was dangerous? Sarah and others had neglected to inform her that Corvin could take away her powers if she allowed him to because it was a taboo in the community. What good did it do to tell her to stay away from him without telling her why?

Maybe other women would have heeded the warning without knowing the reason, but Reg had never been one for blind obedience. She liked to make her own choices based on what she knew and experienced for herself.

And nothing had prepared her for what she would face with Corvin.

"I'll see you next Wednesday, then," Davyn confirmed.

"Right." Reg had made sure to write it down in the appointment book on her kitchen island so that she wouldn't forget about it or schedule a psychic reading for the same time. "See you then."

"No practicing on your own."

Reg hesitated. How was she supposed to get better if she didn't practice? If she only practiced once or twice a week when Davyn was there, her progress would be at a snail's pace. She could advance much further if she could put what she learned into practice during the week and be ready to learn new things when she met with Davyn instead of going over the old ground.

Davyn raised one eyebrow and gave her a hard look. "No practicing on your own," he repeated. "You are not to do this without another fire caster present. You want to burn the whole place down?"

"I wouldn't. I can control it. I did really well today."

"You did well. But you needed to be reminded to focus, and you needed extra control more than once. You are not ready to practice solo."

Reg felt deflated. She thought she had done well.

Davyn patted her on the shoulder. "You will be able to in time," he promised. "Just not yet. You're still a toddler. You're not ready to go running races and climbing the monkey bars."

"Toddlers still get to practice toddling. Walking."

"Give it time. This is a safety issue, Reg. Promise me you won't."

What would he do if she refused to promise? Or promised but then broke her word? He couldn't exactly stop her from doing what she liked once he was gone. She stared past him, not meeting his eyes. "Fine."

"You will not play with fire until I come Wednesday?"

"What constitutes playing with fire?"

"Reg!" His voice was exasperated.

"Can I light candles?"

"No."

"Not even with matches?"

"No."

Reg rolled her eyes and folded her arms.

"Not even matches, Reg."

"Fine."

"What you can work on is meditation. The better you control your thoughts, the easier it will be to keep your fire under control."

"I don't like meditating."

"Use your crystal ball. Get Starlight to help you. If your mind is going every which way, you will not be able to keep your focus on your fire."

"Okay. I'll try."

"Good. See you Wednesday."

He finally walked out the door. Reg stood there, watching him take the pathway up past the big house to the street where his car was parked.

A shadow darted across the yard toward her. With a yelp, Reg jumped back, slamming the door before it could reach her.

Fairy Blade Unmade, Book #7 of the *Reg Rawlins, Psychic Investigator* series by P.D. Workman can be purchased at pdworkman.com

ABOUT THE AUTHOR

Award-winning and USA Today bestselling author P.D. (Pamela) Workman writes riveting mystery/suspense and young adult books dealing with mental illness, addiction, abuse, and other real-life issues. For as long as she can remember, the blank page has held an incredible allure and from a very young age she was trying to write her own books.

Workman wrote her first complete novel at the age of twelve and continued to write as a hobby for many years. She started publishing in 2013. She has won several literary awards from Library Services for Youth in Custody for her young adult fiction. She currently has over 60 published titles and can be found at pdworkman.com.

Born and raised in Alberta, Workman has been married for over 25 years and has one son.

Please visit P.D. Workman at pdworkman.com to see what else she is working on, to join her mailing list, and to link to her social networks.

If you enjoyed this book, please take the time to recommend it to other purchasers with a review or star rating and share it with your friends!

facebook.com/pdworkmanauthor

twitter.com/pdworkmanauthor

instagram.com/pdworkmanauthor

amazon.com/author/pdworkman

bookbub.com/authors/p-d-workman

goodreads.com/pdworkman

linkedin.com/in/pdworkman

pinterest.com/pdworkmanauthor

youtube.com/pdworkman

Lightning Source UK Ltd.
Milton Keynes UK
UKHW021854270521
384511UK00002B/250

9 781774 681329